These [...]
are ready, w [...]
the wild, wild West. Only, they never guess [...]
greatest challenge will be resisting a pretty face!

Cowboy #1
Businessman T. R. McGuinness
thought ranching would be a breeze—
until sexy cowgirl Freddy Singleton *showed* him
how much more he had to learn....

Cowboy #2
Trucker Chase Lavette was looking forward to
having time alone out on the range—until his
former lover showed up with a little surprise....

Cowboy #3
Cop Joe Gilardini had decided to give up law
enforcement—until mysterious "accidents" started
occuring at the ranch. and he found himself
falling for his primary suspect....

URBAN *Cowboys*

Every woman loves a cowboy....

Relive the romance

by Request™

Three complete novels
by one of your favorite authors

Dear Reader,

All of my books are special to me, but there was magic in writing the *Urban Cowboys* trilogy. Maybe it was the setting. I've ridden horseback through the foothills northwest of Tucson, where I decided to "build" the True Love Ranch. I even dragged my editor there on a trail ride recently.

Although the ranch exists only in my imagination, ranches similar to it nestle in a landscape studded with mesquite and palo verde trees, stately saguaros and chubby barrel cactus. I'm crazy about this area, from its rugged mountains to the delicate flowers that bloom on the desert floor every spring.

But the setting wasn't the only magical part of writing the series. I fell in love with the characters, too. Introducing three gorgeous—but clueless—city slickers to the West was more fun than a girl should be allowed. What a hoot these guys turned out to be! They learned to deal with everything from gelding a stallion to falling into a prickly pear cactus. In the process, they became cowboys—irresistible ones!

So, here are Ry, Chase and Joe, my *Urban Cowboys*. Enjoy.

Happy Trails,

Vicki Lewis Thompson

VICKI LEWIS THOMPSON

URBAN *Cowboys*

HARLEQUIN®

TORONTO • NEW YORK • LONDON
AMSTERDAM • PARIS • SYDNEY • HAMBURG
STOCKHOLM • ATHENS • TOKYO • MILAN • MADRID
PRAGUE • WARSAW • BUDAPEST • AUCKLAND

HARLEQUIN BOOKS

by Request—URBAN COWBOYS

Copyright © 2001 by Harlequin Books S.A.

ISBN 0-373-20188-5

The publisher acknowledges the copyright holder
of the individual works as follows:
THE TRAILBLAZER
Copyright © 1995 by Vicki Lewis Thompson
THE DRIFTER
Copyright © 1995 by Vicki Lewis Thompson
THE LAWMAN
Copyright © 1995 by Vicki Lewis Thompson

This edition published by arrangement with Harlequin Books S.A.

Visit us at www.eHarlequin.com

Printed in U.S.A.

CONTENTS

And he thought
surviving on Wall Street was tough…

THE TRAILBLAZER

Prologue

JUST BEFORE the elevator reversed direction and plummeted to the basement, T. R. McGuinnes was thinking about going West. Golden opportunities awaited bold investors who could foresee the direction of growth in the Sun Belt and buy land in its path. As a commodities trader, T.R. prided himself on boldness, but he needed partners. Partners with cash.

Without warning, a relay failed between the second and third floors, catapulting the elevator toward the bottom at a thousand feet per minute. T.R. had approximately three seconds to review his life and wish he'd scheduled his business appointments differently that morning. He looked around and met the startled gazes of the two men who shared the elevator with him, one in jeans, the other in NYPD blues. The man in jeans swore once, loudly, just before the elevator slammed into its concrete base. T.R. was tossed against the elevator wall, cracked his head on the handrail coming down and blacked out.

1

THE GROAN of stressed metal eased into T.R.'s consciousness. He opened his eyes to blackness, breathed in dust and coughed.

"Who's that?" rasped a voice from the back of the elevator.

"Name's McGuinnes." His head pounded. "T.R. McGuinnes. You?"

"Chase Lavette. Are you the cop?"

"No."

"Do you think he's dead?"

"I hope to God he's not," T.R. said. "Are you hurt?"

"Yeah. Something's wrong with my back. It hurts like hell. How about you?"

"I hit my head." T.R. put a hand to the side of his head, but he didn't feel blood, just the jackhammer pain. "Listen, you'd better not move," he said. "I'll check the cop." He got to his hands and knees, wincing at the viselike pressure against his skull. Crawling forward, he brushed something with his shoulder. He reached up and touched the warm surface of a fluorescent light that had been knocked from the ceiling.

"It's getting damned hot in here," Lavette said.

"Yeah." Perspiration soaked his shirt, but it wasn't only the heat making him sweat. It was the thought that he could be approaching a corpse.

"They should be coming to get us out of here pretty soon," Lavette told him.

"Let's hope so." A pinpoint of light from the damaged ceiling allowed T.R. to make out a shapeless mass near the left side of the elevator doors. As he crept toward the body, his knee hit the edge of his briefcase and he wondered if his briefcase, flying through the air, could kill a man. The smell of blood made his gorge rise.

When he reached the cop, he forced himself to place two fingers against the guy's neck. It was wet and he couldn't feel a pulse. Oh, God. He leaned closer. *Breathe, damn you.*

"If you try mouth-to-mouth resuscitation, you're a dead man," the cop said wearily.

T.R.'s breath whooshed out in relief. "Never learned it, anyway." He sat on his heels and reached in his back pocket for a handkerchief to wipe the blood from his hands. Then he shoved the handkerchief toward the cop. "Here. You're bleeding somewhere."

"No joke. How's the other guy?"

"I'll survive," Lavette said.

"Says his back hurts," T.R. added. "I told him not to move."

"Good. Moving a back injury case and severing his spinal cord would top off this episode nicely." The cop eased himself up to a sitting position and winced as he touched the handkerchief to his face. "That briefcase cut the hell out of my chin. What's that thing made of, steel?"

"Brass trim."

The cop snorted. "You got a cellular phone in it, at least?"

"Yeah."

"Then you'd better use it. This has been great fun, but I'm due back at the station in an hour."

T.R. groped behind him for his briefcase. "I suppose almost getting killed is a big yawner for you, isn't it?"

"Killed in an elevator accident? You've been seeing too many Keanu Reeves movies. New York elevators are safer than your grandmother's rocking chair."

"Tell that to my back," Lavette said. "I can't drive with a busted back, and if I can't drive, I can't pay off my rig."

T.R. opened his briefcase, found his cellular phone and snapped it open. "If you can't drive, you'll get an insurance settlement."

"And sit around doing nothing? No, thanks."

T.R. dialed 911, gave their location and problem and hit the Disconnect button. "They're sending a team to get us out," he said. As the news penetrated his numb brain, an adrenaline rush hit his system and he almost dropped the phone. He clenched his fist around it and fought the trembling just as the elevator rumbled and lurched to the right.

"Damn!" Lavette cried out. "Aren't we all the way down yet?"

"We're all the way down," the cop said. "The blasted thing's still settling, that's all. Move your fingers and toes, see if you still have all your motor coordination."

Paralysis. The thought sickened T.R.

Lavette rustled around a little. "I can move everything," he said at last and T.R. sagged with the sudden release of tension.

"Good," said the cop. "What's your name?"

"Lavette. Chase Lavette."

"T. R. McGuinnes," T.R. said, taking his cue.

"Joe Gilardini," the cop supplied. "I wish I could say

it was nice to meet you guys, but under the circumstances, I wish I'd been denied the pleasure."

"Same here," Lavette said.

Sweat dripped down T.R.'s chin and he wiped it with the sleeve of his suit jacket. What they all needed was a distraction, he decided. He scrambled for ideas and came up with the last topic that had occupied his mind before the elevator had crashed. "Either one of you ever been out West?"

"Why do you want to know?" Lavette asked.

"I don't, really. I just think talking is better than sitting here waiting for the elevator to shift again."

"Guess you're right," Lavette said. "No, I've never been out West. Eastern seaboard's my route. Always wanted to go out there, though."

The cop sighed. "God, so have I. The wide-open spaces. Peace and quiet."

"No elevators," Lavette put in.

"Yeah," Gilardini said. "If I didn't have my kid living in New York, I'd turn in my badge, collect my pension and go."

T.R. thought he should probably be locked up for the way his mind was working all of a sudden. Only a crazy person would start putting together a business deal at the bottom of an elevator shaft with his fellow crash victims. Or maybe not so crazy. He'd just been reminded that life is short, and you'd better grab what you can, when you can. A pension and an insurance settlement. It might be enough, with what he could raise. Of course, these guys probably didn't know the first thing about investing, but maybe that was what he needed. His usual contacts knew so much, they'd turn gun-shy on him.

"I just heard about this guest ranch in Arizona that's

up for sale," he said. "One of those working guest ranches with a small herd of cattle. I'm going out there next week to look it over."

"No kidding?" Lavette said. "Think you might buy it?"

"If it checks out."

"Running a guest ranch," Gilardini mused aloud. "You know, that wouldn't be half-bad."

"And after I've had some fun with it, I'll sell it for a nice profit," T.R. said, sweetening the deal. "Tucson's growing in that direction, and in a couple of years developers will be crying out to get their hands on that land, all one hundred and sixty acres of it. I can't lose."

"A hundred and sixty aces," Lavette said with reverence.

"I'm looking for partners."

The cop laughed. "Now I've heard everything. Only in New York would a guy use an accident as a chance to set up a deal."

The elevator settled with another metallic groan.

"Would you rather sit here and think about the elevator collapsing on us?" T.R. asked.

"I'd rather think about your ranch," Lavette said. "I'd go in on it in a minute if I had the cash."

"You might get that settlement," T.R. reminded him.

"You know, I might," Lavette said. "Listen, McGuinnes, after we get out of here, let's keep in touch. You never know."

"I guarantee you wouldn't go wrong on this investment. The Sun Belt's booming."

"I think you're both nut cases," Gilardini said.

"So you're not interested?" T.R. asked.

"I didn't say that. Hell, what else is there to be interested in down in this hole? If the ranch looks good, just call the Forty-third Precinct and leave a message for me."

T.R. shook his hand. "Let me get some business cards out of my briefcase."

"I'd just as soon not think about your briefcase, McGuinnes. Let's talk some more about the ranch. What's the name of it, anyway? I always liked those old ranch names—the Bar X, the Rocking J. Remember 'Bonanza'?"

"I saw that on reruns," Lavette said. "The guy I liked was Clint Eastwood. I snuck in to see *High Plains Drifter* at least six times when I was a kid. Back then, I would have given anything to be a cowboy."

"Yeah, me too," admitted the cop. "So what's the place called?"

T.R. hesitated. These guys were after macho images, and he wished he could give them one. "Well, this spread is named something a little different."

"Yeah?" Gilardini said. "What could be so different?"

"The True Love Ranch."

FREDDY SINGLETON hung up the phone and glared at her younger sister, Leigh, who was perched on the edge of the old pine desk. "Damn. That was Janine at Cooper Realty and she wants us to send the van for that T. R. McGuinnes from New York."

"Do we have to?"

Freddy shrugged. "I'll catch hell from the Westridge corporate types if I don't. They want us to roll out the red carpet for him. They think he's got money. Shoot. I was hoping he wasn't serious. Then maybe Eb's offer would stand."

"Fat chance," Leigh said. "Westridge wants at least

their original investment back." She pushed away from the desk and walked over to study the gallery of framed photographs displayed on the office walls. "Maybe they're hoping for a bidding war between Eb and this Easterner."

"Eb can't go any higher." Freddy tapped a pencil against the desk in frustration. "Just what we need, a greenhorn trying to run the place. Eb Whitlock would just leave me alone to do my thing."

Leigh turned back to her. "Maybe the guy won't be interested once he sees the ranch. We *are* looking a little shabby in spots. And we're low on guests this week. What have we got, eleven? That won't seem like a money-making operation."

"Here's a clue for you, Leigh. It isn't. I've never seen it so slow in May."

"So we'll convert our weaknesses to strengths. Maybe we can scare him off. Don't forget to tell him about the old Indian curse that's supposed to hang over this property."

"Yeah, Westridge has been on my case about all the little mishaps we've had lately. Sometimes I wonder if there really is a curse." Freddy dialed the bunkhouse and asked Duane to make an airport run, then hung up and glanced up at Leigh. "We might as well go down to the corrals and get this morning's chore over with. Are you ready to convince Red Devil that sex isn't all it's cracked up to be?"

Leigh chuckled. "I don't think there's a male animal alive who would accept castration with grace, but I'll do what I can. After all, that's what a head wrangler gets paid for."

Freddy stood and reached for her hat hanging from a

peg on the wall. "You know, I wonder if we really could discourage this T.R. person from buying the ranch."

"He's a dude, right?" Leigh said. "We have ways of handling dudes."

"That we do." Freddy adjusted her hat so the brim settled low over her eyes. "And I'd do just about anything to get rid of this particular tenderfoot."

T.R. WASN'T SURPRISED when the guest ranch van that met him at the airport had steer horns on the hood instead of a standard hood ornament. With a ranch named the True Love, he was lucky the ornament wasn't a valentine heart.

Despite the air-conditioning, it was hot inside the van. He took off his sport coat, making sure Joe Gilardini's home phone number was still tucked in the pocket. He and Joe had been released from the hospital emergency room the same day as the accident, Joe with a broken arm as well as the nasty cut on his chin, and T.R. with a mild concussion. Lavette was still in the hospital with lower back pain and no clear predictions from the doctors on whether he could resume his trucking career, but he was more eager to get in on that ranch deal than Gilardini.

The driver of the van was a certified cowboy named Duane, grizzled and taciturn. His sun-weathered skin made judging his age difficult, but he was probably about forty-five. T.R. gave up on conversation after a few monosyllabic responses from the man and watched Duane navigate the heavy city traffic of Tucson. It wasn't hard to picture him guiding a cutting horse through a restless herd of cattle with the same dedication.

T.R. glanced out the window and grinned. He might

be on a freeway, but there was no doubt he was in the West. Mountains surrounded the city, but the Santa Catalinas dominated it. It wasn't a gentle range.

As they drove, civilization loosened its grip on the landscape and T.R. gazed at hillsides covered with giant saguaros standing fifty-to sixty-feet high, their massive arms lifted toward a sky so blue T.R. took off his sunglasses to make sure the color wasn't an optical trick. It wasn't.

The van turned off the main road where two battered rural mailboxes crouched, one marked Singleton in faded letters, and the other Whitlock. Near the boxes was a small white sign that read True Love Guest Ranch—2 miles. Beneath the lettering was a heart with an arrow through it. T.R. could imagine what Joe would say about that. He had to convince the cop that none of that mattered. The name and the corny heart would disappear in a couple of years, anyway. They could even change the name immediately if Joe insisted on something more...manly.

The van jolted along a dirt road that needed grading, sending a plume of dust behind it. A lane branched off to the right, and a wooden sign announced a turnoff to the Rocking W Ranch—Whitlock's property, T.R. concluded. Several yards down the lane, a gaunt figure in a battered straw cowboy hat supported himself with an aluminum walker as he inched along in the direction of the ranch house. A plastic shopping bag filled with mail hung on one side of the walker.

"Who's that?" T.R. asked Duane.

"Dexter."

As the van drew alongside, Dexter turned slowly and lifted one hand in a salute. Duane raised two fingers from the steering wheel and drove past.

"Aren't you going to give him a ride?"

"Nope."

"Why not?"

"I don't aim to insult Dex."

T. R. glanced back at the old cowboy shuffling along the dirt road. "He picks up the mail every day?"

Duane shifted his tobacco to the other side of his lip. "Yep."

"How long does it take him?"

"Good days, an hour."

T.R. settled in the seat and tried not to think about Dexter's daily trek to the mailbox. It was too personal, too human—the sort of information he'd rather not know, considering his plans for the True Love.

The road forked again, and another sign appeared which read Main House—Registration, and pointed to the right. Beneath that was the word *corrals* and another arrow, this one pointing to the left. And below all that, the darned heart with an arrow through it. These people weren't shy about their sentimentality.

Duane slowed the van at the fork. "Freddy's down at the corrals. I should probably take you there first."

T.R. was impressed that Duane was capable of making such a long speech. "Fine," he agreed. He had to see all of it, so it didn't much matter which end he started with. "What's going on at the corrals?" he asked, not really expecting an explanation.

'Last I heard, Freddy was fixin' to use the emasculator on Red Devil."

T.R. swallowed. From the corner of his eye, he could see Duane watching him for a reaction. He'd never heard of an emasculator, but it didn't take much imagination to figure out what was in store for Red Devil. He adopted the poker face that had served him so well as a deal maker. "Sounds interesting," he said evenly. "Maybe I'll be in time to watch."

"Maybe you will," Duane said, a slow grin spreading across his leathered face as he took the left fork in the road.

T.R. prayed the corrals were a long, long way down this winding road, and that Freddy had already finished the task.

Shortly, however, the corrals appeared. They didn't look very much like the ones T.R. had seen in the movies. The fences were at least a foot thick and made with tree branches laid lengthwise inside upright braces to form a solid wall. The weathered nature of the branches indicated the corrals had been there a long time. One large enclosure containing a least thirty horses was surrounded by several smaller corrals, which were empty. Not far from the corrals stood a large tin barn with two wings, one of tin, and one of stone, looking much older than its counterpart. Across a small clearing was a long one-story building, also of stone, that looked as though it might be a bunkhouse.

A group of cowboys clustered around one of the small corrals. Laughter wafted across the clearing, as if the men were at a party.

"I'll park here, so we don't get no dust over there," Duane said. "Come on," he urged, climbing down from the driver's seat. "We'll get a little closer so you can see."

T.R. took a deep breath and loosened his tie. "Okay." He left his sport coat in the van, deciding a jacket wasn't required at this particular event. Following Duane, he trudged through dust that coated his oxblood wing tips. It sure didn't smell like the city, he thought. But he sort of liked the combined odor of horse manure and animal sweat that hung over the area.

Duane paused next to the fence and found a foothold in the meshed branches. "Just climb up here. You can see, then."

T.R. put his hands on the rough bark, wedged his wing tips in a notch in the branches and hoisted himself up next to Duane. Inside the small corral where the cowboys had gathered, a cinnamon-colored horse lay on the ground, his back leg stretched away from his body with a rope. A blond woman crouched near the horse's head, and a brunette was kneeling by his groin area. T.R. had a sudden uneasy suspicion. "Where's Freddy?" he asked.

"Right there by the business end of the horse. The blonde is Leigh, her sister. She's the head wrangler."

"Oh." He hated surprises. They threw him off his stride.

Duane looked at him. "Freddy's the best boss I ever slung a rope for, mister. And a damned good vet. She took it in school, just so's she could help out with animals around here."

"I'm sure she's very capable," T.R.'s mind raced to assimilate this unexpected information. Freddy had her back to him, her snug-fitting jeans cupping a firm backside, her leather belt cinching in a small waist. Her rich brunette hair was caught with a silver-and-turquoise clip at her nape.

"Leigh calls herself a horse psychic," Duane said. "Some folks laugh about it, but I've known people who could tell what horses are thinkin'. Seems like Leigh can. She's gonna work on Red Devil's self-esteem, I think is what she said."

After that speech, T.R. realized that Duane wasn't

quiet at all. Probably, he just got that way in the unfriendly confines of the city. Out here on the ranch, conversation spewed from him like water from a broken fire hydrant.

But most of T.R.'s attention remained focused on Freddy. Her cooperation would be critical once the purchase went through, because he wanted to continue the guest ranch operation without sinking any more money into improvements. It would be a waste of resources, considering the ultimate fate of the property.

Freddy turned and asked for something and T.R. got a glimpse of her profile. Classic. So she had a face to match her figure, apparently. Now that he'd adjusted to the idea that the ranch foreman was a woman, he liked it. Women were just as good working companions as men. Who knew if Freddy might turn out to be more reasonable about his plans for the ranch than some macho guy protecting his turf. Sometimes women were better at the art of compromise.

"They've sedated him, but they ain't done the cuttin' yet," Duane said, as if he felt obliged to provide color commentary on the event. "Ever seen anythin' like this before?"

"No." T.R. wondered if this was the way Elizabethans used to react to beheadings in the public square—too horrified to watch and too curious to look away. He winced as Freddy began the procedure and fought the urge to put his hands over his own crotch.

"That there's the emasculator," Duane explained, pointing to an instrument in Freddy's hands. "Looks sorta like a nutcracker, don't it? No pun intended."

T.R. wanted to turn his back on the whole thing, but he figured this might be a test, and for some stupid reason, he didn't want Duane to think less of him.

As the operation continued, Duane shifted his weight uneasily. So he wasn't as unperturbed about this as he let on, T.R. thought. "Kinda gets you in the—well, you know," the cowboy said.

"Yeah, I know," T.R. said. He found it interesting that Duane seemed reluctant to mention body parts. He'd heard that cowboys had a chivalrous side and avoided many of the four-letter words tossed out so often by city dwellers. Some of T.R.'s Wall Street friends might launch at the idea that a tabacco-spitting old cowpoke was a gentleman, but that's exactly how T.R. would describe Duane.

At last, Freddy stood, signaling that the operation was over. T.R. realized his jaw hurt, and he relaxed his clenched teeth.

Duane climbed down. "That does it. Might as well take you over to meet the boss. Walk careful and don't stir up no dust. We don't want any on Red Devil's...equipment."

T.R. eased himself off the fence, wiped his sweaty palms on his slacks and started after Duane. As they approached, the blond sister named Leigh noticed them and spoke to Freddy.

The ranch foreman turned and stripped off her gloves. Striding toward them, she held out her hand to T.R. "Welcome to the True Love, Mr. McGuinnes. I'm Frederica Singleton. Please call me Freddy."

T.R. looked into hazel eyes that assessed him with calm intelligence. Her grip was firm, although her skin was temptingly soft. He reminded himself these were the same hands that had just turned a stallion into a gelding. He'd be wise not to underestimate Freddy Singleton.

2

HE HAS NEW YORK *written all over him*, Freddy thought as she took in the pallor of his skin from being indoors too much, the sophisticated cut of his thick brown hair, the bold red-and-blue stripes of his power tie. But his blue-eyed gaze was direct, his smile friendly, even a little sexy. She almost regretted what she was about to do to him. Almost.

"I understand you want to inspect the ranch," she said.

"That's right."

"The best way to see the True Love is from the back of a horse. Can you ride?"

"Yes."

She could just imagine. A little tour around Central Park on a Sunday afternoon, perhaps. But she was glad he'd likely done that much. If he'd never ridden at all, she'd have a tougher time instituting her plan. She surveyed his pristine white shirt and gray herringbone slacks and tried to keep the smile from her voice. "Did you bring anything besides that sort of outfit?"

"No."

Freddy had already anticipated this problem. She dismissed Duane as being too short, but Curtis, who was mending a fence a few yards away, was about T.R.'s height and build. She called him over. "Think you have a pair of jeans and a long-sleeved shirt you could loan our guest? We're going to take a ride around the ranch."

"Around the ranch?" Curtis blinked.

"Yes."

Curtis pushed back his hat and studied T.R. with new interest. "I reckon I have somethin'. What about boots?"

"Listen," T.R. said, "I don't think I should inconvenience—"

"No problem," Freddy interrupted. "What size shoe do you wear?"

"Eleven."

Freddy lifted an eyebrow in Curtis's direction.

He shook his head. "Tens."

"I wear an eleven," Duane said, bending down to pull off one scuffed boot. With no apparent reluctance, he put his sock foot—with a large hole in the toe—on the ground and held the boot out toward T.R. "Try this."

Freddy loved it. She'd bet no one had ever shoved used footwear in T. R. McGuinnes's face, let alone expected him to put it on. He might not realize what a huge favor Duane was granting him, but he was obviously a polite guy. His natural big-city reticence carved grooves beside his mouth as he seemed to be struggling for a graceful way out of taking off his expensive wing tips and trying on the boot. He must have come up empty, because he accepted the boot, walked over to the fence and propped a foot against the rail to untie his shoe.

Freddy considered suggesting that if the boot fit, T.R. could just trade Duane the boots for the wing tips for a few days, but she decided that might be going a bit far.

Besides, Duane wouldn't be caught dead in city shoes like that, not even for a joke.

Duane spat a stream of tobacco in the dirt. "My folks always said I woulda been taller if God hadn't turned up so much for feet," he said with a tobacco-stained grin. "You know he's gonna need a hat," he added in a lower voice. "I'm willin' to loan out my boots 'cause I got the others back at the bunkhouse, but I ain't givin' up my hat, and I don't know any of the hands who would."

"Don't worry. We'll find something in that collection we keep for the dudes who don't remember to bring their own."

Duane made a face. "A man's gotta have a decent hat."

"Only if he decides to stay," Freddy answered with a wink.

T.R. returned wearing Duane's boot on one foot, his pant leg tucked inside, and his dusty wing tip on the other. "They fit fine, but I really think—"

"Perfect," Freddy said, motioning for Duane to take off his other boot.

He complied and held the second boot out to T.R. Then he turned back to Freddy. "Curtis and I can go on up to the bunkhouse, pick up Curtis's clothes for Mr. McGuinnes, here, and meet you at the ranch house in a few minutes."

"Sounds good." Freddy glanced back to where Leigh was standing guard over Red Devil until he came out of the anesthesia. "Let me make sure our patient is okay, Duane. Then I'll bring Mr. McGuinnes up to the house in my truck."

Duane looked at T.R., who was still holding the second boot. "Might as well put'em both on. You look kinda discombobulated like that."

"All right."

As Freddy watched him return to the rail to take off his other shoe, she felt another twinge of conscience. But how else was she supposed to save the ranch from this Easterner if she didn't make him so miserable, he would never want to even *think* about a guest ranch in Arizona? The market was down, so maybe Eb Whitlock could buy the True Love, and life could go on undisturbed.

She walked back toward Leigh, careful not to stir up any dust. In a few days, Red Devil would be ready for use as a saddle horse again, and a much milder-tempered saddle horse he'd be, too.

She squatted next to Leigh, who was stroking Red Devil's neck and murmuring to him. "How's he taking it?" Freddy asked.

"He's still in dreamland. I'm picking up something about a little palomino filly."

"From now on, dreaming's all he'll be doing about that particular activity."

Leigh glanced at her and angled her head toward T.R., who was pulling on Duane's other boot. "So why's Duane giving up his boots?"

"Mr. McGuinnes needs something to ride in if he's going to survey the ranch."

Leigh's eyes widened. "All the ranch?"

"Sure. I figure we'll take a little ride around the perimeter, ending with a trip up Rogue Canyon into the leased Forest Service land, so he can see where we summer the herd."

A slow smile tilted the corners of Leigh's mouth. "That's a mighty long ride."

"I know."

"I doubt you could even finish it today."

"Precisely."

"And unless he's spent a lot of time on a horse..."

Freddy reached down and stroked Red Devil's velvet neck. "Do you think I'm being too cruel?"

"Not if you want to get rid of him."

"I do. And not just for our sakes, either. Belinda and Dexter are too old to deal with an Easterner, and Duane doesn't say much, but I can tell he's worried about keeping his job. Losing it would be the end of the world for him."

"It would," Leigh agreed. "You have to do it, Freddy. But maybe you should take some horse liniment. You don't want to have to call Search and Rescue to haul him out of the canyon."

"Great idea. If he's like most dudes, he'll hate the smell of the stuff, which will suit my purpose nicely. So, can you handle things until tomorrow?"

"Yeah, but you could be back sooner, depending on how much of a wimp this guy is."

Freddy thought of McGuinnes's firm handshake and his clear blue gaze. "No, I think we'll be out there for the duration. He may be in pain, but he'll tough it out."

"Sounds like he might not deserve his fate."

"He probably doesn't," Freddy acknowledged. "If I could think of any other way to keep him from buying the ranch, I'd do that, instead." She gave Red Devil one final pat. "See you tomorrow, big guy."

T.R. FINISHED PULLING on the second boot, took off his tie and tucked it into one of his shoes. Duane and Curtis left, and he hoped Duane remembered the sport coat in the van. Not that he was worried. A guy who would give you the boots off his feet wasn't about to steal a jacket. He chuckled, trying to imagine Duane wearing the navy blazer, even if he did make off with it. Duane would probably sooner be caught in a dress.

Freddy came toward him. "Ready?"

"Sure. How's Red Devil doing?"

"Leigh says he's dreaming of fillies."

"Poor guy."

Freddy smiled at him. "Unless we're planning to stand them at stud, stallions are a liability at a guest ranch. They're either after the mares or trying to pick a fight, which makes them too unpredictable for a guest to ride. The hands don't much like putting up with their shenanigans, either. Around here, we refer to gelding as brain surgery."

"Oh." He tried to appreciate the operation from a business standpoint and failed.

"Let's go," she said. "My truck's under the mesquite tree over there."

T.R. looked at the battered white pickup with the ranch brand stenciled on the door panel. Didn't seem like anyone was wasting money around here. He liked that. "What did you call this kind of tree?" he asked as they walked toward the truck.

"Mesquite."

He surveyed the stand of mesquite, gnarled trunks branching out into a canopy bursting with small, delicate leaves. "Do you sell the wood to restaurants back East? Mesquite-grilled meat is very popular where I come from."

Her glance was not friendly. "No, we don't sell the wood."

"Why not?" he persisted. "Seems like you have a lot of it around."

"The trees protect our privacy. My ancestors used to clear the mesquite to give the cattle more room, but a lot of our guests are birders, and the mesquite bosques attract birds. Besides, I don't much like the sound of a chain saw. It frightens the horses."

"I see." So economics wasn't her top priority, after all. T.R.'s hope that a woman would be more willing to compromise on his plans for the ranch began to disappear. Once the developers finished with this land, there wouldn't be a mesquite bosque to be found.

They reached the truck and he climbed in, dumping his shoes on the floor.

"How are the boots?" Freddy asked as she started the engine.

"Great fit." He'd discovered he liked the boots. With only one on, he'd felt stupid, but with both on, and his pant leg pulled over the shaft instead of tucked in, he felt like a cowboy. He'd always made fun of city people who wore Western clothing as a style statement. But something had happened when he'd put on the boots. He'd walked with more purpose in his stride and had felt more in command of his world. Maybe he'd take a taxi into town and buy some before he left.

Freddy steered the truck past the fork and down the road toward the main house.

"Your ancestors built this place?" T.R. asked, remembering something she'd said earlier.

"That's right. Taddeus Singleton homesteaded the True Love in 1882." After a moment of silence, she continued, "And if you wonder why a Singleton is now only the foreman, and not the owner, after my dad died, I ran into some financial problems and had to sell. The

Westridge Corporation out of Denver bought it. Fortunately, I was allowed to stay on and run the place."

"Considering what you must save them on vet bills alone, I'm sure the corporation is lucky you decided to stay."

She glanced at him, her smile grim. "I'd have to be dragged off the True Love."

He didn't like the sound of that, didn't like it at all. But she was obviously a very intelligent woman. Maybe, as time went by, he'd be able to appeal to her business sense. The True Love property was too valuable to use as a guest ranch. Surely there was other land out in the middle of nowhere that could be had for a pittance. She needed to take a page out of Thaddeus Singleton's book and strike out on her own, carve a new ranch out of some remote wilderness. Maybe he could help her locate that piece of property, give her a business loan to start a new spread. The more he thought about it, the more he liked the idea of being her financial adviser.

The dirt road curved and the main house appeared, surrounded by a low wall of whitewashed adobe that swooped into an arch over a flatstone walk. A border of blue, white and yellow Mexican tile decorated the archway. Cactus that reminded T.R. of giant artichokes stood on either side of the arch, and beyond the wall two large mesquite trees created a filigree of shade over a yard with patchy grass. T.R. noticed a couple of rabbits munching on the grass and wondered how golf courses handled the rabbit situation.

"Here we are." Freddy parked the truck and swung to the ground. "The old ranch house, which was frame, burned down in the thirties, so my grandfather decided to build the new one of adobe—less of a fire hazard. It's grown like topsy over the years, but we've tired to keep Grandpa's basic design." She gestured toward the house. "You're standing at the base of a U shape. Sixteen guest rooms are on the right wing, living and dining room in the middle, and kitchen, storage and family areas on the left. Oh, and we have one little cottage about fifty yards away in a mesquite grove. We use it for honeymooners."

T.R. surveyed the one-story structure that stretched in front of him. *Graceful* was the word that came to him. A developer might want to convert the building into a clubhouse for the golf course because of its charm. The whitewashed adobe contrasted nicely with the red Spanish-tile roof, and a wide porch stretched the length of the building, with potted geraniums blooming under the porch's shade. Shade had quickly become important to T.R., whose shirt was already sticking to his back. He noticed that Freddy seemed barely to perspire.

"Do you have many guests now?"

"Not many this week," she said. "A group of German tourists will arrive on Sunday. The Europeans don't seem to mind the heat, but the bulk of our business is during the winter months, although business hasn't been that terrific recently. Anyway, now's the time we catch up on our chores."

Like castrating poor Red Devil, T.R. thought.

"Let's go in." She started down the flagstone walk, her boot heels clicking on the hard surface. "Duane and Curtis will be along in a minute with your luggage and some riding clothes. In the meantime, I think Belinda can find us each a glass of lemonade."

The suggestion reminded T.R. that he was desperately thirsty. He never remembered being so thirsty in his life.

Freddy grasped the wrought-iron handle set into one of the carved wooden entry doors, opened the door and ushered him inside. He nearly sighed with relief as cool air welcomed him.

She led him through a short tiled hallway into a large room with beamed ceilings at least fifteen feet high. In the far left corner stood a huge beehive fireplace flanked by worn leather couches and two leather easy chairs, also battered. A rough pine coffee table held pewter ashtrays and some back issues of *Arizona Highways*.

Next to the fireplace, a wide bay window looked out on an enclosed courtyard, a kidney-shaped swimming pool and a Jacuzzi. A high rock wall broken by an archway curved beside the pool, and a waterfall spilled from the top of the arch. A mother and her two young children played in the tumbling water. T.R.'s thirst grew.

"Why, there you are, Freddy," called a musical voice.

T.R. turned as a woman he judged to be in her mid-seventies walked into the room. Her gray hair was cut short in a no-nonsense style and she wore slacks and a flowered smock over her ample bosom. She had one of the sweetest faces he'd ever seen.

"You must be a mind reader, Belinda. We could sure use some lemonade." Freddy took off her hat and slapped it against her thigh. "But first, let me introduce you. Belinda Grimes, meet T R. McGuinnes."

Belinda nodded to him politely, but without enthusiasm.

"When the True Love was strictly a working ranch, Belinda was the only cook, but now she supervises a staff of three," Freddy said. "She's been working here for fifty-one years."

"Fifty-two," Belinda corrected in her lilting voice. "I came in March and it's already May."

T.R. received the news uneasily—a foreman whose ancestors homesteaded the ranch and a cook who'd spent at least two-thirds of her life here. There was some serious entrenchment at the True Love. He'd be wise to keep his plans for the property to himself for the time being.

"Dexter came in with the mail a few minutes ago," Belinda said. "I put it in your office."

"Thanks, Belinda."

"Duane and I passed him on the road," T.R. told her. "That seems like quite a hike for a man who has to use a walker."

Freddy's back stiffened. "Dexter Grimes was the best team roper and the finest ranch foreman in southern Arizona until his stroke ten years ago. I think your husband can manage a little walk to the mailbox, don't you, Belinda?"

"I think that walk is what's keeping him alive," Belinda said.

T.R. groaned inwardly. The news just got worse and worse. There was no doubt that Belinda and Dexter Grimes were like a second set of parents to Freddy.

"I'll get you that lemonade," Belinda said. "Anything to eat?"

Freddy glanced questioningly at him.

"No, thanks," he said.

"Maybe some sandwiches for the trail, Belinda," Freddy said. "As soon as Curtis shows up with a change of clothes for Mr. McGuinnes, I'm taking him out for a ride around the ranch."

Belinda paused. "*All* around the ranch?"

"I want to make certain he knows what he's thinking

of buying," Freddy explained. "Don't you think that's a good idea?"

Belinda looked over at T.R., and he had the feeling she was trying not to laugh. Maybe she couldn't imagine that a city slicker like him could ride a horse. "I think that's a wonderful idea," she said, and hurried toward the back of the house just as the front door opened.

Curtis, a lanky blond cowboy of about twenty-eight or nine, stepped inside holding a pile of clothes. Duane followed, carrying T.R.'s suitcase, brass-edged briefcase and sport coat over one arm. He had on another pair of boots, equally as scruffy as the ones he'd loaned T.R.

Duane turned to Freddy. "Where're you puttin' him?"

"In the John Wayne Room," Freddy said.

Duane ambled off down a hallway to the right.

T.R. started after him. "I can—"

"Never mind," Freddy said. "Duane will set you up down there. He knows to check around for scorpions and black widows. You might not know where to look."

T.R. controlled a shudder. "You have much problem with that?"

"Not much," Curtis said. "Except for this time of year. The black widows mate about now and lay their eggs. Once they get what they want from the male spider, they kill him, so if you see a web with this petrified shell of a spider in it, that's the luckless husband, and his widow's around somewhere."

T.R. could do without the explanation, coming as it did on the heels of watching a castration.

But Curtis seemed determined to give a lecture in natural history. "And the scorpions, see, they come out at night. The big ones aren't too bad, but those little ones pack quite a—"

"Now, Curtis," Freddy said, laying a hand on his arm. "Mr. McGuinnes won't be sleeping a wink if you carry on like that."

"Please call me T.R.," he said. He'd had enough of this Mr. McGuinnes stuff.

"Initials seems kind of silly," Curtis said. "What do they stand for?"

"Thomas Rycroft."

"Ain't nobody ever called you Tom?"

The comment hit him like a sucker punch to the gut, but years of practice at hiding pain kept his expression neutral. Only one person had ever used that name, and he wasn't about to let anyone sully that memory. "T.R. is fine," he said. "Are these the clothes you brought me, Curtis?"

"Yep." Curtis held them out proudly. "Brought you my newest jeans and a shirt my brother sent me from Abilene. There's a belt there, and the jacket ain't got no rips or anything, either, and I washed it last week."

"Thanks, but I can't imagine I'll need a jacket."

"Oh, yes, you will," Freddy said. "It gets chilly up in Rogue Canyon. Better take it. And Curtis, would you look in that back closet for a hat? I think one of the guests left a black one that should fit."

Duane reappeared from the hallway. "All set in the John Wayne Room."

Curtis returned with a black hat in one hand and glanced at Duane. "You checked real good for black widows and scorpions, didn't ya, Duane?"

Duane looked blank. Then he grinned at Curtis. "Uh, shore I did. Shore. Only killed two, but of course, this is daytime. They come out more at night, you know."

T.R. vowed he'd inspect the room completely before he turned in tonight. Nobody had said anything about tarantulas, but he seemed to remember they lived in Arizona, too. Funny, but bugs had never shown up on the Ponderosa. He accepted the clothes and started toward the hall. Then he turned. "Did John Wayne really sleep there, or is the name just something to impress the tourists?"

"He really slept there," Freddy said. "He made several movies out at Old Tucson. This was one of his favorite places to stay, and that was his special room."

At last, a piece of good news, T.R. thought as he carried his clothes down the hall. That settled it. The developers should definitely leave the ranch house standing and make use of the John Wayne Room somehow. There also had to be a way to get rid of the damned bugs.

CURTIS TURNED to Freddy after T.R. had left the room. "You know, I'm almost beginning to feel sorry for that tenderfoot. The John Wayne stuff is the only true thing he's heard since he got here."

"That's not so, Curtis," Freddy countered. "Everything we've said is true. The ranch is best seen from the back of a horse. We do sometimes have scorpions or black widows around, although the spraying service works pretty well. And you're one to talk about taking pity on him. You gave him new jeans for the trail ride."

Curtis grinned. "I saw right away what you're tryin' to do. Pretty smart. So if he has a bad time out on the trail, he'll go home, right? And then Mr. Whitlock can buy the ranch."

"That's the idea."

Duane adjusted his hat and chuckled. "You shoulda

seen his face when you cut Red Devil. But I have to hand it to him, he stuck it out and didn't faint or nothin'."

"He's not a bad guy," Freddy said. "But he's an Easterner, and I can tell he's used to running things and wouldn't leave us alone like Westridge has done. He asked me right away why we didn't cut down the mesquite bosques and sell the wood to fancy restaurants back East. If he buys the ranch, he'll have the power to do just that."

Duane's jaw tightened. "Then you'd better take him on a nice long ride, boss. I may cuss those trees when we have to go in there after our critters, but I wouldn't want that wood to be flavoring somebody's beefsteak in New York City."

"Exactly."

"And I can't picture riding for a boss who calls himself T.R."

"It is stuffy." Freddy had noticed that T.R.'s expression had closed down when Curtis had suggested calling him Tom. She wondered if she'd ever learn what caused the sudden reaction. Probably not. By tomorrow, T.R. McGuinnes would be heaving his saddle-sore body back onto a plane bound for New York, and Eb Whitlock would have a clear shot at the True Love.

"Lemonade," chirped Belinda, sweeping in from the other direction carrying a frosty pitcher and glasses. "I heard you boys out here and went back for more glasses."

"Thanks, Belinda," Freddy said. "You didn't have to serve us yourself."

"Nonsense. Feels good once in a while." She held the tray of drinks toward Freddy. "Besides, I wanted to thank you for trying to keep that Easterner from buying the place. I think you've hit on a wonderful idea."

Freddy took a glass from the tray. "I hope so."

"You know," Belinda said, "I could probably adjust, but really if Dexter and I had to leave…"

"I'd do just about anything to keep that from happening, Belinda," Freddy told her.

"I know." Belinda's usually kind expression became flinty. "So would I." She looked over Freddy's shoulder. "And here comes our pigeon now."

Belinda's description made Freddy smile. But when she turned toward the hall, her smile faded. A New York businessman had left the room. Someone with an entirely different aura had returned.

The pearl-buttoned Western shirt, black with a bold gray arrow design across the chest, molded a torso that appeared more muscular than she'd at first suspected. The jeans were snug, too, and looked mighty fine in the front. She didn't need him to turn around to picture how they looked in the back. The black hat was pulled low over his blue eyes, eyes that flashed with a cool kind of fire, as if the clothes had awakened something elemental in him. Sure as shootin', T. R. McGuinnes had turned into cowgirl bait. And she was the one who'd suggested they spent the night together. Her plan had just become more complicated.

3

T.R. LOVED THE FIRST two hours of the trail ride. Despite the heat that baked his back and thighs, he enjoyed the rhythm of the horse beneath him, the acrid scent of sun-warmed bushes and blossom-studded cactus plants, the call of birds and the caress of an occasional cool breeze. The hat shaded his face and the leather saddle cupped his groin in a pleasant grip.

Freddy had assigned him to Mikey, a brown horse with a black mane and tail. Mikey's head bobbed pleasantly as they clopped along the trail behind Freddy's mount, a reddish mare named Maureen, after Maureen O'Hara, one of John Wayne's leading ladies. T.R. had never ridden horseback behind a woman before and hadn't realized how sexy the view could be.

He felt vaguely guilty about his thoughts, but not guilty enough to censor them. Freddy's firm buttocks rested lightly in the saddle as they walked, but brief periods of trotting sent her into a graceful posting motion that was decidedly erotic. His manhood tightened in response to the suggestive movement, but he didn't plan to indulge in anything beyond innocent fantasy. The True Love already had too much emotional baggage for his taste. He wasn't about to add another entanglement by becoming sexually involved with the foreman.

Freddy led him to the south boundary of the ranch,

and from there they rode west, then north toward Whit-lock's property. T.R. glimpsed clusters of cattle, but they were never close enough to get a really good look. The sales brochure had mentioned a herd of about two hundred female Herefords, ten bulls and whatever calves had been born that spring. Freddy pointed out a twenty-acre horse pasture fenced with barbed wire to separate the horses turned loose in the pasture from the cattle that roamed the rest of the property. Farther on was another fenced pasture that held a scattered herd of approximately a hundred red-and-white Herefords.

"Those belong to Duane," Freddy said over her shoulder. "They carry his brand, the D-Bar. He's work-ing on an experimental breeding project, so we keep his stock separated from ours and lease him the land. Ours forage on whatever they can find, but Duane has to feed this bunch."

"Have you had a roundup yet?" he called ahead to her.

She turned in her saddle. "Three weeks ago. That's the one time we're booked solid because we let the guests help."

T.R. nodded. He was sorry he'd missed that.

As they headed east, towards the mountains, T.R. be-gan to feel discomfort. He checked his watch and real-ized he'd expected to be back at the ranch by now. Maybe he'd underestimated his endurance.

A short time later, Freddy gestured to her left. "That adobe building over there is the original homestead built by Thaddeus Singleton."

T.R. stood in his stirrups, glad for a reason to stretch and get his behind out of the saddle. He studied the squat, flat-roofed structure that wasn't much bigger than a single-car garage. A hundred years of sun and rain had battered and bleached the earthen blocks; strong winds and animals had knocked holes in the walls. Yet the pioneer in T.R. admired the spirit of the man who had carved out this foothold in a hostile land.

"I can take you a little closer, if you're interested," Freddy said.

He probably shouldn't agree to detours, considering the condition of his thighs, but he didn't want to seem like a wuss, either. "Sure."

As they drew closer, he noticed that a wooden lintel remained in place over the front door, and the ever-present heart with an arrow through it had been burned deep into the wood. In a far corner of the roofless building, the adobe was blackened, as if by fire. "What caused that?" he asked, pointing.

"Hikers staying here for the night, most likely." Freddy leaned her forearms on her saddle horn and gazed at the ruins. "I've found all sorts of evidence of people camping here. Leigh and I have talked about fencing the building off and eventually restoring it, but the corporation hasn't been interested and Leigh and I don't have the money. My grandfather poured that concrete floor in the thirties, back when the roof was still intact and we used this place for temporary shelter if we were caught out here in bad weather. That's the last improvement the place had."

"I see." He wasn't interested in preservation. Attach too much sentimentality to the place by creating a shrine to the original homesteader, and future developers might run afoul of the historic preservation police. He wanted this prize parcel to be unencumbered when it went on the block.

"Thaddeus's wife, Clara Singleton, once held off a raiding party of twenty Apaches from the roof of that house," Freddy said. "The parapet was about three feet high back then, and she used a ladder to climb up and pulled it after her. She had three guns there, and she crawled around firing them in succession, so the Apaches thought there were more people at the house. Thaddeus was off rounding up strays. She drove off those Apaches all by herself."

"That's quite a story." T.R. had noticed the defiant tilt of her chin, the flash in her eyes as she told it. No one could doubt that Freddy had inherited courage and determination from Clara Singleton. Unfortunately, in this modern-day struggle for control of the True Love, he and his partners would be cast in the role of marauding Apaches, and this time the Singleton women were outgunned.

"Clara was quite a woman." Freddy clicked her tongue and urged Maureen down the trail with a nudge of her heels. "There's a dry wash up ahead," she called over her shoulder. "Want to lope the horses a little?"

"Sure." Maybe a good run would release some of the tension building in him. He'd thought that after fifteen years of commodities trading, he'd be immune to attacks of conscience about making money from the misfortunes of others. The free-enterprise system produced the healthiest economy in the world, but you had to play by the rules. People made money or went broke according to the demands of the market, and woe to the investor who worried about the hindmost.

He eased Mikey down a rock embankment into a wide sandy riverbed littered with tree branches rubbed smooth by rushing water. He'd heard about flash floods and imagined this was the sort of place one would happen. But the sky was an unrelenting blue.

With a whoop and a flick of her reins against Maureen's polished rump, Freddy took off down the wash. With no prompting, Mikey leaped after her, and T.R. grabbed the saddle horn with one hand and his hat with the other.

After the first moment of surprise, he gripped the horse with his thighs, crammed the hat more firmly on his head, and grasped the reins as he leaned into the wind. A fantasy created by years of Saturday-afternoon matinees came true in that moment—T. R. McGuinnes, famous gunslinger, galloped his cow pony under an endless sky, the hot wind flattening his Western shirt against his chest and whipping the horse's mane against the backs of his hands. As he drew alongside Freddy, he looked over at her. She grinned at him, and in that pell-mell moment, with his heart pumping from the excitement of the run, he experienced a rush of emotion that scared the hell out of him. Immediately, he began reining in his horse. Within five seconds, T.R. McGuinnes, commodities trader and emotional conservative, was back in the saddle.

FREDDY NOTICED signs of strain in T.R. by the time they reached the pond that served as a reservoir for the True Love. An earthen dam cradled the waters of Rogue Creek about a third of the way up Rogue Canyon, and it was one of Freddy's favorite spots on the ranch.

T.R. winced as he dismounted and looked longingly at the cool water, as if he'd like nothing better than to strip and immerse himself in it. But to his credit, he didn't complain. Freddy began to wonder what it would take to wring a protest out of him.

Choosing her favorite flat rock under the shade of a large cottonwood, she tethered Maureen to a low branch and dug in her saddlebag for the sandwiches

Belinda had given her. She'd also brought along some dehydrated stew that she'd brew up for their dinner, and each saddle had a bedroll tied to the cantle, but she didn't want to announce their overnight plans yet. She wanted to be far enough into the canyon that T.R. wouldn't consider finding his own way back to a Jacuzzi and a soft bed. She sat down and watched him, wondering how he'd take the news.

T.R. tied Mikey's reins to the same branch Freddy had used for Maureen and gingerly lowered himself to the rock. He'd obviously forgotten to bring his canteen when he'd dismounted, so she offered hers.

"Oh!" He started to get up. "I have a—"

"Never mind." She pulled on his arm to bring him back beside her. "We can share."

"You first," he said.

She took a sip, wiped the rim on her sleeve, and offered it to him. Funny, she'd shared a canteen with riding partners all her life, yet she'd never been so aware of the intimacy of the act. Maybe it was the way he'd glanced at her mouth before he accepted the container of water.

He started to drink, and paused. "Can we refill our canteens from the pond?"

"Yes." She was impressed that he'd thought to ask. Some tenderfeet would have gulped the contents of the canteen and worried about their water supply after it was exhausted. "Besides, I have a couple more jugs in my saddlebag."

"Good." He tipped his head back and swallowed continuously until the canteen was empty. Like a schoolgirl, she watched him, noticing the surprising length of his eyelashes as he closed his eyes and the generous curve of his lower lip as it cupped the mouth of the canteen. A drop of moisture escaped and trickled down his chin. She had the sudden urge to lean over and lick it off. Good thing she'd planned this so he'd most likely be on a plane to New York by tomorrow, or no telling what stupid thing she might do. Her commitment to the ranch allowed no time for romance. Leigh had accused her of throwing herself into ranch work in order to compensate for not having a man in her life, but what did Leigh know?

By the time T.R. had finished drinking, Freddy was busy unwrapping a sandwich. She handed it to him with brisk efficiency and began eating her own.

"Where did the name of the ranch come from?" he asked. "The real estate broker didn't seem to know."

Freddy was offended. In her opinion, no one should be allowed to market her ranch without understanding its history. "When Thaddeus announced he was marrying Clara, the churchgoing people around here had a fit," she began. "Clara was a dance-hall girl, and some said she sold her favors."

"Sold her favors." T.R. smiled. "Such a quaint way of putting it. Do you think she did?"

Freddy looked into his blue eyes and a curl of awareness snaked through her midsection. They were, after all, talking about sex. "Probably. Back then, a single girl could either teach school, take in laundry or entertain men for a living. Clara didn't have any education, and from what I know of her, she wasn't the type to wash other people's dirty shirts."

"Sounds like a feisty woman." There was a note of approval in his voice.

"She was. And Thaddeus was determined to have her, regardless of the wagging tongues. When they were married, he named the ranch the True Love to show those busybodies he didn't give a hoot about their opinion."

"Good for him."

Freddy crumpled her sandwich wrapping. "He was true to her, and she to him, until the day she died, forty-three years later."

"I'll bet he was true to her even after that."

She looked into his eyes and her heart stumbled. Not many men would chance making such a sentimental remark. "He probably was," she said, a bit hypnotized by the depth of emotion in his gaze. She gave herself a mental shake. "If you'll fill the canteens, we can head up the canyon," she said, starting to rise.

"Sure." His slight groan as he pushed himself to his feet elicited sympathy from her instead of the satisfaction she'd hoped to feel. He walked stiffly to his horse, retrieved his canteen and returned slowly to the water's edge with their two containers. He crouched, dipped the canteens in the water and clenched his jaw as he stood. "This is a nice spot," he said, his tone conversational as he glanced at the granite walls rising on either side of them. She could imagine what it cost him to make pleasant comments when his thigh and groin muscles were very likely screaming in protest. "How long has it been here?"

"Thirty years. My dad decided to dam up Rogue Creek and create a pond. He got sick of going to the mountains to fish, so he stocked it with bass."

"Why is it called Rogue Creek?"

"Because it's in Rogue Canyon."

He rolled his eyes.

"The truth is, my great-grandfather had to come up here after rogue cougar. He shot the cougar, but not before the cougar almost killed his horse."

T.R. looked uneasy. "Are there any still living up here?"

"A few." Her conscience prickled her. "But you'll probably never see one. They usually keep away from people."

"Fine with me." He glanced back at the pond. "What if the ranch wanted to tap into this pond?"

"Why would we?"

"Say you wanted to put in more landscape plants, maybe a greater area in grass."

Freddy gave herself a mental slap for softening toward this dude. He was an Easterner, and the first thing most Easterners wanted to do was green up the desert and make it look like the Boston Common. For all she knew, the guy had plans to build the True Love Golf Course out behind the corrals. "We try to keep our watering needs low by using plants that don't require much moisture," she said. "Ready to go? I want to show you the Forest Service land where we summer the cattle."

"Lead on." Only the faintest flicker of his eyelashes betrayed his pain as he settled himself in the saddle once more.

BY FIVE O'CLOCK, T.R. wondered if he'd ever walk normally again. By six, he wondered if he'd ever walk again, period. And his feet weren't the problem. He wasn't a tenderfoot, he was a tenderass. He envisioned Duane and Curtis lifting him from Mikey's broad back with his legs frozen in a permanent bow. He'd have to order a custom-made chair for his office in New York, one with inches of padding and a spacious enough seat to accommodate the new wide-open configuration of his thighs.

They'd climbed for most of the afternoon. Cactus and

sage had given way to something he recognized as belonging to the oak family and a type of evergreen with a fragrant bark, probably some sort of cedar. He supposed it was beautiful, if he could only give a damn. Who would have imagined that riding around the ranch could take this long? Surely they'd have to turn back soon, although he didn't relish the idea of riding downhill and trying to keep his aching private parts from sliding forward against the saddle horn.

He could hardly believe he'd begun this ride having sensual thoughts about the woman in front of him. He couldn't imagine ever using his bruised equipment again. She'd not only crippled him, she'd ruined his future sex life. The crisp jeans that had made him feel like such a stud this morning now felt like chain mail wrapped around his genitals in an imitation of a medieval chastity belt.

One image kept him going; one reward beckoned at the end of this torture trail. He pictured the Jacuzzi he'd seen beside the swimming pool, pictured himself being carried to it, eased into the water and left there for days. The image almost made him weep with longing.

He was so engrossed in his suffering that he didn't notice Freddy had stopped on the trail and he nearly ran Mikey up Maureen's backside. Mikey realized the problem, snorted and backed up a step.

Freddy swiveled in her saddle and smiled at him. "How are you doing?"

Dammit, he wouldn't give her the satisfaction of knowing the truth. "Fine," he said.

"Time has gone by so quickly this afternoon." She gazed out across the mountain slope. "I doubt if we could make it back before dark, so I thought we'd just camp over there, against that cliff."

He tried to clear the haze of pain from his mind. He

could have sworn she'd said they were about to camp.
No Jacuzzi. No bed. Sleeping on the ground. How
could he do that if he couldn't even get off his horse by
himself? Would she notice if he quietly stayed on his
horse and slept in the saddle?

"T.R.?"

He focused on her with effort. "What?"

"Are you okay?" She looked concerned.

He felt his machismo slipping. "Depends on your def-
inition."

"It has been a rather long ride, at that."

"Really? I hadn't noticed."

"Follow me," she said, a gentle note in her voice.

Mikey followed. T.R. had lost the ability to guide
Mikey several hours ago.

"Stay there," she said as she swung down and tied
Maureen's reins to an oak tree. "I'll help."

Pride asserted itself. "I'm fine," he insisted, and in
one brave movement hoisted his leg over Mikey's
rump. Somebody yelled, and as he stumbled to the
ground, he recognized his own cry of pain. Freddy
caught him before he went all the way down and lowered him to a seat on a fallen tree.

"Sit here," she said. "I'll set up camp."

As if he had any choice. He sat and glared at Mikey,
instrument of his undoing. His thigh muscles throbbed,
and the family jewels felt as if Mikey had kicked him
dead center. "Some friend you are," he grumbled at the
horse. Mikey yawned, exposing big yellow teeth. "You
might have warned me that an all-day ride would turn
me into a eunuch."

"Maybe this will help," Freddy said.

He gazed up, bleary-eyed, at the opened flask she extended. "What is it, hemlock?"

"Whiskey. I always carry some in my saddlebag. You never know when it'll come in handy."

"Oh, yeah, for when you have to dig out a bullet after a battle with the rustlers, right?" he said sarcastically.

She pulled the flask away. "If you're going to be like that—"

"No, please. I'd like some." He accepted the flask and took a swig in what he hoped was a manly fashion. The whiskey was strong, at least eighty proof, and he welcomed its punch. He started to hand the flask back to her but she waved it away.

"Keep it. I'll fix us some dinner."

"I suppose you have to go out and shoot it first, this being the Wild West and all."

She stood eyeing him, her hands on her hips. "You do have a wisecracking streak in you, McGuinnes."

"It's either that or hysteria. I thought I'd wisecrack for a while."

A smile tugged at the corners of her mouth. "You told me you could ride."

He straightened as best he could. "I can," he said with as much dignity as he could muster. "For brief periods."

She covered her mouth, where he suspected a smile had broken through. Then she coughed into her fist. "Have a few more pulls on that flask, and when you feel ready, take off your pants."

"Excuse me?"

"So you can massage some Bag Balm into your thighs," she said, barely swallowing a chuckle.

"Bag Balm?"

"Aren't you feeling a bit—uh—chafed?"

"What if I am?"

"This is a lanolin-based product. We use it on the cows' udders to keep them soft and—"

"My God."

Tears of laughter brimmed in her eyes. "Believe me, it will help. And some liniment for your feet and knees will keep you from being so stiff in the morning."

His eyes narrowed as a suspicion worked its way through his pain-clouded brain. "How come you're so well equipped for this emergency?"

"Well—"

"You knew this would happen, didn't you?"

"I suspected it might."

"Is this some sort of greenhorn ritual?"

Her smile faded. "Not exactly. This land tests people, and that's something you should know up front."

"You test people, too, don't you?"

"Maybe I do. But I meant what I said about appreciating the True Love with a ride like this. If you can manage to turn around, you might understand what I was talking about. The only way to really see it is by coming up here on horseback."

The whiskey had dulled the sharp edge of his agony, and with effort he eased his legs over the trunk so he was facing the opposite direction.

The view stole his breath. The valley spread beneath them, honey gold in the setting sun. He picked out the U-shaped roofline of the ranch house with the pool inset like a chip of turquoise. Some distance away, the corrals resembled a tic-tac-toe design against the dun color of the bladed earth. Nearer, a flash of light indicated where the pond lay, its surface gilded by lingering sunbeams.

Land. His land, and his partners' land, if he wanted it enough. He'd never owned even a square foot of anything. He'd lived in leased apartments all his adult life and had never minded the lack of ownership. Until now. Surveying the wide sweep of the True Love's holdings, a new hunger filled him.

"Where's the eastern boundary?" he asked, keeping his gaze fixed on the panorama.

"We crossed it about a mile above the pond. We're standing on Forest Service land, of which we lease a thousand acres."

"That much?"

"We need it to run the herd we have."

"Do you bring Duane's cattle up here, too?"

Freddy chuckled and shook her head. "He'd never let those precious critters run around loose up here. They might lose an ounce or chip a hoof."

A hundred and sixty acres, T.R. thought. And a thousand more leased for grazing. It seemed an immense chunk to a guy who lived in nine-hundred-square feet of space in Manhattan. "It's a lot of land," he murmured.

"Yes, although not compared to seventy years ago. Thaddeus and Clara were able to homestead twice as much, three hundred and twenty acres. But in the time since they died, pieces had to be sold off to take care of debts. Eb Whitlock bought a hundred acres twenty-five years ago."

"To think the ranch was twice this big once. I wish I could have seen it in the glory days of cattle ranching."

Freddy sighed. "I wish I could have, too."

They stood in silence as the crimson sun eased below a horizon trimmed with a rickrack of mountains. T.R. wondered if he'd ever watched the sun set before in all his thirty-five years. He'd had no idea what he'd been missing.

4

FOR AN EASTERNER, T.R. was handling himself pretty well, Freddy thought as she collected wood for a fire. She'd expected him to be in a nasty mood by now, but the whiskey and the sunset over the valley had mellowed him considerably. She'd left him on the log with the flask of whiskey while she completed the routine chores of setting up camp. In short order she'd unsaddled the horses, draped the pads over the saddles to dry and hobbled Mikey and Maureen in a nearby clearing where they could graze.

The altitude and lack of sun was cooling the dry air quickly. Greenhorns like T.R. didn't realize a drop of nearly forty degrees was common in the desert at night. He'd need that jacket he'd been reluctant to bring, and the warmth of a fire, as well. And the Bag Balm and liniment. Considering the lack of privacy the camp provided, she wondered if T.R. would have the nerve to take off his clothes and apply the remedies.

As she crouched next to the fire and stirred the packet of dried stew into a small pot of water, the sound of shuffling footsteps announced his arrival behind her.

"Smells pretty good," said a voice tight with pain.

She glanced over her shoulder. He stood a few feet away, his legs braced and his expression grim beneath the shadow of his hat. He'd finished about half the flask, which probably explained how he'd managed to walk at all. Her heart swelled with remorse. Dammit, she should have known she was too softhearted to pull this off, especially when her target was taking his punishment with such good grace.

"If you'll tell me where the medication is, I'll get it."

"No, let me." She laid the spoon on a piece of aluminum foil, stood and walked over to the pile of gear. After rummaging through the saddlebag, she found the tin of Bag Balm and the liniment bottle. "Here," she said, walking toward him. "It won't work miracles, but it might make the ride out tomorrow more bearable."

He flinched at the reminder that he'd be remounting Mikey in the morning. "Thanks." Keeping the flask in one hand, he cradled the tin and bottle in his other arm while he hobbled back toward the fallen tree.

She watched him go and knew he'd never be able to manage the therapy alone. What had she been thinking? "T.R.," she called, going after him. "Maybe I should ride for help. We could bring a helicopter in here, maybe even tonight if I hurry."

He turned, his expression incredulous. "A helicopter? You've got to be kidding."

"Look, you've proved you can take a beating, so why—"

"Not on your life." Teeth clenched, he eased back to the log and set the flask, the liniment and the Bag Balm on the ground next to him. "Would any self-respecting cowboy call Search and Rescue?" He took off his hat and mopped his damp forehead with his shirtsleeve.

"You're not a cowboy. You're a commodities trader from New York."

He glanced up. "Even commodities traders have their pride, Freddy," he said quietly. "Don't take that away from me."

"But you didn't know what you were getting into! You don't have to tough it out like some stereotypical cowboy. This is my fault, not yours!"

A smile flickered across his face. "I was wondering when you'd admit you deliberately ambushed me."

She averted her eyes. "I wanted to discourage you from buying the ranch."

"Why? Somebody will, sooner or later, and you don't own it now, anyway."

She mustered her composure and faced him. "Eb Whitlock wants it, but he doesn't have the kind of money you do. Eb's a neighbor and a friend. He'll let me keep running the ranch."

"And you thought I'd fire you? After you've proved how valuable you are to the whole operation?"

"You're an Easterner. Who knows what you would do?"

"Never trust anybody who comes from east of the Mississippi, is that it?"

She lifted her chin. "Works for me."

With a sigh, he settled his hat on the log beside him.

"But I'm...sorry I've crippled you," she added. "You didn't really deserve that."

"What if this experience sours me on the True Love and I decide against buying it, just like you planned? Will you be sorry then?"

She looked into his blue eyes, sharp with pain. "Yes, I'll still be sorry. It was a dirty trick and I apologize. Why don't you let me ride down and arrange for a helicopter?"

"No." He took a swig from the flask and contemplated his boots.

"I don't think you can get those off by yourself."

"Of course I can." He leaned slowly forward. "I—

augh!" He straightened and passed a hand over his face. "And to think only this morning I could tie my own shoes."

"Here." Freddy straddled his leg, her backside to him, and took hold of his boot heel. "Resist me on the count of three."

"In this condition., I'll be able to resist you no matter how long you count."

"Very funny. Now get ready. One, two, *three!*" She yanked and he yelled, but the boot came off. "Now the other one." She repeated the procedure, then turned to face him, looking directly into his eyes. "Now the pants."

Defiance flashed in the blue depths. "I can—"

"It'll be faster and easier if I help you." A heavy load of guilt pushed her to press on in this mission of mercy. "This is no time to be modest, T.R. You need that Bag Balm applied as soon as possible. Imagine yourself as a patient in the emergency room of a hospital."

"I usually try to avoid the hospital if I can help it."

"And no woman has even taken off your pants?"

He took another drink from the flask and impaled her with a look. "I didn't say that."

To her dismay, she flushed, which completely destroyed the air of sophistication she'd been striving to maintain, but she barreled on, just the same. "Take off your belt and unbutton your jeans. I'll work them off from the ankles."

He held her gaze while he complied, and she met his challenge for as long as she could before looking away. She suspected the liquor he'd imbibed accounted for the bold stare. The trail ride had been a dumb idea, she decided. She'd thought that by tomorrow she'd be celebrating her victory over the briefcase-carrying businessman who had tried to steal her ranch. Except that T.R. was no longer an impersonal enemy, but a vulnerable man in pain. A sexy man in pain. And that was the crux of the problem.

"I'm ready." He was still regarding her with the same intensity. Only now his jeans were unfastened and his hands were braced on either side of him in what had to be an unconscious gesture of invitation, considering his condition. "Got a bullet for me to bite down on?"

"You've seen too many movies." Taking a deep breath, she squatted between his ankles. As she tugged on the stiff denim, breath hissed between his teeth. She paused.

"Just keep going."

Trying to remain focused on his ankles, she worked the material down. His socks came with the jeans, and finally she was forced to grasp the waistband and pull it past his calves. The job couldn't be done without touching him, but she tried to minimize contact. In spite of her efforts, her fingers encountered firm muscle and the tantalizing brush of hair. She swallowed and wrenched the jeans over his feet with more force than was necessary. He gasped, but didn't cry out.

"There." With a sigh of relief, she got to her feet. Her relief was short-lived. One glimpse and she realized that a half-clothed T.R. McGuinnes, even put out of commission by an all-day ride, was a sight to triple the heart rate of any normal female. From the looks of his powerful legs, he was well acquainted with the inside of a gym. With a new pang of conscience, she realized he'd make a good rider someday, if she hadn't just ruined the experience for him.

He took a glob of Bag Balm from the tin and began dabbing it over the inside of his thighs.

"Not like that," she said before she could stop herself.

He glanced up, a devilish look in his eyes, a crooked smile on his mouth. "You want to show me how?" he said softly.

Now she'd really done it.

"Think of this as a hospital emergency room," he added, holding out the tin of cream.

She'd come this far in her rescue, and if he didn't apply the Bag Balm correctly, it wouldn't do much good. With grave misgivings, she accepted the tin. Kneeling beside him, she smoothed the ointment over the inside of his chafed thigh, applying enough pressure to work it into his skin.

He groaned.

"I have to massage it in a little or it won't penetrate," she apologized. "I know the muscles underneath are sore, too."

"If this didn't hurt so much," he said with obvious effort, "I think it would be lots of fun."

Freddy wasn't about to comment. Instead, she concentrated on covering the reddened area with the ointment. Not far from her circling fingertips, his briefs enclosed an impressive bulge of manhood. She tried to ignore it as she spread ointment on his other thigh. As she settled into her massaging motion, he groaned again. She recognized it as the sound of pain, not ecstasy, but her capricious imagination transformed the low, husky protest into a moan of desire. The image of T.R. making love to her sent tendrils of heat curling through her body.

She looked up into his face. His eyes were closed, his head thrown back, his jaw rigid in response to the pain.

But the expression wasn't unlike that of a man in the throes of orgasm. Her pulse quickened. She remembered the effect he'd had on her when he'd stepped into the living room of the ranch house dressed in jeans, shirt, boots and hat. There had been an air of command about him then. She'd robbed him of that in the past few hours, but if it ever reasserted itself, T.R. McGuinnes would be a man to reckon with.

His hand covered hers, stopping her movement. "That's enough," he said, his voice rough.

She glanced up to find his gaze conveying an unmistakable sexual message. She pulled her hand away and sat back on her heels, her heart pounding.

His smile was wry. "It seems I can't resist you, after all. Maybe you'd better tend the stew while I get myself under control."

One swift look confirmed that he had become aroused during the treatment. She blushed. "I'm sorry. I didn't think—"

"Believe me, neither did I."

"The—the liniment should be put on your knees and feet."

"I'll do it in a minute."

"Then I'll get dinner ready." She jumped to her feet and headed over toward the fire, which seemed cool in contrast to T.R.'s warm gaze. Damn! Her plan to make a fool of this Easterner was in shambles, and in the long run, the fool had turned out to be her.

Two hours later, they'd managed to smooth over the awkwardness between them by ignoring the incident altogether. They sat by the fire drinking coffee laced with the last of the whiskey.

T.R. leaned against the face of the cliff, a bedroll under him and his jacket covering his bare legs. "I suppose I can expect all sorts of poisonous bugs to show up in my bedroll tonight," he said.

"I think the smell of that horse liniment will keep them away."

"So that's why you're sitting on the other side of the fire."

"You've got that right." Actually, the smell of horse liniment didn't bother her all that much. She'd just decided to keep herself as far from temptation as possible during the long night ahead.

T.R. chuckled. "Bag Balm and horse liniment. The funny thing is, I'm having a pretty good time."

"That's because you've finished off that flask."

"Partly. But partly because we're camping out. I've never done that before."

"Not even in Boy Scouts?"

T.R. shook his head. "I got into sports early—Pop Warner Football League, Little League baseball. I didn't have time for Scouts."

"What positions did you play?"

"Quarterback on the football team, pitcher in baseball."

Freddy nodded. "The power positions. They probably called you T.R. when you were nine years old."

He sipped his coffee. "Tommy."

"Really?" She decided to be bold and see if she could unravel one of the mysteries about him. "Then I don't understand why you didn't make the natural progression to Tom."

He gazed into the fire for a long moment. "That's what my wife, Linda, said. She refused to call me by a set of initials. Called it stuffy."

A wife. Somehow, Freddy hadn't thought there was a wife. "She's right."

"Was right," he corrected in a monotone. "She's dead."

"Oh!" Understanding hit Freddy like a blow. She remembered how he'd looked when he'd said Thaddeus must have loved Clara even after her death. Apparently, T.R. still loved his wife. "I'm sorry. I didn't know."

"It's okay. I don't talk about it much."

Freddy stared into her coffee mug. Of course he wouldn't want some cowpoke like Curtis calling him by the name his wife had used. But he wasn't the type to broadcast his personal tragedy, either. Under normal circumstances, she doubted he would have told her, a relative stranger, but there was something about a camp fire that encouraged confidences. And he had consumed most of the flask of whiskey.

She waited without much hope to see if he'd add any details. When he didn't, she refrained from asking. "If it were my choice, I'd call you Ry," she said at last.

"Ry?"

"Isn't your middle name Rycroft?"

"I'm surprised you remembered."

So was she. The number of things that stuck in her mind concerning him were beginning to disturb her. "It's an unusual name, that's all."

"So's Freddy. I thought you were a man."

"Would it have made everything easier if I had been?"

He studied her across the dancing flames. "You tell me. Would a man have trailed me over the ranch until I was so saddle-sore I couldn't stand? Would Thaddeus have done that?"

"If his ranch was at stake, he would have. Duane and Curtis thought it was a terrific idea."

"So everybody was in on it?"

"Why do you suppose you got a brand-new pair of jeans guaranteed to make your ride even more miserable?"

He snorted and shook his head. "You people are tough."

"Out here, we have to be."

"Well, let me tell you something. Wall Street is no baby's playground, either."

"I'm sure that's true, but the stakes aren't as high."

His eyebrows lifted. "You don't consider financial ruin a high-stakes game?"

"Not compared to losing the thing you love most."

The transformation in his expression was dramatic. All the challenge and good humor left his eyes, to be replaced by a stark sorrow that seemed to have no bottom. "You're right, of course."

She felt like hell. What a thing to have said to a man whose wife had died. "Sorry again. I seem to be putting my foot in my mouth on a regular basis."

"Never apologize for telling the truth, Freddy." He finished his coffee and stretched gingerly out on the bedroll. "So you think I should change my name."

"You don't seem like the kind of guy who goes by initials."

"What kind is that?"

She hesitated. "A little on the pompous side."

To her relief, he glanced over at her and laughed. "It's not easy being pompous around you. Maybe I've been heading in that direction, though. Is Ry a good name for a cowboy?"

"An excellent name."

"Then maybe I'll try it for a while." He turned his head to look up into the sky. "I had no idea there were so many stars."

"City lights block them out." Pleased that he'd accepted her nickname for him, she threw another stick on the fire and watched the sparks climb into the cool night air. Then she slipped off her boots and lay down on her own bedroll. "But then, I've never seen the lights of Times Square. I guess each place has its own kind of beauty."

He was quiet, and she wondered if he'd fallen asleep. A series of sharp yips drifted up from the valley. "Are those ranch dogs?" he asked.

"Coyotes."

"I thought they were supposed to howl."

"Most Easterners think that. But they yip. Which makes the dogs go crazy. Can you hear them?"

"Yeah. Noise really travels out here."

Her eyelids grew heavy. "Yes."

"I'm glad you brought me up here, even if your motives weren't pure."

"You've been a good sport."

"Thanks. Good night, Freddy." His voice seemed to caress her name, sending unexpected goose bumps over her skin.

"Good night..." She hesitated. "Ry."

SHE AWOKE to an unidentifiable scream. Bolting from her bedroll, she saw the man she'd recently dubbed Ry crouched against the cliff, a glowing stick he'd plucked from the fire brandished in one hand.

"What is it?" she called.

"I don't know. Get over here."

She was halfway around the fire before she realized she was obeying his command on her territory. The scream came again, followed by the sound of wild snorting and stomping hooves. "It's the horses!" she cried, hurrying back to her bedroll where she pulled on her boots before locating her flashlight and her Smith and Wesson. "Most likely a snake or cougar disturbing them."

"Damn, where are my boots?" he asked.

"Stay put. I'll handle it."

He grunted with pain. "The hell you will."

Ignoring him, she turned on the flashlight and shone it in the direction of the scream. "It's okay, Maureen," she called, setting out through the underbrush. "I'm coming, Mikey. Hang in there." She was counting on the sound of a human voice to discourage whatever critter was after the horses. But if her voice didn't work, her aim with the Smith and Wesson would. She hoped she wouldn't have to use the gun. By coming up this canyon, she knew that she'd invaded the territory of several desert dwellers who had a right to protect themselves, but she had to safeguard her horses.

She found Mikey and Maureen quivering in the clearing where she'd left them, yet a sweep of the flashlight revealed nothing in the area that might have spooked them.

"See anything?" Ry said from behind her.

Freddy sighed in irritation as she continued searching the bushes and overhead branches with the beam of her flashlight. "No, but go back to camp. I don't want to have to worry about you, too."

"No dice."

"Look, you know nothing about the dangers out here. You—where do you think you're going?"

Ry pushed past her and limped over to Mickey. "Shine the light on his hind leg."

She did, and gasped. It was dripping with blood. "Oh, my God." She hurried over and crouched beside the horse, whose flanks were heaving. "Easy, Mikey. Easy, boy. Ry, hold his head so I can check this out."

While Ry stroked Mikey's nose and murmured to

him, Freddy took a bandanna from her pocket and dabbed at the blood until she could see the wound, a jagged cut just above his fetlock. A little deeper and Mikey would have been crippled for life. As it was, he couldn't be ridden back down the mountain. "I'm going to look Maureen over," she said, moving carefully around the quivering Mikey to her own horse.

The whites of Maureen's eyes showed, and she tossed her head when Freddy reached for her, but after a few moments, the mare settled down. She was unhurt, which meant Ry could ride her down while Freddy led Mikey. "Let's take them back to camp and tether them to a tree," she suggested. "I'll lead Mikey if you'll take Maureen."

"I've got Mikey." Ry coaxed the horse forward and the animal complied with an air of trust that astonished Freddy. Both man and horse limped back to camp.

He just might make a cowboy, at that, Freddy thought. He was stubborn enough. And gutsy. After a few hours of being immobilized in sleep, he must have stiffened up considerably, yet he'd torn himself from his bedroll and snatched a weapon before she was fully awake. She had a gun; he had nothing but a stick, and he'd assumed the role of protector without thinking. Definitely the sort of thing a cowboy would do.

After they secured the horses to an oak tree, she cleaned Mickey's wound with water and applied an antiseptic ointment from her first-aid kit while Ry soothed the horse.

"What do you think happened?" Ry asked after they'd built up the fire and were sitting across from each other on their bedrolls, both too keyed up to sleep.

"I'm not sure. I suppose a snake or a cougar could have spooked them, and Mikey might have ripped his leg open on a jagged rock or broken tree limb lying on the ground.''

''Another rogue cougar, maybe?''

Freddy shook her head. ''A rogue would have killed at least one of the horses. We'll probably never know what happened.''

''Is the injury serious?''

''It could have been. As it is, I'll have to lead him down and you'll have to ride Maureen.''

''I'll lead him down.''

''Oh, for heaven's sake. You will not.''

''Yes, I will. It can't be any worse to walk that trail than to ride it again.''

Freddy chuckled. ''And here I was beginning to think you were turning into a cowboy.''

''What's that supposed to mean?''

''A real cowboy will saddle up to ride from one side of his front yard to the other, rather than walk it.''

''That may be true, but if he has to walk so his woman can ride, I'll bet he'd do that.''

His woman. She was certain he'd only used the expression to make a point, and it was a chauvinistic thing to say, anyway. So why did she feel a little glow of pleasure? Why did she turn the phrase over in her mind, listening to it again as if it were a refrain from a favorite song? The pressure of the impending sale must be getting to her. Perhaps, deep in her heart, she longed for a white knight to rescue her and give her back the True Love. Maybe she longed for a white knight, period. Being alone all night with an attractive man reminded her of a seldom-acknowledged emptiness in her life. But if she imagined a commodities trader from New York was the answer to her prayers, she must have accidentally dropped a sprig of locoweed into tonight's supper.

5

T.R. DOZED FITFULLY while leaning against the granite face of the cliff. The rock retained heat from the sun that had bathed it during the day, and the warmth soothed his stiff shoulders. An owl hooting in the gray light of dawn brought him awake, and he glanced across the embers of the camp fire to where Freddy lay with her boots still on, her gun within reach. The owl hadn't disturbed her sleep, probably because she was used to the sounds of wildlife in the desert.

Her hair had come free of the clip and lay spread over her outstretched arm; her lips were parted, her expression relaxed and open. He used to love watching Linda sleep, because it was one of the moments when he glimpsed her soft, vulnerable side. The other was when they were making love.

Linda. She would have hated this trail ride, he realized with a smile. Born and bred to big-city life, she'd barely tolerated outdoor cafés, let alone picnics. Freddy, on the other hand, would feel imprisoned in an office, flail her wings against the walls of a hotel room. In that way, the two women were total opposites, and yet Freddy had that same iron will that had drawn him to Linda. And rarer still, the same sense of fair play. She hadn't been able to pull off her diabolical scheme without confessing, without trying to right the wrong she'd done. She could have pushed her plan to the limit, and without the whiskey and horse liniment, he might have checked out of the True Love today and never looked back.

He was still tempted to give up the whole crazy idea. God, he hurt. He'd become used to the smell of the liniment, but even the slightest movement was agony. Walking the entire trail sounded like torture, but the prospect of riding down wasn't much of an improvement. Freddy deserved every pang of conscience that pricked her, he decided.

But whenever he started plotting revenge, he reminded himself that she'd done him a favor without realizing it. Tough though the journey had been, he treasured his first view of the valley, a view he wouldn't have enjoyed without Freddy's scheming. He wouldn't have slept outside and seen the stars spread over the night sky like fairy dust, or been given a new name, a name that seemed to fit as well and give him as much confidence as Duane's boots.

If Freddy hadn't tricked him, he wouldn't have awakened to the hoot of an owl and breathed cool morning air, a mixture of evergreen and charred cedar smoke that stirred him more than the most exotic perfume sold on Fifth Avenue. He wanted a piece of this land, the right to gaze up at a sky so clear it hurt his eyes, to sit by a smoldering camp fire and watch the pink glow of dawn creep over the valley, his valley. And Joe's, of course. Maybe even Lavette's.

They would sell the True Love eventually because it would be stupid not to. But maybe he'd use the money to buy another piece of the West and play the game all over again.

The owl hooted again. Ry looked up through the twisted branches of a cedar and saw the almond glow

of a pair of eyes. For a few seconds, he met the owl's un-
blinking gaze. Then, with a heavy flap of wings, the
bird lifted above the treeline and soared out over the
valley.

"Are you superstitious?"

Ry glanced across the dying fire and saw Freddy lying on her bedroll watching him. "No."

"Some people think owls are a bad omen."

"Too bad for the owls."

"Have you heard about the curse on the True Love?"

He groaned. "Is this phase two of Get the Greenhorn?"

"I suppose you could say that. But if you're considering buying the place, you should know about all the
skeletons in the closet, don't you think?"

"Are you making it up as you go, or is this a genuine,
certified curse?"

She propped herself up on one elbow. "Okay, I deserved that. But the story has been told around camp
fires since Thaddeus homesteaded the ranch. Do you
want to hear it or not?"

"Guess I'd better."

Freddy lay back on her bedroll and gazed up at the
pink sky. "The story goes that a small tribe of Indians
was massacred on the site where the corrals now stand.
A unit of cavalry swept in and killed a village of un-
armed women and children when the braves were off
hunting. Afterward, when the men of the tribe returned, they put a curse on the land and said no white
man would ever profit from it."

"I'm surprised they didn't stage a little massacre of
their own."

"They tried, but the cavalry handled them easily. It
wasn't one of our finer moments in history."

Ry decided he'd keep that story away from any potential buyers, including his partners. It wasn't a pretty tale, and besides, investors became uneasy when you talked about loss of profit, even if it was connected to something as goofy as a century-old curse. "Seems to me Thaddeus knocked the heck out of that prediction."

"Not really." Freddy laced her hands behind her head, a movement that lifted and defined her breasts.

Ry noticed and chastised himself. Freddy would be his foreman, and he'd known too many businessmen who'd ruined an employer-employee relationship by bringing personal attraction into it. "I thought you said Thaddeus owned three hundred and twenty acres before he died."

"Owned is a relative term. He controlled three hundred and twenty acres, but he was in debt. That's been the story all down the line. In terms of having money left over, making what I would call a profit, nobody's done it yet."

"Not even your father?"

"Especially not my father. After my mother died, he spent more time rodeoing than running the ranch. If it hadn't been for Belinda and Dexter, who knows what would have happened to the place."

Ry heard a familiar note in her voice, the same note of frustration he'd felt when his parents divorced and his world had been torn apart. "When did she die?"

"I was fourteen, Leigh was ten."

"That's rough."

She looked over at him. "Lots of kids have it worse. At least I had a horse of my own and plenty of space to ride. Dexter let me go on the roundups, and I could ride a bronc as well as any of the hands."

"I'll bet you still can."

She grinned. "There's nothing like a good bucking horse to put life into proper perspective." Then her smile faded as she gazed at him. "The True Love is great for making you forget your troubles, but I wouldn't say it's a financial gold mine. That's why Westridge is selling, and all they're after is what they put into it. I could get in trouble for telling you that, but I could get in trouble for this whole stunt, I suppose."

"You're right, you could," he said with a straight face. "You should never have admitted a thing, Miss Singleton. I probably have the power to get you fired."

She didn't flinch. He imagined she wore the same look that gunslingers used in the Old West to face down their opponents. "I reckon you have that power," she said evenly. "And probably the right, too."

"You're a fearless woman, Freddy Singleton."

A corner of her mouth turned up. "Just what I wanted you to think."

Damn, but he liked her. "I won't turn you in. For one thing, it's no secret that the property's price can be negotiated downward. I've studied the profit and loss statements. The resorts built recently in Tucson have hurt business and I know Westridge has a cash-flow problem and is eager to sell. By the way, do they know about this so-called curse?"

"No, not really. They just think the ranch is falling apart from age, which it probably is."

"Do you think it's cursed?"

She shook her head. "I'd planned to tell you I did, to help scare you off, but I think we've just had a run of bad luck."

"If it reduces the asking price, it's good luck for me. All I have to offer is enough to squeeze out Whitlock."

"I see." Her gaze hardened. "Somehow, when you're

hobbling around a camp fire without your pants, I forget that you're a shark in the business world."

She was quick. He liked that, too. "I wouldn't be name-calling after the trick you pulled on me yesterday," he said. "Shall we just agree that we're fighters, and we can both be ruthless when it comes to getting what we want?"

She studied him, seeming to take his measure as he was taking hers. "*Ruthless* is a harsh word. How about *determined?*"

"*Determined* works."

The smile she gave him, fresh as the morning, made his heart ratchet in his chest. "It's a beautiful day," she said. "The birds are singing and the sky is clear. What do you say we call a truce?"

He'd never been at war, but she did seem to perceive him as the enemy. "Okay. Truce."

BREAKFAST WAS coffee and biscuits, which Ry wolfed down with an appetite that astounded him. Somehow he pulled on his jeans and boots without help from Freddy. With luck, they wouldn't have any more intimate encounters like the one with the Bag Balm. He suspected there was some powerful chemistry at work if he could get aroused in the midst of all that pain. Once he'd looked down and seen her head practically in his lap and caught a glimpse of her supple fingers at work, the power of suggestion had made him instantly hard as a rock. Since then, he'd had stirrings in that direction, but he'd kept a rein on his imagination.

He gave her as much help as he could breaking up camp. Moving around was painful, but exercise helped work the stiffness out of his legs. They used the last of their water on the fire and smothered any remaining embers in sand. Freddy paid more attention to putting out the fire than any of the other leave-taking chores.

"No hydrants up here," she said. "Lightning starts enough fires without people adding to the danger."

"Have you had many fires?"

"More than I cared to." Freddy pointed up above the cliff face. "See that grassy area? Lightning started a fire a few years ago, wiped out all the trees on that slope. Seen from the ranch at night, it was almost pretty, with the mountain glowing like a Christmas decoration, until you realized that the decoration was destroying acres of trees, and that if the wind changed, the fire could sweep down and take the ranch."

"What can you do if the wind changes?"

Her expression clouded. "Everything possible, of course. A few times, we've hosed the perimeter when a fire came too close for comfort. But in the end, if you can't stop it, you take your animals and get out."

"Is that what happened to the old ranch house?"

"No, that was a kitchen fire, which was bad enough. A runaway brushfire is our worst nightmare."

Ry gazed down into the valley at the cluster of buildings and corrals, which seemed suddenly small and defenseless against the devastation he could imagine overtaking it. Fire protection might be an issue with developers. But then he thought of all the fires in the canyons outside Los Angeles, of the multimillion-dollar homes that had succumbed to the flames; people still clamored to live at the edge of wilderness, despite the danger.

"I guess that's about it," Freddy said, tightening the cinch of Maureen's saddle. "You're sure you don't want to ride down?"

"Mikey and I will walk. We've bonded."

Freddy laughed. "I do believe you have. Why don't you go first so I can follow and keep an eye on his hind leg?"

"Sure." Holding Mikey's bridle, Ry surveyed the camp one last time. He was reluctant to leave because he knew the walk would be uncomfortable, but that wasn't the only reason.

Freddy settled herself in the saddle and gathered her reins. "Listen, I could still ride down leading Mikey and send a helicopter back up for you," she said. "Nobody would think the worse of you for it, Ry."

"Oh, no?" He grinned and shoved his hat to the back of his head as he gazed up at her. "Can you picture Duane and Curtis watching that helicopter coming in without their making a few choice comments about the dude from New York who thought he could ride a horse?"

"They'd never say anything to your face."

"What a comfort that would be."

"So, shall I send a chopper?"

"No, you shall not. I can make it. I was stalling because...because to tell the truth, I'm sorry the whole thing is over. I had a great time."

Her laughter bounced against the rocky cliff and echoed out into the valley. "The ride crippled you, you smell like a landfill, the horses kept you up all night and you have to walk several miles down a rocky trail to get back home. If this is what you consider a great time, I suggest you get a life," she said, her hazel eyes dancing.

He smiled at her. "I was thinking the same thing." Then he turned and wrapped the end of the reins around his fist. "Come on, Mikey," he said to the horse as they started out of camp. "Let's show the women what grit is all about."

FOLLOWING BEHIND the battered twosome was its own kind of punishment, Freddy decided. The boots Ry had borrowed were made for riding, for occasional dancing, but not for walking down a mountain path. The smooth soles slipped on loose shale, and the heels tilted him forward, sabotaging his balance even more.

A mile down the trail, she called a halt and offered to trade. He wouldn't do it. She was forced to continue behind him and watch the stain of sweat widen across the back of his shirt. She knew he must be thirsty; she certainly was. But they wouldn't be able to drink until they reached the pond, which would take another hour.

He had every right to hate her. If he complained to Westridge and asked for her resignation as a condition of the sale, she couldn't blame him. But the hell of it was, she knew he didn't hate her and wouldn't get her fired. She'd thrown torture after torture at him, and he had the nerve to announce he'd had a great time. Talk about knowing how to hurt a girl!

Ry had his head down watching the trail for loose stones, and Freddy was concentrating so hard on Ry and Mikey that she didn't hear a horse approaching until the little party rounded a bend and Ry came face-to-face with Eb Whitlock's big palomino. Ry stumbled and nearly went down, but he grabbed a bush and kept himself and Mikey steady. Freddy was grateful he'd reached for a smooth-barked manzanita instead of the prickly pear next to it.

"What do we have here?" Eb boomed, reining in Gold Strike.

Freddy smiled. "Eb! What luck. Do you have water?"

"I reckon you need a sight more than water. Your friend looks like he's been rode hard and put away wet."

"I'm okay." Ry pushed his hat to the back of his head and gazed with apparent interest at the man on the palomino. As usual, Eb was decked out in a belt buckle big as a dinner plate and a bolo tie heavy with turquoise.

Freddy realized introductions were in order, although the grapevine had probably already supplied Eb with the identity of the man in front of him. "Eb Whitlock, I'd like you to meet Ry McGuinnes, from New York City."

"Figured as much." Eb handed over his canteen. "Have a drink on me, McGuinnes. Sorry I can't hail you a cab. You look like you could use one." He laughed at his joke, flashing teeth arranged as perfectly as piano keys.

Ry accepted the canteen with a friendly smile. "No problem. Could you hold on to Mikey for a minute?" he thrust the reins into Eb's hand without waiting for a reply, walked over to Freddy and held out the canteen. "Compliments of the man on the very big horse."

Freddy swallowed a burst of laughter. Eb had always ridden huge geldings. Leigh used to say he'd show up on a Clydesdale one of these days. "Thank you," she said, her voice quivering with humor as she met Ry's gaze and accepted the canteen. She could hardly refuse such a gallant gesture, although she was sure Ry needed water more than she did. After one quick gulp, she passed the canteen to him without bothering to wipe the mouth of the jug.

There was a brief flash of awareness in his eyes, as if he'd noticed her omission, before he lifted the canteen to his lips and drank greedily.

She admired the way the trail had toughened his appearance. His cheeks were stubbled with a day's growth of beard and his face had acquired the healthy bronze color of an outdoorsman.

"What happened to Mikey?" Eb asked, breaking into Freddy's absorption in Ry.

"We're not sure," she replied. "Maybe a broken branch or a sharp section of boulder got him."

"Somebody said they saw a big cat up there not long ago."

"If that's what it was, we didn't see it," Freddy said. "We're just lucky Mikey didn't cut himself up any worse."

"I thought I heard a horse scream up here last night," Eb said. "Then this morning, I remembered Curtis or somebody telling me you'd taken the prospective buyer up here, so I decided to investigate, make sure you were okay."

How typical of him, Freddy thought. "You're a good neighbor, Eb."

Eb touched the brim of his hat in a subtle salute. "I try to be, even if it means baby-sitting my competition."

Ry took the canteen from his lips.

"After all, we've known each other for a long time, Freddy," Eb continued. "Why, I remember—"

"Excuse me, but does anybody else want some more water?" Ry asked. "Freddy? Did you get enough?"

"I'm fine." She was amused and somewhat grateful that Ry had broken into Eb's story. Eb was a conscientious neighbor, but he had a tendency to wax nostalgic a little too often.

"Well, then, let's take care of our wounded patient," Ry said. "I believe this is how they do it in the movies." Taking off his hat, he walked up to Mikey and poured the rest of the water into the upended crown of the hat before offering it to the horse. Mikey tossed his head and rolled his eyes. "Come on, Mikey," Ry coaxed, wiggling the hat to make the water slosh inside. "Didn't you ever watch 'Gunsmoke' in reruns?"

Freddy laughed. Ry had just splashed water into a ninety dollar hat, but it probably needed some seasoning anyway. "You have the wrong horse. He's a 'Seinfield' fan."

"Just my luck." Ry adopted a New York City accent. "Try it, Mikey. You'll like it."

The horse snorted and stuck his nose into the hat to suck the water in noisy swallows while Ry exchanged a grin with Freddy.

Eb glanced around and looked impatient. "Tell you what, McGuinnes. You can climb on behind me and I'll lead Mikey down the trail."

"Oh, I couldn't do that, Whitlock." Ry kept his attention on Mikey. "Thanks, anyway."

"Why not? Gold Strike can carry both of us. Hell, he could probably carry a knight in full armor."

"Probably, but I just wouldn't feel right about it." He clamped the dripping hat on his head and handed Eb the empty canteen. "I'll walk with Mikey, if it's all the same to you."

Freddy bit her lip to hide a smile. She figured Ry was telling the literal truth. He'd no more be able to hoist himself up on Gold Strike and spread his legs over that broad back than fly to the moon on gossamer wings.

"Suit yourself." Eb wheeled his big horse, stirring up a cloud of dust that made Ry choke. "By the way," Eb called over his shoulder as he started down the trail, "how do you like the True Love?"

"Love it," Ry called back.

Eb flashed his large teeth again. "Too bad. Oh well, welcome to the neighborhood."

"Thanks, Eb," Freddy called after him. Then she glanced down at Ry. "There you have a real Western gentleman. He wants the True Love so bad he can taste it, but when he finds out you'll probably buy it out from under him, he greets you as his new neighbor."

Ry wiped the grit from his face with the back of his sleeve. "And you could barely tell he hates my guts. What a guy."

"Hates you? I hardly think so! Just because you're both after the same piece of property doesn't mean he takes that personally."

"Oh, it's not just the True Love he's after." Ry wiggled his eyebrows. "He'd like to slap a brand on you, little filly."

"That's ridiculous." She laughed to cover her flush of embarrassment. Leigh had warned her about the same thing, but Eb was old enough to be her father. She wanted to believe his goodwill was motivated by nothing more than neighborly concern. "He's never even asked me to dinner."

"He doesn't have to. He's your neighbor. And he was hoping to buy your ranch. That would put him in a pretty sweet spot, being your boss and all."

Freddy looked away from his penetrating gaze. "You're making some big assumptions on very little evidence."

"I'm sure it seems that way, but I make my living playing hunches. I make a pretty good living, so I've learned to follow my instincts. Trust me, Whitlock hated me on sight, first because I threaten his acquisition of the ranch, and second because he perceives me as a possible threat to his acquisition of you."

Heat swept over her. "Why would he think that?"

"Easy. I just spent the night alone with you, which I'm guessing is more than he's ever done."

"It was only a trail ride!" Not strictly true, she thought. She'd helped him off with his pants and massaged his bare thighs until he became sexually aroused.

"Whitlock isn't so sure." He peered up at her. "Come to think of it, neither am I."

Freddy took a deep breath. "Believe me, when I planned this, I had no intention of—"

"I know. Neither of us could have known." He gave her a long, assessing look. "As I said, I thought you were a man."

"And I thought you were a big-shot businessman."

"That's exactly what I am."

She shook her head. "You're far more than that," she said softly.

"Thank you."

"You've earned it."

He held her gaze for a moment. "You know I'm going to buy the ranch."

"I know."

"Which will make me your boss."

Her heart beat a quick rhythm. "I know that, too."

The fire in his eyes was a controlled blaze. "I've seen personal involvement ruin a lot of business relationships."

"With your experience, I'm sure you have." Her mouth was as dry as the desert floor. "And I want to be the foreman of the True Love for a very long time."

"Then I guess we put our personal feelings on hold."

"Yes, I guess we do."

6

BY THE TIME they reached the pond, Ry's troubles had shifted from his thighs to his feet. He could see no point in toughing it out for the sake of vanity—Freddy had witnessed one of the more vulnerable moments of his life when she'd applied the Bag Balm to his thighs. So when they reached the water, he tethered Mikey and leaned against the tree to pull off his boots.

"Now you understand why cowboys ride instead of walk," Freddy said.

"I do indeed." Without rolling up the stiff cuffs of his jeans, he waded straight into the water. "Good God!" The icy water immediately numbed his feet, and although he tried to grip the algae-covered rocks with his toes, they refused to cooperate. Arms flailing, he landed on his tender rear. On impact, his hat sailed into the water and he grabbed it just before it floated away like a child's toy boat. He slapped the dripping hat on his head and sat there, too disgusted to move.

Freddy dismounted and sauntered over to the pond. "How's the water?"

She was a real smart aleck, he thought. As he sat and fumed, a plot formed in his mind, a plot born of twelve hours of the most extreme discomfort he had ever remembered. Now his butt was numb, which wasn't all bad, but he'd never immersed his body in such cold water in his life. She'd seen what he was about to do. She could have warned him. Now it was payback time.

"Ry?"

From the corner of his eye, he saw her step closer.

"Are you okay?"

The sudden lunge was excruciatingly painful, but worth it. On the football field, his unsportsmanlike tackle would have earned him a flag, but this wasn't a sanctioned game. In two seconds, Freddy was splashing and sputtering next to him in the water.

"Ry McGuinnes, that was the nastiest, meanest—" She started to struggle to her feet and he grabbed her arm to jerk her back down.

"Leaving so soon, Miss Singleton?" He looked her over and noted with satisfaction that her jeans and shirt were soaked. Her hat had flipped backward onto the embankment and water dripped from the ends of her hair. He held her wrist in an iron grip. "The water isn't too *cold* for you, is it? Since you failed to warn me about it, I assumed you'd want to join me in a little swim."

She glared at him. "My boots will be ruined. And I thought you were a gentleman."

"And I thought you were a lady. A lady would have cautioned me about the cold water and the slippery rocks. A lady wouldn't have taunted me once I fell in." He'd begun to notice something else. Beneath the soaked front of her blouse, her nipples shoved against the material in protest against the chill. Now that he'd given in to the need for revenge, other needs began asserting themselves, as if they'd only required the merest crack in his armor of self-control to slip through.

"I'm only trying to save my ranch!" she protested, her chest heaving.

This dunking was either a very good idea or a very

bad one, he thought, longing to unfasten the snaps of her shirt. He looked into her eyes. "And I'm only trying to save my hide," he said pleasantly. She had such beautiful eyes, the same dusky color as the sagebrush growing along the trail.

"Why don't you just give up?" she cried.

"Why don't you?" He studied her expressive mouth. The water was cold as a snowbank, but her mouth would be warm...so warm.

"What do you need this ranch for?" Her eyes misted, dew on sage. "Can't you go buy some more pork bellies or something and be just as happy?"

"Not anymore." He reached up and grazed her lower lip with his knuckle. Had she flinched, he would have released her and climbed out of the water. But she didn't flinch. Instead, her pupils widened in awareness. He sucked in a breath. "Instead of discouraging me, your behavior has only made me more determined," he said.

Her lashes swept down and pink tinged her cheeks. "To buy the ranch?"

He paused, allowing time for her imagination to work. "That's what we're talking about, isn't it?"

"Of course." She said it too softly for the words to carry any conviction. "Anything else would be a mistake. We already settled that."

"Yes, we did." He slid his damp hand behind her neck and she shivered, but whether from the chill or from anticipation, he couldn't know. "But I thought you weren't going to sabotage me anymore, either."

"That wasn't really sabotage."

"No?"

Her gaze reconnected with his and the turmoil in her

eyes betrayed her inner struggle. "Some things just happen."

"So I'm discovering." He guided her closer, watching the battle rage until at last her lashes fluttered down in partial surrender.

Their breath mingled for a long moment as he hesitated. Logic tried for a foothold in his brain and failed. He had to taste her. With the first brush of his lips, her breath hitched, and he knew she was strung as tight as he. Misgivings assaulted him, but the velvet promise of her mouth beckoned. He skimmed over her lips once again and his heart lurched when he discovered them parted in welcome.

Had he imagined anything less from this woman? With a groan, he settled his mouth firmly against hers. And was lost. Her warmth rose to meet him; her passion ignited in concert with his. Her vibrant spirit had led him through hell. Now she offered heaven.

And he took—greedily, angrily, venting hours of frustration with his lips and tongue. She gave without restraint, matching his assault with one of her own. Water sluiced between them as he pulled her close. They might have been naked from the waist up, so drenched were their shirts. His heart pounded as her breasts cushioned the tautness of his chest and he could feel the distinct imprint of her nipples. She wound her arms around his back, pressing, kneading, wanting. Desire defied the icy water as heat spread through him, warming his groin, his thighs, his calves, nibbling on his toes. *Nibbling on his toes?*

He lifted his mouth a fraction. "Do you feel that?"

"Yes." She pressed against him. "Don't stop."

"On your toes?"

"Down to my toes," she agreed, her tone impatient. "Don't talk. Just kiss me like that again."

The rubble came again. "Not *down* to your toes, *on* your toes."

She drew back and frowned. "I have on boots. Two-hundred-dollar boots that may never be the same after this. What are you talking about?"

Ry released her and scrambled to his feet. "Your father's blessed bass! Is every damn thing in this country booby-trapped?"

She sat and stared at him as the sensual haze cleared from her expression and her jaw clenched. "Yes! Yes, it is!" She struggled out of the water, her boots squishing. "Especially to people who don't know the territory. Get that through your thick Yankee head, will you? You don't belong here!"

She'd probably never forgive him for that kiss, he thought. And worse, she'd never forgive herself. He grabbed his boots. "We'll see about that. And by the way, I'm borrowing Maureen for the rest of the trip. This cowboy has walked his last mile."

THEY DIDN'T SPEAK again after that. Which was just as well, Freddy thought as she trudged heavily down the trail toward the ranch's corrals, the wet leather of her boots complaining with every step. Why in heaven's name had she let him kiss her? They could have eventually forgotten about the incident with the Bag Balm, but a kiss was never forgotten. Especially a kiss like that, one that probed deep into the secret canyons of desire they'd kept hidden from each other until now. She was doomed.

Duane was giving a beginning riding lesson in the main corral when they approached. Two men, a woman and two children turned to stare as Freddy led Mikey over to the large metal watering trough. Duane glanced in their direction, pulled his hat lower over his eyes and continued with the lesson. At least he hadn't laughed out loud, and for that she decided to give him a bonus at pay time. If her new bosses would allow it, she thought with a wave of bitterness.

She imagined what she must look like. Eager to end this disastrous trail ride, she'd started down the mountain with her clothes and boots still wet. Along the way, she and Mikey had stirred up the dry dust of the trail, which had caked onto her wet clothes and dried, until she probably looked like an adobe version of a cowgirl.

She held Mikey's reins loosely while he drank. At last, unable to bear the suspense, she flicked a glance back to see if Ry was coming.

He was, slow but sure. Outwardly, he looked better than she did, because he'd at least been riding above the clouds of dust. But the grim set of his mouth told her he wasn't in as good shape as he looked. He walked Maureen over to the trough and let her drink while he stayed in the saddle. Freddy waited for him to climb down. It wasn't nice to stand there waiting for his groan of pain when he dismounted, but in her present frame of mind, she no longer cared about nice. Ry didn't budge.

"Aren't you getting down?" she said at last, unable to contain her curiosity.

He stared straight ahead. "Nope."

"Why not?"

"I think my butt's welded to the saddle."

She bit the inside of her lip to control a chuckle. "I see. Want me to get Duane to help you off?" She figured that would light a fire under him.

It did. He wasn't far wrong about being welded in, though. Moisture, heat and dust had formed something similar to glue between denim and leather. His backside came out of the saddle with a sound like a cow pulling its hoof out of the mud.

Freddy's laughter broke through. She couldn't help it. She'd probably be fired before the day was out, anyway. And once she started laughing, she couldn't stop. She laughed until tears streamed down her mud-caked cheeks.

Ry's bowlegged hobble as he walked over to her made her laugh even harder.

"Think it's pretty funny, do you?" he asked.

She nodded, too overcome with giggles to speak.

He stood there, legs spread and hands on his hips while she gasped and tried to regain her composure, only to have a new fit of hysterics overtake her.

Duane rode over to the edge of the corral. "You got a problem over there?" he called.

"I think she's having a fit," Ry said. "Any suggestions?"

"Nope. Never seen her get like that."

Freddy laughed even harder.

"Only one thing for it," Ry said, coming toward her with his bowlegged swagger.

"Now, Ry," she said, starting to hiccup as she backed away from him.

"This always works in the movies."

He was surprisingly quick, considering his condition. She whooped in protest as he threw her over his shoulder like a sack of feed.

"Put me down!" she screamed, kicking and struggling. But it was too late. Water splashed over her head as he dumped her in the horse trough. After the first shock, it felt surprisingly good and not half as cold as the snow-fed pond. She came up for air slowly and pushed her hair out of her face to find several sets of eyes, including Mikey's and Maureen's, focused on her. The guests seemed fascinated, but Duane looked terrified. He'd never seen anyone toss his foreman in the horse trough before, and he obviously expected all hell to break loose.

Then she glanced at Ry, who was regarding her with his arms crossed over his chest and his gaze enigmatic. She wanted to strangle him for making a spectacle of her. She longed to lash out at him for being a bully and a cad. But the cool water had brought her to her senses. A man who would toss her in the horse trough certainly had enough moxie to clinch a deal on the ranch. That meant he would soon hold her fate in the palm of his hand. And staying on the ranch had always been, and continued to be, the most important thing in the world to her.

She met his gaze. "Thanks," she said sweetly. "I needed that." Then she climbed out of the trough with as much dignity as she could manage, considering she was a walking waterfall. One boot stayed in the trough and she had to fish it out. She poured the water onto the ground, put the boot on and took the other off to repeat the process. Then she reached for her hat floating on the surface of the water and settled it on her head. Water drizzled down her face as if she were standing in the shower. She blew the drops away. "If you'll please unsaddle the horses, I'll go up to the house and change into something dry so I can tend Mikey's wound."

"Be glad to," he said amiably, his blue eyes dancing. There was something deeper burning there, too, something that might have been admiration.

Freddy glanced over to Duane. "Can I borrow your truck?"

"Keys are on the floor," Duane said, looking totally amazed. "Need any help?"

"Not at the moment." Back straight and leaving a dribbling trail of water in the dust, she marched over to Duane's old truck and climbed in.

EAGER TO CALL Joe Gilardini, Ry put off his Jacuzzi and took a quick shower before changing into khaki slacks and a white cotton shirt with the sleeves rolled to the elbow. As physically miserable as he'd been wearing Curtis's and Duane's cowboy garb, he already missed it.

A light snack had been waiting in his room when he'd arrived, probably ordered up by Freddy. She'd apparently had an attitude adjustment since her baptism in the horse trough. Much as he didn't want a continual fight on his hands, he would miss her fiery belligerence.

He ate his food and rehearsed his pitch for bringing Joe into the partnership. Going by the rough figures Joe had given him on the money in his pension fund, the deal could be finalized with that and with what Ry could raise. Lavette would make things easier all the way around, but Joe was the critical part of the transaction.

Yet Joe hadn't been willing to commit himself before Ry had left Manhattan. Over drinks at Joe's favorite bar, the cop had told Ry that yes, he was definitely quitting the force, but no, he wasn't sure a guest ranch was the place to put his retirement money. All he'd promised was that he'd have exact figures on his pension the next time they talked. No promises, no commitment to invest the pension, but he would have the figures.

So this was it. If Joe wouldn't go for the deal, Ry would have to start through his list of contacts until he found someone who'd put up the money. And he'd have to do it fast, before Westridge became tired of waiting and accepted Whitlock's puny offer. In the past twenty-four hours, that possibility had become unacceptable to Ry.

Clearing the tension from his throat, he picked up the receiver of the phone on his bedside table and dialed an outside line. Then he sat on the bed, an antique four-poster, while he punched in Joe's number. As the exchanges clicked through, he gazed out the window. His room was at the corner of the house, with one window facing the mountains and the other looking out on the wide front porch. Holding the receiver to his ear, he walked over to the porch window and leaned against the wall to look out. At the far end of the porch, sitting on one of several old cane-bottomed chairs, was Dexter Grimes, his walker positioned to one side of his chair. Next to him sat Leigh Singleton. A long-haired black-and-white dog rested at their feet, completing the Norman Rockwell portrait.

The line rang, and Joe answered quickly.

"Joe, this is Ry—T. R. McGuinnes. Have you got those figures?"

"Sure." Joe sounded impatient. "But first tell me what the ranch is like."

Ry closed his eyes with relief. He had no idea what had changed Joe's thinking, but from the tone of his voice, the cop was hooked. For the next ten minutes, Ry described the ranch house, the corrals, the horses and the ranch hands, but didn't discuss the True Love curse. He mentioned the John Wayne Room but omitted anything about spiders and scorpions. He described the reservoir stocked with bass but didn't add the story of his personal experience with the fish.

"Have you been out riding?" Joe asked.

"Some," Ry said with a grimace. "There's a beautiful spot above Rogue Canyon where you can see the whole valley."

"Sounds great, just great. What's this guy Freddy Singleton like? Think we can work with him?"

A picture of Freddy coming up out of the horse trough like Venus rising from the sea made Ry smile. "Freddy's a woman," he said. *Is she ever.*

"No joke? Probably one of those leathery old ranch gals, full of vinegar."

His fingers still remembered the softness of her cheek, and his mouth retained the rich taste of her lips. "She's full of vinegar, all right. But she's not what I'd call leathery."

There was a pause on the other end. "Are you telling me that Freddy the foreman is a babe?"

"I wouldn't let her hear you say that, if I were you."

"McGuinnes, you must be the luckiest s.o.b. on the face of the earth. It's not enough that you're out there in God's country. You've stumbled on a ranch with a beautiful woman as its foreman. I suppose she's married, though, probably to the head wrangler or somebody like that."

"No, the head wrangler is her sister, Leigh."

There was a short bark of laughter. "You're putting me on. This is beginning to sound like a fantasy beer commercial."

"Nope. The Singleton women are very real."

"I'm calling Lavette. This'll settle it for him."

"Look, Joe, the women don't have anything to do

with anything. If we buy this place, we'll be their employers. We can't—"

"Yeah, yeah, I know. Still, it beats the heck out of dealing with some grizzled old cowpoke, wouldn't you say?"

Ry thought of all Freddy had put him through and wasn't so sure. A grizzled old cowpoke would have simplified this deal considerably. "I suppose," he agreed, mostly to get off the subject. "We have to start putting this offer together if we want to beat out the neighbor who has already made a lowball bid. Can you give me those pension figures now?"

"You bet. Got them right here." Joe read off the amounts and the method of payment.

Cradling the receiver against his shoulder, Ry scribbled the information on a notepad beside the phone. If they closed the deal in thirty days, Joe would have his pay for unused sick leave and vacation by then. Ry could borrow the rest, with Joe making payments out of his monthly pension checks, but a contribution from the trucker would help a lot in the beginning.

"Have you talked with Lavette recently?" Ry asked.

"Yesterday. The doctors can't guarantee he'll be able to continue his trucking career, and the insurance company wants to settle for a lump sum. Personally, I think he should take the money and run. I'll go see him and fill him in on the ranch details. Maybe that'll help him get off the dime."

"Good idea." Ry walked the length of the telephone cord. "Tell me, why are you so gung ho all of a sudden?"

His question was met with silence.

"Hey, if it's too personal, forget it. I'm glad you're on board."

"It's my kid," Joe said, his tone reluctant. "My ex-wife and her new husband are turning him into a pansy."

Ry struggled to connect this information to Joe's decision to go in on the ranch. "And...?"

"And I figure if I bring him out to the ranch, I can toughen him up some."

Ry bit back his laughter. "No doubt. Just turn him over to Freddy Singleton."

"I mean, he's not a complete weenie yet. He's only seven, but I can see where he's headed and I figure it's up to me to turn him around."

Ry decided to play devil's advocate, to make sure Joe was nailed down tight. "But you wouldn't have to buy the place. You could just pay for a week or two as a guest."

"It wouldn't be the same. If Kyle thinks of me as part owner of the spread, I think I have a better chance."

The spread. Ry loved it. Joe was nailed down, all right. Welcome to the Ponderosa, Joe Gilardini. "You may have a point."

"And it's a good investment, right? We'll make a lot of money when we sell it?"

"I don't see how we can lose, Joe."

7

AFTER RY FINISHED his phone call, he felt restless. He couldn't start negotiating with the bankers until morning, although he itched to start putting the deal together. He called his lawyer about drawing up a partnership agreement, but he'd left the office and Ry decided not to bother him at home.

By consulting an activities schedule left on his pine dresser, he discovered dinner didn't begin until six. He had a couple of hours to kill. He walked back into the main room of the ranch house, which was deserted, and surveyed the pool and Jacuzzi. Both were busy. He decided to postpone his soak until evening, when it was more likely nobody would be around.

Then he headed for the front porch, thinking he might take a walk down to the stables and check on Mikey. Everyone else around here drove between the house and the stables, but the distance wasn't any longer than between his office on Wall Street and Battery Park, where he sometimes walked on his lunch break to enjoy the sweep of the harbor and a view of the Statue of Liberty.

"Mr. McGuinnes," a woman called.

He turned.

Leigh Singleton still sat on the far end of the porch. Dexter and his walker were gone, but the dog remained, curled across her feet. "Need a lift somewhere?" she asked.

He walked back in her direction. "Not really. I was headed down to the corrals. I can walk that."

"I'm sure you can," she said with an easy smile. She wore her honey-colored hair caught back in a clip, as Freddy did. Her faded jeans and work shirt spoke of practicality, but she wore silver hoop earrings decorated with an intricate design. A small turquoise feather dangled from each hoop. And her eyes, golden brown and almond-shaped, seemed exceedingly wise for a woman as young as Leigh. "I would have thought you'd had enough exercise for a while," she added.

He flushed. "I'm a little tougher than you and your sister give me credit for."

"Apparently. But if you were hoping to see Freddy down at the corrals, she's not there. After she doctored Mikey, she rode out to check on one of the stock tanks which seems to be leaking."

Of course he'd hoped to see Freddy, he admitted to himself. "I wasn't going down to see her, specifically."

"I—"

Leigh waved a hand, cutting off his protest. "Any man who spent twenty-four hours with my sister and *wasn't* interested in her would have something wrong with him, don't you think?"

"Depends on whether he's a masochist."

She chuckled. "Freddy's not usually like that. You've threatened her very existence. *Our* very existence, to be exact. Do you blame her for fighting back?"

"I'll probably feel a lot more charitable when my backside returns to normal."

"Yet you were headed down to the corrals because you thought she might be there, doctoring Mikey."

He opened his mouth to deny it, but the all-knowing look in Leigh's eyes made him close it again.

"Care to sit a spell, Mr. McGuinnes?"

"Ry," he said, stepping up on the wooden porch and crossing to the chair next to her.

The dog raised his head, but at a word from Leigh it settled back down. "Ry?" Leigh asked, frowning. "I thought you went by initials. J.R., or TWA, or something."

"Cute. It's T.R."

"I was close. So why the change?"

Then Freddy hadn't told her everything, he thought, gratified. Of course, Freddy might not want anyone to know all the intimate details of their outing. Unless she was a liar, which he sensed she wasn't, she'd have to admit he'd kissed her. Brutal honesty would have required her to add that she'd enjoyed it. "Your sister suggested calling me Ry," he said. "She thought T.R. sounded stuffy."

"Did she?" Leigh gave him an assessing look. "Sounds as if Freddy is somewhat interested, as well. She doesn't assign nicknames to people she doesn't like."

Ry glanced away, afraid those knowing eyes would read too many things from his expression. "If the deal goes through and my partners and I buy the ranch, you and Freddy will become our employees. She and I both understand the politics of that."

Leigh chuckled. "Loosen up, Ry. Out here on the ranch, we don't worry about office politics. People are people. Besides, you don't strike me as the kind who would fire an employee because a love affair didn't work out."

"No, I wouldn't. But she might quit."

"She wouldn't leave the True Love over something like that. But suit yourself. Lord knows, I'm not trying to talk you into anything. I'm glad you decided to take the name she slapped on you, though."

He shrugged and stretched out his legs. The gesture hurt like hell, but he was working hard to appear nonchalant. "No big deal." He wished he had on denim and boots. Out here in the West, denim and boots seemed to telegraph nonchalance much faster than khakis and deck shoes. "I'm pretty burned out with the big-city routine. The new name felt right." He looked over at her. "This ranch feels right."

"You're not the first person to think so. The True Love has been welcoming people home for generations."

Ry straightened in his chair. "That's going a bit further than I intended. I'm just talking about a change of pace. Nothing permanent."

"Oh, I see." She sat quietly, gazing out across the sparse crop of grass.

"What are those earrings supposed to be?" he asked. "They look like a special design."

She reached up to finger one of the silver hoops. "They're called dream catchers. Indian legend has it that the web keeps bad dreams out and lets good ones through."

"What's your take on this curse business?"

She turned those incredible almond-shaped eyes on him. "When something as terrible as that massacre happens, the land bears the mark of it, whether it was deliberately cursed or not. But I like to think the Singletons have been pumping good vibrations into the area for so many generations that the power of the curse is fading." She smiled at him. "After all, Thaddeus Singleton did name it the True Love. Think of the energy inherent in that."

"Energy in a name?" Come on, Leigh."

She gazed at him, her sense of inner calm almost palpable. "I can't believe you would doubt it...Ry."

He gazed at her as a chill ran up his spine. He'd assumed he could buy this ranch, change its name, revamp its purpose and move on, a wealthier man. Why did that assumption seem suddenly naïve?

Leigh nudged the dog from her feet and stood. "If you'll excuse me, I have to drive down to the corrals and saddle a few trail horses. We have a sunset ride scheduled tonight." She glanced down at him. "Want to come on the ride?"

"I—ah—"

She laughed. "Never mind. I was teasing you. Besides, you'd probably better stay here. Last I heard, Freddy had called Eb Whitlock and invited him to have supper in our dining room with her and the other guests, as a gesture of thanks for his coming up to check on you two this morning. You'll probably want to hang around and protect your interests."

He lifted his eyebrows.

"In the ranch, of course," she explained. Then, with a low whistle to the dog, she cut across the yard to yet another battered pickup with the ranch's brand painted on the door panel. This truck boasted an added decoration, however. Over its dark blue fender curved an iridescent rainbow.

FREDDY TOLD HERSELF she'd invited Eb out of courtesy. After all, he had gone out of his way this morning to make sure she was okay. But her pride still smarted from that dunking in the horse trough. She wasn't above needling Ry a little with Eb's presence at her dinner table.

With only eleven guests in residence and five of them out on a sunset trail ride and barbecue, the dining room seemed almost empty. The six remaining guests had all been at the ranch for a week and had become friends, so they commandeered one of the longer pine tables. Freddy ushered Eb to a table set for four with the traditional True Love heart-shaped place mats in red-and-white checks, red napkins and tin plates enameled in red with white flecks.

"I see you've kept the traditions alive," Eb commented, pulling out a chair for Freddy.

"With difficulty." Freddy kept glancing at the door to see if Ry would appear for dinner. "This tinware isn't easy to find anymore."

Eb leaned forward as he pushed her chair closer to the table, and she could feel his breath on her bare shoulders. Her blouse, one Leigh had talked her into buying, had "cold-shoulder" cutouts. The blouse, along with a tiered denim skirt, was her newest outfit, and she'd swept her hair on top of her head and added silver concho earrings. She hadn't been this dressed up in weeks. But a woman who had last appeared climbing from a horse trough had to think of her image.

Of course, Ry might skip dinner. At this moment, he could easily be sound asleep in his room. At least he wasn't in the Jacuzzi—she'd checked.

"I *said*, this sure brings back memories," Eb said, a little too loudly and with a trace of impatience.

Freddy realized she hadn't heard him the first time. "Yes, it does." She smiled at Eb, who had seated himself at right angles to her. "Sorry I haven't had you over sooner, but..."

"Never mind. I know you've had troubles. Seems like all sorts of things have been going wrong."

Although he hadn't touched her, Freddy felt crowded. She'd never realized how Eb seemed to gobble space. "Just a little bad luck is all, Eb."

Manny, one of only two waiters they kept on during the summer months, came by the table with a trayful of salad plates. "Just the two of you at this table, Miss Singleton?"

Freddy sincerely hoped not. She'd invited Eb as a little dig at Ry, but now she was in danger of spending the meal alone with her silver-haired neighbor. Both Leigh's and Ry's assessments of Eb had been weighing on her mind. "I'm not sure, Manny. Why don't you leave another salad, just in case?"

Eb glanced at her. "Isn't Leigh out on a sunset trail ride?"

"Yes."

His expression of goodwill dimmed. "Then I guess you must be expecting your prospective buyer," he said. "Before he arrives, we need to talk. I was hoping your trail ride would discourage him."

"So was I, but he doesn't discourage easily."

Manny put salads in front of both of them. "Where would you like the third one?" he asked.

Eb patted the place mat beside him at the same moment Freddy pointed to the seat next to her. Manny paused as he looked from Eb to Freddy.

"Here, I'll take that from you," Ry said, sitting down next to Freddy. "You look lovely tonight," he murmured to her.

"Thank you." The compliment filled her with pleasure, far too much pleasure for her own good.

"So, McGuinnes, you survived," Eb said.

"So I did. How are you doing, Whitlock?" He reached across the table to shake Eb's hand. "How's Gold Digger?"

"Gold Strike," Eb corrected.

"Oh, yeah." Ry grinned. "You'll have to forgive me. I'm new around here."

"So I noticed. I was wondering how you found your way to the table without a maître d'." Eb gave Ry a wide smile that looked totally insincere.

"We city dwellers learn to be resourceful. I just followed the light flashing off your bolo tie, Eb. May I call you Eb? I'll bet you need a winch to hoist that hunk of silver over your head every morning."

Eb's smile disappeared. "I'm surprised to see you up and about, McGuinnes, much less cracking jokes."

"Yeah, me, too." Ry hoisted his water glass in Freddy's direction. "To the power of...youth."

Freddy knew she shouldn't be enjoying this, but Eb was always so darn full of himself that it was fun to watch someone pricking his balloon of self-importance. In the next moment, she felt guilty. During her father's illness, Eb had almost made a pest of himself with offers to help out. Once, he'd graded the road to the ranch without asking and another time he'd rounded up several of her strays who'd wandered through a break in the fence, returned the cattle and mended the fence. Freddy had been grateful, but Leigh had contended he was building up points toward some future goal.

"I suppose Freddy's told you about the curse on this place," Eb said between bites of salad.

"She has. Fortunately, I'm not a superstitious man."

Freddy glanced at Eb in surprise. "You don't believe in the True Love curse, do you?"

"I didn't used to." Eb pushed away his empty salad

plate. "But consider the run of bad luck you've had recently, Freddy. First your father's cancer. Then you were forced to sell to this big-shot corporation, but the place still hasn't turned a profit. Maybe there's something to that curse business. Even a relatively minor thing like Mikey getting cut up, or your stock tank springing a leak. And remember, too, that calf was stillborn, and pack rats chewed the wiring in two of your trucks."

"Pack rats and stock-tank leaks are just part of living out here in the desert, Eb," Freddy said, irritated by his catalog of mishaps.

"Don't happen that much to me." Eb leaned back in his chair and puffed out his chest.

Or you keep quiet if they do, Freddy thought, and felt uncharitable for thinking it.

Manny replaced the salad plates with servings of T-bone, baked potatoes and beans.

Ry picked up his steak knife. "If I didn't know better, Whitlock, I'd say you're trying to scare me off so you can buy this place for a song. Not that I blame you," he added, cutting into his steak. "Any good businessman would try the same thing."

"Oh, I'm no businessman," Eb said, with a sly nudge of Freddy's knee under the table. "I'm just a rancher."

Freddy felt like a dope. Of course Eb was trying to discourage Ry with all this talk of the ranch's curse. In his typical heavy-handed way, he was trying to help. And she would prefer that Eb buy the place, wouldn't she?"

Manny returned to the table. "Excuse me, but there's a call for Mr. McGuinness."

Ry looked up, his expression alight with anticipation. He turned to Freddy. "Where can I take it?"

"You can go in my office. Just head straight across the main room. The door's open."

After Ry left, Eb heaved a sigh. "I do hate city slickers. I'm surprised he didn't whip out one of those cellular jobs."

"Eb, I thought you just bought one of those things?"

Eb looked uncomfortable. "Okay, I did, but it's just to take out on the range. You should get one, too. It used to be safe for women to ride around this country alone, but not anymore..." He peered in the direction Ry had taken. "Any type of idiot could be out there."

"He's turned out to have spunk, Eb," Freddy said. "I know he's a greenhorn, but he took that trail ride like a man."

Eb gave her a sharp look. "You changing your mind about city guys buying the place?"

"No, not really. Westridge was bad enough, but at least they left me in charge. I have the distinct impression these men wouldn't do that."

"Bet your bottom dollar on it. This McGuinnes is a real wheeler-dealer. He—" Eb didn't finish the sentence as Ry came back into the dining room.

His walk was still a little bowed, and he still grimaced as he sat down, but his blue eyes glowed as he looked at Freddy. "Good news. My third partner is definitely in."

The leap of excitement in her chest caught her totally by surprise.

"And just what does that mean?" Eb asked.

Ry looked across the table at him. "That it's a done deal, neighbor."

FOR THE REST of the meal, Freddy felt like a referee at a sporting event. Eb paraded his knowledge about ranching and Ry parried the rancher's boasting with thrusts of razor-sharp wit. By the time Eb said his goodbyes and drove away in his king-cab dual-wheel pickup, she would gladly have carried him to his ranch on her back.

"Lovely evening," Ry said as he stood next to her on the porch.

She shot him a sideways glance. "I suppose you enjoyed yourself."

"You bet."

"Men," she muttered, lifting her gaze heavenward. "By the way, what are these two partners of yours like?"

He shoved his hands into his pockets. "You know, this is the craziest deal I've ever put together, with the most unlikely characters. A trucker, a New York City cop and me. Can you imagine a stranger combination than that?"

She was unwillingly intrigued. "How did you ever link up with them?"

"We were all in the same elevator accident."

Her stomach pitched. "Were you hurt?" she asked before she could stop herself, before the betraying note of concern could be banished from her question.

He gazed at her, a smile of irony making a brief appearance. "A minor concussion, which is nothing compared to the way I've been battered since I arrived here."

Freddy avoided his gaze. "What about the other two?"

"My briefcase went flying and gashed open the cop's chin, and he also broke his arm. The trucker hurt his back, which put his trucking career in jeopardy but gave him a nice settlement. The cop's quitting the force and sinking his pension into the ranch."

She stared at him in disbelief. "You're using an insurance settlement and someone's retirement fund to buy the ranch?"

"Along with every asset of mine I could liquefy."

"Doesn't that worry you, risking people's nest eggs?"

"No. People thrive on risk. It's playing it safe that ruins them. These two men were both stagnating, needing a challenge but not sure what it should be. I provided one."

From his assured tone of voice, Freddy easily pictured him in a luxurious office in Manhattan, playing the market with nerves of steel, winning and losing small fortunes as if he were using Monopoly money. "And what about you? Did you need a challenge, too?"

"Apparently, I did."

"I suppose your partners will want to come out to the ranch, too."

"Definitely. Chase Lavette, the trucker, plans a trip as soon as the physical therapists have released him, and Joe, the cop, wants to bring his little boy out."

"Of course, the deal isn't finalized," she said. "It could still fall through somehow, or one of your partners could back out."

"They won't."

As crickets chirped in the mesquite branches, Freddy turned this new information over in her mind. She'd been devastated when she'd had to sell the ranch to Westridge, but life around the True Love hadn't changed as much as she'd expected. This time, however, the owners wouldn't be a faceless company. Real people were buying the True Love, people looking for a challenge. God knows what havoc that could create. She felt a headache coming on. "Maybe it's time to call it a day," she said. "We probably both could use some rest."

"Should I check for bugs before I go to bed?"

"No," she said with a weary shake of her head. "We're on a regular schedule with an efficient exterminator. You're safe here."

"I'm almost sorry to hear that."

She looked into his eyes. Had he already developed a taste for danger?

"Good night, Freddy," he said softly. "Sleep well."

Nodding, she retreated inside before the spark of excitement in his gaze could lure her to stay.

TWO HOURS LATER, her headache was worse. Climbing out of bed, she changed into her red tank-style bathing suit, grabbed a towel and headed toward the pool. But once she'd entered the enclosed patio, she paused. Ry was in the Jacuzzi, his head pillowed on a towel, his eyes closed.

She decided to go back to her room, but for a moment she stood and watched him. His arms were stretched out along the lip of the Jacuzzi and his broad chest moved rhythmically as warm water foamed and splashed against his taut belly. Droplets of water clinging to the pelt of his chest hair winked in the light from a nearby gas lantern. Desire eddied through her, but it wasn't just the sight of his naked torso that stirred her senses. It wasn't even the memory of his kiss, although that played a part. But physical beauty and sensuality wouldn't have captured her imagination if she hadn't witnessed the courage with which he'd faced whatever trials she'd thrown at him since his arrival yesterday. He'd responded just like...a cowboy.

Perhaps he'd make a good owner of the ranch, after

all. But he would be the owner, and he didn't believe in compromising his business relationships with personal involvement. She thought it was a wise strategy, herself. She turned to leave the patio.

"Don't go."

She stopped in midstride.

"I owe you an apology."

She swung back, astonished. *"You* owe *me* an apology? How do you figure?"

He'd lifted his head from the towel and gazed at her. "I lost control at least twice today. I shouldn't have dunked you in the horse trough, for one thing."

"I probably had it coming." Her heart pummeled her ribs. "Nobody likes to be laughed at."

He gave her a wry grin. "That doesn't excuse my assaulting you...in the pond."

She wondered if he considered the tackle an assault, or the kiss. Whichever it was, she didn't think they were wise to discuss the incident. "Never mind. I don't hold grudges."

"Good. Because I have a favor to ask." He braced his hands on the edge of the Jacuzzi and lifted himself upward, so he sat with only his feet dangling in the water. His trunks were very brief and very wet. "I noticed you have a fax in your office. I'd like to use it in the morning, if you don't mind. I'll cover the charges."

Freddy gulped and glanced away. "No problem. I have some errands to run in Tucson tomorrow, so I won't be working in there, anyway."

"I see. If my being out here now makes you uncomfortable, I'll go in and let you have the patio to yourself," he said.

She focused on his face and tried to ignore the Chipendale image he presented lounging on the lip of the Jacuzzi. "That's ridiculous."

"I agree. We can't work together very well if you run every time I show up."

"I wasn't—"

"You would have left the patio if I hadn't called you back." He got to his feet. "Do you want the hot tub? I'm ready for a swim."

The last thing she needed was warm, swirling water to stir her senses even more. "I was planning on a swim, myself."

"Think we can share the pool?"

"Of course." She tossed her towel on a chaise, took the pins from her hair and executed a shallow dive into the illuminated water. The cool shock of the water was like a brisk slap in the face, one she probably needed. She swam under the surface to the deep end and glided up beside the diving board. She glanced around to locate Ry, and her breath caught. He stood in the arch behind the waterfall like some Polynesian god, the golden accent lights caressing his muscles as he braced for the dive, pushed cleanly through the cascading water and jackknifed into the pool.

He came up next to her, his hair darkened with water, his eyes seeming to mirror the turquoise blue of the pool. "Want to race?"

She'd do anything that would distract her from the sight of his virile body. "Okay."

"Four lengths of the pool. I'll give you a head start."

"Nothing doing."

"I should have guessed." He hooked both hands over the side and faced the shallow end. She followed suit. "On three," he said. "One, two, *three!*"

Freddy pushed off, but his counting reminded her of

pulling his pants off, which reminded her of massaging ointment into his thighs, which reminded her of what she was trying so hard to forget. She swam, determined to break the languorous hold of her forbidden passions. He pulled ahead, and she redoubled her efforts. She'd taken trophies in school for the Australian crawl.

But she was racing an athlete, she remembered, as he lengthened his lead. And what did it matter, this silly race? After it was over, she could go inside, having proven she could handle close encounters of the sensual kind with Ry McGuinnes.

On his last lap, near the middle of the pool, he went down. She saw the water close over his head and immediately thought he'd had a leg cramp. It would be logical after all he'd been through today. Concerned, she dived for the bottom, following the trail of bubbles. The pool was nine feet deep near the drain. He could drown if she weren't here to haul him out.

She reached him and grabbed his shoulders. He grabbed back and pulled her toward him. She struggled, thinking he was going to drown them both. She wasn't strong enough to break away. He drew her closer, despite her efforts to push him back. Then, just before their bodies entwined, she saw his smile.

Light-headed from lack of breath, she held on as he wrapped his arms around her waist and pushed from the bottom of the pool. As they shot upward, he captured her mouth in a dizzying kiss of conquest.

They burst to the surface, and he threw back his head but didn't release her. She gulped in air just before they slipped beneath the water again and he reclaimed her, thrusting his tongue deep into her mouth. The liquid kiss as they sank to the bottom of the pool made her mind spin and her body thump with need. Sanity deserted her and she wrapped her legs around his hips to press shamelessly against his arousal.

This time when he pushed them to the surface, he kept one arm around her and used the other to maneuver them to the side of the pool.

"You're crazy," she whispered, starting to disentangle her legs.

"You're right." One arm anchored them to the side of the pool, the other kept her close. His blue gaze burned into hers. "You're absolutely right."

Her heart thundered in her ears. "And I'm as bad as you are."

"You looked beautiful tonight. Was that for me?" When she didn't answer, his gaze searched hers. "I keep trying to put you out of my mind, Freddy, but then I see you again, looking so kissable, and all my resolutions go out the window."

She could barely breathe. "But we agreed this would be a mistake."

He tightened his grip. "Then why does it feel so right to hold you?"

Her resistance ebbed as her body melded with his. "You should let me go," she whispered.

"I know." He leaned closer for another kiss.

A cough from the shadows invaded the sensual mood. "What was that?" Freddy asked, her eyes probing the area around the pool.

"I didn't hear anything."

"Well, I did." She pushed him gently away. "And even if I didn't, someone could come along at any time."

He reached for her. "Then we'll go somewhere more private."

"No." She was in control again. "You were right

when you said we shouldn't get involved. It's too risky...for both of us."

The flame slowly faded in his blue eyes and he sighed. "Then I guess you'd better go in. For obvious reasons, I'm staying in the water a while longer."

Her arms trembled as she hoisted herself out of the water. Without looking back, she retrieved her towel and hairpins, slipped into her sandals and left the patio. She'd done some difficult things in her life, and leaving Ry tonight ranked up there as one of the toughest choices she'd ever made.

8

FREDDY DIDN'T show up at breakfast the next morning. If she was deliberately trying to avoid him, he probably deserved it after that stunt in the pool. He'd never before felt the pull of a sensual attraction that completely robbed him of reason. His need for Freddy was disorienting.

After breakfast he walked into her office, half hoping she'd be there, but she wasn't. Last night, he'd been too excited about Lavette's call to take much notice of the office, but now he cast his eyes around the cubicle, intrigued by the little space. The room looked like a converted storage closet; the battered oak desk and chair might have been commandeered from an elementary-school teacher. The same went for the gray metal file cabinet. A computer, a goosenecked lamp and a telephone sat on the desks, and the fax machine occupied the only other piece of furniture in the room, a low bookcase stuffed with ledgers. The room was windowless, which was probably just as well. A window would have taken up too much wall space. Everything in the room spoke of practicality—except for the rogues' gallery on the walls.

The paneling was crammed with framed pictures, each of them a segment of ranch history. A recent color glossy of Leigh on Red Devil nudged against a grainy shot of the old frame ranch house, the surface of the photo cracked and one edge singed. Ry wondered if it had been hastily rescued during the fire Freddy had talked about. Beneath the ranch house picture, women wearing bobbed hair from the twenties posed by the fireplace, and beside that was a portrait of Freddy at about three years of age mounted on a barrel. A closer look showed that the barrel was suspended by ropes. Even at three, she was learning how to ride a bucking bronco.

Ry smiled. All decked out in boots, fringed shirt and hat, Freddy sat straight on the barrel, a wide grin on her face. Ry recognized that grin, the same one she'd given him as they'd raced side by side down the wash two days earlier. It was an expression of pure joy, and he'd felt it, too. Felt it and become frightened. That kind of joy shared with another human being made a person vulnerable to the worst hurt in the world.

He turned from the wall of pictures, walked behind the desk and put his briefcase on its uncluttered surface. Work was the best antidote he'd ever found to that kind of pain. Yet there on the desk, as if to mock him, was a calendar open to May 24, today's date.

The anniversary of Linda's death.

It always ambushed him like a cowardly street thug. Last week, he'd known it was coming, had even realized he'd be in Arizona when it hit. But calendar days didn't seem so important on the ranch, and he'd lost track. That he'd forgotten seemed an act of disloyalty.

Linda would have been the first to criticize him for clinging to his grief. He thought it was the other way around. Grief clung to him like a leech, except when he lost himself in the intense world of commodities trading. And except when he was here. Perhaps that was the magic of this place. Maybe the ranch was the poultice that would draw the agony from him at last.

Well, he'd never know unless he finished putting the deal together. He looked for a wastebasket to rid himself of the piece of paper crumpled in his fist. Then he opened his fingers slowly and stared at the ball of paper. Carefully he pulled it back into shape and grimaced. Without realizing it, he'd torn the page from Freddy's desk calendar. She'd scribbled a couple of things on it—'' auto parts' on the first half and ''Dexter'' on the second. Ry wondered how he'd explain his unthinking vandalism. He'd have to come up with some logical reason.

Stuffing the calendar page into his pocket, he started to pull the chair up to the desk. That was when he first noticed the pillow on the seat. Not a seat cushion, something that might reasonably be on the chair, but a bed pillow, still in its pillowcase.

He wondered who had put it there, and if it was an act of compassion or a taunt. He picked it up and sniffed the case. Freddy's scent, faintly floral, lingered. That devil-woman had taken a pillow from her bed and placed it on her desk chair, expecting him to find it and be reminded that he was a greenhorn who didn't belong here! This was no act of compassion. This was an act of war. His first instinct was to toss the pillow across the room. But, sad to say, he could use the extra padding, although he wasn't as sore today as he had been the day before. He plumped the pillow and settled into the chair. Then he picked up the telephone to begin his business day.

With his first call, he instructed his lawyer to draw up a partnership agreement. Then he spent the rest of the morning haggling with loan officers about interest rates.

Freddy didn't reappear at lunch, either, so Ry used the office again that afternoon when the eager real estate agent arrived at the True Love with the offer typed and ready for Ry's signature. The agent would send the papers to Joe in the overnight mail, and Joe would hand-deliver them to Chase Lavette before shipping them back to Tucson.

Once Ry had put everything in motion toward acquiring the ranch, he sat at the desk tapping the surface with his pen. He had a decision to make. His plane left the next afternoon, and technically he no longer needed to stay in Arizona. The real estate agent would forward the offer to Westridge. Assuming the company accepted it, the closing wouldn't take place for at least two weeks, maybe longer, depending on how efficiently the paper shufflers did their jobs.

But Ry didn't want to go back to New York.

Illogical though it seemed, he felt as if he needed to be physically on the True Love to guarantee the sale. His possessiveness grew with each hour he spent there, almost as if he'd planted a flag in the ground in the same way homesteaders had during the Oklahoma Land Rush.

Besides, now that his butt was healing, he was ready to get back on a horse and toughen himself up. He wanted some jeans and boots of his own to ride in, and he wanted to inspect the ranch in more detail, including the cattle.

And then there was Freddy. He had to figure out how to deal with her. He shouldn't have kissed her again. So what if they were attracted to each other? She didn't want a relationship any more than he did. Romantic involvement would be messy now and possibly disastrous in a couple of years, when the partnership sold the ranch.

Ry was already thinking of ways to soften the blow with better retirement plans for the older employees and financial backing for Freddy and Leigh if they wanted to purchase another ranch. But he wasn't about to buy trouble by announcing those plans now. He just wanted an amiable working relationship with the foreman of his ranch, a relationship that would guarantee a smooth transition when the time came to bring in the developers.

Duane stuck his head in the office doorway, his chewing tobacco making a bulge in his lower lip. "Freddy's not back yet?"

"I haven't seen her."

"Okeydoke." Duane turned away.

"Want to leave her a message?"

Duane swung back, as if Ry had offered a brilliant solution. "I could do that." His smile revealed tobacco-stained teeth. "Leigh asked me to report on Mikey, is all. Looks like he ain't got no infection or nothin'."

Ry tore a fresh sheet of paper from the legal pad he'd been using for his fingers and began scribbling a note to Freddy. "That's great news."

"Leigh wanted me to tell Freddy she was goin' over to Whitlock's to practice team ropin'."

Ry wrote that down, too. As long as he was the messengers boy, he might as well do a complete job.

"She has to go over to Eb Whitlock's, 'cause our arena still needs repairs, but you don't have to put that in the note. Freddy knows that."

"Okay." Ry finished the note, smiling at Duane's obvious enjoyment at having someone take dictation from him.

"See, they was waitin' until somebody bought the place before they asked about gettin' the arena fixed. 'Course, some of the guests been askin' about the rodeo and all, but—"

"The *what?*" Ry glanced up.

"We used to have us a rodeo a few times a year, with some easy events for the guests, if they wanted."

Ry's gut reaction was excitement. Rodeo! Then his business sense kicked in as he thought of the liability. "But now you don't?"

Duane looked hopeful. "We can start again, once the arena's in good shape. We kept the *corrientes*, the steers we use just for ropin'." He adjusted his hat and used his tongue to nudge the chewing tobacco to the other side of his lip. "We was hopin' the new owner would take an interest."

"Did anybody tell you the next owner will probably be me?"

"Well, I figured that. Figured it wouldn't hurt none to speak up about the rodeo, neither. The hands like it. I like it, matter of fact."

Ry felt gratified that Duane accepted him enough to tell him all this, but there was no way the True Love would continue holding rodeos. "Did any of the guests ever get hurt?"

"Their pride, mostly. I think we had one broken arm, and a few sprained ankles. That's the guests I'm talkin' about. We always made 'em sign papers sayin' it ain't the ranch's fault."

"Mmm." Such papers wouldn't hold up a minute if someone died or became permanently injured, he thought.

"The hands git hurt all the time, but they ride hurt, anyways. They don't know any other way of doin' things."

Ry nodded, almost in envy. What he really wanted, stupid as it sounded, was to trade places with one of those hands for a while.

"Ever thought about ridin' a bull?" Duane asked.

Adrenaline shot through him. "You have Brahma bulls at this rodeo of yours?"

"A few. Some of the ranchers 'round here like to keep 'em. Eb Whitlock's got a big one that's never been rode. He's called Grateful Dead, 'cause when you get outta the ring, you're grateful you ain't dead."

Ry could almost taste the danger. And he was far too drawn to it. Better to switch topics. "Duane, where's the best place to pick up some Western clothes?"

"I always like the Buckle Barn. The stuff's not too fancy, but it works good."

"In Tucson?"

"Why, no, it's down the road a piece, in La Osa."

"A shopping mall?"

Duane laughed so hard he almost swallowed his chaw. "I reckon not," he said at last, gaining control of himself. "It's a little town, La Osa is. 'Bout ten miles northwest."

What the hell, Ry thought. Might as well go exploring. "Would it be possible to borrow a truck or something, so I can drive there?"

Duane scratched his chin. "Well, now, I can't think of what you could take. My truck's tore apart, waitin' for the new carburetor Freddy's bringin' from town. Leigh's left already, and she borrowed Freddy's truck 'cause hers needs a new fan belt, which Freddy's also bringin', and Freddy's got the van. There's the stove-up vehicles the hands drive, but I'd be real reluctant to put you in one of them. You could break down, easy. Now, if Freddy was to come back, you could—"

"Did I hear my name?" Freddy appeared in the doorway, a leather purse over her shoulder and a plastic bag in one hand. For the trip to town she'd worn denim shorts and a True Love Guest Ranch T-shirt. Her hair was caught up in a ponytail, and instead of a hat, she'd worn sunglasses, which were pushed to the top of her head now that she was indoors. Ry tried not to stare at the graceful curve of her thighs. With her face flushed from the heat and her informal outfit, she looked like a teenager—a very sexy teenager.

She flicked a glance his way and nodded. "Hello."

"Hello." He hoped this casual greeting fooled her. Had he imagined he'd be able to create an amiable working relationship with a woman who affected him the way Freddy did? One look into the sage-colored coolness of her eyes and he longed to replace that indifference with the hot passion he'd seen there the night before. His hand trembled slightly as he closed his briefcase.

"Here's the fan belt and the carburetor," Freddy said, handing Duane the plastic bag. "Let's hope that's all that has to be fixed for now."

"Let's hope." Duane tilted his head toward Ry. "He wants to go to the Buckle Barn, git him some clothes. Should I gas up the van for him?"

Freddy looked at Ry with raised eyebrows. "You want some Western clothes to take back to New York?"

So she remembered that his plane left tomorrow. She was obviously eager for him to be on it. "Something like that."

"I promised Dexter we'd take him to La Osa this afternoon for an ice-cream sundae," she said. "It's a ritual we have once a week, so I can't loan you the van, but you can ride along."

It wasn't the most gracious invitation he'd ever had, but he'd decided he needed to see La Osa. Anything that might impact on the True Love was important, and he hadn't even known of the existence of a little town near the ranch. If it was quaint enough, it might be a selling point for developers. "Sure, that would be great."

"If you're going, you should know a few things about Dexter," she said. "Because of his stroke, he has aphasia. He understands everything you say to him perfectly, but he can't always find the right word to respond. Some people make the mistake of thinking they can talk in front of him as if he weren't there. But he picks up on everything."

"Boy, ain't that the truth," Duane said. "I think he's sharper now than ever. He can hear better than I can."

"I'll keep that in mind," Ry said.

"Meet you out front in fifteen minutes, then," Freddy said, turning.

"Freddy?"

She glanced back at him.

"The pillow was a nice touch."

Her gaze challenged his. "I didn't want you to be uncomfortable today."

"I feel as if I've been cradled in the lap of luxury. In fact, I feel so much better, I'd like you to take me on another ride this evening and show me more of the spread." God, he was doing it again, looking for excuses to be alone with her. He couldn't seem to stop himself.

"I wouldn't advise that," she said in a superior tone

that maddened him. "You'll just stiffen up again. If Duane fixes Leigh's truck, we can drive."

"I'd rather ride."

She shrugged. "If you insist. You're the boss."

"Not yet."

"No, but I'm certain you will be."

"Until then, you're still free to tell me to go to hell."

"Only a foolish woman would do that, Mr. Mc-Guinnes." She turned on her heel and left.

Duane gazed after her. "Seems like she's still a little upset 'bout that horse-trough dunkin'."

Ry didn't think it was that at all, but he couldn't very well confide in Duane about the kisses in the pool. "You could be right," he said.

But Duane wasn't right, Ry thought when he climbed into the van fifteen minutes later. Freddy was all smiles for Dexter, who was ensconced in the seat next to her. With Ry, she was coldly polite. It should have been a turnoff, but instead he found her frosty behavior challenging.

"We'll drop you off at the Buckle Barn," she said over her shoulder as she pulled away from the ranch house. "It takes us about thirty minutes to finish our ice cream. Then we'll come back for you."

"Okay."

"What's he want?" Dexter asked Freddy in a surprisingly deep voice for someone so frail.

Ry leaned forward to answer, but Freddy beat him to it.

"Everything, I guess," she said. "You know these Easterners."

"Yeah," Dexter agreed with a chuckle. Then he glanced at Freddy and made a kissing sound. "Last night. In the pool."

So he'd been the one who'd coughed and ended the interlude, Ry thought.

Color climbed into Freddy's cheeks. "That was an unfortunate mistake, Dexter. I was hoping nobody saw that."

"I did," Dexter said.

Freddy's cheeks glowed. "It won't happen again," she said through clenched teeth.

"Blame me, Dexter," Ry said. "I tricked her. She hated every minute of it."

"Nope, she didn't," Dexter said cheerfully.

Freddy groaned. "Dexter, I'd count it the biggest personal favor in the world if you would keep what you saw last night to yourself. Mr. McGuinnes is in the process of buying the True Love, and behavior like last night's doesn't reflect well on either of us."

"Why?"

"We're in a business relationship, that's why."

"Seems okay to me." Dexter pointed to Freddy's left hand. "You don't have one of those things. What are those things?"

"A ring?" she suggested.

"That's it. A ring." His face twisted into a scowl. "Remember that guy? Tried to—clap—no—you know." He smacked his lips again. "To Belinda. She has a ring. Mine."

"Eb didn't mean anything by it, Dexter, really. He kissed her on the cheek because she'd baked him his favorite pie."

"Yeah!" Dexter blustered. "Why'd she do that? She shouldn't do that."

Freddy shook her head and grinned at him. "She was being a good neighbor. You are such a jealous husband."

"Have to be," Dexter said. "Belinda's so easy—no—funny—no. What is it? What is it, Freddy? You know."

"Pretty," Freddy supplied.

"Yeah, pretty. Belinda's pretty. I gotta watch. All the time. Watch that guy."

Ry was so fascinated with the concept that Dexter was still protecting his interests after fifty-some years of marriage that he didn't notice they were in La Osa until Freddy swung the truck off the road and into a dirt parking lot. Not that there was much to notice. La Osa was little more than a wide place in the road with three buildings on the right and three on the left.

He rolled back the side door of the van. "Thanks for the lift."

She glanced at him, her sunglasses disguising her expression. "You're welcome. We'll be back in a half hour."

He consulted his watch. "Fine." Then he climbed down and closed the van's side door. As Freddy backed around and pulled onto the road, he took inventory of La Osa.

A giant soft-ice-cream cone angled out over the parking area of a glass-fronted building at the far end of the street. Obviously the ice-cream parlor. Next to it a large tin-roofed structure was, according to the sign attached to the porch roof, Gonzales's Feed And Hardware Store. Above the sign, a life-size statue of a white horse stood on the flat porch roof. Not just a horse, Ry noticed, but a stallion. The horse's gender had been emphasized by some midnight artist who had painted the stallion's private parts bright blue. The third business on the far side of the street was a two-pump gas station.

On Ry's side of the street stood the Buckle Barn, and next to it a low-slung restaurant that promised live country music, well drinks at a dollar each and "The Biggest T-Bone West of the Pecos." The last business on the strip, looking new and distinctly out of place, was a video store. It was probably the only establishment that would survive once the housing development went in, he thought. The pickup trucks parked nose first in front of each establishment would be replaced by Saabs and BMWs. People who drove those kinds of cars wanted a different type of restaurant, a different kind of ice-cream parlor and no feed store whatsoever.

He mounted the wooden steps to the Buckle Barn, barely glancing at the mannequins in the display windows. He had no time for window-shopping today. The scent of leather greeted him as he walked in the door and headed for the rows of boots standing on shelves against one wall. He was one of only two customers in the store, and within twenty minutes he'd found a pair of elkskin boots soft as a glove, three pairs of brushed-denim boot-cut jeans that molded perfectly to his thighs, and six Western shirts in various patterns and colors. He slipped into a dressing room, put on one pair of jeans, a shirt and the boots before he went in search of the final item, the most personal item, a hat.

WHEN RY WASN'T standing outside the Buckle Barn waiting for her, Freddy decided to go in after him. "Just sit tight," she instructed Dexter, who was looking sleepy after his weekly hot-fudge sundae binge. "I'll go fetch that greenhorn."

Dexter smiled lazily. "Awe, you like him."

"For God's sake, don't say anything like that around him, okay, Dex?" Usually, Freddy treasured Dexter's refreshing honesty. It was as if his stroke had stripped life to the essentials and he wasn't capable of lies, not even little white ones. But now he was exposing emotions she wanted to conceal, especially from herself.

"It's okay," Dexter said, pointing to her left hand again. "No ring."

"It's not that simple." She was losing patience. "He's leaving for New York tomorrow, so that will be the end of that. With any luck, he'll be an absentee landlord like Westridge and I'll never see him again."

"Oh, yes, you will."

"Give it a rest, Dex." Freddy sighed and opened her door. "Roll down your window to let in the breeze. I'll be back in no time."

Inside the front door of the Buckle Barn, she breathed in the new-leather scent and looked around for Ry.

Connie Davis, the owner and Duane's steady girlfriend for the past two years, rushed up to her and spoke in a conspiratorial whisper. "Is *he* the one from New York?" She tilted her head toward the back of the store. "The one you were so worried about?"

A giant cardboard cutout of Brooks and Dunn, a popular singing duo, blocked Freddy's view. "I guess. Tall guy, light brown hair, midthirties?"

"Beautiful blue eyes and shoulders that fill out a Western shirt?"

Freddy's breath hitched. She'd rather not think of Ry in those terms. "I suppose."

"You don't have a thing to worry about," Connie said.

"You're probably right. After tomorrow, he'll be back in New York and he can't very well dictate what goes on at the True Love from that distance."

"Going back?" Connie looked confused. "He told me he needed some clothes because he planned to be here at least another week."

Freddy's heart stilled momentarily. "Maybe you were talking to somebody else. Mr. McGuinnes made reservations at the ranch for three nights only."

"We can sure find out. Come on back. This fellow is making a final decision on a hat."

Freddy rounded the Brooks and Dunn display with Connie just as Ry pulled the brim of a black hat low over his eyes. He turned and gave her an easy smile. "Ready?"

She struggled to find a response. Outfitted in borrowed clothes, he'd looked pretty darn good, but nothing compared to the picture he made in jeans that hugged his thighs, supple cotton that moved with each shrug of his broad shoulders and a hat that shadowed his blue eyes, imbuing them with compelling mystery.

She wanted him out of town. "I thought you were leaving tomorrow," she said.

"Freddy!" Connie shot her a glance. "That wasn't very nice."

He regarded her steadily. "I've changed my mind."

"But your reservation—"

"You have available rooms. You said this was the slow season."

And the hot season, she thought, noticing how his chest hair peeked from the open neck of his shirt.

"Don't you need to get back? To Wall Street and everything?"

A corner of his mouth tilted up. "No, not as long as the phone lines work. Of course, I suppose you could go out with your wire cutters tonight and force that issue."

She gasped. "I would never do such a thing."

"Wouldn't you? You've resorted to just about everything else to get rid of me." He turned to pick up the rest of his clothes from a chair by the dressing room door. "But it isn't going to work, so you might as well get used to having me around."

9

AT ABOUT SIX-THIRTY that night, Freddy nudged Maureen into a trot as she and Ry rode along a trail near the southern boundary of the ranch. Freddy knew that Ry's mount, a dark bay named Destiny, would mimic her horse's pace, and she hoped the jouncing would knock some sense into Ry's thick skull. She wondered what he hoped to accomplish by staying on another week. Surely he recognized the volatile situation between them.

To their right, the sun sat like a bronze paperweight anchoring the horizon. Then, as if melting from its own heat, it gradually flattened and slipped out of sight. Above them the sky was clear except for a towering pile of white clouds that looked like a huge serving of vanilla ice cream. As the sun sank, the vanilla turned to strawberry, then raspberry, and finally orange sherbet.

It was Freddy's favorite time of day, when the heat had left the desert air yet there was still enough soft light for a rider to see the trail. A fierce love of this land surged within Freddy as she glanced over at Ry, the interloper. Did he imagine he could really own the True Love? Money wasn't enough to claim ownership.

"When does the real estate agent expect an answer on your offer?" she asked.

"Soon." Despite the trot, he sat on his horse easily, the reins held loosely in one hand, his denim-clad thighs gripping leather as he moved in rhythm with his mount. He pulled his hat brim lower to shade his eyes from the setting sun. "Duane asked me today about reinstating the rodeo."

"And what did you say?"

"I didn't give him a direct answer because I decided to settle it with you, first. We can't take risks like that with the guests, Freddy. No more rodeos."

So it starts, she thought. The greenhorn dictator. "You'll probably lose business," she said. "Lots of people come to the ranch just for the rodeo."

"I don't care. A lawsuit could bankrupt us."

Freddy sighed. That was big-city thinking, all right. And to be fair, he had a point. Her father had loved the rodeo and hadn't worried at all about lawsuits, but her father had been a lousy businessman. Maybe Ry and his partners would be the first to turn a profit from the True Love.

He paused and reined Destiny to the left. "Let's check out that herd of cattle over there."

Freddy surveyed the group of about twenty white-faced Herefords, their rusty coats burnished by the orange light sunset. "That wouldn't be a good idea, Ry."

"Why not?"

Ordinarily, she'd have let him find out for himself, but all this talk about lawsuits had made her jittery. He didn't own the ranch yet, and she and Westridge would be responsible if he decided to sue. "Destiny's been trained as a cutting horse. Get him around a stray animal and he lays down some funky moves."

"Sounds like fun."

"Look, Ry, I don't think you understand. He—"

"Let me try, Freddy." He kicked Destiny into a lope. "How bad can it be?"

"Ry, slow down!" She started after him. "You'll spook them!" she called, too late to stop the cattle from scattering in several directions. They were used to crazy greenhorns, so they wouldn't run far, but any minute, she expected Destiny to spring into action.

He did.

Freddy groaned aloud, but still she loved watching the hairpin turns and dramatic spins of a good cutting horse working cattle. Ry seemed to love it less. First he lost his hat, then his stirrups. Finally, when Destiny sat back on his haunches and wheeled a hundred and eighty degrees after a bolting calf, Ry lost his seat and landed with a thud on the ground, catching part of a prickly pear on his way down. Destiny continued rounding up cattle with even more efficiency now that he'd dispensed with his bothersome rider.

Freddy started toward Ry. It wasn't as if she hadn't warned him, she thought. That should stand up in a courtroom. She leaned from the saddle and snatched his new hat from the branch of a creosote bush.

"Have you noticed that the cactus are in bloom?" she asked. "That beaver-tail prickly pear is especially pretty in yellow, don't you think?"

Ry looked up at her, his hair tousled, his face a grimace of pain.

She dismounted and dropped Maureen's reins to the ground before she walked toward him. One of the prickly pear pads had stuck to his left hip, but he'd avoided landing in the middle of the plant.

"Just think, you can tell all your friends you are thrown by one of the finest cutting horses in Arizona."

He rested his forearms on his bent knees. "I'm going to learn how to stay on that four-legged amusement ride," he said grimly.

"In a week? I don't imagine so. Leigh's a good teacher, but she can't work miracles." She crouched in front of him. "Here's your hat, and you seem to have a piece of prickly pear sticking to you."

His blue eyes met her gaze as he put on his hat. "I'm aware of that."

She didn't dare look into those eyes for very long. He might be a city slicker, but his calm acceptance of disaster was a very compelling trait, and there was no Dexter around to chaperon them this time. "You're lucky you didn't tangle with that cholla over there." She pointed to a jointed cactus with segments the size of hot dogs. "Now that's a cactus with an attitude."

"I'm developing one myself."

"Stay there and I'll help you get the cactus off." She pushed to her feet and looked around for a stick.

"What about my horse?"

She walked over to a dead palo verde. "Destiny will wander back once the cattle are rounded up. He's very well trained." She snapped off a dried branch and returned to where he sat. "Now hold still," she cautioned, crouching next to him again. "We might get all the needles to come out when I pry the cactus away."

"And if we don't?"

She studied the best point to slide the stick under the saucer-size paddle. "Unless you want to ride home this way, and drive the needles deeper, you'll have to take off your pants and hope they stay stuck in the denim."

"Shucking my pants is getting to be a habit around you."

"Trust me, it's not on purpose." She grasped his upper arm for balance as she maneuvered the stick gently between the thorns stuck into Ry's hip. His biceps tensed as the cactus moved, agitating the needles. "You can swear if you want," she offered.

"I appreciate that," he said through clenched teeth.

"I'll wedge the stick in just a little more, and then I'll try to knock off the cactus in one movement."

"Sounds peachy." He sucked in his breath. "You know, in New York, I'm a capable kind of guy. I can hail cabs and—*ouch*—choose good restaurants and anticipate a bull market better than most men. You'd be impressed."

"I'm impressed now." With a quick jerk, she separated the cactus from his jeans.

"God bless America, but that smarts!"

"I know." She studied the dirt-stained denim. "Hold still. There are a couple of thorns I can probably pull out with my fingers, and that may be it."

"Did you mean that?"

"Mean what?" Using her fingernails like tweezers, she gripped one of the two remaining barbs and pulled.

"Sh—sugar! About being impressed."

Had she said that? She'd been concentrating so hard on getting the cactus out of him, she must have spoken without thinking. Gradually, she became aware of her fingers closed securely over his arm, her face inches from his, their bodies hunched together. She glanced at him and found him studying her intently. Her breathing quickened. "One more thorn."

"You know, all along I've thought we couldn't become involved because we would be business associates."

"Exactly," she said, returning her attention to his hip and the last white needle that had pricked through the denim into his skin. She kept her gaze focused on that needle as she gripped it with her fingernails. She must not allow her gaze to wander to his thighs or worse, to the bulge between them. It was like telling herself not to look over the edge of a precipice. She couldn't resist, and a hollow ache began deep within her.

"But thanks to a comment from your sister, I started thinking about how different the rules are out here," he continued. "For instance, in New York, it's manly to swear, even in front of women. But a true cowboy doesn't swear in front of women, does he?"

Even his voice, so close to her ear, was an aphrodisiac. Freddy prayed her trembling fingers would work well enough to pull out the last barb. "You're right. Most cowboys don't swear in front of women."

"And another thing I've noticed. In New York, everybody's scrambling for status and prestige. Out here, nobody wants to lord it over anybody. With the possible exception of Eb Whitlock."

"Oh, for heaven's sake. Eb's not so bad."

Ry made a dismissive sound deep in his throat. "He's probably the only person who would care if we were lovers."

She pulled too quickly and the needle broke off in the middle, leaving only a stub. "Rats!"

"Now what?"

There was one more thing she could do, and it was better than having him shed his pants right now, after that remark about becoming lovers. "I'll use my teeth."

He chuckled. "Oh, Freddy."

"Be quiet, Ry, before I lose my nerve."

"The day you lose your nerve, they'll have to send a national news team to cover it. What do you think of my theory?"

"I think it's dangerous." She took off her hat and laid it beside her.

"I want you, Freddy. And don't pretend you don't want me. It's too late for that."

"All I want is to get this last thorn out." Drawing a deep breath, she marked the spot with two fingers spread on either side of it. Then she leaned down and located the blunt needle with her tongue. The scent of denim, dust and potent male filled her nostrils. Warm rivers of desire coursed through her as she fastened her teeth on the end of the barb. With a twist of her head, she pulled it out and rose to a kneeling position beside him, the needle in her teeth.

"Here," he said softly, reaching to take it. His fingers brushed her mouth and his eyes darkened. He dropped the needle to the ground. She couldn't seem to move, couldn't summon even the faintest resistance as he cupped his hand behind her head and urged her closer.

"You want more than that, Freddy." His lips met hers in soft supplication. All the reasons that she shouldn't be doing this abandoned her with the first touch of those persuasive lips. The slightest feathering of his tongue gained him access to her mouth as she moaned in surrender. Cradling her head in both hands, he tasted her thoroughly. His kiss painted images of skin sliding against skin, of limbs entwined, of bodies thrusting as two become one.

Desire streaked through her like fire through dry brush. She'd chastised herself about responding so readily in the pool, but this was worse. She wanted him with a ferocity that urged her to pull him down to the dusty floor of the desert, rid herself of her restricting clothes and open her thighs to receive all he offered.

Breathing hard, he lifted his mouth from hers. She swayed, and he clasped her by the shoulders, holding her steady as much with his heated gaze as with the strength of his hands. "Open your blouse for me," he murmured.

She hesitated.

"Please, Freddy."

She unbuttoned the cotton shirt with quivering fingers and pulled it from the waistband of her jeans. When the blouse hung open, he stroked down the swell of her breasts and almost negligently flipped the front catch on her bra. Her breath caught as he parted the material, grazing her nipples with his palms.

His voice was husky. "I knew you'd look like this." He tossed his hat to the ground and captured her breasts in both hands. Closing her eyes, she arched upward, anticipating the hot moisture of his mouth. When it came, she sighed with satisfaction and tunneled her fingers through his hair.

Splaying his hand across her back, he held her steady for the onslaught of his lips and tongue and the gentle abrasion of his chin. Thought surrendered to sensation, logic to desire as she gave herself and delighted in the giving. Moistened with need, she begged softly for more.

"Not here," he whispered against her breast. Then, with a groan, he returned to her lips for a penetrating, mind-bending kiss.

A firm bump from the side nearly sent them both toppling over. Wrenched apart by the near fall, they turned in unison and confronted Destiny standing two feet from them, his flanks heaving.

"Go away," Ry said, waving his hand.

Destiny jerked his head up, but he remained where he was. Then he lowered his head and blew through his nostrils, spraying them.

"Ugh." Freddy wrinkled her nose and started mopping her breasts with the tail end of her shirt.

"Let me," Ry said, a trace of humor in his voice as he took the other end of her shirt and began a motion that was more caress than cleanup. "I thought you said he was well trained."

"That's exactly why he's standing there." She struggled to breathe normally, but Ry's touch made that difficult. "He's supposed to return to the spot where he left his rider."

"And blow snot on him?"

She smiled. "No, that's Destiny's specialty. I think he has springtime allergies."

"Remind me to buy him an antihistamine." Ry put his hands under her elbows and lifted her to her feet. "In the meantime, let's get out of the range of fire, go where we won't be so rudely interrupted."

She drew in a deep breath. Destiny had given her a second chance to be rational and she had to take it.

Ry gazed at her. "I see misgivings. Guess I'll have to kiss them away."

"No." She forced herself to step out of his embrace. "I think Destiny just saved us from making fools of ourselves." Avoiding his eyes, she refastened her bra and started in on the buttons of her shirt.

His frustration was evident as he put his hands on his hips and stared at the ground. He lifted his head. "I wouldn't have made love to you on top of a cactus, if that's what you were worried about."

She looked up at the soft gray of the sky, where Venus sparkled next to a sliver of moon. Tucking her shirt into her jeans, she turned and started back toward Maureen. "It's getting dark. We'd better go."

"Whoa, there, little filly." He caught her arm and

turned her to face him again. "Back up for those of us who don't know the territory. A moment ago, you were begging me to love you, and now you're shutting me out. I'm entitled to an explanation. Are you worried about what people will think?"

"Not really. Around here, people mind their own business about things like that. No, the problem is with me."

He frowned.

"If it doesn't work out between us, the fallout could poison my whole existence at the ranch."

"It could also improve your existence at the ranch. Aren't you willing to take a chance that it might?"

She regarded him steadily. "No."

"My God but you're protective of the status quo!"

"You're right. I don't have your appetite for risk." She paused. "But that might be because I've found something worth hanging on to." She pulled from his grasp and walked to Maureen on unsteady legs. "We need to go. It's getting dark."

The dusk-to-dawn light had snapped on by the time Freddy and Ry reached the corral. Freddy noticed that Leigh was back from team-roping practice, and as they rode up, Leigh unloaded Pussywillow, one of her favorite mares, from the horse trailer. Freddy was glad for the company. The less time Freddy spent alone with Ry the better.

Leigh waved a greeting and turned the gray mare into the corral. Then she wandered over to the hitching post as Freddy and Ry dismounted. "Have a good ride?" she asked.

"Ry decided to test-drive Destiny through a herd of critters," Freddy said.

Leigh gave Ry a startled look. "You stayed on him?"

"No." Ry swung down and tipped his hat back as he talked to Leigh. "And I'd like to arrange a few riding lessons, so I'm ready for him next time."

As they discussed scheduling, Freddy pretended to be engrossed in unsaddling Maureen, but her attention remained on Ry. She was amazed at how much he looked like a cowboy now. He'd picked up the mannerisms, the walk, even the aggressiveness of cowboy lovers, she thought as heat rose to her cheeks. She hauled the saddle and blanket into the wing to the right of the barn, an old stone structure reserved for the tack used by the hands. Equipment for the dudes was segregated and kept in the newer tin wing on the opposite side of the barn.

As she started back out, Ry came through the door with Destiny's saddle and blanket. Duane had sponsored Ry's entry into the hands' tack room. She moved aside to let him pass and then started out of the shed as he settled his blanket and saddle on a wooden stand.

"Freddy."

She turned, and before she realized what he meant to do, he'd stepped forward and swept her into his arms. His lips came down quickly, stifling any possible protest, and in seconds he'd shattered her carefully built defenses.

Then he released her. "Think about that," he said. "I'm catching a ride up to the house with Leigh."

Long after he'd left the tack shed, Freddy stood in the same spot where he'd left her, fingers pressed to her love-sensitized mouth. Ry might be lacking riding skills, but his kiss needed no refinements whatsoever. She wanted him more than she'd ever wanted a man, almost more than she'd ever wanted anything...including the ranch.

10

ALL THE WAY BACK to the ranch house, Ry questioned Leigh about her team roping. The more he heard, the more he wanted to try it. Finally, he asked her if she'd teach him that, too.

"Let's improve your horsemanship first," she said with a dry chuckle. "You have to learn to walk before you can run."

"How long do you think it will take before I can start learning team roping?"

"Ambitious son-of-a-gun, aren't you?"

"Always have been, Leigh."

She nodded. "How are things going between you and my sister?"

Ry gazed out the window into the darkness. "She doesn't trust me."

"Should she?"

He couldn't answer that because he didn't know the answer himself. He wouldn't ever run out on a relationship, but that wasn't the issue with Freddy. She wanted a guarantee that she'd always be able to live on her ranch, and he couldn't promise her that. Life involved constant change. Invest too heavily in a certain future and you were bound to lose. He should know that more than anybody.

Leigh parked at the side of the house where Duane was still working on the other ranch vehicles. Ry thanked her for the ride and left her there conferring with Duane about the state of her truck's tires. A country line-dance lesson for the guests was in progress in the main room of the ranch house, the music and laughter spilling onto the wide front porch. A shadowy figure sat in a chair with another shadow at its feet. As Ry came closer, moonlight glinted off an aluminum walker next to the person in the cane chair.

Ry's boots clunked hollowly on the wooden porch as he crossed it—a nice sound, he thought. "Mind if I join you?" he asked Dexter.

"Nope."

The neighboring cane chair creaked as Ry sat down, and the black-and-white dog raised his head. Dexter didn't speak, just reached down and put a hand on the dog's head.

"Is he yours?" Ry asked.

"Yep. A mare. No, a girl."

"The dog's a female?"

"Yep."

"Oh. What's her name?"

"Don't know. Used to know."

Ry wondered what it would be like to have once been the foreman on this ranch, the person in charge of everything, and now be reduced to mail runs, trips for ice cream and lots of porch time. On top of that, it would be an exquisite kind of hell to understand everything going on around you, yet be unable to communicate much of anything without a struggle.

Dexter held up his left hand and pointed to his wedding ring. "Did you ever?"

"Get married?"

Dexter nodded.

Ry settled back in the chair as the lively beat of the

music competed with the steady chirp of crickets. The mingled sounds felt cozy. He relaxed his head against the ladder-back of the chair. "Yes," he said. "I got married."

"Is it broken? I mean, no good?"

"She died."

"Too bad. When?"

"Eight years ago today. May 24."

Dexter was silent. Inside, the music ended, and someone laughed. The instructor said a few things, but Ry couldn't make out the words. Then the music began again.

"Five hundred—no—fifty. Fifty-two years," Dexter said at last.

Ry was beginning to get the hang of talking to Dexter and deciphering his cryptic messages. "That's a long time to be married."

"Yep."

"I envy you that."

"Yep."

Ry allowed himself a rare moment of nostalgic longing. He hadn't been raised to believe in roots and long-term relationships. His father's job had required moving his family many times, and when Ry was fifteen his parents had divorced. Ry and Linda had occupied at least five apartments in their brief marriage, and they'd agreed to postpone having children until they were "settled." Ry had always suspected they wanted to be sure they'd stay together before they took that drastic step.

He'd never had an attic or a basement stuffed with years of collected memories, never had an "old neighborhood" to go back to. He'd prided himself on being pared down, flexible, eager for challenge and change. A marriage that lasted for fifty-two years was almost beyond his comprehension. If he married today, he'd have to live to be eighty-seven to accomplish that. His thoughts drifted to Freddy, whose image was never far from his mind. She was the sort of woman who would expect her marriage to last fifty years.

"Dexter?" A woman came around the end of the house holding a glass in each hand. "Oh, is that you, Mr. McGuinnes?"

He stood. "Please call me Ry, Belinda."

She mounted the porch steps slowly but surely. "Would you like some iced tea?" she asked, holding out the glass.

He was pretty sure she'd intended one of the two iced teas for herself and that she'd expected to join Dexter on the porch. "Thanks, but I was about to go inside. It's been a long day."

"If you're sure," she said in her musical voice. "I wouldn't want to drive you away on such a lovely evening."

"Maybe tomorrow night I'll be more awake and I can enjoy this porch as it should be enjoyed." Sitting here with Freddy wouldn't be a bad way to spend an evening, he thought.

"Oh?" She paused in the act of handing Dexter his iced tea. "Doesn't your plane leave tomorrow?"

"I've decided to stay on a while longer."

"Good," Dexter said.

A pang of conscience assailed Ry as he said his goodnights and walked toward the front door. Dexter wouldn't be so friendly if he knew Ry's ultimate plans for the True Love. And Belinda wouldn't be offering him glasses of iced tea. Duane wouldn't have suggested bronc-riding lessons, and Leigh wouldn't have agreed to help him improve his horse-handling skills. As for Freddy, she would have seen him impaled on a giant cactus before she would have given herself to him as she had tonight. He felt like a fraud, and he didn't know what the hell to do about it.

THAT NIGHT, while going over some figures on the office computer, Freddy noticed that the calendar page for the day seemed to be missing. She hunted around, even checked the wastebasket, but it was definitely gone. It wasn't a big deal, except that it said something about the kind of person Ry was. She'd loaned him her office for the day, and apparently he'd made notes on her calendar. Then he'd torn off the page and taken it with him instead of writing his information on another sheet. It was either insensitive or secretive, and she didn't much care for either trait. She'd been right to repel his advances, she thought as she turned off the computer for the night.

FREDDY SPENT the next few days staying out of Ry's way. Strangely, considering his last kiss, he seemed to be avoiding her, too. Leigh worked with him first thing every morning, and he spent a good part of the day practicing what she'd taught him. During the brief glimpses Freddy had of him, she noticed how tanned his face had become and how his body, already lean, seemed tougher now.

On one hot, cloudless day that heralded the blistering summer to come, she rode out with Duane to check a break in the barbed wire that Duane thought looked deliberately cut. One of the cattle had become tangled in a loose end and had required considerable doctoring.

After assessing the damage, she had to agree with Duane that the wire had been cut.

"Don't you think you should tell Ry about all these things that have been happenin' 'round here?" Duane asked as they rode down the wide lane leading toward the corrals. "They're mostly piddly stuff, but they add up. I don't know if it's the jinx or some harebrained kids tryin' to be smart, but he should know he has a problem if the sale goes through."

"I'll tell him, but my credibility isn't too good these days. After all, I took him on that long trail ride just to get rid of him. Why wouldn't I make up a bunch of incidents to scare him away?"

Duane spat into the dirt. "Then I'll back you up."

"You were in on that trail ride thing. He probably won't believe you, either."

"Yes, he will, 'cause he knows I changed my mind about him. 'Course, we don't know what them partners of his are like, but he's okay. Having him own the True Love wouldn't be so bad. I think I can talk him into havin' a rodeo again."

"I don't think so, Duane. He told me he thought the liability was too great."

"He said that?" Duane scowled. "And here I went and strung up the barrel for him, too."

"You're teaching him to ride broncs? Talk about liability!"

"He wants to. Says he wants to try a bull, too."

"My God, that's insanity!"

"He asked me not to tell you, but I been feelin' bad about that, 'cause I figured you should know. And now I find out he don't want no rodeo. Maybe I jumped to conclusions about that greenhorn."

"Maybe we both did." She glanced at Duane. "What

were you thinking of putting him up on, Grateful Dead?"

Duane shifted his chaw. "Come to think of it, I did mention that particular bull."

Her stomach twisted at the thought. "Duane, I'm sure you've been worried about this change of ownership, just like I have. So I have to ask. Was the bull riding just a way to make him hightail it back to New York?"

Duane shook his head vigorously. "No, ma'am. I swear that wasn't my idea originally. But now that I know he's against the rodeo, it's a thought, ain't it?"

"Absolutely not! The ranch doesn't belong to him yet. He could still sue both me and Westridge." Freddy told herself that was her chief concern. But a picture of Ry beneath the furious hooves of Grateful Dead kept spoiling her calm objectivity. A few riding lessons and a few turns on the bouncing barrel didn't make somebody a rodeo cowboy, but Ry didn't realize that.

She heard the whooping and hollering before she and Duane rounded the bend leading to the corrals. "What the—?" She urged Maureen into a faster trot around the curve. Ahead of her, the hands sat on the top rail of the main corral cheering a wildly bucking bay and its determined rider. Her blood ran cold as she saw who was on board.

"Oh, Lordy, he's on Gutbuster," Duane said.

"Not for long." Freddy leaped from her horse and threw the reins to Duane. "Hold Maureen," she called as she ran toward the corral. She made it just as Gutbuster spun and showed his belly in his famous "sunfish" move. Ry rose in a graceful arc and came down with a sickening thud that plowed his shoulder into the trampled dirt.

Freddy climbed the fence and shoved one of the

hands aside as she jumped into the corral. "Somebody get that damned horse!" she cried as she ran toward Ry.

He lay completely still on his side, his back to her. His cherished black hat rested brim-side up nearby. Fear closed her windpipe. Dropping to her knees, she pressed two fingers against his neck just as he rolled over, bumping into her knees.

"And I thought you didn't care," he said with a wicked grin.

She jerked her hand away. "What in hell do you think you were doing?"

He pushed himself to a sitting position and started brushing the dirt from his shoulder. "Celebrating. And why are you swearing? I thought that wasn't allowed in the Code of the West?"

Anger shot through her, replacing her bone-deep fear. She jumped to her feet. "I should have you horse-whipped! You deliberately waited until Duane was with me and Leigh was out on a trail ride with the guests, didn't you? Of all the stupid, irresponsible, insane—" She paused, remembering something, he'd said. "Celebrating what?"

He stood and gazed at her, his blue eyes sparkling. "Our offer was accepted this morning. The closing's in two weeks. You're looking at the new owner of the True Love Guest Ranch."

"I'm looking at an idiot! The sale's not final yet, and until it is, I'm still the foreman around here. You are *not* to ride one of our broncs again. There's no telling what could happen to you. Although I doubt that anything could crack that hard skull of yours, people have been known to die *coming* off a bronc." To her dismay, she realized the last sentence came out almost a sob.

He leaned down, picked up his hat and whacked it

against his thigh to knock off the dust. "If I didn't know better, I'd think you were sweet on me," he said. Then he put on his hat, adjusted the brim and walked away.

Duane hurried up trailing a litany of apologies. "I shouldn't have fixed him up with that barrel, Freddy. I can see that now. I never dreamed he'd talk one of the boys into saddlin' Gutbuster. Guess I should have knowed it would happen, though. He's the kind that likes provin' himself, but I won't teach him no more. I won't—"

"Never mind, Duane." Freddy gazed after Ry as he walked to the opposite end of the corral and climbed the fence. On the other side stood several of the hands waiting to congratulate him. Covered with dust and looking proud as a peacock, he couldn't be distinguished from the other cowboys who were shaking his hand and clapping him on the back.

"They say he made the eight seconds," Duane said. "Curtis had a stopwatch on him. I wonder if he'll change his mind 'bout the rodeo now."

Freddy barely registered the information. She was too busy assimilating her feelings. When she'd seen him lying so still in the middle of the corral, she'd felt as if someone had ripped out her heart. And until the moment he rolled over, she'd sent a stream of prayers heavenward on his behalf. As foreman of the ranch, she had reason to be upset when someone took foolish chances, but she'd been more than upset. She'd been frantic.

"You won't want to hear this, but I've seen a lot of rodeo cowboys," Duane said. "There's a rhythm to it you can't teach. He's got it. Born with it, probably."

She swallowed the lump of emotion in her throat. "But he's a commodities trader," she murmured, resisting with all her might the urge to run across the corral, wrap her arms around him and beg him not to take such reckless chances.

"Not today he wasn't. Today he was a cowboy who rode a bronc to the buzzer."

THE NEXT MORNING, the ranch van hauled nine German tourists to the True Love, and that afternoon another twelve arrived. Because German groups had spent time at the ranch before, Freddy had picked up enough of the language to get by. So she was able to interpret the complaint when one of the couples said they'd been expecting to sleep in the John Wayne Room. They'd traveled halfway around the world to sleep there, they insisted.

Freddy stood with them in the large living room and tried to explain that they were lucky to get the honeymoon cottage, which was bigger, had a better view and more privacy. The couple shook their heads and began demanding the room they'd dreamed about "for many months."

Ry walked in just as Freddy was starting her fourth polite explanation of why the room was unavailable. He paused to listen and finally sauntered over to the group. Then, in perfect German, he offered to exchange sleeping accommodations with the couple.

The woman practically threw herself into Ry's arms, and the husband beamed and pumped Ry's hand enthusiastically. They chattered so fast in German that Freddy lost most of the conversation, but she would have had trouble following a conversation in English with Ry standing so close and looking so virile, his thumbs hooked through the loops in his jeans. Washing had shrunk them to a delicious fit that defined his shape beautifully. His boots and hat had seen more wear in a week than most cowboys gave them in a month, giving him a rugged aspect that could only be bought with experience on a cattle ranch.

One look into his laughing eyes as he talked with the Germans and she remembered those eyes darkening with passion, those lips capturing hers, those long tanned fingers caressing her. Yet after that last impassioned kiss, he'd made no move in her direction. Was he clever enough to realize that by backing away, he'd make himself even more appealing? Perhaps. Standing next to him now, she had to exercise self-control to keep from laying her hand on his arm, just to see if he'd react.

Partly to distract herself, she snagged a passing maid and gave the woman instructions to move Mr. McGuinnes's belongings to the cottage and prepare the John Wayne Room for new guests. By the time she turned back, the couple were gone.

"Where are they?" she asked Ry.

"I suggested they order a cool drink and sit out by the pool while their room is cleaned. Otherwise, I figured they'd monopolize your time until the maid makes the switch, and you look like you have your hands full."

"Thanks. I do." *With you.* "What were they saying? My German's not that good."

He laughed. "They said I don't look like a guest."

"They're right. You don't. And what were they saying about John Wayne? I thought I heard something about a spirit. Don't tell me they're into seances, or something."

"No. They said I could be a reincarnation of John Wayne, I guess because I'm tall and I'm wearing Western clothes."

"And speaking German. They've probably seen

dubbed versions of his movies. It must have been a fantasy come true to stand here talking to a real live cowboy who speaks German.''

''You think I'm a real live cowboy?''

She didn't dare tell him her exact thoughts, that he was the best-looking stud in the valley. ''Let's just say a tourist would think you were. Where did you learn German?''

''I picked up most of it on business trips.''

She was beginning to get a picture of the astounding reach of Ry McGuinnes. ''Then I assume you know some other languages?''

''*Oui, ma chérie.*'' His gaze probed hers, seducing her as his mouth curved into a slow, sexy smile.

She was losing her composure fast in the spell cast by those suggestive eyes. There were reasons that she hadn't thought it wise to become his lover, but she couldn't think of a single one at the moment. Then she remembered the calendar page he'd apparently destroyed. ''Did you rip a page out of my desk calendar the other day?'' she asked abruptly.

The sensuality faded from his expression. ''Yes, I did. Crumpled it up, too, so I didn't think you'd want it back.''

''Are you in the habit of doing that with other people's possessions?'' she pressed, relieved to have found something to dispel the passion that had begun to materialize between them.

His expression hardened. ''No, I'm not. I still have it. Maybe I can iron it out for you, if it's so important. Now, if you'll excuse me, I have to get down to the corral and lay claim to Red Devil before Leigh changes her mind about letting me ride him.''

''Red Devil?'' She was now fully ready to be perverse. "I'd choose a different horse if I were you. He's thrown two of the hands already. The surgery didn't calm him down much."

His eyes narrowed. "Are you worried about the horse or the rider?"

"Neither, come to think of it," she retorted. "You probably deserve each other. Personally, I don't like riding a horse that gives me a fight."

His teeth flashed white in his tanned face and his eyes gleamed with a wicked fire. "But that's the fun of it, *Liebchen*."

11

RED DEVIL TRIED a little crow-hopping and tossing of his head, but Ry felt in control as he walked the big chestnut horse away from the corrals. Leigh had told him Red Devil had been "cut proud," the cowboy way of describing a gelding who acted like a stallion. Ry liked that. Once the ranch deal went through, he'd own a third of Red Devil, but he'd decided to buy out Chase's and Joe's shares of the horse.

He hadn't made the decision lightly. The commodities market had taken some strange turns in the past few days, and he'd had to scramble to protect his assets. Just before he'd walked out of his room and discovered Freddy embroiled with the German couple, he'd completed a telephone call getting him into the corn market and out of soybeans, both in the nick of time. He'd burned the midnight oil figuring ways to hedge his bets on the gold and silver market so he'd wouldn't have any trouble coming up with his share of the ranch down payment. And through all that, he'd continued to take part in ranch life.

It was a test, to see if he could manage his investments from Arizona. If he could do it without suffering significant losses, he'd be able to spend more on the True Love, more time riding Red Devil, more time polishing his bronc-riding skills. And more time with Freddy. She was resisting him, perhaps from some instinctive sense that he represented change in her life. He wanted to find a way to make her welcome that change, because, try as he might to put her out of his mind, he wanted Freddy.

Just then, a white sedan came down the road toward him, driving fast and sending up a rooster tail of dust. Ry frowned and got a firmer grip on Red Devil's reins. Damned city people. Then he smiled at himself. He was acclimating fast.

The car slowed as it came alongside Red Devil. The horse pranced sideways and arched his neck. Ry reined him in and gripped with his thighs. "Easy, Red. Easy," he murmured.

The tinted window of the sedan buzzed down and a man in suit and tie stuck his head out. The car's air-conditioning wafted around Ry and he found himself thinking the guy was a wimp to need air-conditioning. It couldn't be much over ninety.

The man took off his sunglasses and squinted up at Ry. "Say, cowboy, am I headed in the right direction for the True Love Guest Ranch?"

Being addressed as a cowboy made Ry's day, even though the man's attitude wasn't particularly respectful. "Straight ahead and take a right at the fork," he said, tightening the reins as Red Devil pranced some more.

"That's quite a horse you have," the man said.

"Yep." Ry almost wished he chewed tobacco so he could spit in the dirt after that reply.

"Thanks for the directions." The automatic window buzzed upward and the car took off, spewing fumes and leaving a billowing cloud of dust to settle over Ry and Red Devil.

Cursing and wiping grit from his face, Ry loped away

from the dust and exhaust fumes. Only later, as he traversed the now-familiar western end of the True Love, did he figure out who the guy might be. An environmental engineer was due out any time, to check the water and make sure nothing toxic was buried under the True Love. Ry longed for the necessary paperwork to be finished. Chase had mentioned during his last phone call that he might make it out in time for the closing. It wasn't necessary—everything could be handled by mail—but Ry could understand Chase's eagerness to be part of the process. Besides, without a rig to drive someplace, the trucker seemed to be getting very bored.

Ry thought of the impact the ranch would have on a hot-blooded young rebel like Chase and laughed. If the Gutbuster incident got Freddy's undies in a bunch, wait till she tried to control Lavette.

THE COUPLE WHO'D wanted the John Wayne Room wasn't Freddy's only problem that afternoon. The environmental engineer arrived and she had to provide him with a map of the buildings and outbuildings. Then several of the German guests announced they were vegetarians, precipitating a conference with Belinda on the menu, which was ordinarily built around beef. A young woman started sneezing and insisted her room be cleaned again with damp cloths to pick up all the dust. Freddy suggested allergy medicine, but the woman claimed she never took pills.

"So she comes to a guest ranch in the desert in May," Freddy mumbled to herself as she located Rosa, the housekeeper, and requested the second cleaning.

She'd just ducked into her office to call the bunkhouse and ask for six horses to be saddled for a sunset ride, when Dexter appeared in the doorway leaning on his walker, his best hat sitting jauntily on his head. "Hi, Dex," she said, picking up the phone and punching in the bunkhouse extension. "What can I do for you?"

"Ice cream."

She'd forgotten. She glanced quickly at her calendar and sure enough, today was ice-cream day. One look into Dexter's face alight with expectation and she ditched the idea of putting off the ice-cream trip until the next day. "Sure," she said. "Right after this call."

"Okay." He pivoted his walker and stumped toward the double doors leading to the porch.

In ten minutes, she'd arranged for the sunset ride and had asked Leigh to handle any problems with the guests or the environmental engineer. As Freddy pulled the van up to the arched entryway, Dexter had barely made it down the flagstone path. She guided him in with as little fuss as possible, knowing he hated needing the help. But these days, his ice-cream trip was more important than his vanity.

As they headed toward the main road, a lone rider stood on a rise about a mile to their left. Even from that distance, Freddy recognized Ry on Red Devil. Red Devil tossed his head but otherwise stood quietly. Ry seemed to have perfect control of the big animal, she thought with a pang of resentment. Why should this greenhorn be able to master a horse when some of her experienced hands had failed? Yet Ry sat like a king in the saddle as he gazed out over the land.

Freddy returned her attention to the road, but the picture of Ry surveying the ranch stayed with her. Her father used to do that, and so had she, on occasion. She remembered the possessive feeling of those moments, and she grew uneasy. The True Love belonged to the

Singleton family, no matter who held the deed. At least, that's the way it had always been.

Dexter craned his head backward, still looking at Ry silhouetted on the promontory. "His mother—no—his girl died," Dexter said.

"His wife died," Freddy said. "I know. He told me."

"May 24."

Freddy felt as if someone had dropped ice cubes in her stomach. That was the date on the missing calendar page. But maybe Dexter's comments weren't related to each other. "What about May 24?" she asked.

"She died."

Freddy swallowed. "How do you know that, Dexter?"

"He said."

"He told you his wife died on May 24?"

"Yep."

SOMEHOW Freddy made it through the rest of her duties that day. Ry ate in the dining room, but he'd been appropriated by the couple now sleeping in the John Wayne Room, and Freddy spent most of the meal counseling the young woman with the allergies about not going outside during the early morning and late afternoon, when the pollen count was highest.

Then the sunset-ride crowd came in, and Freddy got caught up in their stories of seeing a pack of coyotes chasing down a rabbit. Some of the riders seemed to think Freddy should do something about protecting the cute little bunnies, so she spent another hour convincing them that they were looking at real nature, not something created as a theme park.

It was almost nine before she broke free. She looked around for Ry, but he was gone. She checked the porch, even asked the couple who had spent most of the evening with him, but nobody could tell her where he was. At last, she decided to try the cottage.

The John Wayne Room couple had blown it, she thought as she approached the small building, which was a miniature of the main house, complete with red-tiled roof, whitewashed adobe and a front porch shaded with a sweet-smelling jasmine vine. Freddy always gave the cottage to honeymooning couples, but none had presented themselves in the German group, so she'd picked at random, thinking she'd offered them a treat.

Ry wasn't sitting on one of the Adirondack chairs occupying the front porch, but a light shone from the window. Freddy tapped on the door.

"Come in," he called, and she opened the carved door, wondering why he hadn't bothered to get up to answer the knock.

He was sitting on the bed talking on the phone, his briefcase open beside him and papers spread over the white comforter. He glanced up, his eyes widening. He covered the mouthpiece. "I'll just be a minute."

She half turned toward the door. "I could come back—"

"No. I'll be through soon."

She pulled out one of the captain's chairs next to a small table in the corner and sat down. She hadn't been in here for a while and had forgotten the charm of the décor. She automatically checked for cobwebs in the beamed ceiling or any yellowing of the Battenburg lace trimming the white comforter and the curtains at the windows. Like most of the beds at the ranch, the one in the cottage was an antique four-poster paired with a dark wood dresser and end table. Ry's hat hung on a post at the foot of the bed, in typical cowboy fashion. His boots were propped in a corner, and his shirt was unsnapped almost to his waist. It was warm in the room, and Freddy wondered if the air conditioner was broken. She'd have to ask.

Everything else looked in good shape. From what she could see of the bathroom, the clawfoot tub looked clean and the towels neatly arranged. The bathroom's tile floor gleamed in the light from the bedroom, and the pine floors of the bedroom looked recently oiled. No stains marred the geometric-patterned Indian rugs on the floors. As Freddy might have expected, Rosa ran a tight ship. Everything was perfect.

"No, I want to get into Eurodollars now," Ry said, running his fingers through his hair. "I know that's risky but I think it'll pay off. I appreciate your handling this for me." He paused and looked over at Freddy. "It's great. Riding bucking broncos and everything." He winked at Freddy. "You bet! Bring Susie and the kids. Okay. Talk to you tomorrow."

He hung up the phone and started gathering up the papers. "To what do I owe this honor?"

Freddy's grip tightened on the arm of the chair. She'd been practicing her apology ever since Dexter had dropped his bombshell. But now words deserted her. She didn't know where to begin. "Isn't your air conditioner working?" she asked instead.

"It's working." He tapped the papers together and tucked them into his briefcase. "I'm just getting used to the heat, I guess. I decided not to turn it on." He snapped the case closed and put it beside the bed.

"So I see."

He glanced down at his unbuttoned shirt. "Does this

offend you, ma'am?" he asked with a deadpan expression.

No, it excited her. She took refuge in a bored tone of voice. "Of course not. I work around a ranch full of men who sometimes, believe it or not, take off their shirts in my presence."

"Funny, but my experience around you has had more to do with pants than shirts."

She flushed, or maybe it was just the heat affecting her. But if he could live without air-conditioning, so could she. After all, she was the one raised in this country; he'd been here less than two weeks. "I didn't mean to interrupt your work," she said, gesturing toward the briefcase. "It must be difficult keeping up with Wall Street when you're this far away."

"It's been difficult, but possible, which is something I wanted to find out. I'll definitely need to spend time in New York, but not as much as I thought at first."

She stared at him. "You sound as if you're planning to take up residence at the True Love."

His gaze was steady. "I am."

"Why?"

"Because I like it here."

She hadn't counted on this. Not by a long shot. "You'd uproot yourself just like that? Change your whole life?"

"I think you advised me once to get a life."

"I was joking. Surely you have ties to New York, people you don't want to leave."

He nodded. "Two couples Linda and I spent time with, and a good friend who works in commodities with me. I just talked to him. You heard me invite him and his family out here, and I'll go back there from time to time. It's not as if I have to spend weeks on a stage-coach to keep in touch."

"But life out here is so *different*."

"Which is why I like it. I've discovered I'd rather ride Red Devil than play handball with the guys at the gym."

She swallowed the nervousness rising in her throat. "What about...girlfriends?"

"Why do you want to know?" he asked with a smile. Heat rose to her cheeks. "Never mind. I don't want to know."

"Yes, you do. I've dated in the past few years, but nothing's ever clicked. In other words, I don't have a lover waiting for me back home, Freddy." The warmth of his gaze made her look away in confusion.

"We have a limited number of guest rooms," she said, studying the pattern of the Indian rug. "I'm not sure where you will be able to stay. We already have several weekends booked solid for the winter season."

Ry appeared unfazed by her objection. "Then I'll sleep in the bunkhouse. I noticed not every bed is in use down there. If necessary, I'll set up a cot in the tack shed. Don't worry. I won't take up much space."

"The bunkhouse?" She glanced up. "That doesn't seem like the right place for one of the owners."

"Don't worry about it. Besides, I can't very well make you or Leigh sleep there, although the hands would think it was a fine idea. According to Duane, most of them get up every morning with a song of happiness on their lips because they work for those good-looking Singleton sisters."

Freddy examined a worn spot on the knee of her jeans. "Duane talks too much."

"He talks a lot more than I would have given him

credit for when he picked me up at the airport. I guess he really hates big cities."

Freddy chuckled and looked up. "He sure does. He says if we ever give him his walking papers, we might as well shoot him and get it over with. He needs to stay near Tucson because his ex-wife and two kids are here, and there aren't a lot of ranching jobs in the area, he'd be stuck looking for a job in town. Can you imagine Duane flipping burgers?"

"No." He paused. "Duane's not too happy with me at the moment. I guess you told him I wasn't in favor of reinstating the rodeo."

"I didn't think it was a secret."

"It isn't." A corner of his mouth turned up. "But now he's threatening to put my saddle in the greenhorn tack shed."

"I'm not surprised. There are two people you don't want to get on the wrong side of around here. Duane's one, and Belinda's the other."

"Belinda?" He raised his eyebrows. "She's the sweetest lady I've ever met."

"Cross her and see how sweet she is. She'd do anything to protect those near and dear to her. So would Duane, for that matter."

"Then it looks as if I'd better find a way to pacify Duane."

"By having a rodeo?" she asked.

"No."

"But you love riding broncs!"

"And I can't very well sue myself, can I?"

Freddy knew she was stalling, putting off the moment she'd have to apologize for making an issue of the calendar page. Facing this subject was much tougher than rising with dignity out of the horse trough. She looked down at her hands and laced her fingers together as she tried to remember how she'd planned to word her statement.

"What is it, Freddy?"

Startled by the nearness of his voice, she lifted her head and discovered he'd left the bed and crossed the room to stand in front of her. "I owe you an apology," she said softly.

"What for now?"

She frowned. "That wasn't nice."

"Sometimes I'm not nice." His eyes had darkened to navy as he stood before her in his bare feet, his shirt open just enough for her to follow the downward spiral of his chest hair to the waistband of his jeans. The scent of horse, male sweat and musk assailed her.

"I didn't realize when I made such a thing of that calendar page that you...that it was the day when...Ry, I didn't know. Dexter told me. If I'd only realized..." She trailed off, failing miserably to make the smooth statement of regret she'd practiced so many times in her head.

"I know," he said gently. "And I wasn't man enough to tell you the reason I ripped it out. It's not your fault."

She swallowed and looked away. He was man enough for anything she could imagine.

"Was that why you came here?"

She nodded. "I felt terrible. You must still love her very much."

He gazed out the window and shoved his hands in his pockets. "I'll always care about her, but that isn't why I mangled your calendar page," he said at last.

Freddy sat very still. She sensed the slightest movement or word from her might send him back behind the wall he'd built around this tragedy.

When he spoke, his voice was a strained monotone. "Even after eight years, I hate being reminded of that day because I keep thinking I should have been able to do something to keep it from happening." He looked at her, his expression tormented. "Punks, that's all they were! Not one of them with a tenth of her potential. When she wouldn't give them her briefcase, which was typical of Linda's defiant attitude, they shot her." He snapped his fingers. "Gone, like that, all that talent, beauty, sense of humor." He began to pace the length of the room. "When the cops finally got them, they couldn't understand the big deal! They had no idea what they'd done with that one, impersonal bullet." His voice dropped to a whisper. "No idea."

Freddy got to her feet, her heart beating a slow, painful rhythm. No one should have to endure something like this, she thought. And certainly not alone. "It was random violence," she murmured, crossing to him and resting her hands lightly on his arms. "You couldn't have stopped it."

He met her gaze. "Maybe not. But when we were first married, I'd meet her at her office and we'd walk home together. Then our schedules got crazy and I stopped doing it. If I'd kept it up, then—"

"She would have accused you of overprotecting her," Freddy said, tightening her grip on his arms.

The anguish in his eyes eased a fraction and he nodded. "Probably."

"I would have," she continued. "I'd never stand for some man chaperoning me everywhere, implying I couldn't take care of myself."

His hands came up to cup her elbows and he smiled faintly. "I know. You remind me of her sometimes."

Freddy relaxed her grip and stepped back. Was that

what this was all about? She didn't want to be a reminder of his late wife.

"And you didn't appreciate my saying that, did you?"

She crossed her arms in front of her chest. "I guess no woman wants to be a stand-in."

With a short humorless laugh, he reached for her, grabbing her arms and pulling her resistant body close enough that his breath feathered against her face. "That's the last thing I'd ever label you, Frederica Singleton. You're unique, and you've been driving me crazy since the day I saw you."

She lifted her chin. "Because I'm like Linda?"

"I'm attracted to strong women. You fit in that category, and so did Linda, but that's where it ends, Freddy." His voice grew tender as a caress. "When we kiss, it's you I'm kissing." His fingers kneaded the pliant flesh of her upper arm. "When I ache for a lover, you're the one I want." His words became a whisper. "You, Freddy."

Her pulse raced as she gazed into the flame-bright depths of his eyes. The heat pouring from him liquefied the brittle shell that had surrounded her for so long, she'd almost forgotten what it was like to be drenched in desire, to feel the surge of that warm river swelling against the moist confinement of its banks, threatening to overflow.

"And now I'll ask you again," he murmured. "Is your apology the only reason you came here tonight?"

12

"No," FREDDY SAID. Ry's question opened a new freshet of passion within her. "No. I wanted to see you. Be with you."

"Ready to risk a little?"

"Maybe."

His gaze smoldered. "We don't have any excuses this time. There's nothing wrong with me. I don't need doctoring because I'm saddle-sore or full of cactus. You're dealing with a completely healthy male animal, no handicaps to slow me down."

Heart pounding, she deliberately moistened her lips. "Then if you don't need doctoring...what do you need, cowboy?"

His reply was husky. "I thought you'd never ask."

If he hadn't held her steady, she might have crumpled like a rag doll when his demanding lips found hers. But she needed his mouth against hers, needed it with a ferocity that made her wind both arms around his neck and hang on, moaning at the sweet invasion of his tongue. The heat of the room seemed fitting, matching the heat inside her, calling forth moisture that slicked her skin, readied it for love.

He snapped open the clip holding her hair and dropped it to the table beside them. Then, as he kissed her into oblivion, he combed her hair with his fingers, starting at her scalp and stroking downward. It was one of the most sensuous feelings she'd ever known, being kissed while he caressed her hair.

Slowly he released her and guided her back to the chair, where he got to one knee and pulled off one of her boots. Then, holding her gaze, he tugged off the other. Her breathing grew shallow.

"We'll have to be inventive," he said. "I'm not...prepared for this wonderful gift you've given me."

"Oh!" And she, a grown woman, wasn't, either. Embarrassment crept up her cheeks. "Then maybe we shouldn't—"

"Yes, we should. Within boundaries."

"Ry, I think I should go."

"No you don't." Taking her by the elbows, he brought her upright and pulled her close. "Only a man with no imagination would let you go out that door tonight."

"But—"

"I'm not that man." Cradling her bottom in both hands, he picked her up. Despite her misgivings, she wrapped her legs around him, tightening the contact. His manhood, held captive in snug denim, swelled in response.

"Ry, this is crazy. We should—"

"Quiet, madam foreman." He sat on the edge of the bed, holding her firmly in his lap, keeping her pressed tight against him. He kissed the corners of her mouth, her chin, the base of her throat, detonating land mines of sensation everywhere he touched. "From the first day, when I rode behind you and watched your tempting backside posting up and down in the saddle, I've dreamed of touching you like this, and I'm not waiting. I know what I'm doing."

She couldn't argue that one as he popped open the first snap of her shirt and eased her back just enough to flick his tongue against the widening vee he'd created. With a sigh, she bared her throat in surrender.

"And then you massaged ointment on my thighs," he murmured as snaps gave way to his questing fingers. "Do you have any idea the image you created, bending over my lap like that?"

"I didn't want you...to be in pain." She was having a hard time thinking as he reached for the front clasp of her bra and her breasts began to ache in anticipation.

"There are many kinds of pain, *ma chérie.*"

"Some can be...sweet."

"If you know that someone will soon relieve it." He lowered his head and took her nipple between his teeth, biting gently. She moaned.

He cradled her breast and licked the heated surface. "You're so cool-looking on the outside, but on the inside—" he nibbled at the turgid peak once more "—you're so hot, you could burn a man."

Desire roughened her voice. "Are you afraid?"

"No." He lifted his head to look into her eyes. "I love the fire." He unhooked her belt and pulled it through the loops. "I love to build it and I love to see it burn."

Through eyes heavy-lidded with passion, she met the challenge in his gaze. Astraddle him like this, she was already open to him, completely vulnerable to his plans, save for some insignificant layers of material. He unfastened her jeans and pulled the zipper down. They were old jeans, soft and pliable from long wear. They easily accommodated the hand that Ry slipped inside the opening. Unerringly, he found her sensitive spot with the heel of his hand and pressed against the damp cotton of her underwear.

She caught her lower lip between her teeth, holding back a small cry.

"Oh, no," he said. "We'll have none of that. Not in this secluded little cottage. Not when the guests are all inside with their air conditioners running." He rotated the heel of his hand against her with lazy precision that wound the spring ever tighter. "I want it all, Freddy. Lose it for me. Let me see the tigress in heat."

She closed her eyes and whimpered.

"That's better." A breath later, he'd pushed aside the cotton barrier and slipped his fingers deep inside her. "Now let's turn up the flame."

She moaned as he initiated an insistent rhythm.

"Yes." His breathing quickened. "More, Freddy." He rubbed her tight knot of desire with his thumb. "Give me more."

She didn't recognize the small cries of need he wrung from her. It was as if she had no choice but to moan and sigh as his clever fingers probed pressure points she'd never guessed existed. The flames licked around her, through her. She gripped his shoulders as the only anchor in a whirling maelstrom where she wondered if pleasure had the power to make her fly apart into a million pieces. She sensed the moment coming, almost heard it like the rumble of a distant waterfall, and then she was pitched headlong past all restraint, flung gasping into the convulsing world of release.

As she shuddered in his arms, he kissed her back to sanity, cupping her face and stroking her hair away from her damp forehead. "You are so beautiful," he said. "I thought so before, but now that I've seen you like this..."

Dazed, she laid her head on his shoulder. "Oh, Ry."

He cuddled her, holding her like a precious artifact. "I knew there was that kind of passion in you."

"I didn't," she murmured.

"You didn't?" The male satisfaction in his voice made her smile.

She lifted her head so he could see that smile. "You wanted me to lose it. I sure did."

"I wanted just what I got, you in a frenzy, so wet and flushed, so willing for me to..." He trailed off and sucked in his breath.

The desire in his eyes told her most of what she needed to know, and a quick glance downward supplied confirmation. He needed her, and she wanted to give. Ry wasn't the only one who'd had fantasies.

She began slowly, reaching inside the open front of his shirt to find his nipples buried in a swirl of chest hair. She scratched across the tips lightly with her fingernails and was rewarded with another sharp intake of breath.

She gazed into his eyes. "I think you might need doctoring, after all."

The look he gave her was hot enough to start a fire in wet kindling. "Could be."

Her shirt was damp. She flicked open the snaps at her wrists. "Let me slip into something more comfortable." With a shrug of her shoulders, the shirt slipped to the floor. She flung her bra after it. "There." When she glanced at Ry to gauge the effect, she was rewarded by the flash of primitive lust in his gaze.

Still astride him, she rose to her knees, her hands cupping her breasts. "See anything you like, cowboy?"

With a groan, he pulled her close, tasting, nipping, suckling. She'd thought to tease him, to drive him a little crazy before she gave him relief, but his teeth tugging at her nipples renewed the fire deep in her loins, and she began to quiver with her own need. She pulled away, breathing hard, and applied herself to the task of unfastening his belt. He pulled her back, toppling them both to the bed as he ravished her breasts.

Before she realized it, he'd nudged her out of her already unfastened jeans and stripped away her panties. Free of restriction, she wanted him in a way that threatened to destroy all reason. Had she imagined she could control a conflagration this powerful?

No longer caring about anything but bringing him inside her, she opened the fly of his jeans and reached beneath the elastic of his briefs. Stroking the fullness there, she begged him to love her. Now.

Gasping, he looked into her eyes. "You tempt me, wicked woman."

"Love me, Ry. Please love me."

He took a long, shuddering breath. "Fantasies first. That time, when you were putting on the ointment, you gave me a picture that won't go away. Give me the reality."

Of course she would. She would do anything for him, despite the aching, driving passion clamoring for his attention.

He lifted his hips and she divested him of his clothes. He was magnificently, achingly aroused. Her fingers closed over the hot shaft. She leaned down, knowing he was watching her. Her tongue tasted salty desire, and the need to love him overrode her need to be loved. His groan as she enclosed him made the sacrifice of her own satisfaction pale to nothing.

He shifted position, but she was so involved in his pleasure that she didn't realize his purpose until he touched the burgeoning point of her own excitement and a spasm of pleasure zinged through her. Then his mouth was there, loving her with a thoroughness that made her dizzy. Somehow, despite the exquisite distraction, she ministered to him, too. His moment came first, and she rejoiced in the great shudders that shook his body. Soon after, he lavished her with an equal gift that left them sated and panting.

He eased up beside her and pulled her close. Silently, they held each other, knowing words could add nothing to such unabashed sharing of pleasure. They breathed in unison, as if they'd synchronized all their responses.

"Stay the night," he murmured at last.

"Isn't that dangerous? We might forget and—"

"If I didn't forget that time, when I could hardly see from wanting you, I won't forget. Stay."

"I'll stay." She snuggled closer.

"But don't expect to sleep much," he murmured, his voice husky in her ear.

"We only have about seven hours until dawn. Will that be enough time for what you have in mind?"

"No. But I can't do everything I have in mind. Tomorrow, we'll pick up what we need to expand our horizons, and we can take it from there."

A delicious tightening in her groin was followed by a realization that it might not be so easy to buy the supplies he was referring to. "We can't get them in La Osa," she said.

"Tucson, then. Because tomorrow night, I intend—"

"I'm sure you do," she said, laying a finger over his lips. "I'll buy some in Tucson. I'll find some excuse to make the trip."

"I'll go with you."

"We'll see. If not, what size shall I buy?"

"You don't know?" he said, laughing. "Why, *muy grande*, of course."

She reached between them and found him hardening again. "Unless they have a larger size than that," she said with a low, sensuous chuckle.

THE NIGHT PASSED as one of sweet challenge for Ry. All his instincts screamed at him to possess this woman in the most basic way, yet he managed to forestall his instincts, promising them full rein in less than twenty-four hours. It was backward from the way he'd always started a sexual relationship. The experimental part usually took place after the first wild coupling that joined two bodies. But he hadn't expected Freddy to show up in his room practically asking for a night of love, and there weren't drugstores on every corner out here in the desert.

Not that he was complaining. In fact, the lack of condoms gave him a wonderful excuse to learn every inch of her fantastic body, and she seemed inspired to do the same with him. He'd discovered he could bring her to completion simply by suckling her breasts. And as for him...she'd found some very creative ways of manipulating his lower anatomy to hurl him over the brink. They'd immersed themselves in the clawfoot bathtub where he'd had some interesting results with the running water, once he'd talked her into getting into a most provocative position. And he'd found out the potency that a few inches of lukewarm bathwater could add sloshing against him while she... He repressed the memory, which was having a predictable effect on him.

She'd just fallen asleep, and although it was nearly dawn, she might be able to catch an hour or so of rest. After all, he didn't want her to be too exhausted to enjoy tonight. Everything they'd done had been fun, but he still wanted...just wanted. He closed his eyes. He should sleep some, too. He wasn't an eighteen-year-old anymore, although last night he'd sure as hell felt like one. He touched her hand and her fingers curled around his in her sleep. With a smile of sweet exhaustion, he drifted off.

THE PHONE WOKE HIM to broad daylight and no Freddy. Dammit, he hadn't wanted her to sneak off like that, as if they'd been doing something shameful. And here he slept like a typical greenhorn long after the ranch day had officially begun.

He picked up the receiver impatiently and came close to snarling his greeting, until he realized it could be Freddy. "Yes?" he said.

"Mr. McGuinnes, this is Jose Ballesteros at Frontier Savings and Loan. There's a potentially disturbing development that may affect your financing on the True Love Guest Ranch. I started to discuss it with Miss Singleton earlier today, but she had to take care of another matter and will call me back. So I decided to call you."

Ry tensed. "What is it?"

"We have reason to believe there may be some petroleum drums buried on the property. E.P.A. standards being what they are these days, we'll have to locate those drums and ascertain the environmental risk before the sale can go through."

"Reason to believe?" Ry's eyes narrowed. "Who has reason to believe, and why?"

"Apparently, the environmental engineer who inspected the property yesterday talked to a neighbor, a Mr. Ebenezer Whitlock?"

"Mr. Whitlock seems to remember that Mr. Singleton

buried the tanks he used back in the days when he was fueling up his own vehicles, before the gas station was put in at La Osa."

"Are you aware that Whitlock had bid on the property, at a much lower figure than mine?"

"Well, yes, we are, but that doesn't change the situation. We need to talk to Miss Singleton to see if she can shed any light on the possibility of buried drums. But I wanted you to be aware, since you're staying at the ranch and she might bring it up."

"Don't have anybody call her. I'll handle it. We'll be in today with the information. How's that?"

"That...that would be fine, as long as you're sure that you and she won't get into any difficulties over—"

"Not at all. Thanks for the call, Mr. Ballesteros."

Ry showered, shaved and dressed with the speed inbred from years of working at a New York pace. He was standing in Freddy's office in less than twenty minutes, but the desk was occupied by Leigh, who was on the telephone.

"No, we're not blaming you, Mr. Gonzales," she said. "But it was the alfalfa we picked up last week, so you might want to check with some of your other customers." She glanced at Ry and held up one finger to indicate she'd soon be finished. "Yes, I think the horse will be fine. Freddy knows what she's doing. I'll keep you posted. Goodbye."

She replaced the receiver and gazed at him with speculation in her golden brown eyes. "Looking for Freddy?"

"Yes." He didn't evade her scrutiny. "Where is she?"

"Down at the corrals. One of the horses got into some moldy alfalfa and bloated. Want me to run you down there?"

"Yes." He didn't feel like being polite and making sure she wasn't too busy.

Leigh pushed her chair back. "Let's go."

She kept up with his rapid strides as they walked to her truck parked beside the ranch house. The crystal that hung from her rearview mirror flashed rainbows as they drove toward the corrals.

"Freddy's different this morning," Leigh said, looking straight ahead. "Do you happen to know anything about that?"

"Did you ask her?"

"Didn't have a chance. So I'm asking you."

Ry hesitated. But Leigh had been a friend to him so far, so he told her, "We spent the night together."

"I thought so. Been expecting it for days now."

Ry shook his head and chuckled. "Then you were way ahead of me."

"Haven't you heard that I'm psychic?"

"I thought that was with horses."

"Oh, I dabble in people, too. Besides, I know Freddy a little better than you. Or at least I did until last night," she amended with a smile. "You've probably caught up some by now."

Ry rolled down the window. It was getting warm in the cab. "We—ah—didn't spend a lot of time talking."

Leigh whooped and pounded on the steering wheel. "By God, Rycroft, you'll make a cowboy yet."

"Tell me about her, Leigh."

"Her love life, you mean?"

"Yes."

"She hasn't been serious about too many guys." Leigh paused. "Maybe I shouldn't assume it's serious between you two, either."

"Assume it."

She glanced at him. "I see. Well, her past loves, and there were only two she contemplated marrying, were both high-energy types like you. Like her, for that matter. Once you decided to stick around, I figured it was only a matter of time."

"What happened to those other high-energy types?"

"Oh, it usually boiled down to the same old argument in the end. Her whole mission in life has always been to run the True Love. None of the guys thought they'd enjoy hanging around to watch her do that." She glanced at him again. "Of course, with you, she has a different problem. You may want to run the ranch yourself."

"Not really." No, the problem was bigger than a mere power struggle, he thought.

"That's nice to know. Then maybe you could make a go of it. I'd like to see her find a man good enough for her."

He gave her a lopsided grin. "Are you implying I might be?"

"Maybe." She braked the truck to a stop under a mesquite and opened her door. "For a greenhorn, you're not so bad." She paused and turned back to him. "And I'll just bet you're dynamite in the sack," she added with a wink.

With a snort of laughter, Ry left the truck and followed Leigh to the same small corral where Red Devil had met his fate. Freddy stood inside, rubbing the nose of a small dun mare. Duane and Curtis hung over the side of the corral, along with a couple of the other hands.

Seeing Freddy sent a jolt of adrenaline through Ry, which mellowed into a misty-eyed tenderness as he drew closer. He was pretty sure what those reactions meant, although he and Freddy had been careful not to use the word last night. They might have abandoned themselves to each other physically, but emotions weren't so easily exposed for people like them. That was okay. They had some time.

He just hoped this petroleum drum business didn't become a major obstacle to the sale of the ranch. That could screw up a lot of his plans for the future, including his future with a certain dark-haired woman who was very inventive in the bedroom.

Duane turned as he and Leigh approached. "She's doin' okay," he said, reaching for his can of tobacco in his hip pocket.

Freddy pushed herself to her feet and turned, her eyes widening slightly when she saw Ry. "I think she'll be fine now." She picked up her kit of medical supplies and handed it across the fence to Curtis. Then she walked over to lean against the gate to the corral. "Did you call Gonzales?" she asked Leigh.

She looked tired, Ry thought with a pang of guilt.

"Yep," Leigh replied. "He was upset, but I told him we weren't holding him responsible. And I warned him to check with anybody else who bought some of that grain."

Freddy nodded. "Good." Her gaze traveled to Ry and she smiled gently.

The smile made him dizzy. He longed to whisk her off to some private spot and soothe away the lines of fatigue shadowing those sage-colored eyes.

"Then I guess we'd all better get back to work," Duane said, slipping a plug of tobacco under his lip.

Curtis glanced at Duane's tobacco can as he shoved it back into his hip pocket, where a permanent faded circle had been formed by the pressure of the can. "Did I ever tell you folks about the New York City gal who wanted to go to bed with a cowboy?" Curtis started to laugh at his own joke and pointed to the impression of the tobacco can in Duane's pocket. "When she saw the size of their condoms, she plum chickened out!" Curtis slapped his thigh and chortled.

Ry's shoulders shook with laughter. One glance into Freddy's eyes, brimming with helpless merriment, and he looked away, across the corals. If he shared this joke too intimately with her, the whole crowd would know what Leigh knew, and he wasn't ready to go that public yet.

"Thank you, Curtis," Freddy said, opening the corral gate and walking out to join them. "I don't know how we'd make it around here without a few of your jokes to keep us going."

"Nothin' to it,' Curtis said over his shoulder as he headed for the tack shed.

"Well, I'm due to take some German folks out for a trail ride in a half hour," Leigh said. "Freddy, I assume you can give Ry a lift back to the house?"

Freddy looked at Ry. "You didn't come down here to ride Red Devil?"

"I came down here to see you."

"Oh." She lowered her eyes and a faint dusting of pink tinged her cheeks.

"Come on, Duane," Leigh said, grabbing the grizzled cowboy's arm as he stood gaping at Freddy and Ry. "You and I have horses to saddle and dudes to enter-tain."

"Shore, Leigh." Duane followed Leigh, but he stopped several times to glance over his shoulder.

Freddy gazed up at Ry with a captivating shyness

lurking in her eyes. "Nothing stays private long at the True Love, I'm afraid."

"That's okay." He traced the line of her jaw with one finger. "I got up this morning and expected the news to be written across my forehead. Which reminds me, why did you leave without waking me up?"

"You looked so peaceful, and I knew there was nothing you absolutely had to do, so I let you sleep."

"While you had to get up and work. I feel like a selfish jerk."

"Don't." She laid a hand on his arm, then abruptly took it away, as if the contact had burned her fingers.

"Be careful," he teased. "I'm barely in control of myself as it is."

The shyness had left her eyes. "Me too, cowboy," she murmured in the sexiest voice he'd ever heard.

The sensual impact of the stoked fire in her gaze took his breath away. He struggled to remember why he'd needed to see her. Nothing seemed as important as what he was contemplating right now, and that involved naked bodies and soft sheets.

"Shall we go back to the house, then?" she asked. "I have a call I need to return."

Of course, he thought. The phone call. "That's what I came to talk to you about. Ballesteros called me after he tried to talk to you. He wants to know what you can tell him about old petroleum drums buried on the property."

She frowned. "There aren't any. Dad had them all dug up and hauled away when the gas station was built in La Osa."

"Then why the hell is Eb Whitlock telling the environmental engineer they're still down there?"

Freddy looked startled. "He did?"

"Yesterday. And unless I miss my guess, this is a deliberate tactic on his part to keep my partners and me from buying the ranch."

"That's stooping pretty low, Ry. I can believe he'd carry on about the curse to discourage you, but lie about petroleum drums? I doubt it."

Her defense of Whitlock irritated him. Whitlock wasn't really a rival, but Ry wished Freddy would be a little less generous with her opinion of the guy. "Then I'd appreciate it if you'd set him straight. Unless you want to help him in his obstructionist cause." He paused, then said, "Maybe I should ask that first, and not make any faulty assumptions. How do you stand on my purchase of the True Love?"

Hurt shone from her hazel eyes. "Do you really have to ask?"

He was instantly contrite and reached for her. "I'm sorry. Really sorry," he said, pouring his heart into his gaze. "If you still wanted to stop me, last night wouldn't have happened."

"No, it wouldn't."

So now she trusted him, with herself and her ranch, which were almost the same thing. He felt a sharp stab of guilt that she still didn't know his ultimate plans. He'd look for a good time to tell her and make her see that selling the ranch was the most sensible course of action for everyone concerned. Somehow, he'd work through her initial resistance to the idea. He had to. Too much was at stake now.

"We'll go to the house and call Eb," she said. "I'm sure this is a big misunderstanding."

Ry didn't think so, but he kept his opinion to himself this time. He'd love to be proven wrong.

13

WHEN FREDDY ENTERED her office and walked around behind her desk, Ry remained leaning in the doorway, his hat shoved to the back of his head. They hadn't talked much on the way back to the ranch house, as if each knew an argument could easily break out over the subject of Eb's character.

She picked up the receiver and glanced at him. "I know what you think, but Eb would not say something like this unless he believed it was true."

Ry's expression gave nothing away, but he didn't agree with her, either.

Freddy punched in the Whitlocks' number. She knew it by heart. She'd spent hours over there as child, back when Eb's wife, Loraine, was still alive. Eb and Loraine had been childless, and so they'd become honorary aunt and uncle to the Singleton girls, especially after Freddy and Leigh's mother died. Ry didn't know all that history, and besides, he was from New York. New Yorkers were famous for their suspicious natures.

Eb's housekeeper, Doreen, answered the phone. "Sure, I'll get him, honey," she said. "He's just out back working on the horseshoe pit he wanted to put in before the next party."

Freddy smiled. Eb loved to entertain, and he usually invited at least a hundred people. His barbecued beef was legendary in the valley.

In a few moments, his voice boomed into her ear. "Freddy! Gonzales called me about that alfalfa. Your horse okay? I meant to phone you, but I got distracted. Which one was it?"

"Tumbleweed, our little dun mare, and she'll be okay. Luckily, we got to her in time."

"I found mold in my alfalfa, too, but I hadn't given any to my horses, thank God," Eb said. "Gonzales is giving us credit on a new load, of course. I made sure he'd do that for all of us."

"Thanks, Eb. Listen, I understand you talked to the environmental engineer who was out here yesterday."

"Just happened to run into him while I was out riding fence. Nice fella. Hated to tell him about those drums, but he was asking questions, and I'm a lousy liar."

"Well, I think your memory's playing tricks on you, Eb." Freddy put a smile in her voice. "Dad had those hauled out when we stopped using them. Nothing's buried at the True Love."

"Freddy, you were only a little thing then. I believe I remember better than you do. He decided not to go the expense. We didn't have so many regulations back then, of course."

"I was ten years old, Eb, and I remember the trucks coming in to haul them away."

A cajoling note came into Eb's voice. "I would do anything for you. You know that. But I have to tell the truth. Those drums are still there."

"Eb, they're not, either!"

"Well, I hope you have some paperwork to prove it, sweetheart, or somebody will have a little digging to do."

Freddy sighed. "I'll look through the files. Talk to you later, Eb."

"Good luck. By the way, you and Leigh are coming to the party next week, aren't you?"

"We'll be there," she said. "Goodbye now." She replaced the receiver and stared at the phone. "I *know* Dad had the drums taken out."

"I'm sure he did, too," Ry said from the doorway. "Old Whitlock's trying to screw up the deal."

She glared at him. "Stop assuming that, Ry! We're talking about something that happened twenty-two years ago. He could have forgotten, and in all honesty thinks he's telling the truth."

Ry folded his arms. "Pretty convenient that he happened to run into the engineer yesterday, wouldn't you say?"

"He was checking his fence for breaks. Is that a crime?"

"I wouldn't think a fellow of Whitlock's stature would be inspecting his own fence. Doesn't he have hired hands to do that?"

Freddy pushed away from the desk and rounded it to open a file cabinet drawer. "You have to understand old cowboys. They can't sit around, and sometimes the most satisfying work is the most mundane. I can easily imagine Eb worrying about his own fence. Now, if I can just find some record of those drums being hauled away, we'll take it into town and clear up this business once and for all."

"You think there might be a receipt in there?"

She shoved the stuffed files apart. "I think there might be."

"Looks like you could use a second file cabinet."

"You're right. But I'd have to find another battered one like this, so they'd match. A brand-new one would spoil the ambience."

He laughed and walked over to brace one arm against the top of the cabinet. "At least we have a great excuse to go into town today," he said in a low voice.

Heat washed over her, but she kept her head down as she closed one drawer and opened another. "Do you think so?"

"When I first came down to the corrals and saw you, I completely forgot about Ballesteros. And you know how important this deal is to me. But one look at you, and all I could remember was last night."

Freddy realized her hands had stilled and she'd been staring sightlessly at the mashed files for several seconds.

"I've never spent a night like that in my life, Freddy."

She risked looking into his eyes. What she saw there made her grip the edges of the file cabinet to keep from throwing herself into his arms. She swallowed. "You'd better go find something to do for a few minutes or I'll never finish this search."

The corner of his mouth tilted up.

"I mean it, Ry. And don't forget, this office is in the middle of all the activity around here. People come and go constantly. We may not be able to keep our relationship a secret, but I'd rather not flaunt it."

He smiled softly. "You're right. Another five seconds and I'm liable to throw you down on the floor and rip your clothes off."

She believed every word of it. "Take a hike, cowboy."

He tipped his hat. "I'll be on the front porch," he drawled.

A half hour later, Freddy gave up. If the receipt was in the bulging file cabinet, she wouldn't be able to find it without going through every piece of paper in every aging folder. That could take hours, even if she enlisted some help. She went looking for Ry and found him sitting with Dexter and Chloe, Dexter's dog.

"It's like the old needle in a haystack," she said, dropping into a chair next to Ry. "I tried all the logical places, but no luck."

"Dexter remembers the drums were hauled away," Ry said.

Freddy leaned around Ry. "You do? The day those big trucks came and took the drums, the ones Dad used for gas?"

Dexter nodded. "Yep."

"I sure wish Eb Whitlock remembered it."

Dexter made a face.

"Oh, Dex!" Despite her frustration, Freddy laughed. "You just don't like him because he kissed Belinda." She glanced at Ry. "Let's go see Mr. Ballesteros. On the way, I'll try to remember the name of the trucking company. They might have records. Do you remember the name, Dexter?"

"Nope. Used to."

"Yeah, me too." Freddy reached across Ry's ankles to pat the dog. "See you later, Chloe."

"Chloe," Dexter said, nodding. "That's it. That's her name.

"What about Duane?" Ry asked. "Has he been here long enough to remember the trucking company?"

"No, but Belinda has." Freddy jumped up and headed for the kitchen.

"I'll come with you," Ry said.

But to Freddy's disappointment, Belinda had been too busy with cooking chores back then to take note of the removal of the drums.

"Let's drive in and see Ballesteros," Ry suggested as

they left the kitchen. "Maybe he'd take a notarized statement from you."

Hope filtered through her gloom. "You think so?"

"It's worth a shot."

"Okay." She took her leather purse from a bottom drawer of the desk. "Let's go."

Ry looked surprised. "That's it? You don't have to fix your face, or anything?"

She paused in confusion. "Why, do I have a smudge of dirt on my nose?"

"No, you're perfect, but I've never known a woman who'd walk right out the door without taking time to primp a little."

Freddy hooked her purse over her arm and grinned at him. "That's because you're used to city girls. Welcome to the country, greenhorn."

THEY TOOK Freddy's truck into town. "Let's hit the drugstore first," Ry said. "I don't want to forget the most important part of this trip."

"As if you would."

He loved the warm color on her cheeks and wondered if he could intensify it. "Actually, there's no chance I'll forget. There is a chance I'll try to seduce you somewhere along the way, and I want to be prepared." As he'd hoped, she blushed even pinker.

"Ry, for heaven's sake. It's broad daylight and we're heading into the heart of the city."

"Which presents a challenge, I'll admit, but I'm getting used to that with you."

She wheeled the truck into the parking lot of a strip shopping center that contained a chain drugstore. "Okay, Mr. One-Track Mind. If you'll make the purchase, I'll use that pay phone to call Ballesteros and tell him we're on our way. It's getting close to lunchtime and we don't want to sit and cool our heels waiting for him."

"Good point."

Moments later, he returned to the truck with a small plastic bag. "All set with Ballesteros?"

She leaned one arm against the steering wheel and gave him an assessing glance. "If I didn't know better, I'd say you planned this, but I guess it would have been virtually impossible, even for a man of your imagination."

"I don't understand what you're talking about."

"Ballesteros has left for lunch, and after lunch, he has an appointment that will keep him occupied until two."

Awareness flickered in his blue eyes. "Really?"

"We could drive home and come back, but that would take almost an hour by itself."

"I see." Ry turned casually and peered down the road. "I could take you to lunch."

"That's a possibility."

He pointed to a hotel a few blocks down the road. "Ever been there for lunch?"

"They don't have a restaurant."

He turned back to her, his gaze intense. "Exactly."

Tension coiled within her. "Ry, I've never checked into a hotel for two hours in the middle of the day. I'd feel like—"

"Someone's lover?" He didn't touch her, but his glance caressed her with bold intimacy. "You are."

Her fingers trembled as she turned the key in the ignition. "I suppose you're used to this sort of interlude, a big-city boy like you." She checked the rearview mirror and backed out of the parking space.

"Right. Two-hour lunches with the well-stacked secretary are commonplace with me."

She hit the brake. "They are?"

He chuckled. "No, Freddy."

She pulled into traffic with the deliberate care of someone who'd had one too many drinks, which was the way she felt—high. "But I'll bet you've done this before."

"I think I can handle the registration and checkout without blushing, if that's what you mean," he said.

"Won't they ask you about luggage, and when you'll be checking out, and stuff like that?"

"I'll tell them the luggage is in the truck and we'll be checking out in the morning. Then when we leave, I'll explain that we had a sudden change of plans."

"But they'll *know*. The maids will see the bed's been..."

"Well-used?" he supplied.

She nodded as her heart pounded furiously.

"Does that mean you'd rather find a coffee shop and have lunch?"

She took a deep breath. "No." She flipped on her turn signal and swept into the hotel's drive-through entrance.

"Want to come in with me while I get us the room?" he asked.

"No."

He chuckled again. "Be right back."

Freddy sat in the truck trying to figure out what she'd say if anyone came by who recognized her sitting there in plain sight with the True Love Guest Ranch brand on the truck's door panels. She ran a guest ranch. Why would she be parked at a hotel in town? She thought for a minute. She was...comparing room rates. That was it.

She and a friend were checking out the going rates in Tucson, to decide if their own pricing structure was reasonable.

But no one came by, and within minutes Ry was back, a key in one hand. "Drive around behind the place," he said, climbing in. "I thought you'd rather not park the truck where anyone on the road could recognize it."

Freddy let out a breath. "Thank you."

"I want to give you pleasure, not embarrassment."

Pleasure. The word echoed in her mind as they parked the truck in the nearly deserted lot behind the hotel. The rooms all opened to the outside, and Ry guided her toward one on the ground floor, put the key in the lock and opened the door. She stepped into the cool interior with a shiver of anticipation.

Behind her, the lock clicked into place and the curtains swished closed, throwing the room into twilight. The air conditioner hummed in a unit beneath the window. In front of her was a king-size bed, quilted spread neatly tucked under the pillows. Now that they were here, alone and undetected, the thrill of being sinful took hold.

"Stay there," she said to Ry, her command coming out in a sultry murmur, "while I redecorate."

"Be my guest."

She laid her hat on the built-in that held the television set as she walked past it to the far side of the bed. In one movement, she swept back the spread and the top sheet, destroying the atmosphere of neatness. Then she plumped the pillows against the headboard.

"Finished?" Ry stood watching her with his thumbs hooked through his belt loops.

"Just getting started." She reached down and pulled

off her boots. "Do you come into town often, cowboy?" she asked as she began undoing the snaps on her shirt.

"Not often enough, obviously."

"Gets lonely out on the trail, I imagine." She held his gaze while she popped the snaps at her wrists and took the shirt off with sensuous rolls of her shoulders.

"You can't imagine how lonely." Passion blazed in his eyes.

She unbuckled her belt and pulled it slowly through the loops. "Days without the soft comfort of a woman's body can take its toll on a man."

"It can make him crazy."

"And are you going crazy?" The jeans slithered over her hips and she kicked them away.

His reply was husky. "Insane."

"Good." She unhooked her bra. "That's how I like my men."

"So I figured."

She dropped the bra to the floor and cupped her breasts. "How long has it been since you touched a woman?"

"Too long."

"Well, I hope you have some staying power." She smoothed her hands down her rib cage, hooked her thumbs in the elastic of her panties and tugged them down her body in one continuous motion. "I'd hate for everything to be over prematurely." She held her panties dangling by two fingers. "If you know what I mean." Then she tossed them across the room toward him.

He caught them without taking his gaze from hers. "I don't think you'll have any complaints."

"Now, that sounds promising." She stretched out on

the bed and propped her cheek on her fist. "Would you care to make good on that boast, cowboy?"

He took off his hat and dropped her panties into the crown before setting the hat next to hers on the built-in. "Reckon I would."

He leaned against the built-in to pull off his boots. Then he rounded the end of the bed, working on his shirt buttons as he walked. She lay back against the pillows as he came to stand beside her and placed the box of condoms at the precise center of the bedside table. "Your underwear was damp," he said.

Her heartbeat thundered in her ears. "Is that so? I wonder what could have caused that?"

He unbuckled his belt and gave her a tight smile. "I think we're about to find out, *Liebchen*."

"A cowboy who can speak German. Oh, my." Freddy ran her tongue over her dry lips as he eased the zipper past the bulge of his arousal. Her heart was chugging like a freight train going up a rise, and the ache within her grew with each bit of magnificent man Ry revealed. When his manhood sprung free, so ready for her, she sucked in her breath.

All his clothes gone, he placed a knee on the bed and leaned toward her. "Is that how you want me to make love to you, little lady? In German?"

"No, cowboy," she murmured, reaching to cup his face and pull him down for a long-awaited kiss. "I want to understand every word you say."

But he didn't need many words to tell her how much he wanted her. Braced above her, he roved her face and neck with his hungry lips. She reached upward to receive his kisses at her breasts. His touch had already become achingly familiar, and she responded with lush abandon as he stroked her hips, her thighs, the backs of her knees. When he caressed her between her thighs, he groaned softly. "I think we've found out why your panties were drenched, *chérie*."

She gasped with longing and gripped his shoulders as he probed deep. "Love me, Ry."

He braced his elbow beside her head as he reached for the box. "And what else did you ask for?" he murmured in her ear. "Staying power?"

"That might not...be necessary."

"Ah, but it would be more fun." He nibbled at the lobe of her ear. "Help me with this, *chérie*. I want to feel your hands on me."

She took the packet and ripped it open with shaking fingers. Then he whispered instructions in her ear as she fumbled with the task, bringing them both to a fever pitch of excitement. Finally, she managed, and in a breathless voice announced her success.

His response was hoarse with need as he moved between her thighs. "Never has incompetence felt so good." Poised above her, he smoothed her hair back from her face. "We've made love in so many ways, but this was what I really wanted." He eased forward. "This."

"Yes." She lifted her hips to meet him, tension throbbing through her, demanding release. "Please, Ry."

He slipped both hands beneath her hips, and with a sharp intake of breath he plunged deep. At that first thrust she erupted into a dazzling climax, calling his name as she writhed in his arms. He moved with each spasm, heightening her pleasure until she became delirious with sensation.

Gradually, she regained the ability to breathe, and her heartbeat slowed a fraction. Yet he was still within her, the sweet pressure producing tiny aftershocks, and a renewed curl of tension. She looked up to find him smiling gently as he gazed at her.

"Good?" he asked.

"Oh, yes." Good didn't begin to describe the pleasure he'd given her, but she had no idea how to tell him that she'd never reacted so quickly and thoroughly with anyone.

"There's more." Lacing his fingers through hers, he stretched her arms above her head, lifting her breasts for his mouth. Nuzzling her pert nipples, he began a slow rhythm with his hips.

Each sensuous thrust set off a responding pulse beat within her, fueled even more by the flick of his warm tongue against her breasts. Sanity slipped away again, to be replaced by the ever-tightening grasp of need. He had pleasured her well the night before, but now he touched elements far more basic as he again and again probed her moist center, claiming his place there. With a cry of surrender, she arched upward as he pushed her once more into the shattering world of release.

Before she'd completely recovered, he wrapped his arms around her waist and rolled to his back, carrying her with him and holding her tightly locked against him. She braced her hands on his chest and absorbed his hot gaze as it traveled over her breasts and down to the juncture of their thighs. He glanced back up into her eyes. "Love me," he murmured. "Ride me, *chérie*."

With a smile of female anticipation, she rose slightly on her knees and settled back down over his heated shaft. He moaned. Her palms flat against his chest, she repeated the motion in a faster rhythm. He clutched the sheet in both hands as his breathing grew labored. Faster she moved, and faster, until he was gasping. She gave him no mercy. She wanted his surrender to be as complete as hers.

His shout of release seemed torn from his soul. As she leaned down to kiss him, he looked into her eyes and she knew he was hers.

14

AT FIVE MINUTES before two, Ry and Freddy walked into the lobby of Frontier Savings and Loan. He'd assured her that after a shower at the hotel and the use of a comb and lipstick from her purse, she didn't look as if she'd just spent two hours making love.

More specifically, a stranger wouldn't know it, he amended to himself as he ushered her past a large Remington sculpture of a cattle stampede and over to a cluster of desks to the right of the teller windows. He had only to gaze into her languorous eyes to read the aftermath of passion written there. The merest brush of her sleeve against his and scenes flashed through his mind—Freddy tossing her underwear across the room, Freddy stretching out on the bed and inviting him to make good on his boast, Freddy arching in surrender at the moment of climax. They'd discovered paradise in that hotel room, and he still carried a bit of it with him.

"We'll wait," Freddy said, nudging him. "Won't we, Mr. McGuinnes?"

He snapped out of his daze long enough to realize Freddy had been communicating with the loan officer at the desk nearest Ballesteros's empty one. And Ry had been out to lunch—literally. He cleared his throat. "Of course."

"Would either of you care for coffee?" the woman asked.

He glanced at Freddy, who shook her head. "No, thanks," he said. "We'll just have a seat until Mr. Ballesteros arrives." Ry wondered if Ballesteros was engaged in a little rendezvous of his own. Probably not. Just because Ry was in an erotic fog didn't mean everyone else was.

As they sat in imitation-leather chairs, Freddy leaned toward him. "You'll have to sharpen up, there, McGuinnes," she said in a low voice. "If you stand around staring off into space, people will wonder what you've been up to."

He gave her a crooked smile. "You're a powerful force, Miss Singleton. I'm not sure I realized what I was letting myself in for."

"Ah." She studied him, a wary look in her eyes. "Second thoughts?"

"Yes. I was trying to figure out how we could have managed this meeting with simply a phone call so we wouldn't have had to leave the room."

Her lips curved provocatively. He wanted to kiss off every bit of her newly applied lipstick.

"Miss Singleton? Mr. McGuinnes? I'm Jose Ballesteros. Sorry to keep you waiting."

Ry looked up as a short, round man with an olive complexion held out his hand. Apparently, they'd missed his entrance into the building. They really would have to pay better attention to the world around them.

"No problem." Ry stood and shook his hand firmly.

Freddy followed suit, and Ballesteros took a seat behind his cluttered desk. "Were you able to find out anything about the petroleum drums?" he asked, pawing through the papers on his desk.

"The drums were taken out," Freddy said, leaning

forward. "I was there. I saw the trucks loaded with the drums pull away and drive down the road."

"Well, that's good," Ballesteros said cautiously, glancing up at her. "Do you have any documentation as to when that was done?"

Ry shifted in his seat. "We're running into some difficulty with that and we thought you might be able to take a notarized statement from Miss Singleton."

Ballesteros met his gaze. "Not a good idea. We can do that, but she'd have to sign a statement that she's responsible for anything that's found buried there, ever. That kind of liability is too broad, in my opinion."

"You're right." Ry shook his head in frustration. "I guess we have to find that receipt."

"What if we don't?" Freddy asked.

"Then I'm afraid, in order to get financing, we have to dig."

"Who's we?" she persisted.

"Well..." Ballesteros obviously wasn't enjoying his role as the bearer of bad news. "The present owners claim they have no responsibility in the matter, and technically they don't. I'm afraid the expense of either proving the drums aren't there, or getting them out and cleaning up the area if they are, will fall to the person who was the owner at the time the drums were installed."

Ry had figured that one out, but he wanted Ballesteros to deliver the message instead of him. And he wanted her to realize just what a jerk Whitlock was turning out to be.

"So, since my father and mother are dead, the responsibility falls to me," Freddy said in a surprisingly calm voice.

Ballesteros steepled his fingers. "I'm afraid so. If I

were you, I'd do everything I could to find a receipt or locate the trucking company. In the meantime, the financing decisions will be put on hold. I'm sorry. This is a very hot subject right now. And you'd better hope that if the drums are down there, they didn't pollute the water supply."

"They're not down there," Freddy said, an edge to her voice.

"Let's hope not."

Ry stood. "We'll find a way to prove it. Thanks for your time."

As they left the building in a much less euphoric mood than when they'd arrived, Ry reflected that there was nothing that spoiled paradise quicker than a snake.

On the way back to the True Love, he glanced at Freddy's rigid profile. "Now do you see what your friend and neighbor has done? He's not only thrown a monkey wrench into the sale, he may have set you up for a very costly procedure."

"Which I couldn't begin to pay for on what I make as foreman of the ranch."

"You won't pay for it. I will."

'That's crazy. It's not your responsibility, and it's bad business besides! I won't let you do that."

"I want the ranch, Freddy." *And the foreman, if she'll have me.* "Whitlock may think this will discourage me from pursuing the sale, but he's mistaken."

"I still can't believe that Eb—"

"Be realistic, Freddy. This was all calculated by him. He knows the drums aren't there, but my partners and I don't. If you can't pay to have it checked out, then we'd have to, and we have no idea what sort of pollution problem we might run into. Any logical business-person would back out of a sale with that sort of snag. If the drums have polluted the groundwater, the property's value will drop drastically."

"But none of that's true!"

"I know, and the one thing Whitlock didn't count on was that I'd credit the memory of a ten-year-old girl over that of a grown man."

Her voice softened. "And you do?"

"Absolutely."

"Thank you."

"Don't thank me," he said with a chuckle. "It makes sense. A couple of weeks ago, you would have resorted to almost anything, including rumors of buried petroleum drums, to scare me off the True Love. If you really wanted Whitlock to have the property, you'd agree the stuff was down there, and I'd ride off into the sunset."

Her throat moved convulsively. "I guess I don't want that anymore."

"Good." His heart squeezed. She hadn't made a passionate declaration, but it was a beginning. He had a long way to go, however, and he still hadn't confessed his plans for selling the property. Guilt nagged him, but caution held him back. Before he confessed, he wanted her to care more about him than she did about the True Love Ranch.

THERE WERE four drawers in the aging file cabinet. Freddy directed Ry to pull them all out and carry them to the dining room, where no one would need the tables for at least two hours. She called Leigh down at the corrals and asked her to come up and help. Then she enlisted Belinda, so there was one person to a drawer.

"Anything that looks like a trucking company receipt, or a hauling receipt, or trash removal, or anything remotely sounding as if it could be what we need, sing out," Freddy said as they began the search.

An hour and a half later, several possibilities had been found then discarded. The tables were piled with folders, and the drawers were almost empty. Leigh slapped her hand on the table in frustration. "Eb Whitlock is a horse's ass! I have half a mind to ride over there and tell him so."

"He's just being an aggressive businessman," Ry said. "Unfortunately for his plans, he's also dealing with one. I'll call in the morning and get somebody out here with a backhoe. Can you pinpoint the location for me, Freddy?"

Freddy's chest tightened with anxiety. "I sure hope so."

He frowned. "What do you mean, you hope so? If he had gas pumps, the drums would be right under that area, so you must remember where the pumps were."

"I do. Somewhere behind the big corral."

"Somewhere behind the big corral?"

Tears threatened. She'd been on an emotional roller coaster for too many days, and it was taking a toll. "I was ten, Ry! I don't remember exactly."

He rose from his chair. "Hey, it's okay." He crossed the room and wrapped his arms around her, in full view of Leigh and Belinda. "We'll dig up whatever we have to in order to satisfy those creeps."

She started to struggle away, but he held her tight. "Belinda and Leigh don't care if I give you a hug," he said gently. "And you look like you could use one."

"Hey, kiss her if you want," Leigh said. "It's been a long afternoon."

Ry chuckled. "I just might."

"Don't worry," Belinda said. "I think I can remember

where the pumps were. And Dexter can remember, too. We'll find the right spot."

"Somebody's talking about me."

Freddy peeked over Ry's shoulder. Dexter stood in the doorway of the dining room. Balanced on his walker, he surveyed the stacks of files with disapproval. "What a mess!"

"We're trying to find the receipt from that trucking company," Freddy said.

"They are." Dexter swept an arm toward Leigh and his wife. "You're not."

Freddy laughed. "No, I'm hugging Ry."

Dexter nodded. "Good."

"Yeah." Freddy leaned back and smiled into Ry's face. "He's one of the good guys."

"That's it!" Dexter exclaimed, clomping into the room with his walker. "Good guys! Good guys!"

Freddy disentangled herself to turn and stare at Dexter.

"Dragging!" Dexter said, obviously very excited. "No, lifting! Big. Real big! Round! Thataway!" He pointed in the direction of the road.

Leigh pushed herself up from the table, her attention focused on Dexter. "Are you talking about the drums, Dex?"

"Yeah! Good guys!"

Disappointment swept over Freddy. She had thought maybe Dexter was remembering something significant, when he was only making a comment about the men who had done the hauling. Apparently, he'd liked them. "I'm sure they were good guys, Dexter. But we need the name of the company."

Belinda jumped up so fast, she knocked over her chair. "That *was* the name of the company. There was a trucking company back then that called themselves Good Guys!"

With a gasp, Freddy ran for the Yellow Pages. She hurried back, flipping through the book. Then her shoulders sagged again. There was no Good Guys Trucking Company. "I guess they've gone out of business."

"Or somebody else bought them out," Ry said, reaching for the book. "Give me a few minutes in your office, *chérie.*"

"Ooh la-la!" Leigh said as he left the room. "Big sister, my hat's off to you for catching a stud who speaks French."

"Good Guys," Dexter said again, nodding. "I remembered."

"Yes, you did." Freddy walked over and squeezed his arm. "It's not your fault they're out of business."

Belinda started reloading files into a drawer. "We'll have to clean this up pretty quick. Dinnertime's almost here."

"Right," Freddy agreed. She and Leigh lifted stacks of files and settled them in the drawers. Leigh started to pick up a drawer that was full. "Let Ry do that when he comes back," Freddy said.

Leigh set the drawer down with a grin. "My, how quickly you've become used to having a big, strong man around."

Freddy gazed at her sister. "It's a little scary, isn't it?"

"I think it's lovely," Belinda said, patting her last files into place. "Now, I'd better go see how everyone's coming along in the kitchen."

"Thanks, Belinda," Freddy said. "We couldn't have—"

"I found them!" Ry strode into the room waving a

piece of paper. "Cunningham Trucking bought out Good Guys sixteen years ago."

Freddy was almost afraid to ask. "But do they have any records that go back that far?"

Ry's jubilant grin provided the answer. "The senior Mr. Cunningham saves everything, according to a disgruntled secretary. She promised she would have no trouble locating the receipt, and she was glad that there was some justification, at long last, for keeping all those dusty files. I gave her your fax number. She expects to send it within the hour."

Freddy had hurled herself into his arms before she realized it. She kissed him soundly, and whirled away to pump Dexter's arm. "You did it," she said, grinning at both of them. "What a team."

Both Dexter and Ry looked immensely pleased with themselves. Ry turned to the old man and held out his hand. Dexter shook it with enthusiasm.

Leigh sauntered up, eyes sparkling. "Congratulations, and all that. But it's time to get back to work, Ry, my friend. Freddy says you're the man to call when it comes to hefting file drawers, and we'll have dinner guests coming in any minute now."

"No problem. I'll—"

"In fact," Leigh said, glancing around Ry, "someone just came through the front door with a suitcase. Freddy, were we expecting another guest tonight?"

"Not that I know of." She looked at the man silhouetted against the open doorway, a battered suitcase in his hand and a cowboy hat on his head. "Maybe he's looking for a job," she said in a low tone. "I'll go see."

But before she could approach the stranger, he plunked down his suitcase and strode into the dining room, his boot heels hitting the pine floor with a confident thump. "T.R. is that you? Didn't recognize you without your briefcase and three-piece suit."

Ry turned in surprise, and his eyes widened. "Lavette! Where did you come from? Why didn't you let us know you were heading in?"

"Thought I'd surprise you." He shook Ry's hand.

Freddy assessed the man's clothes, dusty but new, and smiled. Another urban cowboy had arrived. He looked less than thirty years old, with a devilish gleam in his green eyes and a dimple in his cheek. Thick dark hair reached to his collar. She was already figuring out which horse to put him on, when Ry turned to her.

"Chase Lavette, I'd like you to meet Freddy Singleton, the foreman," he said.

"Glad to meet you." He offered his hand in a firm grip.

"And Freddy's sister, Leigh Singleton, the head wrangler," Ry added.

Leigh responded to his handshake with a smile. "Welcome to the True Love. Do you speak French, Mr. Lavette?"

"Nope." His grin was disarming. "I only know how to kiss that way."

"Easy, Lavette," Ry said, winking at Leigh. "These women can rope and hog-tie you in under thirty seconds if you're disrespectful."

Chase touched the brim of his hat. "No disrespect intended. Can't afford it with my back."

"How's the healing coming along?" Ry asked.

"Pretty well. Sometimes I have good days, sometimes not so good. Today's been good, so far."

"What'd you do, walk from New York?" Ry asked, peering at the dust on his friend's clothes.

"Just from the main road. Hitched from the airport,

for the fun of it. If I'd had a saddle on my shoulder, it would've been perfect." Chase laughed. "I see what you mean about the way the city's moving in this direction, McGuinnes. This land is solid gold."

As if in slow motion, Freddy looked at Ry. She saw the flash of panic in his eyes and her heart began to freeze. Then he turned from her and put his hand on Chase's shoulder, as if to guide him away.

But Chase seemed determined to deliver his observations, oblivious to the dead silence that had settled over the room. "I'm sure that before long, this will be a subdivision, like you predicted, T.R., so I figured bad back or not, I'd better get out here and enjoy the place while I can."

15

FREDDY BROKE and ran. She and Ry had left the truck parked in front of the ranch house, and the keys were on the floor, where she always put them. She heard a shout as she gunned the engine to life. Slamming her foot to the floor, she peeled out, glancing in the rear-view mirror. She'd covered Ry in a shower of dust. She considered backing up and running him over.

The tears didn't start until she reached the corrals and started saddling Maureen. Fortunately, she could saddle and bridle the mare blindfolded, so it didn't matter that she was crying so hard she couldn't see. Duane came over when she was nearly done.

"Freddy, darlin', what's the matter?" he asked, more tenderly than she'd remembered Duane ever speaking in his life.

"Sorry," she said, her voice choked. "Can't talk about it."

"Gonna ride it out?"

"Yep."

"Be careful. Don't poke Maureen's leg in no gopher holes 'cause you're not lookin'. And hold on. Don't want to hafta scrape you off no barrel cactus, neither."

"I'll be careful." Freddy vaulted into the saddle and slapped Maureen's rump with the reins. As if the little mare understood the need for haste, she took off at a lope.

Freddy sent Maureen down the path leading toward the wash. Branches whipped past, and Freddy ducked under them, anchoring her hat to her head with one hand as she drove her heels into Maureen's sides, urging her on. Maybe if she rode fast enough, she could outrun her thoughts. Maybe if she cried hard enough, her tears would wash away the pain of betrayal.

Maureen took the descent to the sandy wash in one graceful leap. A less experienced rider might have pitched forward and sent the mare to her knees, throwing the rider headfirst into the wash. Freddy anticipated the weight change and glided with Maureen to the dry bed. She leaned over and whispered into Maureen's velvet ear, "Run like hell, baby."

Maureen's haunches bunched and she bolted as if from a racetrack gate. Freddy kept her body low over the horse's neck, relishing the snap of the mare's mane against her wet cheeks. Her hair worked its way loose from the clip, which tumbled to the sand as her tresses rippled like a flag in the wind. Maureen's hooves pounded the dry creek bed, sending up grainy geysers as she stretched her legs in a dead run.

The hot wind dried Freddy's tears as soon as they fell, and the fierce joy of riding full speed partly replaced the pain in her heart. But the late-afternoon sun beat down on her shoulders, and she realized that no matter what she needed, she couldn't expect Maureen to continue at this pace for long. Already the mare's breathing was labored, her neck dark with sweat. The wash narrowed, and Freddy pulled gently on the reins, slowing the animal to a lope. A hundred yards farther on, she guided Maureen into a trot, and finally slowed her to a walk.

"Thanks, girl." Freddy cleared the residue of emotion from her throat and patted the horse's lathered neck.

"I'll make it up to you. I promise I will." Then, with a whimper, she laid her cheek on the wind-whipped mane. "Once a city slicker, always a city slicker, Maureen. Don't ever forget it." New tears threatened, and she sniffed them back. "No more tears. No more tears for Mr. T.R. McGuinnes."

But she had to think what to do. He would buy the ranch, he and his city slicker friends. She couldn't stop it now. She'd even helped him do it.

She reined Maureen to the right, back up the bank and along a trail that led toward the old homestead. She had always been able to think better there.

Still excited by the run, Maureen pranced and blew through her nostrils as they navigated the trail. Her gyrations startled a family of quail—mother, father and six little babies the size and shape of golf balls. As the parents herded their charges to safety in the underbrush, Freddy's heart wrenched with a new wave of pain. With a cry of anguish, she faced the death of dreams she hadn't even known she'd had until she saw the quail. Ry had awakened urges for a family of her own, children to teach in the ways of the ranch, to instruct in the legacy of the True Love.

"The place *is* cursed!" she shouted, causing Maureen to throw back her head in alarm. "And I'm a fool for trying to hold on," she said, gazing sightlessly at the trail ahead as she quieted her horse.

Maureen picked her way without guidance along the familiar trail she'd taken countless times with her mistress. Eventually, she halted in the clearing across from the ruins of the small adobe homestead. Freddy roused herself and dismounted, letting the reins drop to the ground so Maureen was free to graze.

As Freddy approached the crumbling adobe building, a green-collared lizard scurried across her path. She checked for spiders and scorpions before sitting on a portion of the ruined wall shaded by a large palo verde.

Taking off her hat, she ran the back of her sleeve across her face and sighed. Apparently, Ry and his partners only wanted the land the True Love occupied, not the ranch itself. She'd feared the dangers of a failed love affair, but this was worse, so much worse. She'd vowed to stay on the ranch until she was tossed off, but she couldn't imagine continuing as foreman knowing that Ry and his co-owners would sell to the first big developer who came along. Leigh might choose to stay on for a while, and Belinda might have no choice, considering Dexter's needs.

Dexter. Freddy's hands closed into fists and she longed to punch Ry in the face. Had he considered what destroying the ranch would do to Dexter? The old man would be dead within a year. And Duane. Where would he keep his precious herd now? He'd planned to use what money he earned with that herd to send his kids to college. His life would be in shambles if the ranch disappeared.

How could Ry do this? Yet, to be fair, she had to admit he'd never promised to preserve the ranch, only to buy it. She'd been blinded by lust into believing he had only the best of intentions toward her and the True Love. And he'd taken advantage of that attraction. God, how she hated him for that.

She gazed out at the desert—the prickly pear decorated in yellow, blossoms wide open, drinking in the afternoon sun. She'd opened herself like that for Ry, thinking to sun herself in his warmth. And she'd been burned.

She thought of Clara Singleton, a woman who'd known how to survive, how to give sexual favors without surrendering her heart, until she found a man like Thaddeus, who offered true love. Then Clara had reaped her reward, perhaps sitting near this very spot and admiring the cactus flowers. She must have appreciated the triumph of a cactus flower, beauty thriving amid harsh conditions, like Clara herself. Clara would most likely have pointed a 30-30 at a land grabber like Ry and ordered him off her spread.

Freddy's jaw clenched. So what was she doing? Meekly handing in her resignation and scuttling away? Giving up?

No, by God!

Freddy leaped to her feet and slapped her hat on her head. This homestead was a proven historical site, and somebody might give Mr. McGuinnes and his partners a really hard time about destroying it. And what about the John Wayne Room? What about the other famous people, some still alive, who had stayed there? There might be enough public sentiment attached to the entire ranch to hold up his development plans for years!

"We'll fight him all the way, Clara," she muttered, glancing at the old house. "You and I."

As she started toward Maureen, a rumble of thunder sounded in the distance. She glanced up into the cloudless sky. Probably a squadron of fighter jets from the air base, she thought, continuing toward her horse.

The rumble grew louder, and Maureen's head came up.

"What is it, girl?" Freddy asked, reaching for the mare's bridle.

Uncharacteristically, Maureen jerked her head away from Freddy's outstretched hand.

"Hey, it's probably a bunch of helicopters on maneuvers," Freddy said, following her uneasy horse. "It's probably—"

A Hereford crashed through the brush and headed straight for Maureen. The horse bolted just as another cow thundered past, and the ground began to shake.

"Maureen!" Freddy cried, running after the horse. But Maureen was gone, plunging wildly down the trail away from the stampeding herd. A heifer bumped Freddy from behind, almost sending her to the ground. She scrambled erect as a powerful shoulder brushed against her and spun her around to face a wall of russet-and-white faces surging toward her.

She lost a precious second as she stood paralyzed. Then she turned and ran for the edge of the clearing, grabbing a branch of the first mesquite she reached. Thorns bit into her palms as she braced a foot in the crotch of the tree and hauled herself up, losing her hat in the process. Just as she got her other foot off the ground, the first wave rushed past, shaking the trunk and rattling the branches. Her hands slipped, and she tightened her grip despite the thorns. Blood trickled down her wrist and soaked into the cuffs of her shirt.

She hauled herself higher, praying the tree was strong enough to hold her weight. A branch cracked but didn't fall as the cattle surged beneath her. Then the massed animals began banging into the trunk, jolting her with each impact.

Slowly, the tree began to lean.

"Help!" she shouted, knowing it was no use, knowing she was absolutely alone. But she shouted, anyway. "Help me! Please help me!"

"Freddy!"

Someone was there. She squinted through the dust as

the tree leaned closer to the trampling herd. "Over here!"

Then she saw him, riding low over Red Devil's neck as the big horse plowed through the river of cattle. No, it should not be Ry. He wasn't a good enough rider to make it through a stampede. He would die trying to save her. "Go back!" she screamed. "I'll make it!"

She glimpsed the grim set of his mouth. He was coming for her. Her heart swelled in response to this show of courage. Foolish, foolish courage. *Oh, Ry! Please go back,* she begged silently, knowing it was no use. If she allowed him to pick her off the tree, as he obviously intended, they'd probably both fall under the churning hooves and be killed. But if she held back, he'd probably fall off trying to reach her and then they'd both die. A no-win situation.

He veered toward the tree, his arm extended. She poised herself for the pickup.

"Now!" he shouted, grabbing her by the belt.

She landed facedown across the front of his saddle, the impact knocking the air from her lungs. She stared straight into the wild eyes of a Hereford running beside Red Devil as she started to slip forward headfirst into the herd.

"No, dammit!" Ry shouted, jerking her back by her belt. "No!"

Gradually, Red Devil's pace slowed. The herd thinned, until Ry was able to rein the horse in. Red Devil stood snorting and shaking as Ry hauled Freddy upright and settled her facing him, her thighs resting across his.

Freddy gasped for breath. Ry's face was a mask of dust, and his chest heaved. He picked up one of her blood-encrusted hands and examined her palm. Then he placed a soft kiss there.

Tears welled in her eyes, and she was about to blubber out her gratitude, when she recalled why she'd ridden out here in the first place. Taking an unsteady breath, she lifted her chin and looked him square in the eye. "I hate your guts," she said.

"I know." He smiled.

"Furthermore, you're not getting away with this, you and your pack of thieves from the big city. I'm fighting you every inch of the way, buster. You haven't seen the last of Freddy Singleton!"

His smile widened.

"What are you doing, sitting there grinning like an idiot? Don't you realize what I'm saying? This is war!"

"I wouldn't expect anything less from you."

"So what's the big smile for, mister?"

"You're alive."

She stared at him, then cleared her throat. "Thank you for saving my life," she said stiffly.

"No thanks necessary. You did me a favor."

"I beg your pardon?"

He reined Red Devil in a circle and started toward the homestead. She was forced to grab hold of his waist to keep from falling off. Even worse, the movement of the horse, balanced as she was up against Ry's crotch, awakened some potent memories she would rather forget.

He held her gently with one arm around her waist, his chin hovering just above the crown of her head. "You see, Freddy, I came to Arizona feeling like a failure. Maybe I'd done well in the paper world of stocks and bonds, but I had no confidence I could make it in the nitty-gritty of real life. Deep down I was afraid that if I'd been faced with those punks who killed Linda, I might not have known what to do. It sounds corny, but my manhood had never been tested."

Ry was a lot harder to hate up close like this, she thought. She found herself hugging him tighter, and then she had to remember to relax her arms and back away as much as possible in this confining position.

"I think that's part of what buying this ranch was all about," he continued. "I wanted to come out here and test myself."

That statement helped renew her fury. "So we were a proving ground for you? How nice. Now you can turn the True Love into a suburban housing development because it's served your purpose."

He tightened his grip around her waist. "We need to talk about that."

"I'm not much in the mood for talking. I think I'd rather cut your heart out."

He sighed. "You may get your chance at that, too. But I—" He paused and pulled back on Red Devil's reins. "My God."

"What?" Glancing up, she saw him staring over Red Devil's head. She swiveled to follow the direction of his gaze, and her breath became trapped in her lungs.

Where the little homestead had once stood as a silent tribute to Clara and Thaddeus Singleton, nothing remained but a pile of rubble. Only the concrete slab had survived in one piece. A lump rising in her throat, Freddy held on to Ry as she wiggled her way out of the saddle and down to the ground. Slowly, she approached the trampled ruins as tears made tracks through the dust caking her face.

She leaned over, picked up a piece of an adobe brick and held the fragment tight in her fist as she imagined

Thaddeus building the wooden forms for the adobe, hauling the sand, mixing the straw and the mud. Brick by brick he'd forged his place in the wilderness, built it for his beloved Clara. Freddy searched the debris for the lintel and found it smashed beyond repair. The heart with an arrow through it was in two pieces.

She picked them up and tried to fit them together, putting a splinter through her finger for her efforts. She'd always meant to have the site stabilized, meant to erect some barrier around it. Now it was too late. The home Thaddeus had built, the home Clara had risked her life fighting for, was gone.

"I'm sorry." Ry put an arm around her shoulders.

She wrenched away and whirled to face him. "How *dare* you say you're sorry? You want to bulldoze the whole place someday!"

Agony was etched on his face. "No, I don't."

"Really?" She saw him through a red film of rage. "Then where were you planning to put the subdivision? What about the golf course? Now I know why you were so interested in the water supply and landscaping. You, you *rapist!*"

He stepped forward and grabbed her. "Listen to me!"

"No!" She tried to twist away and the two pieces of wood fell from her grasp.

"Yes! I meant to do those things when I came here. I admit it! But I've changed, Freddy. You've changed me. Just now, I risked my life to save yours. And I succeeded." He gave her a little shake. "I succeeded! Do you understand how that makes me feel?"

"No," she said tightly.

His touch gentled. "For the first time in my life, I feel like a man. You gave me that. You and the True Love."

He released her. "I don't want it to disappear any more than you do."

She stepped away from him, away from the seductive pull of his touch. "Then let Eb Whitlock buy it."

His eyes narrowed. "I can't do that."

"Why not?"

"Something's going on around here. I'm not convinced all the so-called accidents are accidents."

Even in the heat, she felt a chill run over her. "You think somebody's sabotaging the ranch?"

"Maybe. And Whitlock's one of my candidates."

"Oh, for heaven's sake! That thing with the petroleum drums was a case of bad memory."

"It could have been, but he seemed pretty focused to me. And then there's the question of Duane."

"Duane?"

"Did you see whose brand was on those cattle?"

She tried to remember, but the only thing that surfaced was a mass of heaving bodies with the power to kill her. "No, I didn't."

"I didn't either until the last two ran by me. They both carried the D-Bar on their left hip, Freddy."

"My God, Duane will be furious that his cattle got out and stampeded like that."

"Unless he stampeded them."

"What? You *are* paranoid, Ry McGuinnes!"

"Am I? When I got to the corrals, Duane was on the phone, and I think he was talking to Leigh. We can assume Leigh told him about the subdivision thing. When I saddled up, he came out and asked where I was headed, and I told him over by the old homestead."

She gasped. "Just what are you implying?"

"You're the one who said Duane would do anything to protect his own. He could have figured you could handle yourself in a stampede if you happened to be around, but he may have reckoned I might not."

"No." She shook her head. "You're definitely wrong about this."

"Then what's the explanation for all the accidents? The True Love curse?"

"I'd accept that before I'd accuse anyone I've known and trusted most of my life."

He sighed. "I can understand that, but deep in your heart you know something's wrong around here, and you'll have to agree that several people have a motive for devaluing the property with these accidents. Besides, you don't strike me as the superstitious type."

"I refuse to be the suspicious type, either."

"Not even when you almost died?"

Freddy shoved her hands in the back pockets of her jeans and gazed down at the ground. A short distance away was the tree she'd climbed. It lay broken at the base, toppled over, its leaves and branches crushed. Nearby was a flat, grayish blob that was probably what remained of her hat. She shivered. Was it possible that someone was sabotaging her beloved ranch? If so, she needed an ally she could trust. She leveled a look at Ry. "You've said you don't want the ranch to disappear, but you haven't said you'll work to save it either. Looks like I don't have any good options."

He rubbed the back of his neck. "It's not an easy situation. I can't buy it alone, and I've promised both partners we'll sell to developers and make a huge profit. That's why they're coming in with me."

Freddy's first reaction was despair. But she took a deep breath and thought about the way Chase Lavette had arrived today, decked out in boots, jeans and hat, all dusty from a walk down the road. And hadn't Ry said something about the third partner wanting to bring his son out to the True Love, to give him the experience of being a cowboy? She studied Ry and compared him to the man who had arrived in wing tips and tie.

"Are you sure that's why they're coming in with you on this deal?" she asked. "To make big money?"

"Sure. Why else?"

"You didn't come here just for that. You've just confessed you wanted to test yourself."

"Yeah, but—"

"Ry, what if they're both like you, needing the True Love for some personal reason but not quite ready to admit it? So they use an acceptable excuse, such as making money, to be a part of a ranch, to live a different sort of life."

The corner of his mouth tilted up. "Are you saying we should get them out here and convert them to the idea of keeping the ranch?"

"It seems to have worked with you."

"Yeah, but my case is a little different."

"How?"

The smile left his face and he regarded her with an intensity that sent a quiver through her. "I fell in love."

The earth seemed to drop away beneath her feet.

"Unfortunately," he said, "she doesn't feel the same way about me."

She gazed at him and remembered the emotion that had gripped her when she saw him riding through the stampede to save her. She'd been ready to give her life to save his. Even knowing how he'd deceived her about the ranch, she'd loved him enough to sacrifice herself. Even then. "Don't be too sure," she said unsteadily.

"Oh, I'm sure. You see, this lady's already given her heart away, and that love will always be her first priority. I'd have to accept second place. I'm not satisfied with that."

A pain sharper than she'd ever known knifed through her. "You would make me choose?" she whispered.

"Yes."

"Why?"

"Because I can't promise you that I'll be able to keep the ranch as it is. I can try, and we can hope my partners want to try, but the city could still grow around us, choking us out. We could lose zoning fights. We could go bankrupt. Even Thaddeus Singleton couldn't promise Clara that they'd always have the ranch. He could only promise his love. That's the one sure thing, Freddy." His hands clenched at his sides. "And it has to be enough."

A door swung open in her heart, a door rusty and unused.

"Let it be enough, Freddy," he murmured.

Joy shouldered its way through the door, filling the space where fear had reigned for so long. Happiness made it almost impossible to speak. But she had to say the words, had to give him what he sought. "I love you, Ry."

Intense emotion blazed in his eyes. Then he leaned down and picked up the two pieces of wood. "I think this can be fixed," he said gently. "It's more portable now," he added with a soft smile. "It can go wherever we go." He closed the distance between them. "Will you marry me, Frederica Singleton?"

"Yes."

He pulled her roughly into his arms and kissed her, dust and all. The pieces of wood in his hand imprinted themselves against her back as he tightened his hold.

Clara would have approved of this moment, Freddy thought fleetingly. Then Ry's kiss deepened, and she abandoned thought altogether.

What's more irresistible than a cowboy?
A cowboy and his baby!

THE DRIFTER

Prologue

JUST BEFORE the elevator reversed direction and plummeted to the basement, Chase Lavette was thinking about Amanda Drake. Had she become pregnant that night they'd spent in his truck? Surely she would have contacted him by now. Yet he couldn't shake off the suspicion that she might not, and he'd finally decided to see for himself. There was no way she'd be able to hide the fact at eight months. He didn't welcome the idea of being a dad, but he'd really hate to be one and not know it.

Without warning, a relay failed between the second and third floors, catapulting the elevator toward the bottom at a thousand feet per minute. Chase had approximately three seconds to wish Amanda's office had been on ground level. He looked around and met the startled gaze of the two men who shared the elevator with him: a business type and a New York City cop. He swore once, loudly, just before the elevator slammed into its concrete base. It felt as though somebody had swung a sledgehammer against the balls of his feet as he went down, pain knifing through his spine.

1

HE WAS ALIVE. Twenty years ago, a social worker had told Chase he was a survivor, and apparently the lady had called it right. He started to move and clenched his teeth in pain. He was alive, but something major was wrong with his back.

The air was hot and close. It even smelled hot, like sizzled circuits. He strained to hear any sound of movement from the other two men in the darkness of the crumpled elevator car. Nothing. His stomach felt as if he'd stripped a gear. He'd seen fatalities on the highway, plenty of them, but that hadn't made the prospect of death easier to handle. Still, he was conscious and they didn't seem to be. It was up to him to help.

The groan of stressed metal discouraged him from trying to get up. Then somebody coughed. Thank God. They weren't both dead. "Who's that?" he asked, his throat rusty from fear.

"Name's McGuinnes." A pause. "T. R. McGuinnes. You?"

"Chase Lavette. Are you the cop?"

"No."

Chase grimaced. The cop would probably be of more use than some Wall Street paper pusher. "Do you think he's dead?"

"I hope to God he's not. Are you hurt?"

"Yeah. Something's wrong with my back. It hurts like hell. How about you?"

"I hit my head. Listen, you'd better not move. I'll check the cop."

Chase had no intention of moving if somebody else was volunteering to be the hero. Damn, it would have to be his back. A trucker's nightmare. Of course, the cop might be dead, a thought that put his back problems into perspective real quick. He listened as McGuinnes crawled across the buckled floor of the elevator. As Chase's vision adjusted a little to the darkness, he noticed that the ceiling had partially collapsed and a light fixture dangled near the floor. His heart pounded as if he'd been running and his sweaty T-shirt stuck to his chest. "It's getting damned hot in here," he said.

"Yeah."

"They should be coming to get us out pretty soon." Chase said it more to reassure himself than anything.

"Let's hope so."

Chase held his breath as McGuinnes moved toward the cop.

"If you try mouth-to-mouth resuscitation, you're a dead man," mumbled a voice.

Chase relaxed against the wall, feeling giddy with relief. Thank God there wouldn't be any corpses in this elevator.

"Never learned it, anyway," McGuinnes said, handing the cop a handkerchief out of his pocket. "Here. You're bleeding somewhere."

The cop sounded weary. "No joke. How's the other guy?"

"I'll survive," Chase said.

"Says his back hurts," McGuinnes added. "I told him not to move."

"Good," the cop said. "Moving a back-injury case and severing his spinal cord would top this episode off nicely." The cop pushed himself to a sitting position. "That briefcase cut the hell out of my chin. What's that thing made of, steel?"

"Brass trim," McGuinnes said.

Chase rolled his eyes.

There was a snort from the cop. "You got a cellular phone in it, at least?"

"Yeah."

"Then you'd better use it," the cop said. "This has been great fun, but I'm due back at the station in an hour."

"I suppose almost getting killed is a big yawner for you, isn't it?" McGuinnes asked.

"Killed in an elevator accident?" the cop said. "You've been seeing too many Keanu Reeves movies. New York elevators are safer than your grandmother's rocking chair."

"Tell that to my back," Chase said. "I can't drive with a busted back, and if I can't drive, I can't pay off my rig." He thought of the black Peterbilt 379—all-aluminum hood, stainless-steel grille, Cummins 500E engine. It held a shine like patent leather and handled like the thoroughbred it was. Silver pinstriping on the cab door announced his CB handle—*The Drifter*. Eight months he'd had it. The rig had been a bare three days old when he'd rescued Amanda Drake from a snow-drift in Upstate New York, and Amanda had helped him christen it, in a way.

"If you can't drive, you'll get an insurance settlement," McGuinnes told him.

Chase pulled his thoughts away from that long, snowbound night with Amanda and considered the situation. McGuinnes was probably right. He grimaced. He couldn't imagine life without a gray ribbon of road unwinding in front of him. "And sit around doing nothing? No thanks."

While McGuinnes contacted 911, Chase thought about Amanda, working in some office above him at this very moment. It looked as if he wouldn't be able to see her, after all. He'd ignored her wishes by coming here, but he just wanted to be absolutely sure she wasn't eight months' pregnant with his baby. Or maybe that was the excuse he gave himself because he craved another look at that bonfire of red hair that tumbled past her shoulders. He could still feel it bunched in his fist, still see the light in her blue eyes just before he'd kissed her.

"They're sending a team to get us out," McGuinnes said, snapping the phone closed.

Chase had just opened his mouth to say that was good, when the elevator rumbled and lurched to the right. "Damn!" he yelled. "Aren't we all the way down yet?"

"We're all the way down," the cop said. "The blasted thing's still settling, that's all. Move all your fingers and toes, see if you still have your motor coordination."

Chase felt dizzy at the thought of paralysis. He almost didn't want to put the idea to the test, but he had to know. He wiggled his right hand, his left, and both feet. Then he closed his eyes in gratitude. "I can move everything," he said.

"Good," the cop said. "What's your name?"

"Lavette. Chase Lavette."

"T. R. McGuinnes," the guy in the suit said.

"Joe Gilardini," the cop added, completing the introductions. "I wish I could say it was nice to meet you guys, but under the circumstances I wish I'd been denied the pleasure."

"Same here," Chase said.

McGuinnes remained silent. "Either one of you ever been out West?" he asked finally.

Chase's eyes snapped open. What an off-the-wall question. "Why do you want to know?"

"I don't, really. I just think talking is better than sitting around waiting for the elevator to shift again."

Chase understood the logic. "Guess you're right. No, I've never been out West. Eastern Seaboard's my route." He decided it was up to him to add something to the conversation. "Always wanted to go out there, though."

The cop sighed. "God, so have I. The wide-open spaces. Peace and quiet."

"No elevators," Chase added, trying to lighten things up.

"Yeah," the cop said. "If I didn't have my kid living in New York, I'd turn in my badge, collect my pension and go."

All three were silent for a while, and Chase decided that was the end of the chitchat.

"I just heard about this guest ranch in Arizona that's up for sale," McGuinnes said a few minutes later. "One of those working guest ranches with a small herd of cattle. I'm going out there next week to look it over."

That got Chase's attention. He'd always wished he knew somebody who owned a ranch. "No kidding? Think you might buy it?"

"If it checks out."

"Running a guest ranch," the cop mused out loud. "You know, that wouldn't be half-bad."

"And after I've had some fun with it, I'll sell it for a

nice profit. The city's growing in that direction, and in a couple of years developers will be crying to get their hands on that land, all one hundred and sixty acres of it. I can't lose."

"A hundred and sixty acres," Chase said, letting his mind play with it. He loved open spaces.

"I'm looking for partners."

A ranch, Chase thought. Riding the range, roping cattle, camping under the stars. Chase hadn't called himself *The Drifter* by accident. He was a city boy and had never imagined he could be anything else, but the life of a trucker came about as close to riding the range as anything he could imagine.

The cop laughed. "Now I've heard everything. Only in New York would a guy use an accident as a chance to set up a deal."

The elevator settled with another metallic groan.

"Would you rather sit here and think about the elevator collapsing on us?" McGuinnes asked.

"I'd rather think about your ranch," Chase said. "I'd go in on it in a minute if I had the cash."

"You might get that settlement," McGuinnes said.

"You know, I might." He'd hate to sell his rig, but if he had to, then buying into a ranch might take the sting out of it. "Listen, McGuinnes, after we get out of here, let's keep in touch. You never know."

"I guarantee you wouldn't go wrong with this investment. The Sun Belt's booming."

"I think you're both nutcases," the cop said.

"So you're not interested?" McGuinnes asked.

"I didn't say that. Hell, what else is there to be interested in down in this hole? If the ranch looks good, just call the Forty-third Precinct and leave a message for me."

McGuinnes stirred. "Let me get some business cards out of my briefcase."

"I'd just as soon not think about your briefcase, McGuinnes," Gilardini said.

Chase smiled. Gilardini was okay.

"Let's talk some more about the ranch," Gilardini continued. "What's the name of it, anyway? I always liked those old ranch names—the Bar X, the Rocking J. Remember 'Bonanza'?"

"I saw that on reruns," Chase said. "The guy I liked was Clint Eastwood. I snuck in to see *High Plains Drifter* at least six times when I was a kid. Back then, I would have given anything to be a cowboy."

"Yeah, me, too," Gilardini admitted. "So what's the place called?"

McGuinnes didn't answer right away. "Well, this spread is named something a little different," he said at last.

"Yeah?" Gilardini said. "What could be so different?"

"The True Love Ranch."

COMING UP WITH the ad copy for the Russian Tea Room wasn't going well. Amanda had felt queasy since five that morning, and detailing the wonders of blini and borscht didn't help. She'd also had abdominal twinges, but it was too early for labor pains—a good four weeks too early. Dismissing the twinges, she focused on her computer screen.

By noon the pain had become more intense, and she laid a hand on her swollen belly. "Stop it, Bartholomew," she lectured. "Go back to sleep so I can finish this copy." She couldn't in good conscience feel sorry for herself. She'd chosen to accept this complication in her life, and most of the time she felt like a kid waiting for Christmas. An ultrasound had provided knowledge of the baby's sex, and she had everything ready, from his name to his non-gender-specific nursery. No son of hers would grow up to be a male chauvinist.

Her desk phone buzzed just as another pain hit. She grimaced and reached for the receiver.

"A call for you from a Mr. Chase Lavette," said Bonnie, the receptionist. "He won't say what it's in reference to. Do you want to take it?"

Fear closed her throat. So he'd tracked her down, after all. She'd been a fool to tell him where she worked, but that had been before things had become...more personal. Thank God he'd called instead of coming to see her. And she'd better take the call, or he might show up on her doorstep.

"I think he has something to do with the Big Brothers campaign we're putting together," Amanda said, trying to sound casual so as not to create more interest. "I'll take it." She didn't want anyone in the office to remember the name of Chase Lavette.

"I'll put him through, then."

Bracing herself, Amanda listened to the phone line click open.

"Amanda?"

His voice took her by storm. At the sound of it, everything came back—the terror as her Mercedes slid into a snowbank, the relief at being rescued by somebody in a huge black truck and the excitement of being snowbound in the cab all night with a man like Chase, the type of guy she'd never had reason to know before and never expected to see again.

"Hello, Chase," she said. Another pain ran through her abdomen and she winced. "What a surprise."

"Listen, I was on my way up to your office this morning and the craziest thing happened."

Her glance swung to the door, half expecting him to walk in at any moment. She had to keep him away.

"The elevator crashed," he continued. "I'm in the hospital and something's wrong with my back."

She sagged against her chair in relief, then immediately bolted upright as she realized that her reaction wasn't appropriate. "That's terrible," she said. "Are you in a lot of pain?" Another spasm took her breath away.

"It's not so bad. I thought I'd broken something, but it could just be muscle damage. They've given me stuff for the pain. You know, Amanda, I haven't been able to get that night we spent together out of my mind."

Damn! Just what she'd been afraid of. "Really? I'd practically forgotten until you called just now."

He was silent.

She'd hurt him, but she couldn't help it. She didn't dare tell him that she'd never had such great sex in her life and that she'd forever compare other men to him when it came to lovemaking. She couldn't give him that information, because he might decide to renew the acquaintance, and she couldn't afford to see him again. A sense of obligation might make him insist on things— marriage, perhaps, or a role in raising Bartholomew. "Well, if you'll excuse me, I need to get back to work." She gritted her teeth to keep from moaning as another pain twisted within her. "Nice of you to call."

"Dammit, Amanda, I have to know." His gentle tone had been replaced with the macho snap she would expect from a trucker. "A condom's never broken on me before. Did you get pregnant that night?"

"I said I'd let you know if I did." She gripped the edge of her desk as sweat beaded on her forehead.

"Yes, you did, but I—you didn't have an abortion, did you?"

"No." She'd debated the issue until it was too late.

"Look, I just want to take care of my responsibilities."

"Well, you have none."

"Apparently not." There was a note of regret in his voice. "Sorry to have bothered you, Amanda."

"Goodbye, Chase." She hung up, disconnecting herself from the father of her child just as her water broke.

THREE WEEKS LATER, Chase stood in the lobby of Amanda's office building staring at the elevator. Except for the hospital elevators, where he'd been strapped to a gurney and given no choice but to ride, he hadn't been inside one since the accident. He didn't much like the idea now, but the Artemis Advertising Agency was on the twentieth floor.

His back was behaving itself today. When the spasms hit, he was damn near immobilized, but this morning he'd felt so good he decided to finish his original mission—to find out if Amanda was pregnant. Yet, after fifteen minutes of watching people surge in and out of the elevator, he was no more ready to ride than when he'd walked into the lobby. He glanced around, found the sign for the stairs and was halfway across the lobby when he paused. Then, with a muttered oath of resolution, he strode back to the elevator just before the doors closed, shoved them open and stepped inside.

The trip up made his stomach pitch. He glared suspiciously at the three women and four men in the elevator with him and wondered if any of them would be prepared with a cellular phone in case of an emergency.

His jaw clenched, he watched the flashing numbers above the door. When the twentieth floor appeared, he wanted to shoulder his way past the others who were getting off, but he held back, forcing himself to face the fear. Once free of the elevator, he flexed his shoulders with a sigh and a little smile of triumph. He'd ridden the damn thing.

He stuck his head in the first office that bore the Artemis name on the door and flashed the famous Lavette grin complete with dimple. "I'm looking for Amanda Drake."

The receptionist, a woman in her forties, reacted as most women did when he smiled at them. Pink rose to her cheeks, and the pupils of her eyes widened. Chase had had that effect on women ever since he'd reached puberty, and it was a nice perk in a life that hadn't presented all that many.

"Do you know where I might find her?" he prompted, knowing that sometimes women took a moment to pull themselves together before they answered. According to the nameplate on her desk, this one was named Bonnie Chalmers.

She blinked. "Miss Drake's on extended leave," she said as if reciting her times tables.

Chase thought that over. There was one obvious reason for her to be on extended leave, but his trucking buddies had told him that women in this day and age didn't slip off quietly and have babies. They demanded child support, his buddies had said, and plenty of it.

"She's not sick or anything, is she, Bonnie?" Chase asked.

At the use of her name, Bonnie flushed pinker. "No, she's fine. She'll just be out of the office for a while."

It was all very mysterious, Chase thought, but he

didn't know how things worked in the city. He had no doubt Amanda had a high-powered career, both from what she'd told him on that snowy night, and from the evidence of her material success. He'd noted the late-model Mercedes first. Then he'd caught a whiff of unfamiliar cologne, which he'd later identified by checking out a display in Lord and Taylor.

Then there was the matter of her clothes. He'd had the pleasure of discovering the softness of her cashmere coat as he'd taken it off. He hadn't been paying attention to labels when he'd removed her wool suit and silk blouse, but later, when the clothes were lying around the cab, he'd noticed names like Calvin Klein and Chanel. And her underwear...he could still get aroused thinking about those fragile scraps of lace that had to have been imported from Paris. Maybe she was in Europe right this minute, picking up more of that fancy underwear.

He walked over to the desk. "I guess I'll just leave her a message, then."

"That would be fine. Do you have a card?"

Chase laughed. "No, Bonnie. I don't even have a piece of paper. Is there something I could write on?"

"Certainly." She whipped the top page from a notepad beside her telephone and held it out to him, along with a pen. "I'm sure she'll be sorry she missed you."

Chase wished he could be as sure about that as Bonnie. Amanda had been very cool three weeks ago when he'd called. But three weeks ago he'd simply been a trucker, and an injured one, at that. Today, his back was slowly mending, and soon he might be part owner in a ranch. In a few years, according to McGuinnes, he could be rich. That prospect had given him the courage to come here to issue an invitation to Amanda to come out to Arizona as his guest.

He hoped she would, even though she'd told him straight-out that she didn't think they had anything in common besides sex. And she was probably right. It was a damn strong suit, though. He'd made love to a lot of women, and he'd had a pleasant time with most of them. Yet that night with Amanda had shaken him to a depth he'd never reached with anyone. Her eyes, her soft body and her flame-colored hair had haunted him during eight months of long nights on the road. Knowing that Amanda would probably reject him if he asked her out, he'd tried to forget her with a lusty waitress in Atlanta and a sophisticated bartender in Hartford. And still he burned.

As THE 747 cruised on in to Tucson International Airport, Amanda jiggled Bartholomew in her arms in an attempt to stop his wailing. This was such a bad idea, she thought, looking down at the desert, which at this altitude looked like the browned top of a crumb cake just out of the oven. The pilot had already announced the temperature in Tucson—one hundred and five degrees. She hated to think of how the heat would affect her, let alone a two-month-old baby.

But she had a problem, one she hadn't figured out a way to solve except by coming here. Her family had been shocked and embarrassed by the news of her pregnancy, but her concocted story of going to a sperm bank to get pregnant on purpose had mollified them. That had a classier ring to it than the word *accident*, not to mention the longer version of the truth—a one-night stand with a trucker. Her story had remained viable until the day little Clare, daughter of her best friend, Janice, was diagnosed with diabetes.

"Thank God we knew what to look for," Janice had said when she broke the news. "It runs in the family, so we got on it right away."

In that moment, Amanda's carefully constructed house of cards had tumbled down. This little dark-haired imp who in the past two months had become the center of her world could have a predisposition for any number of life-threatening diseases. She couldn't position herself as his protector unless she knew what to fight. Only one person had the answers—the person waiting in the terminal to take her out to the True Love Guest Ranch.

His move to Arizona had been a convenient one for her. Living so far away, he was less of a threat to her independence, and she could come out here, question him and return to New York without anyone back home being the wiser. She hadn't told Chase about the baby when she'd written her letter telling him of her impending arrival. She didn't think it was the sort of thing one revealed in a letter.

But now, as the plane's wheels bumped against the runway, she wished she had. The prospect of meeting Chase again for the first time since that snowy night was nerve-racking enough. To meet him while carrying his child in her arms might be more than either of them could handle.

The plane taxied to the gate and Bartholomew stopped crying for the first time in two hours. Amanda remained in her seat fussing with his blanket and checking his diaper while passengers filed past her. At last she and the baby were alone with the flight attendants and she had no choice but to gather him in her arms, hoist the diaper bag over her shoulder and start that long walk down the jetway.

She paused at the door of the plane and looked into Bartholomew's blue eyes that already held a hint of green, like Chase's. "Well, kid," she said, taking a deep breath. "Time to meet your daddy."

CHASE SHIFTED his weight from one booted foot to the other as he watched passengers funnel out of the jetway. Amanda would appear any minute now. He adjusted his hat and flexed his shoulders, feeling like a teenager on a first date, with the same sweaty-palmed excitement, the same nervous hopes for the night ahead. Well, perhaps greater hopes than a teenager on a first date might have, he thought with a smile. After all, he and Amanda had become lovers ten months ago.

Her handwritten note had been short. *If it's convenient, I'd like to take you up on your offer.* Except for listing her flight number and arrival time, that had been it. He couldn't consider it a proposition, exactly, but why else would she come to the ranch? She could afford to vacation anywhere in the world. Copying her style, he'd sent a short note back—*I'll meet your plane.* Maybe he and Amanda didn't need words between them. Their bodies had done most of the talking the night they'd met.

He was glad she hadn't come out six weeks earlier, when he'd first arrived at the ranch. Thanks to laps in the pool and massages by the head wrangler, Leigh Singleton, his back was in much better shape. He would have hated it to spasm at some awkward moment, like in the middle of making love. He'd asked Freddy Singleton, Leigh's sister and the ranch foreman, to reserve the little honeymoon cottage for Amanda. Marriage was the last thing on his mind, but the cottage stood in a mesquite grove several hundred yards from the main house, which gave it lots of privacy. Not as much as the curtained bunk of an 18-wheeler on a snowy night, but more than the guest rooms in the main ranch house.

The steady flow of people from the plane slowed to a trickle. With a sick feeling of disappointment Chase wondered if Amanda had changed her mind. Maybe she'd read the weather reports for Tucson and decided her fair skin wasn't suited for the desert summer. He'd worried about that and had planned to make sure she wore hats and long sleeves when she was outside. In the six weeks he'd been on the ranch, his skin had bronzed to a rich brown, but Amanda's skin was so much more delicate.... He licked dry lips and stood on tiptoe to peer deep into the empty tunnel leading to the plane. Maybe he should ask someone if she'd been on the flight.

Then he saw a flash of red hair as a woman came out of the gloom toward him. His heart hammered in his chest. She looked exactly as he'd remembered, only perhaps more beautiful. Her face had the most wonderful glow to it, and her hair was the color of an Arizona sunset. He'd have to remember to tell her that.

He couldn't see the rest of her very well. She had a large piece of luggage slung over one shoulder and was carrying something, holding it close to her chest. He stared at the bundle. It looked a lot like...

The breath rushed out of him and he grabbed the back of a chair for support. Slack-jawed, he stared as the bundle in her arms squirmed. Oh, God. Oh, God!

She came forward slowly, her blue gaze fastened on him.

He braced himself as if standing against a stiff wind. *She'd had a baby! His baby!* An explosion of wonder left him weak and dizzy.

As she drew near, fragments of questions formed and disappeared in his mind like campfire smoke. At last he focused on the fire itself, the burning anger of betrayal.

"Hello, Chase." She sounded out of breath.

Fury made him tremble as he glared down at her. "Liar," he said in a voice gone dead with shock. The baby began to cry.

NOT A GOOD BEGINNING, Amanda thought as she hurried to keep up with Chase's long strides on the way to baggage claim. His expression reminded her of the hurricanes that sometimes buffeted her parents' summer cottage on Long Island. He looked different—taller, more muscular and definitely more tanned than she remembered. The cowboy outfit suited him, but she'd bet his prizewinning smile wouldn't appear today, or the dimple in his cheek that had fascinated her so.

"If you'll let me try to explain," she said, raising her voice above Bartholomew's wailing.

"Not here," he snapped, glancing at the luggage circling the carousel. "What do your suitcases look like?"

"Burgundy leather, Louis Vuitton," she said. "And there's an infant seat, too."

His laugh was harsh. "I suppose that's made by Calvin Klein. All I really had to do was look for the most expensive stuff on the belt."

Amanda turned away to hide the sudden tears that spilled down her face. Here was the true reason behind her plan to keep Bartholomew a secret from Chase. She'd always sensed they wouldn't be able to bridge the social gaps between them. He obviously didn't respect the way she lived and probably the reverse would be true, although she tried not to be a snob. She held her wet cheek against Bartholomew's, and gradually he stopped crying and began to nuzzle against her skin, seeking food.

"Let's go," Chase said from behind her.

She glanced over her shoulder to where he stood hoisting her two large suitcases as if they were filled with air, the infant seat tucked under one arm. She walked toward the entrance, where the sunshine met her like a bank of floodlights.

"Cover the baby," Chase ordered.

"I was planning to." Shielding Bartholomew's face with the blanket, she gasped as they stepped into the ovenlike heat. Landscaping outside the terminal consisted of a few lacy-leaved trees and a desert garden, dominated by a giant cactus that looked like a missile with arms. Amanda had seen pictures of a cactus like that, and she tried to remember its name.

Chase looked over his shoulder before he started across the street. "Don't you have a hat or something?" he asked, his tone brittle.

"No." She lowered her head against the glare. "And my sunglasses are in the diaper bag."

With a deep sigh he set down the suitcases and infant seat before leaning over and opening the bag hanging from her shoulder. The brim of his hat brushed her arm and the air around them filled with the scent of baby powder as he searched through the bag until he located her glasses. He found them, spread the earpieces and slid the glasses over the bridge of her nose. As he leaned close, her gaze dropped to the open neck of his shirt where a small medallion on a pewter chain nestled against a dark swirl of chest hair. She remembered that medallion, remembered thinking it looked vaguely familiar, though she couldn't have said why.

"There." Chase backed away from what under different circumstances might have been a tender moment. A woman passing by looked at them and smiled.

Amanda bit her lip to stifle a little sob of despair. She'd been sniffling a lot lately, and she needed to stop. Her friends with children said crying jags were typical with new mothers, but Amanda didn't want to be typical. Tears were inconvenient and demonstrated far too much vulnerability for her taste. She was a single mother and wanted to keep that status. She had to be tough.

Chase directed them past the cactus garden to a battered van with steer horns where a hood ornament should be. He opened the passenger door where True Love Guest Ranch was stenciled above a heart with an arrow through it. If she'd been in the mood for laughing, Amanda would have gotten a kick out of that. What a joke.

She put one foot on the running board and immediately realized she'd never be able to climb into the van while holding Bartholomew. Then, before she could figure out another way to get in, Chase placed his hands at her waist and lifted her, baby and all, into the seat. And she remembered his touch—a combination of gentleness and strength that had, many months ago, made her beg for his caress.

The interior of the van was stifling, and she loosened the blanket around Bartholomew, who was beginning to squirm and wrinkle his face in preparation for a good long howl of protest. There were two heavy thuds as Chase heaved the luggage into the back of the van and closed the doors.

"I'll strap the infant seat right behind you," he said, coming back to the passenger door and opening the side of the van. "We have child-restraint laws in Arizona. The baby needs to be buckled up."

She turned and watched him secure the infant seat. "I don't need a law to tell me that. How long before we get to the ranch?"

"More than an hour, depending on traffic."

"He's very hungry," she said. "I really should feed him before we start."

Chase's hands stilled. "It's a boy?"

"Yes."

He lowered his head for a moment, without speaking.

"His name's Bartholomew," she ventured.

Slowly, he lifted his head and gazed at her. "Bartholomew what?"

She swallowed. "Drake."

He nodded and turned away to finish securing the infant seat. By the time he climbed behind the wheel of the van, Bartholomew was crying. "I'll get us out of here and find some shade," he muttered, gunning the engine and switching on the air conditioner full blast.

In a few minutes he'd wheeled into the parking lot of a hotel near the airport. Amanda was surprised to see grass and large trees instead of cactus surrounding the hotel. Chase pulled into a shaded parking space near a bubbling fountain and rolled down his window. She shifted a wailing Bartholomew to her left arm and tried to roll down her window, too, but it was stuck.

"Here. I'll do it," Chase said, sounding disgusted as he leaned across her lap and forced the handle until the window lowered. A breeze, cooled by the fountain, wafted in. He straightened, but not before Amanda caught a whiff of his after-shave, a scent she associated exclusively with Chase. The men she usually dated wore designer fragrances. The minty aroma of Chase's inexpensive after-shave was now indelibly paired in her mind with mind-blowing pleasure and powerful climaxes. Just the faintest trace of that scent could arouse her. It was a fact she never intended him to know.

"Thank you," she said, reaching for the buttons of her blouse.

He glanced away as she unfastened her nursing bra and gave her nipple to Bartholomew, whose cries transformed immediately into soft sucking sounds. Amanda began to relax a little as the baby nursed. The gentle breeze and the splash of the nearby fountain suggested coolness, even if drops of perspiration gathered between her milk-heavy breasts.

She looked at Chase, who stared fixedly out the window, his elbow propped against the opening, his chin in his hand. "I'm sorry to spring this on you so abruptly," she said. "But a phone call or letter didn't seem like the way to tell you."

"You've known how to reach me ever since that night," he said, not looking at her. "We could have met for coffee months ago, if you'd wanted to tell me face-to-face."

"The truth is, I didn't plan to tell you at all."

His jaw tightened. "That sucks, Amanda."

"But I didn't know you!"

Her loud retort startled Bartholomew, who lost his grasp on her nipple and began to cry. She guided him back, murmuring assurances. When she looked up, Chase was watching her, a yearning in his green eyes that made her catch her breath.

"Didn't you?" he said.

Yes, she'd known him. That night in the truck, she'd sensed a will of iron, one that would probably have clashed with hers when it came to this baby. "When I first found out, I planned to have an abortion," she said.

His whole body went rigid. "Without telling me?" he asked too quietly.

"I was afraid you'd try to talk me out of it."

"So what?" Beneath the mildly voiced question lay a band of steely anger. "I had a right to know, to take part in the decision. I asked for that right, remember? We talked about it, and you promised to tell me if you were pregnant."

She sighed and stroked Bartholomew's downy hair. "Well, as you can see, I couldn't go through with it, anyway."

"When was he born?"

"The day you called."

He jerked toward her. "The day I called? But that was only eight months!"

"He was premature by a month. They kept him in the hospital for a week after I was discharged, but he's caught up now." She couldn't help the pride in her voice as she glanced down at the nursing baby. "The pediatrician says he's right where he should be for a two-month-old."

"Or you could be lying again, and he's somebody else's kid."

Her head snapped up. "How dare you imply such a thing?"

His harsh laugh made Bartholomew twitch in her arms, but she managed to quiet him again.

"You haven't given me much reason to trust you. Either you lied to me on the phone that day, or you're lying now. Which is it?"

She longed to tell him to take her back to the airport, but she kept thinking of Janice and little Clare. She had to withstand whatever Chase dished out, for Bartholomew's sake. "This baby is your son." She focused on Bartholomew's contented face. "All you have to do is look at him to know that."

Chase met her statement with silence, then a shaky sigh. She glanced up to see him staring out the windshield again. His throat moved in a swallow and his voice sounded strained. "Why didn't you tell me?"

She mentally prepared herself, knowing this issue would be the most difficult. "Because no one knows about that night in the snowstorm, Chase. And I'd rather they didn't."

He didn't respond right away, and when he did, his tone was rough. "What'd you do, trick some other guy into thinking Bartholomew was his?"

She gasped and looked up. "I would never do that."

"Why, because it's dishonest?" Sarcasm dripped from each word.

She held on to her temper and met his look of disdain. "I've done what I thought best for all of us. Once you get over the first shock of finding out about Bartholomew, you'll see I was right."

"And what have you done, Amanda?"

"I told people—" She paused and cleared her throat. "I told people I'd gone to a sperm bank, that my biological clock was ticking and I'd decided not to wait for the right man to come along before I became a mother."

"Good God."

"It's for the best! We're from different worlds. I thought we settled that when you dropped me off at my apartment the next morning. A baby doesn't change that fact.''

''The hell it doesn't! We were talking about whether to *date*. I don't remember giving up my rights as the father of our child.''

Her throat felt tight as tears threatened. ''Oh, Chase, you don't realize how my parents would react. I can't tell them that I...''

''Gave yourself to a disreputable trucker in the middle of a freak snowstorm?''

''That's not—''

''Yes, that's exactly what you mean.'' His green eyes flashed with something that looked like pain, and then his expression became hard. ''And I can see that a woman like you would never admit to a one-night stand in the cab of a truck. What was I thinking?''

''You make me sound like a snob. I'm not.''

His laugh was bitter, his tone suddenly coarse. ''That night you weren't, lady. In fact, I really believed I had a full-blooded woman on my hands. Instead, I discover you're a cowardly little girl. But that's okay. You were still the best lay I've ever had.''

Tears filled her eyes. ''You're being crude on purpose.''

''I'm a trucker, sweetheart. We're all crude. Haven't you heard that?''

She turned away from the taunt in his eyes. With her back to him she transferred Bartholomew to the other breast.

''So tell me.'' He ran a finger up her spine over the damp material of her thin cotton blouse and she shivered. ''What brings you to Arizona? Got a hunger for some of that trucker loving?''

She fought down her rage so that she wouldn't

frighten Bartholomew again. "If my hands were free, I'd slap your face for suggesting that," she snapped.

"That isn't the reason you flew all the way out here? Shucks, I'm just a dumb trucker, so I can't imagine any other reason. You don't need money, and you don't want my name. What else could you be after besides my body?"

"Will you stop that?" she hissed.

"Listen, Ms. Drake, and listen good. You've just stepped off that plane with my baby and announced that everyone thinks his daddy is some sperm-bank donor. You just lost the right to dictate to me! Now tell me what you came for and save us both some time. Then I can put you on the next plane to New York and get on with my life."

She shuddered. If she'd thought he would react in the easy, civilized way her other male friends might have, she'd sadly miscalculated. In her heart she'd known what to expect, though. A man who could love with such thoroughness could hate just as thoroughly. She kept her back to him and took a deep breath. "I need to know something about your family's medical history. An incident with a friend of mine convinced me that's it's irresponsible of me to raise Bartholomew without knowing if he's genetically predisposed to any life-threatening diseases."

"I'm surprised you didn't send me a form to fill out."

She'd thought of it. "I was afraid you'd ignore a form." Or barrel back to New York and confront her. "Also it seemed a little...cold."

"Really? So instead, you traipse out here, dangle my son in front of me while you get your information and whisk him away again. You're all heart, Amanda."

Amanda gritted her teeth and prayed for the strength

to get the information she needed without killing the man who possessed it. "I've tried to handle this so that it's best for all of us. Someday you might even realize that."

"I assume you didn't tell anyone the real reason you decided to come out to Arizona, then," he said.

"I said I needed a vacation and I'd heard good things about this guest ranch."

His dry laugh held no humor. "Your friends and family must be even dumber than I am to fall for that one. An Arizona ranch in July? With a baby?"

"I've always had a fascination with the West. My maternity leave isn't up for another two weeks, and the agency suggested I take a little trip. My mother thought I should go to Colorado instead, but I told her I wanted to see one of those giant cactus with the arms, like the one they have back at the airport." She remembered the name she'd been trying to think of. "Saguaros."

"You pronounce the name with a silent g," he corrected.

"Oh."

His voice gentled. "But I said it wrong when I first got here, too."

Bartholomew's tug at her nipple grew gradually weaker. Amanda eased him away from her breast and refastened her clothing before holding him against her shoulder and patting his back. Soon his burp came, loud as a bullfrog's mating call.

"My God, was that *him?*"

She glanced at Chase, a smile tugging at her mouth in spite of herself. "Are you suggesting it was me?"

Amusement flickered in his eyes. "He sounds like a trucker with a belly full of beer."

"He does, at that." The moment of shared delight

took her breath away. She'd had no idea what she'd been missing. As tears welled up in her eyes again, she averted her gaze and rubbed Bartholomew's back until he relaxed into sleep. "Are you willing to give me the information I need?" she asked without looking at Chase.

There was no reply.

"I'm sure you're upset, but the medical background is really important. Just tell me if you know of any diseases I should watch out for."

Still no answer.

She glanced sideways and found him staring straight ahead, his arms draped over the steering wheel. She could read nothing from his expression. "There's a notebook in the outside pocket of the smaller of my two suitcases," she said. "If you'd be willing to get it and write down the information, you could take me back to the airport and I'll book a flight home. I can see that I shouldn't stay here any longer than necessary."

"Is there someone else?" he asked at last, without changing position.

"Someone...you mean another man in my life?" Her heartbeat quickened at the personal nature of the question, and the implication of his asking it. As furious as he must be, she was astonished that he'd want to know. "No. I haven't dated since I found out I was pregnant. Starting a relationship seemed an unnecessary complication."

He glanced over at her. "Did you mean it about wanting to see saguaros, or was that just another lie?"

"Dammit, I do not habitually lie," she said, hurt by the unexpected accusation. "I swear, if I didn't have a sleeping baby in my arms, I'd—"

"If you didn't have a sleeping baby in your arms, you wouldn't be here, would you?"

"No, I wouldn't," she admitted.

"My giving up trucking and investing in this ranch wouldn't have made any difference to you."

"Why would I start a relationship with a man in Arizona? I have a career based in Manhattan." She wondered why the explanation sounded restrictive today, when she usually took great comfort in the foothold she'd gained. "Besides, we have nothing in common, Chase. We established that ten months ago."

His glance flicked to Bartholomew.

"Okay, one thing."

He met her gaze with bold assessment in his eyes. "Oh, I think we have two things in common, Amanda. Even you can't deny that. We spent several hours proving it to ourselves."

She blushed. "Sex is not enough to base a relationship on. You know that as well as I do."

"I always figured it was a damn good start. But I wouldn't want to meddle with your prejudices."

Her heart thudded erratically as she tried to maintain her poise. Despite the joyful outcome of having Bartholomew, she'd been a fool to give in to her impulses that night in the storm and she mustn't let good judgment desert her again. She just needed her information and she'd be on her way back to her ordered life. "Don't worry about the notebook," she said. "Just tell me what you can. I have a good memory."

"I don't."

Her chest squeezed. "What do you mean?"

"I can't just spew this stuff out. I'll need some time to think, maybe check with a few people. So, did you want to see the saguaros or not?"

She could see where this was leading. "It's not important. I think it would be better if we ended our association as quickly as possible. A letter would be fine. Now that you know what I need, you can send a letter to the agency."

"Scared, Amanda?"

Her pulse raced. "Of what?"

His knowing smile, this time including his dimple, was the only answer required.

"Of course not!"

Chase opened his door. "Then let's strap the baby in the infant seat and start out to the ranch. Along the way, I'll show you a few saguaros."

3

BARTHOLOMEW SLEPT the entire ride to the ranch, leaving Amanda free to gawk at the unfamiliar countryside. And gawk she did. Used to the gentle slopes of the Adirondacks, she stared in amazement at the rough-hewn peaks of the Santa Catalina Mountains towering above Tucson. The route to the True Love curved around the backside of the range, and by the time Chase had guided the van onto a dirt road marked True Love Guest Ranch, Amanda had seen enough saguaros and other prickly plants to last her a lifetime. She had the urge to encase Bartholomew in a suit of armor to protect his soft baby skin from the bristling terrain.

Chase drove in silence, his expression as austere as the landscape. If she didn't so desperately want the information about his family, she'd consider calling a cab when she arrived at the ranch and returning to the airport. His question about whether there were any other men in her life made her wonder if he had ideas of renewing their sexual relationship. If so, he'd be disappointed—she had no intention of letting that happen. Or maybe he just wanted a little more time with Bartholomew. She could hardly deny him that, considering her request for his medical background, but she hoped he wouldn't become too attached to the baby.

The van jounced over a pothole in the dirt road and Chase muttered a curse under his breath.

"Is it your back?" she asked, recalling belatedly that a couple of months ago he'd been in a hospital bed.

"No. I didn't want to wake the baby," he said.

She was unexpectedly touched. "Don't worry. He'll probably sleep until the van stops. How is your back?"

"Not bad."

She decided to press the point. "But you gave up your truck-driving career because of your back, didn't you?"

He nodded. "The physical therapists said it would be at least a year before I could get through a day without pain, and the doctors doubted I'd ever go back to trucking. But I've had a sort of miracle cure out here. Four weeks ago, I started riding, and now, on a good day, I can stay in the saddle for several hours."

It wasn't hard to picture him galloping through this rugged country. The role suited him in the same way driving a powerful 18-wheeler had, and both images stirred her sexually. But she'd already indulged herself in the fantasy once, and the price had been high. Indulging again could threaten her whole way of life. "I imagine the climate would help a bad back." She lifted her hair to let the air-conditioning find the nape of her neck.

He glanced at her, and his gaze warmed. She remembered too late that he'd once commented on that gesture, calling it "damn sexy." Self-conscious, she released the weight of her hair to her shoulders. She hadn't meant to be provocative. She didn't want him to want her.

"The warm weather helps," Chase said after a moment. "And the head wrangler, Leigh Singleton, well, she has some amazing massage techniques."

"Oh." The jolt of jealousy that hit Amanda caught her

completely off guard. She had no right to those kinds of emotions. And they were a dangerous sign that she might have been fooling herself about why she'd come to Arizona. "You're lucky to have found someone like that," she said.

"Leigh is a fascinating woman. I never believed in psychics or natural healing before, but Leigh's changing my mind."

Amanda didn't trust herself to speak. It was one thing for her to decide their relationship had no chance. It was quite another to hear Chase praising the "fascinating" attributes of another woman. Yet she could hardly expect a man with Chase's sex appeal to remain without a woman for very long.

"Well, here we are," Chase said, pulling the van to a stop.

Amanda had a brief glimpse of a low wall that arched over a wrought-iron gate. Behind the wall was a large one-story structure of whitewashed adobe with a red-tiled roof and a wide front porch splashed with red geraniums in pots.

Bartholomew started to whimper in the seat behind her, cutting short her inspection.

"I'll get him," she said, opening her door. By the time she'd extricated Bartholomew from his infant seat, Chase was already striding down the flagstone walk carrying her luggage. Leaving the van door open, she followed him.

The lightweight designer blouse and skirt she'd chosen for the trip had seemed sensible enough at the airport, but now she could see they belonged at a beach cottage, not a ranch. Her open-toed sandals collected dirt and small stones that bit into the soles of her feet and threatened to destroy her nylons.

Shielding Bartholomew from the relentless sun, she hobbled up the walk toward the porch, where an old cowboy sat in a cane chair with a black-and-white dog at his feet. Except for the aluminum walker beside him, the old man looked like something out of a Norman Rockwell painting. Amanda could imagine using him as part of an ad campaign for the True Love, and automatically began composing copy to describe the timeless appeal of a shady porch on a summer afternoon.

Chase set the luggage down on the porch and touched the brim of his hat. "Afternoon, Dex."

The gesture of respect charmed Amanda more than she cared to admit. She remembered the crudeness with which he'd described her as "the best lay he'd ever had," and wondered which was the real Chase, the rough-edged trucker or the gallant cowboy.

"Who's this?" the old man asked with disarming bluntness.

"I'd like you to meet Amanda Drake," Chase said, turning toward her. "And...her son," he added, glancing away.

"Your girl?"

"No, she's...someone I knew in New York. Amanda, this is Dexter Grimes. He used to be foreman of the True Love."

Amanda stepped onto the porch where the shade enveloped her in coolness. She shifted Bartholomew to the crook of her left arm and held out her right hand. "Glad to meet you, Mr. Grimes."

"Likewise." He gripped her hand firmly just as Bartholomew began to fuss.

"Excuse me." She extracted her hand and began to

jiggle the baby against her shoulder. "He's had a long trip."

Dexter held out his arms. "Here."

She stared at the old cowboy. Relinquish her precious baby to a man so uncoordinated he needed a walker to get around? "That's okay, Mr. Grimes. I'd better just take him inside."

Dexter lowered his arms, his gaze sad. "Too old."

"Oh, no!" Sympathy washed over her. "I just..." She glanced at Chase for help, but he returned her gaze without saying a word. Slowly, she turned back to Dexter. Mentally crossing her fingers, she leaned over to offer him her squirming child. "He's a handful," she said cautiously, lowering Bartholomew into Dexter's arms.

"Yep." Dexter cradled the baby as if he'd been holding children for years, and an expression of delight spread over his leathery features. Bartholomew stopped fussing and stared up at the old man. "Pretty," Dexter said.

Amanda's eyes misted. She hadn't received such an uncomplicated expression of joy from either of her own parents. "Yes, he's very pretty," she said.

"Stinks some," Dexter said.

Amanda's chuckle mixed with the lump of emotion in her throat. "I think he needs a change."

Dexter laughed softly as he looked down at the baby. "Could be." He brushed a finger under the tiny chin. "Could be."

And then something happened that took Amanda's breath away. Bartholomew grasped the old man's finger tight in one small fist, and smiled.

She grabbed Chase's arm. "Did you see that? Bartholomew smiled! Chase, he's never done that before. It's the first time!"

Chase glanced at her hand on his arm and she quickly removed it. "Guess he likes ol' Dex," Chase said easily.

"Likes me." Dexter played a gentle tug-of-war with the baby.

Behind them the carved double doors opened. Amanda turned at the creak of hinges and discovered a gray-haired woman with an ample bosom standing in the doorway. "What are you folks standing out in the heat for?" she asked in a lilting voice.

"Foal...no...little...baby!" Dexter said. "There! I said it! Baby!"

"What?" The woman circled Chase, the luggage and Amanda to stand in front of Dexter. "Sakes alive! It is a baby!"

"I said so."

Chase cleared his throat. "Belinda, this is Amanda Drake. Amanda, this is Belinda, Dexter's wife and the person who supervises the kitchen."

Belinda glanced quickly behind her with a smile and a nod. "Nice to meet you," she said before returning her attention to Bartholomew. "But who is this, Dexter?" She reached for the baby and Dexter handed him up to her.

"Baby," he said.

"I can *see* that." Belinda cradled Bartholomew in the crook of her arm and beamed down at him. "And a beautiful baby you are, too," she crooned. "Look at those big eyes! And such curly hair. And a cute little button nose, and rosy cheeks! You are a charmer, you are!"

Chase shifted his weight and hooked his thumbs through the loops of his belt. "That's Amanda's son." He coughed into his hand. "Bartholomew."

Amanda knew in that moment that Chase didn't like

the name she'd chosen, and disappointment pricked her. Not that she should care if he liked the name or not, she told herself.

Belinda looked up at Chase. "Why, he looks just like *you*, Chase," she blurted out. Then she blushed. "Goodness, I probably shouldn't have said that."

"It's okay, Mrs. Grimes," Amanda said. "Chase is technically the father."

Chase spun toward her. "Technically? What kind of ridiculous statement is that?"

Heat rose in Amanda's cheeks. A moment ago, she'd been enjoying the response of these two sweet old people to her baby, almost as if she and Chase had brought Bartholomew home to adoring grandparents. Now the illusion was shattered. "Simply that I don't expect you to shoulder any of the responsibilities of being a father," she said.

Bartholomew, as if he were a barometer of the mood, began to cry.

"I need to take him in and change him," she said, holding out her arms toward Belinda.

"Of course." Belinda leaned down to drop a kiss on the baby's forehead before she gave him up. "He's so sweet."

"Stinks some," Dexter said.

"I'll just go inside and take care of that," Amanda said. "Mrs. Grimes, where would be a good place for me to change him?"

"Come with me. And call me Belinda." The older woman picked up the diaper bag, circled Amanda's waist with one arm and guided her toward the open door. Then she glanced over her shoulder. "Chase, take Amanda's luggage out to the cottage. I think we have an old cradle in storage. Get Rosa to help you find it and clean it up."

Amanda couldn't help smiling at Belinda's tone. She didn't speak to her boss as if she were an employee. Amanda suspected it had been many years since Belinda had felt like anyone's hired help.

They entered a high-ceilinged room that was blissfully cool.

"That was kind of you to let Dexter hold your baby," Belinda said. "Ever since his stroke, he's been so frustrated—can't always find the right word, can't move around as well as he used to. He was such a vital man. It's heartbreaking."

Amanda met the older woman's gaze. "I can imagine it would be," she said gently.

"He was delighted with that baby." She gave Bartholomew a wistful smile before gesturing toward a door to the right. "This way. We'll change him in Freddy's office."

Amanda surveyed the room as they started across it. Directly opposite the front door, a huge picture window revealed a landscaped patio with a pool and a Jacuzzi. A low wall swooped up to an arch, where a waterfall cascaded into the pool, transforming the surface of the water into dancing points of sunlight.

It would have been an idyllic setting except for the cowboy and cowgirl arguing heatedly beside the pool. Intrigued, Amanda paused. She couldn't tell what they were saying, but from the arm-waving and belligerent stances of both, she knew they were furious.

Belinda noticed Amanda's preoccupation. "Never mind them. They're in love."

"Doesn't look like it."

Belinda laughed. "It's been like that between those

two ever since T. R. McGuinnes came to the ranch. Now, of course, we all call him Ry instead of T.R. That was the first thing Freddy did—got rid of those stupid initials and gave him a name you could say without laughing."

"Freddy's a woman?" Amanda had assumed the office they were heading for belonged to a man.

"I'm sorry. I forgot that you don't know who anybody is around here. Ry is one of the three owners of the ranch, and Freddy's the foreman. They're getting married in two days, so we don't have any regular paying guests staying here just now, only members of the wedding party. I guess that's why Freddy and Ry feel free to carry on like that by the pool. When we have paying guests, they usually save their spats for the corrals or the open range."

Just then, the dark-haired woman out on the patio pushed the broad-shouldered cowboy into the water.

"They're getting married?" Amanda jiggled Bartholomew on her shoulder to buy a little time so she could watch the exciting show outside. She'd never known anybody who acted this way, and she was fascinated. "But she just pushed him in the water, clothes and all!" The cowboy swam awkwardly to retrieve his floating hat while the woman stood back, arms crossed, and watched.

"They'll make up. Wait and see."

The woman named Freddy turned on her booted heel and marched, head down, toward the French door leading into the room where Belinda and Amanda stood. She opened the door and turned to shout over her shoulder. "They could rope me with barbed wire and drag me to the altar and I still wouldn't marry the likes of you!" Then she closed the door with enough force to rattle the panes. She obviously didn't notice she had an audience until she turned her attention away from the man still groping for his hat in the choppy water.

"Oh!" she said, her hand going to her throat. "Sorry about that."

"Freddy Singleton, meet Amanda Drake and her son," Belinda said. "I didn't catch the baby's name, Amanda."

Amanda lifted her chin. "Bartholomew."

"What a lovely name," Belinda said, earning Amanda's immediate loyalty.

"I'm pleased to meet you," Freddy said, coming forward with her hand extended.

Amanda barely managed to return the handshake as Bartholomew began wriggling and protesting. Amanda could read questions in Freddy's eyes, but the woman voiced none of them.

"We need your office as a place to change this little boy," Belinda said.

"That's fine." Freddy glanced out toward the pool as the cowboy hoisted himself out. "I think I'll be going now, anyway."

Belinda smiled. "I would, if I were you. I doubt if the water cooled him off any."

"He is so pigheaded!" Freddy said, edging toward the front door as a dripping Ry McGuinnes headed purposefully in her direction. "Well, see you later. Gotta run."

As she dashed out the front door, her wet fiancé entered through the back, his jaw rigid. "Freddy!" he called. Then he glanced over at Belinda and Amanda. "Afternoon, ladies." He tipped his hat, sending a stream of water to the tiled floor.

"Ry, this is Amanda Drake and her son, Bartholomew," Belinda said. "Amanda, this is Ry McGuinnes."

His intense blue eyes widened as he looked at the tiny baby squirming and squalling in her arms. He started to say something but closed his mouth again.

"We have to get this baby's diaper changed," Belinda said, turning Amanda toward an office off the main room. "And you'll need to dry off or get back outside. We can talk later."

"Sure." Ry touched the brim of his hat. "Nice to have met you, Ms. Drake."

Amanda followed Belinda toward the office. Behind her she heard the front door open and Ry bellow Freddy's name again. It didn't sound to her like the call of a lovestruck fool, but what did she know? She had obviously left the familiar world of Eastern manners and conventions for the wild, wild West.

AFTER BARTHOLOMEW had a clean diaper and a more pleasant disposition, Amanda felt ready to view her accommodations.

Belinda walked her over to the little cottage. Chloe, Dexter's black-and-white dog started to follow them, but Belinda ordered her back to the ranch house. "Did you bring any other kind of shoes?" she asked as Amanda struggled along the rutted road toward the cottage.

"They all have open toes, if that's what you mean," Amanda said. "I knew it would be hot, so sandals seemed like the obvious choice." She looked at Belinda's leather running shoes. "Apparently not."

"Out here you're better off in these or boots. But don't worry. I'll bet we can find something you can borrow. You should have seen Ry McGuinnes when he first got here. Polished wing tips, designer tie, the works. Freddy fixed him up in no time."

"I'll bet Chase didn't arrive in wing tips."

Belinda laughed. "No, he didn't. Looked like a catalog cowboy at first, but he broke in those new duds real fast. He's taken to ranch life like a duck to water, especially now that Leigh's put him on a program to keep his back limber and healthy."

Leigh again, Amanda thought sourly. And if Leigh looked anything like her sister Freddy, she'd be very attractive.

"In fact, Chase has become such a cowboy, I doubt he could be happy living back East now," Belinda said.

Amanda got the message. "Don't worry, I'm not here to drag him back there," she said.

"I'm very glad to hear that, because I think it would break his heart to have to choose between his obligation to you and his love of the ranch."

"As I've told Chase, he has no obligation to me or Bartholomew."

Belinda met the comment with silence broken only by the crunch of their shoes on the path and the drone of insects in the nearby bushes. "I see," she said after a moment.

Amanda expected a question about why she was here at all, but none came, and for that she gave Belinda credit.

As they neared the cottage, Amanda's artistic sense was aroused by the quaint adobe structure, whitewashed like the main house, with the same red-tiled roof and a miniature porch shaded by several gracefully arching trees. Two Adirondack chairs on the porch reminded Amanda of her parents' beach house and made her feel more at home.

"I didn't expect so many trees in the desert," she said to Belinda as they reached the porch.

"Many Easterners don't." Belinda mounted the single step to the porch and produced a ring of keys from the pocket of her cotton trousers. "The ones with the avocado-green trunks and branches that look like feather dusters are palo verde, and the ones with the gnarled black trunks and delicate leaves are mesquite. Out here we prize our trees, because we prize the shade."

"I can understand that." She was drenched in perspiration. "Is the cottage air-conditioned?"

"Oh, yes." Belinda opened the door and cool air poured out, beckoning Amanda inside. "And fortunately, Chase had the good sense to turn it on for you when he brought over your bags," she added, stepping inside and walking over to adjust a crooked window shade.

Amanda followed her in and closed the door of the one-room cottage. The high-beamed ceiling and whitewashed walls gave it an open, airy look. Amanda's practiced eye noted genuine antique furnishings, and the comforter on the black walnut four-poster was trimmed in Battenburg lace. On a bedside table sat an imitation 1920s phone, and through the open bathroom door she glimpsed a clawfoot tub.

Belinda cleared her throat, and Amanda realized she expected a comment on the cottage. "It's lovely," she said, and meant it.

Belinda smiled. "Most think so, even the ones who've stayed at fancy hotels. We're proud of the True Love. Did Chase tell you that John Wayne used to stay at the ranch when he was filming in Old Tucson?"

"No, he didn't."

"Shame on that boy. Then he probably didn't tell you how the ranch got its name, either."

Amanda sank to the edge of the bed and hoped it wasn't a long story. Belinda had been so good to her, but she was very tired, and Bartholomew would want to nurse again soon. "No, he didn't."

"Thaddeus Singleton—he's the one who homesteaded the ranch in 1882—fell in love with a dance-hall girl and decided to marry her. Well, the proper ladies of Tucson thought it was scandalous and told him so. He married Clara anyway, and called the ranch the True Love, just to show those old busybodies. His brand is a heart with an arrow through it."

"I've seen that logo." Amanda was unwillingly drawn into the tale. "Did they live happily ever after?"

"Absolutely. Thaddeus built Clara a little adobe house, not much bigger than this cottage, over near what's now the north boundary of the ranch. He even burned that brand into the lintel above the door."

"How sweet."

"Up until six weeks ago, you could still see the ruins of it, but there was a stampede that leveled it. Freddy and Ry found the lintel, split in two, and Ry had it pieced together and framed. They're mounting it on an easel for the wedding ceremony out by the old homestead."

"The wedding's going to be outside?" Amanda had a tough time imagining it in this heat.

"Outside, and on horseback," Belinda said.

"Really!"

"It should be interesting, what with Ry's best man being a dude and all. He's a commodities trader from New York who says he can ride, but we've all heard that before."

To her surprise, Amanda discovered that she wanted to see that wedding, especially after witnessing the pool incident between this intriguing couple. But she probably wouldn't be around day after tomorrow.

Bartholomew began to wiggle and make squeaking sounds.

"Looks as if the little fellow wants something to eat, so I'll leave you alone," Belinda said. Then she glanced around and scowled. "I just noticed Chase doesn't have that cradle in here yet. I'll go ride herd on him and find out what he's doing with all his time."

Amanda started to rise to bid Belinda a proper goodbye.

"Sit down, sit down," Belinda said, waving her hand at Amanda. "You must be exhausted. I'll have that cradle over in a jiffy, and then you and the little one can take a nap before dinner. We eat at six. Will you be able to find your way back to the main house?"

"I'm sure I will. And thank you for all your help, Belinda."

Belinda cast a fond look at Bartholomew. "I didn't realize I was so eager to have a baby around. We don't accept guests with children that young, so I don't get much chance to see really little ones. They brighten up the place. I guess I'll have to start pestering Ry and Freddy about having one." She paused to gaze at Bartholomew again. "Well, I'd better go hunt down that Chase Lavette." With a smile, Belinda left, closing the door firmly behind her.

Still holding Bartholomew, Amanda propped pillows against the headboard of the bed and kicked off her shoes before she unbuttoned her blouse and allowed him to nurse. With a sigh, she relaxed against the soft pillows. Maybe it was exhaustion, as Belinda had suggested, but she felt more relaxed than she had in a long time. She hadn't realized keeping secrets could be so stressful. Here at the True Love her secret was out, and nobody had shunned her, which brought more relief than she could have imagined. Chase had been upset, but who could blame him?

Maybe all he needed was a little time to see that she'd done the right thing. Perhaps she wouldn't have to cut off all contact. As long as Chase planned to stay in Arizona, she could bring Bartholomew out here once in a while for visits and nobody back home would ever have to know the truth. Of course, that would depend upon Chase and what he'd agree to, but it seemed like an ideal situation. Eventually, she might even tell her friends and family about Chase, when time had softened the scandalous nature of her behavior in the cab of that big black truck.

She and Chase had produced such a beautiful baby that night, she thought, stroking Bartholomew's downy head as he suckled on her breast. Had she gone to a sperm bank as she'd told everyone, she couldn't have found a finer candidate to father her child. A memory of Chase floated up, not the angry Chase she'd dealt with today, but the daring man who'd dug through three feet of snow to free her from her car and had carried her, shivering and scared to death, back to his truck. She closed her eyes and felt the warmth of the truck, the warmth of his arms.

He hadn't kissed her then, or made any sexual advances. Once he'd settled her safely in the cab with a cup of coffee in her hands, he hadn't touched her except to rub her feet to make sure they weren't frost-bitten.

Then when he was convinced she was okay, he'd pulled the big truck onto the snowy road, determined to drive them both safely back to the city. They'd talked as he'd battled the treacherous road conditions for another hour, until finally he'd given up and pulled into a rest stop. That's when it had dawned on her that she was about to spend the night with this sexy truck driver, that prim and professional Amanda Drake had never had a one-night stand in her life and that it was an extremely tempting possibility.

Bartholomew's suckling grew less vigorous and she eased him away from her breast. It didn't look as if Chase would arrive with the cradle in time for the baby's nap, and she didn't trust putting him on the bed now that he'd begun to roll. Lifting him in her arms and reaching for a diaper to protect her shoulder, she climbed off the bed and studied the room while she burped him.

The floor would do, she decided, pulling the comforter off the bed and folding it awkwardly with one hand. Finally, she'd created a soft padded surface that would cushion Bartholomew as he slept. A nap would be nice for both of them, she thought with a sigh as she settled him on the comforter.

On her hands and knees, she was stroking his back when a movement from the bedskirt caught her eye.

The bedskirt, also made of Battenburg lace, fluttered gently. She wondered if a draft from the air conditioner had caused it. The lace fluttered again. But there is no breeze down here, she thought, her heart pounding, her hand reaching for Bartholomew.

From beneath the lace darted a forked tongue.

4

AFTER NEARLY a half hour of looking, Chase and Rosa found the cradle behind boxes of Christmas decorations in a little-used storeroom. With a dustcloth Rosa gave him, Chase cleaned the cobwebs from it and in the process noticed the handholds carved into the headboard and footboard were in the shape of a heart. He wiped the dust from the handholds with care.

Rosa returned with a clean quilt that she folded into a serviceable mattress. After thanking her, Chase picked up the cradle, his fingers fitting perfectly into the hearts on either end, and started for the cottage. Carrying a cradle wasn't how he'd pictured this little trip to visit Amanda, he thought with a grimace. Now the scenes he'd imagined taking place in the cottage weren't likely to happen, unless he'd completely misread the signals she'd been giving him.

About a hundred yards from the cottage he heard a screech. He dropped the cradle and started forward just as the door flew open and Amanda bolted out, barefoot, with her blouse undone and Bartholomew clutched against one shoulder, screaming lustily.

"Snake!" she cried above the sound of Bartholomew's screams. She ran toward him, her eyes wide, her face the color of snow.

His blood froze in his veins. "Where?"

"Under...under the bed!"

He tasted the metallic flavor of fear. "Did it bite you?" He reached for the wailing child. "Is the baby—"

"No!" She stepped out of reach. "We're not bitten! Get it out, Chase! Just get it out!"

He glanced around for a stick and broke a forked one off a palo verde. "Stay there."

"Don't worry." She gasped for breath. "I'm never going back in that place."

He approached the door of the cottage with caution and listened, trying to tune out the baby's crying. Rattlers didn't always rattle, he'd learned, but if he heard the buzzing sound first, at least he'd have a better idea what he was dealing with. The cottage was silent. He knocked the stick against the open door. He heard nothing but the baby's ratcheting complaint.

With slow, even steps he walked through the door and cast a look over the polished oak boards covered with Indian-patterned throw rugs. On the far side of the room a white comforter lay folded on the floor, an indentation in the middle where the baby had obviously been lying. He shuddered. Amanda should have put him in the bathtub, but then, she didn't know. A New York copywriter would have no experience with snakes.

Not that a snake was even supposed to be in here. A maid had cleaned the room just that morning. He wondered if the reptile could have slipped through the door when he'd brought Amanda's suitcases over earlier, but he doubted it. He might be a little distracted by Amanda and the baby's arrival, but not *that* distracted.

Since the snake wasn't coming out to greet him, he supposed he'd have to search for it. Too bad it was probably hiding under the bed. He didn't relish putting his face down there at striking level to find out whether or not it was a rattler. Using the stick to lift the bedskirt at the foot of the four-poster, he hunkered down and peered into the shadows. His gut tightened. There was something under there, all right. Something big. He sure wished he had a flashlight.

Bartholomew's crying lessened, then stopped. Chase didn't like the idea of the little guy's being out in the sun too much longer. Time to get the damn snake out from under the bed. He rounded to the side, lifted the skirt with one hand and began to poke the thick body. If it was a rattler, it might come charging out at him. Despite the air conditioner blasting through the cottage, he began to sweat as he poised on the balls of his feet, ready to react.

With a dry whispering sound the snake began to uncoil. He waited, heart pounding, to see which side it would choose. It started moving away from him. Chase eased onto the mattress and inched to the other side, the forked stick poised. The shape of the head would tell him everything, but he hadn't been able to see it in the murky light sifting under the bedskirt. He held his breath.

The bedskirt moved, and the snake started out, its body thick as a baseball bat. Chase shoved the stick down hard just behind the creature's head, which was oval, not triangular like a rattler's. The intruder was a very large, very harmless, bull snake.

Weak with relief, he had a hard time holding the stick steady. Fortunately, the snake had become as motionless as a length of cable, as if complete stillness would keep it safe. It was several seconds before Chase gathered the coordination to reach down and grasp the snake behind the head where his stick had kept it pinned.

He wriggled off the bed and hauled the snake up. Chase was nearly six feet tall, and he had to hold the snake head-high before its tail no longer touched the oak floor.

"I have the snake, Amanda," he called out the door. "It's big, but it's harmless. I'm coming out. Don't be scared. It won't hurt you."

"You mean it's still *alive?*"

"You shouldn't kill them," Chase said, walking toward the door as the snake undulated in the air. "They help keep things in balance around here."

As he walked out on the porch, she gasped and stumbled backward, nearly running into Chloe, Dexter's dog poised right behind her. Chloe's ears pricked forward and she gave a sharp bark.

"Careful," Chase warned. The upended cradle lay a few feet beyond where she stood. "You could trip over the dog, and if you fall, there's a lot of prickly stuff you could land in."

"Of course there is. *Everything* around here is dangerous. I'm in the middle of 'Wild Kingdom'!"

Chloe wagged her tail and sat down next to Amanda. Chase could have sworn the dog, a golden retriever and sheepdog mix, had decided to guard Amanda and the baby.

"Maybe you'd better go back inside while I take this guy out and let him go," he said.

"Oh, God. You're letting it go?"

"I'll walk pretty far out." Chase stepped off the porch and Amanda backed up another step, nearly landing on Chloe's tail. "Besides, this fellow attacks rodents, not people. This snake is no threat to you or the baby. I promise. Now go on inside and wait for me. I'll be back real soon."

She shook her head.

He controlled his irritation. "Amanda, it's safe now, and the baby should be out of the sun. Chloe will react if there's anything else in there to be afraid of."

"I won't go in, and stop calling him *the baby!* If you can call a dog by her name, you can call him by his name, which is Bartholomew!"

God, how she tested his patience. "But I didn't get any say in that choice, did I?"

"And you hate his name." Her lips quivered as her gaze remained riveted on the snake he held aloft.

"No, I don't hate it. I just—aw, hell, Amanda. It's hot and I'm holding a very athletic snake. Can we discuss this later?"

"Just get that thing out of here," she said, her voice strained.

"You should go inside."

"No."

She looked pretty close to hysteria, so he decided not to insist. "Okay. You and...Bartholomew wait here. Chloe, stay with Amanda." The dog wagged her tail in response.

Chase started off through the desert as quickly as he could walk, considering he was wearing boots, avoiding cactus and carrying a six-foot snake that very much wanted to be loose. "Take it easy," he told the snake. "You were probably more scared than she was." Although he doubted it. Amanda had been pretty freaked-out.

She was right about his reaction to the baby's name. He didn't like it. Maybe that was because he'd had no say in naming the kid, but more than that, he thought "Bartholomew" sounded too long and involved for the kind of son he'd like to have, a sturdy little boy who lived to run and throw balls and eat ice cream. A kid who—

Chase brought his imagination to a halt. Where had all that come from? He'd never wanted a kid. Or had never admitted it. But then Amanda had arrived with his son, and unexpected dreams were surfacing. Dreams of a family. For all the good those dreams would do him. Just as Amanda hadn't given him any say in naming the baby, she hadn't invited him to help raise the boy, either. He'd have to fight for that right, and he didn't like the idea of what that might do to Bartholomew.

About two hundred yards from the cottage, he figured he could set the snake free. He lowered it slowly to the ground, released the head last and stepped away. In five seconds the snake was gone, taking off through the creosote bushes. Chase turned and hurried back to where Amanda still stood in the path, Chloe stationed right beside her.

"Where did it go?" she asked.

He tried a smile out on her. "Packed a bag and lit out for Texas."

"Don't try to joke about it. That snake was headed straight for Bartholomew."

"I guess I would have jumped out of my skin myself if I'd been there," he said, softening his tone. "Now let's get him back inside."

"Not until you check everything in the cottage." Her blue eyes still reflected full-scale panic.

"Then at least wait up on the porch in the shade," he said, taking her elbow.

She was stiff, but she allowed him to guide her to the porch. Chloe followed right beside her, panting loudly in the heat. "I don't belong here," Amanda said. "I want you to give me your medical history now, so I can take a flight out. Maybe I can even leave tonight."

"We'll talk about it in a minute." His first concern was getting them all into a cool environment. He left Amanda and the baby on the porch and took Chloe with him into the cottage. "Check it out, girl," he said, and Chloe seemed to understand, because she circled the perimeter of the room and sniffed every corner. Then she snuffled under the bed, obviously still smelling traces of the snake. Chase scoured every nook and cranny, including a closet, all the dresser drawers and a cupboard in the bathroom. He found only one small spider, a harmless kind, which he captured and tossed out the door as he came back to the porch.

"All clear," he said.

She entered slowly, her gaze sweeping the room several times.

"I'll get the cradle," Chase said. "I hope I didn't break it."

"It doesn't matter. I'm not staying."

Chase went after the cradle, anyway. He sincerely hoped he hadn't broken it when he'd dropped it. It had probably been built for a Singleton baby somewhere back in time, and he'd bet both Freddy and Leigh had been rocked to sleep in it. For a reason he didn't want to explore too thoroughly, he wanted Bartholomew to sleep in it, too. And he hoped Amanda wouldn't take the next plane out of town. Not because he wanted anything more to do with her, but because he couldn't say goodbye to his son just yet. Maybe in a few days he'd have it all worked out in his mind, but for now, he wanted that baby around.

The cradle was still in one piece, but the quilt had fallen in the dirt. He shook it out and tucked it under his arm. He'd noticed an extra blanket in the closet that he could use instead. Tossing the quilt on one of the porch chairs as he walked by, he carried the cradle into the room and shut the door behind him.

Amanda stood by the table jiggling Bartholomew against her shoulder as she stared out the window. "I'm sorry I blew up, but I want to go home, Chase," she said softly. "This isn't my type of place. Will you help me get back?"

"Not yet."

She looked up at him, rebellion flickering in her eyes. "I can just call a cab. I haven't even unpacked."

"I thought you needed information before you left."

"Maybe it's best if we communicate by phone."

His gut twisted. She could leave, and he had no power to stop her. He swallowed. "Please don't leave yet."

She studied him for several moments. "Chase, a snowstorm brought us together," she said finally. "Otherwise, we'd never have met because our lives were so different. They still are, even more so now that you're out here. Give me what I need and let me go. It's the best thing we can do with a situation we didn't ask for."

He struggled with the urges coursing through him. He'd never felt possessive about a woman in his life. Easy come, easy go had been a motto that had served him well for years. Yet he couldn't imagine watching Amanda walk out of his life. She was the mother of his child. That created a bond he couldn't take lightly. A shrink would probably say it was because in his own case, that bond had been so carelessly broken. At any rate, apparently Amanda didn't feel connected to him; she could hardly wait to get away from the True Love.

"I told you, I'm not very good at remembering

things," he said. "I need to make some phone calls before I can give you what you've asked for. I haven't had a chance to do that yet."

"Can you do it now?"

"Maybe." Once he figured out where to start. He'd been out of touch for so long, he might find only dead-end streets. "I'll make some calls, Amanda, but I can't promise I'll get you quick results. If you really want to fly out now, I could mail you something, but I'm lousy at writing stuff out. I'd probably miss some detail you'd want."

She heaved a long, shaky sigh. "You're right. It's late, and we're both tired, and Bartholomew's been through enough for one day. I should at least stay until tomorrow, but..." She raised her eyes to his. "That snake frightened the daylights out of me, Chase. I don't know if I can sleep in this cottage tonight."

He almost offered to stay with her, but he thought she might misunderstand the offer. Maybe he didn't even mean it so innocently. Scared as he'd been when she ran out the door and shouted the word *snake,* he'd still noticed her unbuttoned blouse and had glimpsed her bare breast. Sometime during the incident, she'd refastened her blouse, but that didn't eliminate the air of sensuality that still clung to her like morning dew on clover. He might not love her, but he definitely lusted after her. "I'll bet Dexter would let you have Chloe for the night," he suggested.

At the mention of her name, Chloe sat between them and looked up, her tail thumping the floor.

Amanda gazed doubtfully at her. "I've never had a dog."

"Neither have I. But that doesn't matter. Chloe doesn't think she's a dog."

"She really knows when something's wrong?"

"Why do you think she came dashing down here? She heard you scream."

"Really?" Amanda reached down with her free hand and touched the dog's head. "Did you come to help me, Chloe?"

Chloe whined and thumped her tail faster.

"That's amazing. She doesn't even know me."

"I think it has something to do with the way Dexter reacted when you handed him Bartholomew. Chloe was watching all that, and I think she decided that he would be her responsibility, too."

Amanda fondled Chloe's head and scratched behind the dog's ears without looking at Chase.

When Chase heard a sniff, he guessed Amanda was crying. "Amanda?"

"Don't mind me," she said, her voice choked. She sniffed again. "I hear new mothers are sometimes emotional."

Chase had never met a crying woman he hadn't tried to comfort. He drew Amanda, baby and all, into his arms, careful to accommodate Bartholomew as he guided Amanda's head to his shoulder. She began to sob softly, her tears seeping through his shirt. Chase laid his cheek against her wondrous red hair and massaged the small of her back.

He wasn't being smart, he thought, but needy people always got to him. And Amanda had seemed that way from the beginning. Beneath the career-woman image, he'd sensed a hunger very much like his own. She might have thought all they shared in the cab of his truck that night was sex, but he'd always suspected it went much deeper than that.

Before they'd made love, she'd announced that she

considered it a one-night stand, and he'd gone along with the idea. He hadn't been about to turn away from a woman as tempting as Amanda, and he'd been curious, too, wondering what it would be like making love to a woman who dressed in cashmere and drove a Mercedes. Soon, however, he'd forgotten everything about her except the light in her eyes and warmth of her body.

In the morning as they'd driven into the city, he'd made the mistake of asking when he could see her again. That's when he'd discovered that she really did consider him a one-night stand. Oh, she was grateful he'd saved her from the snowbank, and she'd had a terrific time—her exact words—but she didn't think they were at all suited to each other. His pride had made him agree with her. Yet he'd always thought she would reconsider, once the effects of that night had sunk in. She might have, he thought, if she hadn't been pregnant. Had he sensed all along that's what had happened? Probably.

She stopped crying and leaned weakly against his shoulder. Bartholomew had remained quiet the whole time, as if subdued by his mother's tears.

"I'm sorry, Chase," she murmured thickly.

"For what?"

"Everything." She sighed. "Just everything. I've tried to do what was best, but I didn't know that would be so hard on everyone."

"I wish you'd have let me help."

"I don't believe in saddling people with unwanted obligations."

"Amanda, I—"

"People hate obligations!"

His hand stilled in the act of rubbing her back. "Maybe I wouldn't think of it like that."

She lifted her head and met his gaze. "I'm not taking the chance that you would," she said with a vehemence that surprised him. "When I was sixteen, I worked part-time in my dad's law office and I overheard him telling his secretary he couldn't get a divorce because of his *obligation* to his wife and children. *I* was the reason he couldn't be happy, the reason he turned into a martyr who couldn't love anyone! Bartholomew's never going to have that feeling if I can help it."

Chase was silent. To be truthful, he wasn't sure how he would have reacted if she'd begged him to marry her and be a proper father to their child. Maybe like a martyr, just as she'd said. Marriage had never figured into his plans. But that didn't mean he wanted to be kept away from his baby, either. What, exactly, did he want? He wasn't sure. He'd trained himself not to want much of anything from life so that he was seldom disappointed.

But he was a father now. He couldn't drift along and take whatever came his way this time, or he'd lose contact with his son. He needed a plan, but clearheaded planning was difficult while he held Amanda in his arms. Her body pressed against his, the scent of that expensive cologne she wore and the memory of their shared night in the truck cab were working on his imagination. For the first few weeks after the elevator accident, he'd been in too much pain to think about sex, but his back didn't bother him much now. He'd been dreaming of this woman for ten months, and after her letter had arrived, he'd fantasized with great pleasure about undressing her again and making love to her in the antique four-poster bed next to where they now stood.

Slowly he released her and stepped back. She looked

at him through reddened eyes. He supposed he should have been turned off by her puffy, tear-streaked face. Instead, he wanted to tuck the baby in the cradle and tuck her into bed, with him right alongside her. She had the fullest, most kissable mouth he'd ever seen, and it was parted now, just wide enough to allow his tongue to slip inside. There was an awareness in her eyes, a vulnerability that he recognized from that night in the truck.

"There's a blanket in the closet. You can use it as a mattress for the cradle," he said.

"All right." She didn't move, just kept holding the baby against her shoulder like a shield against the emotion shining in her eyes.

"You *are* afraid of me, aren't you?"

She swallowed. "Of course not."

"Then get the blanket and put the baby down."

Still she didn't move.

Muttering a soft oath, he looked away. "We're more alike than you think, Amanda. Neither one of us knows what to do about this problem. The difference is that I'll admit it." He started for the door, then glanced back at the dog sitting attentively beside Amanda. "I'll tell Dexter you're borrowing Chloe for a while." Then he stepped into the hot sunshine and quickly walked away from the little cottage while he could still resist the seductive light in those blue eyes. He wondered if she realized it was there.

SHE HADN'T EXPECTED to want him so much, Amanda thought as she took a deep breath and turned away from the door. She found the blanket he'd mentioned and arranged it in the cradle with one hand, not willing to put Bartholomew on the floor for even an instant.

She certainly remembered Chase as a very appealing guy, but she'd always thought his sexual magnetism had been heightened by the novelty of making love in the bunk of an 18-wheeler. Apparently, that hadn't been the secret of Chase's attraction for her. Once she'd sobbed out her frustration in his arms just now, she'd become aware of his strong arms wrapped around her. Very aware. Had she not been holding Bartholomew.... But she had been, and that had helped her focus.

Chase had told her he was a rambler, a lone wolf, proud of the fact he had no strings to tie him down. He'd even had *The Drifter* stenciled on his truck cab as a general bulletin of the fact. She'd worked hard to create a secure niche with her job and her career-oriented friends. Her parents boasted about her all the time, just as they boasted about her brother, Jason, who was with the diplomatic corps in Spain. They'd boasted a little less about Bartholomew, but as her father had said, "At least you didn't link up with some bum just so you could be a mother."

Remembering that statement and her father's years of sacrifice out of "obligation," Amanda had resisted the urge to throw herself into Chase's arms again. Barely.

Lowering Bartholomew into the cradle, she sat on the edge of the bed and used her toe to rock him gently to sleep. Chloe settled down at the foot of the cradle and put her head on her paws.

When at last Bartholomew's eyes drifted closed, Amanda lay back on the bed. Chase had been right about having Chloe there. Amanda was able to relax, knowing the dog was on duty. But she couldn't sleep. Not when all she could think about was the way Chase had looked at her before he left, his smoky green eyes heavy with passion.

5

CHASE OPENED the back gate leading into the patio and stormed through, not sure where he was headed. He almost ran into Eb Whitlock, who was carrying a potted rosebush in each hand. Eb's ranch, the Rocking W, bordered the True Love on the north, and Freddy had asked him to give her away during the wedding ceremony.

"Hey, cowboy!" Eb said in his typical boisterous bellow. "Somebody set your tail on fire?"

Chase wasn't in the mood for Eb Whitlock's corny brand of humor. The rancher usually laughed at his own jokes, and when he displayed his choppers, Chase was reminded of the grille work on his Peterbilt. "Didn't mean to run you down, Eb," he said. "I guess we're all rushing around these days, with the wedding coming up."

"Exactly. That's why I'm here with these." Eb plopped a container on either side of him, took off his hat and reached for a bandanna in his hip pocket. "Saw them in a nursery in town and couldn't resist." He mopped his forehead and smoothed the sides of his white hair before replacing the bandanna and repositioning his hat. "I have six more out in the truck. Thought they'd look good for the reception. Belinda said to find a place for them out here around the pool."

He walked over by the waterfall. "Maybe one here. What do you think?"

Chase had to admit the roses were a nice thought, although it was typical of Eb to act on his own, without consulting anyone, when he wanted to do something generous. More than once, Chase had heard Ry mutter that he wished Eb would mind his own damn business.

"I don't know the first thing about flower arranging," Chase said, starting to edge away.

"Me neither. I'm just an old cowpoke trying to do a good deed." Eb walked around behind the waterfall. "I'll just put one on the other side, here."

"Well, I'd better be going." Chase eased toward the house, determined to escape while he had the chance.

"Say," Eb called out from behind the waterfall, "how's that little gal of yours, the one that was coming in from New York?"

Chase definitely didn't want to discuss Amanda—or the baby—with Eb. "Well, she—"

"Chase!" Leigh called, bursting from the main room of the house. "What's this I hear about Amanda's... baby. Oh, hi, Eb. I didn't see you out here."

Thanks, Leigh. But he couldn't be angry with her. Not Leigh. When he'd first arrived at the True Love, he'd been attracted by her looks—dark blond hair and a face that reminded him of the Mona Lisa. To his surprise, he and Leigh had become friends instead of lovers. He trusted her, which made their relationship very special indeed.

"A baby?" Eb set the second potted bush on the other side of the waterfall and walked toward them with a grin big enough to eat New York. "Don't tell me you took a bite out of the Big Apple before you left?"

"To be honest with you, Eb, this was as much a surprise to me as it is to you," Chase said.

Eb clapped him on the shoulder. "Then I think it's time we had a talk, man to man. It's dangerous to be ignorant of the birds and the bees, son. Isn't that right, Leigh?"

Leigh's almond-colored gaze was contrite as she looked at Chase. "Oh, I think Chase understands the birds and the bees. In fact, I think he might have written the manual on the subject. Anyway, if you'll excuse us, Eb, I need Chase to help with some chores down at the corrals. Ry was supposed to do it, but he's not available."

Eb winked. "What's wrong, bridegroom jitters?"

"Oh, I hardly think that's the problem, Eb. Nice roses. Too bad Freddy's allergic to them."

"She is?"

"Something terrible. Maybe you can plant those over in your garden."

"But Belinda never said anything about Freddy being allergic."

"With all the food preparation for the reception and thinking about that little baby, Belinda's a basket case. Trust me, Eb. A few minutes with those roses and we'll be toasting Freddy, the red-nosed bride. Nice idea, though. Come on, Chase. We have work to do." She pulled him toward the French doors leading into the main room of the house. "Sorry about that," she said as soon as they were inside. "I didn't see his truck out front and he was hidden behind the waterfall."

"Don't sweat it. Knowing Whitlock's sources, he'd have found out by sundown, anyway. Is Freddy really allergic to roses?"

"Not yet, but she will be if Ry finds out who trundled

them over here unannounced. Their big fight this morning was over whether to have Eb in the ceremony. Ry doesn't want him."

"I don't blame him. Whitlock reminds me of a few truck drivers I've known—big belly and big mouth to match." Chase also knew that Eb had been an unsuccessful bidder for the True Love and hadn't taken well to defeat when Ry had closed the deal.

"The problem is, Freddy promised our father before he died that she'd ask Eb to walk her down the aisle if she ever got married. I think it was a dumb promise, but Freddy will never go back on it."

Chase glanced back at Whitlock, who had retrieved the rosebushes and was walking toward the door. "Let's get out of here." He took Leigh's elbow and they headed out the front door toward her truck. "By now, he's probably thought of a dozen questions about this baby business."

"I'll bet he heard a rumor about the baby and bought the roses so he'd have an excuse to come over and check it out. I'm getting mighty sick of the way Eb uses his little favors and gifts as a manipulation." She gestured toward the passenger door of her truck. "Hop in. You look like a man who could use some therapeutic shoveling."

"You read my mind, as usual." Chase climbed into Leigh's dark blue truck with the rainbow painted on the fender and a crystal hanging from the rearview mirror, which cast more rainbows around the interior. Leigh was one of the few people he allowed to drive him anywhere.

"I'll bet you've missed your swim today," Leigh said as she started down the road.

"I'll get it in tonight," Chase promised. He wasn't

about to skimp on the rehabilitation program she'd set up for him, no matter what Amanda threw at him.

"Stress can zap those muscles, you know."

Chase leaned back against the tattered seat. "What makes you think I'm stressed?"

"Who wouldn't be? I doubt it's every day you have women show up with babies they claim you fathered."

"I did father this one, Leigh."

"I know. Belinda says he looks just like you." Leigh shifted into third gear. "But I can't understand what Amanda is doing out here if she doesn't want you to pay child support or anything."

"She wants information on my family's medical background."

Leigh looked skeptical. "She could have asked you that on the phone."

"And I might have hung up on her. Can you imagine getting a phone call like that?"

"I suppose you have a point, but she should have warned you."

"Yeah, she should have."

Leigh swerved to avoid a rabbit. "Something else is going on here, Chase. My intuition lights are flashing like crazy."

"Well, if you figure it out, tell me." They arrived at the corrals and Chase reached for the door handle. "In the meantime, I have some serious shoveling to do."

"Nothing like cleaning out a corral or two to lower the stress level." Leigh smiled. "Ry thinks we should bill it that way and charge the dudes a fee for the privilege of shoveling."

Chase laughed as he climbed from the truck, but he had to admit it was a good idea. "Are you joining me?"

"I'm not stressed. Besides, I need to check on Penny Lover."

"You're spoiling that mare," Chase said, rounding the truck and starting toward the tack shed.

Leigh was already on her way to a small corral at the far end of the clearing. "Expectant mothers deserve to be spoiled," she called back.

Chase silently agreed with her. And he hadn't been allowed to do that for Amanda, something else to add to his growing burden of regrets. He grabbed a shovel and rake from hooks on the tack-shed wall and headed toward the largest corral. He had the place pretty much to himself, except for the horses and the ever-present flies. Several of the hands had the day off, and there was no sign of Duane, the top hand, who was probably napping in the bunkhouse.

Chase raked and shoveled steadily for nearly thirty minutes, tossing manure into an open trailer used to haul it away. Finally, sweat-soaked and much calmer, he leaned against the shovel and took a breather. He loved being down here, surrounded by corrals built a century ago. They weren't the sort of corrals he'd expected when he'd pictured the ranch, though. Instead of open rails, the fences were made of gnarled mesquite branches stacked between upright supports to create a solid barrier. In Chase's opinion, they were part of what gave the True Love its own character, and he liked just looking at them.

Leigh walked over and leaned against the top of the fence. "Had enough?"

"I guess so. You ready to go back up to the house?"

Leigh nodded. "My maid-of-honor outfit needs a few finishing touches."

"Okay." Chase propped the rake and shovel against

the side of the trailer and pulled off his gloves. "Let me wash off in the horse trough and I'll be right with you." Shoving the gloves into the back pocket of his jeans, he hung his hat on the rake handle and rolled up his sleeves.

"You're getting to be more of a cowboy every day," Leigh said. "A greenhorn wouldn't think of putting horse-trough water on his face."

"You'd better smile when you go comparing me to a greenhorn." Chase leaned over the trough and scooped water into his cupped hands. Splashing it over his face, he sighed at the welcome coolness.

Then his eyes began to burn. Seeking relief, he washed them with more water, but the burning grew worse. "Damn! My eyes!" he cried.

Leigh was over the fence and beside him in a flash. She cupped some water and stuck her tongue in. "Yuck!" She flung the water to the ground. "Something's wrong with this water! Go wash in the bunkhouse and send Duane out here. I'll keep the horses away from the trough."

Eyes streaming, Chase fumbled his way out the gate and ran toward the bunkhouse. "Duane!"

Duane opened the screen door and peered out. "What's wrong?"

"The horse trough is contaminated. Leigh needs help with the horses."

"Damnation," Duane muttered, and started toward the corrals at a bowlegged trot.

Chase caught the screen door before it slammed and barreled inside, his eyes stinging. He jogged the length of the barracks-like structure, deserted at this hour, to the bathroom at the end. After several applications of water from the sink's faucet, his eyes felt a little better.

Grabbing a towel, he mopped his face and headed back outside.

By the time he'd returned to the corrals, all the horse troughs were draining. Duane was mounted on Destiny, the ranch's premier cutting horse, keeping the horses in the biggest corral away from the trough. Leigh was managing to distract the few horses in the smaller corrals.

"We'll need to get Freddy down here to check all the horses," Leigh called out to him as she maneuvered two geldings away from a draining trough. "Dammit! What could be in the water?"

"What about a sample?" Chase asked.

"Oh, God, yes! There should be a jar in the tack shed. Scoop some water out of that main trough before it's all gone."

Chase ran across the clearing, found an empty mason jar in the tack shed and managed to get back to the corral before the trough there was empty. He barely had time to get a sample of the water before the last of it drained into the mud.

"Did you get it?" Leigh hurried up beside him, with Duane close behind.

"Some, at least."

"Thank heavens you thought of it. When the horses are in danger, I really lose it." She pressed her fingers to her temples. "Let's see. We'll take the jar back up to the house, and Ry can run it into town to be analyzed while Freddy, you and I help Duane check the horses for any signs of poisoning."

"I thought Ry was unavailable."

She glanced at him, a suggestion of a smile easing the tension in her face. "He and Freddy had hung a Do Not Disturb sign on their door while they made up after their fight. But I think this warrants disturbing them." She turned to Duane. "Did you notice anything suspicious around the corrals today?"

Duane reached in his back pocket for his can of Red Man. "Nope."

"We're shorthanded this afternoon, so someone could have ridden in without being noticed."

Chase glanced at her. "Are you saying someone deliberately poisoned the water?"

"It's possible."

"Lots of things been happenin' around here." Duane stuck a plug of tobacco under his lower lip.

Uneasiness rolled in Chase's stomach. "Like what?"

"I'll tell you on the way back," Leigh said. "Let's get going."

"I'll drive."

She gave him another half smile. "Thanks, my trucker friend. I'd appreciate it this time."

"OKAY, let's have it," he said as they started down the road in her truck. "What's going on?"

"I was hoping it was over, but I guess not. Right before you three bought the ranch from the Colorado corporation, we were plagued with all sorts of accidents— leaking stock tanks, cattle tangled in barbed wire, stuff like that. Then there was that stampede the day you arrived. Freddy and Ry were almost killed."

"And we found out the gate had been accidentally left open. People make mistakes." Boy, did he ever know the truth of that one.

"Ry still thinks Duane might have had something to do with that stampede."

"You've got to be kidding!"

Leigh sighed. "I can't believe it, either. But I have to

admit he might have a reason. He knows you guys are thinking about selling the ranch to developers. That would put an end to a way of life for Duane, not to mention screw up the breeding program he's conducting on the side, using True Love land. If the accidents drive you away, or at least devalue the property so you can't get a decent price, things might not change for him. And, after all, it was his herd that made up the stampede."

"But Duane wouldn't poison a horse trough."

"Well, Eb Whitlock is always another possibility. He still wants the ranch. And Ry even suspects Belinda."

Chase gave her a startled glance. "Belinda? Why in hell would he be suspicious of Belinda?"

"Because she's so protective of Dexter. Ry thinks she'd do anything to keep him sitting safely on that front porch. She hates the idea of your selling to developers. So do I, for that matter."

Chase fought panic. "But if we don't sell the ranch, we won't make the profit Ry told us about."

"Oh, come on, Chase! Do you mean to tell me you're still interested in getting rich? I've seen how you react to this place. You love it!"

He became aware of a hollow ache in the vicinity of his heart. "I've trained myself not to love any place too much."

Leigh was silent for a long moment. "That's the saddest thing I've ever heard you say," she murmured said at last.

DESPITE HER CONVICTION that she wouldn't sleep, Amanda eventually drifted off. She awoke feeling cozy, a remarkable feat considering the snake episode, she thought. Bartholomew remained asleep, and she enjoyed the luxury of washing her face and deciding what to wear to dinner without carrying a baby around while she did it. Chloe stayed at her post, merely lifting her head when Amanda walked past to open the suitcases.

She'd brought one pair of designer jeans and she decided on a white silk blouse that was tailored enough to be almost western in style. And she wouldn't make the mistake of wearing nylons with her sandals this time.

She barely made it through dressing before Bartholomew woke up, a little before six. He didn't seem particularly interested in nursing, so she changed him, put him in the infant seat and started out the door, with Chloe at her side. Then she paused. Beside the door sat a pair of boots, very nice brown leather boots, with a note tucked in the shank of one.

Belinda said you might be able to use these and figured we were about the same size. You're welcome to borrow them during your stay.

Leigh Singleton.

Amanda glanced from her open-toed sandals to the boots. Leigh's boots. Fantastic Leigh, who could read minds and had massaged Chase to health. Then Amanda gave herself a mental shake, feeling thoroughly ashamed of herself. Despite the fact she'd had Chase's baby, she'd relinquished all claim to him. What kind of woman discarded a man yet resented his attention to someone else? Amanda knew what kind, and it rhymed with witch.

She took the boots inside and changed out of her sandals. They were a perfect fit. As she walked to the main house with the boots lending her added height and

Chloe trotting by her side, she almost felt as if she belonged at the True Love Ranch.

Retracing the path she'd taken with Belinda, she entered the patio through a back gate. Dexter sat in a shady corner across the pool, his walker by his side along with a dish of dog food. Chloe's head went up and her nose twitched. She glanced at Amanda.

"Go ahead," Amanda said. "I'll catch up with you later."

Chloe bounded toward Dexter, who greeted her with such affection that Amanda felt guilty about borrowing the dog for the night. But not guilty enough to refuse. Chloe would bring greater safety to Bartholomew, and that was Amanda's first priority. She waved at Dexter. "Thanks for loaning me your dog."

"Yep."

"Aren't you coming in to dinner?"

"Nope."

"Well, I'm starved," she said. "See you later."

"Yep."

The dining room was bustling, with Ry and Freddy at the center of all the activity. Amanda slipped in unnoticed and chose a table by herself, figuring the wedding guests, none of whom had brought children, would prefer not to have a baby around during their meal. She propped Bartholomew's infant seat on the chair next to her and gave her order to the young waiter who'd appeared.

Ry and Freddy had pushed three tables together to accommodate their crowd of well-wishers. Bartholomew dozed in his infant seat, so Amanda amused herself by figuring out who was who. The man who seemed to be an older version of Ry was definitely his father, but from body-language clues Amanda decided the woman with the elder McGuinnes wasn't Ry's mother. Ry was much more affectionate with another woman in her sixties, who sat with a different man. Divorced parents, Amanda concluded. After that, she had more trouble sorting out who might be friends, siblings or in-laws. Chase was nowhere around.

But Ry and Freddy had definitely made up. Wistfully, Amanda observed their affectionate interplay.

"How are the boots?"

Amanda turned to find a stunning blonde standing next to her table. Soft brown eyes with a hint of mystery complemented a face that would have delighted the Renaissance masters, Amanda concluded. "You must be Leigh." She stood and extended her hand. "Thanks for the boots. They fit as if they were made for me."

"How lucky." Leigh smiled and glanced over at Bartholomew. "Sweet baby."

On cue, Bartholomew began to fuss.

"He's probably hungry," Amanda said, reaching for him. "His timing leaves much to be desired."

"Since your dinner's not here, why don't you feed him?"

Amanda was taken aback. "Oh, I think this is too public a place. I can walk over to the cottage."

"Nonsense. Nursing is a natural part of life. If anyone's sensibilities are disturbed, that's their problem. Besides, if I sit here and screen you from view, nobody will even notice. Go ahead."

"Well...okay." Amanda hadn't yet nursed Bartholomew in a restaurant setting, and she felt self-conscious, but Leigh's comments made sense. As unobtrusively as possible, she unfastened the first few buttons of her blouse, unhooked the cup of her nursing bra, and guided Bartholomew to her nipple. She glanced at Leigh, who watched with a gentle smile. "Thank you for your understanding."

"If he's a typical little Taurus, food is very important to him."

Amanda laughed. "I read that. And so far it's really true. I'll have to make sure he doesn't turn into a little chub."

"I doubt he will. Neither you or his father—" Leigh paused. "Sorry. Maybe you'd rather I not talk about Chase."

"I'd...rather you did. I think I've handled the matter of Chase poorly. Maybe you can help me."

"I can try." Leigh glanced over Amanda's shoulder. "Excuse me a minute." She rose from her seat and intercepted the waiter who approached with Amanda's dinner. He headed back toward the kitchen. "I told him to keep it warm for five minutes."

"Thank you." Amanda decided Chase was a lucky man to have found someone as thoughtful as Leigh. She was determined to be happy for him, even though it hurt—unreasonable though that might be—to think of him making love to someone else.

Leigh resumed her seat. "First of all, what do you want from Chase?"

"Just his family's medical history, so I can be prepared for anything."

"That's all?"

"Absolutely, Leigh. Don't think I'm any threat to you. Once I have the information, I'll disappear with Bartholomew and—"

"Whoa! Back that pony up a minute. Threat to *me*?"

"Not that you're acting threatened," Amanda hurried on. "In fact, you're being far more generous than I would be in similar circumstances. I think Chase is very lucky to have someone like you."

Leigh grinned. "You think Chase and I are lovers, don't you?"

"You're not?"

"I know it's hard to believe, given that Chase is a very sexy-looking guy, but the chemistry isn't there between us. He's like the brother I never had, and to his great surprise, he thinks of me as a sister. Neither of us would dream of jeopardizing that."

"Oh."

"You should see the relieved look on your face, Amanda. Are you sure you came out here just for a medical history?"

Amanda looked away. Bartholomew seemed to be losing interest in nursing, so she nudged him away from her breast and concentrated on refastening her clothes. "It wouldn't work," she said finally, glancing up at Leigh. She placed a napkin over her shoulder and held Bartholomew there while she patted his back. "I've finally established myself in the New York advertising world. In my spare time I enjoy concerts and gallery openings, or discovering new ethnic restaurants. Can you picture Chase living that kind of life?"

"No."

"Then there's the extra psychological baggage of getting to know each other when a baby is already part of the equation. I don't think any relationship should begin under that kind of pressure."

"Probably not, but we live in an imperfect world." Leigh turned as the waiter arrived with Amanda's dinner. "Why don't you let me hold Bartholomew while you eat?"

Amanda tensed. "I couldn't impose on you like that. I can just put him in his seat."

"Where he may or may not want to stay. Let me take him. If you knew me better, you'd realize that I don't offer to do things I don't want to do."

Amanda gazed at her steaming plate of barbecued ribs and realized she'd need both hands if she intended to do the meal justice. And she was starving. "Okay. Bring him back if he's any trouble." She placed Bartholomew in Leigh's outstretched arms.

"Oh, we won't have any trouble, will we, Bartholomew?" Leigh smiled down at the baby. "Come and tell Auntie Leigh all your secrets."

Amanda watched in wonder, and more than a little jealousy, as Bartholomew smiled back at Leigh. So far, he'd reserved that expression for Dexter and Leigh. Amanda might not fit in at the True Love, but her son seemed to be a natural.

"Now, dive into those ribs," Leigh said and carried Bartholomew away.

Amanda fought a moment of panic. No one had ever taken her baby away from her before. Her mother wasn't the type to take charge of a squalling infant, and her friends had apparently sensed Amanda's proprietary attitude toward her baby and hadn't reached for him, either. Amanda had been just as glad. Deep down, she believed that if she allowed Bartholomew out of her sight, something terrible would happen to him. It wasn't a rational belief, and she'd have to conquer it if she expected to continue her career, but she wasn't always rational when it came to her son.

Leaving her plate untouched, she craned her neck to see what Leigh was doing with the baby. Showing him off, apparently. Leigh circled the large table of wedding guests, presenting Bartholomew to them all as if he were an heir to the throne. Bartholomew seemed to love it.

"I take it he doesn't get out much."

Startled, she looked up into Chase's green eyes, and her heart began to race. "He's only two months old, after all," she said. "Time enough for him to become a party animal."

"He already has it down. Look at him waving his arms around."

Amanda glanced in Leigh's direction and laughed. "You're right. He seems to love the attention. See how he tried to grab that napkin?"

"He almost got it, too. The kid's got fast hands."

"Maybe he'll grow up to be a magician." Amanda realized they sounded like fond parents at a family gathering. It gave her a disturbingly nice feeling.

Chase turned his back on the scene. "Your dinner's getting cold. And Belinda makes a mighty fine barbecue sauce. Some say Eb Whitlock's is better, but I vote for Belinda's."

"How about you?" She looked up at him. "Have you eaten?"

"Is that an invitation to sit down?"

"Um, sure."

Chase tipped his hat. "Thank you, ma'am." Then he pulled out the chair next to her where Leigh had recently sat and levered his lanky frame into it. "Did you get some rest?"

"Yes, I did." Amanda picked up her knife and fork and began separating the ribs before she attempted to carve off a piece of meat.

"I hope you're going to use your fingers on those. This isn't the Plaza, you know."

Amanda surveyed her plate and regarded her white silk blouse with grave doubt.

"Here's how you handle that problem." Chase took a napkin from the other side of the table, snapped it open and tucked it deftly into the vee of her blouse.

The brush of his fingers against her cleavage lasted a fraction of a second, but it was enough for her to remember that was exactly how he'd begun touching her that fateful night. He'd taken her hand and led her back to the bed built in behind the seats. Then he'd kissed her, taking his time. After all, there was no rush. Almost lazily he'd brushed his knuckles against the vee of her blouse, a blouse like this one, before he'd slipped the first button from its hole...

Shaken, she gazed at him.

His eyes reflected the flame blazing in hers. "God, Amanda," he murmured.

6

HER HEART RACING, Amanda averted her gaze.

Chase's voice was gentle. "You can't wipe out what happened between us, can you?"

She shook her head.

"If it's any comfort to you, neither can I," he said. "Now, eat your dinner before it gets cold."

She did, because it was the only way she could demonstrate that she'd gained a measure of control. And she used her fingers.

Chase's plate arrived, and he tucked his napkin into the neck of his shirt, gave her a wry smile and began his own meal. A couple of times she sneaked a look at him, and he seemed to be enjoying the food. He polished off a rib and licked his fingers. She remembered all too well how that agile tongue had felt when he'd...

She couldn't think about that. "This is very good," she said in an almost-normal tone.

"Told you so."

"Did you have any luck calling today?"

His jaw tightened just a little. "Didn't have time. Leigh needed me to—ah—do some work down at the corrals. By the way, she also said she loaned you some boots. Want to take a ride tomorrow?"

"I could be leaving tomorrow if your phone calls go well tonight."

"Maybe, but if not, you should see some of the country."

The invitation beckoned, and she fought the sinful temptation to spend the day alone with Chase. "I can't go. Don't forget about Bartholomew."

"That's not likely." He pulled his napkin from his shirt and wiped his hands. "But I'll bet we have something around here we could use to carry him in."

"No. It's too dangerous."

"I doubt it." Chase leaned back in his chair. "Besides, don't you need some tourist-type stories to tell your friends back in New York? Otherwise they'll wonder what you spent your time doing out here. You said you wanted to see the saguaros."

"I saw a bunch of them on the way here today."

"Looking out the window of a van is no way to appreciate the desert." He paused. "But then, maybe you don't know how to ride."

"I can ride." She'd once had her own horse, a gorgeous Thoroughbred named Sultan. Her parents still had the ribbons and trophies she and Sultan had won. "I just don't think it's safe to take Bartholomew on a—"

"Let me check into it." He tossed his napkin on the table and pushed his chair back. "I saw Leigh heading into the kitchen. She and Belinda might have an idea how we could transport him. And by the way, when you're ready, I'll walk you back over to the cottage."

"That's not necessary."

He hesitated. "Snakes come out at twilight, Amanda."

She stared at him and shuddered.

"I'm sorry if that scares you. But the more you understand the dangers, the safer you'll be, just like in the city. And personally, I'd rather watch out for these kind of snakes than the two-legged ones that live in New York."

She tossed her head. "I'm not afraid in New York."

"You should be." He stood, a flash of anger in his eyes. "The next guy who hauls you out of a snowbank might not have the good manners to ask before he pulls your clothes off."

CHASE WALKED toward the kitchen where he'd seen Leigh and Bartholomew go through the door a moment ago. He wasn't often so short-tempered, but it had been a long time since he'd felt this level of frustration, this much lack of control over his destiny.

Late in the afternoon, he'd learned from Ry that the horse troughs had been contaminated with crushed blister beetles, a substance that could have killed some of the horses if they'd taken in enough of it. Apparently, none of them had, and Freddy had only dosed a few for stomach upset. Ry believed the poisoning was sabotage, but he didn't want to call in the police and risk adverse publicity for the True Love. Chase felt helpless to combat the sabotage if it existed, helpless to protect his investment.

On top of that, Amanda seemed hell-bent on leaving once he gave her the precious information. He'd suggested the ride as a delaying tactic, and it might buy him another day. After that, he was out of ideas to keep her in Arizona. Life had been a damn sight less complicated when he was on the road. Of course, it had been a little lonely, but at least he'd been in control.

Through the steam and bustle of the kitchen he saw Leigh and Belinda standing in a corner seemingly oblivious to the hubbub around them as they cooed at Bartholomew. Chase dodged a waiter carrying a trayful of dirty dishes and eased around one of the cooks spooning barbecue sauce into a plastic storage container. Finally, he made it over to the two women.

"Anybody would think you'd never seen a baby before," he said, putting an arm around Leigh's shoulders.

"That's almost true," Leigh said as she rocked Bartholomew. "Belinda was just saying we don't allow the guests to bring babies, and my wrangling duties don't attract infants, either. So when would I ever be around them?"

"Well, you'd better not get too attached to this one."

Leigh dropped a kiss on Bartholomew's forehead. "It's too late. He won my heart the moment I laid eyes on that dimpled smile."

"He smiles just like his daddy," Belinda said. "Isn't that right, Bartholomew?"

"Stop it, both of you," Chase said. "He's leaving in a couple of days, so just cool it."

Leigh caught him in the pull of her all-knowing eyes. "I'm surprised at you, Chase Lavette. You never struck me as a quitter."

"What do you mean by that crack?"

"You don't want this baby to leave any more than we do. Are you going to let Amanda run off with him without a fight?"

Chase knew there was no point in pretending to Leigh that he didn't want to keep the baby around. She'd been able to read him from the first day they'd spent together. "If you mean take her to court and demand my rights, no, I'm not going to do that."

Belinda stroked the baby's cheek. "I don't know why not. What makes her think she can keep this little bundle all to herself?"

Chase sighed. "Think it through. Amanda's job is in New York. All my money's tied up in this ranch. Let's say I won visitation rights. I'd have to move back to New York, get some minimum-wage job and just hang around. And, on top of it all, I know absolutely nothing about babies. Put me in charge of this kid for a couple of hours and it's panic city."

"Then it's time you got your feet wet." Leigh plopped Bartholomew in his arms. "I have to get ready for a date soon, anyway. And stop limiting your thinking, Chase. There are usually more than two answers to any question, you know."

Leigh's comments barely registered as Chase struggled to adjust his arms around this tiny, squirming human being that was his son. He tried to get his elbow under the baby's head, but Bartholomew kept flopping around. "He's gonna fall," Chase said, his voice rising as Leigh and Belinda giggled. "You women stop your cackling. Leigh, take him back. I don't know how. He's gonna—"

"Easy." Leigh helped him reposition the baby. "Just get your right arm under him and cup his head in that big hand of yours. Good. Then wrap your left around him on the outside. See?"

"I don't know." But Chase did know. As his arms found the new position and the baby quieted, Chase met Bartholomew's rapt gaze. The shock of recognition zinged down to his toes. His son. His flesh and blood. His grip tightened and a lump lodged in his throat.

"Don't let her rob you of this baby," Leigh murmured.

He couldn't speak for fear his voice would crack and give him away. Bartholomew looked like him, for sure, but there was something about the baby's deep stare that stirred a long-dormant memory. His mother, leaning over him...just before she walked away.

Bartholomew picked that moment to scrunch up his face and let out a long wail.

"Oh, God." Chase swallowed the lump in his throat and thrust the baby back toward Leigh and Belinda. "I hurt him. I squeezed him too tight. Take him, one of you."

"Stuff and nonsense," Belinda said. "He might be hungry, or need a change, but you didn't hurt him. Babies are tougher than you think. Just carry him back to Amanda."

"Like this? Screaming?"

"I'm sure she's heard it before," Leigh said.

"Yeah, but she's never let me hold him. So the first time she sees me with him, he's crying. What's she going to think of that?"

Leigh smiled. "She might think you're man enough to hold a squalling baby without getting flustered."

"Well, I'm not. I'd rather drive a runaway diesel."

Leigh nudged him toward the kitchen door. "Work on it."

Chase was nearly to the door when he remembered his reason for coming into the kitchen in the first place. He swung around. "Do we have anything around the ranch I could use to carry him on my back? In case Amanda and I take a ride tomorrow," he added when both women looked confused.

Leigh's eyebrows arched. "Now you're talking, cowboy. But I don't know what we might—"

"I do," Belinda said. "Back when you and Freddy were babies, your daddy made a cradleboard, just like the ones the Indians used to carry their little ones. I'm sure it's around here somewhere."

"I haven't a clue what a cradleboard is," Chase said. He'd begun jiggling Bartholomew, and the squalls eased up. Maybe he had to find the right touch, like working with a sensitive clutch.

"It'll work fine," Belinda said. "Just set up your ride."

"Take her up to the pond," Leigh suggested.

"Now, don't you two start getting ideas." Chase swayed gently, soothing the baby even more. "I just thought she should see some of the country as long as she's out here."

Leigh's eyes widened innocently. "Why, I certainly agree, Chase. And I promise not to take any of the dudes on trail rides in that direction tomorrow, so you won't be disturbed while you're showing her the country."

Chase shook his head and started out the kitchen door. Then he turned back again. "You said you have a date tonight? Who with?"

"Edgar."

"The barber? That guy has the personality of a socket wrench, Leigh."

"I know, but I haven't seen a movie in months and it's obvious you won't take me any time soon."

"Somebody needs to improve the quality of your social life."

Leigh waved a hand dismissively. "Feel free to take on my problems after you straighten out your own."

Chase rolled his eyes and turned to leave.

"Nice job with the baby," Leigh called. Her throaty chuckle and Belinda's musical laugh followed him as he used his shoulder to edge out the swinging door into the dining room.

The wedding guests had left, along with Ry and

Freddy. Amanda, sitting with her back to the kitchen door, was the only guest still in the room. The clatter of dishes being cleared muffled Chase's approach, allowing him to pause and observe her for a moment. She took a sip of coffee, put the mug down and ran a manicured finger around the edge. He remembered the gesture from the night in the truck.

Despite her jeans and boots, she'd never be mistaken for a cowgirl, he decided. Her hands were the color of milk instead of tanned as a cowgirl's would be, and her jeans were cut too baggy—probably a fashion statement in New York but not in Arizona. He'd become accustomed to the tight jeans Freddy and Leigh wore, which were far more revealing and sexy, yet Amanda's loose-fitting clothing made her all the more mysterious and desirable.

He thought again of how she'd raced from the cottage earlier, barefoot and half-clothed, desperate to save her baby. In that moment, he'd known she would protect Bartholomew with her life. That kind of devotion had a powerful effect on Chase, maybe because he'd never experienced it. But although he admired her protective instincts, they made her vulnerable and in need of protection herself. And that's where, in a perfect world, he would come in. But this wasn't a perfect world.

With a muted sigh, he approached her table.

She turned in her chair, her eyes widening as she noticed he held Bartholomew.

"Leigh...told me to bring him to you."

Her gaze softened and he held his breath, wishing he could find a way to keep that tender expression on her face. When she looked like that, hope replaced confusion in his heart. She stood and held out her arms. He'd give a lot to have her do that when he wasn't holding a baby.

"I'd better take him back to the cottage."

He settled Bartholomew in her arms, which couldn't be accomplished without a lot of touching, because he was petrified that he'd let go before Amanda had a firm grip.

Amanda's warm breath caressed his cheek. "I've got him," she murmured.

"Right." He stepped back reluctantly, already missing the weight of his son cradled against his chest.

"Apparently you've held babies before," she said, adjusting Bartholomew's T-shirt over his round tummy.

Chase was immensely pleased. "Some."

"I thought I heard him crying in the kitchen, but you seem to have calmed him down."

"He's probably hungry or needs a change."

"Probably." Amusement lit her eyes. "You sound like the voice of experience. Did you have little brothers and sisters?"

"Uh, no." He glanced away as sudden anger at his mother overtook him. He thought he'd forgiven her for dumping him into the world with no safety net, but apparently he hadn't. "Ready to go?"

"In a minute. Let me put him in his seat."

"Oh, yeah." He watched her position Bartholomew in the plastic carrier. "Belinda says she has something called a cradleboard that I could strap on my back if we want to take that ride tomorrow."

"Is it safe?"

"Freddy and Leigh's father made it for them when they were kids, so I guess it is. The Indians used to carry babies that way."

Amanda lifted the carrier in her arms. "Bartholomew's no papoose."

"He'll be okay. Babies are tougher than you think."

She narrowed her eyes. "If you've never had little brothers or sisters, how come you know so much about babies?"

"I pay attention. Here, let me take him." He relieved her of the infant seat before she had a chance to protest, and felt a rush of pleasure that he had his son back in his grasp. This father business was dangerously habit-forming.

On the way back through the patio he spotted Dexter sitting in his usual corner with Chloe at his feet. "Let's go pick up your bodyguard," he suggested as he walked toward Dexter.

Chloe lifted her head and thumped her tail against the concrete.

"Baby," announced Dexter with a grin.

"Yeah, and its time for him to turn in," Chase said, crouching next to Dexter's chair so the old man could get another look at Bartholomew. "Is it still okay if Chloe stays at the cottage tonight?"

"It's okay." Dexter tucked a bony knuckle under Bartholomew's chin. "Smile, some?"

Bartholomew responded with a gummy grin.

Chase's heart swelled. He could see what Leigh meant about losing her heart to that smile. "He's sure taken a shine to you, Dex."

"Yep."

"Guess we'd better get him tucked in, though."

"Yep." Dexter gave Bartholomew another chuck under the chin before Chase stood, lifting the infant seat.

He grunted as pain squeezed his lower back.

"Chase?" Amanda's forehead puckered with worry.

Great, just what he needed, to wimp out now and show he couldn't even carry his own kid around. "I'm fine," he said.

"It's your back, isn't it? Let me—"

"No, I'm really fine. See you later, Dex."

"Yep."

"And thanks for the loan of Chloe." Chase whistled and the dog came instantly to his side.

"Are you sure you're okay?" Amanda asked as they crossed the patio in the pink light of sunset.

"Yes." The spasm was easing a little, but he desperately needed to get into the pool and swim the laps he'd missed today. Leigh had said stress would make things worse, and as always, she was right.

"Why didn't Dexter eat in the dining room tonight?" Amanda asked.

"He can't take too much confusion. The stroke messed up the circuits in his brain, and he has to concentrate really hard to find the words he wants. He has something called aphasia. When a lot of people are talking, it's an overload situation. Quiet routine is the best thing for him."

Amanda nodded. "And so you just let him stay on, even though he doesn't have a specific function at the ranch. I think that's wonderful. Some efficiency expert would have Dexter out of here in no time."

"But then we'd lose Belinda, and I don't know if the ranch could function without her."

"You mean if something happened to Belinda, Dexter would be out on his ear?"

The idea took Chase by surprise. "No, I guess not. Dexter's as much a part of this ranch as anyone."

"Exactly as I thought. It's nice to see business partners with heart."

Chase fell silent. Affection for the ranch and the people who lived here was sneaking up on him, muddying his thinking. He needed to remember that he still wanted to sell the place one day soon, even if Ry seemed to be waffling on that point these days. Chase had figured out that if he made enough profit on the ranch sale, he might be able to return to New York in style and claim his place as Bartholomew's father. But selling the ranch meant ripping people like Belinda and Dexter out of the only home they'd ever known, as Leigh had so cleverly pointed out today. She knew good and well that would bother his conscience.

They walked along the path, lit by ankle-high landscape lights, the silence punctuated only by the chirp of crickets in the creosote bushes.

"It's beautiful out here this time of day," Amanda said after a while. "I've never seen sunset colors like that, so fiery."

Chase remembered he'd intended to tell her that her hair reminded him of the colors in the evening sky. But that was when he thought they'd be strolling back to the cottage for a night of lovemaking. "It's nice."

"Are you watching for snakes?"

"Sure am. So is Chloe. Guess I could have sent you back with her." He should have thought of that, but of course he'd been determined to protect her himself, while he still had the chance. And he might be about to pay the price. The weight of Bartholomew in the infant seat began to pull at his back muscles. He shifted the burden cautiously.

For the first time in weeks, his back seized up on him. "Damn!"

"What?" She clutched his arm. "A snake?"

"No." He spoke through clenched teeth. "My...back.

Take the infant seat." When she'd relieved him of it, he doubled over.

"I'll get help."

"No. Just...give me a minute." He hoped to hell a minute would do it. Chloe nuzzled his hand.

"Can you walk?"

He groaned. "Maybe."

"Then come this way. We're closer to the cottage than we are to the house."

The pain made him too weak to resist as she guided him, hobbling like somebody Dexter's age, up the path. Commanding Chloe to stay with him, she hurried inside the cottage and returned a short time later to help him up the steps and through the door. She closed it behind him.

If he didn't hurt so damned much, he would have laughed. He was inside her cottage at night with the door closed, and he was barely capable of moving, let alone making love. He sank to his hands and knees on the Indian rug, and his hat toppled to the floor in front of him.

Chloe circled him once, obviously unsure whether to help him or guard the baby.

"Go lie down," he rasped. She trotted to one corner and plopped to the floor.

"Tell me what I can do to help," Amanda said just as Bartholomew started to cry.

Chase forced the words out past his pain. "Take care of the baby. And don't step on my hat."

"But you—oh, damn. Okay. I'll change him." She whisked Chase's hat off the floor and out of his sight.

He tried the imaging techniques Leigh had taught him and pictured himself cradled in warmth while gentle fingers worked lovingly at his tortured muscles. The picture wouldn't hold through the steady wailing of his son.

"I guess he's still hungry." Amanda sounded upset. "Let me call someone. Maybe Leigh could—"

"Feed him," Chase muttered. "Leigh's gone for the night."

"All right. I'll feed him."

Chase closed his eyes and imagined himself sliding into hot mineral springs. Hell, he might as well imagine someone handing him a cold beer. Might as well picture Amanda, wearing a string bikini, sliding into the mineral springs with him.

"I have one hand free."

He glanced sideways to see her kneeling on the rug, the nursing baby balanced in the crook of her left arm.

"I can massage with one hand," she said almost impatiently, as if talking to someone who wasn't very bright. "Just tell me how Leigh does it."

Not with her blouse open and a baby at her breast, he thought. But her concern for him had apparently overridden her modesty. And maybe she could ease the bunching of his muscles. "Okay." He took a shallow breath. "The heel of your hand, circular motion, above my belt."

He hadn't expected her to pull his shirttail out to do it, but that was her first move. He found himself dealing with the sweet pressure of her soft hand on his bare skin, and he wanted to weep with frustration. He'd spent hours recalling the intimate nature of her caresses. He'd loved imagining those caresses being repeated, expanded....

"Here?"

"Yes. Harder."

She bore down, and he gasped.

"Too much?"

"No. Keep going." He lowered his head and tried to help with deepening breaths and a conscious loosening of his muscles. Close to his ear the sound of soft sucking reminded him of the nursing baby and unfastened buttons, velvet breasts and firm nipples. As Amanda rose higher on her knees to reach across to his right side, the silk of her blouse brushed against his bare back. Despite his pain, his mouth moistened with need. Then there was the scent of her—that expensive cologne mixed with baby powder and the tantalizing fragrance of mother's milk. He wondered if he'd go insane right here in this little cottage.

"Is it getting any better?"

"Some." Or maybe the intensity of his desire was making him forget the spasm in his back.

"Good. Let me switch Bartholomew."

His peripheral vision had always been excellent, which had been a plus when he'd driven trucks. Now that talent taunted him with a pretty good view of Amanda sitting back on her heels, undoing the other cup of her nursing bra, and giving her right breast to Bartholomew. She didn't bother to fasten the left side.

Maybe she thought he was blind with pain, but if so, she was very mistaken. He took in every detail of each creamy mound, traced with delicate blue veins and crowned with moist tips darkened to burgundy. He'd never realized that a mother nursing her child could be such a turn-on. Sore back or not, he had to get out of here before he humiliated himself by begging.

Clenching his jaw, he brought one booted foot under him.

"What are you doing?"

"Leaving." Sweat stood out on his forehead as he got

to his feet. He couldn't stand straight, but he could stand.

"You're in no condition to walk. Let me—"

"You've been a big help," he said, staggering toward the door. "I'll be fine."

"You won't! Let me work on those muscles some more."

He paused, his back to her. "And then what?"

There was a significant silence. "What do you mean?"

"After you've finished the massage, will you refasten your blouse and send me on my way?"

Another silence lengthened between them. "Chase, I was only trying to take care of you. I wasn't trying to seduce you."

"Then I guess the seduction was a bonus. Congratulations." Standing as tall as possible, he hobbled out the door.

7

IT WAS THE WORST NIGHT of Chase's adult life. The only good news was that Ry and Freddy had organized the wedding guests for a boisterous game of Trivial Pursuit and he had the patio to himself. He soaked in the Jacuzzi until his toes wrinkled and then forced himself to swim ten laps. He repeated that routine until he was loose enough to sit through a few telephone calls, but the hour he spent on the phone in his room yielded no answers to Amanda's questions. Finally, he went into the kitchen, pulled a six-pack of beer from the walk-in refrigerator and headed back for some more soaking and laps. Ry came out once to ask if he wanted to join the group and he begged off in the name of pursuing his therapy.

Eventually, the game broke up and everyone trailed off to bed. Chase was sitting in the Jacuzzi, working on his fourth beer and feeling extremely sorry for himself when Leigh arrived home and strolled out to the patio.

She glanced at the beer.

"Help yourself," he said.

"Sure you can spare it? Looks like you need all six."

"Be nice to me, Leigh."

She unhooked a can of beer from a plastic ring and popped the top. "Your back went out tonight, didn't it?"

"Among other things. How was your date?"

"Boring." She pulled up a chaise longue and sat on the edge of it. "We didn't laugh at the same jokes in the movie."

"Bad sign."

"Yeah." She stood up and patted the chaise. "Come on up here and let me work the kinks out for you."

"You don't have to."

"Don't be an idiot, Lavette. That macho pride doesn't cut any ice with me."

"Okay, okay." He climbed out gingerly, using the steps and the rail. Yesterday he would have been able to hoist himself out using his arms. "I hate this."

"I suspect you were a little too proud of your male physique, my friend. The universe has a way of evening things out."

"The universe has been chopping away at me ever since the day I was born." Chase eased himself face-down on the chaise. "I'm so far from even, it's pathetic."

"My, we are into self-pity tonight."

Chase muttered an oath.

"Well, pain does put people in a foul mood," Leigh said, sounding more sympathetic. She dropped to her knees and began an expert massage of his back.

At her touch, Chase could feel the healing begin. "You have a real gift for this, Leigh. You could set up a clinic and charge people." He congratulated himself on coming up with the perfect solution to what Leigh would do once the ranch sold. He'd been thinking about that tonight, as if he didn't have enough to worry about.

"Nope." Leigh leaned into the massage. "I have a theory that once I started charging, I'd lose my abilities. Did you know I'm also a water witch?"

"A what?"

"I can find water with a forked stick. I've been able to do it ever since I was a little girl. But my dad warned me never to charge for the service, or I'd lose the gift. I think it's the same with massage."

Chase sighed. Another of his great plans down the drain. But his back was improving radically. He considered it one of the great mysteries of nature that Leigh could give him a rubdown and he felt no sexual arousal at all. One soft caress from Amanda, however, and he was a basket case.

Leigh paused to sip her beer. "Did Belinda find that cradleboard?"

"I don't know, but it doesn't matter. I wouldn't dare take Amanda and the baby out."

"Why not?"

"Look at me! What if my back seized up out on the trail?"

"I guess you could ride home facedown over the saddle."

"Not funny, Leigh." *Ride home.* How easily she'd said that. Home wasn't a foreign concept to Leigh, but it was to Chase, who'd never allowed himself to call anyplace home. When an apartment got too cozy, he moved, just to keep in practice. He'd become very good at leaving.

"I'd give it a try," she said.

He had to think for a moment to remember what she was talking about. Oh, yeah. The horseback ride with Amanda.

"I gather you don't have much time to settle things between you two," Leigh added.

"That's right."

Leigh resumed the massage. "The way I see it, your best hope is to get her to bring Bartholomew back to the ranch every few months. If she has a good time here, she might be more willing to do that."

"Define a good time."

Leigh chuckled. "Oh, no. I'll leave that up to you. But it's evident your charms worked on her once before."

"Are you telling me to seduce her?"

"I'm telling you to make use of your strong points, cowboy." She gave him a sharp whack on the butt. "Now get back in the pool and do ten more laps. I'm going to bed."

WHEN AMANDA AWOKE the next morning, the first thing she saw was Chase's black Stetson dangling from the bedpost where she'd tossed it the evening before. Bartholomew had gotten her up once during the night to nurse, and now he and Chloe were sound asleep. As the room filled with pink light, Amanda snuggled under the covers and contemplated Chase's hat. The black felt bore scuff marks on the crown, as if it had landed in the dirt a few times, and the brim dipped down in front, as if molded that way when Chase had repeatedly tugged it low over his eyes.

She remembered her first glimpse of him in the hat when she'd stepped from the jetway. On a virile man like Chase, a black Stetson was almost overkill. Now that she thought about it, she could trace her loss of detachment from her first encounter with his hat.

Then he'd compounded the hero effect by charging in after the snake, and after that, by holding her while she'd cried. But maybe she could have dismissed those incidents, even turned her back on the desires he'd stirred in her, if only he hadn't walked toward her, still wearing that darned hat, and carrying Bartholomew.

She hadn't anticipated how she'd feel seeing their son in his arms.

Had Chase and Bartholomew been strangers, it still would have been a compelling picture—a rugged cowboy whose big, work-roughened hands cradled a tender little baby. But they were not strangers. Chase was the man who had made such beautiful love to her months ago, and Bartholomew was the stunning result. The image of Chase holding their child would haunt her for the rest of her life.

On the bedside table the telephone buzzed. She reached for it quickly.

"Good morning, Amanda."

She closed her eyes at the sound of his voice and curled the cloth-covered telephone cord around her finger. "Good morning, Chase."

"I know it's early, but we ought to beat the heat if we're going up into Rogue Canyon today."

"Are we? What about your back?"

"My back's fine. Belinda found the cradleboard and she's packing us a lunch. I'll have Duane bring the horses up to the house so we don't have to fool with driving down to the corrals. How soon can you be ready?"

"I, ah, imagine because of your back you didn't have a chance to make any calls last night."

"Actually, I did. I thought we could talk about it up in the canyon. It's a beautiful spot, Amanda."

She hesitated, then succumbed. "Give me twenty minutes."

"Great."

"Unless Bartholomew's poky about eating. Then I might need longer."

"I'll be waiting in the dining room with a cup of coffee for you."

"That would be nice." She played with the telephone cord, pretending she was in an old black-and-white movie. "I take sugar."

"I know." He sounded as if he might be smiling. "Tons of sugar."

Then she remembered the cups of coffee they'd shared in the cab of his truck and how he'd teased her about the amount of sugar she put in hers. And later, when he'd sampled nearly every inch of her body, he'd said, "I know why you taste so sweet. It's all that sugar you put in your coffee."

"Amanda? Are you still there?"

She took a shaky breath. "Yes, I'm still here." She glanced up at the bedpost. "I have your hat."

"Wear it. I have another one. See you soon." Then he was gone.

Amanda held the phone to her ear a moment longer as she gazed at the hat. He loved that hat. Even in the midst of his agony the night before, he'd warned her not to step on it. Her heart beat faster. Perhaps she was being wooed.

Probably because she was impatient to get out the door, Bartholomew seemed to nurse more slowly and wouldn't burp for her. Accustomed to meeting deadlines and arriving on time for appointments, she was irritated at being five minutes than she'd estimated when she dashed out the door with Chloe trotting by her side. She'd thrown a clean diaper over her shoulder to protect her blouse in case Bartholomew decided to burp or worse on the way to the main house.

Instead of braiding her hair as she'd intended, she'd settled for the quicker solution of tying it back with a silk scarf. Chase's hat was slightly big, but she loved the way it looked when she pulled it down in front, the way Chase wore it. And the brim offered wonderful protection from the sun, which already felt warm on her shoulders.

When she opened the patio gate and stepped inside, she was greeted with bedlam as Belinda supervised the stringing of thousands of tiny white lights, the placement of tables and chairs and the arrangement of baskets of huge paper flowers from Mexico. Some of the guests were attempting to help, while others had abandoned the idea in favor of a swim, which caused more commotion as they were warned not to splash and damage any of the decorations.

Dexter sat in a shady alcove watching the proceedings. Chloe's breakfast was in a dish beside him.

"Go on, girl," Amanda said, stroking the dog's head. "And thanks." As Chloe navigated the crowded patio toward her owner, Amanda waved at Dexter. "Thank you," she called. "She made me feel much safer."

Dexter waved back. "Yep!"

Belinda turned, a string of lights in her hand, and smiled at Amanda. "The cradleboard's all ready."

"Are you sure it'll work okay?"

"Absolutely. Freddy and Leigh spent hours in it when they were babies. Now go have fun."

Amanda had noticed how Belinda doted on Bartholomew, and took heart from the woman's confidence in the cradleboard. "I'll do that," she said, returning Belinda's smile.

She skirted a man carrying a ladder and nearly bumped into Leigh and Freddy, who were walking across the patio deep in discussion.

Leigh surveyed Amanda's outfit and nodded in satisfaction. "You're looking more and more like a cow-girl. I guess you're going on that ride."

"I guess I am. And I'm late."

"Don't sweat it," Freddy said. "With Chase still around, Ry had an excuse to hide out in the dining room and drink coffee instead of coming out here to help decorate."

Amanda adjusted Bartholomew against her other shoulder. "Did Chase mention he had a problem with his back last night?"

"Yes," Leigh said. "And as his unofficial nurse, I urged him to go. He's borrowing Ry's cellular telephone, so if you have any trouble you can call the ranch for help."

"Oh!" Amanda hadn't expected such amenities as cellular phones at a place like the True Love. Her anxiety level dipped considerably. "That's a terrific idea."

"The phone works even up in Rogue Canyon," Freddy said. "I didn't want to get one, but Ry insisted and now I love it."

"It makes me feel a lot better about going up there with Bartholomew," Amanda said, "although I hate to leave you with all this work and take Chase away, on top of it."

Freddy waved a hand dismissively. "The work will get done, and you shouldn't go back to New York without a ride up to Rogue Canyon. Besides, it's cooler up there."

"If you're sure..."

"We're sure," Freddy said. "Go find Chase. And tell Ry he's needed out here."

"Cancel that last part," Leigh said. "Freddy and I have to get something straight before her beloved groom shows up. Just go, Amanda, and have a great time."

"Thanks." As Amanda started toward the French doors leading into the house, she overheard a few words as Leigh turned to Freddy.

"Before he comes out, promise me you'll tell him you're allergic to roses."

"But then I'll never get roses my whole married life!"

"Maybe he'll go for diamonds, instead."

Amanda decided against trying to puzzle out the meaning of the exchange as she headed for the dining room.

Sure enough, Ry and Chase were in a far corner hunched over coffee mugs, a third one steaming by Chase's elbow right next to the cellular phone. A disreputable-looking brown hat pulled down over Chase's forehead made him look more like a rogue than a gentleman, but his idea of using the cellular phone showed that he was obviously taking his responsibility for her and Bartholomew seriously. A rogue who took his responsibilities seriously. It was a tantalizing combination.

Both Chase and Ry glanced up and started to rise as she approached.

"Please don't get up," she said, touched by the courtly gesture.

Ry sank back to his seat but Chase moved toward her.

"Let me hold him so you can drink your coffee." He'd extricated Bartholomew from her arms before she could protest.

"You'd better take this diaper to protect your shirt." She tried to hand it to him but he shook his head. "Chase, you—"

"I'll be fine." His eyes had a stubborn gleam.

"If you say so." She sat down in the chair he'd just vacated. "Good luck."

"I don't need special equipment just to hold you, do I, son?" Chase hoisted Bartholomew to his shoulder with a manly heave.

Bartholomew responded by upchucking down the back of Chase's shirt.

Chase's eyes widened but he kept his grip on the baby. "Damn. I think his radiator just overflowed."

Amanda tried not to laugh, but Ry was chuckling gleefully, and finally she couldn't help herself. "I warned you. You'd better put that shirt in to soak and get a clean one." She held out her arms. "I'll take him so you can go do that."

"No, *I'll* take the little buckaroo," Ry said. "But I'm not too manly to wear a diaper over my shoulder while I do it. Give him to me, Chase. I might as well get in shape. I have a feeling Freddy's going to be in the market for a couple of these pretty soon."

"Hold him real careful," Chase said, relinquishing control of the baby with obvious reluctance. "Get both hands under him. Support his head. Not like that, like this." He adjusted the baby in Ry's arms.

Amanda brought her coffee mug to her lips to hide her smile.

Ry frowned as Chase kept repositioning his grip. "Hell, Chase, I think I can hold a baby without you giving me lessons."

"Don't cuss in front of him, either."

"Why not? You did when he barfed on you."

"He caught me by surprise. No, move your arm a little the other way. He likes it better if you—"

"Will you *leave*?" Ry glared at Chase. "I never knew you were such a fussbudget, Lavette."

"I'm leaving." Chase backed away and adjusted his hat. "Don't drop him."

"Oh, for crying out loud."

After Chase left, Ry shook his head. "The boy's gone haywire. By the way, do you want anything to eat? The kitchen's a disaster, but I'm sure we can round up a cinnamon roll or something."

"Coffee's fine." She took another drink of the warm liquid, which was the perfect temperature and sweetened exactly as she liked it.

"I envy you two riding out of here today," Ry said. "If I didn't think Freddy would have my head on a pole, I'd go with you."

"She did mention something about your hiding out in here so you wouldn't have to help," Amanda said.

Ry grinned, and Amanda glimpsed the good humor that Freddy must have fallen in love with. "I don't stand a chance," Ry said. "That woman's had my number since day one."

"It looks like an pretty even contest to me."

Ry gazed at her, his smile softening. "All I know is, she's the one. I'm a lucky man to be marrying Freddy Singleton tomorrow."

An unexpected lump formed in Amanda's throat at the tender admission. "I wish you both the best."

"Just keep your fingers crossed that the horses don't buck. I should have my head examined for agreeing to this wedding on horseback. At least you'll have something unique to tell your friends in New York."

"I...may not be here for the wedding."

"Oh? I thought your reservation here ran through the week."

She glanced away from him. "It does, but I think it would be best for all concerned if I left sooner. Chase said he had some information for me on his family's medical history. He thought I should see the canyon before I go, and he'll give me the information while we ride, I guess. I'll probably catch a night flight out."

"Have you made plane reservations?"

"No." She looked at him and her chest tightened. "Perhaps I should do that now."

His gaze was speculative. "No rush. Flights usually aren't crowded this time of year."

The tightness in her chest eased. "I suppose not. And I don't know exactly when we'll be back from the ride."

"Or how it'll go."

She swallowed. "That's not really—"

"For the record, I think Chase deserves a chance to be a father to this baby."

She gasped at his directness. The charming good humor was gone from his expression and she remembered he was also a high-powered commodities broker. In retaliation, she adopted her big-city, don't-mess-with-me attitude. "I don't believe that it's any of your business."

"He's my partner." Ry's blue eyes narrowed. "That makes it my business. I've advised him to take you to court if necessary, and I'm in contact with lawyers who could win the case, hands down, but he won't discuss that option, so I'm appealing to you. Do the right thing, Amanda."

"I believe I am doing the right thing!"

"Then I guess we have a difference of opinion on the matter." Ry stood and walked around the table. "If you'll excuse me, I think I'll go out and help Freddy with the decorations." He handed Bartholomew to her with care, but there was no smile on his face. "Chase would have wanted a connection with his son even if he'd never seen him, but now that you've brought the baby out here, you can't just snatch him away. If Chase is the man I think he is, he won't allow it. Have a nice ride." Then he tipped his hat and left the room.

Bartholomew began to fuss and Amanda rocked him against her as she tried to regain her composure. It was difficult. Everything Ry had said had struck a nerve and challenged her sense of fair play. And he was right that she'd have the same moral dilemma whether she'd come to Arizona or not. The trip had simply brought it to a head sooner.

"Where's Ry?" Chase asked, striding into the room.

"He, um, decided to go out and help with the decorations."

"You're kidding." Chase glanced in the direction of the patio. "He told me he'd rather shovel a corral of manure than arrange paper flowers in a basket." He shrugged. "Oh, well. Ready to go?"

She could tell him she'd changed her mind and insist that they talk about the medical history now. Then she could book a flight out this morning and leave the True Love and all the conflict it caused within her. Except she knew her problems couldn't be solved that simply anymore.

8

A HALF HOUR LATER, Amanda had plenty of time to contemplate the wonders of a cradleboard as she rode on a gray mare named Pussywillow. Ahead of her, Chase, mounted on a bay gelding named Mikey, carried Bartholomew on his back. Chase had assured her that Mikey was the steadiest horse the True Love owned.

Amanda had been introduced to Rosa, the head housekeeper, who'd shown them how to wrap Bartholomew securely in a blanket and lace him inside the cradleboard, which was made of leather, not wood as she'd imagined. He looked like a little mummy with only his face peeping out. Even that was protected from the sun with a leather hood projecting from the top of the board. Apparently, the arrangement suited Bartholomew. After a huge yawn, he fell asleep.

A western saddle felt cumbersome to Amanda after riding English all her life, but she loved having a horse under her again. Pussywillow had a soft mouth and responded to Amanda's slightest pressure on the bit. Amanda knew instinctively the little mare would be terrific at a fast lope, and she battled her impatience at the slow pace of the ride.

But slow was the only way to take Bartholomew along, so she settled back and savored the rolling gait of her horse and a luxurious sense of freedom. It had been months, ten to be exact, since she'd been on an outing with an attractive man. Raising her son alone had seemed like a liberating thing to do until she'd actually had the baby and realized how drastically her life had become circumscribed by her new role. She had no idea how she'd successfully resume a career that required the same single-minded dedication her son demanded.

This morning, however, with Chase carrying Bartholomew, she felt unencumbered, a little less like an overburdened mother and a lot more like a woman—a desirable woman. The pleasant friction of the saddle against her thighs and the constant view of Chase's broad shoulders and narrow hips drew her thoughts once again to that night in the truck cab.

She and Chase seemed destined to meet during temperature extremes. That night she'd been in danger of freezing to death. Today perspiration trickled between her breasts. She unfastened her canteen, unscrewed the lid and took a drink. Then she dabbed some water on her neck and between her breasts. A swim in the pond would be nice, but of course she'd brought no bathing suit....

Wanting to hear the sound of Chase's voice, she cast around for a neutral topic of conversation. "Does it ever rain here?" she finally asked.

"They tell me it does," he replied over his shoulder. "But I've never seen it. Sometime after the Fourth of July it's supposed to rain nearly every afternoon, and that goes on until September, but here we are in the middle of July and not a drop. The desert's dry as a tinderbox. Leigh keeps threatening to stage a rain dance."

"After the wedding."

Chase laughed. "Yeah. After the wedding."

She liked his laugh. She hadn't heard it all that much since she'd arrived.

He guided his horse into a clearing dominated by a pile of clay-colored rubble. "And speaking of the wedding, this is where it will take place at nine in the morning. Almost twenty-four hours from now, as a matter of fact."

"Here?" It seemed a most unremarkable spot to her.

"It's the original homestead of Thaddeus and Clara Singleton. Leigh told me it was built in 1882 and the walls were still standing until a couple of months ago. A stampede flattened the house the day I got here."

"Belinda told me about the stampede. And the smashed lintel with the True Love brand on it. Aren't they mounting it on an easel or something for the ceremony?"

"Yeah." Chase adjusted the cradleboard straps over his shoulders.

"Is your back okay?"

"So far, so good." He surveyed the clearing. "You know, it doesn't seem like much of a place for a wedding. When I was living on the road, I saw the perfect wedding church in Upstate New York, sitting smack-dab in the middle of a green meadow. White clapboard siding, stained-glass windows, a steeple and a bell. I thought about stopping, but I was late for a delivery. Didn't matter, anyway. I never planned on getting married."

Some of her sensual fog slipped away. "I know. You told me that."

He glanced over at her. "I did? When?"

"After we...while we were driving home, when we discussed whether we should see each other again. I didn't think it was a good idea, and you said I was probably right, because I looked like the type who might get serious, and you had no intention of letting that happen with any woman."

He studied her for several moments. "Is that one of the reasons you didn't tell me about the baby?"

"Yes."

He dropped his gaze and swore softly.

Hope ignited by Ry's statements earlier burst into flame within her. "Did I misunderstand you?"

He raised his head and gave her a long, level look. "No, you didn't," he said at last. He reined his horse around. "We'd better go on. It's getting hot."

Amanda rode along the path lined with bleached-out bushes and bristling cacti and wondered what she was doing on this stupid outing. She usually liked being right, but in this case it hurt like hell. Chase was exactly what he'd proclaimed himself to be in the first place, a drifter who wanted no entanglements. He might expect some contact with his son, on his terms, but he wasn't about to beg her to marry him and establish a traditional home together. And she also had to face an unsettling truth about herself. Increasingly, she wanted him to do exactly that.

Not that she'd come to Arizona with that in mind, at least not consciously, but every moment with Chase had made the idea seem less crazy, especially when she saw him with Bartholomew. Then he'd practically insisted on this ride so they could be alone, and he'd offered her his hat to wear. Silly her, she'd thought he might be moving in the same direction she was. Obviously not.

The trail wound upward as they worked their way into the canyon along a dry creek bed. Granite cliffs rose ever higher on either side of them. There was no sound save the crunching of the horses' hooves in the sand, the creak of leather and the muted drone of insects. Amanda realized she'd never been out of reach of traffic noise. Lured by the absence of civilization's clamor, Amanda began to fantasize what it might have been like for a frontierswoman and her man carving out a life in the desert.

It would have been physically very difficult, but that might have forged a stronger bond. Men and women seemed to depend on each other more back then. Except for the drifters, she thought with a grimace. The frontier had fostered its share of those, too, and Chase Lavette was a throwback if ever she'd seen one. He needed the equivalent of a string of dance-hall girls and no children whatsoever. Ry McGuinnes could think what he wanted, but Chase wasn't the type to be tied down by a wife or a baby.

"The pond's just over there, up where those cottonwoods are," Chase said, pointing.

She sighed in audible relief at the sight of a swath of emerald green tucked into the canyon ahead of them.

He turned slightly in his saddle. "Are you going to make it?"

She straightened, not wanting his concern. "Of course. I rode Thoroughbreds in competition when I was a teenager. It's not the riding. It's the heat. I can't believe Bartholomew's still asleep. I bet he'll be soaked with sweat."

Chase faced forward again. "I guess it wasn't such a good idea, coming up here."

"Then why did you suggest it?"

"God knows, Amanda. But we're almost there, so we might as well spend some time near the pond and cool off a little."

The horses apparently smelled the water and quickened their pace. Within minutes, they'd climbed past the rock-and-earth dam barricading the creek, and Amanda caught her first glimpse of the pond. Huge cottonwoods, their trunks dappled gray and white, grew beside the sandy bank, shading the oasis created by the pond. Amanda had already learned the dramatic difference between sun and shade. Shade next to water looked like heaven.

They dismounted and tethered the horses to a low-hanging branch.

"Let me help you get that cradleboard off," Amanda said as she crossed to Chase.

"Thanks." He lifted the straps away from his shoulders and Amanda took the weight of baby and carrier. She noticed the dark stain of sweat covering Chase's back before she returned her attention to her baby. Bartholomew opened his eyes and blinked.

"Hello. Trip's over, sweetheart." Amanda settled the board on the sand and unlaced the fastenings.

"Is he okay?"

"Just a little sweaty and hungry," Amanda said without glancing up. The cool shade had improved her mood a bit. "He'll be fine after I change and feed him."

"Then I think I'll take a swim if you don't need anything right now."

"Oh." She glanced up and saw him already stripping away his shirt. The pewter medallion winked in the sun. "That sounds wonderful. Do you swim here often?"

"Whenever the pool in the patio is too crowded to do my laps."

Sweat trickled down her back and she cast a look of longing at the pond.

"You can go in after you've fed Bartholomew. I'll watch him."

"I...didn't bring a suit." She pulled Bartholomew out of the wrapped blanket and stood, holding his damp little body against her shoulder.

"Neither did I." He sat on a rock and pulled off his boots. "Didn't think I'd go swimming, but I should have figured I'd need it after carrying the baby."

"Well, I have no suit and no excuse of a bad back."

He stood and unbuckled his belt. "So what? Swim in your underwear and sit in the sun until it dries." He unbuttoned his jeans and shoved them over his hips. Then he glanced at her. "You're staring, Amanda."

Her face grew hot and she turned toward her horse, where she'd packed extra diapers in the saddlebag. "I'm just not as casual about these things as you are, I guess."

"The hell you're not. At least not around me, for some reason."

She jerked her head up to meet his challenging gaze. "If you're referring to last night—"

"Yes, I'm referring to last night. I've been thinking about that, and I've decided you knew, on some level, how you were affecting me, breastfeeding while you gave me a back massage. You were flirting with me, Amanda."

"I was not! It was an emergency and I couldn't come up with any other solution." But a guilty conscience pricked her. Perhaps she had enjoyed teasing him, just a bit, under the guise of ministering to him. Maybe she'd enjoyed it a lot. And she was furious with him for figuring it out.

"Well, this is an emergency and I can't come up with any other solution." Chase kicked away his jeans and walked toward the pond. She drew in a quick breath. The last time she'd seen him, his body had been white as sculpted marble, but weeks of swimming and sunning at this pool had transformed him into a bronzed god. He strode into the water, flexed his back muscles and executed a shallow dive. He was, she concluded, definitely flirting with her. And the effect was exactly what he would have wished.

While Chase swam, Amanda changed Bartholomew and found a large cottonwood tree to sit against. From her position slightly above the pond, she watched Chase's steady, clean strokes through the water while she nursed the baby. The pond was bigger than she'd expected, at least fifty or sixty yards at its longest point. Chase swam to within a few feet of the shore, where he turned and started back across. Patches of sunlight gilded his shoulders, and the reeds bordering the far edge of the pond swayed in the current he created.

His graceful movement seduced her with memories of the fluid surge of his hips as he'd loved her. That night in the truck nothing had seemed important but the melding of two bodies. Now that she had time to reflect, what amazed her was the effortless way they'd come together, how synchronized their rhythm had been from the start.

That rhythm seemed to have followed them to this glade. It echoed in his purposeful stroke through the water, the pulsing buzz of insects, the suckling of their child at her breast. The air smelled warm and ripe, and she vibrated to the subliminal beat, unable to stop herself from slipping into the sensuous cadence.

When he left the water, she wasn't surprised when he walked toward her with deliberate strides, as if in time to the unheard rhythm. He dropped to one knee beside her, his gaze on the nursing baby. He reached out to stroke the downy head, and she sighed.

"Amanda. I don't want to fight with you."

She lifted her head slowly. "Then let's not fight."

His hand still cupping the baby's head, he looked at her, his eyes as green as the sunlit canopy of trees. Slowly, he reached behind her and gently untied the scarf from her hair. It floated to the ground as he used his fingers to comb her hair forward until it shimmered in a fiery curtain just above where Bartholomew clung to her breast. His eyes grew shadowy with desire as he gazed at her, and her breathing quickened.

Carefully, he leaned toward her. Her eyelids drifted closed in surrender when his lips, cool from the pond, touched hers with no more pressure than a falling leaf fluttering to the ground. She met his gentleness with her own, warming his mouth as if in apology for all the hurt they'd showered on each other. She leaned into the kiss, balancing herself with one hand against the powerful bulge of his biceps. It flexed beneath her touch, coolness turning to heat. Then, before the heat could turn to fire, he pulled away.

She opened her eyes again. His gaze probed hers. "You were right," she whispered, her lips tingling, wanting more. "I am afraid of you."

He brushed her cheek with his knuckles. "I don't want to make problems." His voice was husky. "But I can't let you walk out of my life and never come back."

She thought of what Ry had said. "Because...because of Bartholomew?"

He hesitated. "No, not just because of Bartholomew."

"But a little while ago you just said you don't want entanglements." Her heart hammered as she gazed into his eyes.

He slid his hand behind her neck and massaged gently. "Yeah, and I'll probably say it again at some stupid moment. For years I've guarded my freedom like a junkyard dog. Old habits die hard."

"Sometimes they never die."

"Just bear with me a while, Amanda."

With a shuddering sigh, Bartholomew drew their attention down to where he clung to Amanda's breast.

"I love watching you nurse him." Chase outlined the curve of the baby's cheek with one finger. "That's another thing I shouldn't have said. Maybe you were flirting with me last night. Maybe you were just acting natural. Whichever it was, I'd never want you to be embarrassed about doing this in front of me."

"For some reason, I haven't been," she murmured. "Not even that first time in the van."

"Good." He traced a path along Bartholomew's chin and continued the caress over the fullness of Amanda's breast.

She gasped and looked up at him.

His gaze was fathomless as he continued to trace soft patterns over her breast. "I've never wanted a woman the way I want you," he said softly. "I haven't wanted to admit that, for fear I'd jeopardize my precious freedom, but it's true. I know it's not convenient for either of us, but you're driving me crazy." His mouth curved in a smile and his dimple flashed. "From the look in your eyes, I think you feel the same way."

She had trouble breathing. "Chase, we can't—"

"I know." He glanced down at Bartholomew. "But I couldn't resist touching you, just this once." He levered himself away from her with a sigh. "And once is about all I can manage without forgetting myself."

She almost moaned in frustration. He was right,

though. They couldn't keep playing with fire when they had a baby to consider. Bartholomew loosened his grip on her nipple and gazed up at her, as if to remind her of that fact. He needed to be changed, and she had to figure out where he could be settled for a short nap. "Where's a safe place for him to sleep?" she asked as she refastened her nursing bra.

"That depression between the exposed tree roots should make a perfect bed for him."

She studied the spot Chase had indicated and decided it would work. "There's another blanket and a clean diaper in my saddlebag, if you wouldn't mind getting them."

"I'll do better than that. I'll change him for you."

"You will?" She looked up and discovered he was already halfway across the clearing.

"Sure," he called over his shoulder. "With those sticky tab things instead of pins it should be a cinch."

Amanda was touched by his eagerness to participate. She'd read once that a new father's willingness to help could be destroyed if the mother hovered around offering suggestions. Difficult as it would be for her, she'd let him change Bartholomew without interference.

Chase returned with the blanket and diaper. He folded the blanket and arranged it in the natural depression between two cottonwood roots, put the fresh diaper to one side, and held out his arms for the baby. She gave him Bartholomew with what she hoped was an encouraging smile.

"Okay, buddy," Chase said, settling the baby on the blanket and pulling at the tabs fastening the old diaper. "Time for an oil and lube job."

Amanda kept quiet as he wrestled with the fastenings. When he leaned closer, his medallion dangled within Bartholomew's reach. Gurgling happily, the baby grabbed it and pulled, nearly throwing Chase off-balance. Amanda pretended not to notice.

The diaper came off in shreds, but Chase finally removed it. "This doesn't seem very wet," he said, glancing at Amanda. "We may have wasted a perfectly good—"

"Chase, look out." But the warning came too late. A steady stream rose in the air as if from the nozzle of a miniature fire hose.

As it splattered against Chase's neck and ran down his chest, he yelped in surprise. "It's a gusher!"

Amanda couldn't hold her laughter another second. "I forgot to warn you," she gasped, holding her sides. "Sometimes when fresh air hits, he—"

"No kidding." His attempt to look stern was marred by the amusement dancing in his green eyes. "At least I know the equipment works."

"I'll finish up if you want to go wash in the pond."

Chase got to his feet with a show of dignity. "Guess I'll take you up on that. Next time I'll be ready."

Next time. Amanda smiled at the pleasant sound of that promise as she diapered Bartholomew while Chase cleaned off in the pond.

Soon he was back. "You can swim now if you want," he said, kneeling next to Bartholomew.

She considered the welcome treat versus the wisdom of undressing in this sensually charged atmosphere. "I don't think that's a good idea."

He glanced up. "If you think I'll be tempted to make love to you if you take off your clothes, you're right. But if you think I'll forget about Bartholomew and seduce you on the spot, you don't know me very well."

She couldn't resist a smile. "That's the whole point. I don't know you very well."

"Then it's time to learn. The water's cool. And you look—if you'll excuse the expression—hot."

And so she was. She wanted to take off her clothes, all right. But not necessarily to go swimming. Considering their obligation to keep a watchful eye on Bartholomew, swimming was the safer option. "All right," she said, turning toward the pond.

She walked down to the narrow strip of sand beside the water and unbuttoned her blouse. She didn't look to see if he was watching, pretty certain that he would be. A large boulder provided a seat while she pulled off her boots and stuffed her socks into them before placing them next to Chase's on the sand. Then she wriggled her bare toes in pleasure. Before she'd come to Arizona, she'd treated herself to a pedicure—the salon hadn't minded that she held Bartholomew on her lap during the procedure—and her toes were tipped in cranberry. Of course, her decision to get a pedicure had nothing to do with the fact that Chase had remarked on her delicate feet the night they'd made love. Of course not. She was beginning to wonder just how much she'd been fooling herself.

As she stood and unfastened the waistband of her jeans, she felt a little like a nightclub stripper performing for a single customer. She was unsettled to discover the idea exciting. She remembered that she'd worn a favorite pair of silk bikinis under her jeans. Cut high, they were trimmed around each leg with a ruffle of Belgian lace. When she stepped out of her jeans, she imagined she heard Chase catch his breath. But it could have been a lizard moving through dry leaves beneath the trees. She'd seen several today, harmless little creatures with no teeth. Still, she walked toward the water as if she were a model on a runway, admitting to herself that she wanted him to want her.

At the edge of the pond, sand gave way to mossy rocks, and her graceful entrance into the water was marred by some hobbling until she finally launched herself with a satisfying splash. Ah. For a moment, she forgot about Chase as she slipped along in a slow crawl, her self-made current swirling past her body and cleansing away the dust and sweat of the ride. She'd only been swimming in private pools and Long Island Sound, and she kept expecting either the taste of chlorine or salt. This water held neither, and she rolled to her back like an otter, reveling in the pond's crystal perfection. No wonder Chase loved swimming here.

She floated for a while, her hair billowing out around her, and gazed up through the leaves to the blue sky beyond. Life at the ranch was the complete opposite of her life in the city. Work there was indoors and cerebral; work at the ranch was outdoors and physical. She'd probably be bored in no time out here. It was okay for a change of pace, but she needed intellectual stimulation, the thrill of business competition, the—

Something yanked at the hem of her panties. After her experience the day before, all she could imagine were water moccasins. She flipped over in a panic and swallowed some water. Another yank, this time from the front. With a yelp, she propelled herself through the water. "Chase!" she burbled, scrambling over the rocks. "Chase!"

He ran to meet her, catching her by the elbows and hauling her up onto the bank.

"Something tried to bite me," she cried, her arms automatically going around him as she shivered. "I think it was a water moccasin."

He enclosed her in arms warmed by sunlight and brought her against his chest. She laid her cheek there. As she listened to the rapid thud of his heart, her gaze rested on the pewter medallion that moved gently with his breathing. He'd put his jeans back on—she felt the brush of denim against her bare legs and wished he hadn't, wished...but that wasn't wise. As she slowly stopped shivering, she realized he was shaking with silent laughter.

"I forgot to tell you about the fish," he said, chuckling. He tugged playfully at the Belgian lace decorating her panties. "They were probably after this."

She sagged in his arms. "Fish," she mumbled, feeling stupid. "I can deal with fish."

"There's nothing dangerous in that water." Chase had abandoned the lace and now cupped one hand under her bottom. "I wouldn't have let you go in if there had been."

She stayed very still as he pressed her closer and his heartbeat grew louder. Beneath his jeans he was hard as stone.

"But there is danger right here," he murmured against her wet hair. "Because now that I have you in my arms, I don't want to let you go."

9

HEAT SEARED through Amanda's veins, bringing a flush to her chilled skin. She moaned softly. Then she lifted her head and gazed upward into Chase's passion-filled eyes. "Bartholomew," she whispered in a voice heavy with disappointment.

"Yes, Bartholomew." With a sigh he released her and averted his eyes. "I'll get the sandwiches and canteens if you'll go check on him. When you called from the pond, he was still asleep."

Biting her lower lip in frustration, Amanda picked her way across rocks and sandy ground toward the tree where Bartholomew lay cradled between the exposed roots. He was still fast asleep and looking like an angel with his little snub nose and his tiny mouth pursed as if ready to give her a kiss. Except that Bartholomew's kiss wasn't the one she wanted at the moment. She loved her baby, loved him to distraction. But she hadn't anticipated the vigilance he'd require. Or the sacrifices.

She sat on a large section of root and combed her fingers through her wet hair as Chase came toward her, a canteen slung over one tanned shoulder, a bag of sandwiches in one hand and his shirt in the other.

He handed her the shirt. "I'd appreciate it if you'd put this on. You don't have to button it or anything, just...put it on."

She glanced down at her damp underwear and understood his point. When wet, the silk items didn't disguise much. She slipped her arms into the sleeves and pulled the shirt over her shoulders. Immediately, she was assailed by the scent of Chase—his mint aftershave and the tang of male sweat. Her nipples tightened beneath her damp bra and tension collected at the juncture of her thighs. She looked up at him. "Better?" The question came out sounding like a throaty invitation to share more than lunch.

Chase stared at her, his gaze tortured. "Not a hell of a lot, but I don't know what else to do short of tying myself to my horse." He tossed the sandwiches and canteen to the ground and hooked his hands at his beltline. "We're either going to have to do something about this or I'll have to put you on a plane very soon."

Desire had turned her into a temptress. "And which would you rather do?"

He made a noise deep in his throat and pulled her to her feet. His mouth came down hard on hers and his tongue thrust forcefully, claiming her. The blood sang in her ears and desire pounded through her. His tongue probed deeper, and he wrenched open the cup of her nursing bra to capture her breast in his calloused hand. He kneaded her soft flesh with the experienced touch she'd craved that night they'd spent together in the truck, the forbidden touch she'd dreamed of for months afterward. Then he released her and backed away, panting. "Does that answer your question?"

She brought a hand to her lips. He'd nearly bruised her mouth with the force of his kiss. That night in the truck he'd never come close to being that rough, but then he'd never been pushed to the brink of frustration, either. She understood the forces that drove him to kiss her that way. They were the same forces that made her relish his demands.

He shook his head, his voice husky. "I knew that bringing you on this ride would be a temptation, but I thought I'd handle it better than this. I didn't realize how maddening it would be for us to be alone and yet...not alone."

"No, we're not alone."

He leaned down to retrieve the canteen and bag of sandwiches. "Well, we lugged food all the way out here. If we don't eat it, Belinda will be highly insulted."

"Then let's eat." She refastened the cup of her bra and lowered herself, still shaking, to the smooth tree root. They sat on opposite sides of the sleeping baby while they ate. Chase didn't seem in a hurry to reopen the conversation, and she didn't know where to begin with all the questions swirling in her head.

"Chase?"

He swallowed a mouthful of food and looked at her.

"I don't know what comes next. Where we go from here."

He regarded her with a steady, yet heated gaze. "I have some ideas we might be able to live with."

"Such as?" Her mouth was dry with anticipation.

"I can't expect you to give up your career and life back in New York, and I'm stuck out here for the time being, but you could schedule trips out to Arizona as often as possible. I'd want to help you with expenses, especially all the traveling."

She started to tell him that was ridiculous and he held up his hand.

"I know you don't need my money. That you're even afraid it comes with strings attached. That's not true."

He gave her a wry smile. "Okay, one string. I'd want to share your bed when you came out."

A new wave of heat washed over her. "What...what would I tell people about all these trips I'd be taking?"

He was very quiet. "You could try the truth," he said at last.

She struggled with that concept. It would be tough facing her family and friends and explaining that she'd lied about the sperm donor when in fact her lover in Arizona was the father of her child. The whole truth would have to include that Bartholomew had been conceived in the bunk of an 18-wheeler. Her best friends would stick by her, but her parents...she shuddered to think how they'd react to that story, and to their grandson after they'd heard it. But maybe it was time to come clean. Maybe—

"Or not," Chase said, his tone bitter and impatient.

Amanda had the feeling a door had just slammed in her face before she'd been able to see what was on the other side. "Chase, maybe—"

"I don't really care, I guess. What does it matter what everybody else thinks?"

She glanced at him and tried to gauge his sincerity, but his expression was unreadable.

"Tell them you've developed a crush on the True Love Ranch," he continued. "Or tell them you're working on a big advertising campaign for us. Tell them you come here to have an out-of-body experience. Or to get laid by a cowboy."

"Chase!"

"Too crude, Amanda? Or too close to the truth? Forget pretending you don't want to go to bed with me again. That little cat's out of the bag."

She looked away, knowing her cheeks were pink.

"That's okay, sweetheart. You can blush and be coy to your heart's content, just so you'll let me enjoy that tempting body of yours. So what do you think? Can we work something out?"

Although she didn't like the cynical tone he'd adopted, he was offering her a way to keep her reputation intact. She'd flit out to Arizona once in a while, let him be with his son, make passionate love when Bartholomew was otherwise occupied and go back to her life in New York when the vacation was over. She should love the idea. She didn't. "What if I don't like that plan?"

A hint of vulnerability shone in his eyes as his mood shifted subtly. "Consider it, Amanda. We...might get to know each other that way."

"Why?" His statement about never getting married jangled in her memory. "Why get to know each other?"

He held her gaze, and the light slowly died in his eyes. He turned away. "Hell, I don't know. You're not interested in someone like me, no matter what. I don't know why I keep banging my head against a stone wall. Forget it. Just agree to bring Bartholomew out a few times a year and I promise never to lay a hand on you again."

It was the exact opposite of what she'd hoped for. "That isn't—"

"Oh, I know you want me, but you hate wanting me because you don't think I'm good enough for you." He stared into space. "You've made that very clear."

She was stung by his conclusions, but she could hardly blame him for drawing them. She had rejected him before, and that rejection had carried an unspoken implication that she didn't consider him good enough. He had no way of knowing how her feelings had changed in the past two days and she wasn't sure how she could tell him now that he'd become so defensive. Swallowing a nervous lump in her throat, she chose her words carefully. "Let's back up a minute. Were you trying to say that someday, if we discovered we got along really well, we might...make the arrangement between us...permanent?"

He glared at her. "Pretty stupid idea, right? You don't even know how stupid."

"No, it's—"

"You see, I'm not good enough for you. My pedigree has some serious problems. Last night, I spent an hour on the phone, got in touch with all the people I could think of who might be able to track down my mother. No luck. I'm not surprised—this isn't the first time I've tried to locate her. Maybe she doesn't want to be found. Maybe she's going by a different name. Maybe she's even dead. She always had lots of men around, so God knows if she could identify my father in the crowd, anyway." He sneered. "There's your family history. Pretty picture, isn't it?"

Amanda's heart wrenched with remorse at her insensitivity. How she'd pounded him with questions about his family. How those questions must have hurt him. "Chase, I'm so sorry. I didn't—"

"Save it." He didn't look at her. "I was a cute little kid. I always got into foster homes real easy. Some kids didn't."

"How...old were you?"

"When Mom checked out?" He picked up a stone and examined it as if it were the Hope diamond. "Three."

Three. Not even able to read. Barely able to understand what was happening. But understanding enough.

Her chest tightened in grief. "How many foster homes?"

"I lost track after the first six." He threw the stone in a long arc. It landed in the pond with a loud plop and sent out ripples that made the reeds on the far shore dance. "Doesn't matter, anyway. Some were nice, some weren't so nice. They just all kind of ran together after awhile."

She didn't realize she was crying until a tear dropped onto her sandwich wrapping. Maybe before she'd had Bartholomew she wouldn't have been stabbed with so sharp a pain at the idea of a little kid left to fend for himself. But now she could hardly stand the thought. She wiped at her damp cheeks and gazed at his rigid profile.

"You're pretty quiet over there, Amanda. Guess you're about to pack up the kid and hightail it back to New York." He turned to her. "Right? You—Aaw, hell!" He stormed to his feet and towered over her. "I can take just about anything you have to dish out, babe, except pity."

"It's not pity! I feel terrible about hounding you for details of your family, when you—"

"And in my book, that adds up to you feeling sorry for me," he cut in, scowling down on her. "Spare me, little rich girl. I can do without your tears!"

Bartholomew began to cry.

"How about his tears?" She scooped him up and got to her feet. All sense of control and decorum had left her. "If you're so eager to be a daddy, how about taking care of a crying kid, huh? You woke him up with all your blustering about pity, so take some pity on this little baby, who didn't ask for any of this and was only trying to get a little sleep!"

Chase stared at her, his expression thunderous as Bartholomew's cries grew louder. Then his gaze dropped to the squalling infant in her arms and the anger drained from his face. When he spoke, his voice was hoarse but gentle. "Yeah, none of this is his fault. Come here, little guy."

She was surprised that he took the baby, but she loosened her hold and allowed Chase to lift him from her arms.

"Hey, Bartholomew," Chase murmured, cuddling the baby against his bare chest. "Take it easy, buddy. We'll work it out."

Bartholomew's cries slowed.

"That's it, buddy. Listen, kid. Bartholomew's a pretty long name for such a little guy. How about if I call you Bart instead?"

The baby snuffled and rubbed his nose against Chase's shoulder.

Amanda looked at them and her heart cracked down the middle. "I'll be glad to bring him to Arizona as often as I can," she whispered in a broken voice.

Chase glanced at her, his gaze impersonal. "Good. Because you may not need me, but he does."

I need you, too, she thought. He probably wouldn't believe her.

"Now that we have that settled, it might be better if you catch a plane out of here tonight and give us both a chance to cool down a little before we see each other again."

She could barely speak around the lump in her throat. "I suppose you're right."

After a brief moment of eye contact, Chase returned his attention to his son. "Hey, Bart, when was the last time you went fishing? Come on and I'll show you some big ones." He turned and started walking toward the pond. "Once you can hold a fishing pole, buddy, we'll have some great times up here, you and me. Early morning's good. You like to get up early? I do."

Amanda clutched her stomach and sank onto a rock. Chase and Bartholomew made an idyllic picture down by the lake—the tanned muscular father crouched by the shore balancing his tiny son on his denim-clad knee. Bartholomew waved his arms and gurgled at the sun striking sparks on the surface of the water. Such a beautiful picture. And just like that, Chase had shut her out of it.

THEY DIDN'T TALK MUCH as they packed up and headed toward the ranch. Amanda couldn't think of anything to say that wouldn't be misinterpreted as pity for Chase's childhood. She hadn't agreed to his proposal of regular visits right away because she was beginning to think she wanted more from this relationship. Apparently, he'd thought her hesitation meant she didn't want to have anything at all to do with him, and he'd shut down his feelings for her.

He'd probably had a lot of practice cutting himself off emotionally from people, she thought as they rode in silence. That skill would be a requirement for anyone being jerked from one foster home to another. And she'd had the nerve to whine because her father hadn't been as loving as she would have liked. Chase probably would have been willing to trade places with someone like her any day.

The long ride back to the ranch gave her a lot of time to think, and her thoughts weren't cheerful ones. She cringed at the knowledge that at one time, she'd been ready to deprive Chase of his son, the bundle riding trustingly like a little papoose on his back as they made their way down the canyon. She'd awakened to the realization that to take a man's child away would be unfair in most cases, but particularly unfair to a man who'd never had any family. She could see now that he'd avoided connections because he didn't believe people would honor those connections. Which would make him all the more determined to honor his to this child he'd fathered. Somehow she would keep her part of the bargain and bring father and son together as often as possible, no matter what the cost to her own aching heart. She feared she was falling in love with a man who didn't believe it could happen.

They were about a mile from the house when they heard the siren.

Chase straightened in his saddle and Bartholomew's eyes snapped open. "Amanda!" Chase called back to her. "Do you see smoke?"

"No!" Her heart began to race. She didn't know the people at the ranch well, but in the short time she'd been there, she'd come to care very much what happened to them. "What could be wrong?"

"I don't know. I hope it's not Dexter." His voice was tight with worry. "Listen, I can't ride any faster than this with the baby on my back, but you can. Go on ahead. Maybe they need an extra hand with whatever's happening. I'll be there as soon as I can."

She didn't need any more urging. Digging her heels into Pussywillow's ribs, she leaned forward and clucked her tongue at the little mare. Pussywillow shot ahead of Chase. Amanda anchored her hat on her head with one hand and moved as one with the galloping horse. She'd never wish problems on anyone at the ranch house, not even that pesky Ry McGuinnes, but oh, it was glorious to have a legitimate reason to ride full tilt up the lane. The bonds of responsibility that had begun to chafe her soul loosened temporarily, and she longed to shout with the joy of release.

CHASE WATCHED in amazement as Amanda hurtled down the road ahead of him as if she'd been launched from a slingshot. He hadn't taken her comments about her riding skills very seriously, but he could see now that the woman was a natural. Why she'd chosen to spend her life in a stuffy office when she could ride like that was beyond him.

The whine of the siren died down, and he figured whatever the emergency vehicle was, it was sitting in front of the ranch house right now. God, he hoped it wasn't Dexter. Belinda swore he'd outlast them all, especially because he walked all the way to the main road every day to get the mail. "That's more walking than any of the rest of you cowboys get," Belinda often said. "And he's eating chicken while you stuff down the steak. His heart's in great shape." Chase sure hoped so. He'd broken one of his cardinal rules and allowed himself to grow very fond of old Dex.

Yet when he trotted Mikey up to the front of the ranch house, paramedics were loading someone into the back of a Rural-Metro ambulance. And Belinda was climbing in after the stretcher.

Heart thudding with dread, Chase nudged Mikey into a trot and arrived at the back of the ambulance before the paramedics closed the doors. "Belinda?"

She turned, her eyes bright with unshed tears.

Chase had to work to get the words out. "Is it his heart?"

Belinda shook her head. "They don't think so. They think it's something he ate."

"Stomach hurts!" Dexter bellowed from inside the ambulance.

"What the hell?" Chase peered at Belinda.

Belinda swallowed. "The paramedics think we all have...food poisoning."

"Excuse us," said a paramedic as he closed the back doors of the ambulance and blocked Chase's view of Belinda and Dexter. "We need to get going."

Food poisoning? Chase stared after the ambulance as it started out of the driveway, red dome-lights whirling. Belinda ran a spotless kitchen. She boasted that the board of health sent restaurant owners to see her if they couldn't figure out how to keep their facilities clean, and Chase personally knew of a time a restaurant owner had come out to the True Love for that very purpose.

Maybe Dexter had some other problem, Chase thought as he dismounted by the hitching post where Pussywillow was tethered. Amanda was nowhere in sight. After tying Mikey's reins to the post, Chase adjusted the shoulder straps on the cradleboard and started toward the house. A stepladder stood on the porch, and a strand of tiny white lights hung from the rafters, as if someone had been stapling the lights across the length of the porch and had taken a break.

Inside, the main room was deserted, as well as the patio. Chase glanced into the dining room and found a sight he'd never seen before. Dirty dishes from lunch remained on the tables at nearly two in the afternoon. That never happened. The whole place had a ghost-town feel about it.

"Amanda!"

She appeared from his right, coming from the hall that led to the guest rooms. "Chase, thank God you're here! Everyone has food poisoning."

"Everyone?"

"Except Belinda, because she was too busy to eat lunch. At least that's how the paramedics diagnosed the situation. I called the board of health and someone's coming out to test the food that was served, but the symptoms are typical—stomach cramps, vomiting. Belinda called an ambulance for Dexter because she didn't want to take any chances, and because she feels so responsible, I guess. That kitchen is her whole identity."

"I know."

"Here." She walked around behind him. "Let me help you with the cradleboard and I'll tend to Bartholomew while you call Duane down at the stables."

Chase lifted the straps over his arms as Amanda relieved him of the weight of the board and Bartholomew. "Are the hands all sick, too?"

"Freddy doesn't think they will be because they didn't eat the same thing for lunch that people at the main house did. And somebody has to finish cleaning and decorating for the wedding tomorrow."

Chase turned back toward her. "Are you feeling okay? Our lunch came out of that kitchen, too."

She'd laid the cradleboard on a leather sofa to unlace it. She glanced up into his eyes and looked away again just as quickly. "I'm fine, but it's nice of you to ask."

It had been his first thought. His second had been that if she got sick, she might pass the problem on to Bart through her breast milk. But her welfare had been his first thought. The realization stunned him.

"I guess the sandwiches we took didn't have anything in them that was contaminated," she said as she pulled a wiggling Bartholomew out of his swaddling blanket. "Unless you're feeling sick?"

Not from the food, he thought. "No, I'm fine, too. I guess we shouldn't feel lucky, but I'm glad we weren't here for lunch. So everybody's down and out?"

"Everybody." Amanda stood and held Bart against her shoulder. "Freddy asked me to go check on the wedding guests for her, because she and Ry are in no condition to do it. I'd just finished making sure nobody wanted a doctor when you called to me."

"How about Leigh?"

"Leigh seems to be hit pretty bad. Apparently, she stuffed herself at lunch, claiming she had to keep up her strength for all the decorating. Even the maids and the handymen are done for. They all went home. The paramedics seem to think everyone will be okay in the morning, but we can't wait until then to finish the work. It's up to you, me, Duane and the rest of the hands."

"Then I'd better go call him." Another mysterious disaster, Chase thought as he headed for Freddy's office. He wondered if Eb Whitlock had been around today. Later he'd ask. He couldn't believe that Belinda would be behind something like this, but Duane had been spared the ordeal. Chase wondered if that was a bit too convenient. Then again, maybe this was just an accident. Everyone had been busy getting ready for the wedding. Maybe Belinda's quality control had slipped slightly, just enough to allow something in the kitchen to spoil.

Chase picked up the phone and dialed the number for the corrals. The main goal was to get ready for the wedding. It was the least he could do for Ry and

Freddy. Then he realized that Amanda had sounded as if she planned to pitch in with everyone else. It looked as if she wouldn't be getting on a plane tonight, after all.

10

A REPRIEVE. Amanda wasn't sure what that would mean. Perhaps nothing at all. But the food-poisoning incident made it important for her to stay through tonight, and no one would expect her to leave first thing in the morning when the wedding was taking place. The soonest she'd be expected to fly out would be in the evening, after the reception. In the meantime, maybe she could find a way to convince Chase that she was no longer the snob that had stepped off the plane two days ago.

She and Chase divided up the duties. Because of her advertising and artistic background, Amanda volunteered to supervise three of the hands in completing the decorating of the patio and front porch. Chase would take the other four, including Duane, and direct them in the cleaning.

"It may not be up to Rosa's standards," Chase said, "but we'll get the worst of it."

The afternoon passed quickly. Chase brought the infant seat over from the cottage so Amanda could set Bartholomew in the shade while she moved around the patio with a critical eye. Chloe appeared soon after Amanda settled Bartholomew into the carrier and lay beside it, as if resuming her duties.

Amanda thought of the close bond between Dexter and the dog. She crouched and scratched behind

Chloe's ears. "Dexter will be okay, Chloe," she murmured. "He'll be back soon."

The dog thumped her tail on the flagstone and looked up at Amanda with soulful eyes.

"I think Bartholomew needs a dog like you," Amanda said. Then she wondered how on earth she'd accomplish that. Pets were banned in her apartment building.

Curtis, a tall blond cowboy who was one of the three assigned to Amanda, sauntered toward her. "What do you want us to do first, ma'am?" he asked.

"I guess we'll finish stringing the lights." She stood, and in the process noticed Curtis casting an appreciative eye over her figure. She couldn't imagine what he found to look at. Her clothes were rumpled from her ride up the canyon, and she hadn't done anything with her hair except tie it back with the silk scarf. Her makeup was nonexistent by now. Yet Curtis seemed entranced.

With a mental shrug she turned her attention to the work at hand. "Let's start over there at the far end of the patio," she said.

Curtis motioned to the other two cowboys, Rusty and Jack, and the work commenced.

Amanda liked the Mexican-fiesta motif that Freddy and Ry had planned to execute with tiny lights, large paper flowers and several colorful *piñatas*. When it came time to stuff the *piñatas* prior to hanging them, Amanda had to keep a close eye on Rusty and Jack to make sure they didn't eat too much candy while they worked. Curtis followed Amanda around with more devotion than Chloe had shown to Bartholomew. And although Curtis was handsome in a lean sort of way, Amanda felt not a twinge of attraction. That didn't seem to penetrate Curtis's romantic fog. In his eagerness to help, he accidentally stepped on one empty *piñata*, smashing it before its time.

Eventually, the patio was finished to Amanda's satisfaction. The folding tables and chairs were in place, each with a pottery *luminaria* anchoring a scarlet tablecloth. The paper flowers bloomed in several large baskets, and the *piñatas* danced in the breeze, ready for the moment when someone would swing a baseball bat at them and spill the contents onto the flagstone beneath. When darkness arrived, the area would wink with thousands of white lights.

Amanda picked up the infant seat with Bartholomew in it. He'd begun to squirm and make little mewling sounds that told her it was nearly time for him to nurse. "Okay, guys. Let's take a break," she said. "I'll meet you on the front porch in twenty minutes so we can finish up that area, and then we'll be done."

"I'll carry the baby for you, ma'am," Curtis volunteered. "Just tell me where you're aiming to take him."

"Thanks, but it's nearly his suppertime," Amanda said.

"Oh." Curtis flushed. "Then let me get the door for you." He opened the French door into the main room of the house.

She had to assume word had gotten around the ranch that she and Chase weren't formalizing their relationship and she was therefore a free agent. That would be the only explanation for Curtis's obvious interest, considering Chase was his boss. "Thanks, Curtis," she said, choosing not to smile and encourage him any further.

"You're welcome, ma'am." Curtis touched the brim of his hat. "I'll see you on the front porch in a little bit."

"Right." She turned and walked into the room to be

greeted by the sight of Chase, his legs planted apart, his fists on his hips and his expression grim beneath a hat pulled dangerously low over his eyes. The effect of outraged manhood was marred slightly by the feather duster he clutched in one big hand. Amanda pressed her lips together to keep from smiling.

"What's Curtis so chummy about?" Chase asked.

"He's a polite cowboy, that's all." Amanda took Chase's show of jealousy as a promising sign. He couldn't be jealous if he'd shut off all his feelings for her.

"The way he looked at you as he closed the door was a darn sight more than polite, if you ask me."

"I didn't," she snapped, but his possessiveness felt wonderful. "Now, if you'll excuse me, I need to find a private place to nurse Bartholomew."

At that moment, Duane came into the room pulling a canister vacuum cleaner by the hose. The cord and plug snaked out behind. "I done the hall." Duane waved the hose, to which was attached the slim tool used to clean crevices and baseboards. Amanda wondered what he could have accomplished using that narrow attachment. Duane shifted his chaw of tobacco to the other side of his lower lip. "What's next?"

Chase glanced around, looking somewhat bewildered. "Everything, I guess." He made a wide sweep with the feather duster that took in the entire main room.

Amanda bit the inside of her cheek to keep from laughing and wished she had a camera. The picture of her big, tough cowboy waving a feather duster through the air was priceless.

"If you say so." Duane located an outlet and pulled the plug toward him as if reeling in a fish hand over hand. He shoved the plug into the outlet and the vacuum surged to life. Apparently, he felt using the on-off switch was wasted labor. Stooping down, he swung the crevice attachment across the tiled floor as if it were a metal detector.

Amanda glanced at Chase, who shrugged. Shaking her head, she walked over to him. "Hold Bartholomew for a minute."

Chase stuck the handle of the feather duster in his back pocket and accepted the infant seat.

Amanda turned and approached Duane. "Can I make a suggestion?" When he didn't respond, she raised her voice. "Duane?"

"Huh?" He glanced up.

"Can I make a suggestion?"

Duane grinned, showing tobacco-stained teeth. "Shore!"

"Let's turn off the machine first!"

"Oh! Shore!" He grabbed the cord and yanked the plug from the wall in the same motion he might have used to tighten the noose on a steer's horns.

Amanda winced but said nothing about the wear and tear on the plug. This would probably be Duane's only experience with this vacuum cleaner. "Your method is great, but I'll bet there's a special attachment for these floors somewhere," she began.

Duane took off his battered hat and scratched his head. "This here's the one that was on it. You mean there's another one?"

"Probably several more."

"I'll be hornswoggled." Duane repositioned his hat on his head. "What do you make of that, Chase?"

"It's not my area."

"Mine, neither," Duane agreed.

Amanda controlled her amusement with difficulty as she turned to Chase. "If you'll show me where the cleaning supplies are kept, maybe I can find the other attachments."

"Okay. It's a storeroom just past the kitchen. I'll go with you."

"What d'ya want me to do in the meantime, Chase?" Duane asked.

Chase held the infant seat firmly in one arm as he reached behind him for the feather duster. He tossed it end over end to Duane.

Duane caught it by the feathers and nearly choked on the black cloud of dust that flew out. "What do I do with this?"

Chase paused. "Use your imagination," he said finally.

On the way through the dining room to the kitchen, Amanda could no longer control her chuckles. "You guys don't know the first thing about cleaning this place, do you?"

Chase looked offended. "Sure we do."

"What were you using the feather duster for?"

He hesitated. "To sweep out the fireplace?"

Amanda nearly choked on her laughter. "Is that an answer or a question?"

"It worked," he said with an air of injured pride.

"I imagine it did." She stifled a giggle.

"Well, I sure couldn't handle the decorating part, and you couldn't do everything, so—"

"Chase, you're doing a fine job," she said, suddenly contrite. "We're all managing the best we can, under the circumstances. By the way, I saw you talking to the inspector from the health department. What did she say?"

"It was the chicken soup."

"You're kidding." She held the swinging kitchen door open wide enough to accommodate Chase and Bartholomew in the infant seat. "Chicken soup is supposed to cure what ails you."

"I know, but somehow Belinda brewed up a toxic batch. Everybody here had some. Belinda's famous for her chicken soup. She was planning to take a kettle of it down to the bunkhouse to feed the hands, but she didn't get around to it."

"Lucky for us," said a cowboy wearing a tea towel around his waist as he worked over a sinkful of suds. Nearby, a man with his stomach sagging over his belt buckle wielded a drying towel. Amanda had never seen kitchen help wearing Stetsons, but the men seemed to know what they were doing.

"That's Ernie up to his elbows in dishwater," Chase said by way of introduction. "The guy drying is Davis."

Davis nodded. "Ma'am." Then he turned to Chase. "This food poisoning's going on the True Love's record. Think that's going to hurt business?"

"Let's hope not," Chase said.

"Ernie here's been telling me about the True Love Curse," Davis continued. "Guess I missed that story somewhere along the way, but it sure seems like the ranch has had a mess of accidents lately."

"The True Love Curse?" Amanda glanced at Chase. "What's that?"

"An old wives' tale, most likely," Chase said, sending a quelling glance in Davis's direction. "You know how superstitions get started. Come on, let's get those attachments for Duane."

"Okay. Nice to meet you both." She surveyed the clean dishes stacked on a large cutting board. One counter was filled with recently washed champagne flutes. "Keep up the good work."

Chase inclined his head toward the flutes. "I told them to get those out and clean them."

"Great idea," Amanda said as they started down the hall toward the storeroom.

Chase grinned, flashing his dimple. "You mean I'm good for something?"

She caught her breath. She loved his smile, she realized, and she hadn't seen it nearly enough in the past two days. "You're good for many things," she said.

"Oh, really?" His voice sounded a little richer, a little deeper.

Her heartbeat accelerated. "Really."

"This door on the left is the storeroom."

She opened it, found the light switch on the right wall next to the door and walked in. He came in behind her. She heard the door close as she walked over to a shelf of cleaning supplies. The scent of lemon oil permeated the windowless room, lined with shelves on all sides. Enticed by the privacy of the tiny space, she searched for the vacuum attachments with trembling hands. From behind her came a sound that could have been Chase setting the infant seat on the floor. Or it could have been Chase bumping his elbow against something on one of the shelves.

He came up behind her, too close to have Bartholomew still in his arms. "Care to expand on that last statement?"

She turned, a vacuum attachment clutched in each hand. "Where's Bartholomew?"

"Stuffed him in the mop bucket."

She gasped.

"No, I didn't. Good grief, Amanda." Chase swung

aside to give her a glimpse of Bartholomew sitting in his infant seat on the tiled floor. "Seems to be having a great time examining his feet. He's fine." He turned back to her and his gaze traveled over her face. "You, on the other hand, have a large smudge on your nose."

She started to reach up with the back of her hand and he caught her wrist.

"Let me." He brushed at her nose with two fingers, then chuckled as he looked at his soot-blackened hands. "Now your nose is really dirty."

She remembered that soft chuckle, remembered the sound of it in her ear as he'd made love to her in the truck cab where they'd found themselves literally bouncing off the walls. "I always did have trouble keeping my nose clean," she said.

He looked deep into her eyes. "Especially with jokers like me around." He reached out and grasped the shelf behind her head with both hands, imprisoning her between his outstretched arms. His lips curved in a lazy smile. "I have to admit I hated it when Curtis looked at you like he was ready to take a bite."

She lifted her face to his. "You did?"

"'Fraid so. It doesn't speak well for my character, does it?" He leaned closer and his breath feathered her lips.

"Curtis means nothing to me."

"But someday, some guy in New York might look at you that way, and he might mean something." His lips hovered nearer; his eyes were half-closed. "I've never allowed myself to be jealous of anyone before. Now I can't seem to help it." His voice roughened. "God, Amanda, you're tearing me apart."

The vacuum attachments clattered to the floor. "Then let me put you back together, cowboy," she whispered, sliding her hands along his beard-stubbled jaw and bringing his mouth down to meet hers.

He groaned as she slipped her tongue between his teeth and stroked the roof of his mouth. Nipping and teasing his lips, she reached down and snapped open the fasteners of his shirt so she could run her hands over his chest.

"I hope you know what you're starting," he murmured against her mouth.

"I have a general idea." Stroking down over the pewter chain, she tunneled her fingers through his wiry chest hair and scratched her fingernails lightly over his hard nipples. His chest heaved and he deepened the kiss. Amanda opened to him, inviting him to delve into the moist recesses of her mouth. Inviting him to dare yet more.

When she reached down to the fly of his jeans and stroked him there, the contents of the shelf he was clutching began to rattle.

He wrenched his mouth from hers with obvious effort and stared down at her, his eyes glittering, his breath coming in great gasps. "You were supposed to be on a plane by now."

She rubbed the heel of her hand over the bulge in his jeans. "Is that what you want?"

He stared at her for what seemed like forever. Finally, his answer came, low and full of tension. "I want you to leave your door unlocked tonight."

She trembled, her body already heavy with need. "All right."

"And snap up my shirt. If I do it, I'll leave soot marks everywhere and people will think I've been massaging my own chest in here."

Triumph and desire surged through her as she refastened his shirt with slow, sensuous motions, taking time to caress him as she did so.

"Amanda, you're taking a big chance, playing around like that. You're liable to end up on your back on this concrete floor with soot marks all over that white skin of yours."

Holding his shirtfront with both hands, she stood on tiptoe to brush his lips with hers. "I just don't want you to forget to come by tonight. For my bedtime story, you can tell me about the True Love Curse."

He made a sound deep in his throat. "I have a slightly different bedtime story in mind." He leaned down and ravished her lips once more before pushing away from the shelf with a resigned sigh. "We'd better get out there before Duane uses the feather duster on the white drapes."

Amanda's eyes widened. "Would he?"

Chase's mouth curved in a smile. "Well, I told him to use his imagination. Duane is a good old boy, but he has the imagination of a hubcap."

"Judging from that night in the truck, that's not one of your shortcomings."

"And I was working in a limited space, too."

She caught her breath as erotic images assaulted her.

"Don't give me that look, you devil woman. As it is, I'll have to stagger out of here bowlegged." He leaned down and scooped the vacuum attachments from the floor. "I'm taking these to Duane. This might be the most private place to feed Bart, if you want to stay. There's a folding stool in the corner."

"Are you coming back?"

"Knowing you're in here with your blouse undone? Not likely." His eyes took on a wicked gleam. "Shall I tell Curtis you'll be a little later than you thought coming out to the porch?"

She put a hand to her throat, where her pulse was beating madly. She'd completely forgotten about the rest of the decorating job. Completely forgotten about Curtis and his hopeless crush. A smile of feminine delight touched her lips as she realized that was exactly what Chase had intended. "Please," she said.

"Shall I tell him why you'll be a little late?"

"I doubt that will be necessary. I've discovered nothing's a secret for long around here."

Chase stood with his hand on the doorknob as his gaze raked her possessively. "Good."

11

CHASE MOVED through the rest of the cleaning and decorating in a daze. Freddy, Ry, Leigh and the wedding guests kept to their rooms and couldn't be tempted to come out for the makeshift dinner, which consisted of peanut butter and jelly sandwiches washed down with beer. None of the hands complained. Chase figured it was because peanut butter wasn't known for giving anyone food poisoning. During the meal, Belinda called from the hospital and said Dexter was better but the doctor wanted to keep him overnight. They'd be back first thing in the morning.

After dinner, Chase sent Amanda back to the cottage with Chloe as escort while he and the hands tidied up. Then he walked with them out to the front porch just as the last russet glow was fading from the sky. "Thanks, guys," he said.

"You're shore welcome," Duane said as he started down the flagstone walkway to the rusty pickup he'd used to haul the hands up from the bunkhouse. Then he turned and grinned at Chase. "'Course, you know my dang manicure is ruined."

Davis sashayed up beside him, flung an arm around his shoulders and spoke in falsetto. "You should use rubber gloves, dear. I always do, and it keeps my hands so nice."

"I wanna know why I didn't get to wear an apron

with ruffles," Ernie complained. "I always liked aprons with ruffles."

"I'll get you one for Christmas," Curtis said. "Red-and-white-striped, to match your eyes."

Laughing and trading insults, the cowboys piled into the back of Duane's pickup.

Just before he drove off, Duane leaned out the window of the truck. "I used to think that high-dollar woman of yours was a waste of your time," he said. "But she's okay. Purty little filly, too." Duane beeped the horn and drove away.

A high-dollar woman. Good description, Chase thought. He had a feeling Amanda was going to be very expensive indeed, and the cost would have nothing whatsoever to do with money.

Fifteen minutes later he was showered, shaved, dressed and on his way through the patio when a voice called from the shadows.

"What's your hurry, cowboy?"

Chase spun around and saw Ry lying on a chaise longue. "Hey. You scared the crud out of me. Feeling any better?"

"Some. I was getting cabin fever in my room."

Chase walked back toward the chaise, a smile tugging at his mouth. "And bridegroom jitters?"

"How should I know?" Ry grumbled. "I expect bridegroom jitters and food poisoning feels about the same."

"I wouldn't know. Never had either one. Never plan to."

"Yeah, you're such a free man you can hardly wait to get over to that little cottage."

"Uh..."

"Don't try to get high and mighty with me, Lavette.

You're as lovestruck as I am. If Amanda offered to stay at the True Love and wash your socks for the rest of your life, you'd jump at the chance."

Chase adjusted his hat and looked away. "Yeah, well, I can guarantee she's not gonna do that, buddy."

Ry laughed. "You're not giving yourself much credit. The night's still young."

"That's not what I'm looking for, going over there."

"You're not looking for sex?"

"That's *all* I'm looking for." Chase thought it sounded good, just the sort of thing the old Chase would have said. But the old Chase was fast disappearing in the force of this driving passion. "The last time was a one-night stand for her. Now it's my turn," he added, as if smart remarks could stop the momentum of his downward slide into neediness. Fat chance.

Ry chuckled. "If you say so." Then his voice lost its playful tone. "What do you make of this food-poisoning business?"

Chase hooked his thumbs in his belt loops. "Could somebody deliberately cause something like that?"

"I don't know why not. Just drop some tainted chicken in the kettle. It could have been anyone who had access to the kitchen."

"Which was damn near everybody, today," Chase said. "Was Whitlock over here?"

"I don't think so. But did you notice who didn't eat any soup?"

"Yeah, but come on, Ry. Belinda wouldn't poison her own husband."

"How do you know he was poisoned? Those two old people are crafty. She could have coached him on how to react."

Chase shook his head. "I just can't buy it. I saw her

face just before she got in the ambulance. You know, Duane didn't eat any soup, either. None of the hands did, for that matter. Maybe somebody has a grudge you don't even know about."

Ry heaved a sigh. "Anything's possible. Damn, but I hate having these suspicions."

"Davis mentioned something today about a 'True Love Curse.' What's that all about?"

"That's more Leigh's department than mine, but the way I heard it, some cavalrymen killed a village of Indian women and children on this spot back in the 1800s. The men of the tribe supposedly put a curse on the land and said no white man would ever profit from it."

Chase gazed uneasily at the shadowy mountains towering above the ranch house. "Did you hear this before we bought the place?"

"Yeah, but I don't believe in superstition, so I didn't see the point in repeating the story to you and Gilardini. We may have a problem on the True Love, but it sure as hell isn't on account of some century-old curse. It's because some flesh-and-blood trickster wants to drive us off of this land. I just wish I could catch somebody in the act."

"I think you should forget it for tonight, buddy, and try to get some rest. Tomorrow's your big day."

"And what if someone tries to ruin that, too?"

Chase couldn't very well promise there wouldn't be any accidents on Ry's wedding day. "Let's just hope our friends outnumber our enemies tomorrow," he said, turning to go. "See you in the morning, bridegroom."

"Yeah. Good luck tonight, cowboy."

Chase raised a hand in acknowledgment of the remark. He didn't comment that a guy who didn't believe in superstitions shouldn't be wishing anyone good luck, either. As he walked toward the cottage, a pewter sliver of moon hung in the western sky with Venus dangling off its tip like a diamond pendant. He'd wished on a star exactly once. Nothing had happened. After that, he'd relied on himself to get what he wanted. And if he couldn't get it, then he'd convince himself it wasn't worth having.

No light shone from the cottage windows, and his heart beat faster. She was already in bed. Waiting. Or else she'd changed her mind, locked the door and turned out the light to warn him away.

In the pale gleam from the crescent moon, he could make out Chloe stationed outside the door on the porch, instead of inside the cottage. That was a promising development. Chloe stood and wagged her tail as Chase drew near.

"Come here, girl," Chase called softly. Chloe trotted down the steps toward him and shoved her nose against the palm of his hand. He scratched behind her ears and lifted her muzzle to look into her eyes. "Go find Ry," he commanded. "You stay with Ry tonight. I'll be on duty here." Chloe whined. "Go find Ry," Chase said again. The black-and-white dog bounded down the moonlit path to the main house.

Chase stepped up on the porch, wondering if Amanda could hear the sound of his boots on the weathered pine above the soft purr of the air-conditioning unit. He held his breath and turned the knob.

It opened.

He stood in the doorway, his heart hammering, as his eyes adjusted to the darkness. There was music, unfamiliar music with violins, playing on the radio. Gradually, like a Polaroid picture developing, the four-poster came into focus with its expanse of lace-edged sheets. And there, reclining against a mound of fluffy pillows, the sheet pulled up over her breasts, her shoulders bare and her glorious hair spread around her, was Amanda. His throat went dry.

"The baby?" His question came out as a feeble rasp.

"Stuffed him in a mop bucket," she murmured in a low voice.

"I see."

"I hope you don't mind the music. It helps him sleep."

"No." He'd listen to somebody with a pocket comb and a kazoo if he could make love to Amanda while it was playing. He was a country-and-western fan, himself, but this music seemed to suit Amanda. Unwilling to abandon the sight of her stretched out in bed, Chase reached behind him to close and lock the door. Then he took off his hat and sailed it toward a bedpost. It caught and spun around once, almost in time to the music, before settling there.

"Good aim."

"I've practiced."

She muffled her laughter against her hand.

He walked toward the bed, unfastening his shirt as he came. "I figured that any cowboy worth his spurs should be able to do that before he climbs into a four-poster bed with a woman." His arousal pushed painfully against his clothing.

"I agree," she said softly. "What else have you been practicing?"

"Lately? Not much." And he hoped he wouldn't pay for his lack of recent sexual activity by taking her like some rutting animal. He'd have to be careful. He wanted her so much he was beginning to shake. If he could pace himself to that gentle music, he'd be okay.

"If you tell me you've been celibate since that night in the truck, I'll know you're a liar," she said.

He leaned on the bedpost to pull off each boot in turn. "Then I won't tell you that."

"Who was she?"

He paused in the act of unhooking his belt from the buckle. In the past he would have shut down that line of questioning real quick. But that was because he'd made it a rule never to ask those same questions of the women he'd slept with. He'd already broken that rule with Amanda. He'd broken several of his rules with Amanda. "A waitress and a bartender," he said as he pulled his belt through the loops. "Very nice ladies."

"Two? At once?"

He controlled his laughter because of the baby. "Never tried that. Always thought it would be too confusing." He dug the condoms out of his pocket before he stepped out of his jeans.

"Did they...know about each other?"

"No." He walked to the head of the bed and deposited the condoms on the table beside it. "But then, they didn't ask." He was close enough to see the shine of her eyes in the dim light. Her gaze was fastened on him, and under the sheet her breasts moved up and down in time to her rapid breathing. He reached for the elastic of his briefs.

"Did you ask them if they'd had other lovers besides you?"

"No, I didn't."

She met that admission with a satisfied smile and asked no more questions. He figured she was remembering that he'd asked about other men within an hour of seeing her again. He'd told Ry he was here for a one-night stand, and the stupidity of that statement was already becoming obvious. He pushed his briefs down and released his straining erection.

Her glance swept downward, then back to his face. She caught her lower lip between her teeth and he clenched his hands to keep from flinging himself on her. The music. He had to use the rhythm of the music to stay calm. He took the sheet back slowly when he longed to rip it away from her body. The movement of the sheet stirred the scent of her perfume, which reached out to him with memories he'd never erase.

His breath came out in a long, shaky sigh and he cursed his lack of schooling. He wanted to tell her how beautiful she looked lying there naked against the white sheets, her body almost glowing, but he'd never be able to find the right words, especially when he needed her so much he couldn't think straight.

He returned his gaze to her face as he slid into bed beside her. He lay there, not touching her, just drowning in those eyes and feeling like a novice, a beginner, a virgin. His next move was too important. After loving so many women that he'd lost track of the number, he had no idea where to begin.

She took the decision away from him. Slipping a hand up the curve of his jaw, she guided him down with subtle pressure until their lips hovered a breath apart. "Get this straight, Lavette. I don't share," she whispered just before she kissed him. It was a kiss that shattered what was left of the wall he'd tried to build around his heart. It was a kiss of complete, utter surrender.

With a groan, he pressed deep into her mouth and

took that surrender, burying himself in the limitless passion she offered. Now he knew what to do.

As violins teased him to even greater awareness, he found the curve of her neck with a sure touch, followed it over her shoulder, into the tender crook of her elbow, down past the delicate bend of her wrist until at last he laced his fingers through hers. That clasp of hands felt more intimate than any touch he'd ever shared with a woman. She gripped his fingers as if she'd never let go. He returned the pressure as he moved his lips to the hollow of her throat. He'd forgotten how perfectly his tongue fit there, and how she shuddered as he trailed the moist tip over her collarbone and down the slope of her breast.

He remembered the silken texture of her skin, the exotic taste of scented lotion, but this time she swelled beneath him with more urgency than before. He listened to the rhythm of the music, circling the pebbled areola slowly, making the music part of the caress. Her fingers tightened in his, and he took her nipple into his mouth.

The taste of her milk stirred him as nothing had in his life. He felt as if her essence had passed into him, bonding them in a way he'd never be able to untangle. And didn't want to. He kissed his way to her other breast, eager for her, unashamed to let her know how he craved this closeness. She moaned and tunneled the fingers of her free hand through his hair.

Memories of their long night in the truck came rushing back. He'd learned about her then, and the imprint was still fresh, as if it had been only days instead of months. He retraced the path between her breasts, heard the familiar catch in her breathing as he caressed the gentle valley between her ribs. There was a ticklish spot—his tongue found it again—that he'd loved to lick just to hear her gasp of laughter. When her laughter bubbled out on schedule, his heart rejoiced in rediscovery.

And now, the most beloved and best-remembered part of the journey, through the thicket of curls that would glow like burnished copper if he could only have light. Her musky woman-scent rose to meet him, signaling how much she wanted him, and he longed to shout his delight. Instead, he paid homage to that need in ways that made her writhe beneath him. He pinned her thighs with his forearms and settled in, his heart beating in fierce triumph as he brought cries to her lips, cries muffled against a hastily grabbed pillow.

When she began to tremble and clench beneath him, he rose, wanting the end to come when he was deep inside her. Usually adept at putting on condoms, he fumbled this time. The music filtering through the labored sound of his breathing mingled with her soft plea to hurry, hurry. Please hurry. No. He forced himself to rejoin her with exquisite slowness, in time to the music. Always in time to the music.

She lay back among the tousled pillows, her hair in disarray, her legs spread, her breath shallow. "I don't remember wanting you...this much." Her voice was like the sigh of wind through the leaves in Rogue Canyon.

"You didn't." He braced himself above her and took the time to comb her hair away from her face. This moment would be over soon enough. He didn't have to rush it. The music. He'd move with the music. "I didn't want you this much, then, either. We've had a long time to think about it."

She didn't deny that she'd been thinking of him all that time, and he took satisfaction from that. She might not have liked that she was obsessed with him, might have fought it with all the strength of her upper-class background, but she'd lost the fight. If she hadn't, she wouldn't be lying beneath him now, her hands reaching for his hips, wanting this union more than anything in the world.

"Wait," he whispered. He caught her hand and brought it over her head. Then he pulled her other hand there, too, and circled both wrists in the fingers of his left hand. "Let it build."

She arched like a bow, her wrists and her hips anchoring her to the bed. "Chase...I need you now."

"You'll need me more in a little while."

"No." She moved her head back and forth on the pillow. "I couldn't want you more than this. I feel like screaming."

"Don't." He leaned down and covered her mouth with his, but he didn't push into her, much as his aching loins begged him to. He left room for his right hand, his gearshift hand, he thought wryly, to bring her to another level of awareness. He absorbed her moans into his mouth as he fondled her breasts—cupping their weight, massaging their fullness, caressing the nipples until his fingers were sticky with milk.

He trailed his knuckles between her ribs to her navel, where he pressed gently, knowing she was sensitive there. The music surged around them, through them, as he moved the knuckle of his index finger lower, finding the jewel buried in a thicket of curls. He rubbed gently, then with more force as she lifted her hips. When she was wild with sensation, he stopped, letting her fall gradually back to earth as he kissed her.

"You are insane," she said against his mouth.

His heart thundered as if he'd just survived a pileup on the freeway. "I think you're right."

"When, Chase? When will you give me what I want?"

"Now." He thrust deep, catching her by surprise.

She gasped and her eyes flew open. He gazed down at her, wanting her to remember his face for the rest of her life. "It may never feel like this again, Amanda." He released her hands.

"Chase…"

His mouth curved. "As they say on the bumper stickers—'get in, sit down, shut up and hang on.'"

He abandoned the rhythm of the sedate music now. It was too tame for what was about to happen between them. He drew back and pushed in tight again, a movement that brought her hands to his shoulders and her nails into his skin. He didn't care. This was worth bleeding for.

His next movement was more forceful, and she bucked when he applied pressure to that tiny spot that controlled so much of her. Yes, Amanda. We might wake the baby this time. Again he came in, and again, always on target, while the momentum built in him just as surely, just as potently. Again. Oh, Amanda. He'd meant to stay in control until she crossed the line. He'd planned this all in his head—until the moment when his control snapped, and he plunged into her with a frenzy that mocked him with its power.

She rose beneath him calling his name as spasms shook her. It was all he needed to explode like a gasoline tank touched by a match. He was flying apart, yet anchored to safety, all at the same time. It was a pedal-to-the-metal ride of passion, and he'd never known anything like it.

THROUGH THE DELIRIOUS haze of pleasure that settled over Amanda in the aftermath of Chase's loving, came the soft croaking sounds of Bartholomew, waking up. It was her fault, she knew. She'd tried to be quiet, but Chase had robbed her of reason.

Chase lay against her, his chest hair causing delicious friction against her breasts, the pewter medallion making a remembered imprint on her skin.

"I have to get him," she murmured.

"I know. We woke him up."

"I did."

"I did my share of making noise," Chase said. "Want me to get him and bring him to you?"

It was a novel, beautiful concept that had never occurred to Amanda before. "Yes. Please."

Chase eased out of her, made a quick trip to the bathroom and then lifted Bartholomew from his cradle. "Hey, Bart," he crooned. "How's it going, big guy? Is the neighborhood a little rowdy for you?"

Amanda propped her head on her fist and watched them in the pale light that drifted in the window. Chase looked like a statue by Rodin as he stood silvered by moonlight. Bartholomew stopped his hiccuping little cries and seemed to study the new situation—being rescued from his bed at night by this person with a deep voice and gentle hands.

Perhaps not so gentle, Amanda thought as she remembered how he'd exacted his toll, wringing the last bit of response from her as if he wanted nothing to remain inside. Ah, but he'd miscalculated. No sooner had he left her bed than she'd begun to yearn again, and that yearning had started the cycle all over. He'd said it might never be like that again, and perhaps he was right, but she'd like to find out.

However, first there was Bartholomew to deal with. "Bring him here," she murmured.

"Want to go see Mom? I guess so. You won't find what you're looking for here."

Chase's soft laugh tickled down Amanda's spine. She was lost and she knew it. The cowboy had won her heart.

He walked over to the bed and laid Bartholomew in her arms. "He's no dummy. He knows where the good stuff is."

Right in this room, Amanda thought with a rush of emotion. *All I need to be happy is right in this room.* She nestled Bartholomew against her and gave him her breast.

Chase stood silhouetted against the window, his back to her. "That is the sweetest sound."

"What?"

"Him nursing. I love to hear it."

And babies nurse for such a short time, Amanda thought. Perhaps by the time she returned to Arizona, Bartholomew would be weaned. But she didn't say that. The moment was too perfect to spoil. She stroked her baby's head and admired the sturdy outline of his father standing at the window.

Chase turned and walked back to the bed. "I want to stay the night, Amanda."

"I expected you to."

"I wasn't sure." He eased back into bed. "You're used to your space."

"It's nice having you here." She sighed. "God, we sound so polite."

He chuckled. "Kind of silly, isn't it? One minute we're as close as two people can be, and the next we're talking like strangers who happen to be sharing a table at a crowded restaurant.''

"That's because this is so backward. We made love for one night and became parents. How are two people supposed to handle that?''

"It's been confusing, all right." He trailed a finger down the side of her breast, stopping just short of her nipple, where Bartholomew was fastened, his pudgy hands pressing against the fullness. "But I wouldn't want to change any of it."

She met his gaze over the top of Bartholomew's fuzzy head, and time seemed to stop. At the moment, that was all she wanted.

12

AMANDA HAD WONDERED if Chase would be jealous of the baby's needs. Yet he lay with his chin propped on his hand and watched with an indulgent smile as she nursed Bartholomew. Then, true to his word, he helped change him, all the while holding the palm of his hand ready to deflect accidents.

"Pretty impressive equipment, Bart," he said with obvious pride as he gazed down at the naked little boy squirming on the bed between them.

"As if that's the measure of a man." Amanda fastened the adhesive tabs on the diaper and reached for the soft cotton shirt she'd laid on the bedside table.

"Hey, it's a start." Chase leaned toward the baby and whispered, "Don't let her kid you, Bart, old buddy. They all say they don't care about size and pretend it's our hang-up. But I've seen *Playgirl* magazine. They care."

Bartholomew gurgled and grabbed Chase's nose. Chase cried out in mock pain as Bartholomew crowed and tugged harder. Amanda laughed and wished she had a camera. Then she realized that she'd just had the urge to record Chase and Bartholomew together on film. If anyone saw that, one picture would be worth a thousand words.

"So you think you can lead people around by the nose?" Chase eased the baby's fingers loose. "I'll bet your mother taught you that trick." He glanced up at Amanda and gave her a wink.

"I beg your pardon." She tried to adopt his bantering tone as she popped the shirt over Bartholomew's head. But her heart was too full from watching them together.

"Then again, maybe it hasn't been my nose you've been leading me around by," he said softly, his teeth flashing white in the pale light as he smiled at her. "It might be something a bit lower. I wasn't very good at anatomy in school."

She scooped Bartholomew up and slid out of bed. "But I imagine you were very good at anatomy after school was out." She turned toward the cradle.

"No comment. But what about you, Amanda? Did you kiss the boys and make them cry?"

She adjusted the blanket in the cradle, not feeling very comfortable talking about her romantic past, or lack of it. "My story is pretty dull. You'd get bored in a heartbeat." She settled Bartholomew down on the blanket and rocked him gently with one hand.

"Try me."

"I was quiet, a bookworm. Always writing, drawing, reading. When I wasn't doing that, I was riding my horse. And I was—still am—a feminist. I saw dating and marriage as a trap for women, so I didn't aim in that direction."

"Never even engaged?"

"Once. It didn't work out." She gazed down at Bartholomew. She'd never seen him so relaxed, as if the doting attention of both parents was exactly what he needed. Gradually, his eyes drifted closed. She rocked a while longer before standing and walking back to the bed. "From the way I acted in the truck that night, you probably thought I was a real swinging chick, but I'm not. I'd never behaved that way before."

He reached out and caught her hand, drawing her back down to the bed. "That's what made you different," he murmured, curving his arm around her waist and urging her against him until they were pressed together in sweet tension. "You were scared and excited at the same time." He massaged the length of her spine as he talked. "I figured the only times you'd ever been to bed with a man were after you'd known him a long time."

"That's true." Barely tamped desire flared at his touch, sending heated signals that tightened her nipples and moistened the pulsing channel he had so recently explored. "You were an adventure," she said. "My one chance to be a naughty girl."

Chase cupped her bottom with both hands, kneading her flesh. "And was I wild enough for you?"

Her body grew languorous and willing as his erection pressed against her belly. "You were...very nice."

"The hell with nice." He adjusted his body to hers, positioning her so that his shaft separated the folds of her femininity. "Nice is what those other guys were, the ones you had dinner with a million times before you let them touch you like this." His movements were subtle but powerful as he eased up and down, connecting with her most sensitive spot without entering her.

She grew breathless with the mounting tension. His ability to bring her to flashpoint so quickly was unnerving. "You were incredible," she managed to say.

"So were you," he said in a gruff voice. "Inexperience isn't necessarily a bad thing."

"Chase." She gripped him urgently. "Kiss me, Chase, before I wake...the baby."

He muffled her cries with his mouth as a climax shattered the last of her reserve. As the quivering subsided, he moved from her lips to the curve of her ear. "Are you getting warmed up?" he whispered.

She sighed. "I think so."

"I was hoping you were. There are a few things I'd like you to do for me." Then he murmured his requests, requests that turned the blood that was already singing through her veins into molten lava. His loving had removed all shame. Rising over him, she satisfied the first of his wishes by trailing her fiery hair over him, tickling and tantalizing his chest, his inner thighs, his quivering erection. She wrapped her hair around that throbbing shaft and drew it away slowly, judging the effect by the rasp of his breathing and the clenching of his hands.

Then she used her tongue on his muscular body, laving his tanned skin until he was quivering in anticipation. His control was incredible. When she touched his shaft with the tip of her tongue, all she heard was an intake of breath—between clenched teeth. She took her time. After all, he'd asked her to. But at last she heard a muted plea of "enough."

She slid up to kiss his mouth and he rolled her to her back in a fierce embrace.

"Any more experience and you'll be dangerous," he gasped, looming over her, his eyes glittering.

She laughed softly, triumphantly, and arched her breasts upward in invitation.

With a moan he accepted the invitation, sending reverberations spiraling downward to her heated center as he sucked.

"Come to me," she begged, abandoning all modesty. "I want you inside me."

He lifted his head and gazed down at her, his

breathing harsh. "I've never wanted anyone this much."

His words set off skyrockets in her head. "Neither have I. Oh, Chase, what are we going to do?"

The corner of his mouth tilted up. "I know what we're going to do right this minute." He reached for one of the condoms on the table.

Bartholomew stirred and started to cry.

Chase paused in midmotion. "Maybe not just this minute."

"I'll try rocking him." Battling her frustration, Amanda rolled to her stomach and reached for the edge of the cradle. She rocked it slowly, easing Bartholomew back into sleep. Behind her, cellophane crinkled, and she trembled just thinking of Chase sheathing himself, Chase waiting for her.

He trailed a finger down her backbone. "How's he doing?" he murmured.

"Going back to sleep." She stopped rocking as Bartholomew's breathing grew steady. At last she removed her hand from the edge of the cradle with a sigh.

"Time to go off duty for a while," Chase said. Caressing her bottom, he slipped his hand between her thighs and probed gently until he gained the entrance he sought. With deft fingers he stroked, and she unconsciously lifted herself into the caress.

His breath caught. His knee brushed hers as he moved behind her and guided her farther upward, caressing, encouraging her with soft endearments. Heart racing, body pounding with urges outside her experience, she complied, rising to her knees and offering herself in a way that reached back beyond the rules of civilization, to a time of caves, flickering fires and base needs satisfied.

When he eased into her, she gasped at the primitive carnality of the gesture. The lust of animals flowed through her, and she took her lip between her teeth to keep from crying out her fevered response. His hips tight against her buttocks, he slid his hand over her thigh and into the moist valley where her pleasure point lay. And she dimly recognized that this was the difference that separated such a basic act from the mating of animals—he would give while he took. She became sensation itself as he moved rhythmically inside her and coaxed her to greater heights with firm pressure from his fingers.

As the tempo increased, she fought to be silent, knowing from muffled groans that he waged the same war. When the moment came, she pressed her lips together and whimpered. She heard his gasp, his final, shuddering thrust, and she absorbed the pulsing impact of his climax. They trembled together for a moment before he withdrew and she sank to the cool sheets, her body sapped of the will to move.

He left the bed for only a moment, and soon he was back, lying beside her and smoothing her hair from her face.

She gave him a sated smile. "I think that qualifies as wild enough."

He smiled back, a lazy, contented smile. "Did I shock you?"

"A little."

He brushed a finger across her lower lip. "Good."

"Are you setting out to shock me?"

"I'm setting out to show you what you've been missing."

AS LONG AS the room remained dark, Amanda could allow feelings to override thoughts, touch to supplant words. But toward dawn, as objects in the room took on a sharper edge, so did the meandering of her mind. Chase dozed beside her, an arm flung over her waist. She liked the weight of it there far too much. She still had no idea if this drifter lying beside her had decided to change his wandering ways, and what it meant to her future if he had.

The passion they'd generated through the night could all be the work of an accomplished lover seducing a woman who'd lived like a nun for almost a year. Yet she suspected something far more complex had happened in the large four-poster bed. Originally, Chase had been no more than a fantasy figure, a sexy blue-collar worker willing to provide earthy, inhibition-shattering sex. But in the past two days he'd become so much more to her—a man who'd struggled against the odds to establish an identity, a father capable of incredible gentleness toward his child and a tender partner in lovemaking, a partner willing to put aside past hurts for present pleasure.

By some miracle, Chase Lavette had emerged from his unhappy background with a generous spirit. Far more generous than hers, Amanda admitted with chagrin. Yet in the warmth of Chase's arms, her reservations melted away and she began to dream of ways they could be together, all three of them. And as well, she wasn't ready to abandon the search for his family. The information was still important for Bartholomew's sake, but she thought it was important for Chase, too. Everyone had some good news in their background. She wanted to help Chase find his.

The telephone rang, startling her out of her reverie. She picked up the antique handset and answered in a muted voice.

Ry was on the other end, sounding frazzled. "Amanda? I hate like the devil to bother you this early, but is Chase there?"

The realization that everyone on the True Love would know Chase had spent the night gave her a mild shock. She wasn't used to people knowing her intimate business. "Yes, he is." She covered the mouthpiece and glanced at Chase, who lay with his head on his outstretched arm, looking at her with an unreadable expression. "It's Ry." She handed him the receiver.

Chase took it and rolled to his back, tugging the cloth-covered cord across Amanda. "This better be important, bridegroom." He turned his head to look at Amanda and noticed the spiral cord stretched across her bare breasts. With a little smile he eased the cord back and forth across her nipples, which snapped to attention at the casual contact.

How easily he demonstrated his power over her. She would have resented that power if she hadn't glanced down and noticed his penis stir and gradually stiffen as he gazed at her breasts.

"Sure, I'll do that," Chase said. "No problem. How is everyone this morning?" He drew the cord across her breast more slowly this time. "Glad to hear it. Yeah, I'll pick them up by seven and be back before eight. Don't worry, nobody wants to miss watching you get branded, buddy. See you soon." He took the receiver from his ear.

She reached for it, disappointed that he'd referred to Ry's marriage vows as "getting branded." Maybe she'd better rein in her thoughts of a close relationship with this drifter. They'd had good sex. Perhaps that was all they were to have together. "Want me to hang that up for you?"

"Not when things are becoming interesting." He propped himself on his elbow and dragged the cord over her nipple one more time. "Maybe not at all. We don't need any calls right now."

Her breathing quickened. "Don't you have to leave?"

"Not yet." He curled the cord around the fullness of her breast. "Ry needs me to pick up Belinda and Dexter at the hospital, but it's only a little after five now." He pulled the cord a little tighter and looked into her eyes. "How come the phone didn't wake up the little guy?"

"He's used to that noise, I guess." Her eyes widened as he drew the cord down between her legs. "At the apartment I get a lot of calls..." She gasped as he slid the cord into the cleft of her femininity. "...from work."

"Sounds like you needed this vacation." He laid the receiver between her legs and drew the cord gently upward, making sure each ascending spiral teased her to a higher level of arousal. Then he picked up the receiver and drew the cord down again.

She was aflame for him. "Chase, you'll get the telephone cord—"

"Wet? Looks like it."

"But the management..." She moaned as he eased the cord back down.

"I am the management, sweetheart." He pulled the cord in a little tighter. "There, that should mark my place for a minute. Don't move." He kept his gaze on her as he put on the condom. She didn't move, but her body hummed like an engine that had been started and needed only the slightest touch on the throttle to leap forward.

Then he was back, moving between her thighs, replacing the telephone cord with his fingers, but leaving the receiver beside them on the bed, off the hook. "Just where I left off," he whispered. "Good morning, sweet-heart."

"Good...morning," she whispered back, arching into his caress. She'd thought this morning they'd talk, but he didn't seem to want to leave time for that.

Lifting her hips still more he slid into her effortlessly.

Through a sensuous haze she looked up into his face. Unspoken words of love trembled on her lips, words that might drive him away. After all, he wouldn't want to risk being branded like his partner Ry. "You're very good at this, cowboy," she murmured instead.

A shadow seemed to cross his expression, almost as if she'd insulted him, somehow. His jaw tensed. "You bet I am, babe," he said, his tone almost harsh. Then he loved her hard, wringing a response from her, taking his own pleasure, and leaving her feeling strangely empty. He departed the cottage with few words. Amanda stared at the closed door as tears burned her eyes and the dreams she had begun to weave hung in tatters around her.

BETWEEN BRINGING Dexter and Belinda home and help-ing the hands with the horses, Chase kept busy prior to the wedding. But he still had time to think and cool off a little. Amanda probably hadn't meant her remark the way it had sounded, but after she'd said it, he'd thought she saw him as just another hunk of meat, the way women had been reacting to him all his life. Not so long ago that had been okay, and had even given him brag-ging rights with the truckers he knew. But for the first time in his life he wanted more than sex from a woman. He wanted lovemaking. He had no practice asking for that, and it took so little to send him running for cover.

Maybe sometime during the day he'd work up the courage to talk to her, really talk.

As his last chore before the wedding, he'd volunteered to drive a buggy from the corrals to the main house while Duane and the hands led the string of horses. The buggy was for Dexter and Belinda, so they could make it out to the homestead site.

When he arrived, the wedding party was milling around in the front yard, men and women separated into same-sex groups while Duane and Leigh tried to keep some order. The men wore brightly patterned western shirts, while the women had opted for broomstick skirts and fluffy blouses. All except Amanda, whose turquoise dress was probably a designer number from Fifth Avenue. She stood talking to Belinda with Bartholomew held against her shoulder.

As she turned to shade the baby from the sun, the light caught in her red hair and Chase's heart wrenched with longing. He wanted to go over and apologize for his abruptness this morning, but now wasn't the time, not with so many people around. Amanda spoke to Freddy, who moved restlessly though the crowd of women. She wore a dress of snowy lace decorated with long white fringe that danced as she walked. Ry had told him that Freddy's outfit had been modified from a dress that had belonged to her grandmother. Freddy had added a white Stetson draped with a white scarf and white lace-up granny boots.

It wasn't much of a mental stretch for Chase to imagine Amanda in bridal white, but he shoved the image aside, frightened by the unfamiliar desires it produced in him. Wanting something you might never have was dangerous.

Ry stood in the center of the group of men. He looked

hot, but he'd insisted on wearing a black western jacket over his white shirt and black western-cut slacks. Love did crazy things to a man, Chase thought. Dexter stood nearby, balancing himself on his walker.

Duane's call for attention got nowhere. Finally, he hopped up on the three-foot wall surrounding the yard and whistled through his teeth. "That's more like it," he said as everyone turned in his direction. "Now, I got to tell everybody—you're responsible for yer own horse." He paused, and notwithstanding his new shirt and bolo tie, spat into the dirt. "They're all saddled and ready to go, but some of 'em tend to blow out, so before you get aboard, check that cinch. Everybody know how to do that?"

A chorus of confirming shouts made Chase grin and shake his head. These dudes would sooner die than admit they didn't know their way around horses. He could identify. Six weeks ago he'd been the same way. He made a mental note to check Amanda's cinch, although she might be the one greenhorn who would know how. She'd had her own horse, after all. Probably was also given a sports car when she was sixteen and had tuition paid to a fancy college. He needed to remember all that when he was spinning fantasies involving Amanda.

"Now, as soon as Eb Whitlock shows up, we'll start on out to the homestead," Duane said.

Chase realized then that Eb's big palomino wasn't tied up to the hitching post, and Eb wasn't part of the crowd of men clustered around Ry. He could guess how steamed Ry must be, considering he didn't want Eb to be part of the wedding in the first place.

"Here he comes!" shouted someone as Eb's dual-wheeled pickup and horse trailer rumbled down the road sending up clouds of dust. Eb braked to a stop and the dust cloud settled over the wedding party and the horses Duane and Curtis had so carefully groomed for the event. Men brushed at their shoulders, women at their skirts as Eb, wearing a pearl gray western coat, vest and matching hat, climbed down from the air-conditioned cab of his truck with a politician's wave and his truck-grille smile.

"Howdy, folks," he said. "Nice day for a wedding, ain't it? Hey, Duane, give me a hand unloading Gold Strike," he called as he started back toward the trailer.

"Shore." As Duane passed Chase in the buggy, he paused. "Guess you and Leigh might as well get the rest of 'em mounted up while I help unload the wonder horse," he said in a low tone.

"He knew better than to ask me," Leigh grumbled as she came up beside the buggy. "You just watch. That gelding will be covered with horse jewelry."

Chase laughed. "What?"

"Silver on every inch of leather except the seat of the saddle. Just wait and see. In the meantime, we'd better divvy up these ponies. Give Amanda Pussywillow."

Chase climbed down from the buggy. "I thought Ry's stepmother wanted her."

"She did, but she doesn't ride as well as Amanda."

"How do you know how well Amanda rides?"

"I was out in the yard holding my stomach and watching for the ambulance when she tore in here yesterday." Leigh looked up at Chase from under her pink maid-of-honor Stetson. "She has the makings of a cowgirl, you know."

"Yeah, right. I'm sure she'd give up her big paycheck in New York to come out and wrangle for the True Love."

"You never know until you ask."

Chase's stomach flip-flopped at the idea and he changed the subject. "Okay, Ry's best man will be on Mikey, right?"

"Right. He wanted Destiny, but forget that. He thinks he's a hotshot around horses, but he doesn't have a clue."

"What's his name again?"

"Stewart. Stewart Hepplewaite. Now let's see." Leigh tapped her finger against her chin. "We'll put Ry's stepmother on Bobby. He's steady. And Ry's mother on Billy."

Chase forced himself to concentrate as she rattled off the rest of the horse assignments he was supposed to handle. He started toward the group of people on the lawn just as a collective gasp made him turn around to see what they were all staring at. He was nearly blinded by the reflected light coming off Gold Strike's saddle, headstall and breastplate as the big horse backed out of the trailer. But Leigh hadn't been entirely right about the horse jewelry. The trim on the leather wasn't silver. It was gold.

Chase chuckled and continued with his duties. As he was approaching Stewart Hepplewaite to give him the bad news that he'd be riding Mikey and not Destiny, Ry caught his arm.

"Did you see that s.o.b.?" he muttered.

"Meaning Whitlock," Chase said, holding back a smile.

"He's trying to impress Freddy, and convince her she's making a mistake marrying me instead of him."

Chase couldn't resist. "Think it's working?"

Ry scowled. "Oh, hell, of course not, but the guy's so damned irritating." Ry lowered his voice. "I'd love to nail him for these ranch accidents, just for the pure satisfaction of it."

"Just don't let the fact that he's a jerk get in the way of clear thinking, buddy. I hope it's him instead of somebody close, like Duane or Belinda. But that's not always the way things work." He clapped Ry on the shoulder. "Time to mount up, bridegroom. Red Devil looks almost as antsy as you do, so be careful. We'd all hate to see you land on your butt during the ceremony."

"If it happens, I'm blaming Whitlock. Between that gold tack and the shine on his teeth, he could signal passing aircraft. I'll be amazed if he doesn't spook somebody's horse."

"Hey, you two, get a move on," Leigh called over to them.

Ry glanced at Chase. "Okay, I'm going."

"You could look a little happier about it," Chase called after him. Then he went in search of Stewart Hepplewaite.

Twenty minutes later, the procession jingled and clopped down the road toward the homestead. The wedding would be late. Ry and Freddy led the way, so they wouldn't get too much dust on their wedding clothes. Leigh and Duane had set up the procession like a cattle drive, with each of them riding point. Curtis and Ernie manned the middle as swing riders, Davis and Rusty rode flank and Chase rode drag with Jack, behind the buggy. Belinda handled Clyde, the ranch's big draft horse, with ease. Between her and Dexter sat Chloe, whose tongue was hanging out, ears alert. Propped behind the seat was an easel and the framed lintel from the old homestead.

Chase had asked to be in the back, because he

thought it was the safest place for Bart, who was laced into the cradleboard on his back.

Ahead of him Amanda rode next to Stewart Hepplewaite and the two of them were laughing and talking like old friends. Stewart was her kind of guy, no doubt, a polished New Yorker who could probably name every damn tune that had played on the radio the night before. Chase felt like strangling Stewart Hepplewaite.

Miraculously, the procession arrived without incident at the clearing where the homestead had once stood. Duane dismounted and set up the easel with the framed lintel propped on it. Positioning his horse beside the easel, the minister turned to face the group while Ry and Stewart Hepplewaite arranged their mounts on his left and Leigh guided her horse to the minister's right. The horses snorted and stamped some, but none of them acted up except Red Devil, Ry's big chestnut. He kept throwing his head back, and Chase wondered how long it would be before Ry caught it on the chin.

Freddy and Eb Whitlock moved to the back of the group, which assembled on either side of the clearing. Now that Hepplewaite was otherwise occupied, Chase maneuvered next to Amanda. Curtis untied his guitar from his saddle and began to play the wedding march as Freddy laid her hand on Eb's arm and they nudged their horses into a rhythmic walk.

Chase hadn't expected the ceremony to get to him, but his eyes began to burn and his throat closed up. He glanced at Amanda and discovered she was looking straight at him, her eyes shining with unshed tears. He felt as if he'd been kicked in the gut by Gold Strike. Caught in the brightness of her blue eyes, he couldn't look away as Curtis played the final note on the guitar and Freddy and Ry began exchanging their vows.

Chase had attended a few weddings, mostly for truckers he knew. He'd always thought the language was ridiculous. Everyone knew people didn't stay married "until death do us part" anymore.

And yet...

This time, looking into Amanda's eyes, the words took on a luster he'd never heard. Maybe it was because he knew Freddy and Ry would make it. They had love and grit enough to last until death took them. And if one couple could make it...

Amanda's gaze softened, and Chase would have bet money she was thinking the same thing. Then she smiled, and that smile sent sunshine pouring into his aching heart. Maybe, just maybe...

A ripple of laughter from the group brought his attention back to the ceremony. He blinked, not realizing at first what had happened. Then he remembered Duane's instructions about tightening cinches. Apparently, Stewart Hepplewaite hadn't followed orders. As he'd leaned toward Ry to hand him the ring, his saddle had begun to rotate.

Everyone stared in mesmerized silence as Stewart clutched the horn and rode the saddle slowly down. Gravity pulled it toward the underbelly of the horse, which is where he would have ended up if Ry hadn't reined Red Devil in closer at the last minute, stopping the fall when Stewart was perpendicular to the ground.

Stewart landed with his head in Ry's lap.

13

THE LOOSE CINCH ended the run of good luck. Red Devil tossed his head back for the hundredth time, but Ry's attention was on Stewart reclining in his lap and Red Devil knocked Ry's hat off. The hat spinning to the ground spooked Maureen, Freddy's mare, who reared, her hooves coming down on the easel holding the framed lintel.

Both Ry's mother and stepmother started screaming. That noise, added to the splintering of the easel, sent the minister's horse into a bucking fit that dislodged the minister, who slid from the horse's rump onto a small but very thorny hedgehog cactus. Chloe leapt from the buggy, her usual restraint destroyed, and raced around barking. Eb Whitlock spun in ineffectual circles on Gold Strike, seemingly unable to control the horse as sunlight flashed off the gold tack until Chase saw spots in front of his eyes.

Chase backed his horse away from the general pandemonium, not wanting to endanger Bart. But Amanda waded right in on Pussywillow. Chase watched in open admiration as she grabbed Gold Strike's bridle and halted the palomino's spin. Chloe miraculously obeyed Amanda's command to return to the buggy, and then Amanda worked side by side with the cowhands soothing mounts and reassuring edgy riders.

Eventually, Stewart was sitting upright on Mikey

once more, the ring was placed on Freddy's finger, and the minister, who chose to stand, pronounced them husband and wife. They kissed as passionately as their restless mounts would allow, and Curtis played a recessional as they straggled back to the ranch house, the minister riding high in his stirrups for the duration of the trip.

By the time they returned, the clearing around the ranch house looked like a used-truck lot. Ranching friends from all over the valley had arrived for the reception, and they crowded around to congratulate the bride and groom. Chase reined his horse past the well-wishers and headed for the hitching post. Bart was beginning to fuss.

As Chase dismounted, Amanda rode up on Pussywillow. "I'll take him now," she said, swinging down and tethering Pussywillow.

Chase eased the leather straps off his shoulders as she stood behind him to take the cradleboard. "Got him?"

"Yes."

"I think he's getting hungry." Chase turned. "If you'll hold him, I'll unlace this thing. I don't think you want to try and carry him through that mob still strapped in."

"Probably not." Amanda held the board steady while Chase pulled the laces free. "He was good though, during the ceremony. I was afraid he'd cry and spoil it."

Chase laughed as he pulled Bart from the wrapped blanket. "And goodness knows, we wouldn't have wanted to spoil the ceremony. It was so picture perfect."

Amanda chuckled. "Can you believe the way Stewart slid around into Ry's lap? What an idiot."

"I don't think he tightened his cinch, do you?" Chase

said with a grin as he hoisted Bart to his shoulder. Life was turning out pretty well, after all.

"Nope." Amanda's eyes brimmed with merriment. "I wouldn't have missed that wedding for the world. What a hoot."

"Sure was." He couldn't stop gazing into her eyes. "You did a great job settling people down. Leigh must be right. She predicted that you'd make a good cowgirl."

"Did she?" Amanda looked pleased, and his hopes soared higher. "Coming from Leigh, that's a big compliment."

He hesitated. "Amanda, we need to talk. I—"

Bartholomew's cry interrupted him.

"We'll talk," Amanda said. "Later."

"Is that a promise?"

"Yes." She held out the cradleboard. "Trade you."

He held Bart in one arm and took the cradleboard with his free hand. "I'll be waiting."

"Me, too." Then with a smile that turned his insides to mush, she took the baby from him and left.

AMANDA KEPT EXPECTING the wedding reception to wind down, but the party seemed to gain momentum as afternoon turned into evening. Freddy and Ry showed no signs of leaving on their honeymoon—a week in the pine forests of Mount Lemmon, little more than an hour's drive away. The guests obviously felt that as long as the bride and groom remained, the party should continue in full swing.

Amanda surveyed the patio, proud of the way everything looked and her part in making it that way. While strolling *mariachis* played, people ignored the heat, drank beer and margaritas and ate Belinda's food as if no one even considered the possibility of food poisoning. Yet Amanda couldn't help wondering if they would be so unconcerned once they'd heard the gossip that would inevitably spring up surrounding yesterday's disaster. A rumor of food poisoning in one New York restaurant had damaged its reputation beyond what any of her ad campaigns had been able to repair. She didn't want that happening to the True Love. She had to admit her growing fondness for the place, or maybe it was the tall cowboy who was one-third owner she was growing fond of.

Bartholomew seemed to enjoy the color and activity of the party. She alternated between putting him in his carrier, where he sometimes dozed off, and holding him. She slipped into Freddy's office twice to feed him, but otherwise she kept him in the thick of things. He acted like a magnet for the guests, and nearly everyone came by to admire and coo. Everybody except Chase, that is. But that was okay. The promise of talking to him before the day ended shone like a beacon for Amanda. She hadn't been mistaken. The wedding ceremony had stirred him as much as it had her. Whatever misunderstanding had caused him to stomp off this morning would be ironed out.

Not that the problems would end there. She'd decided to tell her family about Chase, but she didn't expect them to react well. And the logistics of a future relationship would be tricky, unless Chase agreed to the plan she'd dreamed up this afternoon. She could hardly wait to tell him about it. And then there was the medallion. She'd finally figured out where she'd seen one like it.

Duane came by her table, a beer in one hand and an empty coffee can in the other. "Havin' fun?"

"Yes, I am," she said with a smile.

"Jest wanted to thank you for helpin' with the commotion out there." He angled his head in the direction of the road to the old homestead. "Didn't know you was so handy with horses."

"I'm glad I could help."

"You recall how Red Devil was tossin' his head?"

Amanda nodded. "He's pretty high-spirited."

"Not that high. When we took off his bridle, we found a big old burr under there. Must've been drivin' him crazy."

"That was unlucky."

"More'n unlucky." Duane scowled and spat a stream of tobacco into the coffee can. "That don't happen 'round here. The hands are real careful about stuff like that." Duane eyed her. "I think some low-down snake put it under there on purpose."

"You mean as a wedding prank?"

"Maybe more'n a prank." He gave her a dark look. "Did Chase tell you about what's been goin' on?"

"No." She grew uneasy. "I don't know what you're talking about."

Duane nodded and glanced away. "Guess he didn't want to worry you none."

Alarm ran through her and she thought immediately of the snake under her bed. "So what is going on?"

"I'd best let Chase tell you." Duane reached out and wiggled Bartholomew's foot. "See you later, cowpoke."

"Duane—" She closed her mouth as he walked away resolutely. Now she had a second reason to talk to Chase. If this place was booby-trapped, she wanted to know it. She had a child to protect.

CHASE LOVED HIS SON, but the more he thought about this critical talk with Amanda, the more he wanted to have it without the distraction of a baby. He studied the situation in the patio and finally approached Belinda, tossing his empty beer can into a bin of recyclables on his way.

She glanced up with a twinkle in her eye. "I hope all the festivities are giving you ideas, Chase."

He grinned at her. "Could be, Belinda. Matter of fact, I'm here to ask a favor. I need to talk to Amanda alone, and I wondered if you'd watch Bart for a little while. Last time I checked, he was sound asleep, so I don't think he'll be much trouble."

"That little baby would never be too much trouble. Dexter's been wanting to see him. I'll take Bartholomew over and sit with Dexter and Chloe for a while."

"That's only if it's okay with Amanda. I haven't asked her yet."

Belinda smiled, and for a moment she looked like a young girl again. "You leave her to me. I'll set it up. Where would you like her to meet you?"

Chase sorted through the possibilities. Guests clustered everywhere—the patio, the main room of the house and the front porch. "Out in back, I guess, just beyond the gate. I'll wait for her," he said.

"How romantic. I'll send her out to you." Belinda turned and headed for the table where Amanda sat talking to Ry's mother.

Chase mentally crossed his fingers and strode toward the back-patio gate. On the way he tried to figure out what to say to her. The word *love* buzzed around in his brain like a honeybee. He wasn't sure he was ready for that word yet, but he was ready to tell Amanda that she meant a lot to him and that he didn't want to lose her. He wondered if he'd have the nerve to ask her to stay in Arizona. Leigh thought he should. Maybe there was work in her field in Tucson. She'd seemed pleased about being called a cowgirl. She got along with everybody. Maybe she was beginning to like it here, and if not, he'd make love to her so often, she wouldn't have time to think about where she was living.

He glanced up at the sky as he slipped through the gate, leaving it open a couple of feet. A few clouds remained clustered around the mountains, and once in a while they'd light up as if somebody had turned on a switch inside them. But it didn't look as if it would rain tonight, after all. Selfishly, Chase was glad. It gave him this chance to be outside in the warm summer night, waiting for Amanda. He moved into the shadows near the thick adobe wall. The laughter and music from the reception breached the wall, but the adobe buffered the noise just enough so that he and Amanda would be able to talk.

The trouble was, when she opened the gate and stepped through, with moonlight gilding her hair as she glanced around for him, he no longer wanted to talk. "Over here," he said, his voice stretched as tight as the fabric of his jeans. He stepped from the shadows and she came toward him, moving quickly.

When she was within reach, he pulled her close with a groan, his mouth seeking hers. He thought his chest would explode when he realized she was grabbing at him with an equal hunger, her fingers digging into his back, her pelvis pushing hard against his erection.

He kissed her mouth, her cheeks, the curve of her throat. "I need you, Amanda."

"I need you, too," she whispered desperately. "Why did you get so angry with me this morning?"

"It was stupid." He leaned down and kissed the swell of her breasts above the scooped neckline of her dress. "When you told me how good I was, I thought you only wanted me for sex, like every other woman I've ever taken to bed."

"Oh, Chase." There was amusement in her voice as she stroked his hair. "You thought I considered you a sex object?"

"Something like that." He unfastened the top two buttons of her dress and slipped his hand beneath her bra.

"And you wanted me to think of you as more than that."

"Yes. I—" As he stroked her warm breast heavy with milk, he lost his train of thought and picked up a new one. "Ah, Amanda, you feel like silk. Let's forget about the reception. I'll get Bart and we can head back to the cottage."

She arched against his palm. "What if I feel like a sex object?"

"It's not like that, and you know it."

"I do?" she said softly.

His hand stilled and he gazed into her eyes. "I don't know if I can be any good at this, but I...want to work something out. I want to be with you...somehow."

"That's an interesting thought." Her lips curved. "Half-formed, but interesting."

"I'm glad you think so." He massaged her breast and leaned down to nibble at the corner of her mouth. "Now let's go get Bart and head for the cottage so we can work out the details."

"You know if we do that we won't work out any details, and we have so much to talk about, so much we don't know about each other." She slipped her fingers under the chain around his neck. "Like this. Where did you get it?"

He lifted his head to gaze down at her. "Not from some other lover, if that's what you're worried about."

"Considering your independent nature, I didn't think so, either. Did the medallion belong to your mother?"

He released her and stepped back, suddenly wary. "Why?"

"Because if it did, I might know where it came from. My mother has one just like it. It was a citizenship award in eighth grade from a school in Brooklyn. She told me once that there's also a plaque at the school with the name of everyone who's ever won that award."

His chest tightened. When he was younger, he'd wondered what the little medallion meant and why his mother's name was inscribed on the back, but as he'd grown older, he'd just accepted it as the only part of her he had left. At fifteen, he'd bought a chain for it and he'd become so used to feeling its weight around his neck, he'd forgotten it was there.

When he started to speak, he realized his throat had seized up on him. He cleared it and tried again. "I...I guess that would be nice to know. Where it came from, I mean."

She grabbed his arm. "It could mean more than that. Maybe that school is a place to start, a way to find her."

He glanced away from the excitement in her expression. "Maybe. I know you want the information for Bart's sake, but I—"

"I want it for your sake."

That got his attention. "Me? Why me?"

"Chase, you didn't come from nowhere. You have grandparents, great-grandparents, aunts, uncles and cousins. You have family. Everyone does. Some good, some bad. One of my great-grandfathers was a horse thief. So what? That doesn't mean I'm a horse thief. The point is, you have connections. We should find them."

He drew her slowly back into his arms. "We?"

"I want to help."

"You might not like what you find."

"You weren't listening. You're not responsible for what's in your family tree. But wouldn't it be nice to know you had one?"

The concept was a little mind-boggling, and he was pretty sure if they located his mother it wouldn't be a pretty sight, but she looked so happy about the prospect of digging into his background he decided to go along with it. "Sure. Sure it would." He leaned closer, needing her lips against his. "Now, let's—"

"Wait. I have to ask you something else."

"Remind me never to give you a whole day to think about things."

She looked up at him earnestly. "Is there a problem here at the True Love?"

"Yes. Too damn many activities, when all I want to do is this." His mouth descended again.

She leaned away from his kiss. "I'm serious. Duane hinted at some trouble but he said you should be the one to tell me."

Thanks, Duane. Great timing. He sighed. Then he cupped her face in his hands and gazed down at her. "I don't know if there's trouble or not. We've had some incidents."

Anxiety shone in her eyes. "Like what?" she asked.

"Most of it's the sort of thing you could expect around a ranch. Stock tank leaks, breaks in the fence, gates left open. But the morning you got here, somebody contaminated the water in the horse troughs.

Thank God we discovered it before any horses got sick. And then there was the food poisoning. Ry doesn't think that was an accident, either."

Amanda's eyes were wide. "Duane found a burr under Red Devil's bridle when he turned him into the corral. Duane thinks it was put there on purpose, to louse up the wedding."

"Or maybe one of the hands screwed up," Chase said.

"What about the snake?"

"Oh, I don't think—"

"Why not? If someone wants to ruin the True Love's reputation or bring down the property's value, all of that makes sense. Would anyone have reason to want the True Love to go under?"

Chase released her again and rubbed the back of his neck. A headache was lodging at the base of his skull. That indicated tension, which could bring on a back spasm. And the way the party was going, he wouldn't be swimming laps tonight. "The three of us, Ry, me and Joe Gilardini, the cop, bought this place as an investment, figuring to sell it in a couple of years to developers."

Amanda drew in a sharp breath. "Do Freddy and Leigh know that? Does Belinda?"

Chase nodded. "Nobody liked the idea when they heard it. There's a steady campaign to get each of us to change our mind and become a gentleman rancher, instead. But Ry thinks somebody is going beyond that to outright sabotage. If the ranch isn't worth much, we might sell just to get out from under. Then someone else, someone who wants to keep it as a ranch, could buy it."

Amanda shivered. "If someone could be hurt, or

worse, I say let them have the ranch, whoever they are, if they're that desperate."

Chase was amazed at how he rebelled at that idea. "In the first place, we don't know who's doing it, and in the second place, speaking for Ry and me, we're not about to give up the True Love that easy."

"I thought you planned to sell it to developers eventually, anyway."

Chase massaged his neck and chuckled, mostly at himself. "Yeah, that's the way it was supposed to work."

"You don't want to sell, do you?"

It was an interesting question, and Chase didn't have the answer yet. "I guess that depends. There's a little more to the decision now than there was a few days ago. When I think of you and Bart, I have to consider the money angle. As a guest ranch, the True Love hasn't ever made a lot of money."

She cocked her head and gazed at him. "Then I guess this is the perfect time to tell you my idea. It finally hit me that cowboys are all the rage right now. If you come back to New York with me, I could set up modeling agency interviews. I know this business, Chase, and with that cowboy look you've developed, you'd be making more money than you ever dreamed of in no time at all." She paused. "And we could be together, which is something you said you wanted."

He stared at her and wondered if maybe he'd misunderstood. "This isn't a cowboy look, Amanda. This is what I am, now. It's what I was meant to be, I think, even when I was driving truck."

"Exactly! So you're authentic, and that would shine through in the ads. You'd be a huge success, Chase. I've been watching the way you move, and you'd be a natural in front of the camera. I don't know why I didn't think of it sooner."

He couldn't believe that such a warm, sexy woman could come up with such a harebrained idea. Rounding up members of his family tree he could go along with, but parading around in front of a camera pretending to be a cowboy instead of being out here on the ranch actually living that life would be the worst kind of hell he could imagine. Couldn't she see that? "It's not for me, Amanda."

She looked as if he'd slapped her. "You're rejecting the idea just like that? Without thinking about it?"

"Doesn't take much time to think about an idea like that. I'd hate it."

She spoke slowly, carefully. "Then what did you think we would do?"

And he saw it all very clearly, then. She'd come up with that plan because it would allow her to stay in her world and make him an acceptable part of it, in the bargain. He wouldn't be a trucker or a cowboy tied to some ranch in the middle of nowhere, he'd be a celebrity model. A prize. He shook his head. "God knows, Amanda. Certainly not anything like that."

"Then what?" she persisted. "Both of us stay here and watch this ranch go down the tubes? From what you've said, this is a very risky venture, with saboteurs lurking in the wings. Is that what you want for yourself? For me and your son?"

She made it sound pretty foolish, when she put it like that. But he couldn't change his basic nature to make her happy. And apparently she couldn't change hers. "No, I wouldn't want that for you or Bart," he said quietly. "But I'm willing to take the risk for myself. So I guess that about takes care of our talk, Amanda. If you'll just promise to bring Bart out West once in a while, so I can see him—" Chase's throat closed and he couldn't go on. The thought of Amanda and Bart leaving hurt too bad to think about, but they would leave.

"Dammit, Chase, is that really all you have to say?"

He looked away from the tears in her eyes. "Guess so." From the corner of his eye he could see her rebuttoning her dress with trembling fingers. Then she straightened her shoulders and lifted her chin. She had guts. He'd give her that.

"I'll make plane reservations for tomorrow. I'm sure Duane will be taking a load of people out to the airport, anyway, so I'll just ride along."

He didn't say anything. He was afraid if he opened his mouth, he might start begging, which wouldn't do any good, anyway. She didn't want the life he had to offer, so he might as well save himself the humiliation.

Leigh stuck her head around the partially open gate. "Hey, you two lovebirds! Freddy and Ry are finally leaving for Mount Lemmon. Get in here and help us pelt them with rice!" Then she disappeared.

Chase looked at Amanda. He hadn't known he could hurt this bad. "I owe them a good sendoff," he said, his voice cracking. "But you don't have to do this if you don't want to."

"I want to," she said, and whirled away to stride purposefully through the gate.

Chase had never seen her look more beautiful.

AMANDA COULDN'T BOOK a flight out of Tucson until midafternoon the next day. Afraid she would start screaming if she had to hang around the ranch all morning being pleasant, she decided to go somewhere more private. She called the bunkhouse and asked the cowboy who answered to saddle Pussywillow for her.

"Is Chase going with you?" said the hand, who sounded like Curtis.

She realized she'd never get away if she didn't lie. "No, but I'm only going down to the main road and back. I don't need Chase for that."

"Okay. I'll bring her up for you."

Amanda laced Bartholomew tightly into the cradleboard and lifted it onto her shoulders. It was heavier than she'd expected, but she figured she could manage. She thought of making up some excuse to take the cellular phone, but that would arouse suspicion. A ride to the mailbox and back hardly required a phone connection. As she started down the flagstone path leading away from the house, she saw Curtis riding up the road, leading Pussywillow. So far, so good.

"Where you goin'?" asked a deep male voice.

She turned to see Dexter sitting on the porch, Chloe by his side.

She tried to sound casual. "For a little ride."

"No one? By—alone?"

"Nope." She smiled. "Bartholomew's going, too."

"You need Chase."

No, she didn't. Not anymore. Not ever again. "I'll manage just fine, Dexter."

"Take the dog."

Amanda considered that for a moment and rejected the idea. A dog on the trail might be more trouble than she was worth if she spent time chasing rabbits and gophers. "I'm really not going that far," she said, gritting her teeth to keep from shouting her impatience to be off. She glanced back toward the road. "Well, here's Curtis with Pussywillow. See you later, Dexter."

She hurried down the walk and out the gate to the hitching post where Curtis had dismounted and was holding his horse and Pussywillow by the reins.

He looked doubtfully at the cradleboard. "Didn't know you were takin' the baby."

"He's very light," she fibbed. These Western men were a little too overprotective for her taste.

"I should probably go with you." He glanced uncertainly around the yard. "Where's Chase?"

"I don't know for sure." She smiled her brightest smile. "He partied pretty hard last night."

Curtis nodded. "Like the rest of us. My head feels like a barrel cactus this mornin'."

"I didn't want to bother him, but I longed for another ride on Pussywillow. She has such a nice gait."

"She's a good one, all right." He studied her. "And I've seen you sit a horse. You know what you're doin'. Guess it's all right." He grinned. "Besides, if I rode with you, I'd probably get into trouble with Chase."

Not anymore, Amanda thought. "I really don't need an escort," she said. "But thanks for being concerned."

"I'll help you up, at least."

She accepted the two cupped hands he offered and placed her booted foot in them. The cradleboard threw her off-balance just enough to make mounting from ground level difficult. She'd have to find a fallen log when she remounted. She settled herself in the saddle and smiled down at Curtis. "Thanks."

"As long as you don't get off again until you get back, you'll be fine." He adjusted his hat. "Guess I'll go in and trouble Belinda for a cup of coffee. Maybe I'll still be here when you get back. That way I can help you down again."

"Maybe." She reined Pussywillow around. "Thanks

again," she called over her shoulder as she started down the lane at a slow walk so she wouldn't jostle Bartholomew.

CHASE TOOK a cup of coffee out to the patio and squinted up at the sun. Must be damn near eleven in the morning. He rubbed a hand over his bristled chin. He felt as if somebody had hit him over the head with a tire iron. Switching from beer to margaritas after Freddy and Ry left might not have been such a great idea, but it had kept tension from attacking his back muscles. He remembered dancing with Rosa, who was old enough to be his mother, and smashing the hell out of a *piñata*. He even remembered asking Curtis to saddle up Gutbuster, the True Love's most dangerous bronc. Curtis had refused, thank God.

Some perverse impulse drew him out the back patio gate to the scene of the crime. Funny, but the spot where his whole future had collapsed didn't look much different from the rest of the surrounding desert. He glanced up the trail in the direction of the cottage and wondered if she was in there packing. Or hiding.

A cloud eased over the sun and the wind picked up. Maybe today the rain would start, but Belinda had told him they'd probably get a lot of wind, first. She'd also told him to go back to his room and shave, but he didn't much feel like it. Duane was the one driving to the airport, not him. And he was one of the owners of the place, wasn't he? An owner should be able to walk around unshaven without the cook chewing his behind about it. Belinda was just ticked because Amanda and the baby were leaving. Maybe Belinda even thought he could do something about that, but the time was long past.

The wind almost took his hat, and he pulled it lower over his eyes. He gazed out over the desert, where a couple of dust devils whirled across the desert floor like columns of smoke. Then he picked out a third, a bigger one, looking more gray than tan. He narrowed his eyes. Wait a minute. That wasn't a dust devil.

He dashed his coffee in the dirt and sprinted back into the patio. Wrenching open the French doors, he bellowed out Leigh's name.

"In here!" she called from Freddy's office. "And keep your voice down, cowboy. Some of us have headaches from last night, you know."

He covered the distance to the office door in three quick strides. "There's a fire," he said, breathing hard. "Looks like it's near the mouth of Rogue Canyon."

14

LEIGH JUMPED from the desk chair uttering a very unladylike oath. "You're sure? It's not just a dust devil?"

"I'm sure."

Leigh swore again and punched in the Rural-Metro Fire Department's number on the telephone. After consulting with the dispatcher, she hung up and called the bunkhouse. "We've got a fire up at the mouth of Rogue Canyon," she said. "Rural-Metro's going to see if they can line up some choppers with buckets. Have Curtis, Rusty and Jack start hosing down the corrals. The rest of you get shovels and mount up." She replaced the receiver and glanced at Chase. "Could you tell which way the wind was blowing?"

"East, I'd say."

"So unless the wind shifts, the ranch won't be in danger, but an easterly wind could blow that sucker up the canyon, right toward our summer pasture and our herd. Ever fought a brushfire before?"

"Nope." He relished the challenge of protecting the True Love. As a bonus, fighting the fire would take his mind off Amanda.

"Go get on your oldest clothes and meet me back here in five minutes." Leigh grimaced. "I hate to do this, but I'm calling Ry and Freddy on Mount Lemmon. They'd want to be here. Happy honeymoon."

"Yeah." Chase started to say something about the True Love Curse, but the ringing telephone stopped him.

Leigh grabbed it. "Yeah? Just a minute. I'll check." She covered the mouthpiece with one hand. "Curtis wants to know if Amanda and the baby are back from their ride yet."

Fear whacked him in the chest. "Their what?"

"Ride. You didn't know about it?"

"No, I didn't know about it. Let me talk to him." Chase crossed to the desk and took the receiver from Leigh. "What's this about a ride?"

"She said it would be a short one, Chase. But that was almost three hours ago." Curtis sounded scared. "Took the baby in that cradleboard. I thought about tagging along, but I thought you'd get mad."

Chase didn't want to waste time debating that issue. "I'll find her." He pressed the disconnect button and dialed the cottage. No answer. He dumped the receiver into the cradle. "Let me check out front. Maybe she's just coming in or something," he said to Leigh before dashing toward the front porch.

He willed her to be riding down the lane as he flung open the front door. She wasn't. He stepped out on the porch and strained to see down the dusty road. No Amanda. The little bit of coffee he'd drunk tasted like acid on his tongue.

"Went that way," Dexter said.

Chase whirled and glanced at the old cowboy sitting in his cane chair, Chloe at his feet. "Which way, Dexter?"

"That way." Dexter jerked his thumb over his right shoulder in the direction of Rogue Canyon.

Chase tried to calm his rolling stomach and deny

what he knew in his bones to be true. "How do you know? You can't see the fork in the road from here."

Dexter gestured toward his walker. "I visited... no...followed her. She went slow."

Leigh came out on the porch, her truck keys in one hand and Ry's cellular phone in the other. "No sign of her?"

Chase felt his chest tightening, his back threatening to spasm. He couldn't allow that now. "I think she might be up in Rogue Canyon," he said quietly.

"Oh, God. The fire."

Dexter clutched her sleeve. "Fire?"

"There's a fire at the mouth of Rogue Canyon, Dex," she said. She laid a hand on Chase's arm. "Maybe she's on her way back."

"Maybe." He spoke in a monotone, afraid any emotion might start a reaction inside that would leave him screaming with the terror he felt at the possibility that Amanda and Bart were trapped in the canyon by the fire.

"Forget changing clothes," Leigh said. "We can always get new clothes. We'll just go to the stables. I'll bet she'll be there when we arrive."

"Yeah. Let's go." Chase jogged to the truck, his gut filled with tension.

Leigh was right behind him. They both piled in and she started the truck. The back tires spit dirt and gravel as she peeled out. "I'm sure she's out of there by now, Chase."

"And I think you're trying your damnedest to deny what we both know. Be honest with me, Leigh. You're supposed to have these psychic powers. Where is she?"

Leigh wouldn't answer him, which was as good as an answer.

He slammed the door panel with his fist. "What did she have to go off like that for, with the baby? Talk about stupid!"

"You drank yourself silly last night and she took a ride this morning. We all handle stress differently, Chase. She's a good rider. It wouldn't have been risky except for this fire."

He was desperate for someone or something to blame. "But I told her the desert was dry as a bone! Why didn't it rain yesterday, Leigh? Where is the damn rain?"

"You'll get her back, Chase."

Chase's throat felt as if he'd swallowed road tar. "I have to. I couldn't live if she..." He couldn't finish the sentence.

Leigh shot him a look. "Does she know that?"

"No." He stared sightlessly down the road. "Because I didn't know. Until now."

Leigh took a curve fast enough to throw him against the door. "Then make this fire count for something," she said.

Moments later they arrived at the corrals and Chase scanned the busy area. There were lots of people, lots of horses. No Amanda. He clenched his teeth. He knew what he had to do.

As he got out of the truck, Chloe jumped from the back and ran up to him. "Hey," he called after Leigh as she headed for the hitching post. "What's Chloe doing here?"

Leigh didn't pause. "Dexter sent her along," she said over her shoulder. "Didn't you hear him tell her to come with us?"

In three long strides he'd caught up with her. "No, and I think she'll only be in the way."

"You have to understand what this is like for Dexter. His range is burning and he can't do anything but sit and wait for the news. He did the only thing he could. He sent Chloe." Leigh glanced at him. "I'd advise you to take her with you when you ride up into the canyon."

He stared at her. "You won't try to stop me from going?"

"No. If Amanda's smart, she's waiting up by the pond. A helicopter can't land there. But if somebody goes up on Mikey, they can bring her down. We got Mikey from the forest service and he's old, but he's fire-trained. Pussywillow isn't, but she likes Chloe. Chloe may be able to settle her down. It's worth a shot."

"Thanks, Leigh. I thought I'd get an argument because of my back."

She smiled gently. "I know you have to go. Remember the deep breathing to keep your back relaxed. Take two blankets from the bunkhouse and soak them in the horse trough before you leave." Her brown eyes glowed with encouragement. "You'll make it."

Fifteen minutes later, Chase held on to Leigh's confidence like a talisman as he started along the trail at a brisk trot, the wet blankets tied to the back of his saddle dripping water down Mikey's flanks. His shirt and jeans were already starting to dry, and the blankets would dry out quickly, so he had to get there before that happened. He loped the horse when he could, always aware of Chloe racing by his side. Fortunately, she was in good shape. He carried extra canteens of water, and he'd douse her with them when they reached the fire line.

With the wind blowing away from him, he didn't smell it until he was close to the billowing brown smoke, but he could hear it crackling, popping and hissing as water stored inside the saguaros and barrels began to boil. Mikey twitched his ears and danced nervously, but he kept going.

Then Chase saw the fire ahead of him on the trail, the flames licking through the sage and creosote, leaving glowing twigs as it passed. The heat rolled toward him, but the fire moved away, carried by the wind upward toward the canyon. Toward Amanda and Bart. He had to outrun it.

Mikey nickered and tossed his head when the flames came into view. And he's the fire-trained horse, Chase thought, dismounting and calling Chloe over to douse her with water. He gave Chloe a drink from his cupped hands before he poured the contents of the canteen over her black-and-white fur. "Stay close, now," he said, mounting up and untying one of the blankets to wrap around his shoulders.

He poured another canteen over Mikey, concentrating on the animal's mane and tail. Then he pulled the still-damp blanket around his shoulders. The smell of wet wool, wet horse and wet dog mingled with the sharp bite of charred desert as he started picking his way around the ragged edges of the fire, working his way to the head of it. Adrenaline pumped through him, sharpening his senses and delaying fear. He had to get through and he had to come back with Amanda and Bart. He had no choice.

Mikey pulled at the bit and shied whenever a small creature bounded past them in panicked retreat. A slithering rattlesnake momentarily distracted Chloe, who stopped to growl and raise her hackles. But the snake slipped out of sight before Chloe could get very excited. None of the creatures seemed to care much about a dog and a man on a horse. Survival hung in the balance as they raced from the flames.

At last Chase made it back to the main trail, just yards from the entrance to the canyon. He was ahead of the blaze now, and smoke billowed around him, making him cough and choke. Through watering eyes he tried to gauge the distance the fire had to travel before it blocked the canyon entrance. As he saw how quickly the escape route could be closed, even adrenaline couldn't prevent the cold sweat of fear.

Whipping off the blanket and holding it under one arm, he concentrated all his energies on getting Mikey up the trail as quickly as possible. Canyon walls that had seemed so sheltering now closed in like a prison. Except for the crackling behind him, the air was hushed. No birds sang, no insects buzzed—they'd already evacuated the area.

He rose above the level of the smoke, took a deep lungful of clean air and glanced at Chloe scrambling up the trail ahead of him. "Find Amanda!" he called, and Chloe's answering bark was a reassuring sound in the stillness. She bounded up the trail, slipping on loose shale but always regaining her balance and hurtling on. Soon she was out of sight.

AMANDA WONDERED if she'd imagined the bark as she sat on a rock next to the pond and cuddled Bartholomew. She'd tried not to convey her fear, but he'd picked it up and was wailing pitifully. Pussywillow, tied securely to a cottonwood, snorted and pawed the ground. Every once in a while she shuddered, rattling the metal fittings on her saddle and bridle.

Dread and blame vied for dominance in Amanda's churning stomach. She'd been so sure she could handle this ride, so sure it wouldn't jeopardize the safety of her baby. She'd made this trip to Arizona for his safety! And now she'd stranded him in a canyon with a brush-fire licking at the canyon mouth. She would have made it out if she could have controlled her mount better, but riding with a cradleboard on her back wasn't the same as riding alone, and Pussywillow had spooked at the sight of the fire.

Amanda's only concern after that was staying on as the gray mare had spun in her tracks and bolted back up the trail. Being thrown on this morning ride hadn't occurred to her. But it should have. She was a stupid woman, an irresponsible mother, she thought misera-bly. Once she'd realized that Pussywillow wouldn't carry them out, Amanda had decided to wait by the pond. If the fire came up that far, the pond was the saf-est place to be. She'd wade out in it if necessary. She prayed it wouldn't become necessary.

The bark came again, closer this time, and she stood, her heart beating with hope. Someone was coming! "I'm here!" she called, her voice cracking on the words.

A moment later, a bedraggled Chloe bounded up the path and skidded to a stop in front of her. Tears sprang to Amanda's eyes as she stooped down toward the dog. "Chloe!" A lump lodged in her throat. "Did you...did you bring someone with you, girl?" *Chase. Oh, God, let Chase be with you. Please don't have come up this canyon on your own.*

Chloe licked her hand and nuzzled at Bartholomew, who had stopped crying and was staring at the dog. Then he reached both pudgy hands out, and Chloe licked those, too. Bartholomew made a little gurgling noise and waved his arms.

Tears streamed from Amanda's eyes and landed on

Chloe's matted coat. "You've brought someone, haven't you," she whispered, refusing to believe otherwise. "I hope so, because we're in bad straits here. I'm very glad to see you, but I'd be even happier to see Chase. Is he with you?"

Chloe whined and wagged her tail.

"Let's go watch for him." Amanda straightened, took a calming breath and walked toward the trail. "Chase!" she called. A hot wind blew up through the canyon and seemed to carry her shout behind her.

"Amanda!" came a reply from below her, down the trail. "Stay there, babe!"

Half crying, half laughing, she hugged Bartholomew to her. "I will!" she called in a choked voice. "Your daddy's coming," she murmured to the baby as she rocked him back and forth. "Your daddy's coming to save us!" She stood on tiptoe, straining to see the winding trail obscured by rocky outcroppings and scrub oak. At last she made him out, moving along the trail, the most wonderful man in the world. "I see you!" she called, waving. Her words echoed against the canyon walls.

"Are you okay?" came the echoing response.

"Yes!"

"Is Bart okay?"

She didn't miss the order in which he'd asked. "Yes! Is the fire bad?"

"We'll make it," he called after a moment.

We'll make it. The echo bounded back and forth, surrounding her, suffusing her with hope and energy. He'd said the same thing when he'd carried her through waist-high snowdrifts to the truck of his cab. Fate had sent her this warm and caring man to love and protect her from harm, and all she'd tried to do was drive him away. Yet here he was again, determined to bring her to safety.

Warm emotions coursed through her, emotions begging to be released as she watched him climb steadily toward her. Soon he was close enough to glimpse his unshaven face beneath the battered old brown hat. His clothes looked as if he'd slept in them. She'd never seen anyone so handsome in her life.

"I love you," she called, her voice echoing down the canyon toward him.

His head snapped up in surprise. "You what?"

"I love you!" she shouted, making the canyon walls ring.

"Well, I love you, too, you headstrong woman!" He sounded a little angry, a little tense, but he'd said it. He'd said it!

She laughed.

After a moment, his laughter joined hers, rippling through the trees, bouncing off the granite walls. He was still laughing when he dismounted beside her and pulled her into his arms. "Of all the stupid times for you to say that."

"I know." She looked up into his shining eyes.

"You realize we'll have to get married."

"If we get out of this canyon alive, that is."

"Amanda, just shut up and agree to marry me. Let me worry about getting us out of here."

"I'll marry you, but what about—"

He kissed her swiftly. "That's all the time we have for that. We have to douse us all in water and get going."

"Yes, but we haven't settled—"

"We will. Come on. You're going in the pond with me, and so is little Bart. And so is Chloe. Get everything wet."

"Even your hat? You love this hat."

He gave her a crooked smile. "I guess that gives you an idea of how much I love you, now, doesn't it?" he asked softly. "Get in the water."

Amanda followed his directions and they all started down the trail dripping wet, with Chase carrying Bartholomew on his back and leading the skittish Pussywillow.

"We'll leave her if we have to," he said over his shoulder. "We'll try to have you ride her out, but if she won't go, even with Chloe's help, I'm taking you on behind me and sending her back up the canyon."

"Chase, I don't want to leave—"

"You will, if I have to strap you on behind me like a gunnysack. Is that understood?"

She should have been outraged that he'd order her around like that. She wasn't. With every word out of his mouth since he'd appeared on the trail, he'd emphasized that she was the most important person in the world to him. She'd never been that before, with anyone except the little baby riding on Chase's back. It felt wonderful. She still had no idea how they'd work out the details of living together. Giving up her career wasn't an option. *We'll make it,* he'd said. She had to believe they would.

Pussywillow began to tremble as the smoke reached them. Chloe stayed where the gray mare could see her, and Pussywillow kept putting one foot in front of the other. Amanda wrapped herself in the wet blanket as Chase had instructed. As she pulled it over her mouth and nose, Chase adjusted his blanket around Bartholomew.

"There's not much space, but we're going through,"

he shouted back to her over the roar and snap of the fire.

Pussywillow whinnied and tried to rear. Chase pulled down hard on her reins. "Come on, Pussywillow! Carry that woman through this fire! Chloe's here. Follow Chloe!"

As if in response, Chloe barked, taking Pussywillow's attention away from the flames. As Amanda leaned forward and stroked the gray mare's neck and murmured encouragement, the horse put one shaking leg forward, then another.

Coughing and gagging, they inched along. It's like walking through hell, Amanda thought as she pulled the wet wool blanket over her nose and mouth. Her eyes streaming from the smoke, she kept her gaze fastened on Chase's blanket-shrouded form. *Whither thou goest.* He had never led her astray.

At last the smoke began to clear. When they were several yards from the edge of the blaze, Chase swung the blanket from his shoulders and pulled on Pussywillow's reins to bring Amanda alongside him. "Check on Bart," he said.

Amanda took off her own blanket so she could lean over and peer under the hood of the cradleboard. Bartholomew stared back at her, his eyes solemn, looking for all the world like a green-eyed Indian baby. "You okay, sweetheart?" she murmured, touching his cheek and giving him an encouraging smile.

Bartholomew smiled back.

"He's fine." Tears poured from her eyes. "No thanks to me, he's fine."

Chase turned in the saddle. "Don't you dare blame yourself. You're the best mother I've ever seen."

"I nearly got him killed."

"No, the fire nearly did that, not you."

"But if you hadn't come to save us...."

He smiled. "The thing is, I did. Now let's get out of here before Pussywillow acts up again." He started off, leading the mare behind him.

The thing is, I need you. Bartholomew and I need you, Amanda thought as they rode south and put more distance between them and the fire.

Finally, Chase led them to the top of a rise and pulled Amanda alongside him again. He gazed at her without speaking for a moment. Then he cleared his throat. "Did you...mean what you said back there in the canyon?"

Sudden fear struck at her. Maybe it had only been the drama of the moment that had made him say he loved her, that had made him propose and cast away his role as a drifter. "Did you?"

The corner of his mouth twitched a little at that. "Dammit, woman, I asked you first."

She lifted her chin. All right. Let her be a fool, then. "Yes, I meant it. I love you. And I can see that you belong here, not in New York posing for ads. I don't know where that leaves me. Leaves us. But I won't ask you to change anything for me. And I know you think marriage is the equivalent of being branded, so I won't hold you to that offer, either. You're a drifter, but I love you, anyway."

"Does that mean you're going to tell your family the truth about me and about Bart?"

She gazed into his eyes and nodded. "I was pretty mixed up, but love has a way of straightening out a person's priorities. I'll tell them as soon as I get back."

"But I don't want you to go back, Amanda."

Her heart beat faster.

"People drift because they don't expect life to give them anything permanent. My expectations have changed." He reached out and touched her cheek, brushing a fleck of soot away. "When the fire started, I had to fight it because the True Love's become the first home I've ever had. And when I figured out you were up in that canyon, I had to find you because..." His gaze searched hers. "...you're the first woman I've ever loved."

She caught his hand and held it to her cheek. "Oh, Chase."

"Does that sound like a drifter to you?"

Her eyes misted with happy tears. "No." Holding on to the cantle of his saddle, she raised in her stirrups, leaned over and kissed him.

He kissed her back, his fingers combing through her hair and cradling her head. "I love you," he murmured against her mouth. "But I can't ask you to leave the career you love, just to be with me."

She leaned away from him a fraction. "You let me soak your favorite hat."

"That's not the same—"

"There they are! Kissing like damn fools!" The shout came from their far left. They turned to see Leigh bearing down on them, the rest of the hands behind her.

She reined up alongside Amanda. "Honest to Pete, couldn't you have saved that for later? We've been frantic!"

"Sorry, Leigh," Chase said with a grin. "But we had some things to work out."

"Well, work them out somewhere else. There are helicopters on their way, and each one is carrying about a hundred thousand gallons of water to dump on this fire. Their aim is good, but I can't guarantee it's perfect.

Unless you want to experience a hundred-thousand-gallon shower from fifty feet above, I suggest you move it!"

Chase handed Pussywillow's reins to Amanda. "Guess we'd better do what the lady says."

"Guess so."

Leigh led them all a half mile away before turning back toward the fire. "We can watch from here. It should be pretty spectacular. Here they come."

Amanda was transfixed by the sight of one of the helicopters carrying a giant yellow bucket suspended from a long cable. When the helicopter was positioned over the fire, the bucket opened from the bottom and water cascaded over the fire. The blaze hissed and steamed, exactly as if it were a giant campfire. A second helicopter came in and repeated the process on a different section.

"They'll go back and reload, and do it again. With that and the trenches we dug, I think we'll be okay," Leigh said. "The air tankers are standing by in case we need to drop a fire retardant, but we may not need it." She turned to Chase. "So what did you two have to work out that was so important?"

"How we can maintain a marriage when Amanda's working in New York and I'm out here."

Leigh rolled her eyes. "Is that all? Ry and I have that figured out."

"Oh, have you?" Chase shoved his hat to the back of his head. "And when did you do that?"

"I wandered out to the patio the night we all had food poisoning. Ry said you'd gone to the cottage, so we started brainstorming. We figured you two had your minds on less-practical matters."

To Leigh's left Duane gave a snort.

"Go on," Amanda said.

"Ry needed something to do the morning of the wedding. He was driving us all crazy from five on. We didn't want to let him be the one to pick up Belinda and Dexter at the hospital for fear he'd run the van into a tree, so I finally told him to call Amanda's ad agency in New York. He hired them to beef up the True Love's image—something it really needs after all these so-called accidents."

Amanda's jaw dropped. "He's hired Artemis?"

"With the provision that you'll do all the work, and we recommended you be on site. I realize it's not a complete answer to your problem, but it's a start."

"I'm astounded. I don't know what to say."

"You can thank Ry when you see him. He's the one with the mind for these things. I never thought I'd say that a New York mentality would be good for something, but apparently it is."

"You can thank him now," Duane said. "Here he comes, with Freddy right behind him. He musta driven that mountain like he had a burr under his saddle to get here this fast."

Ry charged up the hillside and wheeled Red Devil to look out over the charred desert. "Is it under control?"

"I think it will be soon," Leigh said. "Sorry about the shortened honeymoon."

"No problem." Ry stared at the smoke, which grew lighter in color as the fire began to go out. "Duane, why don't you and the hands ride around to the north and make sure everything's okay in that direction."

"Shore, boss." Duane motioned to the other hands and they trotted away just as Freddy rode up.

"Where are they going?" she asked.

"I sent them off so we could talk in private," Ry said. "Anybody have any ideas how this started?"

No one said anything.

Ry glanced at Chase and Leigh. "Do you think it was set?"

"Could be," Leigh said. "I didn't see any lightning over this way last night."

Ry absently rubbed Red Devil's neck. "And nobody's come across Whitlock this morning?"

Leigh shook her head. "He partied pretty late, too, but you'd think somebody over at his place would have seen the fire and come running."

"Eb wouldn't do this," Freddy said, earning a skeptical look from her husband. "I can't imagine anyone deliberately setting a fire. Even if you could devalue the True Love, it isn't worth the risk."

"It is if you're desperate," Ry said. "I'm beginning to think there's more at stake here than the land."

Leigh sighed. "My instincts tell me you're on to something, much as I hate to admit we have a problem. Look, we've fooled around long enough. How about getting your buddy Joe Gilardini out here to conduct a quiet little investigation? This sort of thing has to stop or we'll lose the True Love."

"That can't happen," Amanda said with a conviction that surprised her.

"Is that so?" Chase's dimple flashed as he glanced at her. Then he turned to Freddy. "Looks like you've won more support for your cause, Mrs. McGuinnes."

Ry coughed. "You all realize that if Joe wants to sell the ranch, we have to sell it." He glanced apologetically at his wife. "I gave my word."

"All the more reason to get him out here," Freddy

said. "We'll give him a horse to ride and a mystery to solve. What more could he want to keep him happy?"

"Oh, I can think of something," Chase said with a wink at Amanda.

As if on cue everyone turned toward Leigh.

She held up both hands. "Oh, no, you don't. A New York City Cop? Not in a million years!"

She longed to be held
in the strong arms of the law...

THE LAWMAN

1

A MAN WAS ABOUT to kiss him.

As the guy's breath began to tickle his mustache, Joe blinked and tried to clear the fog from his brain. "If you try mouth-to-mouth resuscitation, you're a dead man," he mumbled, giving him the benefit of the doubt.

"Never learned it, anyway." The guy—Joe realized it was the business type who had been in the doomed elevator with him—sat back on his heels and loosened his tie with such apparent relief that Joe decided maybe he'd been wrong about the other guy's intentions. But these days, you just didn't know.

"Here." The businessman reached into the inside pocket of his suit coat and handed Joe a handkerchief. "You're bleeding somewhere."

"No joke." Joe could feel it dripping from his chin. He pressed the snowy-white handkerchief, no doubt monogrammed, against the gash. Visibility was poor in the crumpled elevator, which was hot and smelled of dust and fried wires. He'd never liked small spaces. "How's the other guy?"

"I'll survive," said a voice from the back wall.

"Says his back hurts," volunteered the businessman. "I told him not to move."

What a genius. "Good," Joe said aloud. "Moving a back-injury case and severing his spinal cord would top this episode off nicely." Still holding the bloody handkerchief to his chin, he struggled to a sitting position, wincing at the sharp pain in his left forearm. Probably broken. Great. Why couldn't it have been his right arm, so he'd be able to get out of writing reports for a while?

He would have landed better if something hadn't bashed him on the chin and knocked him out. The floor had buckled on impact, and a fluorescent fixture dangled nearly to the floor, but he didn't think that was what had clipped him. The briefcase the businessman had been carrying was now lying up against the elevator doors. Aha. "That briefcase cut the hell out of my chin," he said, hazarding a guess. "What's that thing made of, steel?"

"Brass trim," the guy replied.

Joe snorted. "You got a cellular phone in it, at least?"

"Yeah."

Joe would have bet a month's salary on the answer to that one. Unfortunately, he'd left his own radio in the cruiser. "Then you'd better use it. This has been great fun, but I'm due back at the station in an hour."

"I suppose almost getting killed is a big yawner for you, isn't it?" the businessman asked, an edge to his voice.

Joe almost laughed. "Killed in an elevator accident? You've been seeing too many Keanu Reeves movies. New York elevators are safer than your grandmother's rocking chair."

"Tell that to my back," said the guy in jeans. "I can't drive with a busted back, and if I can't drive, I can't pay off my rig."

"If you can't drive, you'll get an insurance settlement," the businessman said.

"And sit around doing nothing?" the trucker said. "No thanks."

Joe considered commandeering the businessman's phone and calling in the accident himself but when the businessman picked up the phone to call, Joe figured he might as well continue. Anyway, with his luck the phone was some upscale model that required either a Ph.D. or the mind of a seven-year-old to work it. His son Kyle loved technology—he'd even shown Joe how to program his new VCR last weekend. Joe wouldn't have bought the thing except Kyle liked to rent movies on the rare occasions he spent time with Joe. And they were always the same movies—*Star Trek* I through VI. The kid loved Spock.

"They're sending a team to get us out," the businessman said, snapping the phone closed.

Beam me up, Scotty, Joe thought just as the elevator rumbled and lurched to the right.

"Damn!" the trucker yelled. "Aren't we all the way down yet?"

"We're all the way down," Joe said. "The blasted thing's still settling, that's all. Move all your fingers and toes, see if you still have your motor coordination." In the silence, Joe said a little prayer for the trucker. Paralysis was a tough hand to be dealt.

"I can move everything," the trucker said.

"Good. What's your name?"

"Lavette. Chase Lavette."

"T. R. McGuinnes," said the businessman.

"Joe Gilardini," Joe supplied. "I wish I could say it was nice to meet you guys, but under the circumstances I wish I'd been denied the pleasure."

"Same here," Lavette said.

McGuinnes remained silent. "Either one of you ever been out West?" he asked a few minutes later.

"Why do you want to know?" Lavette asked.

"I don't, really. I just think talking is better than sitting around waiting for the elevator to shift again."

"Guess you're right," Lavette said. "No, I've never been out West. Eastern Seaboard's my route. Always wanted to go out there, though."

Joe sighed. "God, so have I. The wide-open spaces. Peace and quiet."

"No elevators," Lavette added.

Joe smiled in the darkness. The trucker had a sense of humor. "Yeah. If I didn't have my kid living in New York, I'd turn in my badge, collect my pension and go." But he didn't dare leave town with Darlene's rich lawyer hubby filing petitions to legally adopt Kyle. Joe had been on his way up to his lawyer's office to discuss the reply to that petition. "Hell, no," hadn't been quite the reply his lawyer had recommended, but that was the tone Joe wanted to convey to Emerson J. Pope, alias Kyle's stepfather.

Joe had met the esteemed Mr. Pope once. He dressed a lot like McGuinnes and was the kind of stuffed shirt who could give Kyle video games by the truckload, send him to space camp and computer camp and quite possibly turn him into a nerd.

"I just heard about this guest ranch in Arizona that's up for sale," McGuinnes said, breaking into Joe's thoughts. "One of those working guest ranches with a small herd of cattle. I'm going out there next week to look it over."

Lavette leapt on it. "No kidding? Think you might buy it?"

"If it checks out."

"Running a guest ranch." Joe smoothed his mustache. "You know, that wouldn't be half-bad." God, he'd love to take Kyle out to a place like that, let him ride horses and play in the sunshine like a real boy for a change. A father and son could really get to know each other on a ranch .

"And after I've had some fun with it, I'll sell it for a nice profit," McGuinnes continued. "The city's growing in that direction, and in a couple of years developers will be crying to get their hands on that land, all one hundred and sixty acres of it. I can't lose."

"A hundred and sixty acres," Lavette said.

Joe liked the sound of it, himself, although he wondered why McGuinnes was telling them all this.

"I'm looking for partners," McGuinnes said.

Joe laughed. That answered his question, all right. "Now I've heard everything. Only in New York would a guy use an accident as a chance to set up a deal." The elevator settled with another metallic groan, jostling Joe's bad arm. He grimaced.

"Would you rather sit here and think about the elevator collapsing on us?" McGuinnes asked.

"I'd rather think about your ranch," Lavette said. "I'd go in on it in a minute if I had the cash."

"You might get that settlement," McGuinnes said.

"You know, I might."

Joe listened with interest. No question that Mc-Guinnes was a born deal-maker, which was probably why he had lots of money and Joe didn't.

"Listen, McGuinnes," Lavette said. "After we get out of here, let's keep in touch. You never know."

"I guarantee you wouldn't go wrong with this investment. The Sun Belt's booming."

"I think you're both nutcases," Joe said, but underneath his sarcasm he wasn't so sure. All his life he'd struggled with finances, but he just didn't seem to have a talent for making money. McGuinnes obviously did.

Besides that, a ranch in Arizona sounded damned appealing right now. Emerson J. Pope didn't have a ranch in Arizona, now, did he?

"So you're not interested?" McGuinnes asked.

Oh, he was smooth, Joe thought. "I didn't say that. Hell, what else is there to be interested in down in this hole? If the ranch looks good, just call the Forty-third Precinct and leave a message for me." He calculated his unused sick and vacation days. That would raise a chunk of money. If he took out a loan using his pension as collateral, he might be able to get in on this deal. Then again, it was taking a hell of a financial risk.

McGuinnes stirred. "Let me get some business cards out of my briefcase."

"I'd just as soon not think about your briefcase, McGuinnes," Joe said. "Let's talk some more about the ranch. What's the name of it, anyway? I always liked those old ranch names—the Bar X, the Rocking J. Remember 'Bonanza'?"

"I saw that on reruns," Lavette said. "The guy I liked was Clint Eastwood. I snuck in to see *High Plains Drifter* at least six times when I was a kid. Back then, I would have given anything to be a cowboy."

"Yeah, me, too," Joe admitted. "So what's the place called?"

McGuinnes didn't answer right away. "Well, this spread is named something a little different," he said at last.

"Yeah?" Gilardini said. "What could be so different?"

"The True Love Ranch."

JOE SAT at a fork in the dirt road, his 1983 Chevy Cavalier groaning from an overworked air conditioner. Kyle sat perched in the passenger seat, a model of the bridge of the *Enterprise* on his lap. He wore new cowboy boots, jeans, a snazzy Western shirt and Spock ears. He'd worn those damned ears the entire road trip from New York. Joe was afraid some sort of fungus might be growing under them, but every time he tried to coax them off, Kyle had a fit.

At the fork in the road a wooden sign indicated Corrals to the left and Main House to the right. Underneath each sign was burned what was apparently the True Love's official brand, a heart with an arrow through it. Joe stared at the heart and stroked his mustache. And he'd hoped to make a man out of his son in this place.

"What ya say we check out the corrals first, son?" he asked, figuring that would set the right tone for the visit.

Kyle shrugged. "I guess."

"Before we do, how about if you take off your Spock ears and put on that cowboy hat I gave you?"

Kyle clapped his hands over the pointy ears.

"Come on, Kyle. Cowboys don't have Spock ears."

"I'm not a cowboy." Kyle's blue eyes grew stormy. "I'm the second in command of the starship *Enterprise.*"

"Okay, let's pretend we just beamed down to the planet Arizona, where everybody wears cowboy hats and boots, and you're here on a secret mission, so you have to look like the natives."

Kyle craned around in his seat and surveyed the unfamiliar trees, bushes and prickly cactus plants. Then he gazed up at the craggy mountains towering above them. "It looks a lot different from home, that's for sure."

"That's because it's the planet Arizona." Joe reached over to the back seat and picked up the black hat he'd bought for Kyle the week before, a miniature version of the one he was wearing. "Here. Just take off the ears, and—"

"Nope." Kyle pressed his hands against his ears and shook his head.

Joe sighed.

Kyle peered up at him, looking worried. "Are you mad at me, Dad?"

"No, not really."

"I'll wear the hat *with* the ears." Joe handed him the hat and watched him position it carefully, so that the ears curved up against the underside of the brim.

He glanced at his father. "How's that?"

It wasn't exactly how Joe had pictured Kyle looking when the boy stepped foot on the ranch where his father was one-third owner, but it would have to do. "Fine," he said, and turned the wheel toward the left.

He'd never had much use for planes—total lack of control—so he'd decided to drive out to Arizona from New York. That way he could also see some of the country and give himself more time to spend with Kyle. McGuinnes hadn't liked that. He'd wanted Joe to come out immediately to investigate the "incidents" they were having on the True Love. Joe figured McGuinnes was letting the excitement of the wild West fire his imagination. Besides, Joe was officially retired from police work, but McGuinnes had claimed that Joe needed to protect his investment. He was a persistent son-of-a-gun, Joe had to admit. McGuinnes had pursued the purchase of this ranch and the financial cooperation of his partners with a single-mindedness that impressed Joe.

And he'd married the foreman, Freddy Singleton. Lavette had tied the knot recently, too—some gal from

New York he'd accidentally gotten pregnant during a wild night in his truck cab. "You guys are taking this True Love name a little too literally, aren't you?" Joe had commented when he'd heard about Lavette. "You got aphrodisiacs in the well water or something?"

"Maybe. Wait'll you see Freddy's sister, Leigh."

"Hey, that's the *last* thing I'm looking for when I come out there."

"Then you'd better stick to beer," McGuinnes had said, laughing.

The corrals came into view, solid fences of weathered tree branches laid on top of each other between parallel supports. Beyond the corrals was a metal-sided barn with two wings, one made of the same sheet metal and the other, looking older, built of rock. Several pickup trucks clustered around the barn and corrals, and something was obviously happening. Cowboys were hanging on the fence, and considerable dust was rising from inside.

Joe drove partway into the clearing and parked the Chevy under the shade of a feathery-leaved tree with green bark. "Let's go see what's going on," he said. He was all the way around the car before Kyle climbed reluctantly from his seat. Joe scooped him up and held him so he could see into the large corral to their right, where about twenty horses milled around or stood and dozed. Joe felt a rush of pride. Those were his horses. He was standing on his land. He took a deep whiff of dry desert air scented with horse manure. No car exhaust. No rotting garbage. It had taken all of his unused sick leave, all his vacation pay and a big chunk of each monthly retirement check, but it was worth it. "Pretty good-looking animals in that corral, wouldn't you say?"

"They're big."

"They won't seem so big when you get used to them," Joe said. From the far corral came shouts of encouragement from the cowboys lining the fence. He put Kyle down and took his hand. "Come on. Let's go over there and find out what the fuss is all about."

As they started across the clearing, brakes screeched behind them. Joe turned quickly to make sure the vehicle was under control, and saw both doors of a dark blue pickup fly open. A blonde leapt from the driver's side and a brunette from the passenger's side.

"Ry's going to kill me for telling you about this!" shouted the blonde.

"I would have killed you if you hadn't!" the brunette shouted back.

Neither paid any attention to Joe and Kyle as they raced for the far corral.

"Daddy, who are those ladies?" Kyle asked as they followed the two women across the dirt yard.

"I think those are the Singleton sisters," Joe said. Even running pell-mell across the clearing, they lived up to McGuinnes's description. Freddy, the brunette, was the taller of the two. Leigh, the head wrangler for the True Love, had the more voluptuous figure.

Kyle pointed to Freddy as she ran toward the corral, her boots kicking up little explosions of dust. "That one is real mad."

"I think—"

"Ry McGuinnes, don't you dare!" Freddy pulled herself up on the fence and leaned forward. "Get off of there this minute!"

Joe wondered who the hell Ry was until suddenly he remembered that T.R. had officially changed his name, saying that Ry suited him better now that he lived in the West.

That wasn't all that had changed about McGuinnes, Joe decided as he neared the corral. A makeshift bucking chute had been constructed on the left side of the structure. McGuinnes—a tanner, leaner McGuinnes in worn jeans, a dirt-stained Western shirt and a battered cowboy hat—crouched above the chute, ready to lower himself to the broad back of a Brahma bull.

McGuinnes flicked a glance over at Freddy, his bride, and touched the brim of his hat in salute. Then he lowered himself to the bull's back and gave the signal to open the gate.

"You idiot!" yelled Freddy, and smacked her hat on the ground.

Leigh climbed onto the fence for a better view. Her backside wasn't far from Joe's cheek, but she didn't acknowledge his presence. All her attention was focused on the man and animal in the bucking chute.

Joe followed the direction of her gaze as the bull stood trembling for a moment, then hurled itself into the corral. Cowboys cheered as the bull spun around, the bell strapped to its chest clanging like a fire alarm. Then the animal bucked and landed forefeet first while it kicked out viciously with its hind legs. McGuinnes whooped and stayed on.

Across the corral Joe spied Lavette. The ex-trucker was yelling and punching his fist in the air. Lavette looked different, too—bigger, stronger. Ranch life had also treated him well, it seemed.

The bull spun again, its eyes wild, with mucus flying from its nostrils. All four feet came off the ground at the same time, and when they landed, Joe winced at the jarring impact.

"Ride him, McGuinnes!" Leigh shouted.

McGuinnes stayed on.

"Dad." Kyle pulled on his hand. "What's happening?"

Joe picked him up so he could see. "My partner is riding that bull," he said with a wide grin. Ranch life was going to be more fun than he'd thought.

Kyle took one look at the heaving, snorting animal and buried his face in Joe's shoulder, nudging off his hat. "I wanna go home!"

"Kyle, it's okay."

Leigh glanced briefly in his direction.

"It's like a rodeo," Joe continued, embarrassed by Kyle's reaction. He was seven, after all—old enough to handle something like this. "Haven't you seen rodeos on TV?"

The bull bellowed and lifted itself into the air with the grace of Michael Jordan making a jump shot. Still in the air, it twisted, and that twist sent McGuinnes flying. Joe tensed.

"Daddy," Kyle whimpered, still hiding against Joe's shoulder. "I wanna go! I'm scared."

McGuinnes hit the dirt hard. He didn't move.

"Get that bull away from him!" yelled Freddy, who was already climbing the fence as if she intended to play the part of rodeo clown herself.

A grizzled cowboy grabbed her by the belt and pulled her off the fence. "I'll git him," he drawled. He was inside the corral in record time and whistling to get the bull's attention. "Haul Ry outa there while I supervise this critter!" he called to the cowboys at the opposite side of the corral.

"Gotcha, Duane," someone yelled.

Duane taunted the bull, waving his hat like a matador's cape to get the bull to charge. Meanwhile, the other cowboys hauled a groggy McGuinnes to his feet and helped him over the fence.

"He's safe!" shouted a cowboy to Duane.

"I don't need to be told twice." Duane feinted left and charged right, leaping for the safety of the fence only inches ahead of the bull. He scrambled over right in front of Joe, who stepped aside and held tight to a quivering Kyle.

"'Scuse me," Duane said. "That bull's a bit upset."

As if to underscore the statement, the bull bellowed and charged the fence at the point where Duane had just climbed over. Wood splintered and flew in all directions as the fence gave way.

With another bellow, the bull charged through the opening and veered, coming straight at Joe.

2

SPLIT-SECOND TIMING was Joe's specialty. In one unbroken motion he hoisted a screaming Kyle up to Leigh and reached for his gun. Except there was no gun.

With a curse, he leapt aside just as the bull charged. People yelled all around him, but he ignored the noise and focused on the animal, which for some perverse reason had chosen him as a target. The bull whirled and Joe headed for the first available cover, the far side of his road-weary Chevy.

As the bull bellowed and charged, he realized his mistake. He should have hurled himself behind the ranch truck, instead.

The rampaging animal hit the passenger side with a crunch of metal and an explosion of glass. At the moment of impact, Joe remembered with deep regret that he'd dropped his comprehensive insurance coverage. The Cavalier rocked but didn't go over. He eased up and looked through the shattered window to discover the bull, apparently unhurt, backing up and pawing the ground as if preparing for another charge.

Before the bull could accomplish more vehicular damage, two ropes sailed out. One settled around its horns and the second looped one hind foot. A moment later, a third loop dropped over its horns and a fourth snagged his other hind foot. Joe recognized Duane stretching one of the ropes. Equally experienced-looking cowboys held tight to the other three. Joe cautiously stood up behind his car.

"Git the bull rope and strap off him," Duane said, directing a fifth cowboy who moved in on the wild-eyed bull. "That'll settle him down some."

Joe noticed with some surprise that the fifth cowboy was Lavette. The ex-trucker deftly removed the chest rope holding the bell and another strap down by the bull's genitals. When Joe saw where the second strap had been chafing the bull, he figured the animal had a right to be mad as hell. Joe just wished he'd picked a different target.

As Duane led a considerably more docile bull away, Lavette glanced toward Joe, then gazed at the car. The passenger door was caved in and the window glass sprayed over the interior. Lavette shook his head. "Welcome to the True Love," he said in a rough imitation of Lorne Greene.

Joe cleared his throat. "You folks know how to do it up right. Is McGuinnes okay?"

"He's fine now, but I wouldn't give you two cents for his hide after Freddy's through with him."

"I'd better go see about my kid." Joe glanced toward the corral where Leigh Singleton was climbing down, Kyle still in her arms.

Leigh. He recalled that in that sliver of a second when he'd handed Kyle up, her gaze had locked with his. It had probably been just the drama of the moment that had given their exchanged glance such importance. But in that moment when he'd entrusted Kyle to her, he'd imagined...no, that was stupid. He didn't believe in any of that New Age nonsense about fate. He started across the clearing.

Kyle had a hammerlock on Leigh's neck as he looked

fearfully from the departing bull to the smashed car. Once the bull was out of sight behind the barn, Leigh said something to Kyle and gave him a squeeze. Then she lowered him to the ground and retrieved his hat. When she tried to hand it to him, he shook his head and started toward Joe at a run.

Joe cursed to himself. This little episode wasn't going to help Kyle adjust to ranch life. The child could easily demand to go home this very minute. As Kyle came nearer, Joe squatted so he'd be at his son's eye level. He greeted Kyle with a nonchalant smile. "Pretty exciting stuff, huh?"

Kyle regarded him with a solemn expression. His voice came out as a whisper. "He smashed our car, Dad."

"Nah. Just a little dent." Over Kyle's shoulder Joe could see Leigh approaching with Kyle's hat in her hand. "I can pound it out."

"Dad, can I go—"

"Listen, Kyle." Joe hoped to avoid the embarrassment of having everyone witness his son begging to leave the ranch. He clasped Kyle by the shoulders and gazed into his eyes. "I know this was a little scary, but don't bail out on me yet, okay? I think if you give this place a try, you'll like it a lot."

Kyle fidgeted. "But, I—"

"We drove all the way out here to see Arizona." Joe's impatience grew as he longed to instill some grit in the timid boy. "You don't want to turn around and go back before you know what ranch life is like, do you?"

Kyle's soft blue gaze looked distressed. "But can I go—"

"Just a week, Kyle. Give it a week. Seven days. I know you can do that."

"But can I go to the *bathroom*?"

Leigh's soft chuckle let Joe know she'd heard most of the exchange. Feeling like a fool, he glanced up, straight into her liquid brown eyes. And he forgot to breathe.

"I have to go really *bad*," Kyle said, hopping up and down.

"Okay, buddy." Joe stood, commanding himself to look away from Leigh's compelling gaze. Damn. And he hadn't even had a sip of the well water around here yet.

"You can take him into the bunkhouse," Leigh said.

"Where's that?"

"Right over there." She pointed toward a one-story rock building that reminded Joe of an army barracks. "Want me to take him?"

"No." Joe glanced at her but didn't allow himself to fall headfirst into that deep gaze again. "I mean, no, thanks. And I really appreciate your grabbing him when the bull broke through the fence. Not everyone has that kind of quick reaction in an emergency."

"No problem." She held out her hand. "I'm Leigh Singleton. You must be Joe."

"That's right." He'd been shaking hands with women ever since he'd hit puberty. Sometimes he'd felt the sensuous pull of a potential lover in the simple gesture, sometimes just the touch of a future friend. But when he enclosed Leigh's hand in his, a connection was made that surged through him with the power of a .357 Magnum. Drawn back into the fathomless mystery of her eyes, he was stunned into speechlessness.

"I...I'm sorry about your car." Her voice had a husky edge to it, as if she felt the incredible energy between them, too. Whether she did or not, she hadn't pulled her hand away and he seemed incapable of releasing it.

"It just needs a little bodywork," Joe said. Bodywork. Two bodies, working together in perfect—

"Daddy!" Kyle grabbed his arm and forced Joe's attention back to his son.

If he hadn't, Joe wondered if he would have remembered Kyle was even there. "Sure thing." He released Leigh's hand and looked down at the boy, who was holding his crotch and dancing around.

"Here's his hat," Leigh said, handing it to Joe.

"Thanks. Guess I'll be seeing you around."

"Considering the condition of your car, you'll need a lift to the house. I can take you if you want."

"Sure." He twirled Kyle's hat, trying for nonchalance, and had to make a grab for it as it flipped out of his hand. "That would be great."

"I'll be here."

"Great." With Kyle tugging on his arm, he sort of backed away from her and damn near tripped himself up before he finally turned around and walked to the bunkhouse facing forward, like a sane person. That's what he'd been until five minutes ago. He'd embarrassed himself badly. After all, he was a man who would turn forty-two in November, a man who'd taken several women to bed and been married for six years. He considered himself experienced when it came to women. He considered himself in control. He'd never believed in attraction more powerful than reason.

Until now.

LEIGH TOOK a deep breath and fingered the crystal hanging on a velvet cord around her neck. Her whole body was on red alert. She'd always known this would happen to her someday, but she'd never have guessed the feeling would be brought on by a New York cop.

Funny thing was, with his jeans, boots and a Stetson, he looked more like Pat Garrett or Wyatt Earp, especially with the fresh scar across his chin. Leigh could easily imagine him facing down a gunslinger. She pictured how his steel gray eyes would narrow as his face became an impenetrable mask. Not even a twitch of his mustache would betray him until the moment a gun appeared in his hand.

Leigh shivered. If this was the man with whom she was psychically linked, the cosmos certainly had a sense of humor.

"Hey, Leigh!"

She turned to face Ry, who was walking unsteadily toward her. Remembering that he might be angry because she'd told Freddy about his decision to ride the bull, she held up both hands. "Look, she was suspicious and finally asked me a direct question about whether you planned to ride that bull today. You know I'm no good at lying, especially to my own sister."

"Oh, that." He dismissed the topic with a wave of his hand. "It'll blow over."

"I don't see her hanging on your arm like an adoring bride."

"No, I think she caught a ride back to the house with Lavette. Said something about not wanting to ride in any vehicle I was driving."

Leigh repressed a smile. "Then I guess it hasn't blown over yet."

"It will. She has something more important on her mind than me riding a bull, as I'm sure you know."

"I do?"

Ry stared at her in astonishment. "She didn't tell you?"

"How should I know? I don't even know what you're

talking about. I think getting thrown from that bull addled your brains."

Ry took off his hat and ran his fingers through his sweat-matted hair. "I figured she'd tell you first." A smile softened his lips. "But apparently, she didn't. I'll be damned."

"Will you tell me what the heck you're babbling about?"

Ry adjusted his hat and looked at her with a jubilant light in his eyes. "Freddy's pregnant."

Leigh whooped and launched herself at him, forgetting he'd been thrown from a bull not long ago. "I knew it!"

Ry groaned and set her gently away from him. "You did?"

"Well, I didn't *know*, in the sense that she'd told me, but I had a feeling. She made a mysterious trip into town yesterday, but she didn't tell me why."

"Oh." Ry's pleased expression returned. "Then I must have been the first one she told."

"She told you just now, after the bull ride?"

He looked sheepish. "I think she was planning to save the news for a more romantic moment, like over dinner in La Osa or a moonlight ride out to the pond. Instead, it sort of—came out. I was a little groggy, but I vaguely remember her saying that a man who was about to become a father had no business risking his ass on a bull. Something like that."

Leigh chuckled. "At least you still were the first to know."

"Yeah," he said softly. "I like that. By the way, where did Joe and his son go? I saw you talking to them, but by the time I looked over here again, he was gone."

"He took Kyle to the bathroom in the bunkhouse. I'm sure they'll be back any minute."

"Good. When they get back, will you distract his son for a little bit? I want to show Joe the corral fence, and there's no point in scaring that little kid any more than we have already."

A familiar dread gripped Leigh. "What's scary about the fence?" She could almost predict what he was about to say. The corrals were nearly a century old, but they were strong. A solid wall of mesquite shouldn't splinter and give way, not even when assaulted by an angry bull.

"Some of the branches were sawed through," Ry said. "Not just at that point, but in several places. I need to get Lavette down here with me later on today to check all the corrals."

Leigh's stomach clenched at the thought that someone had taken a saw to the mesquite logs, which had been framing the True Love corrals for generations. "Why don't you ask Duane to do it?"

Ry blew out a breath. "Because I can't trust him."

"Ry! Duane just saved your ungrateful hide from that bull!"

"I know." Ry looked unhappy. "He's the one who taught me how to ride him, too."

"Not to mention the fact that he's our top hand. I've known him for fifteen years, and he's not capable of something like that."

"Depends on how threatened he feels by the idea of us selling the ranch to developers one day. If he hates the idea as much as I think he does, he has a motive, and he sure as heck has the opportunity. I think that Joe will agree that—" He paused and glanced over Leigh's shoulder. "Well, here comes our investigator, now. How're you doing, Joe?"

Joe grasped his hand. "You know, McGuinnes, every time I'm around you, things coming flying at me. First your briefcase and now your Brahma bull. It's an upsetting pattern."

Goose bumps rose on Leigh's arms at the sound of his voice. It's timbre resonated through her, as if she'd been listening to it all her life. Her first impulse was to stare at him. To avoid doing that, she focused on Kyle, who had his hat back on with the Spock ears poking out under the brim.

"Romeo's your bull, too," Ry said to Joe with a grin. "Just let me know when you're ready to ride him."

"I should have guessed the True Love would have a bull named Romeo."

Leigh thrust her hands into her hip pockets. "He was already named when my dad won him in a poker game," she said.

Joe glanced at her. "I suppose you'd call that fate."

"I suppose I would." She could feel him testing the link between them the way a high-wire artist tests a tightrope.

"We've considered selling him," Ry said, "but the guests like to have their pictures taken with him."

"And every once in a while some fool climbs aboard to prove his manhood," Leigh added.

Joe nodded and looked at Ry. "I'll admit I was impressed. From the bull market to a real live bull is quite a stretch for a commodities broker, wouldn't you say?"

"Wait until you've been here a while," Ry said. "This place inspires you."

"I'm sure Joe's not crazy enough to follow your example." Leigh said that for Kyle's sake, but in actuality she figured Joe was at least that crazy. She sensed he was attracted to risk, and for all his feigned nonchalance she'd bet he was already picturing himself on that bull. He probably didn't even realize his son was standing next to him trembling with fear at the same picture. To end the discussion, she implemented Ry's plan. "Listen, I know you two have a few things to catch up on, so why don't Kyle and I unload your car and put everything into the back of my truck while you talk?"

"Great idea," Ry said. "As a matter of fact, I did want to consult with you, Joe. Something's happened concerning that subject I mentioned when I asked you to come out here."

Joe hesitated and glanced at Kyle. "Is that okay with you, son?"

"Daddy, you aren't gonna ride that...that Romeo, are you?"

"Not today, that's for sure."

"You might ride him some other day?"

Joe put a hand on his son's shoulder. "I doubt that, Kyle. Don't worry about it. I'd appreciate your helping Miss Singleton get our stuff while I talk to Mr. McGuinnes."

"You mean her?" Kyle pointed to Leigh.

"Yes. Miss Singleton."

"She said to call her Leigh."

"Oh." Joe's glance flicked to Leigh and she nodded. "Okay." He dug in his pocket for the car keys and handed them to her. "Thanks, Leigh."

She'd waited a lifetime to hear her name spoken with that subtle intonation that hinted of future passion. "You're welcome." She took the keys, her fingers brushing his. The texture of his skin was tantalizingly familiar. As she'd have expected, the key ring was plain with no whimsical identification hanging from it. A unicorn dangled on her key chain. "Come on, Kyle." Leigh held out her hand, and after another apprehensive look in his father's direction, Kyle put his hand in hers. As she started away from Joe, she could feel his gaze on her and knew from an abrupt absence of warmth the very moment he turned away and returned his attention to Ry.

"I take it you like 'Star Trek,'" she said to Kyle as they neared the battered car.

He nodded vigorously.

"How about 'The Next Generation'?"

Kyle glanced up at her in surprise. "Have you seen that show?"

"Yes. I didn't watch all the episodes, but I've seen a few."

"I've seen them *all* but what I like best is the movies."

"And your favorite character is Spock."

Kyle's eyes widened. "How did you know?" When she smiled, understanding dawned on his face. "Oh, yeah. My ears."

"That was my first clue."

"Dad wanted me to take them off, but I didn't."

"You mean those aren't your real ears?"

He giggled. "No. 'Course not. I'm not a Vulcan really."

"Well, they *look* real."

"They sure do." He gazed up at her with the sunniest expression she'd seen since he arrived. "You know what I have in the car?" he said. "The bridge of the *Enterprise!* I'll show it to you." He started to pull away from her.

"Wait a minute, Kyle." She gently tugged him back. "Let me go inside the car first. There's broken glass, and

I don't want either of us to get cut." She led him around to the driver's side of the Cavalier and opened the door.

"It should be on the seat." Kyle bounced around behind her, trying to see inside. "That's where I left it."

"Let me check." Leigh picked a couple of pieces of glass from the driver's seat and put her knee down gingerly. When no hidden glass bit into it, she held the passenger seat headrest for balance and leaned over, searching for Kyle's toy. Nothing occupied the seat but a shower of glass.

"Do you see it?"

"Not yet. I'm looking." She peered on the floor, but only found more glass, a discarded Big Mac box and a map. With a sinking sensation in her stomach, she leaned farther across the seat so that she could see into the caved-in space between the seat and the door. A crumpled piece of multicolored plastic was wedged there. She'd never seen a model of the bridge of the *Enterprise,* but she was pretty sure she was looking at the ruins of one now.

"Is it in there?" His voice was pitched higher now, as if he'd guessed the fate of his treasure.

She longed to tell him she couldn't find it, unload the trunk and let Joe handle this. She backed out of the car and crouched to Kyle's level. "I'm afraid the bridge is done for, Kyle. It fell between the seat and door, and when the bull—"

"I wanna see!" He made a lunge for the interior of the car and she caught him just in time. "I wanna see!" he cried again, struggling in her arms.

"You can't. There's glass everywhere. I'm sorry, Kyle."

"Spock is in there!" From Kyle's tragic wail Leigh

could almost imagine Leonard Nimoy himself squashed in the wreckage.

"We'll get him out," she said, holding fast to the squirming boy. "But it might take a crowbar to get that door open. And I don't know what you'll find."

Sobbing, Kyle collapsed against her. "My bridge. My bridge."

Leigh held him as tears misted her own eyes. Poor little guy. He'd have a hard time living up to the rough-and-tough image his father seemed to hold in such esteem.

"What's he crying about now?"

She glanced up to see Joe standing less than a yard away, his legs braced apart, his hands bracketing his hips, his expression clearly annoyed. But it was his use of "now" that set her off. "He just discovered his favorite toy was smashed in the door when the bull charged," she snapped. "And he has every right to cry about that, in my opinion."

Joe's eyes narrowed, just as she'd imagined they would when facing down a gunslinger. "I don't remember asking your opinion. Kyle, come here."

Kyle slowly disengaged himself from Leigh's arms, turned and walked toward his father, his head bowed.

Joe crouched. "We'll get another bridge, Kyle."

Kyle sniffed. "I want Spock," he said brokenly.

"Stop crying and be a big boy."

Leigh clenched her teeth in frustration. She glanced around for Ry, but he must have found an errand elsewhere. She'd have to deal with Mr. Macho on her own.

"I want Spock!" Kyle cried.

"We'll get another Spock."

Kyle's head came up as if his father had uttered a blasphemy. "No, Daddy! We have to get him out!"

"Kyle, it's just a plastic—"

"Oh, for heaven's sake." Leigh stormed around the car and grabbed the handle. Focusing all her strength on the task, she yanked the door. It came open, the remaining window glass tinkling as it spilled to the dirt. A little figure in a blue tunic toppled out. She picked him up. He had a couple of nicks, but at least he wasn't missing any body parts.

Joe had come around the car, Kyle's hand firmly gripped in his. Leigh avoided his gaze as she handed the tiny figure to Kyle.

"Thanks, Leigh," he whispered, holding Spock against his chest. Then his glance fell on the mangled bridge smashed up against the seat and his lower lip trembled.

"That's enough, Kyle. Go on over by the blue truck while we unload the car."

The little boy started over. Once, he turned back and gazed with grief-stricken eyes at his beloved bridge, but at a nod from Joe he trudged on.

"Don't you see that it's more than just a piece of plastic to him?" Leigh asked.

"That's what bothers me. He's in tears at the drop of a hat."

"And I don't suppose you've ever cried, have you?"

"Not since I was a lot younger than he is. Not that it's any of your business, if you'll pardon my being blunt."

"If you'll pardon my being blunt, Kyle is nothing like you. He's a sensitive, imaginative little soul who needs careful nurturing."

His jaw muscles tensed. "If he is, it's because he's been mollycoddled."

"I suppose you consider what I just did mollycoddling?"

"Yes." When she started to protest, he cut her off.

"Kyle is my son," he said with fierce emphasis. "*My son.*"

"You sound as if I mean to take him away from you!"

"That's ridiculous!" He walked quickly past her toward the car. "We're wasting time. Let's get the stuff out of the trunk."

Her anger drained away. So *that* was it. Although he'd moved rapidly to hide his response, she'd seen the flash of stark fear in his eyes. He was a divorced father afraid of losing touch with his only child. Leigh wondered if it had already happened, or if fate had tossed them all together just in the nick of time.

3

As Joe rode with Leigh and Kyle up to the ranch house, rainbows flashed in his face from the crystal she'd hung from the rearview mirror. Damned distracting and probably a road hazard, he thought. He'd noticed a rainbow painted on the fender, and a unicorn hung from her key chain, swaying with every jolt of the rutted dirt road. So she was into the New Age scene. Next she'd be asking him what sign he was born under so she could figure out why he was such a mean father.

He wondered if things could possibly be worse. Kyle was afraid of everything about the ranch, except, of course, for his new idol, Leigh Singleton. As they drove, Leigh pointed out a jackrabbit and a roadrunner to Kyle, who seemed entranced with every observation Leigh made. Joe would be lucky if he'd get any time alone with the kid now. Kyle would be Leigh's shadow for the next week.

On top of that, Joe had begun to believe there really was a sabotage problem at the True Love. Apparently, he'd given up New York felons in exchange for Arizona saboteurs. Had he really been naive enough to imagine he'd find a different world out here? And his car was smashed in, not to mention Kyle's favorite toy. He'd felt bad about that, but pampering Kyle wouldn't help the kid grow up. The world was a rough place, but Kyle wouldn't learn that from Emerson J. Pope. Teaching Kyle those lessons was up to Joe.

"Did Ry send you any pictures of the ranch house?" Leigh asked, glancing at Joe.

"No." He decided to tack on a little more explanation so he wouldn't sound belligerent. Leigh had already caused him to display his feelings more than he cared to. "But he did describe it as whitewashed adobe, so I have a mental picture."

"Leigh, what's adobe?" Kyle asked.

Joe noticed which adult Kyle asked for information.

"It's building blocks made of mud and straw," she said. "In the old days, they baked the blocks in the sun, but now they fire them the way you would a clay pot."

"Could I make some adobe blocks and bake them in the sun?"

"Sure. I mean—" She shot a look at Joe. "We'll have to see how the time works out. I'm sure you have a lot of things planned to do with your father."

"Not really."

Joe clenched his jaw. "Leigh's a busy lady, Kyle. She's the head wrangler for the ranch, which means she has to take care of all the horses. I don't know if she'll have time to—"

"I have time." Her voice had an edge to it.

Joe felt as if she'd just drawn a line in the sand with the toe of her boot. "So do I," he said.

"So do I!" chortled Kyle. "We can all do it together."

A dry chuckle came from Leigh's side of the cab. Then she steered the truck around a bend in the road and the ranch house came into view. "Well, here we are."

A small smile of satisfaction came unbidden to Joe's lips. The graceful one-story ranch house, shaded across the front with a wide porch, looked exactly as he'd pictured it. Pots of red geraniums and a line of cane chairs occupied the porch, although no one was sitting there in the heat of early afternoon.

"That's a big house," Kyle said. "How many people live in it?"

"That depends." Leigh parked the truck in front of a low wall that embraced a front yard of grass and two large trees. "We don't have many guests this time of year. August is always slow. But when all the guest rooms are full, we have close to sixty people here."

"Then it's just like an apartment," Kyle said. "Only stretched out flat instead of stacked up."

Leigh turned to him and smiled. "That's right. We have room to stretch out on the True Love."

She had a way with double meanings, Joe thought. And that smile. He'd never seen one quite like it. It warmed and welcomed, yet hinted of untold secrets. He was a sucker for secrets.

"Belinda makes the best lemonade in the valley," Leigh said, opening the door of the truck. "Who's ready for some?"

"Me!" Kyle said. "Who's Belinda?"

"She's been in charge of the kitchen for more than fifty years."

"Wow." Kyle slipped under the steering wheel and got out on Leigh's side. "I need my backpack."

"I'll get it," Joe volunteered. "You two go ahead. I'll bring the suitcases." He wanted some time alone to savor the setting as well as a few minutes to neutralize Leigh's effect on him. In spite of his earlier anger and her instant camaraderie with Kyle, he was drawn to her. If he didn't exercise some care, he'd soon be following her around just like his son.

He watched the two of them go up the flagstone walk as if they'd known each other for years. Kyle grabbed Leigh's hand and pointed, with obvious excitement, to a pair of cottontails munching on the grass. Crouching next to him, Leigh said something Joe couldn't hear and Kyle nodded solemnly. His heart heavy, Joe turned away and walked around to the truck's tailgate to retrieve the luggage. Kyle was supposed to be responding to him like that, instead of to some woman who had been a stranger only two hours earlier.

He slung Kyle's backpack—a Star Trek model, of course—over one shoulder and hefted a suitcase in each hand. He hadn't brought much, figuring Western clothes would be cheaper out here than back in New York. He'd sublet his apartment, leaving it furnished; it had been no trick to turn his back on that depressing little place. Leaving the station had been tougher than he'd imagined, though. He couldn't quite believe he was no longer a cop. After twenty years, it felt weird to be a civilian, to know he wouldn't be putting his life on the line every day.

But the charging bull had thrown him right back into the old adrenaline rush, and he had to admit he'd missed it. He wouldn't go back to police work just to get some excitement in his life, but becoming a bull rider... With a faint smile of anticipation, he headed up the flagstone walk.

His boots clomped satisfyingly on the wooden porch as he crossed to the heavy set of carved doors. He set down one of the suitcases, opened one of the doors and propped his shoulder against it. But as he reached down to retrieve the suitcase, Lavette appeared and grabbed it instead.

"Just in time, Joe," Lavette said. "We're trying to get

everybody together so Amanda can report on the ad campaign for the True Love Rodeo."

"The what?" After some quick thinking, Joe remembered that Amanda was Lavette's wife's name, but this was the first he'd heard about a rodeo.

"We have to do something to improve business," Lavette said. "We decided to hold a rodeo." He set Joe's suitcase down on the brick-colored tile and glanced around. "What do you think of the place?"

Joe put down the other suitcase and took in the high-beamed ceiling, beehive fireplace, massive leather furniture and huge picture window looking out on a sparkling pool. To his left, through an archway, was a dining room with several rugged-looking tables flanked by ladder-back chairs. "I can't imagine why business isn't booming," he said. "This is fantastic."

Lavette lowered his voice. "It's the damned accidents. The True Love's getting a bad reputation. Ry called up here from the corrals and told me about the fence. We're hoping you—" A baby's lusty wail interrupted him. Lavette grinned and looked toward a doorway off to the right. "The kid's got a good set of lungs."

Joe recognized fatherly pride in Lavette's tone. "Must be the famous baby I've been hearing about."

"Yeah." Lavette turned to Joe and his grin widened. "That's Bart, the wonder baby, conceived in the cab of the prettiest Peterbilt you've ever seen. Amanda's in Freddy's office changing his diaper. She'll bring him out when he's decent."

Joe envied Lavette, just starting out with his son. Chase had a chance to do it right, while Joe wondered if he'd ever make up for the years he'd lost with Kyle. "Speaking of kids, where's mine?"

"Leigh shuttled him to the kitchen for lemonade and cookies."

Joe swung the backpack from his shoulders. "I'd better take him this."

"Just go through the dining room. The kitchen is beyond the swinging door on the right. The working end of the ranch house is all in that wing and the guest rooms are on the other side. While you're gone, I'll find out where these suitcases go and have them transferred."

"Thanks." Joe started toward the archway leading into the dining room.

"Joe?"

"Yeah?" Joe turned back toward Lavette.

"Maybe Belinda should keep your son in the kitchen while the rest of us talk out here. Ry's on his way up and wants to go over the incident with the fence. No use scaring your son with stories about what's been happening around the ranch."

"Sure." Joe started through the dining room and fought his irritation with Lavette. Didn't anyone credit him with any sense about being a father? Of course he wouldn't let Kyle hear their discussion. Introducing him to horses and cowboys was one thing. Exposing him to adult violence was quite another. But Lavette was new to this parenthood business and probably thought he knew more than anyone else. Joe remembered a time when he'd felt that way, too.

He pushed through the swinging door into the kitchen, a large room equipped with a commercial-size stovetop, two wall-mounted ovens, numerous cupboards and wide counters. At a small table to his right sat Leigh, Kyle and an older couple. An aluminum walker stood next to the old fellow's chair. An animated discussion came to a halt as everyone glanced up when he came in.

"Hi, Dad," Kyle said, his mouth full. "The cookies are *great*. You should have one."

"Maybe in a little while. I thought you'd want your backpack." Joe couldn't remember a time in the past three years when Kyle hadn't been frantic to have his backpack next to him.

"Sure." He put down his cookie and slid unhurriedly from his seat before coming toward Joe to take the pack. "Thanks."

Leigh stood. "Joe, I'd like you to meet Belinda and Dexter Grimes. Dexter was the foreman here for years."

"But a blood clot zapped into his brain, Dad." Kyle shouldered his backpack and walked over to stand next to the aging cowboy, who gazed at Kyle with a bemused expression. "He can understand everything, but he can't talk so good, right, Dexter?"

Dexter nodded and patted Kyle's shoulder with a gnarled hand. "Right."

Kyle looked at Leigh and Belinda. "You know, if Dexter was on the *Enterprise*, they could fix him right up."

"Kyle," Joe began, "the *Enterprise* isn't—" He'd been about to say "isn't real," until he caught Leigh's frown. "—isn't available," he finished instead, gaining Leigh's approving smile. Not that he sought that. God knows he didn't care whether she approved of him or not. But there was no need to get into an argument with Kyle in front of this nice old couple.

"It's nice to meet you, Joe." Belinda, plump and grandmotherly, had a musical voice and an angelic quality that would typecast her as a fairy godmother if such imaginary beings existed, Joe thought. And Dexter seemed like a nice old guy. Kyle obviously liked them, and Joe could see why. Kyle had struck out in the grandparent game. Joe's folks were dead, and Darlene's parents lived in a social whirl that left them little time for their only grandchild.

"It's nice to meet both of you," Joe said. "I appreciate your making Kyle feel so at home."

"Funny things," Dexter said, touching Kyle's Spock ears.

Joe braced himself for Kyle's indignant response.

Instead, Kyle giggled. "Dexter's never *heard* of Spock." He glanced back at his father. "I'm gonna have to teach him *everything.*"

"While he teaches you how to make adobe," Leigh added.

"Right," Kyle said, returning to his chair and zipping open his backpack. "Wait'll I show you what's in here, Dexter. All kinds of good stuff."

Leigh directed her gaze at Joe. "I take it we're wanted in the main room? Chase said we'd have a little meeting when you got here."

"Just leave Kyle with us," Belinda offered before Joe had a chance to ask. "I'm curious to see what's in that backpack, myself."

"You're sure he won't be any trouble?" Joe asked.

"Don't be silly." She waved him toward the door. "You and Leigh go talk about important matters with the others. We'll be fine in here."

"Thank you. Kyle, I'll be back soon, okay?"

"Okay." Kyle was digging in his pack and didn't seem the least concerned about Joe's whereabouts.

Joe held the door for Leigh and followed her out. She passed close enough that he caught a whiff of wildflowers that made his pulse race. Was there *anything* about this woman that wasn't desirable?

"They'll take good care of him," she said when the door closed.

"I have no doubt of that. It's just—" He caught himself before he said anything stupid.

She paused and looked up at him. "He's very proud of you, Joe. He told us about all of your citations for bravery from the New York Police Department."

Joe blushed, which embarrassed him more than the mention of the citations. "He found them in a drawer when I was cleaning out the apartment before we left." He damn sure didn't want her to think he'd bragged to his son about his accomplishments.

Leigh nodded. The corner of her mouth tilted up as she considered him for a moment longer. "Funny how such a brave guy can be so scared," she said softly.

"Now wait a minute. I—"

She touched his arm, effectively silencing him. "We can hash that out later. Right now we need to get this powwow over with."

Joe wondered exactly what they'd hash out, especially considering the urges flowing through him every time he looked at her. As he followed her into the main room, he marveled at how his arm still tingled where she'd laid her fingers for only a second. If he believed in magic spells, he'd swear she'd put one on him. Darlene had often complained that she'd never known what he was thinking. He had the uneasy feeling that Leigh understood his every thought.

When he and Leigh walked into the room, the other four were already seated, waiting for them. Ry and Freddy McGuinnes sat at opposite ends of a large leather sofa set at right angles to the fireplace. They weren't looking at each other, and Joe guessed the bull-riding episode was still a problem between them. Lavette sat on the arm of an overstuffed leather chair, his arm possessively draped across the back. Ensconced in the chair was a delicate-looking woman with long curly hair the color of firelight. The baby asleep on her lap had a shock of black hair like Lavette's.

Lavette stopped talking to Ry as Joe and Leigh came in. "There they are. Probably been stuffing themselves on Belinda's cookies."

From her seat on the far end of the sofa, Freddy held out her hand. "Hi, Joe. I'm Freddy. Sorry about the disaster when you arrived. It should never have happened." She flicked a glance toward Ry, who seemed not to notice.

Joe walked over to shake her hand. "I'm getting used to that kind of thing when I'm around your husband."

Ry glanced at Joe and lifted an eyebrow but said nothing.

"I'm sure glad I wasn't there," said the redhead.

"That makes two of us," Lavette said. "Joe, this is Amanda...and Bart." The loving tone he lavished on those two names told Joe everything he needed to know about that relationship.

Amanda smiled. "I'd shake your hand, Joe, but my arms are full."

"No problem." Joe looked around for a place to sit. All that remained in the fireplace grouping was a love seat across from the sofa. If he and Leigh shared it, they'd be quite close together. Across the room stood a table and four chairs that were probably used for card games. Joe crossed to the table, snagged one of the wooden chairs and carried it over in front of the fireplace. Turning the chair around, he straddled it and crossed his arms over the back. A quick glance told him Leigh had taken the love seat. A second glance confirmed the amusement sparkling in her brown eyes. Let her be amused, he thought. Let her consider him a coward. It was better than trying to concentrate on this meeting with her sitting inches away from him.

Ry leaned forward, hands clasped and elbows on his knees. "What do you know? All six of us in the same room at last. This is what we've needed to get the True Love on solid footing—all of us working on the problem. Amanda, what's happening with the rodeo publicity?"

Joe tried to listen to Amanda's detailing of media coverage for the rodeo, which would take place in ten days, but his attention kept straying to Leigh. She was toying with a crystal she wore around her neck on a black silk cord. When she let it go, it nestled into the unbuttoned vee of her Western shirt, a cool talisman against creamy skin that would be so warm to the touch...so warm....

"What plan of action do you propose, Joe?" Ry asked.

Joe snapped to attention. He had to assume they'd abandoned the rodeo topic and had started on the sabotage. Ignoring the laughter in Ry's expression, Joe gathered his thoughts. "You realize I've spent most of my time in uniform, not playing detective," he said.

"You're still our best hope," Lavette said. "If we call in the Pima County Sheriff's Department, we'll stir up a bucketload of publicity. You've had more experience than the rest of us, so you're elected."

A sense of excitement in the pit of his stomach told Joe he'd take on the challenge. There was a secret to be discovered. He'd complained to Ry about not wanting a working vacation, but after a long, uneventful ride in the car with Kyle, he could use some activity. The bull had taught him that. His pulse quickened as he started mapping out a strategy for catching the saboteur. "I'm not very good on a horse," he said, "and whoever investigates should probably be able to ride, so he can cover the entire ranch easily. Can somebody help me brush up on my riding skills?"

"Amanda and I can't," Lavette said. "Our plane for New York leaves in the morning, and we'll be gone a week."

Joe stared at them. "You're leaving?"

Lavette glanced down at Amanda. "The timing's not great, but we can't put it off any longer." He looked back at Joe. "We got married in a quick Las Vegas ceremony last month, and Amanda's parents are going nuts because they've never met me. That's one piece of business. The other is settling Amanda's job situation. She's going to try and convince her ad agency in New York to open a branch in Tucson and let her run it."

"Freddy and I will have our hands full getting the arena built for the rodeo," Ry said. "But Leigh's one of the best riders in the valley. She can teach you everything you need to know. She can also serve as your guide around the ranch."

The suggestion was inevitable, he thought. No matter which direction he turned, there was Leigh, singing her siren song. She was right about his being scared. He had no experience with the kind of emotions she fostered in him. She was too poised, too beautiful, too sexy. The more time he spent in her company, the better his chances of making a complete fool of himself.

"Don't forget that Joe brought his son out here for a vacation," Leigh said. "It's not fair to expect him to abandon that little boy so he can conduct our investigation."

Kyle. Joe turned to look at Leigh. In the excitement of an impending investigation, he had forgotten about his responsibility to Kyle, but Leigh hadn't. He couldn't decide if she was taunting him with his insensitivity or shining a light to direct him. Either way, she was demonstrating her superiority over him. He gritted his teeth.

"That's easily solved," Freddy said. "Leigh can teach both you and Kyle at the same time. He can go with you while you familiarize yourself with the ranch. We have a gelding named Mikey who is the gentlest, steadiest horse in the world. We'll keep him reserved for Kyle."

Joe relaxed a little. Kyle's presence would keep him from doing anything too dumb. "Sure, that'll work. I wanted Kyle to see some of the country from horseback, anyway. I hear there's bass in the pond. Maybe we can take a break for some fishing."

"That's not a bad idea," Ry said. "I'd like this investigation to be as subtle as possible. We've spread the word that you're sick of police work so that the culprits, if they're around, won't be so suspicious of you."

"Oh, they're around," Joe said. "A mysterious cattle stampede, poisoned horse-trough water, a brushfire, booby-trapped corrals—everything you've told me points to an inside job."

Freddy laughed. "Present company excluded, of course."

Joe's gaze made its way around the circle of faces. "At the beginning of an investigation, a smart cop doesn't eliminate any suspects," he said. He recorded the flash of angry fire in Leigh's eyes, and he met it with steady assessment. The investigation had begun now, as far as he was concerned, and it might as well begin with Leigh. She had as much motive as anyone. As a good cop, he had to put emotion aside and admit he really had no idea what she was capable of. Yet.

4

RY TRIED to make a joke out of Joe's statement...and failed. But after twenty years on the force, Joe was used to the kind of tension he'd just created. Unperturbed, he rose from the chair. "If somebody will tell me where Kyle and I are sleeping, I'd like to settle in there. Then I'm going back to the corrals and clean the glass out of my car."

"You're in the John Wayne Room," Freddy said sarcastically. "It's the corner room on the front of the house. We took the double bed out and put in two twins." She sounded almost resentful of the effort she'd expended on his behalf.

Joe smiled to himself. The John Wayne Room. He might not be popular now, but if he uncovered the saboteur, he'd be a hero. Unless, of course, the perp turned out to be one of the Singleton sisters. That would be messy, but he couldn't be responsible for the fallout. He'd been asked to do a job, and he intended to do it to the best of his ability.

"I'll show you where it is," Ry volunteered as the gathering dispersed.

"Okay." Joe figured Ry wanted a chance to defend his wife and sister-in-law, and he wasn't disappointed.

No sooner had they stepped into the John Wayne bedroom than Ry launched into his protest. "Listen,

Freddy and Leigh have nothing to do with the sabotage. I'll vouch for them."

Joe leaned against the antique pine dresser set against one wall. "How can you?"

"Because I know them, dammit." Ry shoved his hat to the back of his head. "They would no more do these things than—"

"That's the kind of blind loyalty that muddies up clear thinking, McGuinnes. Didn't you tell me some ancestor of theirs homesteaded this place?"

"Yes, and I know what you're thinking. They'd do anything to keep it from becoming a housing development. The truth is, they *are* doing a lot to keep that from happening. They're hoping to make each of us love the place so much we aren't willing to sell."

Joe's eyes narrowed as Leigh's sexual allure took on a deeper meaning. "Is it working?"

"Well—" Ry scratched the back of his neck and glanced out the window. Then he turned back to Joe. "It's a hell of a place. It gets into your blood, changes you. You'll see what I mean in a few days."

"You mean, when Leigh's had a chance at me?"

Ry had the decency to look uncomfortable. "I'll admit Freddy and I considered that you two might hit it off, but Leigh just laughs at us. She says a New York cop is the last man she'd fall for. Besides, you just killed your chances, by insinuating that she was a suspect."

"She is. So's your wife."

Ry groaned.

"Maybe you'd rather hire somebody else to conduct this investigation, somebody who'll handle it the way you dictate."

Ry settled his hat over his eyes with a heartfelt sigh. "No. I'll just get used to sleeping down at the bunkhouse until this is cleared up. Freddy has already suggested I might want to take my belongings over there. In fact, I think she suggested I sleep in Romeo's pen." He glanced at Joe. "I've invited our neighbor Eb Whitlock over for dinner tomorrow night so you can get a look at him. Now, there's a suspect worth your time. I know for a fact he wants this place."

"So, we have your top hand, Duane, who needs the ranch as a continued source of employment and a place to raise his experimental herd. We have Belinda, who is fiercely protective of Dexter and wants him to live out his days at the True Love and we have our neighbor, Whitlock. Anybody else?"

Ry managed a smile. "Would you believe a bushy-haired stranger?"

"Nope. Our perpetrator is somebody very close by."

"I'd sure like to convince you that Freddy and Leigh are innocent."

"They'll have to do that for themselves."

"They will. And for the sake of my marriage, I hope it's fast." He started for the door and turned back. "Let me know when you're ready to go down and clean the glass from your car. I'll give you a lift."

"You're not going to con Leigh into doing it?"

Ry grimaced. "After what just happened, I'll be lucky if she agrees to give you a riding lesson tomorrow, even if she's the logical one for the job. Besides, the more you're around her, the sooner you'll eliminate her as a suspect. But to be on the safe side, I'd probably better make up a list of the mean horses. Don't let her put you up on any of those, or you're roadkill."

"Sounds like this will be a challenge."

"That's a slight understatement. Did I mention that these two women are quite...independent?"

"You didn't have to. I got the picture the minute I arrived."

Ry shook his head. "All this because of a freak elevator accident. I checked with a few people who know elevators, and that kind of thing almost never happens. With all the safety precautions these days, the odds against it are tremendous. If I didn't know better, I'd say fate had a hand in it."

A shiver rippled down Joe's spine. "I don't believe in fate," he said firmly.

LEIGH KEPT TRACK of Joe's whereabouts for the rest of the day so she wouldn't have to run into him. She wanted to abandon the riding lesson the next morning, too, but the thought of Kyle kept her from doing it. She figured Kyle would be afraid, and she didn't trust Joe to deal sensitively with that fear.

So by breakfast the following morning, she'd resigned herself to spending a few hours in Joe's company. Wanting the experience to get off to a positive start, she approached Joe and Kyle as they ate breakfast in the dining room. She noticed that Kyle had on a *Star Trek* T-shirt today and his Spock ears still poked out under the brim of his Western hat.

"Ready for a ride, cowboy?" she asked him with a reassuring smile.

Kyle looked up from his plate of scrambled eggs, and his blue eyes were troubled. "Hi, Leigh," he said in a subdued voice. "You won't make me go, will you?"

She shot a quick glance at Joe. His expression was tense. "Make you? Of course not."

"If he'd just go down to the corrals with us, I'm sure he'd want to try it," Joe said.

"I don't *like* the corrals, Dad."

"It's the bull you don't like, Kyle," Joe said. "The bull will stay in his pen, right, Leigh?"

"Yes. And Romeo's normally very tame. It's the ropes they tie around him that upset him."

"There, you see?" Joe pushed back his chair. "Let's go check out those horses, buddy."

Kyle's lower lip quivered. "No, Dad. Please."

Joe blew out an exasperated breath. "Kyle—"

"Excuse me, Joe," Leigh interrupted. "Even if Kyle decides to go, I can see he's not quite finished with breakfast. I'd hate to take a cowpoke out on an empty stomach."

Joe opened his mouth to say something, but Leigh barreled on.

"Do you know anything about engines? The truck's making a funny sound. It's parked right out front, so maybe while Kyle finishes his eggs, you could take a look."

Joe gave her a glance of disbelief but he got up from the table. "We'll be back soon, Kyle."

"I really appreciate this," Leigh said as they left the dining room.

"Right." When they reached the deserted front porch, he turned to her. "Now, why don't you tell me why you really brought me out here? I doubt you want me to fix your truck."

"Actually, I do need someone to look at it, although I don't think there's a serious problem. The truck can wait. I got you out here because I have a suggestion about Kyle."

"I am surprised."

Leigh sucked in a breath and prayed for patience. It would be far simpler to hit this man alongside the head with a two-by-four, but tact was required if she intended to protect Kyle. "I agree he needs to get over his fear of the corrals. But I don't think forcing him to go down there is the answer."

"And you do know the answer?"

God, he was maddening. And infuriatingly attractive. His steady gaze had a way of making her forget what she'd been about to say, and the movement of his lips beneath that tantalizing mustache made her want to.... She swallowed and focused on a point beyond his left shoulder. "My Appaloosa mare, Penny Lover, is in foal."

"How nice for her."

"Dammit, will you drop that bored-cop manner of yours for five minutes?"

"What makes you think I can?" he asked quietly.

She stared into the gray depths of his eyes. There had to be a passionate, warm human being hiding behind that granite facade. That was the only explanation for her instinctive need to reach out, no matter how obnoxious he seemed on the surface. "You'd better hope you can," she said. "There's a lot riding on it."

Emotion flickered in his eyes for a second, but was quickly masked.

She soldiered on. "I suggest you take a riding lesson without Kyle so he doesn't feel pressured. When you get back, you can tell him about my mare being due to have a foal soon. Kids are usually fascinated by that. I'll bet Kyle will want to come down and see her himself tomorrow."

"But I want him to learn to ride. We only have six days left."

"Does he have a reason to be afraid of horses?"

"Oh, sure." Joe turned away and propped his hands at his hips while he stared at the mountain-draped horizon. "He has a reason to be afraid of a lot of things, because my ex-wife taught him to be. One of my buddies was a mounted patrolman and he tried to take Kyle up on his horse once. Darlene went ballistic and snatched him down, screaming that he could be killed. He was only three, but I'm sure it made an impression on him."

"Then we need to take it slow. Please don't drag him to the corrals this morning. It would be a miserable experience for all of us."

Joe glanced back at her. "You said yourself I shouldn't abandon him to do my own thing."

"Not for the whole stay, but you can leave him with Belinda and Dexter for a couple of hours. Maybe he'll even miss you and wish he'd gone along."

He hesitated. "I wish I could believe that."

Her heart leapt at this small evidence of a crack in his armor. "Take a risk, Joe," she said. "Believe it." Then she turned and walked into the house. If he'd met her suggestion with an expression of cynicism, she didn't want to see it.

DISAPPOINTMENT OVER Kyle's refusal to come down to the corrals hung over Joe for most of the trip in Leigh's battered truck. But as the weathered fences came into view, Joe's excitement grew. He'd always secretly wanted to be with the mounted unit in New York City, but his superiors had insisted they needed him in the Bronx. As a teenager, he'd ridden a few times in Central Park and had loved it, but once he got on the force, there didn't seem to be any time for hobbies like horseback riding.

After Leigh parked the truck, they got out and started toward the tack shed. She set a brisk pace, her boots thudding rhythmically across the dirt as she called out greetings to the hands who were working on reinforcing the fence in all the places it had been sawed through.

It would be a hot morning's workout. Already Joe's shirt stuck to his back, but physical discomfort had never bothered him much. He took a deep breath, savoring the musky odor of animals and warm earth. "Who are you going to start me on?" he asked. Ry had clued him in as to which horses to avoid, and he wondered if Leigh would try to sneak one of them in, just to humiliate him.

"We'll put you on Mikey."

"Mikey? Isn't he a kid's horse?" Joe realized the hands would be watching this lesson and his pride kicked in. "I think I can handle something a bit more spirited than that."

Leigh gave the brim of her straw cowboy hat a little tug. "Mikey has plenty of spirit, but he's also completely trustworthy. It's a good combination of qualities—for horses and people."

"And extremely rare."

Leigh spun to face him, her eyes dark with fury. "That may be true where you come from, but out here it's the norm," she said in a low voice. "I realize you consider me one of your prime suspects, but you'll have to trust me, at least for the next two hours, or I won't be able to teach you a damn thing."

He gazed at her flushed face, her slightly parted lips, the little drop of moisture that had gathered in the hollow of her throat. She was magnificent. "Well said," he murmured, and tightened his hands into fists to keep from reaching for her.

The fire in her eyes glowed bright for a moment, then

gentled into a soft warmth as the corner of her mouth tilted. "Thank you. Now let's get to work."

He helped her carry saddles and bridles to the hitching post. Then he leaned against it while she grabbed two lead ropes and went into the corral after the horses. She moved with assurance through the herd of powerful animals, laying a hand on a muscled shoulder, slapping a shining rump, passing out pieces of carrot, laughing as the animals nuzzled her back pockets for more treats. This was what Joe had wanted Kyle to see, but in a way, he was glad Kyle wasn't here. Joe felt more free to indulge in fantasies that would have seemed inappropriate with his son around.

And Leigh inspired fantasies, with hair the color of honey, a voice shaded with mystery and movements as fluid as a woodland sprite's. She was a seductress in worn denim and scuffed boots. Joe couldn't take his eyes off her.

Finally, she came through the gate leading a bay gelding and a gray mare. All the anger and frustration he'd been so used to seeing in her expression was gone, as if contact with the horses had cleansed her of negative emotions. She held out the lead rope for the gelding. "Here's Mikey."

"I had that one figured out." Joe took the rope and walked Mikey over to the hitching post.

"It doesn't pay to go by names." She tied the gray mare next to Mikey. "We have a mare called Georgina, but mostly we know her as George."

Joe rubbed the white blaze on Mikey's nose. "To confuse the dudes?"

"Well, it does have a way of uncovering the real greenhorns. When someone rides George and says, 'He's a great horse,' we know they didn't check their cinch like they were supposed to. If they had, they'd have noticed that 'he' was missing some necessary equipment." She disappeared into the tack shed, but not before he detected a blush on her cheeks.

When she came back, she had a brush in each hand. She gave him one. "Some of the old cowboys make fun of me for grooming the horses and tell me I'm babying them, but I do it anyway, and I insist the guests do, too." She moved around to the far side of the gray mare, so he could only see her hat. "The horse deserves some pleasure out of the experience," she said.

His groin tightened. All this talk of male equipment and pleasure, combined with the sight of Leigh moving around in snug jeans, was getting to him. "Sounds fair." He concentrated on Mikey's rich mahogany coat that rippled in reaction with each stroke of the brush. Brushing the horse only seemed to enhance the sensuous images assaulting him. He didn't think Leigh was deliberately tormenting him, but maybe she was. Maybe she considered it fit punishment for the suspicions he held about her.

"Be careful around his belly," she warned. "He's ticklish there, just like a lot of people."

"Are you?" He wished the question back immediately.

After a beat of hesitation, she answered, "Sometimes."

He knew if he asked when that was, he was a dead man. He brushed so hard, Mikey stepped sideways and swung his head around as if to ask what maniac was trying to scrub his hide from his body. Joe gentled his motion.

By the time he'd worked his way around to Mikey's right side, Leigh was on the gray mare's left. They worked back to back, and inevitably, as they leaned over, touched backsides. He registered the rounded firmness of her buttocks in that one casual encounter and his mouth went dry. "I think that's good enough," he said, returning to the safety of Mikey's other side.

"Have you ever saddled a horse before?" She sounded slightly out of breath.

"No."

"Then I'll talk you through it." She ducked under Mikey's neck and came to stand next to Joe on Mikey's left side. "The saddle blanket goes first, of course. I'm sure you know that."

"Right." In his present state of mind, he wondered if he would have known anything, including his own name. Somehow, he followed her instructions for positioning the blanket, placing the saddle on Mikey's broad back and drawing in the cinch. But every time her hand accidentally touched his or her breath fell warm on his cheek, he fought the urge to turn and take her in his arms. No matter that there were cowboys all around, or that he needed to maintain his objectivity where this woman was concerned. He was fast becoming obsessed with the need to taste her lips, to feel her body pulled tight against his, to...

"You can mount, now."

He stared at her.

"Mikey's ready," she said.

His heart hammered in his chest. "What about you?"

"I'll get you mounted first, and then I'll saddle up."

Of course that's what he'd been referring to. Of course. Like hell. And the color was high on her cheeks. She knew. With shaking hands, he reached for the saddlehorn.

"No." She laid a hand on his arm. A branding iron

wouldn't have given off more heat. "If you're going to grab something, take a handful of mane instead."

Oh, he wanted to grab something, all right. He clutched a fistful of Mikey's black mane, shoved his booted foot into the stirrup, and swung up with as much grace as he could muster considering the condition of his swollen manhood.

"Very nice," she said.

He didn't dare look at her. He fumbled with his right foot and managed to slip it into the stirrup on that side.

"The stirrups are too short. Take your feet out and I'll adjust them."

"They feel okay." And he didn't think having her fooling around by his thighs was a good idea at all.

"They're too short. This is western, not English. You're not going to start questioning my judgment at this stage, are you?"

With a small sigh of resignation, he slipped his feet free and eased back on the saddle. But he couldn't ease back far enough to escape the push of her shoulder against his sensitized thighs. He clenched his jaw and tried to think of boring things—traffic duty, paperwork, cold coffee at three in the morning. Nothing erased the sensation of sitting in a warm saddle with all his senses aroused while a bewitching woman stood nudging his inner thigh with her face nearly level with his crotch. She moved to the other side and he held his breath while she puttered with his right stirrup and the denim of his jeans bound him tighter and tighter.

"There." She backed away. "Try that."

I think you know what I'd like to try, he thought, thrusting his feet into the stirrups.

"Now stand in them."

Standing was a great suggestion. It relieved some of the pressure.

"Okay. Looking good. Just give me a minute and we'll head over to the round pen."

He needed at least a minute. He wondered if she'd noticed what a state he'd been in, and if she took satisfaction in the way she affected him. Probably yes on both accounts, although he'd been unwilling to meet her gaze and find out. Then there was the flip side of the question—how she was responding to him. If she was toying with him without investing any of herself in the exchange, he could find the courage to turn away. But if she wanted him with even half the intensity he felt... He shook his head and swore softly. There would be no escape.

5

LEIGH SAT on Pussywillow and watched Joe canter around the aluminum pen they used for training horses and riders. "Keep your heels down," she called. "Grip with your thighs. That's it." A teacher had to keep a close eye on her pupil, she told herself, all the while knowing that images of Joe Gilardini would appear in her dreams tonight. Images this potent always did. His broad shoulders filled out a yoked Western shirt to perfection, and the ripple of powerful thigh muscles beneath his jeans drew her attention more than once. Back in New York, he must have been one tough cop.

He was also a quick study—his lean body had already absorbed the rhythm of the gently loping horse.

"Reverse direction," she called.

His reflexes were lightning fast. She'd known that from the first day when in one economical motion, he'd protected his son from the bull and saved himself. Yet she was amazed at the ease with which he shifted his weight, reined in a tight circle and started off in the other direction. True, he lost a stirrup in the process, but in seconds he had it back. As a teacher, she was gratified. As a woman, she couldn't ignore the sexy tilt of his pelvis as he rocked in the saddle. Her body warmed, remembering how he'd responded to her during the saddling of his horse. But he'd probably choke before he'd acknowledge it. She was a suspect in his investigation, after all. If he was determined not to crack, she wouldn't, either. He'd only think she was trying to seduce him out of his suspicions, anyway.

A wind had sprung up, swaying the mesquite branches at the edge of the round pen. Rain clouds snagged by the mountains would provide a cooling afternoon deluge, but at ten in the morning, it was still well over a hundred degrees, and Mikey's coat was dark with sweat.

"That's enough work for Mikey this morning," she called. "Slow him to a trot and then we'll take him out on the trail for a little cool down." She rode toward the gate and leaned down to open it. As she fumbled with the latch, a gust of wind blew a bit of dried weed against Pussywillow's foreleg. The mare leapt in fright, and Leigh grabbed a hunk of mane as she started to slide sideways.

"Easy." Joe pulled alongside and clamped a hand on her arm.

She would have been able to right herself, but acting on instinct she allowed him to do it instead. The imprint of his strong fingers burned through the sleeve of her shirt.

"Okay?" he asked, slowly releasing her arm. Very slowly.

She tilted back her hat and gazed at him without speaking for a long moment. Almost independent of their wills, their bodies found excuses to touch and be touched. Perhaps they wouldn't have as much control over this conflagration as she'd thought. "Thanks," she murmured. "I'm fine. Pussywillow's a skittish little mare."

His gaze held hers. "Then why did you choose her to ride?"

"She has a wonderfully soft mouth."

Joe's gray eyes darkened and his glance drifted to Leigh's mouth. Then, as if catching himself, he turned away. "Let's go," he muttered, wheeling Mikey around.

Shaken, Leigh led the way out of the round pen. This was getting too heavy. She should definitely lighten up. She would advise Joe to do the same, but she didn't think it was in his nature.

She decided to take him out to the site of the old homestead. The trail there was fairly level and wide enough to ride two abreast, so she could keep an eye on his technique. At least that was the excuse she gave herself for watching how he moved in the saddle. "You're doing well, but you could ease up on the reins a little," she said.

He relaxed the reins a fraction. "Thanks."

"How does it feel?"

Unexpectedly, he flashed her a smile. "Great."

The smile caught her like a blow to the stomach. God but he was attractive when he did that. His mustache gave his smile a rakish look that took her breath away, and for the first time, she contemplated the enormous appeal of Joe Gilardini having fun.

For the next few minutes they rode in a silence broken only by the call of quail and the chatter of cactus wrens. Yet the atmosphere felt anything but peaceful to Leigh, as her sensitized awareness recorded the rhythm of Joe's breathing, the slightest movement of his hands, the direction of his gaze. She even imagined she could hear his heart beat. When he let out a satisfied sigh, she felt as if the air had been pushed from her own lungs.

"I don't understand what could be scary about all

this," he said. "When I was a kid, I would have given anything to ride a horse and be a cowboy."

"Seems like the kid grew up to do exactly that."

He gave her a wry smile. "I guess you're right. And I thought that Kyle would be as excited about it as I am."

"Give him time."

Joe sighed again. "Time. I can't believe he's already seven. If I don't connect with him soon, it's going to be too late."

"I'll tell you a secret. Out here, time isn't something to be bludgeoned into submission the way it is back in New York."

"Is that so?"

"Ask Ry McGuinnes if you don't believe me. When I first met Ry, he was hell-bent-for-leather, just like you. Wanted me to teach him riding the first day, team roping the second. That's an Easterner's way of attacking life, trying to cram too many things into each hour. Ry's beginning to understand that most worthwhile things can't be accomplished that way."

"I've never been real long on patience, myself."

Leigh nodded. "That's okay. You've come to the right place for learning some." She pulled Pussywillow to a halt as they entered a clearing. On the far side, a cracked concrete rectangle and a few scattered pieces of adobe were all that was left of the homestead.

Joe leaned on his saddlehorn and looked around. "So this is the site of the stampede that almost killed Freddy and Ry."

"This is where everything began, when Thaddeus Singleton built the homestead, brick by brick, back in 1882."

Joe swung down from the saddle. "I want to look around. Should I tie him somewhere?"

"Just drop the reins to the ground. Mikey will stay put. Unless there's another stampede." Leigh dismounted and tethered Pussywillow to a nearby mesquite before she walked over toward Joe.

He turned. "Think there will be another stampede?"

She paused and met his gaze. "If you're implying I lured you out here to cause some accident to befall you, then come right out and say so, Officer."

"No, I don't really think that." He walked over to the cracked concrete and gazed at it. A gray green lizard about eight inches long scurried across the surface, paused for a few lizard push-ups and scuttled away into the desert beyond the slab.

"This concrete hasn't been here since 1882," Joe observed.

"The concrete was poured in the thirties to help stabilize the house. Even though no one had lived in it for several years, the hands still used it as a place to get out of the sun or the rain. But by the sixties there was no roof to speak of, so it was abandoned to the elements."

Joe wandered the perimeter of the ruin. "Why did Thaddeus pick this spot?"

"Supposedly because there wasn't as much caliche here, and his wife Clara wanted a small garden. Dexter told me that. Clara didn't die until a few years after Dexter and Belinda came to work at the ranch, so they both knew her."

"What's caliche?"

"Layers of mineral deposits hard as granite. I've seen my dad take a stick of dynamite to make a hole through it so he could plant a tree."

Joe stood, his hands in his back pockets, and gazed around him. "Why wasn't the next ranch house built here, then?"

"Privacy, I suppose. The son and daughter-in-law probably wanted some distance between themselves and the old folks. But Clara hung on to this place as long as she could, I'm told, even without plumbing and electricity. My grandfather said she cried when she was forced to move into the big house. I guess I can understand it."

"I'm sure you can." His gray eyes were assessing. "But I expect you'd do something more active than cry if you were put in the same position."

"I am in the same position, as you very well know."

"What if I said, right now, that I don't want the True Love sold to developers," he said quietly. "Would the sabotage stop?"

She matched him, squint for squint. "I have no idea." She hesitated, but the question was too important not to ask it. "Now that you've seen some of the area, how do you feel about the sale of the ranch?"

"I have no idea."

Frustration made her spin away from him and stare up at the mountains towering above them. "What colossal arrogance! The True Love has been nurturing families for over a hundred years, yet here you come, some city slicker from New York, and imagine you have the right to snap your fingers and relegate it to the bulldozers, all because you hold the almighty purse strings! I find that kind of irreverence incomprehensible." She took a deep breath, knowing she had to cool it. She was already a prime suspect. An emotional outburst would tighten the noose around her neck.

Joe remained silent for several moments, as if allowing her to collect herself. "Well, at least we've established one thing."

She turned back. "We have?"

"You're not going to try and sweet-talk me into deciding to keep the ranch."

She watched the flicker of amusement in his eyes. A sheepish smile made its way through her anger. "Guess not."

"That's a shame."

Her heart, slowed from its angry pounding of a minute ago, began to beat to a brighter rhythm. "It is? Why?"

Joe's mouth curved. "There's a good chance you could have done it." Turning away, he walked toward his horse and swung himself into the saddle.

JOE NOTICED that Leigh didn't have much to say on the ride back. He helped her brush the horses and turn them into the corral, and all the while aware that she kept sneaking looks at him. Maybe she was regretting not trying to seduce him. Inadvertently she almost had, but he vowed she'd never know how close he came to pulling her into his arms at the homestead site. Her passionate defense of the ranch had colored her cheeks and lit dark flames in her eyes, making her nearly irresistible. But he did resist. She was too loyal to her ancestral home to be dismissed as a suspect. At the end of this investigation, someone would go to jail, and that someone could still be Leigh.

"If you're up to it, we can go out again tomorrow and see more of the ranch," she said as they drove back to the ranch house.

"That pond in Rogue Canyon sounds like a great place to take Kyle," he said. "If there are some poles around, we might do a little fishing."

"I can find you some poles, but I wouldn't set my heart on taking Kyle up there yet. He'd have to ride a horse, and I'm not sure he'll agree to it so soon. Just getting him down to the corrals will be a victory."

"We'll see." Joe wondered if she really thought Kyle wouldn't want to come, or if she wanted another crack at being alone with him now that he'd admitted his vulnerability to her charms. Joe was determined to take Kyle on that ride the next day. His son would be the perfect chaperon.

When they arrived at the ranch house, he reached for the door handle on the truck. "Thanks for the riding lesson," he said as he climbed down. "In exchange, I'll check that funny noise in the engine. Could be just a speck of dust in the carburetor."

"That's okay," she said quickly, hopping to the dirt. "Duane can look at it later."

"But I can look at it now." He snared her with a glance across the truck's dark blue hood. "Sort of even things up between us."

"What's the matter? Are you afraid to be indebted to me?"

"Maybe."

She tossed him the keys. "You do make things tough on yourself, Officer. You can bring these back to me when you come in for lunch. And thanks."

"Anytime." The little unicorn's horn bit into his palm as he caught the keys. He watched her walk away without a backward glance, her hourglass figure beckoning him with every step. At first he'd thought she didn't want him nosing around her truck, but then she'd let him have the keys with such nonchalance he decided he'd been wrong.

After opening the hood, he started the truck and took off the air filter. He used his handkerchief to clean the butterfly valve on the carburetor and the hesitation in the engine seemed to go away. The whole procedure had taken less than five minutes, so he left the truck running and climbed back into the cab. The glove compartment contained the usual ownership and insurance papers, a few colored stones and a worn copy of a book called *Creative Visualizations* by somebody named Shakti Gawain. He sniffed the book. It smelled vaguely of incense, of mystery, of secrets. As he opened it, he felt that he was peering into the fascinating labyrinth of Leigh's mind.

Glancing around to make sure no one noticed, he flipped through the book and read a few underlined passages. They spoke of going with the flow and not forcing issues, letting life unfold. Joe shook his head. Damned passive philosophy as far as he was concerned. It also didn't fit with the type of person who would commit sabotage. He closed the book and put it back in the glove compartment, arranging everything as he'd found it. Then he turned off the engine and pocketed the keys, unicorn and all.

As he walked in the front door of the ranch house, the hum of voices from the dining room told him lunch was already in progress. He ducked into his room to wash up and noticed Kyle's backpack lying open on his bed, his Star Trek figures strewn about. The kid had apparently spent some time in the room by himself playing with the plastic toys when he could have been in the fresh air learning a new skill. Well, Joe would see that didn't happen two days in a row.

When he reached the arched entry to the dining room, he noticed Kyle and Leigh sitting together at a table. Kyle's fair head so close to Leigh's honey-colored one made them look remarkably like mother and son. Had Kyle really been Leigh's, he wouldn't be so lacking in courage, Joe thought. Leigh had the heart of a lioness. She spotted him and spoke to Kyle, who swiveled in his chair and waved wildly.

"Over here, Dad!"

He strode over, determined to convince Kyle to go fishing with him the next day. There had to be some significant change in the way this vacation was going.

"Did you know Leigh's horse is going to have a baby?" Kyle said before Joe could form the first part of his argument.

"Yes, I did, and I think—"

"I'm going down there with you guys tomorrow morning," Kyle said. "I want to see that mother horse. Leigh said the baby could be born *any day.*"

Joe glanced at Leigh, who looked somewhat wise and smug, but then she had a right to, he supposed. He opened his mouth to tack on a suggestion for the fishing trip, but the exhortations from Leigh's book drifted through his mind. Not that he believed in that stuff, but maybe this time he wouldn't push for more just yet. He'd stick the fishing poles in the back of the truck, just in case, though.

"When you checked the truck, did you find anything?" Leigh asked.

He blinked, giving away far too much information for someone of Leigh's perceptive abilities. "It was probably dust in the carburetor," he said, digging her keys out of his pocket. "Seems okay now."

"Thank you for investigating."

He was sure she knew exactly what he'd been up to, poking around through her glove compartment, looking for anything that would shed light on the strange occurrences at the ranch. She was either innocent or very smart. Then there was the outside possibility she was both.

He turned to Kyle. "I'm going to pound the dents out of the car this afternoon. Want to help me?"

"Dexter and me, we were gonna play Junior Scrabble." Kyle looked worried, as if he suspected this might not be the right response.

Joe swallowed his disappointment and sat down at the table with a determined smile. Go with the flow. "No problem, Kyle. What's for lunch?"

THE AFTERNOON rain played havoc with Joe's plan to pound the dents out of his car. He'd never seen a storm come on so fast. He barely had time to cover the broken window with a tarp before it hit, sluicing down as if from a giant bucket. Carrying his tools, he ran for cover under the front porch, only to watch his tarp blow away from the window and the rain pour in, drenching his seat covers. Then, as quickly as the storm swept in, it departed. Determined to finish the job, Joe trudged back out and worked in the mud for another half hour before the storm, growling like an angry dog, turned and headed back at him. This time, instead of running for cover, he continued to work as rain dripped from his hair, eyebrows and nose.

Pounding furiously on the caved-in steel, he didn't hear anyone approach until Leigh yelled in his ear. He dropped the mallet in the ooze at his feet and whirled, his hand automatically going for his weaponless hip.

She leapt back and nearly fell in the muck. He grabbed her just in time, his fingers slipping, then tightening on the yellow raincoat she was wearing.

"You crazy idiot!" She shook away his grasp and adjusted her floppy yellow rain hat.

With her hair in a braid down her back and her rain boots peeking out from under her coat, she looked about twelve years old. He smiled in spite of himself. "A *grinning* idiot, no less! Don't you hear that thunder? You could be struck by lightning out here!"

Apparently, she'd donned rain gear to come out in the thunderstorm to warn him. Probably for Kyle's sake, he thought sullenly.

"I'm almost done!" he yelled back. "Five more minutes, tops!"

She grabbed him by the shoulders and tried to shake him, but she didn't make much headway. "Didn't you hear me? You could get hit!" A flash followed by an explosion of sound sharp as the crack of a rifle punctuated her statement. "Come inside this minute!"

The next flash nearly blinded him, and instinctively he grabbed her and pulled them both through the open door of the car onto the soggy driver's seat as the crash made him temporarily deaf. When he could hear again, he realized his elbow was on the horn. Leigh was wedged on top of him as they sprawled half in, half out of the car. He didn't think the bolt had struck the Cavalier, but if it had, at least the tires would have grounded them.

He moved his elbow and the horn stopped its blaring. The rain, too, seemed to lessen at the same moment. He looked into Leigh's eyes, wide with shock. Her rain hat was gone, knocked into the mud at their feet, most likely.

"You're right," he murmured. "It's dangerous out here."

She opened her mouth, but no words came out, and she closed it again. She was so close, he could count each individual rain-damp eyelash and admire the subtle shades of gold and brown in her eyes. He watched her pupils widen with awareness as he cradled the back of her head and brought her the last two inches necessary to mold her lips to his.

With that velvet touch, he forgot the gearshift jabbing his right side and the rain soaking his jeans. He forgot that he should keep his distance from this woman who could be guilty of sabotage, who might monopolize his son, who might jeopardize his sanity with her crazy view of the world. There was only the soft, moist temptation of full lips that tasted of some exotic spice that his fevered brain couldn't identify. But he wanted more. Much more. With a groan, he pressed deeper and she opened like a tropical flower in the heat of the jungle. He dipped his tongue inside her mouth and grew drunk with the pleasure he received there. Nothing mattered but this. So rich, so lush, so—

"What's the deal, here?" boomed a voice from outside the car. "Leigh, what're you doing hanging half-out of that heap of tin? You two look like a couple of sardines that refused to be canned!" The last was followed by a bark of laughter.

Leigh struggled out of Joe's arms, and he let her go. Whoever the bastard was who'd ended that kiss would pay for it one day, Joe vowed.

"Well, hello, Eb," Leigh said with a show of dignity that impressed Joe no end. She stood beside the car and straightened her raincoat. She offered no explanation, either, which Joe liked even more. "Ry and Freddy told me you were coming for dinner. I'd like you to meet Joe Gilardini."

Joe hauled himself out of the car and held out his hand to Eb Whitlock, one of Ry's prime suspects. He was a large man, dressed dramatically in a black shirt with silver embroidery on the yoke. A heavy silver and turquoise bolo tie hung around his neck and an equally large and expensive-looking buckle graced his expansive belly. Joe could understand why Ry wanted this guy to be the saboteur. There was a lot to dislike about Eb Whitlock.

"The third partner." Eb flashed a set of large teeth and gave Joe a bone-crushing handshake. Joe crushed right back and had the satisfaction of seeing Eb wince. Eb retrieved his hand and adjusted his bolo tie, while managing to show off a silver and turquoise watchband at the same time. "I understand you're a cop."

"Was," Joe said. "Now I'm just a private citizen, like the rest of you."

Eb gestured toward the Cavalier. "Must not have paid you much."

"I got by."

"Come on into the house, Eb," Leigh said, starting toward the flagstone walk, shiny with rain. "Dinner will be in a half hour, Joe," she said over her shoulder.

"I'll be there." He would cherish every minute of putting Whitlock on the hot seat.

Leigh glanced at Eb as they started up the walk. "I was just having some Bengal Spice tea with honey. You're welcome to join me."

Bengal Spice with honey, Joe thought. So that was the exotic taste that had captivated him so. Except he wasn't sure it was entirely the tea she'd been drinking that had made her so inviting.

"You and your herb tea," Eb said, putting an arm around Leigh's shoulders. "Got any good Scotch?"

Joe clenched his fists. One kiss gave him no rights. No rights whatsoever. Just before they stepped up on the porch, the sun burst out from behind a cloud and splashed the yard, making the potted geraniums glow with passion. A stray sunbeam reached up and fingered a tendril of Leigh's hair that had escaped from the braid. Something about seeing the sun in her hair made his throat hurt. He leaned down and picked up the yellow rain hat and carefully brushed away the mud.

6

As Leigh took off her muddy boots on the porch and shook out her raincoat, she kept up a normal conversation with Eb Whitlock about the number of inches of rain they'd had so far this season. Yet nothing would ever be normal again. She could still sense the power behind the lightning strike, still feel the electricity singing through the air, sizzling against her lips, igniting a passion that would never sleep again. The drumming of the rain on the car roof had echoed the drumming of her heart as he'd closed the gap between them....

"If you were smart, you'd have that cop investigate all the little accidents you've had around here," Eb said as he held the carved wooden door open for her.

Leigh pulled her thoughts together with difficulty and gave the response she and Ry had agreed upon. "Joe's on vacation while he's out here. All he wants to do is relax. In fact, tomorrow I'm taking him up to the pond for a little bass fishing."

"Sounds like fiddlin' while Rome burns, if you ask me." Eb followed her into the main room of the ranch house. "Don't tell me you're not hurting for business. How many guests you got right now?"

"Five. But it's usually slow in August. Sit down, Eb," she said with thinly disguised irritation as she waved him toward an overstuffed leather chair. "I'll order us something to drink."

"I'll take a glass of ginger ale," Freddy said, coming out of her office. "How are you, Eb? Hope the drive over didn't get that new truck of yours too muddy."

"A truck like mine's built to take a little mud. Just last week I drove it across the riverbed after some strays, and it didn't get stuck once. They don't make them any better than that model."

Leigh hurried from the room before she had to hear another story about Eb's marvelous truck. She might have been more tolerant if Eb had earned the money to finance his materialistic tastes, but his wife had inherited the tidy sum that had allowed Eb to buy a hundred acres from Leigh's father twenty-five years ago. When Loraine Whitlock died, Eb seemed to focus completely on his possessions and made no bones about wanting to add the True Love to his list of things to brag about.

She found Manny, one of two waiters they kept on in the summer months, arranging place settings in the dining room. She gave him the drinks order and he nodded.

"Thanks, Manny," she said. "Maybe you'd better bring a beer for Ry, too. He should show up soon. Make that two beers," she added. "I imagine Joe Gilardini will be joining us, too."

Manny grinned. "That little kid of his has been playing Scrabble all afternoon with Dex. Belinda loves it, because Dex is using words he couldn't remember before. The kid taught them how to do high fives, and every time Dexter uses a new word, there are high fives all around. You should see Belinda and Dexter doing a high five. It's hilarious."

Leigh's chuckle was tinged with admiration. "Kyle's a great kid." If only Joe could appreciate his son's strengths instead of focusing on his weaknesses, she thought sadly. She thanked Manny again and returned to the living room, where Ry had joined the group. Down the hall, the door to Joe's room was closed. She suspected he was inside cleaning up. Taking off his clothes. Taking a shower.

With an effort, she pushed those thoughts aside and smiled at Ry and Freddy, who had apparently settled their differences and were tucked into the love seat with Ry's arm draped possessively over the leather back.

Eb glanced at Leigh as she chose a seat on the long sofa. "I've just been telling Ry and Freddy what I told you, Leigh. You folks can't go on this way. Admit it, your bookings are down for the fall season."

"The rodeo will generate more business," Freddy said. She paused as Manny came in and served the drinks. "Once we have the arena set up, we can schedule another rodeo in November and perhaps even a third in February. Amanda has some dynamite ideas for promotion. We'll be okay."

Ry picked up his bottle of beer and took a swallow. "And speaking of the rodeo, Eb, we'd like to rent Grateful Dead for the bull-riding competition."

Freddy almost spilled her ginger ale as her glance snapped toward her husband. "And who, pray tell, plans to ride that monster? Don't tell me. I think I can guess." Putting down her glass, she stood and walked over to the fireplace, where she turned back to face Ry. "I'd hoped Romeo had knocked some sense into that thick skull of yours."

Ry shrugged. "I rode him."

Freddy threw up her hands in a gesture of frustration. "I give up. My baby's destined to be the child of a cripple."

"Baby?" asked Joe, who walked in just in time for

Freddy's last statement. His hair still damp and curled from the shower, and attired in a fresh Western shirt and jeans, he made Leigh catch her breath. His gaze rested warmly on her for a brief second before he turned to Freddy. "What's this about a baby?"

"We're going to have one." She paused to glare at her husband. "Although I'm beginning to think men as hardheaded as Ry McGuinnes shouldn't be allowed to reproduce."

Joe grinned and addressed Ry. "Congratulations." His gaze swept to include Freddy. "That's great news...isn't it?"

Freddy gestured toward Ry. "Go ahead. Tell him what a fool you are."

Ry reached for the extra beer on the coffee table and handed it to Joe. "Eb here has a Brahma bull that's never been ridden to the buzzer."

"And why you keep him I'll never know," Freddy put in.

"Because he's the best," Eb said with a Chesire-cat smile. "I get offers from rodeo stock people all the time who want to buy him outright, but I'm not selling. If you want to try ridin' him, McGuinnes, be my guest. I might even waive the rental fee, seeing as how we're neighbors."

"How charitable of you," Leigh murmured. Eb would love to see Ry knocked six ways to Sunday. A disabled Ry would improve the rancher's chances for acquiring the True Love. "I agree with Freddy, Ry," Leigh said. "That bull is a tough customer. Romeo is a sweetheart unless you put the bull rope on him, but Grateful Dead is another story."

Eb laughed and glanced at Joe. "Know why he's

called Grateful Dead? Because after he tosses you, you're grateful you ain't dead."

"Nobody can deny he'd be a great draw for the rodeo," Ry said, taking another swig of his beer.

"The Christians and the lions were a great draw for the Roman-coliseum crowd, too," Freddy said. "I never figured you for a martyr, though."

"I've decided you're all martyrs," Eb said. "Flying in the face of the True Love Curse."

"And what is that, again?" Joe asked. "I never can get these superstitions straight."

"The cavalry massacred some Indians on this land, so the Indians cursed it and said no white man would ever make a profit here," Eb said.

"Is that so?" Joe gazed at Eb. "Then why are you—" He stopped speaking as Kyle ran into the room.

Kyle skidded to a stop and glanced uncertainly at his father. "Belinda told me to wash up for dinner."

"Who's this?" Eb boomed, leaning over the arm of his chair to stare at Kyle. "And what're those funny things on his ears?"

Joe walked over to Kyle and placed a hand on the boy's shoulder. "This is my son, Kyle," he said in an even tone. "Kyle, this is Mr. Whitlock, who owns the Rocking W Ranch right next to ours. I guess he's not a 'Star Trek' fan."

Eb blinked. "'Star Trek'? Oh, I see. That weird guy with the ears, Dr. Spock or something."

Kyle drew himself up straighter. "*Mr.* Spock," he said.

Ry joined the exchange, a challenging gleam in his eye. "You have to forgive Mr. Whitlock, Kyle. At his age, it's tough to keep up with things."

"Now, wait a minute," blustered Eb. "I never wanted to keep up with all that space stuff."

"Exactly Ry's point," Leigh said. "Space is the wave of the future, a concept for the younger generation."

Kyle's gaze swung from Ry to Leigh. Leigh winked at him and a slow smile spread across his face.

"Better go wash up, buddy," Joe said, squeezing Kyle's shoulder gently.

"Okay." Kyle turned to Eb with new confidence. "Nice meeting you. I'm sorry you're so old."

Leigh bit the inside of her lip to keep from laughing as Kyle skipped from the room. A glance into Joe's twinkling eyes told her he'd enjoyed the interchange as much as she had. And he'd acknowledged his son, Spock ears and all. She raised her tea mug slightly in salute. He responded with an almost imperceptible lift of his beer bottle and his teeth flashed beneath his mustache in a brief smile. Leigh felt giddy with hope, and the beginnings of a deeper emotion she dared not give a name to.

o

ALL JOE WANTED was five minutes alone with Leigh to apologize. Wonderful though the kiss had been, it never should have happened. He'd put her at risk. He'd been so determined to finish the damn car door that he'd ignored his own safety, which wasn't too smart, considering his responsibility to Kyle. He hated to think he'd developed such a taste for personal danger over the years that he'd welcome a lightning storm.

But regardless of his own stupidity, he'd almost caused injury to Leigh. He hoped she'd forgive him, although he doubted he'd ever forgive himself.

The dinner with Eb Whitlock dragged on forever, it seemed. When the festivities moved from the dining room to the living room, Joe excused himself to put Kyle to bed. When he returned, Eb was back in the overstuffed chair he seemed to prefer, drinking coffee with Leigh, Freddy and Ry. Two of the guests, a couple from Japan, had joined the group and seemed entranced by Eb's stories.

Joe stood in front of the fireplace and observed Eb. No doubt the guy was acquisitive, not to mention obnoxious, but Joe had a hard time imagining he'd stage all the accidents just to add another hundred and sixty acres to his holdings. The bragging value didn't seem high enough for that, and owning the True Love wouldn't change Eb's life appreciably. Time and again Joe had to consider who had the most at stake—Belinda, Duane, Freddy...and Leigh. Under normal circumstances none of them would react this way, but he, Ry and Chase had backed them into a corner, and that could produce dangerous behavior.

When Eb finally left, Ry cornered Joe and indicated he wanted a powwow on the patio. Joe spent a half hour explaining to a very disappointed Ry that he didn't think Eb was the culprit.

"You said yourself these were desperate acts," Joe said as they sat in lounge chairs. The pool, lit from beneath the water, glowed in its tiled setting like a smooth turquoise. The rain had cooled the night air until it was almost crisp, and no evening swimmers marred the glasslike surface.

"The brushfire was definitely the act of a desperate person," Ry said. "And I might add that my wife was nowhere near the ranch when it broke out."

Joe waved aside the comment. "People can be hired. She could be in league with Belinda, Dexter or Leigh. My point is, all of those people have reasons to be desperate. Whitlock doesn't. I can see why you'd like to nail him. He's an irritating son of a bitch, but unfortunately that's not against the law."

"You sound like Lavette. He keeps telling me not to let my dislike of Whitlock get in the way of my judgment. But I keep thinking there might be something we don't know, something that would make Whitlock willing to commit those acts. I think he's vicious enough. He can hardly wait to get me on that bull of his."

"Yeah, what's that all about? Do you have a death wish or something?"

Ry grinned. "That bull will probably toss me six ways to Sunday, but having him perform will be good publicity for the rodeo, and I'm about the only guy willing to get aboard. And who knows? Maybe by some miracle I'll stay on for eight seconds. It would be sweet if I could make it to the buzzer and wipe that damned smirk off Whitlock's mug. But all of that's secondary, really."

"And what's primary?"

"The real reason I'm riding that bull is that I can't ever let Freddy think she's tamed me. She's a hell of a strong woman, and once I start saying, 'Yes, dear,' our relationship will go downhill fast. I have to keep that balance."

Joe laughed and shook his head. "Watching you two is sort of like watching King Kong and Godzilla battle it out."

"I wouldn't let Freddy hear you say that. I doubt she'd feel flattered to be compared to either of those characters, especially after she starts getting a little rounder, if you know what I mean." Ry pushed himself up from the chair. "Well, I can see you're not going to support my case against Whitlock, so I'd better go find that wife of mine and see if she'll welcome me into her bed tonight. It's never a sure thing."

"Sounds like a rough way to live."

"Nah. I love a challenge." Ry adjusted his hat and walked inside.

After he left, Joe went looking for Leigh. She wasn't in the living room or dining room. When he poked his head in through the swinging door of the kitchen, Belinda looked up from the table where she was busy making out a shopping list.

"Still hungry, cowboy?" she said in her lilting voice.

He liked being called that. "No, thanks. Dinner was great. Have you seen Leigh?"

Belinda's eyes twinkled. "Try the front porch. She likes to sit out there with Dexter and Chloe."

As Belinda had predicted, Joe found Dexter and Leigh sitting in the shadows with Dexter's black-and-white dog curled at their feet. Dexter said something in a low voice and Leigh laughed softly. Joe's heart turned over at the inviting sound of it.

The dog noticed him first and raised her head.

Then Leigh glanced toward the door, her delicate silver earrings winking in the light spilling from a nearby window. She'd combed her hair free of its braid and it hung free down her back. "Hello, Joe."

The sound of his name coming from her lips was sweet torture. "Hi."

"Dexter was telling me about the Scrabble game with Kyle. I guess they had a great afternoon together."

"Great," Dexter echoed.

"Glad to hear it." Joe wondered how to describe his afternoon. Earth-shattering, perhaps.

The front door opened behind him and Belinda stepped out. "Bedtime, Dexter," she said.

"You're sure?" Dexter asked.

"I'm sure," she replied firmly.

"Okay." Dexter reached for his walker. "Come on, dog. What's her name, again?"

"Chloe," Leigh said.

"Chloe," Dexter repeated. "Why can't I remember?"

"You will," Leigh said gently. "Every day you're getting better, Dex. Keep playing Scrabble with Kyle."

"Great game," Dexter said as he pulled himself erect and moved the walker across the wooden porch toward his wife. "High fives."

"Kyle was so sweet to play with Dexter all afternoon," Belinda said to Joe. "He's a nice boy."

"I'm sure he enjoyed it, too," Joe said.

"I hope so. Good night, you two."

"Good night," Leigh and Joe said together.

Joe held the door for them as they went inside, Belinda following Dexter's measured progress and Chloe trotting behind Belinda. Then he quietly closed the door.

"Kyle accomplished quite a feat this afternoon," Leigh said.

"What's that?" So aware of her that his skin tingled, he sat on the chair recently vacated by Dexter.

"With that Scrabble game, he's found a teaching tool that might help Dexter overcome some of his communication difficulties. And a boy with an empathetic personality like Kyle's is perfect for working with Dexter."

"That's great, of course, but—" He paused, knowing they were dealing with thorny issues, wishing he could just sit here and absorb the magic of the night a little longer.

"But?"

"Kyle spends too much time indoors, as it is. I was hoping this vacation would be different for him."

A tense silence followed his comment. "There are times when it's prudent to be indoors," she said at last.

So she regretted the moment they'd shared, he thought with a sinking sensation in his stomach. "You're right. That's why I came out here, to apologize for this afternoon. I should never have—"

"Kissed me?" The question had a harsh ring.

"That's—"

"I'm sure you regret giving in to your impulses." She stood and walked to the edge of the porch. "A good lawman doesn't let emotion interfere with his judgment like that, does he? And certainly not with the suspect in a crime."

He ran his finger thoughtfully over his mustache as he gazed at her profile, cold and unyielding in the pale light from the stars. "No, I wasn't acting very professionally this afternoon," he said.

She crossed her arms and looked up at the night sky, free of clouds now, although there was no moon. "I'm guessing you're a Scorpio."

"Which, I suppose, explains everything."

"It explains a lot." She didn't even gloat over the fact she'd been right about his sign.

"Don't try to pin labels on me, Leigh."

She turned back to him, her face shadowed. "Not labels. Human traits. Human frailties. You do have them."

He pushed out of the chair and stepped closer. "I realize that. I just said I made some mistakes this afternoon."

"Mistakes you plan to correct, I take it."

A soft breeze carried her wildflower scent to him. His

heart pounded as desire stalked him like a jungle cat. "You tell me. You have all the answers."

"So do you." Her voice caressed the air around him. "You just don't realize it."

"Probably not. I'm not as subtle as you." Need tightened his chest, making breathing a chore.

"Ah. It's not a big step from subtle to devious, now, is it?"

"Stop it, Leigh. I didn't say that."

"But I expect you were thinking it. How inconvenient for a man of your sensibilities that you're attracted to someone who could turn out to be your criminal." She leaned against a post and wrapped her arms behind it in a provocative gesture that lifted and defined her breasts beneath the soft material of her blouse. "I should take pity on you and keep out of your way, I suppose. But it's too much fun trying to get a rise out of you, so to speak."

He lost the battle. Muttering an oath, he slid one hand behind the small of her back and the other behind the nape of her neck. He took some small satisfaction in the knowledge that she was trembling.

"My goodness." Her voice was raspy, which excited him all the more. "Are we about to be unprofessional again?"

"You witch." He pulled her roughly against him and took her mouth in a kiss meant to punish. Yet when she opened to him, the lush promise of her lips drowned his anger and replaced it with blinding passion. All of her teasing dissolved into the most honest response he'd ever experienced from a woman. She held nothing back, and in seconds he was fully, achingly aroused.

Yet now was not the time to finish this. Maybe the

time would never come. Steeling himself for deprivation, he released her and backed away.

She leaned against the post again, her chest heaving. Then she ran her tongue slowly over her lips, and he groaned. "Coward," she whispered. He turned away, not trusting himself to reply to her taunt.

"Sleep well, cowboy," she murmured.

He heard her move from the post and walk across the porch to the front door. When at last it closed behind her, he let out a long, shaky breath. Sleep well. What a laugh.

7

LEIGH WAS DETERMINED that the trip to the corrals the next morning would be a good experience for Kyle. If Joe wasn't satisfied with the way everything turned out, that was too damn bad. Joe needed an attitude adjustment, and she was just the woman to give him one.

All three of them rode down in her truck with Kyle sitting between Leigh and Joe. She'd located a couple of fishing poles and lures that Chase Lavette had used on his last expedition to the pond, and Belinda had packed them all a lunch, just in case Kyle agreed to the trail ride. But Joe would not force the issue. Not on her watch, she'd decided.

"Do you think Penny Lover could have her baby *today?*" Kyle asked as the truck bounced along the road, rattling the fishing poles in the back.

"I don't know," Leigh said. "After I check her this morning, I'll be able to tell you."

"I wish she would. I've never seen a real baby horse before." Kyle looked up at Joe. "Have you, Dad?"

"Just in the movies," Joe said.

"They're pretty cute," Leigh said, "trying to stand on those wobbly legs, their stubby little tails wiggling around for balance. As far as I'm concerned, the birth of a foal is the most exciting thing that happens on the True Love."

"I think so, too," Kyle said, his voice full of reverence.

As they reached the corrals and Leigh stopped the truck, he scrambled to his knees, digging the toe of his boot into her thigh in the process. "Which one is she?"

"You can't see her too well from here. I have her in one of the far corrals by herself." She opened her door. "Ready?"

"Yep."

Leigh smiled to herself. The afternoon spent with Dexter had made an impression. Kyle was beginning to sound like a cowboy. Except for the Spock ears, he looked like any other little boy who'd grown up on a ranch, with his red plaid Western shirt and a belt cinching his jeans tight so they wouldn't slide down over his skinny hips. But when his booted feet hit the ground, his city roots became obvious. A ranch boy would have taken off running for the corrals. Kyle looked over at the milling herd of horses, which looked more imposing now that he was out of the truck. He shrank back and grabbed Leigh's hand.

She wished he'd grabbed Joe's hand instead. Joe had his stoic mask in place, as if he hadn't noticed Kyle's gesture, but she'd bet money he had, and was hurt by it. The day Joe Gilardini surrendered completely to his human emotions would be a glorious one indeed. Leigh wondered if she'd be around to see it.

Leigh gave Kyle's hand a reassuring squeeze. "Let's go see Penny Lover."

Kyle nodded, too overwhelmed by his surroundings to speak.

When they neared the corral, the Appaloosa spotted Leigh and shoved her nose over the fence. Leigh fed her a carrot from her pocket and scratched behind the horse's ear. "How's my little mother today? I brought you some visitors."

"All I can see is her head," Kyle complained.

Leigh had anticipated that Kyle wouldn't be able to see over the solid mesquite fence, but she'd decided against picking him up. Like any young animal, he needed to start learning how to get around on his own.

"Here's how you climb up, Kyle." She demonstrated by placing her foot in a crevice and pulling herself up.

Kyle looked at her doubtfully. "I might fall."

"Not if you choose your footholds carefully. You can do it."

Kyle took a deep breath and stepped up to the fence. His progress was slow, but Leigh resisted the urge to help. At one point, she glanced at Joe. He returned her glance and mouthed the word *thanks*. She felt inordinately pleased with herself.

Kyle reached the top and peered over. "Wow, she's *fat*."

Leigh and Joe laughed, and Penny Lover tossed her head.

"She won't be fat much longer," Leigh said. Unlatching the gate, she slipped inside the corral, another piece of carrot handy to calm the horse. "Easy, girl. She's a Blanket-hip Appaloosa," she explained as she stroked Penny Lover's swollen belly. "That means the front part of her is solid, in this case brown, and her rump and hips are flecked with white."

"Will her baby look like that?" Kyle asked.

"I sure hope so. That's the gamble. We never know if the offspring will carry the Appaloosa markings or not." She took another piece of carrot from her jeans pocket and walked toward Kyle. Penny Lover followed. "Want to give her a piece of carrot?"

Fear and yearning vied in his blue gaze.

"She won't bite you. Just hold your hand flat and she'll take the carrot off with her lips."

Slowly Kyle extended his hand, palm up, and Leigh placed the carrot in the center. Penny Lover's ears pricked forward and she took a step toward Kyle. He jerked his hand back. Joe, leaning against the fence, sighed, and Leigh could have kicked him.

"Keep your hand steady," Leigh instructed. "Carrots are like candy to her. Give her a piece of carrot and she'll love you forever."

Eyes wide, Kyle extended his hand again. Penny Lover walked forward, her nostrils flared.

"She looks scary," Kyle said. But he didn't move his hand.

Leigh's voice became almost a croon. "She won't hurt you. Easy. Easy. That's it."

The Appaloosa stretched her lips over the carrot and picked it up.

Kyle giggled and snatched his hand away. "She *tickled* me." Then he gazed with pride as Penny Lover crunched the carrot between her teeth. "Is that good, Penny Lover?" The horse tossed her head, and Kyle giggled again. "Can you tell if she'll have her baby today?" he asked.

Leigh had been evaluating Penny Lover the entire time she'd been inside the pen. "I doubt if it will be today," she said.

"Aw," Kyle said, his face cloudy with disappointment.

"Since she won't have her baby today, how about a picnic?" Leigh suggested as she let herself out of the corral and latched it behind her.

Kyle called a last goodbye to Penny Lover and climbed carefully down from his perch. "Where?"

"There's a beautiful little canyon with a pond not far from here. We could all go if you want."

Kyle looked at Joe. "Do you want to?"

To his credit, Joe tried to appear nonchalant. "Sure."

"How will we get there?"

He was a smart little kid, Leigh thought. "We'll take a trail ride."

Kyle shook his head. "I don't think so."

"You could ride the horse I had yesterday," Joe said. "Mikey's very gentle. You'd like him."

Kyle shook his head again.

"What if you rode Mikey with me?" Joe asked. "I could make sure you don't fall."

Kyle stood for a long moment, considering. "I'd ride with Leigh," he said at last.

Leigh's heart wrenched at the sadness that flashed in Joe's eyes before he covered it with his usual calm expression. "Okay," he said.

Leigh crouched next to Kyle. "Your dad's a terrific rider," she said. "Why don't you—"

"I said it was okay," Joe interrupted. "Now let's get going."

HIS SON WAS on a horse. Joe tried to take comfort in that as he followed Leigh and Kyle up the narrow trail into Rogue Canyon. The trouble was, Leigh was responsible for all the progress with Kyle. She had the pregnant mare that had lured Kyle to the corrals and she'd been the one to coax Kyle to climb the fence and feed carrots to Penny Lover. Now Kyle was riding a horse because he trusted Leigh to keep him from falling off. Joe was glad for all of it if that meant Kyle would begin to love the ranch, but as Leigh skillfully handled each situation with Kyle, Joe's feelings of inadequacy deepened. If there was one emotion Joe hated more than any other, it was that one.

Both fishing poles were stashed in his saddlebags. With his luck, Leigh would be a better fisherman than he was too. It was a petty thought and he brushed it aside, irritated with himself. He was probably looking for a reason to be upset with Leigh so he could distance himself from her. After their encounter on the porch, he'd tossed and turned all night. It was against his personal policy to become entangled in a relationship as complicated as this one threatened to be.

Along the trail he watched Leigh carefully as she pointed out the scarred acres blackened by the brushfire a month earlier. She seemed genuinely distressed by the destruction, but he wasn't letting her off the hook yet. He'd keep watching her, along with Freddy, Belinda and Duane. Somebody would get careless eventually.

The horses picked their way up into the canyon, their hooves clipping the rocks embedded in the trail. Joe took off his hat and wiped his forehead with his sleeve. The humidity from yesterday's rain turned the canyon into a giant sauna, but Joe didn't mind the heat. Better canyon walls than New York skyscrapers, better a hawk circling in the breeze than a flock of pigeons. Despite all his emotional turmoil since he'd arrived, he didn't regret a penny of his investment.

At last a bouquet of green farther up the canyon announced the location of the pond. When they rounded another bend, Joe could make out the rock-and-earth dam that sat astride the dry creek bed. Leigh urged Pussywillow up a steep bank to the right of the dam and he followed on Mikey, who smelled the water and nickered.

"Look, Dad!" Kyle pointed with excitement to the pond cradled by the dam. Its surface caught the reflection of cobalt sky and a crowd of majestic cottonwoods rimming the oasis. An orange dragonfly skimmed the water and barely escaped the fish leaping after it.

"Looks great, Kyle." Joe noted the size of the fish and immediately picked out two spots for casting—the sandy beach on the left side of the pond and a large rock on the back side. From either spot he should be able to avoid the reeds that swayed on the pond's far right bank.

Nudging Mikey, he rode up beside Leigh and dismounted, dropping the reins to the ground. "I'll take Kyle," he said, ducking under Mikey's neck and reaching for his son. Kyle came into his arms without hesitation, and his heart jerked with pleasure. "How'd you like the ride, buddy?" he asked as he set him on the ground.

"It was awesome!"

Joe flashed a smile at Leigh. It didn't really matter that she'd been the one to bring Kyle up here. They'd made it, and Kyle would be more than ready to go again. He returned to Mikey and opened the saddlebag. "Hey, Kyle, ready to do some fishing?"

"Okay."

Joe's happiness quotient increased. A day fishing with his son. Everything was going to be fine, just fine.

Leigh dismounted and opened her saddlebag. "I'll set up the picnic under that cottonwood tree, and we can eat whenever you want to."

Joe suddenly realized he'd only brought two poles. How stupid. "Do you want to fish? You can have one pole and Kyle can have the other. I really don't need to—"

"Don't be silly. You two go do your thing. I'll sit over here and be lazy. I brought a book, anyway."

He wondered if it was the same one he'd found in the glove compartment of her truck. "If you're sure."

"I'm sure." She gave him that mysterious, mind-bending smile of hers, the one that knocked him right on his rear. With that smile alone, she made him want her.

"Okay. Come on, Kyle. You're going to love this." As he assembled the poles and threaded the line, he wondered why he hadn't thought earlier of fishing as an activity to share with Kyle. There was nothing scary about fishing. Just a lot of thinking time, talking time. He attached a lure for Kyle and helped him cast the line out into the water.

"Now what?" Kyle asked.

"I'll cast mine out, and we'll sit and wait for the fish to come."

"Oh." Kyle stood patiently holding his pole while Joe got his line in the water. When Joe sat, Kyle sat, in exact imitation.

"Did you see how that horse Penny Lover took my carrot?" Kyle asked.

"I sure did."

"Horse lips feel funny." Kyle sat there staring at the water for a while. "I wonder what cow lips feel like. Or elephant lips."

"Or bird lips."

Kyle glanced at him, then saw he was teasing and laughed. "*Bird lips.* What about..." His rolled his eyes and pursed his mouth. "What about *bug* lips?"

"Don't you think ladybugs have lips?"

"No!" Kyle laughed again. Still smiling, he gazed across the pond. "I like this, Dad."

"Good. Me, too." Joe glanced over at Leigh, propped against the tree reading her book. She'd taken off her hat and sunlight filtered down through the leaves to dapple her golden hair. Joe's heart swelled with gratitude, and something else that was linked to desire, but wasn't quite the same. Something he hadn't felt in a very long time.

"She's a nice lady," Kyle said.

Joe brought his attention back to Kyle, who had noticed the direction of his glance. "Yes, she is."

"I think—"

But Joe never learned what Kyle thought. Kyle screeched as his fishing rod was nearly jerked from his hands.

"You've got a fish! Hold tight! Leigh, come hold my rod!" Joe didn't understand her peal of laughter until much later. He was too busy issuing instructions to Kyle to notice sexual innuendos.

"It's pulling really hard, Dad!" Kyle had staggered to his feet and was struggling to hold on.

Leigh arrived and Joe handed her his fishing pole. Then he crouched behind Kyle and wrapped his hands around Kyle's. "We'll pull him in gradually. Let me help you turn the reel. That's it." Joe's voice quivered with excitement. His son's first catch, and he was there. Maybe they should have the fish mounted.

"He's jumping around, Dad. Here he comes! Here he comes!"

Joe reached for the line and hauled in the bass, a respectable size for a first catch. He held it suspended by the gills as its tail flipped wildly back and forth. "A beauty, Kyle. You did great!" He bestowed a proud smile on his son. Then he blinked. Kyle's face was white, his eyes wide with horror. "What's wrong, buddy? This is a great fish!"

"The hook's through his mouth, Dad! And he can't breathe. He's dying!"

"Kyle, it's a fish. We catch fish. We eat fish."

"Not me!"

"Where do you think fish sticks come from? Or those tuna sandwiches you like?"

"They don't look like that!"

"Once they did."

Kyle's lower lip quivered. "Put him back, Dad. Please. Take the hook out and put him back, so he can breathe."

Although Joe had his back to Leigh, he could feel her eyes on him. Hell, he could hear that soft, compelling voice of hers inside his head telling him to release the fish. She should stand by him on this. She lived on a ranch, for God's sake. Where did Kyle think hamburgers came from?

A tear dribbled down Kyle's cheek, making a track in the dust he'd picked up on the trail. "Please, Daddy."

Joe blew out a long, exasperated breath. The hook was imbedded pretty deep. As he tried to work it free, the bass jerked and he jabbed his thumb. Cursing under his breath he kept working, his blood mingling with that of the fish. Finally, the hook was out, and he tossed the fish back into the pond with a loud splash. It flipped its tail and disappeared beneath the surface. Kyle let out a gigantic sigh and plopped to the sand as if his legs wouldn't hold him another minute.

"I guess that's it for fishing," Joe said as he turned to Leigh. "I might as well reel that line in, too."

She handed him the fishing pole with a sympathetic glance.

"I'm leaving the issue of cows up to you," he said in an undertone.

She shrugged and gave him a small smile.

"Don't tell me you're a vegetarian."

"Pretty much."

"Swell. What's for lunch, cucumber sandwiches?"

"Roast beef for you, cheese for me and peanut butter and jelly for Kyle." She walked over to where Kyle sat on the sand and stared at the water. "The fish will be okay, Kyle."

"I sure hope so."

"Come on and help me get the sandwiches out." Leigh glanced up at the sky. "The clouds are moving in, so we'd better eat and mount up."

Joe looked up at the thunderheads forming against the mountains at the end of the canyon. After yesterday, he accorded them a lot of respect. He reeled in the line quickly and hurried to where Leigh had lunch laid out. "You're right," he said to her, tipping his head toward the clouds. "We'd better eat and run."

"I think we can stay ahead of it."

"Good. One encounter with lightning is enough for me."

She caught his eye for a moment and then quickly looked away again. "I understand."

He knew from her expression she'd read more into what he'd said than he'd intended. "I'm a simple man, Leigh. Don't look for hidden meanings."

Kyle gazed at his father. He hadn't spoken directly to him since they'd let the fish go. "What are you talking about, Dad?"

Joe couldn't imagine how he could give Kyle an explanation that would make any sense to a seven-year-old, so he didn't try. "Nothing, Kyle."

"Oh." Kyle returned his attention to his sandwich.

"Your dad thought I misunderstood him, but I don't think I did," Leigh said. "Now finish your sandwich quickly so we can get going. He's right. We don't want to get caught in the storm."

Moments later, as Joe was stashing the poles in the saddlebag, he thought he saw something move beyond the trees. A deer? He peered through the foliage, but whatever it was seemed to be gone. He turned to Leigh, who was mounting up. "Do you have deer up in this canyon?"

"A few. Why?"

"I may have just seen one."

"A deer?" Kyle gazed around. "Where?"

"It would be unusual to see a deer this time of day," Leigh said. "They prefer early morning or twilight."

"I must have been mistaken," Joe said. "Come on, buddy, and I'll lift you up in front of Leigh." He decided against suggesting Kyle ride down with him. No matter what he tried to do with the boy, it never worked out right. Apparently, he wasn't cut out to be a father to a boy like Kyle.

8

THE DARK CLOUDS advanced, but not fast enough to explain Leigh's uneasiness. She tried to identify the source of her worry. Maybe it was the bad business about the fish. She'd known in her heart that Kyle wouldn't like the final outcome of fishing, but she'd pushed the knowledge aside and hoped she was wrong. Joe so desperately wanted something to share with his son.

Pussywillow seemed to share Leigh's nervousness, but it could be a residual reaction to the fire. When Amanda and the baby had been trapped up in this canyon during the brushfire last month, Amanda had been riding Pussywillow. Leigh thought the gray mare had been cured of her fear of the canyon, but maybe not. Pussywillow balked on the trail several times and tossed her head.

"Leigh, what's the matter with her?" Kyle asked. He was wedged in front of her on a saddle Leigh had chosen for its roomy seat.

"Oh, she just gets twitchy sometimes." Behind them, thunder bounced across the mountain peaks, but the trail was still in sunshine.

At a switchback, Leigh glanced up at Joe following behind on Mikey. Joe had a tense set to his shoulders and a frown cut a groove between his eyebrows. The thunder rolled again, and he leaned back to study the clouds.

Leigh fought a sense of urgency. A good rider didn't push a horse down a steep trail. There was plenty of time to make it back to the ranch before the storm hit, so she had nothing to worry about. But her instincts told her she did. She scanned the empty trail ahead of her for some sign that there was a problem but could find nothing unusual. A cactus wren scolded them from the top of a saguaro, and a chipmunk skittered away from the approaching horses and riders.

"I hope Dexter wants to play Junior Scrabble today," Kyle said.

"I'm sure he's counting on it," Leigh replied. "That game really helps him remember words."

"It's fun talking to Dexter. Sometimes I pretend he's an alien trying to learn our language."

Leigh smiled. "He does have to learn a lot of things over again. They're all locked in his head, and he can't get them out."

"*I'm* going to help him get them out."

"Yes, I believe you are." Somewhere above them in the mountains, lightning hit a tree with a loud crack, and Pussywillow threw up her head. "Pat Pussywillow's neck," Leigh told Kyle. "Tell her everything's okay."

"It's okay, Pussywillow," Kyle crooned. "We're right here."

Leigh watched him and felt a moment of unexplainable terror. Kyle was so small. A lump formed in her throat and she glanced back at Joe. She wished he were following a little closer. She drew in Pussywillow's reins. "Come on, Joe," she called. "You're lagging back there."

He looked over his shoulder at the storm, then turned toward Leigh. "Mikey's doing his best. You know, I don't know what it is, but I have this funny feeling that—"

Boom!

The explosion shook the ground and careened off the granite walls. Kyle screamed, and Leigh fought with Pussywillow to keep her head down as the terrified mare tried to rear.

"Leigh!" Joe shouted. Rocks clattered off the edge of the trail as he propelled Mikey toward them.

"We're okay!" she shouted back, all her attention on her plunging horse. "Don't run into us!" She brought the mare to a shivering standstill just as Joe skidded next to them. She wrapped an arm around Kyle, who had a death grip on the saddle horn and was whimpering softly.

"What the hell was that?" Joe asked, staring up the canyon in the direction of the explosion.

"Shh! Listen!" Leigh said. A soft roar grew steadily louder. When she realized what it had to be, her stomach pitched and she glanced wildly around them. They had to get up the side of the canyon. In less than a minute, a wall of water would reach them, sweeping away everything in its path.

She looked at Joe. "The dam just broke."

Panic was allowed only a temporary place in his eyes before it was replaced with fierce resolution. "We'll make it out."

"You take Kyle with you. Mikey's a stronger horse, and he's better in chaotic situations."

Joe's jaw flexed. "Then you and Kyle get on him and I'll take Pussywillow."

"No." The roaring grew louder, accompanied by ripping noises as undergrowth was torn from the canyon floor. "We don't have time to argue. I'm a better rider."

"All the more reason for you to take him on Mikey! We're not going to argue, because I'm telling you—"

"I wanna stay with Leigh!" Kyle wailed.

"See?"

"Just do it, Joe. I don't think I have the strength to hold him while we go up." Birds flew down the canyon, animals sought higher ground as the earth trembled.

His expression was grim. "All right. Come here, Kyle."

"No!"

"Now, Kyle!"

Leigh leaned close to the trembling boy. "This is an order from your captain, Mr. Spock," she murmured, holding him tight, trying to convey strength. "The success of the mission depends on it. I'm counting on you. And you'll have to be very quiet, so you don't scare Mikey."

After a tense moment, he nodded.

She lifted him from the saddle and into Joe's arms. She had to shout to be heard above the deafening sound of the water that was nearly upon them. "Get Mikey up the side of that hill! I'll be right behind you!" She hoped. Mikey was steady and well-trained enough to go up the hill. She wasn't so sure about Pussywillow.

Joe clamped an arm around Kyle, pointed Mikey at the hill and dug in his heels. The horse plunged upward, scrabbling to gain its footing on the loose rock. Leigh held her breath and silently urged them on. She'd made the right decision. She didn't have Joe's upper-body strength and she would never have been able to keep her seat and hold on to Kyle at the same time.

Snorting and heaving, Mikey gained a yard, two

yards, slid back a foot, gained another two. Joe's shoulder muscles bunched as he kept a tight hold on Kyle with one arm and grasped the reins in the other hand.

After what seemed like hours, enough room opened up behind them and Leigh pointed Pussywillow in the same direction. The mare wouldn't budge. Leigh stroked and patted, crooned and demanded. The sound of rushing water grew close, very close.

"I should leave you here, you bag of bones," Leigh muttered. "But I won't. We'll try this another way." She dismounted and started up the hill, the reins in her hand. They tightened as Pussywillow continued to balk. "Come on, girl," Leigh called. She clucked and whistled, promised treats and apologized for calling the mare a bag of bones. Then the roar became deafening, and she looked up the canyon and saw the water.

Suddenly, all she could think of was the old movie clip of Moses parting the Red Sea. The water advanced down the narrow canyon, a ten-foot-high blade scraping everything clean as it passed. Nothing could survive being carried along in the torrent.

"Come on!" Leigh shouted, yanking on the reins.

Pussywillow took a step forward, then another.

"That's it!" Leigh climbed higher, pulled harder. Pussywillow followed, but she was going too slow. "You stupid horse," Leigh cried, pulling until she thought her arm would come out of its socket.

Then a strong hand wrenched the reins from her. Joe was beside her, hauling the horse up the slope, yelling at her to go on up to Kyle.

She glanced at the wall of water bearing down on them and shook her head.

Joe's eyes blazed. His shout was nearly obliterated by the oncoming water as he tugged on the terrorized horse's reins. "Go! He needs you more than he needs me!"

"That's not true, you bullheaded dope! There's no dealing with you, is there?"

Joe stared at her. Then his mustache twitched as the corner of his mouth lifted in a half smile and he shook his head. "Go," he murmured. For good measure, he gave her a swift whack on the behind.

Recognizing the stubborn Scorpio will in action, she started up the slope. Kyle couldn't be left alone, and Joe would wrestle with that horse until the water arrived. She knew that more surely than anything else in the world. Grasping at bushes and outcroppings, she climbed toward the ridge where he'd left Kyle and Mikey. She could see a portion of the bay horse, but no sign of Kyle. He must be petrified.

"We're coming, Kyle!" she called, not knowing if he'd be able to hear her over the crash of the torrent below or if the term *we* was accurate.

When she was nearly to the ledge, she looked back. Joe had made some progress, but not enough. The water surged just below him, gradually slicing the ground from beneath Pussywillow's hind feet.

"Joe! Leave her!" she screamed.

He dropped the reins, but instead of abandoning the mare, he lunged for the bridle and yanked. For once, Pussywillow acted in her own interests and leapt forward just as the last bit of support slid from behind her. Horse and man scrambled, slid back, scrambled some more.

And made it.

Leigh sat down where she was, covered her eyes and began to weep. Slowly she became aware of a small arm around her shoulders, and a hand patting her arm.

"Don't cry," Kyle said, sounding as if he would burst into tears himself at any moment. "Don't cry, Leigh."

She sniffed and wiped at her eyes just as Joe reached the spot where she sat.

He adjusted his grip on Pussywillow's bridle and gazed down at her without speaking. Finally, he cleared his throat. "Why aren't you two up on the ledge with Mikey?"

Kyle looked up at his father. "I came to be with Leigh."

An immense sadness filled his eyes and he looked away. "Yeah, I can see that, buddy. I can see that plain as day."

THE DANGER WAS OVER so quickly it seemed incredible to Joe that it had ever existed. In a matter of minutes the water level began to recede, until finally only the creek bed ran full. But a shadow passed over the sun, and Joe remembered that they still had an impending thunderstorm to worry about.

"Let's go." He started the laborious process of turning Pussywillow around.

"The trail will be wiped out," Leigh said. "Want me to lead?"

"I can handle it. You bring Kyle on Mikey." He made himself say it, feeling the pain of knowing that Leigh was a better choice for taking care of his son than he was. If she hadn't told him to, Kyle wouldn't have ridden with him up the hill. Kyle depended more on a woman he'd known three days than on Joe, his own father. Sometimes Joe found it difficult to believe Kyle was really his son, although he didn't doubt the biological fact of it. But there seemed to be nothing of Joe's spirit in this boy, nothing to connect them except for a last name. And Emerson Pope would love to change even that. Maybe Joe was wrong to fight it.

The trip back was tough as they worked their way around uprooted trees, their roots reaching into the sky like sea anemones, and boulders the size of sedans wedged against piles of debris. Any minute, Joe expected the thunderstorm to strike, but instead the clouds edged north along the mountains, moving gradually out of range, grumbling as they departed.

When the bedraggled group was nearly out of the canyon, Joe heard a shout and answered it. From around a dislodged boulder Ry and Freddy came riding toward them, their faces taut with strain.

"Thank God!" Freddy cried, urging her horse forward. "We heard the explosion and rode out to investigate. When we saw the water in Rogue Creek, and no sign of you..." She swallowed. "Where were you when the dam gave way?"

"On the trail coming back," Joe said, his gaze swinging toward Ry, who looked grim as death.

Freddy gasped.

"Hey, sis," Leigh said, coming up beside Joe. "Am I glad to see you."

Freddy's eyes brimmed. "I'm pretty thrilled about it, myself. Come on, let's get you all home again so I can have a nervous breakdown."

Joe glanced at Ry. "It doesn't look as if we'll have that storm this afternoon, so if you have the time, I'd like you to come back up the canyon with me," he said.

"Sure thing. Freddy can go back with Leigh and Kyle." Ry sounded casual, but Joe knew by the set of his jaw that he was anything but relaxed.

Freddy looked from her husband's stern expression to Joe's determined one and nodded. "Let me switch mounts with you, Joe. Pussywillow looks done in. You'll do much better on Maureen."

Joe rubbed the gray mare's neck. "I'm sure Pussywillow would appreciate that. She's had a bad day." He swung down from the saddle.

Kyle turned wide blue eyes on him. He hadn't spoken since they'd climbed down the hill and started home. "Will the water come back again, Dad?"

Joe paused. "No, Kyle. That was all the water from the pond, and it's drained now."

Kyle drew in a sharp breath. "The fish! What about the fish?"

Joe heaved a sigh. He didn't believe in holding out false hopes to anyone. It only prolonged the agony. "I don't think they made it, buddy. I'm sorry."

"Daddy!" Kyle's cry was almost an accusation. "Can't you save them when you go back up there?"

"I don't think we can, son."

"Your father saved *us*, Kyle," Leigh said. "And didn't you see the way he pulled Pussywillow up the hill? If he hadn't done that, she would have been swept away too."

Joe knew she was only trying to help, but it was humiliating that she even had to try. He sought her gaze. "I'd appreciate it if you'd just get him home for me," he said softly.

"I will." Her eyes were deep with unspoken sympathy.

"Thanks." He turned away. Taking the reins that Freddy handed him, he swung up on Maureen and followed Ry up the canyon.

Viewing the damage after the adrenaline rush was gone made his stomach turn, especially when he thought of what could have happened to Kyle and

Leigh. In the Bronx he'd seen the rubble left when a ten-ement house had been bombed as part of gang retalia-tion. This was a little like that, except the bodies were of animals caught in the destruction instead of people. Joe could easily imagine people instead. Specific people. That was the difference between a cop's imagination and a civilian's, he thought. A civilian might be afraid of death, but in general terms. A cop had seen enough to make those terms very specific.

"What do you think we'll find when we get up there?" Ry asked over his shoulder.

"I hope we'll find evidence of dynamite. Maybe some footprints, hoofprints of a horse. I saw something when we were up there for our picnic, something I thought was a deer. I think it was our guy."

"Unfortunately, you're not going to be able to prove much from footprints or hoofprints. The True Love has traditionally given hikers and trail riders access into the mountains through Rogue Canyon. Matter of fact, I think Duane brought a breakfast ride up this morning. The pond's a popular spot. At least it was a popular spot."

"Then Duane could have planted a timed explo-sive?"

Ry didn't reply right away. "I guess he could have."

"Whoever did this is a reckless bastard," Joe said. "Maybe he'll also start getting careless."

"I hope this incident convinces you it couldn't have been Freddy or Leigh."

Joe had been giving that some thought. He didn't an-swer right away.

Ry swiveled in his saddle. "Joe? Come on, man. Leigh could have been killed today, along with you and

Kyle. You saw how Freddy reacted, too. And you just suggested the person is a man."

"I don't think either of them executed this, if that's what you mean. But suppose they started something they don't know how to stop? Suppose they hired somebody in the beginning, and that person has decided to take command of the operation?"

Ry shook his head. "Freddy couldn't keep something like that from me this long. I'd sense it, or she'd break down. If I thought she was capable of hiding a secret that horrible, I'd have to question the validity of our whole relationship."

Joe gazed up the canyon. Was it the aftermath of battle, or only the beginning of the fight? "I hope that won't become necessary," he said.

"It won't."

"And maybe Freddy doesn't know anything. Maybe it's Leigh who started the ball rolling." The words sat bitterly on his tongue, but he had to say them.

"You're wrong, Joe. Leigh has a reverence for life. Even if your original supposition was true, and Leigh had hired someone to make mischief around the True Love, she'd have exposed that person after the brushfire, no matter what the consequences to her." Ry swept his arm to encompass the battered canyon. "She'd have gone to jail before she would have allowed something like this to happen."

Joe wanted to believe him, but Ry wasn't a reliable source. He'd fallen in love with the ranch and its foreman. "Well, this joker has my full attention, now," Joe said. "I'm on this case full-time. I'm even considering sending Kyle back to his mother, since I can't spend time with him."

"I would hate to see you do that," Ry said. "I know

how much it meant to you, bringing him out. Maybe you'll wrap this up quickly. Belinda and Dexter can keep an eye on him, and Leigh seems to have taken a real shine to him."

"Yeah. A real shine." Joe hesitated. "The thing is, even if I could spend time with Kyle, he probably wouldn't want me to."

"Hey, I doubt that."

"We just don't operate on the same wavelength, Ry. I've tried, but we keep missing the connection. I'm making us both miserable."

Ry didn't respond right away, and the silence was filled with the crunch of the horses' hooves in the streambed. Finally, he said, "This is going to sound corny as hell, but I'll say it, anyway. The True Love has a way of helping you sort out stuff like this."

"Now you sound like Leigh."

"I know it. A few months ago I would have choked before admitting that a place could have...well, like a *healing* effect on people. Living with asphalt and concrete all my life, I couldn't imagine what a ride through the desert on a good horse could do for me."

Joe laughed. "The way I heard it, you ended up so saddle sore you could barely stand up."

"That, too." Ry guided his horse carefully over a fallen tree. "Who knows, maybe it won't happen for you. I was just a paperpusher back in New York, but out here..."

"I know what you mean. It's the way the dust smells, the way the shadows change on the mountains."

"The sunsets."

"The thunderstorms," Joe said. He'd loved that storm yesterday, he realized now. It wasn't very rational to tempt lightning that way, but he hadn't been operating rationally, especially after Leigh arrived.

"It's up to you, of course, but I wouldn't send Kyle back just yet," Ry said. "Give it some time. I don't think you'll regret it."

"Hell, I have so many regrets now, a few more wouldn't matter, anyway."

9

LEIGH UNDERSTOOD that Joe had to make the investigation top priority. He and Ry had found evidence of dynamite at the ruined dam, and the whole future of the ranch was at stake. Yet, she thought Joe was carrying his absorption in the case too far. For the past three days, he'd spent virtually no time with Kyle. True, he spent his days and some of his nights talking to anyone who might have information he could use, and he had reason to be tired and distracted. But Leigh suspected Joe was using the admittedly legitimate excuse of the investigation to avoid painful contact with a son he didn't understand.

Kyle made do, Leigh noticed. He played Junior Scrabble with Dexter a lot and swam in the pool under Belinda's watchful eye. Leigh set up the adobe block project, and she and Dexter spent an afternoon out behind the patio wall teaching Kyle how to make the sun-dried bricks. They'd had to erect a plastic tent to keep the adobe dry during the afternoon rain, but the blocks had turned out fine. Kyle had used them to build a shelter for his Star Trek action figures.

To someone who didn't look closely, Kyle might have seemed perfectly happy, but Leigh watched Kyle with the empathy of a kindred spirit. She noticed each time he looked longingly after his departing father, and the slump to his shoulders after Joe had dismissed an overture for attention by saying he had to discuss something with Ry.

Apparently, Joe had decided to ignore Leigh, too. His words to her were few, and if from time to time he glanced her way, he turned his head the minute she tried to meet his gaze. After two earth-shattering kisses, he'd closed himself off. Textbook Scorpio—stubborn and wary. But knowing that didn't ease the ache in her heart.

Still, she thought she and Kyle were coping well under the circumstances and she'd decided not to make an issue of Joe's behavior. Until today, however, when she looked out the living room window and saw Kyle fishing in the swimming pool with a fishing pole made from a stick, a string and a rock tied to the end of it. Chloe, Dexter's dog, lay beside Kyle, her head on her paws. The sight of that lonely little boy sitting cross-legged by the pool pretending to fish broke her heart.

She walked through the French doors onto the patio and Kyle looked up, his Spock ears still resting on the underside of his cowboy hat. Leigh smiled whenever she saw those ears. Joe didn't realize it, but Kyle's stubborn insistence on wearing the ears was evidence enough he was Joe's son.

"Hi, Leigh," Kyle said. Chloe lifted her head and smacked her shaggy tail on the concrete.

"Hi, yourself." She took a deep breath of the rain-scented air. A storm had passed through a few minutes earlier, washing away the intense heat. Scattered clouds remained, blocking out the punishing afternoon sun. "It's nice out here. Mind if I join you and Chloe?"

"No, but I only got one fishing pole."

"That's okay." Leigh grabbed a plastic chair cushion

and set it down next to Kyle on the damp concrete. "Isn't your behind getting wet?"

"Yeah." Kyle grinned. "I don't care. Chloe doesn't care, either."

"I guess you're both tougher than I am, then." Leigh lowered herself to the cushion and sat quietly, waiting to see if Kyle would talk.

"This is the part of fishing I like," he said at last. "You can just sit and think. Or if somebody's with you, you can talk a little bit. I've been talking to Chloe."

Leigh's heart squeezed. "That is a good part of fishing."

"I don't like the catching fish part."

"Me, neither."

Kyle sighed, and it was much too grown-up a sound to have come from a seven-year-old.

Leigh waited, letting him choose his moment, his way of communicating his problem.

"Like I've been telling Chloe, my dad sure is busy," Kyle said at last.

"It takes a lot of time, trying to find out who blew up that dam."

"Don't worry. Dad will catch them. He's the best."

Leigh gazed into the turquoise water of the pool. "I'm sure he is."

Kyle raised his pole a little and the stone tied to the end bobbed to a different spot on the bottom of the pool. He sighed again. "The trouble is, my dad hates me."

Leigh gasped and turned to him. "Oh, no, Kyle! He loves you more than anything!" That much she knew. Joe couldn't express his love, but she never thought for a moment it didn't exist.

But Kyle shook his head. "He thinks I'm a wimp because I like Star Trek stuff, and I'm scared to ride a horse by myself, and I don't like catching fish. I bet he wishes he had a different boy.''

Leigh wrapped her arm around his shoulders. ''More likely he wishes he could be a different kind of dad.''

''Different?'' Kyle looked at her in surprise. ''But he's perfect the way he is!''

A lump lodged in her throat. ''So are you,'' she murmured.

''No, I'm not. I get scared. I get scared a lot.''

She gazed into his blue eyes and debated how much to say. ''Everybody gets scared sometimes.''

Kyle returned his attention to his fishing pole. ''Not my dad.''

''Even your dad.'' Instinct made her glance toward the living room window. Somehow, she'd known Joe would be there, watching them. She caught the bleak yearning in his expression before he realized he'd been discovered and walked away from the window.

Apparently, Kyle had been too wrapped up in his misery to notice the figure at the window. ''My dad's not afraid of anything,'' he maintained, his chin jutting out.

He looked so much like Joe at that moment that Leigh had a sudden insight. What if Joe had been a sensitive little kid, just like Kyle? Maybe he'd been teased, hurt, disgraced somehow. Someone with a protective instinct as developed as Joe's would want to make sure his son didn't suffer the same fate. The only way to do that was to toughen the kid up and help him build a shell around himself just like his father had.

''Kyle, I'm going to tell you something about me, something I don't talk about with people unless I trust them. Can I trust you?''

Kyle turned to her and nodded so hard his hat flipped off. He grabbed it and put it back on, careful not to crush the Spock ears.

"All my life I've been able to...sense things. I'm sort of like a radio that picks up waves. If I tune in, I can sometimes tell what people are thinking. If I really concentrate, I can tell what animals are thinking."

"Cool! What's Chloe thinking?"

Leigh hesitated, then focused on the dog. She smiled. "She's thinking that damp concrete feels good. And that she likes the way you smell."

Kyle laughed and scratched behind the dog's ears. "I like the way she smells, too. We can't have a dog in my mom and stepdad's apartment, but I sure would like to have Chloe live with me. Would you like that, Chloe?"

Chloe licked his hand.

"I don't think she would," Kyle said, looking back at Leigh. "No rabbits to chase, no horses, no Dexter."

"You see? You can figure out what animals are thinking, too."

Kyle looked startled. Then he shook his head. "I was just guessing."

"I think with practice you could do more than guess."

"Wow. That would be cool."

Leigh smiled down at him. She could really grow to love this kid. "I had a specific reason for telling you about this ability I have. First of all, do you believe me?"

Kyle nodded.

"Then listen very carefully. Your dad doesn't hate you. He loves you very much. He'd like for you and he to be better friends, but he hasn't figured out yet how to make that happen."

Doubt struggled with hope in Kyle's blue eyes. "You saw that in his mind?"

"Absolutely."

Hope won, and a tiny smile played at the corners of his mouth.

"So think about that while you and Chloe are fishing, okay?"

"Okay."

"I have a few things to take care of, but I'll see you at dinner." Leigh pushed herself upright and picked up the chair cushion.

"Yep," Kyle said happily, his face lit with joy. "See you at dinner."

LEIGH HURRIED toward the French doors. With luck Joe was somewhere nearby, and he was going to listen to what she had to say if she had to rope him and tie him to a post to keep him in one spot.

Joe was no longer in the living room, but Rosa, the head housekeeper, was there supervising a new girl who was cleaning the cobwebs from the high, beamed ceiling.

"Did either of you see where Mr. Gilardini went?" Leigh asked.

Rosa propped her hands on her hips. "Out on the porch, I think. *Sí.* The porch."

But Joe wasn't there anymore, either. Leigh gazed around in frustration. Then she started down the flagstone walk. She'd told Kyle she could read minds, and many times she could. Right now, she had to connect with Joe's if she expected to locate him. The ranch was a big place.

At the end of the walk she paused and glanced at the sandy ground. There were boot prints in the moist earth and the prints led off to the left. She followed them, knowing that she could be tracking anybody in a pair of cowboy boots. But intuition told her she was following Joe. A path beyond the parking area led to a seldom-used picnic spot in a grove of mesquite trees. Leigh had vague memories of family picnics there when she was very young and her mother was still alive. But with one rickety picnic table and no fireplace for cooking, it wasn't a practical spot for feeding ranch guests, and few people knew it was even there.

The tang of wet creosote bushes spiced the air. The green bark of a nearby palo verde tree gleamed as if it had been shellacked, and in its branches hung a cobweb woven with diamonds. Bring water to the desert and amazing things happened, Leigh thought. Flowers bloomed where only thorns had been before. If only such a transformation could be wrought in people. Perhaps what some people needed was a cleansing storm.

Her boots crunched along the sandy path as she walked toward the picnic area. She made no attempt to approach quietly. She was through pussyfooting around Joe Gilardini.

He sat on the table, his feet propped on the attached bench. His expression was guarded as he watched her come toward him. "There must be some Indian blood in your ancestry," he said. "Tracking me all the way out here."

She stopped and braced herself for the fray. "Maybe I should just stake you over an anthill and pour honey on you, come to think of it."

Joe nudged his hat back with his thumb. "And to what do I owe this flood of hostility?"

She threw her anger at him as if hurling a bolt of lightning. "Your general stupidity."

"That comes as no surprise. I never claimed to be a genius."

She aimed again, determined to crack his armor. "How about a father? Did you ever claim to be that?"

His eyes darkened and he stepped down from the table. "I should have known this would be about Kyle. I saw you out there having a little talk with him while he fished with that stick of his."

"Don't you dare make fun of that fishing pole."

He came closer. "If I don't, some other kid will. The way I look at it, it's my job to—"

"Make him tough?"

"Somebody has to."

"And make him think you hate him?"

He recoiled as if she'd slapped him. His mask slipped. "What?"

"That's what he thinks. And considering all your macho instructions, your disapproval, your long absences lately, it's no wonder. He has every reason to suppose that—"

Joe grabbed her by the shoulders, his eyes reflecting the storm in hers. "How could he think I hate him? Did you plant that in his head? Because if you did, so help me, I'll—"

"*You* planted it in his head, you idiot! You've given him the idea that there's something wrong with him because he's not as fearless as you are. He doesn't realize that *you're* the cowardly one, running away from any show of emotion, running away from anybody who might make you *feel* something." She gasped for breath, drawing the warm, wet air into her lungs, the scent of ripe earth into her nostrils. Her heart fluttered like a bird's.

A muscle worked in his jaw as he glared down at her.

"You're nothing but trouble. I figured that out the first time I saw you."

"You think *you* have trouble with *me?* I wish you'd never set foot on this ranch! Of all the men in the world, it had to be you—a proud, suspicious, stubborn *Scorpio.* Fate couldn't send me a gentle Pisces or a fun-loving Libra, or a kindhearted Aquarius. No, I have to end up with you!"

He gave her a shake. "End up with? What in hell are you talking about?"

"This." She stood trembling in his arms, drowning in the sensation of his touch. "Don't tell me you can't feel what happens whenever we get within ten feet of each other."

His grip tightened and flames danced in his eyes. "That's the dumbest thing I've ever heard. Maybe there's some basic animal attraction between us, but I'm no victim of fate. Neither are you."

"Then let go of me," she murmured, knowing he would not, could not.

"In a minute." He drew her closer, swept her hat from her head and tossed it on the table behind him.

"Why not now?" she taunted as her mouth moistened for his kiss and her body tightened and throbbed for even more.

"Because I choose not to."

She closed her eyes. "That's what you think."

His mustache tickled her upper lip as he paused. "Shut up, Leigh," he said softly.

Then he was there, and nothing mattered but this. He pulled her in, setting her heart in motion as surely as the moon swelled the tides. His tongue sought entrance and she gave it—unable to resist giving whatever he called forth in her. Exchanging breath for breath, they kissed deeper, and deeper yet, strengthening the connection made in that first glance, that first touch.

She arched against him, feeling the familiar imprint of his body. She didn't know when they would make love—perhaps not even in this existence. But they would make love. It was inevitable. She would smooth the rough, raw edges of his soul with the nectar of desire; he would slake her thirst for cataclysmic passion. Because at last she understood. She was not destined for a gentle love filled with soft sighs and dewy looks. She was born for the whirlwind.

He'd unfastened the first two buttons of her blouse before his hand stilled and his mouth lifted from hers. He was breathing hard. "There's no such thing as star-crossed lovers," he managed to say.

She greeted his statement with a soft laugh.

He moved his hand from the buttons of her blouse up the column of her throat to her chin, where he tilted it back so he could look into her eyes. "You're beautiful and I want you, simple as that. A normal man-woman thing."

She struggled for breath. "And you always have this strong a reaction to the beautiful women you meet? In a city like New York, where fashion models walk down the street every day, you must be in a perpetual state of arousal."

"No, I don't, but the pressures are different there. The pace is faster. There's not as much time to think about..." As he gazed down at her, he seemed to lose his train of thought. Naked passion flared in his eyes. "All right. I've never wanted anybody like this," he admitted. "I want to rip your clothes off and take you right here on the picnic table."

"Why don't you?"

He caught his breath. "God, you're sassy."

"Get used to it, cowboy."

"That's like asking a horse to get used to a burr under his saddle."

"I couldn't have said it better. When are you going to let loose and take that saddle off? Burrs aren't a problem if you ride bareback."

He groaned and pulled her tight against him. "I've tried so hard to stay away from you. I need a clear head for this investigation, and you turn my brains to mush."

"You're making the mistake most cops make, trying to solve a case with logic. If you'd let me help, I could save you a lot of time."

His gaze narrowed. "With your 'powers' you could lead me to the person who's doing this?"

"Maybe. I could certainly tell you who isn't doing it."

"Okay."

She was taken aback. He'd capitulated to her methods too easily. "Okay?"

"Sure. I'll use any information that comes my way. Go ahead."

She backed out of his arms. "You're stringing me along, aren't you?"

"No. I'd honestly like to hear your opinion."

She studied his expression and believed his statement, as far as it went. But something didn't feel right. "We can discuss the case later. The most important issue right now is Kyle. He's probably still sitting out by the pool, and he desperately needs some attention from you. That's what I came out here to accomplish. But somehow, when we're alone..." Her gaze sought his and her body responded to the banked desire in the depths of his eyes. Warmth rushed through her. On this level of communication, she had no doubts.

His hands clenched at his sides and his breathing quickened. "My God, you test a man's control." His look burned as it swept over her, as if making an unspoken promise that the fire raging between them would be dealt with soon. "Go on back. I'll follow in a minute."

Leigh did as he suggested, not because she was willing to comply with his orders, but because, at the moment, a little boy's needs were more important than her own.

When she reached the ranch house, an unfamiliar BMW sat in the parking area outside the low adobe wall. She hurried down the flagstone walk, her instincts on red alert. Opening the front door, she found Kyle and Belinda standing with a chunky man, whose silk tie looked uncomfortably tight around the collar of his white dress shirt. He wore glasses and was beginning to grow bald. But the most important thing about him was the way he rested his hand on Kyle's shoulder.

Belinda glanced at Leigh. Her expression was distraught, but she maintained her poise and spoke with her usual pleasant manner. "This is Emerson J. Pope, Kyle's stepfather," she said, confirming what Leigh had suspected. "Mr. Pope, this is Leigh Singleton, our head wrangler."

Pope turned, but he didn't offer her his hand. "Kyle called his mother yesterday," he said. "His stories of rampaging bulls and flash floods made her hysterical with worry. We're convinced this isn't a safe environment for the boy. I've come to take him home."

10

JOE LEANED his backside against the picnic table with a sigh. Folding his arms, he studied the damp, sandy ground at his feet. Leigh was so tuned in to him that he'd have to be very careful. She wanted to help him with the investigation. This could be her way of leading him to the person she'd hired and ending the destruction without implicating herself. Maybe she was in league with Eb Whitlock. He hated to think it, but he had to stay objective, despite the way she heated his blood. Even despite her good intentions with Kyle.

He now believed she really wanted to help him connect with his son. So, Kyle thought he hated him. Funny, Joe had figured it the other way around. He thought Kyle didn't have much use for his rough, crude father, the fish killer. Every move Joe had made seemed to be the wrong one, so he'd relegated himself to the role of bad guy, the unpopular person destined to teach Kyle about reality. But he didn't want Kyle to think he hated him. He loved the little guy, Spock ears and all. Yet he'd never said so, never felt comfortable with stating his feelings straight out like that. And gushing about love wouldn't help the kid toughen up, which he desperately needed to do if he was to survive.

Joe started up the path and thought about what he could say to Kyle that would convince the boy he didn't hate him. Maybe he could tell him how proud he'd been that Kyle had fended for himself while his dad had been busy with the investigation. That would reinforce self-reliance. Joe could admire the adobe blocks Kyle had made and compliment him on picking up a new skill, which conveyed another good message.

As he reached the ranch house, he felt better about the coming conversation with Kyle. At least he had a plan. He noticed the relatively clean BMW sitting outside the adobe wall and wondered who had driven in from town. Most of the people in the area had pickup trucks, and with all the rain that had fallen recently, the fenders were usually crusted with mud.

Striding down the walk, he went over what he would say to Kyle. He wouldn't make fun of the stick-and-string fishing pole. Leigh had been right about that. Better to keep away from the subject of fishing altogether. He opened the front door and started inside. Then suddenly, he stopped, one hand still on the door handle, and stared at Emerson J. Pope.

Pope stared back.

"What the hell are you doing here?" Joe bellowed.

"You weren't entirely candid about conditions out at this ranch, were you, Joe?" Pope said. "Hardly a place for a small boy, wouldn't you say?"

Joe's gaze shot from Pope to Leigh, who looked upset, to Belinda, who looked grief stricken, to Kyle, who looked cowed. "What do you mean, *conditions?*" he asked, turning back to Pope. "Talk like a normal human being, if that's possible."

Pope's cheek twitched, a tic that had caused him some problems in the courtroom, Joe happened to know. Joe had liked nothing better than quizzing cops who had testified at trials where Pope had been the lawyer for the defense. Especially trials where Pope lost.

Unfortunately, that didn't happen often enough to suit Joe.

"I'm referring to the bull incident," Pope said. "As if that weren't bad enough, you took the child into the middle of a lethal flash flood. Darlene instructed me to bring him back to New York. I'm prepared to get a court order, if necessary."

"You son of a—" Joe remembered Kyle and censored his language. "Is that what Kyle wants?"

"I'm not prepared to let a seven-year-old make that sort of decision. He's coming with me."

"Not if he doesn't want to, he's not."

"Look, Gilardini, don't make me use the power of the courts. I—"

The front door swung open and Freddy burst into the room. "Leigh! I called from the corrals earlier but you weren't here, so I drove up—" She noticed a stranger in the room and paused.

"This is Kyle's stepfather, Emerson J. Pope," Leigh said. "Why did you want me?"

"Penny Lover's showing all the signs. Since it's her first foal, I know it could be a while, but I think you'd better get down there. Duane's with her now."

Kyle broke free of his stepfather's grip and rushed toward Freddy. "Penny Lover's going to have her baby?"

Freddy grinned. "I think so. Want to watch?"

"Boy, do I!"

Pope cleared his throat. "I have return plane reservations for both of us in three hours. That leaves just enough time for Kyle to pack and for me to return the rental car. He won't be able to go with you to the stables, or whatever you're talking about."

"No!" Kyle whirled toward his stepfather. "I have to stay, Em! Penny Lover's going to have her *baby*."

Joe stepped closer to Pope. "He's staying."

Pope adjusted his glasses. "I'm afraid not. I promised Darlene that—"

Leigh edged her way between the two men. "I have a suggestion. Why don't you stay at the True Love tonight as our guest, Mr. Pope? I'm sure you can change your plane reservations, and Kyle's mother can't possibly be worried about him now that you're on the scene. Kyle has been waiting for this foal to be born, and I hardly think you want to deprive him of an educational experience I'm sure you couldn't duplicate in New York City. You're welcome to come down to the corrals, yourself, if you like."

Joe watched with interest as Leigh turned up her compelling gaze to full wattage. Joe knew well the effect of that wise serenity.

Pope squirmed and finally looked away. "I—ah—see your point. The boy is very bright—gifted, in fact. Darlene's family is very intelligent. She's always trying to expose Kyle to new experiences, challenge his intellectual capacity. Let me call her and discuss the situation."

"Leigh," Freddy said, urgency in her voice. "We have to go."

Leigh gave a slight nod and returned her attention to Pope. "By all means, call her. Belinda can reach us down at the corrals if your wife still insists that you and Kyle be on that plane tonight, but I have a hunch she won't." She put out her hand to Kyle. "Let's go."

Kyle took it and looked up at Joe. "Are you coming, Dad?"

"Wouldn't miss it for the world." Joe fell into step beside Kyle as Freddy led the way out the door. Behind them, Belinda directed Pope to the phone.

When they were all safely headed down the walk toward Freddy's truck, Joe glanced over at Leigh. "That was one of the slickest things I've ever seen."

Leigh just smiled, but Freddy laughed outright. "You don't want to get into a verbal contest with my sister."

"But that guy's a trial lawyer!" Joe said.

"But Leigh read his mind," Kyle said. "Didn't you, Leigh? That's how you knew what to say."

Leigh flicked a glance at Joe before smiling down at Kyle. "I could see that your stepfather really had your best interests at heart, so I simply pointed out that in this case, it would be in your best interests to stay and watch Penny Lover give birth. It's true, after all."

"It sure is!" Kyle said, almost skipping along beside her.

"Somebody's going to have to ride in the back of the truck," Freddy said. "All four of us can't squeeze into the seat."

"I'll ride in back," Joe volunteered.

"Me, too!" Kyle said.

"No, I'm afraid not," Joe said. "I don't want your stepfather taking a look outside and discovering I allowed you to ride in the back of a pickup. He has enough charges racked up against me already. I wonder how he found out about the flood and the bull?"

Kyle looked miserable, but he squared his shoulders and faced his father. "I called and told Mom. It's my fault, Dad. All this is my fault."

Joe met the admission with a swell of pride. "It took guts to tell me that, Kyle. Congratulations."

"Then you're not mad at me?"

"Of course not." He gave Kyle's hat a tug. "Now get in the truck. We have business down at the corrals."

Leigh held the door as Kyle clambered into Freddy's muddy white truck. Just before she got in, she glanced back at Joe. Her smile was bright enough to light the universe. Or at least his corner of it. He grinned back and vaulted into the truck bed. He'd never met a woman to equal Leigh Singleton.

TWO HOURS LATER, quite a festive group had gathered around Penny Lover's corral as the mare took her time about going into labor. Joe stood leaning against the fence with Ry and Duane while Duane told stories of previous births and Ry kept wondering aloud if he ought to send somebody into town for cigars. For the moment, Kyle sat on the top rail right next to Joe's shoulder. He alternated between that perch and standing between Freddy and Leigh while the two women stroked and crooned to the expectant mare.

The other hands kept dropping by the corral to check on Penny Lover's progress. Joe's three days of familiarizing himself with everything about the ranch had included learning their names. Curtis was the tall blonde; the guy with the big belly and mustache was Davis; and everyone called the earnest young kid with freckles Rusty.

They all seemed to have adopted Kyle. Curtis and Davis even coaxed Kyle over to pet Romeo in his pen behind the tack shed.

"He's pretty nice, really," Kyle confided to Joe afterward.

Ry had arrived about an hour ago, bringing with him a message from Emerson J. Pope. He and Kyle's mother had decided Kyle could remain another night and witness the birth of the foal. Pope had decided to stay at a resort closer to town, where he could get what he termed "a decent meal." Joe was determined to make the most of this reprieve.

Duane bit off a chaw of tobacco and tucked it under his lip. "Any of you city fellers ever seen anythin' born?"

"Nope," Ry said. "This will be good practice for when Freddy has a baby."

Freddy looked over her shoulder at him. "Does that mean you expect me to give birth in the middle of a corral?"

Ry nudged back his hat and winked at her. "Sure would save a pile of money, sweetheart."

The hands all laughed, and Joe grinned, shaking his head at his partner. He'd bet Ry and Freddy would be trading barbs on their fiftieth wedding anniversary.

"I've never seen anything born," Kyle said. "Have you, Dad?"

"Yep." Joe poked Kyle gently in the middle of his chest. "You."

"You *did*? I didn't know that."

"Best day of my life," Joe said.

"It was?" Kyle's eyes shone with eagerness. "What did I look like?"

"A bright red monkey."

"*Dad.*"

"A handsome bright red monkey." *And I was so happy, I cried when the doctor handed you to me.* But this wasn't the time or place to say that. Joe wasn't sure if there was a good time to admit something so personal. Even Darlene hadn't noticed, because he'd turned away before she could see the tears streaming down his face, the tears that had dripped onto that screaming, bloody, fantastic miracle of life that was his son.

Leigh left her charge for a moment and walked over to the fence where Kyle was sitting. "I'm not sure when things will get started around here," she said, her eyes encompassing both father and son. "Maybe you'd like to go back up to the house and have something to eat."

"I don't want to leave," Kyle said. "I might miss it."

"I could go and get Belinda to pack us a picnic or something," Joe offered.

"That's a thought." She stood in the glow from the setting sun, surrounded by light the color of ripe peaches. Joe had never wanted to kiss someone so much in his life.

"I tell you what we're gonna do," Duane said. He paused to spit on the ground. "Penny Lover would prob'ly appreciate it if we'd move a little distance away and give her a chance to concentrate. We got that fire pit over by the bunkhouse and some mesquite stacked up near it. I say let's have us a barbecue while we're waitin' for this baby to get born."

"Yeah!" Kyle said. "That would be great!"

"Wonderful idea," Leigh said with a smile. "An old-fashioned cowboy camp fire."

"I'll go start the fire," Duane said, sauntering off.

"And I'll run up to the house and get the steaks and the beans," Ry offered, heading for Freddy's pickup.

"This will be fun." Leigh turned to the cowhand named Davis. "How about fetching your guitar?"

Davis hoisted his belt over his large belly. "I can do that."

"Do you know any Lionel Richie songs? My mare is partial to *Penny Lover*."

Davis looked offended. "Lionel Richie is not a country singer, ma'am."

"Just thought I'd ask," Leigh said with a chuckle.

By the time the sunlight faded from the sky, everyone except Leigh and Freddy were gathered around the fire. Ry slapped a few steaks on a huge metal grate and

Duane stirred beans in a cast-iron pot. Beer and soda cans were passed around, and fat chunks of wood were pulled around the camp fire for seats. Joe remained standing next to Ry while he nursed a beer and kept an eye on the corral. And on Leigh, he admitted to himself.

Freddy walked over, looped an affectionate arm around Ry's waist and tucked her hand in his back pocket. "Leigh suggested we take fifteen-minute shifts watching Penny Lover. She's on the first watch, and Duane will be the second. I think Penny Lover did need a little more privacy than we were giving her. She seems much calmer now."

"I'll take a shift," Kyle volunteered.

"Maybe you'd like to come along on my shift," Freddy suggested. "I'm after Duane."

"Sure!" Kyle said happily. "You know what this is like, with everybody together? The crew of the *Enterprise*."

Freddy smiled. "I guess it is, at that. And our mission tonight is to bring a foal into the world."

Joe silently blessed her for agreeing with Kyle so easily. "Can I get you something to drink, Freddy?" he asked.

"A ginger ale would be great, thanks." She smiled at him, but there was a wariness in her eyes. She obviously hadn't forgotten that he considered her a suspect in the sabotage case.

Walking over to the ice chest to get Freddy's soda, he wished he could forget all the lessons he'd learned in his twenty years of being a cop. But perpetrators of crimes were seldom complete strangers, and this case had all the earmarks of an inside job. Yet, as he walked back into the firelit circle and looked around, it seemed impossible that anyone sitting there sharing a meal and swapping stories could be guilty of stampeding herds, setting brushfires and dynamiting dams.

Duane walked over and helped himself to some more beans from the pot. "Ain't this like old times, Freddy?" he asked.

"Yes, it is," she agreed. "A scene like this would have made Thaddeus and Clara Singleton proud, after all the things they went through a hundred years ago to keep this place going."

"What things?" Kyle asked with his mouth full.

"The Apache Indians tried to wipe them out once," Freddy said.

"Really?" Kyle's eyes grew wide.

"And then, there was a summer when it didn't rain much, and most of their herd died. There were some terrible dust storms, too."

"How do you know?" Kyle asked.

"Lots of people kept diaries in those days," Freddy told him. "Leigh and I have Clara's, and another one written by Clara's daughter-in-law, Ellie. After that generation, we don't have as much—a few letters, some scrapbooks."

Kyle chewed thoughtfully. "I'd like to see them."

"I'll show them to you tomorrow," Freddy promised. "Hey, Davis, how about a song?"

"You bet." The paunchy cowboy strummed a few experimental chords on his guitar and began "The Streets of Laredo." Curtis and Rusty joined in, and Duane sang along until he had to leave for his shift with Penny Lover.

By the time Leigh arrived in the circle, Davis had switched to "Red River, Valley," a song about a woman who was leaving the valley and taking the sunshine with her. Joe thought of what this valley would be like with the True Love gone. And Leigh gone. Unimaginable.

He levered himself to his feet and went over to take the tin plate she held in her hand. "Go relax. I'll get you something to eat. I assume you're just having beans and bread."

"And a beer?" she added with a grin.

Joe touched the brim of his hat. "Sure thing, ma'am."

"I do love a polite cowboy," she said, and walked over to sit on a stump beside Kyle.

The casual statement hit him with unexpected force. He didn't want her to be casual with a word like that. Not around him. He wanted her to save a word like that for...what? God, he was getting muddled.

He returned with her food and beer and sat quietly on Kyle's other side while she talked with Ry and Freddy. Then she coaxed Kyle into singing along when Davis launched into "Drifting Along with the Tumbling Tumbleweeds." And with her every smile, her every gesture, the ache in Joe's heart grew. He couldn't figure out what in the hell was wrong with him. Indigestion, most likely.

Eventually, Freddy glanced at her watch and handed her plate to Ry. "Your turn to do the dishes, darling. Kyle and I are due over at the corral for our shift." She motioned to Kyle. "Let's go, buckaroo."

Joe gazed after them. "That kid is having a ball."

Ry nodded. "I'll bet after tonight he's not going to want to go back with your friend Pope."

"He's most definitely not my friend."

Leigh set her plate on the ground. "Is he within his rights to drag Kyle back to New York?"

"He might be if he can prove negligence." Joe finished the last of his beer and crushed the can in his fist.

"The thing that worries me is that he'd like to adopt Kyle and get me out of the picture completely. Somebody who knows the law as well as he does can be dangerous."

Ry clapped a hand on Joe's shoulder. "Don't worry. We can handle him." His eyes gleamed with anticipation. "And after that remark he made about going into town for a 'decent meal,' I'd take pleasure in fixing his little red wagon."

"That makes two of us."

"Three of us," Leigh said. When Joe looked at her in surprise, she winked at him. "Ain't it great to have friends, cowboy?"

"Yes, it is," he said, amazed at how much he meant it.

"Daddy!" Kyle called, running from the corral so fast he nearly tripped. "Daddy, it's time!"

Leigh jumped up, her face luminous, and walked quickly toward the corral. Everyone else around the circle deposited plates, cups and beer cans on the ground and followed her. When she started through the gate, she glanced at Kyle hopping along right beside her. Crouching, she took him by the shoulders and looked into his eyes.

Joe couldn't hear what she said, but Kyle nodded and climbed the fence to his perch on the top rail. Joe found a spot next to him and looked into the corral. "All ready for this, buddy?" he asked, putting an arm around Kyle's waist.

Kyle nodded, his face tight with excitement. "I can't be down there right now, because it's very tricky, but I get to *name* the baby when it's born."

"Hey, that's great." Joe gave him a hug. Then he stared in fascination at what was taking place in the corral. The Appaloosa remained standing while two forelegs and a head encased in what looked like blue plastic poked out. Joe concluded that horses and humans had a slightly different way of giving birth. As the birth progressed, Leigh stationed herself at Penny Lover's head and talked gently to her, while Freddy monitored the foal's progress.

"Leigh knows what that horse is thinking," Kyle said in a low voice.

Next to Kyle, Duane chuckled. "She's thinkin' she'd like to get this business over with."

As if to demonstrate the fact, Penny Lover dropped to her knees, and with a grunt rolled to her side.

Kyle gripped Joe's hand and spoke in an urgent whisper. "Here it comes. See, Daddy? Look, there it is!"

Sure enough, as Penny Lover heaved and snorted, the foal emerged, the placenta shimmering in the floodlight illuminating the corral. A muted cheer went up from the group leaning on the fence.

Freddy cleared the mucus from the foal's nose and peered at the foal's underbelly. Then she turned to Leigh with a triumphant smile. "It's a filly. A fine little filly. Let's stand back and let Penny Lover clean her baby."

Leigh leaned down and hugged Penny Lover around the neck before rising and backing away from mare and foal. Her shoulders quivered and she wiped her eyes with the back of her sleeve.

She's crying, Joe thought, *just like I did.* A lump formed in his throat, and he would have given anything to hold Leigh at that moment.

"I knew I should have ordered cigars," Ry mumbled, and his voice sounded suspiciously husky.

Penny Lover whinnied and turned to her baby. With great swipes of her tongue she cleaned the foal, and as the damp coat became more and more visible, Leigh reached out and gripped Freddy's arm. The little filly's rump was spotted with white, just like her mother's, just as Leigh had hoped, Joe remembered.

As a breathless audience watched, the mare stood and nudged her baby. The filly put her two impossibly long legs in front of her, lunged forward and toppled over. The group let out a collective sigh. She tried again, this time getting her hind legs under her for an instant before tumbling to the dirt again.

"She'll make it this time," Kyle announced.

And she did.

There was much chuckling and backslapping among the hands as the filly staggered toward her mother and began to nurse. Freddy and Leigh hugged and turned back toward the fence where Kyle, Joe and Ry waited.

"Well, Kyle?" Leigh asked, lifting her tear-stained face toward him. "What's her name?"

Kyle didn't hesitate. "Spilled Milk!"

Leigh nodded with satisfaction. "Perfect. Good thing she had the Appaloosa markings, though."

"I knew she would," Kyle said.

Leigh stuck her hands in her back pockets and gazed at him. "Learning how to read minds, buckaroo?"

Kyle grinned at her. "Could be."

11

LEIGH AND FREDDY needed to stay at the corrals with Penny Lover a while longer, but Joe could tell from Kyle's wide yawns that he was ready for bed. Kyle was finally persuaded to leave with Joe and Ry after Leigh promised him he could spend the next morning with Penny Lover and Spilled Milk.

Joe and Kyle rode with Ry in the van back up to the ranch house. Kyle kept drifting to sleep in the back seat, but then he'd rouse himself to talk about the birth of the foal one more time.

As Ry pulled into the parking area, Kyle suddenly jerked fully awake. "Oh, no! He was supposed to take me back tomorrow."

Joe knew exactly who Kyle meant. "Do you want to stay?" he asked quietly.

"Of course I do! Leigh told me I could go see Penny Lover and Spilled Milk. I like being a cowboy. I want to stay here with you, Dad. I have to stay. I just have to." Kyle sounded ready to cry.

"Then you will," Joe said, glancing over at Ry. Ry nodded.

Kyle swallowed noisily, as if fighting the tears. "But he said—"

"Never mind what he said." Joe turned in his seat to look at Kyle. "I'll find out where he's staying and call him. You won't have to go back."

Kyle sighed. "Thanks, Dad. You're the best."

"So are you, son."

Kyle's responding smile lit up the night.

Later, while Kyle got ready for bed, Joe picked up the bedside phone and put in a call to the golf resort where Pope was staying. Pope sounded wary when Joe identified himself.

"I'm afraid you made the trip for nothing," Joe said. "Kyle wants to stay a few more days."

"That's unfortunate, because I'm taking him back tomorrow."

Joe longed to issue his own ultimatum, but he remembered Leigh's approach and decided to adopt it. "He learned quite a bit watching the foal being born tonight. Leigh, our head wrangler, has promised him he'll be able to spend a lot of time with the mare and filly. It's like a minicourse in biology."

Pope seemed to be mulling that over. "Darlene wants him home. She's really worried about him."

Kyle was in the bathroom brushing his teeth, but Joe lowered his voice, to be on the safe side. "Look, Pope, the kid's never even had a dog, and he was allowed to name this filly. You should have seen his face. It's as close to having his own animal as he may ever get. Don't take this away from him. He's safe. You have my word on that."

"Let me talk to Darlene and get back to you."

"Okay." Joe hung up the phone and prayed for patience.

"What did he say?" Kyle asked, coming into the room dressed in his Star Trek pajamas, a ring of toothpaste around his mouth.

"He's checking with your mother."

Kyle nodded. "He always does that."

"Really?"

"He's always asking her, 'Should I wear this tie or that tie? Should I take them to lunch at this place or that place?' Stuff like that."

Joe worked up his courage to ask a question he'd never dared voice before. "What do you think of him?"

"Of Em?" Kyle shrugged. "He's okay, I guess, but he'd never make it on the *Enterprise*."

Joe bit back a smile. "Why not? He's smart."

"In some things, but when stuff goes wrong, like the time one of the apartments in our building had a fire, he gets all goofy and runs around in circles, screaming. Mom has to take over."

"Good thing somebody does." Joe never thought he'd be grateful for Darlene's bossy attitude, but at least she could handle a crisis. He was also beginning to suspect the real culprit behind the move to legally adopt Kyle. All along he'd thought it was Pope's idea.

The bedside phone rang and he picked it up. "Gilardini."

"Do you always have to answer the phone as if you were on a police radio?" Darlene asked.

"Hello, Darlene, nice to hear from you." Joe couldn't keep the sarcasm from his voice. Theirs had not been an easy divorce.

"I'm tempted to come out there myself and make sure Kyle's all right."

Joe squeezed his eyes shut and prayed.

"But as long as Emerson's there, and I'm in the middle of a project at work, I'll let him handle it."

Joe let out his breath. "Kyle's fine, Darlene. We got off to a rough start, but he won't be in any more dangerous situations. He wants to stay and get to know this little filly. It's a great opportunity."

"Let me speak to him."

Joe handed the phone to Kyle. The conversation was mostly on Darlene's side, and Joe suspected she was giving him a list of things to be afraid of. Joe looked away and gained control of his anger so that he wouldn't display it to Kyle.

"I miss you, too," Kyle said at last. "Want to speak to Dad again?" He paused. "Okay, 'bye," he said and re-placed the receiver in the cradle. "I can stay." He didn't sound too jubilant about it.

"And?"

"And Em's staying, too. He's still going to be at that resort, but he'll be driving out every day to keep an eye on me." Kyle glanced at his father. "And you."

Joe groaned.

"Mom said he was an equestrian in college, so he's supposed to teach me the correct way to ride."

Joe gazed at Kyle and digested the news. "An eques-trian?"

"You know, somebody who rides—"

"I know what the word means." A small smile crept over his lips. "And I hope he announces it just that way to the folks down at the corrals tomorrow morning."

DUANE FINALLY CONVINCED Freddy and Leigh that Penny Lover could handle her baby without people hovering around the corral all night.

"I'm so glad we decided to breed her, even if the stud money was hard to justify when we were struggling last year," Leigh said to Freddy as they pulled up in front of the ranch house.

"Me, too." Freddy shut off the engine and sat gazing at the house, its windows spilling light onto the porch. "That little filly seems like a sign that everything is going to work out. Joe's going to find out who's sabotaging the ranch and he's also going to agree we shouldn't sell it to developers."

"I want to believe that, too. But I should warn you, he has his emotions locked in a vault. He's not the sort to be swayed by sentimentality about the old homestead."

Freddy looked at her. "But he *has* emotions, I assume?"

Leigh thought of the restrained power of his kisses. "Yes."

"If anybody can dig them out, you can, baby sister."

"I'm almost afraid to try. The result could be something like the flash flood after the dam was dynamited. People could be swept away."

Freddy contemplated her for a long moment. "But isn't that what you've been waiting for? A great passion destined by the stars?"

Leigh swallowed. "Theoretically. In practice, it's scary as hell."

"All these years you've been telling me you couldn't get serious about this one or that one because he wasn't the explosive lover who could fulfill your destiny. Are you saying that Joe could be that lover, and you're backing away?"

"You don't understand." Leigh's voice dropped to a whisper. "He has the power to break me."

Freddy reached over and squeezed her knee. "The best ones all do, sweetie. Take my word, they're worth the risk. And speaking of that, I'm going inside and commune with that special guy of mine."

Leigh opened her door. "Remember how Dad used to drive out to the homestead every time a foal was born and take a bottle of champagne?"

"I do." Freddy climbed down and started toward the house.

Leigh fell into step beside her. "I bought some champagne last week. I'm going out there and thank Clara and Thaddeus for the gift of Spilled Milk."

"Great idea. I'd join you, but now that I'm expecting, champagne's off limits. And—"

"You need to be with Ry," Leigh finished. "That's okay. I have some thinking to do, anyway." She followed Freddy through the front door and nearly collided with Joe.

"I thought I saw you two drive up," he said. "Listen, I wanted to thank you for...well, everything. Kyle will remember watching that foal being born for the rest of his life. And getting to name her, too.... It was the best thing you could have done for him."

Freddy's glance flicked between them. "Where is the little buckaroo?"

"Sound asleep, with a big smile on his face."

Freddy nodded. "That's nice. Leigh was headed out to the old homestead to drink a bottle of champagne in celebration," she added casually.

"I see. Well, I wouldn't want to hold you up. I just wanted to thank you for giving Kyle such a great experience."

Freddy shot a look at her sister. "Yes, well, we took a big *risk* breeding Penny Lover, but the *reward* was certainly worth it, wasn't it, Leigh?"

Leigh wasn't sure if Freddy had forced the issue, or if the evening was unfolding in an inevitable pattern. Whatever the explanation, this was a crossroads she would have reached sooner or later, with or without Freddy's intervention. Perhaps it was appropriate she face this challenge after receiving the gift of Penny Lover's foal. The universe didn't reward cowards.

Taking a deep breath, she looked up at Joe. "Would you like to drive out to the homestead with me and share the champagne?"

Momentary surprise was soon replaced by a soft glow of awareness in his gray eyes. "Yes."

"I'll go get the champagne from the kitchen, then."

"I'll be here," he said as Freddy and Leigh walked away.

Freddy waited until they were through the swinging kitchen door before she let out a muffled whoop of triumph.

"It's all your fault," Leigh said. "If this turns out to be a rotten idea, I'm going to haunt you to the end of your days, Frederica Singleton McGuinnes."

"Where's your ability to see into the future? You should be able to tell how things will turn out."

"The only way I can do that is when my mind is completely relaxed. When I'm around that man, my mind is anything *but* relaxed."

Freddy grinned. "I've been waiting for this day for years. Now go get the champagne and wait right here. I'll be back in a minute."

Leigh retrieved her bottle from the walk-in food locker and plucked two champagne flutes from a shelf. As she turned from the glassware cupboard, Freddy reappeared from the hallway that led to the private wing of the house.

"Tuck these in your pocket." She thrust several small cellophane packages at Leigh.

"Oh, for heaven's sake!"

"Take them! A man on a vacation with his son should

not be expected to carry birth control around with him."

"Freddy, we probably won't even—"

"Then you can bring them back, can't you? Here." Freddy shoved them into Leigh's pocket.

"What if he finds them? How will I explain the fact that I'm running around with condoms, as if I expected something to happen?"

Freddy smiled. "If he finds them, it will be because something is about to happen. Now, go."

So that was how Leigh happened to be driving out to the old homestead site with a bottle of champagne, two crystal flutes and a pocketful of condoms. Next to her loomed a man who seemed to take up more space than she remembered. He held the flutes in one big hand, the champagne bottle in the other. Every time she reached for the floor shift on the old truck, her hand came dangerously close to his knee. When the truck bounced over a rut, his arm brushed hers. The truck cab filled with the masculine, spicy scent of him, and her heart wouldn't behave.

Compared with Joe, the men she'd dated seemed immature and boring. His profession might have closed off his more tender emotions, but it had also surrounded him with an irresistible cloak of valor. He was a modern-day knight in armor, a protector of those smaller and weaker than himself. His presence made her nervous, yet expectant.

"My father started this custom," she said as the headlights picked out the rutted road in front of them. "He called it 'A Toast to the Ghosts.' Every time a foal was born, he drove out here with a bottle of champagne. My mother was sure he would run himself into a tree on the way back, but he never did."

"Did he drink the champagne sitting on the concrete floor?"

"No, he sat in the back of the truck. That way, he didn't have to worry about snakes while he was celebrating."

"Sounds like an interesting man."

"He was a Singleton," Leigh said. "They've been known for doing things their way."

"So I've noticed."

Leigh pulled into the clearing where the concrete slab gleamed a pale white in the light from the stars. "Well, here we are." The beating of her heart sounded loud in her ears. "I guess we could just sit in the cab and drink the champagne."

"That isn't what your father would have done."

"No, he liked to be able to look up at the stars while he contemplated his good fortune."

Joe opened the door. "Then let's go."

The next few minutes were filled with the business of getting situated. The truck bed was littered with an inch or so of hay left over from the time Leigh had hauled a couple of bales out to Duane's herd. Joe set down the champagne and glasses while he helped her spread an old blanket over the hay. It felt for all the world as if they were making up a bed with fresh linens, and then climbing into it as they settled themselves on the blanket, took off their hats and leaned against the cab. Down in the riverbed, a pack of coyotes yipped and barked as they chased a rabbit. Without a moon, the stars were so thick they looked like a dusting of powdered sugar.

"I feel as if I should take off my boots," Joe said.

Leigh's pulse quickened, and she took a steadying breath. "Go ahead."

As he leaned down and did exactly that, she threw

caution to the winds and took hers off, too, while he opened the bottle. She was impressed with how well he knew his way around a champagne cork.

After he'd poured them each a glass, he sat the bottle beside him and raised his goblet. "To Spilled Milk."

"To Spilled Milk, my wonderful little filly, appropriately born under Leo, sign of royalty." She clicked her glass against his and the chime carried through the clear air.

After they drank, Joe lifted his goblet again. "And to the Singleton nerve."

She touched her glass to his and met his penetrating gaze. "To the Singleton nerve." Then she closed her eyes and took a bigger swallow of champagne. Sometimes the Singleton nerve needed a little help. She settled back against the cab of the truck.

Joe followed suit, his shoulder brushing hers. "You had to think about it before you asked me out here tonight."

"A little."

"Why did you ask me?"

She drank some more champagne before answering. "To seduce you so you won't sell the True Love."

Joe's chuckle was warm and rich.

"What's so funny about that? Are you one of those untouchable cops who can't be bribed?"

"I answered that the other day, if you'll recall. When it comes to you, I'm very touchable."

A shiver of awareness ran up her spine. "So why did you laugh?"

"Because you wouldn't try to bribe me with sexual favors if your life, or even the ranch, depended on it. It's not in your nature."

"How can you be so sure? Didn't anybody tell you I'm descended from a lady of the night?"

Joe laughed again. "No, I can't say they did. Which ancestor was that?"

"Clara Singleton, wife of Thaddeus, the better half of the couple we're honoring here tonight."

"Clara was a prostitute?"

"There's good evidence she was, before she met Thaddeus. But you see, he was a very liberal-minded fellow, and he didn't care who had gone before him, so long as Clara pledged her love to him from that day forward. From reading her diary, I can tell she worshiped Thaddeus for restoring her good name." She took another sip of champagne. "She would have done anything for him."

"Sounds as if Thaddeus knew a good deal when he found one." He reached for her glass and refilled it. Their fingers brushed as he returned the glass to her. The contact was enough to interrupt the pattern of her breathing, but he didn't follow the gentle touch with anything more than a smile.

The champagne was making her reckless. "It was a good deal for him." She took a sip while still maintaining eye contact with Joe. "She wasn't an inexperienced virgin, like most of the brides he might have chosen. From a careful reading of the diary you can tell that Clara knew a lot about making love, and she taught Thaddeus everything she knew."

Desire flared in his eyes, but his voice remained calm. "Interesting." He drank his champagne, but his gaze never left hers. "So getting back to your original statement, you're telling me that you, a descendant of a former prostitute, have the ancestral background to use sex to get what you want. Does that about sum up your reason for asking me out here tonight?"

"It could."

"But it doesn't."

She gulped the last of her champagne.

He took the glass gently from her. "You don't need that to deal with me."

"Oh, yes, I do. I wouldn't mind having the rest of the bottle. I wouldn't mind being totally pie-eyed to deal with you, Officer Gilardini."

He put down his own glass and turned back to her. "Then let's see how you're progressing toward your goal." Rising to his knees, he cupped her elbows and drew her up to face him.

"What are you doing?"

"Administering a field test for sobriety."

"You're going to see if I can walk a straight line on my knees?"

His mustache twitched in amusement. "If you can do that, drunk or sober, we ought to get you on Letterman." He held up his index finger. "Follow the movement of my finger."

"Why?"

He sighed. "I knew you'd be a difficult test subject. This is called horizontal-gaze nystagmus. Now just do it."

She laughed but did as he asked.

"Mmm. Again."

She repeated the exercise.

Moving slowly, he cupped her face in both hands. "I regret to inform you that you are not intoxicated."

Yes, I am. "How could you tell?"

He caressed her cheeks with his thumbs, sending heat coursing through her. "If you had been, your eyes

would have jerked involuntarily while you were following the movement of my finger. Yours didn't." His
voice grew husky. "They're also the most luminous
brown eyes I've ever tested."

Leigh gulped. "I think I need more champagne."

His voice was gentle but firm as he leaned toward
her. "No, you don't," he murmured, holding her captive with the pressure of his fingers. "You're a Singleton." His mouth hovered above hers. "You can take the
heat."

12

JOE KNEW he could be kissing a felon, and it showed how far gone he was that he no longer cared. If Leigh had hired someone to cause the accidents, she'd certainly lost control of the process. If it turned out she was implicated, he'd use everything he'd learned about the law to get her off. Maybe she was guilty of loving the ranch a little too passionately for her own good. Joe understood. It was the same sort of desperate need he was beginning to feel for her.

Her mouth opened beneath his as he'd known it would. She could no more deny him than he could deny her. He took her surrender with a fierce joy, thrusting his tongue deep into her sweetness as he pulled her close. He sought to ease the pounding demand of his body against the softness of her breasts, the valley between her thighs—ah.

Yet she was not close enough. He needed...needed... He opened her blouse, unfastened her bra and groaned with satisfaction as the unbound swell of her breast filled his cupped hand. She arched her back and he pushed the garments from her shoulders, baring her to the glow of starlight. It was her element. Surrounded by the silver glow, she lost all hesitancy and met his gaze with a passion that made him catch his breath in wonder.

He stared at her, dazzled as if confronted by a goddess. His voice rasped in the night. "Who are you, Leigh?"

"The one you came to find."

He shook his head. "But I didn't—"

"Didn't you?"

And he knew then that it hadn't been the ranch or the Old West he'd been seeking. It had been himself, the man he'd lost somewhere on the streets of the city. With this woman, he could be that man.

She reached for his hand, turned it palm up and feathered a kiss there. Then she placed it over her breast so he could feel her pounding heart, beating as rapidly as his. "I am flesh and blood, as you are, and our bodies have a powerful need for each other. But our spirits crave connection even more."

And he knew that, too. He'd known it from the moment he'd first looked into her eyes. He'd been fighting the knowledge because it didn't fit with anything he'd ever believed. But he couldn't deny what his trembling soul told him was true.

She brought his hand back to her mouth and kissed each finger before holding the back of his hand against her cheek. "Make love to me, Joe."

The deepest sorrow he'd ever felt washed over him. He hadn't expected this, not really. Even if he had, there'd been no time to make preparations. And no matter how unearthly the connection between them, it could have earthly consequences. He shook his head.

She released his hand and he mentally prepared himself to climb into the truck cab and ride back to the ranch for a long, agonizing night of abstinence. Instead, she smiled her enigmatic smile and reached into her pocket to withdraw several familiar-looking packets. "Would these help?"

He broke out laughing, a joyous sound that welled up from deep within him. "You are amazing. From fantasy to reality in the blink of an eye."

"Well?"

"Yes, these will help." He scooped them from her hand and tossed them to one side, right where he could find them again. Then he reached for her, holding her close as he gazed into her wondrous eyes. "And I *will* make love to you, Leigh Singleton," he murmured. "And count myself the luckiest of mortals to be allowed that."

She took his face in her hands. "I knew there was a poet in there somewhere."

"You would make a poet out of a stick of wood," he said, leaning down to drink nectar from her lips.

She unfastened his shirt, and he grew dizzy with the first contact of his skin against hers. Were there sparks from the friction, or was it desire exploding behind his eyes like Roman candles? He buried his face against her neck and the scent was of jungles he'd never seen, opulent flowers he'd never touched, yet he knew them as intimately as he would soon know her.

Her skin tasted like spice from the Orient, fruit from a tropical paradise, ambrosia from the depths of his fantasies. She created a world in the circle of her arms and offered it to him. Offered. Never had there been a sweeter word to describe the way she lifted her breasts for his pleasure. And he took shamelessly.

It was not enough. He removed the rest of her clothing that he might touch her essence, know the richness of her craving to be loved. She was lush with need, ripe for him, pulsing with his rhythm. He eased her back on the rough blanket, having only a moment to wish it could be velvet against her soft skin. But overwhelming awe swept away that mild regret as he gazed at her flawless body stretched beneath him.

Her image would be with him forever, yet he stroked her with the fervor of a blind man striving to memorize every nuance with his fingertips. She rewarded his touch with small gasps and moans that tightened his groin until he could stand no more and fought to free himself of his own remaining garments.

Looking into her bottomless eyes, he knew he could have slid effortlessly into her without thought of protection and she would not have resisted. The temptation flavored his tongue and trembled through his taut body, but he curbed it and reached for one of the packets beside her head. Distracted by the tumbled locks of her golden hair, he paused to comb his fingers through them. Then he opened the packet.

She watched him, her lips parted and her breath coming in quick spurts that made her breasts quiver. He leaned down to kiss those trembling peaks, to draw them once more into his mouth and feel the excruciating pleasure against his tongue. Her small, inarticulate cries heated his blood and filled him with visions of burying himself deep within her. He released her and sheathed himself with unsteady movements.

When he glanced back at her, his breath caught in his chest. She opened her arms, opened her thighs in a gesture of giving so complete that he moaned in ecstasy. He moved over her, knowing that he would never be the same man from the moment he joined with this woman. He held her gaze as he moved slowly, taking his time, entering her with the reverence due the most shattering moment of his life.

At last he was there, and she lifted her hand to trace the tears dampening his cheeks.

"Yes," she whispered in sweet benediction. Then she tightened around him, awakening the wildness that lay just beneath the surface.

With a sound deep in his throat that he barely recognized as his own, he drew back and thrust forward again. She rose to meet him with a gasp of approbation. He moved again, watching the light flare in her eyes. He worked with that light, building it into a bonfire that made her body glisten in the starlight. In this moment he would claim what she had offered. And she would no longer be the same woman who lay down beneath him.

Surging within her, he lost all sense of where he left off and she began. Nothing mattered but the entity they were creating together, a fusion born of white-hot heat and primitive rhythms. At the moment she arched and cried out, synergy pulled him into the same spiral of release, and he surrendered as never before, without fear, spinning through time and space, his soul entwined with hers.

THE RISKS OF HEARTBREAK remained the same, but now Leigh had savored the rewards and knew she would dare anything to hold this man in her arms. For a few precious moments, he'd cast aside his protective armor and allowed her a glimpse of the richness of emotion he kept hidden like a casket of stolen jewels. No matter how he closed himself off again, he could never take back the naked passion that blazed in his eyes as he rose over her, or the tears when he claimed her.

He stirred and lifted his head from where he'd nestled in the curve of her shoulder. He gazed into her eyes and his mustache lifted as he gave her a slow smile. "Have we landed yet?" he asked softly.

"We may never touch earth again."

He brushed his lips against hers, tickling her with his mustache. "I don't know astrology from Astroturf, but something weird is going on here."

She nibbled on his lower lip. "People don't always have to believe in things for the consequences to affect them. But in case you're interested, we called down some mighty forces tonight."

"I'd be a fool not to agree with you." He touched his forehead to hers. "I've never had an experience even close to that."

"Of course not. Neither have I."

"Because it's written in the stars?"

"That's right."

"This requires some thinking." He eased away from her and reached for the edge of the blanket. Then he pulled it over both of them as he rolled slowly to his back and gazed up at the spangled sky. "You believe what happened tonight between us was predestined?"

At least he was no longer making fun of the idea, she thought. "What other explanation can you give? You were in an elevator accident, a rare thing in itself, right?"

"Almost never happens these days."

"And you met Ry McGuinnes, who happened to be interested in buying this ranch."

"And I came out here and saw you." He reached for her hand beneath the blanket. "Then the fireworks started."

"And where is the first place we made love? The same place Clara and Thaddeus first made love."

He caressed her palm with his thumb. "You said she wasn't the virginal type, so they might have fooled around someplace else before he built this place."

"Nope. I've read Clara's diary. They didn't make love until their wedding night, when he carried her over the threshold of the adobe house he'd built for her, under the lintel with the True Love brand burned into it. She was very proud of that wedding night, almost as if the abstinence cleansed her of her past."

He lay quietly for a moment. Finally, he brought her hand to his lips and kissed it gently, tickling the back of it with his mustache. "I don't know if I can buy everything you're saying, but when I made love to you just now, I felt like that. It seemed like my first time, as if the other women I'd taken to bed were wiped out of my memory. Burned out, is more like it."

Leigh's chest tightened and tears blurred the clear light of the stars. "Yes."

His breathing quickened. "For you, too?"

"Yes."

He turned on his side and propped his head on his hand so he could look at her. He cupped her face and stared intently into her eyes. "That's wonderful to hear. You can't imagine how wonderful." He paused. "And I know what should come next now that you've confessed how you feel. But the thing is, you'd be getting a bum deal with someone like me."

Although she'd expected him to say something like that, it still made her heart trip and stumble. "I'm willing to accept the risk."

"I doubt you even know the extent of the risk."

"I—"

"Do you know why I decided to leave police work?"

"I suppose because you were sick of the violence."

He shook his head. "That's a good, standard answer, but it's not true. What many people don't realize is that a lot of cops get hooked on the excitement that violence brings, and I was one of them. Looking back, I'm not surprised Darlene left me. I was a terrible husband. Being around her bored me compared to being on the job. Even Kyle's activities bored me, so I wasn't much of a father, either."

Secretly she'd feared this part of his personality, but she grasped at hope with both hands. "Yet you did quit the force. And you're trying to connect with Kyle."

"And making a mess of it, too." He sighed. "There was a time I was a lot like Kyle. But I killed off that part of myself when I was pretty young."

"No, you didn't." She reached up and stroked the soft line of his mustache. "I met that side of you tonight."

He looked down at her, longing darkening his gaze. "I don't want to hurt you," he murmured. "And I can be such a bastard sometimes."

"And an angel sometimes." She smiled. "I—"

He tensed and glanced out into the darkness.

She started to speak and he pressed a hand over her mouth. Then she heard the voice.

"Right there, you dummy!" came the harsh male whisper. "A dark blue pickup!"

She shivered as if someone had thrown ice water over her. Joe slowly extricated himself from the blanket and his hand closed over the neck of the champagne bottle.

"Nobody's in it," said another man.

"But somebody drove it out here," said the first speaker.

Leigh didn't recognize either voice.

She could feel the transformation in Joe. With stealthy movements, he reached for his clothes and put them on with an amazing lack of noise. Excitement radiated from him, and she remembered seeing him this way twice before—once when the bull had charged at him and then again when the dam had burst. So this was the demon within him she had to fight.

"I don't like it," said the first speaker. "Somebody's around. Let's go back."

"He won't be happy if we do," said the second man.

"Who gives a damn if he's happy? Come on."

Joe pulled on his boots too hastily, causing one heel to scrape against an exposed part of the truck bed.

"There!" said the first man. "Someone's here!" His exclamation was followed by the sound of boots scrambling against sand and rocks.

Joe leapt from the truck bed, the champagne bottle in his hand as he started in the direction of the running men.

Leigh peered into the shadows created by creosote bushes and cactus. Joe couldn't run through there without getting something stuck in him, but she knew better than to call out and tell him that. Then came the distinct thud of hooves pounding the desert floor. The men were escaping on horseback.

Soon afterward, Joe reappeared in the clearing and walked over to the truck bed. "They got away. Did you recognize either of the voices?"

"No."

"Where's your flashlight?"

"Under the seat, but the batteries are dead."

"What the hell good is a flashlight with dead batteries?" The question cracked like a whip in the still night.

"Nobody's made a trip into town to get fresh ones recently!" she retorted, struggling into her clothes. "My God, you sound as if having dead batteries were a crime."

"They could *cause* a crime. I can't believe you were

willing to drive out, here in the middle of the night without a working flashlight. There's a dangerous jerk on the loose somewhere on this ranch. What if I hadn't come with you?"

"I wouldn't have to listen to this tongue-lashing!"

"Every vehicle should have a working flashlight," he insisted stubbornly.

"Oh, stuff it, Officer Gilardini. I'll drive you to the ranch so you can pick up your working flashlight, since I'm sure you have one in that Chevy of yours. Then you can come back out here and prowl around to your heart's content, doing your cop thing."

They drove to the ranch in tense silence. When they reached it, she turned off the engine and left the keys in the ignition. "Take the truck when you go out again," she said. "Your Cavalier will bottom out on the ruts."

"Thanks."

Scooping up the champagne flutes from the seat, she opened her door and stepped down from the truck.

"I warned you," he said, opening his door.

She leaned her head against the cool metal of the door. "Yes, you did." She glanced up at him "Did you run into any cactus when you took off after them?"

He shrugged.

"You did, didn't you? I suppose you still have thorns in a few places. Let's go inside and I'll—"

"A few thorns won't kill me. I need to get back out there before anything gets disturbed."

"I'll go with you."

"No."

She sighed. "Yes, you did warn me, didn't you?"

He met her comment with silence. She turned and walked toward the house under stars that suddenly seemed cold and very far away.

EVEN WITH A FLASHLIGHT, Joe didn't find anything of value. The ground was too rocky to have recorded much in the way of footprints or hoofprints. A sophisticated crime lab might have been able to do something, but Ry didn't want Joe calling anyone in on the investigation. Used to dealing with a support system, Joe was discovering just what a hindrance working on his own could be. If only he could have caught one of those guys. Someone had sent them out to the homestead site, and he'd bet good money that the someone was the perp he was looking for. He wondered what the homestead had to do with it all.

Finally, he gave up and drove back to the dark ranch house. He wondered if Leigh was asleep. He doubted it, just as he doubted that he'd sleep much in the hours that were left of the night. He smacked the steering wheel in frustration. A lot of years had gone into making him the man he was. One night of lovemaking, no matter how terrific it had been, couldn't alter how he approached life, no matter how much she might wish it would.

FOR KYLE'S SAKE, Leigh exuded good cheer all through breakfast the next morning. To his credit, Joe made the same attempt. All three of them walked out the front door of the ranch house looking as if they were the best of friends. The falsity of it made Leigh's heart ache.

As they started to get into Leigh's truck for the trip to the corrals, Pope drove up in his rented BMW. He climbed from behind the wheel, and Leigh stared. "I believe we have a catalog cowboy on our hands," she muttered under her breath.

"A what?" Kyle asked.

"I'll explain later," she said.

Pope adjusted his white Stetson and walked toward them. Leigh hoped he'd think her smile came from friendliness and not amusement. It was hard to keep a straight face looking at that pristine white felt. Apparently, Pope hadn't heard that modern-day good guys wore black hats. He walked a little stiffly in his new jeans and didn't seem quite used to the heels on his boots. The boots alone would have attracted Leigh's complete attention, decorated as they were with bucking broncos in amazing shades of red, purple and green against a white background that was supposed to coordinate, she guessed, with the hat.

Joe propped his hands on his hips and gazed at Pope. Then he turned to Kyle. "I think your equestrian's here."

Kyle looked his stepfather over, from the tip of his outrageous boots to the crown of his white Stetson. "Guess so."

Leigh bit the inside of her cheek to keep from laughing. Kyle was definitely picking up a cowboy's gift for understatement.

"I'll take the boy with me," Pope said.

Joe nudged his hat to the back of his head. "I dunno. Looks like you might have trouble driving in that getup."

"I would expect that sort of comment from you, Gilardini. Come on, Kyle."

Kyle looked to Joe for confirmation, and Leigh wondered if Joe would kick up a fuss. Instead, he nodded to his son and Kyle trooped off to the BMW with Pope.

Leigh and Joe got into the pickup and led the way to the corrals. "I was sure you'd insist that Kyle ride with us," she said as they started off.

"No use trying to hang a guy when he looks determined to hang himself. When I found out he was an equestrian, as he puts it, I decided to sit back and watch the fun."

"I hope that's what it turns out to be. To be honest, I don't look forward to putting up with him all morning."

"Probably not any more than you look forward to putting up with me."

She shot a glance in his direction. Dammit, no matter how much he frustrated and irritated her, he still had the power to twist her heart. She wanted to stop the truck, take that stubborn face in both hands and kiss that grim mouth until she connected with the passionate man who had loved her so well the night before.

"For what it's worth, I'm sorry," he said.

"For what?" Once before she'd leapt to a conclusion about his apology. She was determined not to do it again.

"For making an issue of the flashlight."

Her shoulders sagged in relief. "I thought you might be apologizing for making love to me."

"Not in a million years."

The statement squeezed the air from her lungs. "Does...that mean you might be interested in trying it again sometime?"

He groaned.

"Joe?"

"I can't believe you have to ask," he said softly.

"I was afraid that—"

"I would walk across hot coals to take you in my arms again, if you're fool enough to want me."

She gulped as desire pounded through her. "I guess I am that much of a fool." She parked the truck at the corrals and worked to control her trembling.

Joe covered her hand with his as she reached to turn off the ignition. Her gaze swung up to meet the intensity in his gray eyes. He didn't say anything, but he didn't have to. His longing and confusion were reflected there for her to read. She turned her hand over and laced her fingers through his. He gripped her hand tightly and the confusion gradually faded from his eyes. She smiled, and slowly, he smiled back.

"Let's go," she whispered. "We're keeping the equestrian waiting."

"Right." With a final squeeze, he released her.

13

JOE NOTICED that Pope and Kyle had already started toward Penny Lover's corral when he and Leigh left the truck. As Pope walked across the clearing, he collected stares and smirks from the cowboys he passed. Curtis was so busy watching Pope, he tossed a shovelful of manure down the front of Rusty's shirt.

Duane came out of the tack shed carrying a saddle and nearly dropped it when he saw Pope. "Who ya got there, Kyle?" he called when he recovered himself.

"This is my stepdad, Em," Kyle said.

"Glad to know ya," Duane said, his mustache twitching. "Thought for a second there it was Tom Mix hisself showed up at the True Love."

"I'm going to take him to see Spilled Milk," Kyle said.

"Then I'm going to show Kyle the correct procedure for riding a horse," Pope said. "I'd appreciate it if you'd saddle one for me."

"What type ya want?"

"Preferably one with spirit. I don't want some worn-out trail pony."

"Okeydoke." Duane nodded his head wisely. He stood and watched Kyle lead Pope away.

"What do you think of our new equestrian?" Leigh asked as she and Joe approached Duane.

"Is *that* what he is?" Duane spat into the dirt and

hung the saddle over the hitching post. "I was wonderin'."

"How are mama and baby doing this morning?"

Duane's weathered face creased in a wide grin. "Them two made me plum glad to git up this mornin'. Penny Lover's given us a fine little filly. A fine little filly."

"Well, I'm going over for a visit," Leigh said. "Want to come with me, Joe?"

Joe felt like following her to the ends of the earth, but he had to use some discretion. "I'd just as soon wait until Pope clears out of that area, if you don't mind. I'm resolved not to punch the guy, but too much proximity and I might forget that resolve."

"Okay." She sauntered over to the far corral.

"Sweet on her, ain'tcha?" Duane asked.

Joe realized he'd been staring after Leigh and felt a flush creep up his neck as he glanced at Duane.

"Don't blame ya none. 'Scuse me. I have to call up to the house and check somethin' with Ry." He reappeared in less than three minutes. "Jist as I thought. Let's you and me go catch a couple of horses." He tossed Joe a bridle.

Joe was pleased that Duane thought him enough of a ranch hand to assign him a chore. "Which ones?"

"I'm gonna need Destiny so's I can work him some before the rodeo comin' up. You catch Red Devil for our equestrian over there."

"Red Devil? Ry's horse?"

"That's what I jist checked. Asked Ry if he thought Red Devil had enough spirit for this feller who had to stay at a resort last night to git a decent meal. Ry thought Red Devil would do nicely."

Joe grinned. "Isn't Red Devil kind of particular about who gets on him?"

"Yep."

By the time Leigh, Kyle and Pope came back, Joe and Duane had saddled Red Devil. Joe found a piece of straw to chew on, leaned against the rough adobe walls of the tack shed, tipped his hat lower over his eyes and prepared to enjoy himself.

Duane swung a saddle up on Destiny, the ranch's best cutting horse, before glancing at Pope. "That horse should suit ya," he said, tipping his head toward Red Devil.

Leigh raised an eyebrow in Duane's direction, but he pretended not to notice.

"Fine-looking animal." Pope adjusted his glasses and folded his arms."

"Jist go ahead and climb aboard," Duane said. "I got some things to do, but I'll be back to check on ya in a bit."

"No need. I want to put on a little demonstration for Kyle, here."

Duane swung up on Destiny. "Oh, I imagine you'll do that." He clucked to his horse and started around behind the tack shed.

Leigh put a hand on Kyle's shoulder. "Let's go over in the shade of the tack shed while your stepdad shows us what riding is all about."

"Okay." Kyle walked with her over to the shed. After glancing at his dad, he picked up a piece of straw, stuck it in the corner of his mouth and propped himself against the wall in exact imitation of Joe's stance, complete with one booted foot angled against the adobe.

When Kyle tugged his hat down over his eyes, Joe

had to chuckle, but he was secretly thrilled that Kyle admired him enough to copy his behavior.

Pope seemed pleased to have an audience. He untied Red Devil's reins from the hitching post with a flourish and looped them over the animal's neck. Red Devil rolled his eyes and backed up a few steps.

"Whoa, there, big fella," Pope said, shuffling after him as he held the saddle horn.

"Did Ry okay this?" Leigh asked in a low voice.

"Absolutely." Joe realized with delight that Pope was planning to mount Red Devil on the wrong side. He also noticed that Curtis and Rusty were both leaning on their shovels to watch.

"You have to show them who's boss, Kyle," Pope said as he attempted to get his foot in the stirrup on the horse's right side. Red Devil tossed his head and sidled away. "I can see this horse needs to learn a few manners." Pope angled for the stirrup again, but Red Devil circled away from him and the stirrup twisted in his hand. Finally, Pope managed to shove his foot in, but Red Devil kept moving away from his intended rider, forcing Pope to hop after him in a circle, cursing under his breath. His cheek twitched as his tic started acting up.

Joe bit down on his straw to keep from laughing out loud. After a few moments, Pope grabbed the saddle horn and lunged upward. The stirrup untwisted and he landed in the saddle facing Red Devil's rump.

"Is that a trick or something, Em?" Kyle asked.

Joe almost choked on his piece of straw.

Red-faced, Pope managed to clamber down before Red Devil tossed him off, which required some agility, Joe had to admit. The big gelding pawed the ground and snorted menacingly while Pope muttered to himself.

"Comin' through," Duane called, riding out from behind the tack shed. He had a coiled rope in one hand as he casually herded Romeo into the clearing. Pope was concentrating on Red Devil and didn't notice what was coming up behind him.

Joe straightened and put a hand on Kyle's shoulder.

"It's okay," Leigh whispered, laying her hand on Kyle's other shoulder. "He's very tame without that bull rope on him."

"How're you doin'?" Duane asked Pope. "Thought you'd be on that horse by now."

"Nobody taught this bag of bones how to stand still," Pope said, starting to turn around. "I'd advise you to—"

Joe had always thought "his eyes bugged out of his head" was just an expression, but that was exactly what happened with Emerson J. Pope. Then he opened his mouth, but he didn't yell. He didn't even scream. He squeaked. Joe had never heard such a peculiar sound in his life. Pope dropped Red Devil's reins, turned tail and ran as fast as his new boots would carry him toward his rented BMW. His white hat flipped off and landed in the dirt, but he didn't go back for it.

As Joe, Leigh, Kyle, Duane, Curtis, Rusty and even Romeo watched in amazement, Pope spun the BMW in a dusty circle and bounced down the road going much faster over such rough terrain than the rental company would have appreciated.

Kyle shook his head. "He'd never make it on the *Enterprise*."

Joe felt a stab of remorse. Kyle had to live with this guy, jerk that he was, for some of the year, at least. He crouched next to his son and cleared his throat. "And most of the time, that doesn't matter. I'm sure the guy has his good points, too."

"Yeah." Kyle grinned. "But he sure is a dweeb, isn't he, Dad?"

"I'm afraid he is," Joe replied solemnly. "But dweeb or not, I'm going after him to smooth things over." He stood and glanced at Leigh. "Think Ry would mind if I borrowed his horse?"

"I'm sure he wouldn't," Leigh said, her brown gaze warm and encouraging.

Red Devil tossed his head around some, but Joe managed to get aboard. As he started away from the corrals, Kyle ran after him holding Pope's dust-covered hat. Joe leaned down and took it. "Thanks, buddy."

"I don't want him to take me home yet," Kyle said.

"I know. That's one reason I'm going after him."

"Thanks, Dad."

Joe touched the brim of his hat, and Kyle touched his. Then Joe nudged Red Devil into a trot. He figured Pope would drive straight back to the resort instead of going to the ranch house, so he cut through the desert to head him off at the ranch's entrance road. Red Devil was already agitated and seemed happy to pick up the pace. Lying low over the big horse's neck, Joe savored the thrill of the chase. But this time, he wouldn't be arresting someone at the end of it, he reminded himself. Worse yet, if he did his job right, he'd be making amends to a lawyer.

He saw the cloud of dust to his left and coaxed Red Devil into a dead run. Horse and rider came out on the road a hundred yards ahead of the car. Red Devil reared, which nearly tossed Joe in the dirt but managed to get Pope's attention. He braked the car and dust billowed everywhere.

Joe got Red Devil under control and dismounted, keeping the reins in one hand. Pope climbed warily from his car. They eyed each other for several long seconds.

"I'm sorry about what happened back there," Joe said at last as he fingered the brim of the white Stetson. "The bull's really tame, but you didn't know that. The ranch hands have a twisted sense of humor, I'm afraid."

Pope nodded. "Once I was out of there, I realized they were only taunting me because I'm from New York. Is that the same bull that came at you and Kyle?"

"Yeah. That time, they had him trussed up with something called a bull rope, and he was pretty ornery. Even so, the hands subdued him in seconds. The people on this ranch know what they're doing. I realize what you and Darlene think, but Kyle's probably as safe out here as he is in Manhattan."

"Are you going to be spending more time with him?"

The question caught Joe off guard. "What do you mean?"

"When Kyle called us, we got the impression you weren't around much. He said that you were out on some sort of investigation. Darlene and I decided it was the same old story, that you hauled him out here but you didn't plan to spend time with him. That's one of the main reasons I came out, to be truthful."

Joe longed to strike back with some comment about the irony of a lawyer's being truthful, but he thought of Kyle and restrained himself. "Yes, I'll be spending more time with my son," he said, allowing himself to emphasize the last part. "And while we're on the subject, what's this horse manure of you trying to adopt him?"

"Look, I know cops. Darlene didn't have to tell me about all the times you buried yourself in your work and acted as if she and Kyle didn't exist. I thought you might even be relieved to end the charade of trying to be a father."

Joe clamped his back teeth together to keep from commenting on that with all the four-letter words it deserved. "You thought wrong," he said, his voice deadly calm.

"Well, Gilardini, it just so happens I have revised my opinion recently. All the way down to the corrals, Kyle talked about how great it was being here at the ranch with you." He glanced back down the road he'd just driven in such haste, and sunlight glinted off the lens of his glasses. "Doesn't appeal to me in the least, but Kyle seems happy. That's the important thing. I asked Kyle how long he'd like to stay, and he said he didn't want to leave until school started. That gives you another three weeks with him, if you want them."

The idea of accepting favors from Emerson J. Pope didn't sit very well, but Joe realized that he was partially responsible for the situation turning out as it had. He hadn't been the best husband and father in the world, and now it was pay-up time. "I want them," he said.

"Good. Then I'll be flying out today. Can't understand what you like about this godforsaken country."

"It grows on you." Joe stepped forward. "Here's your hat."

"Ah, keep it. I imagine you could use a good hat. Yours looks a little battered, if you don't mind my saying so. You look more like one of your employees than an owner of the place."

"Thank you. You couldn't have given me a better

compliment." Joe tossed the hat toward Pope and he caught it awkwardly. "But you keep the hat. It's not my size."

"I would have thought it would fit perfectly."

"Nope." Joe swung into the saddle. "Way too big. See you, Emerson." Joe touched the brim of his hat and galloped down the road so Pope wouldn't see the grin of triumph on his face. He'd managed to get in the last word, and that didn't often happen with a lawyer. Life was good.

As Joe APPROACHED the corrals, the sight that greeted him made him catch his breath. Leigh had taken Penny Lover out of her pen and was leading her around the clearing, with Spilled Milk following obediently behind. And on Penny Lover's bare back, holding a fistful of mane and looking pleased with himself, was Kyle.

"Hi, Dad," he called, waving. "We're a parade, see?"

"I see." His throat constricted as he realized what Leigh had accomplished by getting Kyle up on the mare all by himself. It was all part of a natural progression to rid him of his fears, and it was working. Another three weeks and Kyle would love the ranch every bit as much as Joe had hoped he would. All because of Leigh. Joe's heart swelled with an emotion he'd skittered away from most of his adult life. And for the first time in a long while, he allowed himself to feel it.

He walked Red Devil over to the hitching post, dismounted and tethered the horse. Patting him on the neck, he walked over to meet Leigh as she circled the clearing again. "Looking good," he said.

"Thanks." Her expression sent him messages that sped up his heartbeat.

"What did Em say?" Kyle asked.

Joe dropped back to walk beside Penny Lover. "He's heading home today, but he can see how much you like the True Love, so you can stay here until school starts, if you want."

"All right!" Kyle swiveled around to the foal ambling along behind. "Did you hear that, Milk?" He turned back to his father. "I call her Milk for short. It's easier."

"I'm all for taking the easy way."

"Three weeks," Kyle said. "Wow. Did you duke it out with him?"

Joe glanced up at his son in surprise. "Why would you think that?"

Kyle shrugged. "I know how mad he makes you. The way he talks and stuff."

"Well, I didn't hit him. And I won't. He's your stepfather, and he cares about you. For that he deserves respect. From me and from you."

Kyle gazed at him and finally nodded. "Okay."

Leigh looked over her shoulder at them. "As long as Red Devil's saddled, how about if we round up Mikey and Pussywillow and go for a little ride?"

"Three horses?" Kyle asked.

"Sure," Leigh said, her tone nonchalant. "If you can ride Penny Lover with nothing to hold on to but a hunk of her mane, you can handle Mikey."

"Pussywillow's smaller," Kyle said. "How about her instead?"

"Okay. Pussywillow it is. I'll take Mikey."

Joe was ecstatic, but he took his cue from Leigh and didn't make a big deal of the decision as they put Penny Lover and Spilled Milk into their pen and then saddled Mikey and Pussywillow. Leigh helped Kyle into the saddle, and although he looked a little nervous, he picked up the reins and nudged the gray mare with his heels as they set off down the road toward the old homestead with Leigh in front, Kyle next and Joe bringing up the rear on Red Devil.

Joe checked for possible problems, but the sky was clear and the breeze almost nonexistent. Leigh held Mikey to a sedate walk and kept up a stream of chatter, turning constantly in her saddle to smile back at Kyle. As they approached the homestead, memories of the night before flooded through Joe. He wondered if Leigh was being affected in the same way. Maybe she'd brought them out here on purpose, to fire his imagination. As if he needed his imagination fired. One look at her in her formfitting jeans and he was a wild man. All he lacked was the opportunity to do something about it.

Leigh rode into the clearing and reined Mikey in a wide circle to head back in. "I think this is far enough for today," she said to Kyle. "How are you doing?"

"Good." Kyle sat straight and proud in the saddle. "It's not so scary. Can we go faster?"

"Next time." She glanced over at Joe. "How are you doing, cowboy?"

He caught the subtle teasing in her question. She knew good and well that being out here was bombarding him with images of their lovemaking. "I'm getting a little hot," he said.

Leigh chuckled. "That's an Easterner for you. Can't take the heat."

"Maybe that's because we haven't learned all the tricks for relieving it," he said.

"Then I'll have to teach you some." She winked at him before she started back down the road.

"What's that piece of paper over there?" Kyle asked.

Joe followed the direction of Kyle's pointing finger. Sure enough, a sheet of white paper was stuck on a cholla cactus. He knew for a fact it hadn't been there the night before when he'd searched the area, but a dust devil could have picked it off the ground and swirled it into the cactus after he'd left.

"I'll get it," Leigh offered. "No point in leaving litter out here." She rode over to the cholla and dismounted.

Pussywillow followed, and Kyle allowed her to go. Joe stayed back, not wanting to crowd the gray mare. Everything had gone beautifully, and he didn't want Pussywillow spooking over a piece of paper. He would have preferred Kyle on Mikey, but Kyle on any horse was a miracle, so he couldn't complain.

He watched Leigh lift the paper carefully away from the thorns. Something moved at her feet. He looked closer and saw a hairy spider crawling slowly toward her boot. It was easily as broad as his spread hand. He tensed, knowing what might happen if Kyle noticed. "Leigh, go ahead and get on your horse now," he said as easily as possible. "Come on, Kyle. I'll lead us back."

Too late. Kyle glanced down, and his scream tore through the air. Before it ended, Pussywillow had grabbed the bit and bolted toward the riverbed.

Joe dug in his heels and Red Devil lunged after the mare. "Hang on!" Joe yelled as Kyle lost a stirrup. "I'm coming!" The little boy bounced in the saddle as Pussywillow careered down the trail, but he stayed on. Joe thundered after him. He knew that when they reached the riverbank Pussywillow would leap the distance to the sandy bottom. Even an experienced rider could be thrown. Kyle would never make it.

Joe gauged the distance to the riverbed. Fifty yards, forty yards, thirty. He drew alongside, reached for Pussywillow's bridle, missed, reached again. Ten yards. He grabbed and held on, pulling back on Red Devil's reins at the same time. Both horses skidded to a stop, their haunches nearly touching the ground. Panting, Joe stared down at the drop-off into the riverbed right below them.

Then he turned to Kyle. His son sat with both hands still gripping the saddlehorn, his face as white as the piece of paper Leigh had dismounted to retrieve. Joe opened his mouth to tell Kyle he should never, *never* scream when he was riding a horse. Kyle swallowed, and tears filled his eyes. He looked as if he expected the rebuke Joe was about to deliver.

Joe took a deep breath. "You did good," he said, reaching across to grip Kyle's arm. "You stayed on."

Kyle's eyes widened in surprise. Color began to seep back into his face and he blinked away his tears. "I...shouldn't have screamed," he whispered.

Joe managed a smile. "That was a mighty big spider."

"That was a *gigantic* spider," Kyle said.

"It was a tarantula," Leigh added.

Joe turned to see her sitting behind them on Mikey.

"They're scary-looking, but pretty harmless," she said. "Some people keep them as pets."

Kyle's shoulders heaved. "Nooo, thanks."

"You two handled that crisis like real cowboys," Leigh said. "Ready to go back, now?"

Joe waited for Kyle to ask if he could ride with Leigh on the way home. He couldn't blame the kid. Bouncing along on a runaway wasn't the best introduction to riding.

Kyle straightened in the saddle and looked Joe in the eye. "Yep, I'm ready."

Joe didn't suppose he could ever be prouder of Kyle than he was at that moment. "Lead the way, son," he said.

14

IT'S HAPPENING, Leigh thought as she led the way back to the corrals. Before her eyes, Joe was emerging from his shell and casting away his need to control. She'd been astounded when he'd decided to go after Emerson Pope, yet it was the right thing to do and he'd apparently handled it beautifully. His attitude toward Kyle had undergone a change, too, judging from his behavior after the runaway. The old Joe would have berated Kyle for scaring the horse. Instead, father and son ended the episode with mutual respect.

The mood was lighthearted as they dismounted, unsaddled the horses and groomed them before turning them loose in the corrals. After a quick visit to Penny Lover and Spilled Milk, they decided to go up to the house for some lunch. Leigh had forgotten about the piece of paper she'd retrieved until she climbed into the driver's side of her truck and the paper crinkled in her back pocket.

She pulled it out and handed it to Joe. "Here's the thing that Kyle saw. I haven't even looked at it."

As they drove, Joe unfolded the paper and studied it. "This is a photocopy of a handwritten document. There's a date here. I think it's June, no, January, abbreviated. January—let's see—could be 1885."

Kyle leaned over to look. "Maybe it's a diary, like Leigh was telling us about last night."

"It reads like that," Joe said. "And it sounds like it was written by a prisoner of some sort. He mentions a guard, and working on a rock pile and taking exercise in the yard."

Leigh wondered if the diary page had anything to do with the men she and Joe had heard the night before, but her rendezvous with Joe wasn't a subject she intended to discuss in front of Kyle. "It could be from a college class," she said. "Students hike out here a lot. Maybe they were studying something from the time period when the ranch was homesteaded, and they dropped some of their papers."

"This is August," Joe said. "Is school in session?"

"I don't know. Maybe a summer class."

"Do you think it's a clue, Dad?" Kyle asked.

"Probably not." Joe folded the paper and snapped open his breast pocket to tuck it inside.

As they pulled up in front of the ranch house, Freddy and Dexter came down the flagstone walkway.

"I've left Ry to supervise construction on the rodeo arena and we're going into La Osa for ice cream," Freddy said. "Anybody want to come along?"

"Me!" Kyle said and started toward the ranch van.

"Hold it, buddy." Joe put out a restraining hand. "You haven't had lunch yet."

"I'll buy him a sandwich first," Freddy promised. "I'm sure Dexter would love it if Kyle came along."

"Yep," Dexter said.

"Okay. Sure," Joe said.

"Great!" Kyle ran over to Dexter and they exchanged high fives.

Joe snapped open his pocket. "Listen, while you're there, could you get a copy of this for me?" He handed her the diary page. "I don't know if it's important, but we found it out by the old homestead."

"Be glad to," Freddy said.

"What's that?" Dexter asked.

"A page from a diary," Kyle said. "I'll read it to you on the way to town, okay?"

"Good," Dexter said, nodding. "Let's go."

Leigh and Joe waved as Freddy, Dexter and Kyle drove off in the van. Then they turned toward each other, their eyes communicating the same silent message. Opportunity had just knocked.

Leigh tilted her head and gazed up at him, her pulse racing. "There's something I need to show you."

"Is that right?"

"One of our secret ways of relieving the heat around here."

"I'm partial to secrets."

"Then come with me." She led him around the side of the house to the back door that accessed the family wing. The prospect of loving him made her blood race, but there was no point in advertising their activities to the rest of the ranch. She suspected Freddy would guess. Freddy might even have suggested taking Kyle into La Osa on purpose. Bless her.

They ducked into the shade of a small porch and in through the back door. Leigh's room was on the end, next to Freddy and Ry's. With both her sister and brother-in-law out of the house, it was the most privacy she and Joe could hope for.

Inside the room she closed the door and pulled the shades, eliminating the rainbow colors flung by the crystals she hung there to catch the sunlight. Then she turned to find him surveying the room with interest. His gaze traveled to the unusual dream-catcher hanging above her headboard. The large webbed circle, at least eighteen inches across, contained a small crystal unicorn in the center. Peacock feathers hung from the edge of the circle.

"You have something like earrings like that," he said.

She nodded. "The legend says that bad dreams are trapped in the web, and good dreams are allowed to pass through."

"Does it work?"

"You're here."

Passion ignited in his eyes and he started toward her. She held up her hand. "Wait."

He paused, lifting his eyebrows in question.

"You'll see." She moved slowly around the room, reveling in his hot gaze as she lit jasmine incense, slipped a tape of soft synthesizer rhythms into the recorder and found the oils she needed. She'd spent years perfecting her massage techniques to relieve pain. She'd never used them to excite a man to unearthly desires. Joe would be the first.

She faced him. "Take off your clothes and lie on the bed. Relax and focus on your breathing while I'm gone."

He gave her a wry smile. "If I'm lying in your bed waiting for you, I doubt I'll be able to focus on my breathing."

"Try." She went into the adjoining bathroom, removed all her clothes and slipped on a white silk toga scented with the aroma of ripe raspberries. Her skin was flushed with anticipation, her nipples tight with desire. She had never brought a man here, to her sanctuary. She'd never allowed a man to touch that part of her being that danced with the powers of the universe. She had been waiting...for this man.

She returned to the room. He'd propped her pillows behind his head and lay watching her as she crossed to him. They'd made love in starlight before, and she hadn't seen him well. She knew there were scars—she'd felt the ridges and absorbed some of the stories they told. He lay against her snowy sheets, a magnificent warrior marked by battle, a man aroused by passion.

He noticed the sweep of her gaze. "It's the body of a street cop," he said.

"The body of a brave man."

"No."

She put one knee on the bed and leaned toward him to run a hand over his chest as she gazed into his eyes. "Yes, brave. Not because of the physical dangers you've faced, and there have been many, but because you've dared to reach out for love. From your son. From me."

He caught her hand and tried to draw her closer.

She backed away and gently disengaged her hand from his. "Not yet."

"I can tell you this much about your secret remedy. I'm not getting any cooler watching you move around in that silk number."

She laughed softly. "Actually, you won't get cooler. The secret is that soon, you'll no longer mind the heat."

"I want you, Leigh."

"I want you, too." She reached for the massage oil. "But there are levels of wanting, levels of pleasure we have yet to explore." She poured a circle of oil in the palm of her hand. It pooled there, warm and moist as the delicate scent of safflower and coconut drifted around her. "Now roll over," she whispered. "And let me worship you."

He held her gaze for a moment, and then he complied. Kneeling beside him, she smoothed the oil over the broad expanse of his muscled back. She anointed several puckered ridges where a bullet or a knife had gouged his flesh, and the violence that had caused the scars flooded into her hands. She took it in, breathing deeply to cleanse herself, and him.

She knew healing physical injuries was possible with her touch, yet now she sought to heal the deeper scars, the ones that didn't show. He moaned as she rotated her palms down his spine, over his firm buttocks. Replenishing her supply of oil, she manipulated the muscles in his thighs and calves. When she reached his feet, she used her thumbs to stimulate, as well as soothe. His breathing quickened.

With long, languorous strokes she returned to his hips, his buttocks, the small of his back, until he grew as pliable as warm clay beneath her fingers, until his breathing synchronized with hers. "Melt for me," she murmured.

Arms flung to the sides, he closed his eyes and surrendered to her rhythm. A slow, steady beat grew through the music, through her kneading fingers. "Give way," she crooned, wanting nothing less than capitulation.

He sighed, a sound wrenched from the depths of his soul.

"Yes." With gentle hands she guided him to his back. He moved with fluid grace born of total relaxation, his eyes closed, lines of care erased from his forehead. She covered his chest with smooth strokes, working the oil into his body, the peace into his soul. And the paradox that she had dreamed of came true. The more he relaxed, the more he surged with desire. His shaft thickened and pulsed. She saved the final massage until last.

Then, when his body obeyed her every pressure, moved in tune with each kneading motion, she swept up that rising expression of his need with one firm stroke, and he groaned the groan of a man carefully, completely aroused.

"I think," she whispered, "that you are ready." Her own preparation had been in tandem with his. Learning his body, she'd schooled her own in the perfect way to fit, to mold, to caress.

Sheathing him became part of the massage as she unrolled the condom slowly, deftly, giving pleasure as she prepared him for greater joy. At last she unclasped the silk toga and allowed it to fall away.

"Open your eyes."

As his lids lifted, the blaze of passion there took her breath away. She had imagined what she was building, but her imagination had failed to conjure up the burning depths in his eyes.

As she rose over him, he grasped her shoulders, his fingers biting into her with a force that stopped just short of pain. His voice was rich with husky desire. "If you've ever loved another man this way..." He paused, holding her tight. "I just might have to kill him."

"No." She drowned in the molten lava of his gaze as she lowered herself, taking him in. "Never another...like this."

He gasped and closed his eyes. "Please," he whispered. "Please."

That he could beg, this man so used to command, was all that she needed to know. Using the rhythm of the ages, she loved him. Desire took him over the edge, pummeling his defenseless body, conquering his will until he arched and cried her name. Over and over. And then, as she melted with him, she called his name, as well, wanting the universe to hear their names spoken together. Then she flew with him across an unbounded and uncharted frontier, a sensuous landscape that would demand no less than all they had to give—forever.

JOE HAD TROUBLE returning to reality—or what he'd always considered to be reality. The mystic world that Leigh offered him when they made love was so powerful that he had to acknowledge its existence, too. How the guys in the precinct would laugh if they saw him now, stretched beneath a woman who believed in crystals, dream-catchers and unicorns. But more important than all of that, she believed in him.

He stroked her shoulder and she stirred, as if coming out of a trance. He'd felt exactly the same way as he'd gradually become aware of birds chirping outside the window and footsteps in the hallway. "Someone may come looking for us soon," he murmured.

"That's likely." She lifted her head and gazed down at him, her hair tumbling around her face and swinging down to tickle his nose.

He ran his fingers through it. "I love your hair."

"I love your mustache." She traced his upper lip.

"I love your eyes." He recognized that they were circling a sensitive topic, playing it safe instead of saying the words they were probably both thinking. But that was okay, for now. They both had a lot to deal with in getting used to such forceful emotions. "I think you've hypnotized me."

She smiled. "A little, perhaps."

"A lot, perhaps."

"I love your eyes, too," she said. "When I first saw you, I thought you looked exactly like a lawman from the streets of Dodge City or Tombstone. I think the right term is *flinty-eyed*."

"You liked that?"

"Sure." She traced the line of his eyebrows. "It showed strength."

"And then I became putty in your hands."

Her smile broadened. "Exactly."

He glanced around the room. "The minute I stepped in the door, I figured out this was your show. What kind of incense is that?"

"Jasmine. For luck...and love."

He looked into her eyes and allowed her to see a depth of emotion that he felt unable to voice. "I like it. The music's nice, too."

"And the massage?"

He laughed. "Not bad." His laughter faded and he touched her cheek. "I'm not good at superlatives, but you were...amazing."

"I want you to know something. I've never brought another man here. To do so seemed too personal."

A primitive satisfaction flooded through him. "I'm honored."

"Yes, you are. And now we really need to see if Freddy's back." She kissed him lightly and moved away.

He fought the urge to pull her into his arms and say the hell with everybody else. Instead, he caught her hand and caressed her wrist with his thumb. "I'm afraid you've turned me into an addict. Do you think we can manage this disappearing trick again soon?"

Her brown eyes twinkled. "In case you haven't noticed, most people go to bed early around here. And my room is right by the back door. I believe, as one of the owners, you have keys to every door on the ranch."

"That I do." Just the prospect of loving her again in this room tonight was enough to bring a response from his eager body. "But right now I think a cold shower is in order."

"Through there."

Her bathroom was stuffed with aromatic lotions and scented soaps. He scrubbed himself with a loofah and experimented with the pulsing jets on her shower. Such unabashed sensuality really turned him on. He might become a New Age enthusiast yet.

While he dressed and she took her turn in the shower, the scent of the soap she used and the rhythmic pounding of the shower jets affected him so much, he had trouble zipping his jeans. She came out of the shower wrapped in a huge fluffy towel. Ignoring her was not an option.

He drew her into his arms, towel and all, and inhaled her sweet fragrance. "You're delicious," he said, savoring the come-hither look in her eyes. "That's the only word to describe you. You're not a woman, you're an entire life experience."

"Most women are, if given half a chance," she said.

"I plan to give you a whole chance, and then some." He nestled her against his chest and stroked her hair. "Look, I want you to know something, too. Just like you've never brought another man in here, I've never said this to another human being." He hesitated, searching for the right words. "Anything you do, or have done, is okay with me. I'm not sitting in judgment. I just want you to know that."

She stiffened. "I'm not sure what you mean."

He tried again. "I respect your reasons for any actions you've taken, and I want to help. I'll do anything to protect you. So you don't have to be afraid to tell me anything."

She pulled away from him and clutched the towel around her. "You're talking about the sabotage, aren't you?"

"Yes."

"And you still think I know something I'm not telling you?"

"Leigh, it's logical that you're involved. You have the strongest motive. What I'm trying to say is that I understand. I'm sure it got out of control and now you don't know where to turn. Turn to me. I want to help you."

Her eyes became dark pools of fury. "Do you imagine I could love you like that—" she swung an arm at the bed "—and still be holding a terrible secret from you?" She began to shake. "That sort of loving means stripping away *everything* false. You can't have that kind of experience if you're keeping things from each other!"

"But—"

"I have made a mistake." Her eyes filled with pain. "I wanted you so much that I imagined you were ready for what I have to give. Obviously you're not."

His mind whirled, trying to grasp that she was rejecting him. No. She couldn't be slamming the door of paradise in his face. It wasn't possible.

"Go."

"Don't do this," he murmured. "I'm only trying to tell you that I—"

"Think I'm a liar?" She lifted her chin with such regal poise that he imagined a goddess preparing to smite some poor mortal with a thunderbolt for his audacity. "As long as you can think that, we have no reason to breathe the same air. Now go."

Breathe the same air. Ah, she had such a way of phrasing things. That was exactly what he wanted to do, for the rest of his life. But he'd poisoned the air between them with his suspicion. He could not take it back. She was right, he did have doubts. By her standards, doubts were not allowed. There was no arguing with that.

He picked up his hat from a chair and settled it on his head. Then he touched the brim. "Ma'am." He didn't look back as he walked out the door.

15

THE FLURRY OF ACTIVITIES in the days preceding the rodeo kept Leigh busy enough for her to submerge her sense of betrayal. She tried to take comfort in the growing intimacy between Kyle and his father. Joe had made progress, astounding progress, really. She'd expected too much from a man used to suspecting the worst from everyone. She assumed that eventually he'd solve the mystery of the accidents around the ranch. When he did, she'd be vindicated, but that would be too late. Joe would have to believe in her on faith alone, before he uncovered the facts that cleared her name, or all was lost.

Two days before the rodeo, Amanda, Chase and little Bart returned from New York. Amanda had convinced her advertising agency to open a branch in Tucson, and Amanda's family had been delighted to meet Chase. Leigh was thrilled for Chase, who had become as close to her as a brother in the months he'd lived at the True Love.

No sooner had Chase and Amanda unpacked than they asked Belinda to watch the baby so they could take a horseback ride with Leigh.

"Are you sure you want me to go?" Leigh asked as they all saddled up. "I can understand wanting to get on a horse again after all that time back East, but you two probably haven't had much time alone since you left."

"Yes, we want you along," Chase said firmly. "We want to go up and see how the reconstruction's coming on the pond, for one thing, and with the hands up there building the dam, we wouldn't have much privacy, anyway. Besides, we have a few things to tell you."

Leigh was secretly glad for any excuse to get away from the ranch for a while. She kept running into Joe, and keeping up a pleasant exterior was becoming increasingly difficult.

On the way up the canyon, Amanda and Chase exclaimed over the damage caused by the flash flood.

"I was hoping Joe would have solved this business by the time we got back," Chase said. "Doesn't he have any idea who's behind the accidents?"

Leigh decided not to mention that she was Joe's chief suspect. "It's difficult working on his own and trying to keep the investigation quiet. When the dam was dynamited, he and Ry talked about putting in an insurance claim, but the insurance company would have sent investigators out here."

Chase sighed. "If Joe doesn't solve this soon, we'll have to call in the police. We've been lucky nobody's been seriously hurt. Or killed."

Leigh shivered. Joe thought she had something to do with incidents that could have cost lives. The concept made her soul ache with the injustice of it.

She, Chase and Amanda inspected the progress on the pond. A temporary dam had been constructed farther upstream, and now the hands were replacing the rocks at the original dam site. All the dead fish had been hauled away, but the scummy bottom of the pond still didn't smell very appetizing.

"Yuck," Amanda said, wrinkling her nose. "Let's go upstream." She turned her horse and started up the canyon.

A muscle in Chase's jaw twitched as he eyed the scene. "I would love to get my hands on the jerk that did this. In fact, I look forward to meeting him. He has a lot to answer for."

"Don't forget that Duane and Belinda are still on Joe's list of suspects."

Chase shook his head. "Neither of them was responsible for this."

"Try telling Joe that." Leigh realized she'd revealed some of her bitterness when Chase glanced at her, a question in his green eyes. She waved a hand dismissively. "Don't mind me. We've had an eventful few days while you've been gone."

"I take it you and Gilardini aren't getting along?"

"You could say that."

"Do you want to tell me about it?"

She gave him a weary smile. "Maybe. But not right now. I agree with Amanda. Let's go upstream."

They found a spot near the temporary dam where a gnarled oak provided enough shade for all three of them. They dismounted, tethered the horses and carried their canteens under the tree.

"Okay," Leigh said when everyone was settled. "What's the big news?"

"We didn't want to make a general announcement, but we wanted you to know," Amanda said. "We found out about Chase's mother."

Leigh's gaze swung to Chase and he nodded, a sad smile playing over his face. Raised in a series of foster homes with no idea who his father was and no knowledge of his mother's whereabouts, he'd been ashamed of his background for most of his adult life. Amanda had encouraged him to confront his past and try to find his mother. "You don't look very happy about what you found," Leigh said.

"It's not a happy story, but I'm glad I know it." He reached for Amanda's hand. "If Amanda hadn't come into my life, I'd have gone on believing my mother wasn't a very nice person."

"You're speaking in the past tense," Leigh said.

"Yeah." Chase sighed. "We found out where she's buried, in a grungy little cemetery. We're buying her a decent headstone. Amanda helped me with the words on it. *Helen Marie Lavette, mother of Chase. She gave everything she had.*" Chase looked up, his eyes bright, his voice husky. "And she did."

As if sensing Chase would have difficulty telling the story, Amanda took up the tale. Through a medallion Chase wore that had belonged to his mother, they'd located Helen's grammar school and eventually one of her old classmates, Suzanne, who'd kept in touch with her. They learned that Helen had been managing to support her only child with a series of minimum-wage jobs, but she had no family, no safety net of any kind. Then she developed cancer and knew she would waste away, possibly traumatizing her small son. She'd put him in foster care before the deterioration started. As long as she had the strength, she'd kept tabs on him, creeping up to the window of the house where he lived or peering over the fence to watch him playing in the yard, until she was hospitalized for the last weeks of her life.

"She must have loved you very much," Leigh said, her throat tight.

Chase swallowed and stared at the toe of his boot. "Yep."

"We're keeping our fingers crossed that our next baby will be a girl," Amanda said, "so we can name her Helen Marie."

Leigh focused on them and allowed her mind to expand beyond this moment under an oak tree. "I think you will have a little girl," she said with a smile.

Chase looked at her. "You think or you know?"

Leigh chuckled. "Actually, I know, but I usually pretend I'm not sure, so people won't freak out."

"We won't freak out," Chase said with a grin. "We know you're weird, and we love you for it." He got to his feet and helped Amanda up. "We'd better get back. We're not keeping the story about my mother a secret, exactly. We just wanted you to be the first to know." He glanced at her. "Unless you knew all this already?"

"No, I didn't." Leigh got up and brushed off the seat of her jeans. "If I had, I would have told you and saved you a heck of a lot of trouble. I don't have unlimited pyschic power. If I did, I'd have figured out who's causing the accidents." Not that Joe would believe her if she did, she thought. Then, for some reason, she remembered the diary page that she'd pulled from the cactus. "You must have had to plow through some old records to find your mother," she said to Chase.

"Amanda did. She's a whiz at that."

Leigh glanced at her. "Joe has something we found out in the desert that looks like a photocopy of an old diary page. If you'd be willing to take it down to the Arizona Historical Society, we might find out what diary it came from. I told Joe I didn't think it was important, but it keeps flashing into my mind. That means there's something to it."

"Consider it done," Amanda said. "I'm hopelessly inadequate at helping build a rodeo arena, so this will make me feel useful."

THE NIGHT BEFORE the rodeo, just before sunset, Joe went with everyone else to admire the new arena and welcome the delivery of Grateful Dead, Eb Whitlock's Brahma bull. Chase, Amanda and little Bart rode the half mile to the arena with Leigh in her pickup. Ry and Freddy took Kyle with them, and Joe rode in the back.

Ever since the afternoon he and Leigh had made love, Joe had prayed for a cleansing vision that would convince him Leigh had nothing to do with the sabotage. Unfortunately, he'd been cursed with a logical mind that preferred careful deductions to cleansing visions. He was ninety-nine percent sure she was telling the truth, but he couldn't say that to her and expect anything but disdain. He had to come to her free of doubt, and he knew it.

The entrance to the arena parking area was on the main road leading to the highway. An arch over the gate announced the True Love Rodeo Grounds, bracketed on either side by a heart with an arrow through it. Ry tooted his horn as he led the way under the arch. An afternoon rain had washed down the arena and the tang of wet creosote bushes mingled with the fragrance of new lumber. Ry had floated a loan to construct the modest structure, which included several holding pens, bleachers, two bucking chutes and a small judges' stand.

While Ry stood by proudly, everyone exclaimed over the finished arena and speculated as to how much revenue it could bring in during the year. But a cloud of dust on the entrance road ended the discussion as all eyes focused on the arrival of Grateful Dead.

"Your nemesis is on his way," Freddy said to Ry.

"The man or the animal?" Ry asked. "I have far more reservations about Whitlock than I do about his bull."

"I found out where that diary page came from," Amanda said as the shiny dual-wheeled pickup came into sight. "The guy who wrote it was named Whitlock, too. Jethro Whitlock."

"Maybe he's related," Kyle said.

"That's probably why the diary page was out there," Joe said. It looked like another dead end. He watched as Eb parked the truck and climbed out. "Some amateur historian found the diary at the historical society and is trying to prove a link between that Whitlock and the one who owns the Rocking W Ranch."

"I'm going to start reading it tonight," Amanda said to Joe. "I'll let you know if anything turns up."

"Can I read it after you?" Kyle asked.

"Sure." Amanda squeezed his shoulder. "But it won't be as sweet as Clara's diary, I'm afraid. This guy sounds like a rough character. Went around robbing banks and stage lines until he was finally caught and thrown into the Yuma Territorial Prison. I guess he died there, which was probably a relief to the citizens of Arizona."

Eb parked the truck with a flourish and climbed out. "Well, I brought your star attraction," he boomed. "How do you like my trailer? You could leave it parked out front to get people's attention."

"Looks big enough for a circus elephant," Ry said, glancing at the large purple trailer with Grateful Dead, The Bull That's Never Been Rode stenciled on the side in gold.

Eb hitched up his belt. "That's so my boys can cross-tie him in the middle and he won't be able to throw himself against the sides and get hurt. See that slot along each side? That's my invention. A cowboy can be on either side of the trailer on the outside and move that bull in slick as a whistle. Had to come up with something. None of my hands would walk into the trailer with him." Eb glanced at the group. "In any case, I'd advise taking the little ones to one of your trucks before we bring him out, just to be on the safe side."

Freddy glanced at Ry. "Isn't it nice to know you're planning to ride an animal like that?" She turned to Amanda, who was holding Bart and looking alarmed. "Let's go, Amanda. Kyle, why don't you come with us into my truck? We'll turn on the radio and sing some songs while these macho guys show how tough they are."

Kyle glanced at Joe and Joe nodded. "Good idea, buddy. This bull is no Romeo, from what I hear."

"Are you staying, Dad?"

"Yes."

Kyle squared his shoulders. "Then so am I."

Joe felt caught in a trap of his own making. He loved the courage that Kyle demonstrated; the little guy had come a long way since the day they'd arrived at the True Love. If Joe ordered him into the truck, Kyle might feel put down, yet this bull made Joe nervous. He glanced at Leigh, seeking some signal, some silent communication that would help him decide what to do. For the first time he could remember since he'd met her, she gave no indication of what she was thinking. She seemed to have withdrawn into herself.

"Just keep the boy out of the way, then," Eb said. "I brought the cattle prod to use on him."

Leigh roused herself. "Don't use the cattle prod."

Eb paused and looked at her as if she'd come unhinged. "What do you mean, don't use it? This animal is hard to control, Leigh. You've seen him."

"Let me talk to him."

"Let you—" Eb stared at her.

"I want everybody away from that trailer," Leigh said. "He hates it when people crowd around."

Ry stepped toward her. "Leigh, you know how much faith I have in you, but this bull is legendary. Let's not take any foolish chances."

She faced him, her expression composed. "The foolishness would be for all of you to converge on him and jolt him out of the trailer with a cattle prod. I can guarantee somebody will get hurt if you do that. Now, I'm going over to the trailer to talk with him." She started across the parking lot. "I'm warning you to stay back," she called over her shoulder.

"Leigh—"

"Let her do it, Ry." Joe was surprised to hear himself say it. He didn't want Leigh to put herself in danger. Why was he so certain that she would be okay? Logically she had no business dealing with a two-thousand-pound Brahma bull.

"Yeah," Kyle echoed. "Let her."

Ry glanced at Chase, who shrugged. "Doesn't seem like a problem if she talks to him," Chase said. "He's still in the trailer. He can't do anything from there."

"No, it's a strong trailer." Eb shook his head. "But you boys humor Leigh far too much with this voodoo hocus-pocus of hers. If you want her to sweet-talk Grateful Dead, be my guest, but it won't accomplish anything."

As Joe watched Leigh move to the front of the trailer

and look in through the metal grille, he could swear she seemed to be standing in a pool of light. He glanced at the setting sun, sure it was a trick of the clouds rimming the horizon, but he couldn't figure out the trajectories that would bring a beam of sunlight to fall directly on Leigh.

She stayed at the head of the trailer for several minutes while the men waited in tense silence. Then she walked to the back. Before Joe realized what she was doing, she had the tailgate unlatched.

"Hey!" Ry called, starting over at a run. Joe followed. Leigh spun and held up a hand. "Stop right there."

Ry skidded to a halt and Joe nearly bumped into him. He felt a body thump into his and turned to see Chase over his right shoulder.

A smile twitched at the corner's of Leigh's mouth. "Will you guys ease up before you hurt yourselves? I can handle this."

Grateful Dead kicked the side of the trailer and bawled out a warning.

"You're not going in there," Ry said.

"How else can I lead him out?"

"With the ropes on the sides, like Whitlock said," Chase suggested.

"He'll try to get away once he's out of the trailer if you treat him like that. He's in a strange place, and he's very nervous." She turned away from them as another metallic thump came from inside the trailer. "I'm going in."

"Aw, Leigh," Chase said. "We can't let you do that."

"*Let?*" She whirled and glared at all three of them. "Six months ago, you three greenhorns had never laid eyes on a steer, let alone a Brahma bull."

"*Greenhorns?*" they chorused.

"Don't think you can tell me how to handle this animal. I have more experience than the three of you put together, with Eb Whitlock thrown in for good measure!"

Ry braced his hands on his hips. "And here I thought you were the reasonable sister. You've got more of Freddy in you than I thought."

"The fact is, we both have a lot of Clara in us. Now back off, all of you."

"No, by God," Ry said, starting forward. "I—"

Joe caught his arm. "She can do it."

Ry turned to stare at Joe. "How the hell do you know? You're the greenest one of the bunch!"

"That's true, but I know Leigh." He felt as if the words were flowing through him, not from him. "If she says she can handle that bull, I believe her."

Ry took off his hat and scratched his head. Then he peered at Joe as if his partner had taken leave of his senses. Yet Joe had never felt more alive, more joyous in his life. He couldn't have explained the exact connection between Leigh's fearless handling of the bull and her truthfulness about the accidents, but there was one. It wasn't logical, but it was real.

Ry put his hat on and tugged it over his eyes. "I don't like this. If anything happens to that woman, I'm holding you responsible, Gilardini."

"All right." Joe gazed across at Leigh. Now, when she looked at him, the mask was gone, and her spirit shone forth so brightly he caught his breath. "I'll take the responsibility," he said.

"Chase, go get a couple of ropes to have ready," Ry said. "Just in case Grateful Dead isn't a true believer in the power of psychic connections."

"What's Leigh gonna do, Dad?"

Joe glanced down to see Kyle standing next to him. If Grateful Dead bolted from the trailer, Kyle would be much too close for comfort. But the bull wouldn't bolt. Confidence in Leigh overrode Joe's fear. "She's going to talk that bull out of the trailer, Kyle. She's connecting with his mind, just the way she does with horses."

"And people," Kyle said.

"Yes, and people." He believed, yet he held his breath as Leigh edged into the trailer, crooning to the bull with every step. When another thump of hooves against metal interrupted her litany, Joe winced.

"I thought you had complete faith in this project," Ry said, eyeing him.

Joe kept his gaze on the trailer. "I do."

"They say love is blind," Ry said.

Joe didn't respond. He'd never been able to see more clearly in his life, but it was a different sort of seeing, and he wasn't about to explain it to Ry right now.

"Here they come," Kyle whispered.

Joe clenched his jaw as Leigh emerged, holding the halter of the ugliest animal he'd ever seen. Horns curved viciously forward above a white death-mask face with dark splotches around each eye. The menacing hump above his massive brindle shoulders swayed as he walked. Next to him, Leigh looked no bigger than a child. Joe had witnessed some unbelievable acts of courage during his twenty years as a cop, but he'd never seen anything more heart-stopping than the picture of this slight young woman leading a beast that could crush her in an instant if it chose to do so.

Leigh didn't break her concentration as she moved slowly down the ramp, her head close to the bull's ear while she kept up a constant flow of soothing words. She walked away from the trailer toward the sturdy pen designated for the bull, and Joe followed her with his eyes, his heart full. Careful to keep her movements steady, she unlatched the gate and led the bull inside. When she latched the gate after her, closing herself inside with the animal, Joe thought he might pass out.

She stood there for long moments scratching the monster's nose. Then she unhooked the lead rope and turned her back on the bull as she unlatched the gate again and walked out. An audible sigh went up from the group watching her.

Joe didn't consciously decide to go to meet her, yet suddenly he was on his way, eating up the space that separated them with long strides. When they were face-to-face, she stared up at him.

"I believe you," he said.

"I know you do." Her bottomless gaze drew him in and her mysterious smile made him tremble with anticipation.

"Leigh, I—"

"Hey, that was some trick!" called Whitlock.

Joe turned to see him barreling over, destroying any chance for Joe to say what was burning in his heart. His buddies knew enough to hang back when they'd figured out what was happening, but not this blowhard. Where was Chase with a rope when a guy needed one?

"I wouldn't have believed it if I hadn't seen it with my own eyes," Eb said as he reached them.

Joe glanced over to where Ry, Chase and Kyle stood. All of them, including Kyle, looked highly amused. Joe wasn't.

Whitlock compounded his boorish behavior by clapping Joe on the back. "You guys sure have been hanging in there with this ranch. I'm surprised, to tell the truth. Thought you'd have given up and cleared out by now, especially with all the things going wrong recently."

Joe gazed down at Leigh. "I'd say everything's going along pretty well right now."

"I suppose you still think you'll make a big profit when you sell to the developers in a couple of years, but with interest rates going up, I wouldn't count on that," Whitlock said. "We could be in for another real-estate slump. Frankly, I think you'd be better off to sell now."

Joe had trouble wrenching his attention away from Leigh, but something in Whitlock's tone niggled at him. He forced himself to look into the guy's eyes. Was it his imagination, or was there a spark of desperation behind the genial smile, the hearty advice? He decided to probe a little deeper. "There's a good chance we won't ever sell the True Love," he said.

Whitlock's smile stayed in place but his eyes narrowed. "That's crazy. You're just city boys playing at running a ranch."

"I wouldn't bet on it." Joe met the challenge in Whitlock's eyes.

Whitlock's smile faded and he looked away, his glance darting everywhere but at Joe. "You'll never succeed. Haven't you heard? The True Love is cursed."

I've got you, you son of a bitch. Now I just have to find proof. Joe stepped over beside Leigh and slipped an arm around her waist. "You know, Whitlock, I have the strongest feeling that curse is about to be lifted."

16

"IT'S WHITLOCK. I just don't have a way to prove it yet," Joe said later that evening as he sat with Ry, Freddy and Chase on the patio. Kyle was out on the front porch with Dexter, and Amanda was putting Bart to bed. Joe had chosen the patio for the discussion because it was fairly private. The number of guests had swelled in the past week due to the publicity about the rodeo, and most of them were gathered in the main room of the house for line-dancing lessons conducted by Leigh.

Joe could see her rhythmic motions through the large window, and they fired his blood. He longed to ditch the investigation and take her back to her room for a night of lovemaking. But he had a job to do, and the job affected her welfare, too.

"You know I agree with you," Ry said. "I've never trusted him."

Freddy shifted in her lawn chair. "I still can't believe it's Eb. Not when we're talking about a dangerous brushfire and a flash flood that could have killed Leigh and Kyle. Eb wouldn't do things like that just to get a piece of land."

"It's more than the land," Joe said. "And once we find out what he's after, we'll have our proof. What about mineral rights? Could there be oil under here?"

Freddy shook her head. "My dad had geologists

come out more than once. There's no oil in the ground, or precious metal in the canyons, either."

"Then it's something else," Joe said. "And we have to come up with it fast. He's liable to create an accident during the rodeo tomorrow. I'm worried about—" Joe paused as Kyle came through the French doors and walked across the patio toward them. "Hi, buddy."

"Belinda says it's time for me to go to bed. The dancing's about over."

"Good idea," Joe said. "Tomorrow's a big day."

Kyle came over and leaned on Joe's chair. "I told Dexter about that Jethro Whitlock guy who wrote the diary Amanda's reading. He got kind of excited."

Freddy laughed. "Dexter hates anybody with the name of Whitlock. He caught Eb giving Belinda a kiss on the cheek once, and he's been jealous ever since."

Joe glanced at Chase. "Is Amanda planning to read the rest of that diary tonight?"

"If she can keep her eyes open." Chase stretched. "We're both still suffering from jet lag."

"I think we all need a good night's rest," Leigh said, coming out to the patio. "I'm beat. You can stay up all night discussing this if you want, but I'm going to bed."

Joe gazed up at her, trying to decide if her announcement was an invitation or a rejection. They'd had no time alone since she'd taken Grateful Dead to his pen, and now she seemed determined to avoid his questioning glance. He stood and turned to his son. "Go get ready for bed, Kyle. I'll come and tuck you in in a minute."

"See you all in the morning," Leigh said, starting toward the back patio gate that would provide a shortcut to her room.

Joe followed her. "Leigh."

She turned just inside the gate. "Yes?"

He lowered his voice, aware they might be overheard by Chase, Ry and Freddy. "We need to talk." *I need to make love to you.*

She laid a hand on his arm. "I can see how involved you are with the investigation, and God knows it needs to be solved, for all our sakes. I'll see you in the morning."

Her rejection knocked the breath out of him. "But—"

"Good night, Joe." She slipped through the gate and was gone, leaving him totally confused. He'd seen the light in her eyes when he'd walked out to meet her at the rodeo grounds. He'd expected clear sailing from that moment on. What the hell had happened?

AN HOUR INTO THE RODEO the next afternoon, Leigh surveyed the crowd from the bed of a open wagon drawn up beside the stands. Belinda and Dexter were sitting next to her on lawn chairs, with Kyle on Dexter's far side, and a vacant chair ready for Amanda and Bart, who were due to arrive at any moment. A canvas awning provided shade. It was Ry's creative suggestion to provide a comfortable spot for Belinda, Dexter, Amanda and the baby. Dexter had requested that Kyle join them. Following her team-roping event with Ry, Leigh had climbed up on the wagon to see if anyone in the group needed anything.

"We're fine," Belinda assured her. "You and Ry were wonderful, by the way. I yelled myself hoarse."

"It was fun." Leigh was proud of the way she and Ry had worked together in their first competition. Pussywillow wasn't as well trained as Penny Lover, but she was adequate. Ry had ridden Red Devil and the big gelding had performed well. They hadn't won the event, but they'd come close.

"Kyle's father certainly has been busy today," Belinda commented.

"He has a lot on his mind," Leigh said. She knew Joe had checked and rechecked every detail of the rodeo to make sure Eb Whitlock hadn't sabotaged anything. He'd kept a constant eye on Eb, who'd spent the day strutting around the rodeo grounds bragging about Grateful Dead's upcoming performance. Leigh had tried to stay out of Joe's way, knowing he was in full cop mode. The strength of her feelings would only interfere with his concentration.

She listened to the rodeo announcer describe the bareback bronc-riding event and searched the area around the bucking chutes, figuring Joe would be down there making sure everything was going smoothly. She couldn't find him. She scanned the crowd and the perimeter of the arena and still couldn't locate him.

The announcer finished his introduction. *"But before we continue the event, I have someone here with something to say to a certain young lady."*

The microphone crackled. *"Leigh, this is Joe. I've been trying to talk to you all day but you keep ducking me."*

Warmth washed over her and she placed a hand over her racing heart. She could feel the attention of everyone in the arena focused on the little wagon beside the stands.

"I'd order you to meet me, but I know Singleton women don't take kindly to orders. So if you can spare the time, come to Grateful Dead's pen immediately. Please."

The stands erupted in laughter and Leigh's face flamed. She glanced at Kyle, who was staring at her with his mouth open. Speechless herself, she could only shrug and give him a silly smile.

"I think you'd better go meet him, sweetheart," Belinda said gently, giving her a nudge. "No telling what message he'll put on the P.A. system next."

Leigh stumbled down from the wagon in a daze. Surely she was dreaming. Joe Gilardini, the man who kept his feelings guarded more carefully than Fort Knox, wouldn't announce his relationship with her over a loudspeaker. As she skirted the arena fence, a few cowboys called out kidding remarks, but then the announcer started the bronc-riding event, and everyone's attention returned to the competition.

Everyone's except for the tall cowboy standing next to Grateful Dead's pen. Joe's gaze, steady and sure, drew her closer.

She shook her head. "I can't believe you did that."

"Can't you? I'm a desperate man. You won't have anything to do with me."

"I'm trying to help!"

"By frustrating the daylights out of me?" He took a stride forward and grabbed her elbows. "Just when I have everything figured out, you're nowhere to be found!"

"You've figured out why Whitlock wants this place?"

"No, you crazy idiot." He smiled gently. "I've figured out that I'm hopelessly in love with you."

She stared up at him in total shock. Of all the ways she'd imagined he'd finally break down and tell her, declaring it in the middle of a crowded rodeo grounds while he was working on the sabotage case was not one of them.

"Well, don't you have anything to say?" he demanded.

"You're at the climax of an investigation!"

His gray eyes danced. "But that's not the climax I keep thinking about."

Desire blossomed in her, but she fought her reaction. "You have to concentrate and forget about me for now," she said with as much firmness as she could muster.

He pulled her close. "I can't."

She tried to put some space between them, but he wouldn't allow it. "Now, Joe, I'm sure that after twenty years you've learned how to block out your emotions at a time like this."

"So I did." He looked down at her, his gaze smoldering. "But you've changed me. I can't block you out. I want to hold you, to make love to you."

She felt momentary panic. What had she done?

"Don't look so scared," he said gently. "I'm still a good cop. I'll figure this guy out. But I can't go it alone anymore. Even if we can't make love this minute, I need to know that we will, and soon. Most of all, I have to know that you're on my side."

She cupped his face in both hands, and her eyes filled with tears. "Oh, yes. A thousand times, yes! I was saving this moment for when we could concentrate completely on each other. I didn't realize..."

"That I needed you?"

"Forgive me, my darling." She blocked out the noisy crowd and the flurry of activity around them. She blocked out everything except the passion in his gray eyes. "I love you, Joe," she said, tears of happiness rolling down her cheeks. "You're the missing part of me, the man I've been searching for all my life."

"And I was such a fool, I didn't know I was searching. But I was." He lowered his mouth to hers. "And I found you," he whispered just before he claimed her lips.

"Joe!"

With a muttered oath, he lifted his head.

"I'm sorry, Joe. Leigh." Chase paused to catch his breath. "But Amanda's found something in that diary. Jethro Whitlock knew Clara Singleton. He mentioned her several times and said something in the diary about going back after what was his. It could have been Clara, but it also could have been a shipment of gold he took from the Butterfield Stage. The gold from that robbery was never recovered, and it would be worth several million now. Amanda thinks it's buried on the ranch."

Joe released Leigh and turned to Chase. "Would Whitlock know about the diary?"

"Just before we came down here we called the Arizona Historical Society. They remembered Whitlock coming in there during the past year, and apparently he was interested in the diary."

"Then we'd better have a little talk with Whitlock."

"That's just it," Chase said. "He's disappeared. Ry's supposed to ride Grateful Dead in about fifteen minutes, so you'd think he'd be around for that."

"Unless he's gone after the gold now, knowing half the valley would be watching his bull pulverize Ry," Joe said.

"There's another thing," Chase added. "Kyle just interpreted this from something Dexter was trying to say over at the wagon. Dexter seems to think the gold could be buried under the old homestead floor."

Joe looked at Leigh. "That's it," he said. "Everything falls into place now. Leigh and I scared off a couple of guys out there the other night. They must have been sent out to start digging."

Chase's eyes narrowed. "And now, while everybody's at the rodeo—"

"Let's go," Joe said. "We'll be less conspicuous on horseback than if we take one of the trucks."

"I'll ride Destiny," Chase said, loping off toward the pens where the cutting horses were kept.

"Take Pussywillow, Joe," Leigh said. "She's fast."

"Good idea." He started off toward the pens just as Ry rode up on Red Devil.

He wheeled his horse in front of Joe. "Amanda just told me the story."

"We think Whitlock's at the homestead. Lavette and I are riding out there."

Ry tugged his hat over his eyes. "So am I."

"You have an event in less than fifteen minutes," Joe reminded him.

Ry grinned. "Maybe I won't have to ride that bull, after all." He held out a hand to Joe. "Hop on. I'll give you a lift to the holding pens."

Joe started to get on without a backward glance. Leigh wondered if he'd forgotten she was standing there. Then he seemed to catch himself and came back to her.

He gripped her arms and his gaze was intent. "Take care of Kyle for me."

She gasped. "Don't say things like that. You're coming back."

He smiled at her. "Of course I am. I meant just for the next hour or so. I don't want him to worry about what we're up to."

"I'll take care of him." She concentrated hard, surrounding Joe with protective light.

"I love you," he murmured. Then he vaulted to the back of Ry's horse and they galloped away.

Leigh knew that if she kept very quiet and focused on what was about to happen out at the homestead, she would know how the coming confrontation would turn out. If millions of dollars was at stake, Eb would be a dangerous enemy. By using her powers, she could find out whether Joe would emerge unscathed...or not. She wiped all thought of the homestead from her mind as she hurried over to the wagon to reassure Kyle.

JOE, Ry and Chase cut across a little-used trail to reach the riverbed, then doubled back toward the homestead, approaching at a slow walk with Joe in the lead. He paused and held up his hand to call a halt. As he listened, sorting through the rustling of animals in the brush and the chirping of birds, he heard the rhythmic sounds of shovels biting into the dirt. Joe reached into his boot and pulled out his .38.

He nudged Pussywillow and motioned the other two men to follow him. He had the only gun, but Ry and Chase had ropes and knew how to use them far better than he did. Joe was counting on the element of surprise to give them an advantage, as well as something less tangible. Whitlock was after money. Joe and his partners cared about something more important than that. They were fighting for their home.

Closer in, he heard voices and held up his hand again. Turning in his saddle, he used gestures and mouthed instructions to send Chase around to his left, Ry around to his right. He'd explained on the way over that he would go in first, gun drawn. If Whitlock and his men offered no resistance, Chase and Ry could ride in afterward and help tie them up. If they did offer resistance, then Joe hoped his partners were as good at roping two-legged critters as they seemed to be with four-legged ones.

Joe started forward again. Through the mesquite branches he could see them—two men besides Whitlock. A battered old truck with a winch on the front bumper was pulled up close to the hole they'd made in the floor of the homestead, and they were straining to get two cables fastened around something in the hole. If they hadn't been totally engrossed in hauling a fortune out of the ground, they would have heard him approach. But buried treasure had made them temporarily deaf.

Whitlock was the only one armed. He had a handgun in a holster on his hip. He stood back and allowed his men to do the dirty work. Joe decided to let them get the gold all the way out before he interrupted their little party. Ingots were damned heavy.

Cursing and sweating, the men positioned the cables beneath the chest and tightened them. The winch whined as one man operated it and the other steadied the rusty black strongbox coming out of the hole. Finally, they had it out, and Whitlock hurried over to throw open the lid. All three men gasped.

So did Joe. The chest was stacked tight with gold bars. Even tarnished a rusty brown with age, they gleamed with promise. Whitlock reached out a hand, and Joe called out.

"Get 'em up, all of you!"

They whirled in his direction, but only one of Whitlock's men lifted his hands in the air. The other grabbed for a shovel, and Joe shot it out of his hand. The man howled and held his bleeding wrist against his stomach.

The distraction gave Whitlock time to draw his gun

and get off a shot. Joe's right forearm burned as the bullet passed through, nicking the same bone he'd broken in the elevator. The force of the bullet flung his gun from his hand. As Whitlock raised his gun for a second shot, a rope sailed over his shoulders and snapped tight, throwing him to the ground. The gun discharged into the air as he landed.

Ry leapt from Red Devil's saddle as the big horse sat back on his haunches, keeping the rope taut around Whitlock. The uninjured man grabbed a sledgehammer. Swinging it over his head, he started for Ry. He never made it. Chase's loop caught him around the ankle, jerking his leg out from under him.

Joe dismounted and ran over to grab Whitlock's gun in his left hand, but as he did, the injured man fled into the brush.

"Destiny and I will get him," Chase said. While Ry covered the guy on the ground, Chase loosened his rope and flicked it from the man's ankle. Then he coiled it and headed into the brush after his quarry.

Joe held the gun while Ry, using his best calf-tying techniques, trussed up Whitlock and his hired hand.

"How'd you know?" Whitlock cried, his face contorted with fury. "How the hell did you guys know?"

Joe gazed at him. "We got the word from Clara."

"Come on." Whitlock spat in the dirt. "You don't believe that claptrap any more than I do." He glared at his hired hand. "One of you guys talked, didn't you?"

"No, but they got a little careless," Joe said.

When Ry finished tying both men securely, he turned to Joe. "You're bleeding pretty bad."

"A pressure bandage ought to do it." Joe glanced down at Whitlock, who was still dressed in the showy

Western shirt he'd worn to the rodeo. "Why don't you tear up Whitlock's shirt?"

"It would be a pleasure."

"That's a fifty-dollar shirt!" Whitlock bellowed.

"Where you're going, they provide free clothes." Joe sat down and trained the gun on Whitlock while Ry ripped off the front of his shirt, created a makeshift bandage and bound it to Joe's arm with strips from the same shirt.

"Same ol', same ol'," Joe said as Ry worked on the bandage. "You realize this is the same damned arm I broke in the elevator. I get hurt every time I'm around you, McGuinnes."

"Yeah, but just like I told you in the elevator, Gilardini, I'm also going to make you rich." Ry tied the last knot and stood just as Chase came trotting in, his prisoner at the end of his lariat.

"Hog-tie him, Ry," Chase said, dismounting and coming over to Joe. "How's the arm?"

"I'll make it."

Ry finished trussing up the last prisoner and ambled over to stand next to Chase. He pushed back his hat. "Damn, but that was fun."

Chase grinned. "Can't remember when I've had a better time with my clothes on."

Joe studied his two partners. "For a couple of civilians, you were passable."

"Passable?" Ry cried. "We were great! The three of us make a hell of a team."

Joe chuckled. "Too bad you have such a small ego, McGuinnes."

Ry turned to Chase. "Weren't we great?"

"I'll tell you who was great. Destiny. I'm riding that horse from now on. He can *move*."

"Give Red Devil another year and he'll be almost that good. Give him five years and he'll—"

"You're not talking much like a guy who plans to turn a profit by selling the place," Joe observed.

Ry and Chase stared at him.

"Wasn't that the idea?" Joe tried to keep a straight face as his two partners grew more and more uncomfortable. "Aw, hell," Joe said finally, breaking into a smile. "I don't want to sell, either. You were right, Ry. The place grows on you."

"I heard that," cried Leigh, reining in Mikey and leaping to the ground. "You have a witness." She ran over to Joe and dropped to her knees beside him. "I would think a man of your experience could avoid getting shot," she said, her voice husky as she examined the makeshift bandage. "Did it go all the way through?"

"Yes, ma'am." He drank in the sight of her. Maybe it was the loss of blood affecting his vision, but he could swear she was surrounded by that darned halo of light again. "I was lucky."

"Lucky? You got shot!"

"Any bullet that doesn't kill you is a lucky bullet," he said. "The way I figure it, someone was watching over me."

She gazed into his eyes and swallowed hard. "Someone was."

"Hey, why are you here, anyway?" Joe asked, remembering his last instructions to her. "I thought I told you to stay and take care of Kyle."

Freddy rode up and dismounted. "You have a short memory, Joe. Just recently, you announced to the world that Singleton women don't take kindly to orders." She unstrapped her first-aid kit from her saddle.

"Where *is* Kyle?" Joe asked.

"With Dexter," Leigh said, stepping back so Freddy could look at Joe's wound. She waited anxiously while Freddy checked Joe's vital signs and examined the bandage. "How bad is it?"

"Not too bad. The bleeding's about stopped. You're a lucky guy."

"Absolutely," Joe said, gazing up at Leigh.

"Wouldn't you just know it? Now here comes Amanda!" Chase cried in an exasperated tone. "After I specifically told her to stay with Bart. Pardon my French, honey bun, but what the hell are you doing out here? And where's our son?"

Amanda swung down from the saddle and tied her horse to a tree. "Our son is with Belinda," she said, striding toward him. "Freddy, Leigh and I had a little talk and decided we had as much right to be out here fighting for the True Love as any of you. Then on the way we heard shots and put on the speed. Leigh outran us. How is he, Freddy?"

"He'll be fine."

"Thank God." Amanda glanced at the rusted chest and did a double take. "Is that *real?*"

Ry turned to Whitlock. "Tell her, neighbor." Whitlock just glared at him. "Aw, he must not be feeling too neighborly," Ry said. "To answer your question, Amanda, I believe you're looking at the gold shipment from the Butterfield Stage robbery pulled off by Jethro Whitlock about a hundred and ten years ago."

Amanda walked over to the chest. "Wow." She gazed down at the gold bars. "Did you notice there's a piece of paper tucked in here?"

"Probably some invoice," Ry said. "But we might as well take a look at it." He crossed to where Amanda stood and peered over her shoulder as she unfolded the paper. "Well, I'll be damned."

"It's a letter," Amanda said, turning toward Leigh and Freddy. "A letter from Clara. Would one of you like to read it? I'm not a relative or anything."

"Read it," Freddy said. "You're one of the True Love women, now."

Amanda's face lit with pleasure. "Yes, I believe I am." She turned her attention to the letter. "It says:

To the person who discovers this gold—On September 19, 1884, Jethro Whitlock and his desperadoes came to my home when Thaddeus was away. They held me at gunpoint while they buried their stolen goods beneath the dirt floor of my home. Jethro will give Thaddeus all the details of my soiled past and implicate Thaddeus and me in the robbery if I tell anyone about the gold. Now that Jethro and his gang has left, I have uncovered the strongbox so that I may insert this note, hoping it will keep suspicion from ever falling on my dear husband. I pray that Jethro retrieves his booty soon and that Thaddeus will never know of its presence in the lovely home he built for me. He risked his reputation to marry a woman of questionable character. I will take this secret to my grave to protect my husband's good name.

In great remorse,
Clara Singleton

Freddy shook her head in wonder. "To think that the True Love has harbored a fortune for years and none of our ancestors knew it. A treasure was right under Clara's feet all the time."

"That's not where the treasure was, Freddy." Leigh's glance rested on Ry and her sister, then moved on to Chase and Amanda. Finally she crouched next to Joe and laced her fingers through his. "And Clara was smart enough to understand that," she murmured, gazing into the eyes of the man she loved.

Epilogue

Frederica (Freddy) and **Thomas Rycroft (Ry) Mc-Guinnes** named their twin girls Clara, after Freddy's great-great-great-grandmother Clara Singleton, and Belinda, after the ranch's loyal cook, Belinda Grimes. Ry eventually rode Grateful Dead to the buzzer, suffering a broken rib and a two-day tirade from his wife in the process.

Amanda and **Chase Lavette** became parents of a girl they named Helen Marie, after Chase's mother. Helen turned out to be a boisterous child who got her older brother Bart into all sorts of trouble. She was nicknamed "Hel" by her proud father, who took over most of the child-rearing duties while Amanda ran an ad agency in Tucson.

Leigh and **Joseph (Joe) Gilardini** presented Joe's son, Kyle, with a baby brother. Kyle was allowed to name the boy, and he chose "Leonard," for his idol Leonard Nimoy. Joe became a successful private investigator largely due to the information he solicited from his psychic wife.

Kyle Gilardini spent all his Christmas and summer vacations at the True Love Ranch and became an accomplished rider who eventually won several junior roping competitions on his Appaloosa, Spilled Milk. Kyle wrote a research paper for school about the True Love Curse, and discovered that the massacre had actually taken place on Eb Whitlock's property.

Ebenezer (Eb) Whitlock spent many years as a guest of the state of Arizona. He claimed that he was no relation to Jethro Whitlock and had merely found the diary by accident while browsing through Arizona Historical Society files.

The Reward for the recovery of the **Butterfield Gold Shipment** provided the True Love Ranch with enough revenue to construct a separate house for each of the partners, with enough left over to rebuild the homestead and open it to the public as a museum. Kenny Rogers's documentary about Clara Singleton and the cache of gold she kept hidden under her floor aired on national television.

The True Love Ranch has become a sought-after travel destination for romantics the world over as word spreads that something magic in the desert air inspires true love. Dexter still fetches the mail every day, but he now pushes a cart to handle the slew of wedding invitations and birth announcements that arrive from former guests. With each new expression of joy, the legend grows....

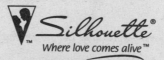

SPECIAL EDITION™
Emotional, compelling stories that capture the intensity of living, loving and creating a family in today's world.

Silhouette®
Desire.
A highly passionate, emotionally powerful and always provocative read.

Silhouette®
Where love comes alive™

INTIMATE MOMENTS™
A roller-coaster read that delivers romantic thrills in a world of suspense, adventure and more.

SILHOUETTE *Romance™*
From first love to forever, these love stories are for today's woman with traditional values.

Visit Silhouette at www.eHarlequin.com

SILGENINT